10—

D1449066

Gaudissart the Great

Photogravure — From an Original Drawing

Illustrated Sterling Edition

THE THIRTEEN

FATHER GORIOT

AND OTHER STORIES

BY

HONORÉ de BALZAC

With Introductions by

GEORGE SAINTSBURY

BOSTON

DANA ESTES & COMPANY

PUBLISHERS

CONTENTS

PART I

PART II

ILLUSTRATIONS

PART I

PART II

THE THIRTEEN

INTRODUCTION

THE *Histoire des Treize* consists—or rather is built up—of three stories: *Ferragus* or the *Rue Soly, La Duchesse de Langeais* or *Ne touchez-pas à la hache,* and *La Fille aux Yeux d'Or.*

To tell the truth, there is more power than taste throughout the *Histoire des Treize,* and perhaps not very much less unreality than power. Balzac is very much better than Eugène Sue, though Eugène Sue also is better than it is the fashion to think him just now. But he is here, to a certain extent, competing with Sue on the latter's own ground. The notion of the "Dévorants"—of a secret society of men devoted to each other's interests, entirely free from any moral or legal scruple, possessed of considerable means in wealth, ability, and position, all working together, by fair means or foul, for good ends or bad—is, no doubt, rather seducing to the imagination at all times; and it so happened that it was particularly seducing to the imagination of that time. And its example has been powerful since; it gave us Mr. Stevenson's *New Arabian Nights* only, as it were, the other day.

But there is something a little schoolboyish in it; and I do not know that Balzac has succeeded entirely in eliminating this something. The pathos of the death, under persecution, of the innocent Clémence does not entirely make up for the unreasonableness of the whole situation. Nobody can say that the abominable misconduct of Maulincour—who is a hopeless "cad"—is too much punished, though an Englishman may think that Dr. Johnson's receipt of three or four footmen with cudgels, applied repeatedly and unsparingly, would have been better than elaborately prepared accidents and duels, which were too honorable for a Peeping Tom of this kind; and poisonings, which reduced the avengers to the level of their victim.   But the imbroglio is of itself stupid; these fathers who cannot be made known to husbands are mere stage properties, and should never be fetched out of the theatrical lumber-room by literature.

La Duchesse de Langeais is, I think, a better story, with more romantic attraction, free from the objections just made to *Ferragus,* and furnished with a powerful, if slightly theatrical catastrophe.   It is as good as anything that its author has done of the kind, subject to those general considerations of probability and otherwise which have been already hinted at.   For those who are not troubled by any such critical reflections, both, no doubt, will be highly satisfactory.

"The third of the series, *La Fille aux Yeux d'Or,* in some respects one of Balzac's most brilliant effects, has been looked at askance by many of his English readers.   At one time he had the audacity to think of calling it *La Femme aux Yeux Rouges*.   To those who consider the story morbid or, one may say, *bizarre,* one word of justification, hardly of apology, may be offered.   It was in the scheme of the *Comédie Humaine* to survey social life in its entirety by a minute analysis of its most diverse constituents.   It included all the pursuits and passions, was large and patient, and unafraid. And the patience, the curiosity, of the artist which made César Birotteau and his bankrupt ledgers matters of high import to us, which did not shrink from creating a Vautrin and a Lucien de Rubempré, would have been incomplete had it stopped short of a Marquise de San-Réal, of a Paquita Valdès. And in the great mass of the *Comédie Humaine,* with its largeness and reality of life, as in life itself, the figure of Paquita justifies its presence."

Considering the *Histoire des Treize* as a whole, it is of engrossing interest. And I must confess I should not think much of any boy who, beginning Balzac with this series, failed to go rather mad over it. I know there was a time when I used to like it best of all, and thought not merely *Eugénie Grandet,* but *Le Père Goriot* (though not the *Peau de Chagrin*), dull in comparison. Some attention, however, must be paid to two remarkable characters, on whom it is quite clear that Balzac expended a great deal of pains, and one of whom he seems to have "caressed," as the French say, with a curious admixture of dislike and admiration.

The first, Bourignard or Ferragus, is, of course, another, though a somewhat minor example—Collin or Vautrin being the chief—of that strange tendency to take intense interest in criminals, which seems to be a pretty constant eccentricity of many human minds, and which laid an extraordinary grasp on the great French writers of Balzac's time. I must confess, though it may sink me very low in some eyes, that I have never been able fully to appreciate the attractions of crime and criminals, fictitious or real. Certain pleasant and profitable things, no doubt, retain their pleasure and their profit, to some extent, when they are done in the manner which is technically called criminal; but they seem to me to acquire no additional interest by being so. As the criminal of fact is, in the vast majority of cases, an exceedingly commonplace and dull person, the criminal of fiction seems to me only, or usually, to escape these curses by being absolutely improbable and unreal. But I know this is a terrible heresy.

Henri de Marsay is a much more ambitious and a much more interesting figure. In him are combined the attractions of criminality, beauty, brains, success, and, last of all, dandyism. It is a well-known and delightful fact that the most Anglophobe Frenchmen—and Balzac might fairly be classed among them—have always regarded the English dandy with half-jealous, half-awful admiration. Indeed, our novelist, it will be seen, found it necessary to give Marsay English blood. But there is a tradition that this young Don Juan—not such a good fellow as Byron's, nor such a *grand seigneur* as Molière's—was partly intended to represent Charles de Rémusat, who is best known to this generation by very sober and serious philosophical works, and by his part in his mother's correspondence. I do not know that there ever were any imputations on M. de Rémusat's morals; but in memoirs of the time, he is, I think, accused of a certain selfishness and *hauteur,* and he certainly made his way, partly by journalism, partly by society, to power very much as Marsay did. But Marsay would certainly not have written *Abelard* and the rest, or have returned to Ministerial rank in our own time. Marsay, in fact, more fortunate than Rubempré, and of a higher stamp and flight than Rastignac, makes with them Balzac's trinity of sketches of the kind of personage whose part, in his day and since, every young Frenchman has aspired to play, and some have played. It cannot be said that "a moral man is Marsay"; it cannot be said that he has the element of good-nature which redeems Rastignac. But he bears a blame and a burden for which we Britons are re-

sponsible in part—the Byronic ideal of the guilty hero coming
to cross and blacken the old French model of unscrupulous
good humor. It is not a very pretty mixture or a very worthy
ideal; but I am not so sure that it is not still a pretty common
one.

The association of the three stories forming the *Histoire
des Treize* is, in book form, original, inasmuch as they filled
three out of the four volumes of *Études des Mœurs* published
in 1834-35, and themselves forming part of the first collection
of *Scènes de la Vie Parisienne*. But *Ferragus* had appeared
in parts (with titles to each) in the *Revue de Paris* for March
and April 1833, and part of *La Duchesse de Langeais* in the
Echo de la Jeune France almost contemporaneously. There
were divisions in this also. *Ferragus* and *La Duchesse* also
appeared without *La Fille aux Yeux d'Or* in 1839, published
in one volume by Charpentier, before their absorption at the
usual time in the *Comédie*.

G. S.

THE THIRTEEN

AUTHOR'S PREFACE

IN the Paris of the Empire there were found Thirteen men equally impressed with the same idea, equally endowed with energy enough to keep them true to it, while among themselves they were loyal enough to keep faith even when their interests chanced to clash. They were strong enough to set themselves above all laws; bold enough to shrink from no enterprise; and lucky enough to succeed in nearly everything that they undertook. So profoundly politic were they, that they could dissemble the tie which bound them together. They ran the greatest risks, and kept their failures to themselves. Fear never entered into their calculations; not one of them had trembled before princes, before the executioner's axe, before innocence. They had taken each other as they were, regardless of social prejudices. Criminals they doubtless were, yet none the less were they all remarkable for some one of the virtues which go to the making of great men, and their numbers were filled up only from among picked recruits. Finally, that nothing should be lacking to complete the dark, mysterious romance of their history, nobody to this day knows who they were. The Thirteen once realized all the wildest ideas conjured up by tales of the occult powers of a Manfred, a Faust, or a Melmoth; and to-day the band is broken up or, at any rate, dispersed. Its members have quietly returned beneath the yoke of the Civil Code; much as Morgan, the Achilles of piracy, gave up buccaneering to be a peaceable planter; and, untroubled by qualms of conscience, sat himself down by the fireside to dispose of blood-stained booty acquired by the red light of blazing towns.

After Napoleon's death, the band was dissolved by a chance event which the author is bound for the present to pass over in silence, and its mysterious existence, as curious, it may be, as the darkest novel by Mrs. Radcliffe, came to an end.

It was only lately that the present writer, detecting, as he fancied, a faint desire for celebrity in one of the anonymous heroes to whom the whole band once owed an occult allegiance, received the somewhat singular permission to make public certain of the adventures which befell that band, provided that, while telling the story in his own fashion, he observed certain limits.

The aforesaid leader was still an apparently young man with fair hair and blue eyes, and a soft, thin voice which might seem to indicate a feminine temperament. His face was pale, his ways mysterious. He chatted pleasantly, and told me that he was only just turned of forty. He might have belonged to any one of the upper classes. The name which he gave was probably assumed, and no one answering to his description was known in society. Who is he, do you ask? No one knows.

Perhaps when he made his extraordinary disclosures to the present writer, he wished to see them in some sort reproduced; to enjoy the effect of the sensation on the multitude; to feel as Macpherson might have felt when the name of Ossian, his creation, passed into all languages. And, in truth, that Scottish advocate knew one of the keenest, or, at any rate, one of the rarest sensations in human experience. What was this but the incognito of genius? To write an *Itinéraire de Paris à Jérusalem* is to take one's share in the glory of a century, but to give a Homer to one's country—this surely is a usurpation of the rights of God.

The writer is too well acquainted with the laws of narration to be unaware of the nature of the pledge given by this brief preface; but, at the same time, he knows enough of the history of the Thirteen to feel confident that he shall not disappoint any expectations raised by the programme. Tragedies dripping with gore, comedies piled up with horrors, tales of heads taken off in secret have been confided to him. If any reader has not had enough of the ghastly tales served up to the public for some time past, he has only to express his wish; the author is in a position to reveal cold-blooded atrocities and family secrets of a gloomy and astonishing nature. But in preference he has chosen those pleasanter stories in which stormy passions are succeeded by purer scenes, where the beauty and goodness of woman shine out the brighter for the darkness. And, to the honor of the Thirteen, such episodes as these are not wanting. Some day perhaps it may be thought worth while to give their whole history to the world; in which case it might form a pendant to the history of the buccaneers—that race apart so curiously energetic, so attractive in spite of their crimes.

When a writer has a true story to tell, he should scorn to turn it into a sort of puzzle toy, after the manner of those novelists who take their reader for a walk through one cavern after another to show him a dried-up corpse at the end of the fourth volume, and inform him, by way of conclusion, that he has been frightened all along by a door hidden somewhere or other behind some tapestry; or a dead body, left by inadvertence, under the floor. So the present chronicler, in spite of his objection to prefaces, felt bound to introduce his fragment by a few remarks.

Ferragus, the first episode, is connected by invisible links with the history of the Thirteen, for the power which they acquired in a natural manner provides the apparently supernatural machinery.

Again, although a certain literary coquetry may be permissible to retailers of the marvelous, the sober chronicler is bound to forego such advantage as he may reap from an odd-sounding name, on which many ephemeral successes are founded in these days. Wherefore the present writer gives the following succinct statement of the reasons which induced him to adopt the unlikely sounding title and sub-title.

In accordance with old-established custom, *Ferragus* is a name taken by the head of a guild of *Dévorants, id est*

Devoirants or journeymen. Every chief on the day of his election chooses a pseudonym and continues a dynasty of *Dévorants* precisely as a pope changes his name on his accession to the triple tiara; and as the Church has its Clement XIV., Gregory XII., Julius II., or Alexander VI., so the workmen have their *Trempe-la-Soupe IX., Ferragus XXII.. Tutanus XIII,* or *Masche-Fer IV.* Who are the *Dévorants,* do you ask?

The *Dévorants* are one among many tribes of compagnons whose origin can be traced to a great mystical association formed among the workmen of Christendom for the rebuilding of the Temple at Jerusalem. *Compagnonnage* is still a popular institution in France. Its traditions still exert a power over little enlightened minds, over men so uneducated that they have not learned to break their oaths; and the various organizations might be turned to formidable account even yet if any rough-hewn man of genius arose to make use of them, for his instruments would be, for the most part, almost blind.

Wherever journeymen travel, they find a hostel for *compagnons* which has been in existence in the town from time immemorial. The *obade,* as they call it, is a kind of lodge with a "Mother" in charge, an old, half-gypsy wife who has nothing to lose. She hears all that goes on in the countryside; and, either from fear or from long habit, is devoted to the interests of the tribe boarded and lodged by her. And as a result, this shifting population, subject as it is to an unalterable law of custom, has eyes in every place, and will carry out an order anywhere without asking questions; for the oldest journeyman is still at an age when a man has some beliefs left. What is more, the whole fraternity professes doctrines which, if unfolded never so little, are both true enough and mysterious enough to electrify all the adepts with patriotism; and the *compagnons* are so attached to their rules, that there have been bloody battles between different fraternities on a question of principle. Fortunately, however, for peace and public order, if a *Dévorant* is ambitious, he takes to building houses, makes a fortune, and leaves the guild.

A great many curious things might be told of their rivals, the *Compagnons du Devior,* of all the different sects of workmen, their manners and customs and brotherhoods, and of the resemblances between them and the Freemasons; but here, these particulars would be out of place. The author will merely add, that before the Revolution a Trempe-la-Soupe had been known in the King's service, which is to say, that he had the tenure of a place in His Majesty's galleys for one hundred and one years; but even thence he ruled his guild, and was religiously consulted on all matters, and if he escaped from the hulks he met with help, succor, and respect wherever he went. To have a chief in the hulks is one of those misfortunes for which Providence is responsible; but a faithful lodge of *dévorants* is bound, as before, to obey a power created by and set above themselves. Their lawful sovereign is in exile for the time being, but none the less is he their king. And now any romantic mystery hanging about the words *Ferragus* and the *dévorants* is completely dispelled.

As for the Thirteen, the author feels that, on the strength of the details of this almost fantastic story, he can afford to give away yet another prerogative, though it is one of the greatest on record, and would possibly fetch a high price if brought into a literary auction mart; for the owner might inflict as many volumes on the public as La Contemporaine.*

The Thirteen were all of them men tempered like Byron's friend Trelawney, the original (so it is said) of *The Corsair.* All of them were fatalists, men of spirit and poetic temperament; all of them were tired of the commonplace life which they led; all felt attracted towards Asiatic pleasures by all the vehement strength of newly awakened and long dormant forces. One of these, chancing to take up *Venice Preserved* for the second time, admired the sublime friendship between Pierre and Jaffir, and fell to musing on the virtues of outlaws, the loyalty of the hulks, the honor of thieves, and the immense power that a few men can wield if they bring their

*A long series of so-called Memoirs, which appeared about 1830.

whole minds to bear upon the carrying out of a single will.
It struck him that the individual man rose higher than men.
Then he began to think that if a few picked men should
band themselves together; and if, to natural wit, and education, and money, they could join a fanaticism hot enough
to fuse, as it were, all these separate forces into a single one,
then the whole world would be at their feet. From that
time forth, with a tremendous power of concentration, they
could wield an occult power against which the organization
of society would be helpless; a power which would push obstacles aside and defeat the will of others; and the diabolical power of all would be at the service of each. A hostile
world apart within the world, admitting none of the ideas,
recognizing none of the laws of the world; submitting only
to the sense of necessity, obedient only from devotion; acting
all as one man in the interests of the comrade who should
claim the aid of the rest; a band of buccaneers with carriages
and yellow kid gloves; a close confederacy of men of extraordinary power, of amused and cool spectators of an artificial and petty world which they cursed with smiling lips;
conscious as they were that they could make all things bend
to their caprice, weave ingenious schemes of revenge, and
live with the life in thirteen hearts, to say nothing of the
unfailing pleasure of facing the world of men with a hidden
misanthropy, a sense that they were armed against their kind,
and could retire into themselves with one idea which the most
remarkable men had not,—all this constituted a religion of
pleasure and egoism which made fanatics of the Thirteen.
The history of the Society of Jesus was repeated for the
Devil's benefit. It was hideous and sublime.

The pact was made; and it lasted, precisely because it
seemed impossible. And so it came to pass that in Paris
there was a fraternity of thirteen men, each one bound, body
and soul, to the rest, and all of them strangers to each other
in the sight of the world. But evening found them gathered
together like conspirators, and then they had no thoughts
apart; riches, like the wealth of the Old Man of the Mountain,

they possessed in common; they had their feet in every salon, their hands in every strong box, their elbows in the streets, their heads upon all pillows, they did not scruple to help themselves at their pleasure. No chief commanded them, nobody was strong enough. The liveliest passion, the most urgent need took precedence—that was all. They were thirteen unknown kings; unknown, but with all the power and more than the power of kings; for they were both judges and executioners, they had taken wings that they might traverse the heights and depths of society, scorning to take any place in it, since all was theirs. If the author learns the reason of their abdication, he will communicate it.

And now the author is free to give those episodes in the History of the Thirteen which, by reason of the Parisian flavor of the details or the strangeness of the contrasts, possessed a peculiar attraction for him.

PARIS, 1831.

THE THIRTEEN

I.

FERRAGUS

CHEF DES DEVORANTS

To Hector Berlioz.

THERE are streets in Paris which have lost their character
as hopelessly as a man guilty of some shameful action;
there are likewise noble streets, streets that are simply honest
and nothing more, young streets as to whose morality the
public as yet has formed no opinion, and streets older than
the oldest dowager. Then there are deadly streets, respectable
streets, streets that are always clean, and streets that are invariably filthy; artisan, industrial, and commercial streets.
The streets of Paris, in short, possess human qualities, so that
you cannot help forming certain ideas of them on a first impression. There are low streets where you would not care to
linger, and streets in which you would like to live. Some,
like the Rue Montmartre, for instance, turn a fair front on
you at the first and end in a fish's tail. The Rue de la Paix
is a wide and imposing street, but it arouses none of the
nobly gracious thoughts which take a susceptible nature at
unawares in the Rue Royale, while it certainly lacks the ma-
jesty which pervades the Place Vendôme. If you take your walks abroad through the Ile Saint-Louis,
the loneliness of the spot, the dreary look of the houses and
great empty mansions is enough to account for the melancholy
which settles on your nerves. The Ile Saint-Louis, a corpse

no longer tenanted by farmers-general, is the Venice of Paris. The Place de la Bourse is garrulous, bustling, common; it is only beautiful by moonlight; an epitomized Paris in broad day, by night a dreamlike vision of ancient Greece.

Is not the Rue Traversière Saint-Honoré plainly a shameless street, with its villainous little houses a couple of windows in width, and vice, and crime, and misery on every floor? And there are thoroughfares with a north aspect, visited by the sun only three or four times in the year; deadly streets are they, where life is taken with impunity, and the law looks on and never interferes. In olden days the Parlement would probably have summoned the lieutenant of police to hear a little plain speaking, or at least they would have passed a vote of censure on the street, just as on another occasion they recorded their dissatisfaction with the perukes worn by the Chapter of Beauvais. Yet, M. Benoiston de Châteauneuf has shown conclusively that the mortality in certain streets is twice as high as the normal death-rate! And to sum up the matter in a single example, what is the Rue Fromenteau but a haunt of vice and murder?

These observations may be dark sayings for those who live beyond the bounds of Paris; but they will be apprehended at once by those students, thinkers, poets, and men of pleasure, who know the art of walking the streets of Paris, and reap a harvest of delights borne in on the tides of life that ebb and flow within her walls with every hour. For these, Paris is the most fascinating of monsters; here she is a pretty woman, there a decrepit pauper; some quarters are spick and span as the coins of a new reign, and a nook here and there is elegant as a woman of fashion.

A monster, indeed, is the great city, in every sense of the word. In the garrets you find, as it were, its brain full of knowledge and genius; the first floor is a digestive apparatus, and the shops below are unmistakable feet, whence all the busy foot-traffic issues.

Oh! what a life of incessant activity the monster leads! The last vibration of the last carriage returning from the ball has scarcely died away before Its arms begin to stir a little at the barriers, and the City gives itself a gradual shake. All the gates begin to yawn, turning on their hinges like the membranes of some gigantic lobster invisibly controlled by some thirty thousand men and women. Each one of these thirty thousand must live in the allotted six square feet of space which serves as kitchen, workshop, nursery, bedroom, and garden; each one is bound to see everything, while there is scarce light enough to see anything. Imperceptibly the monster's joints creak, the stir of life spreads, the street finds a tongue, and by noon it is alive everywhere, the chimneys smoke, the monster feeds, and with a roar It stretches out its myriad paws. 'Tis a wonderful sight! And yet, oh Paris! who has not marveled at thy dark passages, thy fitful gleams of light, thy deep, soundless blind alleys? They who have not heard thy murmurs between midnight and two o'clock in the morning, know nothing as yet of thy real poetry, of thy bizarre, broad contrasts.

There are a very few amateurs, amateurs are they that can keep a steady head and take their Paris with gusto; and these know the physiognomy of the city so well, that they know "even her spots, her blemishes, and her warts." Others may think of Paris as the monstrous marvel, as an astounding assemblage of brains and machinery in motion, as the City of a Hundred Thousand Romances, the head of the world. But for these who know her, Paris wears a dull or a gay face, she is ugly or fair, alive or dead; for them she is a living creature. Every room in a house is a lobe of the cellular tissue of the great courtesan, whose heart, and brain, and fantastic life they know to the uttermost. Therefore they are her lovers. They look up at a street corner, knowing that they shall see a clock-face; they tell a friend with an empty snuff-box to "take such and such a turning, and you will find a tobacco-nist's shop to the left, next door to a pastry-cook that has a pretty wife."

For poets of this order, a walk through Paris is an expensive luxury. How refuse to spend a few minutes in watching the dramas, the accidents, the faces, the picturesque chance effects which importune you in the streets of the restless Queen of Cities that goes clad in placards, yet can boast not one clean corner, so complacent is she to the vices of the French nation? Who has not left home in the morning for the uttermost ends of Paris, and recognized by dinner-time the futility of his efforts to get away from the centre? Such as these will pardon these vagrant beginnings, which, after all, may be summed up by one eminently profitable and novel observation (so far as any observation can be novel in Paris where there is nothing new, not even the statue set up yesterday, on which the street urchin has left his mark already).

Well, then—there are certain streets, unknown for the most part by fashionable people, there are certain districts and certain houses to which a woman of fashion cannot go, unless she wishes that the most cruelly injurious constructions shall be put upon her errand. If she is a wealthy woman with a carriage of her own, and if she chooses to go on foot, or disguised, through one of these slums, her reputation as an honest woman is compromised. If, furthermore, it should so happen that she is seen about nine o'clock in the evening, the conjectures which an observer may permit himself are like to have appalling consequences. And, finally, if the woman is young and pretty; if she is seen to enter a house in one of these neighborhoods; if the house has a long, dark, damp, and reeking passage entry; if, at the end of the passage, a feeble, flickering lamp lights up the features of a hideous crone with bony fingers—then, to tell the truth in the interests of young and pretty women, that woman is lost. She is at the mercy of the first man of her acquaintance who chances to meet her in these foul ways.

And there is a street in Paris where such an encounter may end in a most dreadful and ghastly tragedy, a tragedy of blood, a tragedy in the modern vein. Unluckily, the convincingness of the situation and the dramatic element in it will be lost, like the modern drama, upon all save the very few; and a sad pity it is that the tale must be told to a public that cannot fully appreciate the truth of the local color. Still, who can flatter himself that he will ever be understood? We all die unappreciated. It is the lot of women and of men of letters.

At half-past eight one February evening, thirteen years ago, a young man chanced to turn the corner of the Rue de Pagevin into the Rue des Vieux-Augustins precisely at the point where the Rue Soly enters it. Now, at that time there was not a wall in the Rue Pagevin but echoed a foul word; the Rue Soly was one of the narrowest and least practicable thoroughfares in Paris, not excepting the most frequented nooks in the most deserted streets of the city; and the young man came there by one of those chances that do not come twice in a lifetime. Arrived at this point, he was walking carelessly along when he saw a woman a few paces ahead of him, and fancied that he saw in her a vague resemblance to one of the prettiest women in Paris, a beautiful and modest woman whom he secretly and passionately loved; loved, too, without hope. She was married. In a moment his heart gave a bound. An intolerable heat, kindled in his diaphragm, spread through every vein. He felt a cold chill along his spine, a tingling sensation on the surface of his face.

He was young, he was in love, he knew Paris. His perspicacity would not allow him to shut his eyes to all the vile possibilities of the situation—a young, fair, and wealthy woman of fashion stealing along the street with a guilty, furtive step! That She should be in that filthy neighborhood at that hour of night!

· His love seems romantic, no doubt, and the more so because he was an officer in the Guards. Of a man in an infantry regiment the thing is not inconceivable; but as a cavalry officer high in the service, he belonged to a division of the army that most desires rapid conquests. The cavalry are vain of their uniform, but they are vainer still of their success with women. Nevertheless, the officer's love was a genuine passion that will seem great to many a young heart. He loved the woman because she was virtuous. Her virtues, her reserved grace, the saintliness that awed him,—these were the most precious treasures of his hidden passion. And she, in truth, was worthy of a Platonic love such as you sometimes find like a rare flower on the chronicler's page among the ruin and bloodshed of the Middle Ages. She was worthy to be the secret spring of all a young man's actions; the source of a love as high and pure as the blue heavens, a love without hope, to which a man clings because it never disappoints him, a love prodigal of uncontrolled delight, especially at an age when hearts are hot and imaginations poignant, and a man's eyes see very clearly.

There are strange, grotesque, inconceivable night effects to be seen in Paris; you cannot think, unless you have amused yourself with watching these, how fantastic a woman's shape can grow in the dusk. Some times the creature whom you follow by accident or design seems graceful and slender; sometimes a glimpse of a stocking, if it is very white, leads you to think that the outlines beneath are dainty and fine; a figure, muffled up, it may be, in a shawl or a pelisse, develops young luxuriant curves in the shadows; and as a last touch, the uncertain light from a shop-window or a street lamp lends the stranger a fleeting halo, an illusion which stirs and kindles imagination to go beyond the truth. And then, the senses are stirred, color and life is put into everything, the woman is transfigured; her outward form grows fairer; there are moments when she is a woman no longer, she is an evil spirit, a will-of-the-wisp, drawing you further and further by a glowing magnetism until you reach—some decent dwelling, and the poor housewife, terrified by your menacing approach, and quaking at the sound of a man's boots, promptly shuts the door in your face without giving you so much as a glance.

Suddenly the flickering light from a shoemaker's window fell across the woman in front; it struck just across the hollow of the back. Ah! surely those curves belonged to Her only among women! Who else knew that secret of chaste movement which all innocently brings the beauty of the most attractive shape into relief.

It was the same shawl and velvet bonnet that she wore in the morning. Not a speck on her gray stockings; not a trace of mud on her shoes. The shawl clung tightly about the outlines of her bust, vaguely moulding its exquisite contours; but the young man had seen those white shoulders in the ballroom, and he knew what a wealth of beauty was hidden beneath the shawl.

An intelligent observer can guess by the way in which a Parisienne wraps her shawl about her shoulders, by her manner of lifting her foot, on what mysterious errand she is bent. There is an indescribable tremor and lightness about her and her movements; she seems to weigh less, she walks on and on, or rather she threads her way like a spinning star, flitting, borne along by a thought, which the folds of her dress, the flutter of her skirts, betray.

The young man quickened his pace, passed, and turned his head to look at her—— Presto! She had disappeared down an entry, a wicket with a bell attached slammed and tinkled after her. He turned back and caught sight of her as she climbed the staircase at the end of the passage, not without obsequious greetings on the part of an old portress below. It was a crooked staircase, the lamplight fell full on the lowest steps, up which the lady sprang lightly and briskly, as an impatient woman might do.

"Why impatient?" he asked himself, as he went back to plant himself against the opposite wall. He gazed up, luckless wight, watching every story as narrowly as if he were a detective on the track of a conspirator.

It was a house like thousands of others in Paris, mean, commonplace, narrow, dingy, with three windows on each of the four floors. The shop and the entresol belonged to the shoemaker. The first-floor shutters were closed. Whither had the lady gone? He fancied that he heard the jingling of a door bell on the second floor. And, in fact, a light began to move in a room above, with two brightly illuminated windows, and presently appeared in a third window, hitherto in darkness, which seemed to belong to the parlor or dining-room. In a moment the vague shadow of a woman's bonnet appeared on the ceiling, the door was closed, the first room relegated to darkness, and the two further windows shone red as before. Just then a voice cried, *"Look out!"* and something struck against the young man's shoulder.

"You don't seem to mind in the least what you are about," said the gruff voice. It was a workman, carrying a long plank on his shoulder. He went by. The man might have been sent as a warning by Providence to ask the prying inquirer, "What are you meddling for? Mind your own business, and leave Parisiennes to their own little affairs."

The officer folded his arms; and being out of sight of every one, he allowed two angry tears to roll down his cheeks. The sight of these shadows moving across the windows was painful to him; he looked away up the Rue des Vieux-Augustins, and saw a hackney cab drawn up under a blind wall, at a distance from any house door or shop window.

Is it she? Or is it not? Life or death for a lover. And the lover waited in suspense for an age of twenty minutes. Then she came downstairs, and he knew past mistake that this was the woman whom he loved in his secret soul. Yet even now he tried to doubt. The fair stranger went to the cab and stepped into it.

"The house is always there," thought he; "I can search it at any time;" so he ran after the cab to make quite certain of the lady. Any remaining doubt was soon removed.

The vehicle stopped before a flower shop in the Rue de Richelieu, close to the Rue de Ménars. The lady alighted, entered the shop, sent out the fare to the cabman, and chose some marabouts. Feather plumes for that black hair of hers, with her dark beauty! She brought the feathers close to her face to judge of the effect. The officer fancied he could hear the shopwoman speaking.

"Nothing more becoming, madam, to a dark complexion; there is something rather too hard about the contours of a brunette; the marabouts impart just the fluffy touch which is wanting. Her Grace the Duchesse de Langeais says that the feathers lend something vague and Ossianic, and a great distinction to a face."

"Well, send them to me at once."

With that the lady tripped away round the corner into the Rue de Ménars and entered her own house. The door closed upon her, and the young lover, his hopes lost, and double misfortune, his cherished beliefs lost too, went through Paris like a drunken man, till before long he found himself at his own door, with no very clear knowledge how he came there. He flung himself into an easy-chair, rested his feet on the fire-dogs, and sat, with his head in his hands, while his soaked boots first dried and then scorched on the bars. It was a dreadful hour for him; he had come to one of those crises in a man's life when character is modified; and the course of action of the best of men depends upon the first lucky or unlucky step that he chances to take; upon Providence or Fate, whichever you choose.

He came of a good family, not that their nobility was of very ancient date; but there are so few old houses left in these days, that any young man comes of an old family. One of his ancestors had purchased the post of Councillor to the Parliament of Paris, and in course of time became President. His sons, with a fine fortune apiece, had entered the King's service, made good marriages, and arrived at Court. Then came the Revolution and swept them all away. One of them, however, an old and stubborn dowager, who had no mind to emigrate, remained in Paris, was put in prison, and lay there in danger of her life till the 9th Thermidor saved her, and finally she recovered her property. Afterwards, at an auspicious moment in 1804, she sent for her grandson Auguste de Maulincour, sole surviving scion of the Carbonnons de Maulincourt, and in the characters of mother, noble, and self-willed dowager brought him up with treble care.

At a later day, after the Restoration, Auguste de Maulincour, aged eighteen, entered the *Maison rouge,* followed the Princes to Ghent, received a commission in the Guards, and at three-and-twenty was a major in a cavalry regiment—a superb position which he owed to his grandmother. And indeed, in spite of her age, the old lady knew her way at Court remarkably well.

This twofold biography, with some variations, is substantially the history of every family of émigrés, when blessed with debts and possessions, dowagers and tact.

Mme. la Baronne de Maulincourt had a friend, the elderly Vidame de Pamiers, a sometime Commander of the Order of Malta. It was an eternal friendship of the kind that grows out of other ties formed sixty years ago, a friendship which nothing can destroy, because down in the depths of it lie secrets of the hearts of man and woman. These, if one had the time, would be well worth guessing; but such secrets, condensed into a score of lines, lose their savor; they should furnish forth instead some four volumes that might prove as interesting as *Le Doyen de Killerine*—a work which young men are wont to discuss and criticise and leave unread.

Auguste de Maulincour was connected, therefore, with the Faubourg Saint-Germain through his grandmother and the Vidame; and with a name that dated two centuries back, he could assume the airs and opinions of others who traced their descent from Clovis. Tall, pale, slender, and delicate-looking, a man of honor whose courage, moreover, was undoubted (for he had fought duels without hesitation for the least thing in life)—he had never yet been on a field of battle, and wore the Cross of the Legion of Honor at his buttonhole. He represented, as you see, one of the mistakes of the Restoration, perhaps one of its more pardonable mistakes.

The young manhood of the Restoration period was unlike the youth of any other epoch, in that it was placed between memories of the Empire on the one hand, and of exile on the other; between the old traditions of the Court and the conscientious bourgeois system of training for appointments; between bigotry and fancy dress balls; between a Louis XVIII., who saw nothing but the present moment, and a Charles X., who looked too far ahead. The young generation was always halting between two political creeds; blind and yet clairvoyant, bound to respect the will of the King, knowing the while that the Crown was entering on a mistaken policy. The older men counted the younger as naught, and jealously kept the reins of government in their enfeebled hands at a time when the Monarchy might have been saved by their withdrawal and the accession of that young France at whom the old-fashioned doctrinaires and émigrés of the Restoration are still pleased to laugh.

Auguste de Maulincour was one victim of the ideas that weighed upon the youth of those days. It was in this wise. The Vidame de Pamiers, even at the age of sixty-seven, was still a very lively personage, who had both seen and lived a great deal. He told a story well, he was a man of honor and gallantry, but so far as women were concerned he held the most detestable opinions. He fell in love, but he did not respect women. Women's honor, women's sentiments? Fiddle-de-dee! folly and make-believe. In the company of women he believed in them, did this *ci-devant* "monster"; he brought out their merits, he never contradicted a lady. But among friends, when women were in question, the Vidame laid it down as an axiom that the whole duty of a young man was to deceive women and to carry on several intrigues at once; and that when a young man attempted to meddle with affairs of State, he made a gross mistake.

It is vexatious to be obliged to sketch such a hackneyed character. Where has he not appeared? Is he not literally almost as worn out as the Imperial Grenadier? But over M. de Maulincour the Vidame exercised an influence which must be recorded; he was a moralist after his own fashion, and he used to try to convert the young man to the doctrines of the great age of gallantry.

As for the dowager, she was a tender, pious woman, placed between her Vidame and God; a pattern of grace and sweetness, but none the less endowed with a persistence which never went beyond the bounds of good taste, and always triumphed in the end. She had tried to preserve her grandson in all the fair illusions of life; she had brought him up on the best principles; she had given him all her own delicacy of feeling, and had made a diffident man of him, and to all appearance an absolute fool. His boy's sensibility, untouched by contact with the world, had met with no rubs without; so modest, so keenly sensitive was it, that actions and maxims to which the world attaches no importance grieved him sorely. He felt ashamed of his sensitiveness, hid it beneath a show of assurance, and suffered in silence, laughing in company at things which he alone in his secret heart admired. And therefore he was mistaken in his choice; for by a common freak of Fate he, the man of mild melancholy, who saw love in its spiritual aspects, must needs fall in love with a woman who detested German *sensiblerie*. He began to distrust himself. He grew moody, hugged himself on his troubles, and made moan because he was not understood. And then—since we always desire a thing more vehemently because it is hard to win—he continued to worship women with the ingenious tenderness and feline delicacy of which they possess the secret; perhaps, too, they prefer to keep the monopoly of it. And, indeed, though women complain that men love amiss, they have very little taste for the semi-feminine nature in man. Their whole superiority consists in making the man believe that he is their inferior in love; for which reason they are quite ready to discard a lover when he is experienced enough to rob them of the fears in which they choose to deck themselves, to relieve them of the delicious torments of feigned jealousy, the troubles of disappointed hopes and vain suspense, and the whole train of dear feminine miseries, in short. Women hold Grandisons in abhorrence. What is more contrary to their nature than a peaceful and perfect love? They must have emotions. Bliss without storms for them is not bliss at all. A soul great enough to bring the Infinite into love is as uncommon among women as genius among men. A great passion is as rare as a masterpiece. Outside this love there lies nothing but arrangements and passing excitations, contemptible, like all petty things.

In the midst of the secret disasters of his heart, while he

was seeking some one who should understand him (that quest, by the way, is the lover's folly of our time), Auguste found a perfect woman—a woman with that indescribable touch of sacredness and holiness which inspires such reverence that love needs all the support of a long intimacy to declare itself. He found her in a circle as far as possible from his own, in the second sphere of that financial world in which great capitalists take the first place.

Then Auguste gave himself up wholly to the bliss of the most moving and profound of passions; a purely contemplative love—a love made up of uncounted repressed longings, of shades of passion so vague, so deep, so fugitive, so vivid, that it is hard to find a comparison for them; they are like sweet scents, or sunlight, or cloud shadows, like all things that shine forth for a moment in the outer world to vanish, revive, and die, and leave a long wake of emotion in the heart. When a man is young enough to conceive melancholy and far-off hopes, to see in woman something more than a woman, can any greater happiness befall him than this—of loving so well that the mere contact of a white glove, the light touch of a woman's hair, the sound of a voice, the chance of one look, fills him with a joy outpassing a fortunate lover's ecstasy of possession? And for this reason, none but slighted, shy, unattractive, unhappy men and women, unknown lovers, know all that there is in the sound of the voice of the one whom they love. It is because those fire-laden vibrations of the air have their source and origin in the soul itself that they bring hearts into communication with such violence, such lucid thought transference. So little misleading are they, that a single modulation is often a revelation in itself. What enchantment is poured forth upon a poet's heart by the musical resonance of a low voice! What freshness it spreads through his soul, what visions it summons up! Love is in the voice before the eyes make confession.

Auguste, a poet after the manner of lovers—for there are poets who feel and poets who express, and the former are the happier—Auguste had known the sweetness of all these early joys, so far-reaching, so abundant. *She* was the possessor of such an entrancing voice as the most guileful of women might covet, that she might deceive others at her pleasure; hers were those silver notes, low only to the ear, that peal aloud through the heart, soothing the tumult and unrest that they stir.

And this was the woman who had gone at night to the Rue Soly in the neighborhood of the Rue Pagevin! He had seen her stealing into a house of ill-fame; and that most magnificent of passions had been brought low. The Vidame's reasoning triumphed.

"If she is false to her husband, we will both avenge ourselves," said Auguste. And there was still love left in that *if*. The suspended judgment of Cartesian philosophy is a homage always due to virtue. The clocks struck ten; and Auguste de Maulincour bethought himself that the woman he loved must surely be going to a dance at a house that he knew. He dressed, went thither, and made a furtive survey of the rooms. Mme. de Nucingen, seeing him thus intent, came to speak to him.

"You are looking for Mme. Jules; she has not come yet."

"Good evening, dear," said a voice.

Mme. de Nucingen and Auguste both turned. There stood Mme. Jules dressed in white, simple and noble, wearing those very feathers which the Baron had watched her choose in the shop. That voice of Love went to his heart. If he had only known how to assert the slightest claim to be jealous of the woman before him, he would have turned her to stone then and there with the exclamation, "Rue Soly!" But he, a stranger, might have repeated those words a hundred times in Mme. Jules' ear, and she in astonishment would merely ask him what he meant. He stared at her with dazed eyes.

Ill-natured men who scoff at everything may, perhaps, find it highly amusing to discover a woman's secret, to know that her chastity is a lie, that there are strange thoughts in the depths beneath the quiet surface, and an ugly tragedy behind the pure forehead. But there are others, no doubt, who are saddened at heart by it; and many of the scoffers, when at home and alone with themselves, curse the world, and despise such a woman. This was how Auguste de Maulincour felt as he confronted Mme. Jules. It was a strange position. He and this woman exchanged a few words seven or eight times in a season—that was all; yet he was charging her with stolen pleasure of which she knew nothing, and pronouncing judgment without telling her of the accusation.

Many a young man has done the same and gone home broken-hearted because all is over between him and some woman whom he once worshiped in his heart, and now scorns in his inmost soul. Then follow soliloquies heard of none, spoken to the walls of some lonely refuge; storms raised and quieted in the heart's depths, wonderful scenes of man's inner life which still await their painter.

M. Jules Desmarets made the round of the rooms, while his wife took a seat. But she seemed embarrassed in some way; and as she chatted with her neighbor, she stole a glance now and again at her husband. M. Jules Desmarets was the Baron de Nucingen's stockbroker. And now for the history of the husband and wife.

M. Desmarets, five years before his marriage, was a clerk in a stockbroker's office; he had nothing in the world but his slender salary. But he was one of those men whom misfortune teaches to know life in a very few lessons, men who strike out their line and keep to it persistently as an insect; like other obstinate creatures he could sham death if anything stopped him, and weary out the patience of opponents by the patience of the woodlouse. Young as he was, he possessed all the republican virtues of the poor; he was sober, he never wasted his time, he set his face against pleasure. He was waiting. Nature, besides, had given him the immense advantage of a prepossessing exterior. His calm, pure forehead, the outlines of his placid yet expressive features, the simplicity of his manners, and everything about him, told of a hard-working, uncomplaining existence, of the high personal dignity which inspires awe in others, and of that quiet nobleness of spirit which is equal to all situations. His modesty impressed those who knew him with a certain respect.

It was a solitary life, however, that he led in the midst of Paris. Society he saw only by glimpses during the few minutes spent on holidays in his employer's drawing-room. And in him, as in most men who lead such a life, there were astonishing depths of passion, inward forces too great to be brought into play by small occasions. His narrow means compelled him to live like an ascetic, and he subdued his fancies with hard work. After growing pale over figures, he sought relaxation in a dogged effort to acquire the wider knowledge so necessary to any man that would make his mark in these days, whether in business, at the bar, in politics or letters. The one reef in the careers of these finer natures is their very honesty. They come across some penniless girl, fall in love, and marry her, and afterwards wear out their lives in the struggle for existence, with want on the one hand, love on the other. Housekeeping bills will extinguish the loftiest ambition. Jules Desmarets went straight ahead upon that reef.

One evening, at his employer's house, he met a young lady of the rarest beauty. Love rapidly made such havoc as a passion can make in a lonely and slighted heart, when an unhappy creature's affections have been starved, and the fair hours of youth consumed by continual work. So certain are they to love in earnest, so swiftly does their whole being centre itself upon the woman to whom they are attracted, that when she is present they are conscious of exquisite sensations, in none of which she shares. This is the most flattering form of egoism for the woman who can see, beneath the apparent immobility of passion, the feeling stirred in depths so remote that it is long before it reappears at the human surface. Such unfortunates as these are anchorites in the heart of Paris; they know all the joys of anchorites; sometimes, too, they may yield to their temptations; but it still more frequently happens that they are thwarted, betrayed, and misinterpreted; and only very seldom are they permitted to gather the sweet fruits of the love that seems to them like a power dropped down from heaven.

A smile from his wife, a mere modulation of her voice, was enough to give Jules Desmarets a conception of the infinite of love. Happily the concentrated fire of passion within revealed itself artlessly to the woman for whom it burned. And these two human creatures loved each other devoutly. To sum up all in a few words, they took each other by the hand without a blush, and went through the world together as two children, brother and sister, might pass through a crowd that makes way admiringly for them.

The young lady was in the odious position in which selfishness places some children at their birth. She had no recognized status; her name, Clémence, and her age were attested, not by a certificate of birth, but by a declaration made before a notary. As to her fortune, it was trifling. Jules Desmarets, hearing these bad tidings, was the happiest of men. If Clémence had belonged to some wealthy family, he would have despaired; but she was a poor love-child, the offspring of a dark, illicit passion. They were married. This was the beginning of a series of pieces of good fortune for Jules. Everybody envied him his luck; jealous tongues alleged that he succeeded by sheer good fortune, and left his merits and ability out of account.

Clémence's mother, nominally her godmother, bade Jules purchase a stockbroker's connection a few days after the wedding, promising to secure all the necessary capital. Such connections were still to be bought at moderate prices. On the great lady's recommendation, a wealthy capitalist made proposals on the most favorable terms to Jules Desmarets that evening in the stockbroker's own drawing-room, lent him money enough to exploit his business, and by the next day the fortunate clerk had bought his employer's connection.

In four years Jules Desmarets was one of the wealthiest members of his fraternity. Important clients had been added to the number of those left him by his predecessor. He inspired unbounded confidence; and from the manner in which business came to him, it was impossible but that he should recognize some occult influence due to his wife's mother, or, as he believed, to the mysterious protection of Providence.

Three years after the marriage Clémence lost her god-mother. By that time M. Jules, so called to distinguish him from his elder brother, whom he had established in Paris as a notary, was in receipt of an income of two hundred thousand livres. There was not such another happy couple in Paris. A five years' course of such unwonted love had been troubled but once by a slander, for which M. Jules took a signal vengeance. One of his old associates said that M. Jules owed his success to his wife, and that influence in high places had been dearly bought. The inventor of the slander was killed in the duel. A passionate love so deeply rooted that it stood the test of marriage was much admired in society, though some women were displeased by it. It was pretty to see them together; they were respected, and made much of on all sides. M. and Mme. Jules were really popular, perhaps because there is no pleasanter sight than happy love; but they never stayed long in crowded rooms, and escaped to their nest as soon as they could, like two strayed doves.

The nest, however, was a fine large house in the Rue de Ménars, in which artistic feeling tempered the luxury which the city man is always supposed to display. Here, also, M. and Mme. Jules entertained splendidly. Social duties were somewhat irksome to them; but, nevertheless, Jules Desmarets submitted to such exactions, knowing that sooner or later a family will need acquaintances. He and his wife lived like plants in a hothouse in a stormy world. With very natural delicacy, Jules carefully kept the slander from his wife's knowledge as well as the death of the man that had almost troubled their felicity.

Mme. Jules, with her artistic temper and refinement, had inclinations towards luxury. In spite of the terrible lesson of the duel, there were incautious women to hint in whispers that Mme. Jules must often be pinched for money. Her husband allowed her twenty thousand francs for her dress and pocket-money, but this could not possibly be enough, they said, for her expenses. And, indeed, she was often more daintily dressed in her own home than in other people's houses. She only cared to adorn herself for her husband's eyes, trying in this way to prove to him that for her he was all the world. This was love indeed, pure love, and more than this, it was happy as clandestine love sanctioned by the world can be. M. Jules was still his wife's lover, and more in love every day. Everything in his wife, even her caprices, made him happy. When she had no new fancy to gratify, he felt as much disturbed as if this had been a symptom of bad health.

It was against this passion that Auguste de Maulincour, for his misfortune, had dashed himself. He loved Clémence Desmarets to distraction. And yet even with a supreme passion in his heart he was not ridiculous, and he lived the regular garrison life, yet even with a glass of champagne in his hand he wore an abstracted air. His was the quiet scorn of existence, the clouded countenance worn alike on various pretexts by jaded spirits, by men but little satisfied with the hollowness of their lives, and by the victims of pulmonary disease or heart troubles. A hopeless love or a distaste for existence constitutes a sort of social position nowadays.

To take a queen's heart by storm were perhaps a more hopeful enterprise than a madly-conceived passion for a woman happily married. Auguste de Maulincour had sufficient excuse for his gravity and dejection. A queen has always the vanity of her power; her height above her lover places her at a disadvantage; but a well-principled bourgeoise, like a hedgehog or an oyster, is encompassed about with awkward defences.

At this particular moment Auguste stood near his undeclared lady. She, certainly, was incapable of carrying on a double intrigue. There sat Mme. Jules in childlike composure, the least guileful of women, gentle, full of queenly serenity. What depths can there be in human nature? The Baron, before addressing her, kept his eyes on husband and

wife in turn. What reflections did he not make! In a minute's space he recomposed a second version of Young's *Night
Thoughts.* And yet—the rooms were filled with dance music,
and the light of hundreds of wax tapers streamed down upon
them. It was a banker's ball, one of those insolent fêtes by
which the world of dull gold attempted to rival that other
world of gilded rank and ormolu, the world where the high-
born Faubourg Saint-Germain was laughing yet, all unconscious that a day was approaching when capitalists would invade the Luxembourg and seat a king on the throne. Con-
spiracy used to dance in those days, giving as little thought
to future bankruptcies of Power as to failures ahead in the
financial world. M. le Baron de Nucingen's gilded salons
wore that look of animation which a fête in Paris is wont to
wear; there is gaiety, at any rate, on the surface. The wit
of the cleverer men infects the fools, while the beaming expression characteristic of the latter spreads over the countenances of their superiors in intellect; and the whole room
is brightened by the exchange. But gaiety in Paris is always
a little like a display of fireworks; pleasure, coquetry, and
wit all coruscate, and then die out like spent rockets. To-
morrow morning, wit, coquetry, and pleasure are put off and
forgotten.

"Heigho!" thought Auguste, as he came to a conclusion,
"are women really after all as the Vidame sees them? Certain it is that of all the women dancing here to-night, not
one seems so irreproachable as Mme. Jules. And Mme. Jules
goes to the Rue Soly!"

The Rue Soly was like a disease, the mere word made his
heart contract.

"Do you never dance, madame?" he began.

"This is the third time that you have asked me that question this winter," she answered, smiling.

"But perhaps you have never given me an answer."

"That is true."

"I knew quite well that you were false, like all women——"
Mme. Jules laughed again.

"Listen to me, monsieur. If I told you my real reason for not dancing, it would seem ridiculous to you. There is no insincerity, I think, in declining to give private reasons at which people usually laugh."

"Any confidence, madame, implies a degree of friendship of which I, no doubt, am unworthy. But it is impossible that you should have any but noble secrets, and can you think me capable of irreverent jesting?"

"Yes," she said. "You, like the rest of men, laugh at our purest feelings and misconstrue them. Besides, I have no secrets. I have a right to love my husband before all the world; I am proud of it, I tell you; and if you laugh at me when I say that I never dance with any one else, I shall have the worst opinion of your heart."

"Have you never danced with any one but your husband since your marriage?"

"No, monsieur. I have leaned on no other arm, no one else has come very close to me."

"Has not your doctor so much as felt your pulse?"

"Ah, well, now you are laughing."

"No, madame, I admire you because I can understand.— But you suffer others to hear your voice, to see you, to . . . In short, you permit our eyes to rest admiringly on you——"

"Ah, these things trouble me," she broke in. "If it were possible for husband and wife to live like lover and mistress, I would have it so; for in that case——"

"In that case, how came you to be out, on foot and disguised, a few hours ago, in the Rue Soly?"

"What is the Rue Soly?" asked she, not a trace of emotion in her clear voice, not the faintest quiver in her features. She did not redden, she was quite composed.

"What! You did not go up the stairs to the second floor in a house at the corner of the Rue des Vieux-Augustins and the Rue Soly? You had not a cab waiting for you ten paces away? and you did not return to a shop in the Rue de Richelieu, where you chose the marabouts in your hair at this moment?"

"I did not leave my house this evening." She told the lie with an imperturbable laughing face; she fanned herself as she spoke; but any one who could have laid a hand on her girdle at the back, might perhaps have felt that it was damp. Auguste bethought himself of the Vidame's teaching.

"Then it was some one extraordinarily like you," he rejoined with an air of belief.

"Sir," said she, "if you are capable of following a woman about to detect her secrets, you will permit me to tell you that such a thing is wrong, very wrong, and I do you the honor of declining to believe it of you."

The Baron turned away, took up his position before the hearth, and seemed thoughtful. He bent his head, but his eyes were fixed stealthily upon Mme. Jules. She had forgotten the mirrors on the walls, and glanced towards him two or three times with an evident dread in her eyes. Then she beckoned to her husband, laid a hand upon his arm, and rose to go through the rooms. As she passed M. de Maulincour, who was talking with a friend, he said aloud as if in answer to a question:

"A woman that certainly will not sleep quietly to-night——"

Mme. Jules stopped, flung him a crushing, disdainful glance, and walked away, all unaware that one more such glance, if her husband chanced to see it, would imperil her happiness and the lives of two men.

Auguste, consumed with rage smouldering in the depths of his soul, soon afterwards left the room, vowing to get to the bottom of this intrigue. He looked round for Mme. Jules before he went, but she had disappeared. Here were the elements of a tragedy suddenly put into a young head, an eminently romantic head, as is generally the case with those who have not realized their dreamed-of love to the full. He adored Mme. Jules in a new aspect; he loved her with the fury of jealousy, with the agonized frenzy of despair. The woman was false to her husband; she had come down to the ordinary level. Auguste might give himself up to all the felicity of success, imagination opened out for him the vast field of the transports of possession. In short, if he had lost an angel, he had found the most tantalizing of devils. He lay down to build castles in the air, and to justify Mme. Jules. Some errand of charity had brought her there, he told himself, but he did not believe it. He made up his mind to devote himself entirely to the investigation of the causes and motives involved in this mysteriously hidden knot. It was a romance to read; or rather it was a play to act, and he was cast for a part in it.

It is a very fine thing to play the detective for one's own ends and for passion's sake. Is it not an honest man's chance of enjoying the amusements of the thief? Still, you must be prepared to boil with helpless rage, to growl with impatience, to stand in mud till your feet are frozen, to shiver and burn and choke down false hopes. You must follow up any indication to an end unknown; and miss your chance, storm, improvise lamentations and dithyrambs for your own benefit, and utter insensate exclamations before some harmless passerby, who stares back at you in amazement. You take to your heels and overturn good souls with their apple-baskets, you wait and hang about under a window, you make guesses by the running hundred. Still it is sport, and Parisian sport; sport with all its accessories save dogs, and guns, and tally-ho. Nothing, except some moments in the gambler's life, can compare with it. A man's heart must needs be swelling with love and revenge before he will lie in ambush ready to spring like a tiger on his prey; before he can find enjoyment in watching all that goes on in the quarter; for interest of many kinds abounds in Paris without the added pleasure of stalking game. How should one soul suffice a man for all this? What is it but a life made up of a thousand passions, a thousand feelings, and thoughts?

Auguste de Maulincour flung himself heart and soul into this feverish life, because he felt all its troubles and joys. He went about Paris in disguise; he watched every corner of the Rue Pagevin and the Rue des Vieux-Augustins. He ran like a lamplighter from the Rue de Ménars to the Rue

Soly, and back again from the Rue Soly to the Rue de Ménars, all unconscious of the punishment or the reward in store
for so many pains, such measures, such shifts! And even
so, he had not yet reached the degree of impatience which
gnaws the vitals and brings the sweat to a man's brow; he
hung about in hope. It occurred to him that Mme. Jules
would scarcely risk another visit for some few days after de-
tection. So he devoted those first few days to an initiation
into the mysteries of the street. Being but a novice in the
craft, he did not dare to go to the house itself and question
the porter and the shoemaker; but he had hopes of securing a
post of observation in rooms exactly opposite that inscrutable
second floor. He made a careful survey of the ground; he
was trying to reconcile caution with impatience, his love,
and the secret.

By the beginning of March he was in the midst of his preparations for making a great decisive move, when official duties
summoned him from his chessboard one afternoon about four
o'clock, after an assiduous course of sentry-duty, for which
he was not a whit the wiser. In the Rue Coquillière he was
caught by one of the heavy showers which swell the stream in
the kennels in a moment, while every drop falling into the
roadside puddles, raises a bell-shaped splash. A foot-pas-
senger in such a predicament is driven to take refuge in a
shop or café if he can afford to pay for shelter; or, at urgent
need, to hurry into some entry, the asylum of the poor and
shabbily dressed. How is it that as yet no French painter
has tried to give us that characteristic group, a crowd of Parisians weatherbound under an archway? Where will you find
better material for a picture?

To begin with, is there not the pensive or philosophical pedestrian who finds a pleasure in watching the slantwise
streaks of rain in the air against the gray background of sky
—a fine chased work something like the whimsical shapes
taken by spun glass? Or he looks up at the whirlpools of
white water, blown by the wind like a luminous dust over the
house-roofs, or at the fitful discharges of the wet, foaming

stack-pipes. There are, in fact, a thousand nothings to wonder at, and the idlers are studying them with keen relish
although the owner of the premises treats them to occasional
thumps from the broom-handle.

There is the chatty person who grumbles and talks with the
porter's wife, while she rests on her broom as a grenadier leans
on his gun; there is the poverty-stricken individual glued fan-
tastically to the wall—he has nothing to dread from such contact; for his rags, they are already so well acquainted with
the street; there is the man of education who studies, spells
out, or even reads the advertisements, and never gets to the
end of them; there is the humorous person who laughs at
mud-bedraggled women, and makes eyes at the people in the
windows opposite; there is the mute refugee that scans every
casement on every floor, and the working man or woman with
a mallet or a bundle, as the case may be, translating the
shower into probable losses or gains. Then there is the amiable man, who bounces in like a bombshell with an "Oh! what
weather, gentlemen!" and raises his hat to the company; and,
finally, there is your true Parisian bourgeois, a weatherwise
citizen who never comes out without his umbrella; he knew
beforehand that it was going to rain, but he came out in spite
of his wife's advice, and now he is sitting in the porter's
chair.

Each member of this chance assembled group watches the
sky in his own characteristic fashion, and then skips away for
fear of splashing his boots, or goes because he is in a hurry
and sees other citizens walking past in spite of wind and
weather, or because the courtyard is damp and fit to give you
your death of cold—the selvedge, as the saying goes, being
worse than the cloth. Every one has his own reasons for going, until no one is left but the prudent pedestrian, who waits
to see a few blue chinks among the clouds before he goes on
his way.

M. de Maulincour, therefore, took refuge with a tribe of
foot-passengers under the porch of an old-fashioned house
with a courtyard not unlike a gigantic chimney shaft. There

were so many stories rising to a height on all sides, and the four plastered walls, covered with greenish stains and saltpetre ooze, were traversed by such a multitude of gutters and spouts, that they would have put you in mind of the cascades of St. Cloud. From every direction came the sound of falling water; it foamed, splashed, and gurgled; it gushed forth in streams, or black, or white, or blue, or green; it hissed and gathered volume under the broom wielded by the porter's wife, a toothless crone of great experience in storms, who seemed to bless the waters as she swept down a host of odds and ends into the street. A curious inventory of the rubbish would have told you a good deal about the lives and habits of the lodgers on every floor. There were tea-leaves, cuttings of chintz, discolored and spoiled petals of artificial flowers, vegetable refuse, paper and scraps of metal. Every stroke of the old woman's broom laid bare the heart of the gutter, that black channel paved with chessboard squares, on which every porter wages desperate war. The luckless lover gazed intently at this picture, one of the many thousands which bustling Paris composes every day; but he saw it all with unseeing eyes, until he looked up and found himself face to face with a man that had just come in.

This man was, at any rate to all appearance, a beggar. Not a Parisian beggar, that human creature for which human speech has found no name as yet; but a novel type, a beggar cast in some different mould, and apart from all the associations called up by that word. The stranger was not by any means remarkable for that peculiarly Parisian character, which frequently startles us in those unfortunates whom Charlet drew, and often enough with a rare felicity; the Paris beggar with the coarse face plastered with mud, the red bulbous nose, the toothless but menacing mouth, the eyes lighted up by a profound intelligence which seems out of place—a servile, terrific figure. Some of the impudent vagabonds have mottled, chapped, and veined countenances, rugged foreheads, and thin, dirty locks that put you in mind of a worn-out wig lying in the gutter. Jolly in their degradation and degraded amid their jollity, debauchery has set its unmistakable mark on them, they hurl their silence at you like a reproach, their attitude expresses appalling thoughts. They are ruthless, are these dwellers between beggary and crime; they circle at a safe distance round the gallows, steering clear of the law in the midst of vice, and vicious within the bounds of law. While they often provoke a smile, they set you thinking.

One, for instance, represents stunted civilization; he comprehends it all, thieves' honor, patriotism, and manhood, with the perverse ingenuity of the common criminal and the subtlety of kid-gloved rascality. Another is resigned to his lot; he is past master in mimicry, but a dull creature. None of them are exempt from passing fancies for work and thrift; but the social machinery thrusts them down into their filth, without caring to discover whether there may not be poets, or great men, or brave men, or a whole wonderful organization among the beggars in the streets, those gypsies of Paris. Like all masses of men who have suffered, the beggar tribes are supremely good and superlatively wicked; they are accustomed to endure nameless ills, and a fatal power keeps them on a level with the mud of the streets. And every one of them has a dream, a hope, a happiness of his own, which takes the shape of gambling, or the lottery, or drink.

There was nothing of this strange life about the man who was propping himself, very much at his ease, against the wall opposite M. de Maulincour; he looked like a fancy portrait sketched by an ingenious artist on the back of some canvas returned to the studio.

He was lank and lean; his leaden-hued visage revealed glacial depths of thought; his ironical bearing, and a dark look, which plainly conveyed his claim to treat every man as his equal, dried up any feeling of compassion in the hearts of the curious. His complexion was a dingy white; his wrinkled, hairless head bore a vague resemblance to a block of granite. A few grizzled, lank locks on either side of his face straggled over the collar of a filthy greatcoat buttoned up to the chin. There was something of a Voltaire about him, something too

of a Don Quixote; melancholy, scornful, sarcastic, full of philosophical ideas, but half insane. Apparently he wore no shirt.
His beard was long. His shabby black cravat was so slit and
worn, that it left his neck on exhibition, and a protuberant,
deeply furrowed throat, on which the black veins stood out
like cords. There were wide, dark bruised circles about his
eyes. He must have been at least sixty years old. His hands
were white and clean. His shoes were full of holes, and trod-
den down at the heels. A pair of much mended blue trousers,
covered with a kind of pale fluff, added to the squalor of his
appearance.

Perhaps the man's wet clothes exhaled a nauseous smell;
perhaps at any time he had about him that odor of poverty
peculiar to Paris slums—for slums, like offices, vestries, and
hospitals, have a special smell, and a stale, fetid, unimaginable reek it is. At any rate, the man's neighbors edged away
and left him alone. He glanced round at them, and then at
the officer; it was an unmoved, expressionless look, the look
for which M. de Talleyrand was so famous, a survey made by
lack-lustre eyes with no warmth in them. Such a look is an
inscrutable veil beneath which a strong mind can hide deep
feeling, and the most accurate calculations as to men, affairs,
and events. Not a wrinkle deepened in his countenance.
Mouth and forehead were alike impassive, but his eyes fell,
and there was something noble, almost tragic, in their slow
movement. A whole drama lay in that droop of the withered
eyelids.

The sight of this stoical face started M. de Maulincour upon
those musings that begin with some commonplace question
and wander off into a whole world of ideas before they end.
The storm was over and gone. M. de Maulincour saw no
more of the man than the skirts of his great-coat trailing on
the curbstone; but as he turned to go, he saw that a letter had
just dropped at his feet, and guessed that it belonged to the
stranger, for he had noticed that he put a bandana handkerchief back into his pocket. M. de Maulincour picked up the
letter to return it to its owner, and unthinkingly read the
address:

A Mosieur.

Mosieur Ferragusse,

Rue des Grands-Augustins, au coing de la
                              Rue Soly.
                                        Paris.

There was no stamp on the letter, and at sight of the direction M. de Maulincour hesitated to return it; for there are few passions which will not turn base in the long length. Some presentiment of the opportuneness of the treasure trove crossed the Baron's mind. He would keep the letter, and so acquire a right to enter the mysterious house, never doubting but that the man lived therein. Even now a suspicion, vague as the beginnings of daylight, connected the stranger with Mme. Jules. Jealous lovers will suppose anything; and it is by this very process of supposing everything and selecting the more probable conjectures that examining magistrates, spies, lovers, and observers get at the truth which they have an interest in discovering.

"Does the letter belong to him? Is it from Mme. Jules?"

His uneasy imagination flung a host of questions to him at once, but at the first words of the letter he smiled. Here it follows words for word in the glory of its artless phrases; it was impossible to add anything to it, and short of omitting the letter itself, nothing could be taken away. It has been necessary, however, to revise the orthography and the punctuation; for in the original there are neither commas nor stops, nor so much as a note of exclamation, a fact that strikes at the root of the system by which modern authors endeavor to render the effect of the great disasters of every kind of passion:—

"Henry" (so it ran), "of all the things that I have had to give up for your sake, this is the hardest, that I mayn't give you news of myself. There is a voice that I must obey, which tells me I ought to let you know all the wrong you've done me. I know beforehand that you are that hardened by vice

that you will not stoop to pity me. Your heart must be deaf
to all feeling; is it not deaf to the cry of nature? Not that
it matters much. I am bound to let you know the degree to
which you are to blame, and the horror of the position in
which you have put me. You knew how I suffered for my
first fall, Henry, yet you could bring me to the same pass
again, and leave me in my pain and despair. Yes, I own I
used to think you loved and respected me, and that helped me
to bear up. And now what is left to me? I have lost all that
I cared most about, all that I lived for, friends, and relations, and character, and all through you. I have given up
everything for you, and now I have nothing before me but
shame and disgrace and, I don't blush to say it, want. It
only needed your scorn and hatred to make my misery complete; and now I have that as well, I shall have courage to
carry out my plans. I have made up my mind—it's for the
credit of my family—I shall put an end to my troubles. You
must not think hardly of the thing that I am going to do,
Henry. It is wicked, I know, but I can't help myself. No
help, no money, no sweetheart to comfort me—can I live? No,
I can't. What must be, must. So in two days, Henry, two
days from now, your Ida will not be worthy of your respect;
but take back the solemn promise I made you, so as I may
have an easy conscience, for I shall not be unworthy of your
friendship. Oh, Henry, my friend, for I shall never change
to you, promise to forgive me for the life I'm going to lead.
It is love that gives me courage, and it is love that will keep
me right. My heart will be so full of your image, that I shall
still be true to you. I pray Heaven on my bended knees not
to punish you for all the wrong you have done, for I feel that
there is only one thing wanting among my troubles, and that
is the pain of knowing that you are unhappy. In spite of my
plight, I will not take any help from you. If you had cared
about me, I might have taken anything as coming from friendship; but my soul rises up against a kindness as comes from
pity, and I should demean myself more by taking it than him
that offered it. I have one favor to ask. I don't know how

long I shall have to stop with Mme. Meynardie, but be generous enough to keep out of my sight there. Your last two visits hurt me so that it was a long time before I got over it; but I don't mean to go into any particulars of your behavior in that respect. You hate me; the words are written on my heart, and freeze it with cold. Alas! just when I want all my courage, my wits desert me. Henry dear, before I put this bar between us, let me know for the last time that you respect me still; write to me, send me an answer, say that you respect me if you don't love me any more. I shall always be able to look you in the face, but I don't ask for a sight of you; I am so weak, and I love you so, that I don't know what I might do. But, for pity's sake, write me a line at once; it will give me courage to bear my misery. Farewell, you have brought all my troubles upon me, but you are the one friend that my heart chose, and will never forget.   IDA."

This girl's life, her disappointed love, her ill-starred joys, her grief, her dreadful resignation to her lot, the story summed up in so few words, produced a moment's effect upon M. de Maulincour. He asked himself, as he read the obscure but essentially Parisian tragedy written upon the soiled sheet, whether this Ida might not be connected in some way with Mme. Jules; whether the assignation that he chanced to witness that evening was not some charitable effort on her part. Could that aged, poverty-stricken man be Ida's betrayer? . . . The thing bordered on the marvelous. Amusing himself in a maze of involved and incompatible ideas, the Baron reached the neighborhood of the Rue Pagevin just in time to see a cab stop at the end of the Rue des Vieux-Augustins nearest the Rue Montmartre. Every cabman on the stand had something to say to the new arrival.

"Can *she* be in it?" he thought.

His heart beat with hot, feverish throbs. He pushed open the wicket with the tinkling bell, but he lowered his head as he entered; he felt ashamed of himself, a voice in his inmost soul cried, "Why meddle in this mystery?"

At the top of a short flight of steps he confronted the old woman.

"M. Ferragus?"

"Don't know the name——"

"What! Doesn't M. Ferragus live here?"

"No name of the sort in the house."

"But, my good woman——"

"I'm not a 'good woman,' sir, I am a portress."

"But, madame, I have a letter here for M. Ferragus."

"Oh! if you have a letter, sir," said she, with a change of tone, "that is quite another thing. Will you just let me look at your letter?"

Auguste produced the folded sheet. The old woman shook her head dubiously over it, hesitated, and seemed on the point of leaving her lodge to acquaint the mysterious Ferragus with this unexpected incident. At last she said, "Very well, go upstairs, sir. You ought to know your way up——"

Without staying to answer a remark which the cunning crone possibly meant as a trap, M. de Maulincour bounded up the stairs and rang loudly at the second-floor door. His lover's instinct told him, *"She* is here."

The stranger of the archway, the man who "had brought Ida's troubles upon her," answered the door himself, and showed a clean countenance, a flowered gown, a pair of white flannel trousers, and a neat pair of carpet slippers. Mme. Jules' face appeared behind him in the doorway of the inner room; she grew white, and dropped into a chair.

"What is the matter, madame?" exclaimed Auguste, as he sprang towards her.

But Ferragus stretched out an arm and stopped the young man short with such a well-delivered blow, that Auguste reeled as if an iron bar had struck him on the chest.

"Stand back, sir! What do you want with us? You have been prowling about the quarter these five or six days. Perhaps you are a detective?"

"Are you M. Ferragus?" retorted the Baron.

"No, sir."

"At any rate, it is my duty to return this paper which you dropped under an archway where we both took shelter from the rain."

As he spoke and held out the letter, he glanced round the room in spite of himself. Ferragus' room was well but plainly furnished. There was a fire in the grate. A table was set, more sumptuously than the man's apparent position and the low rent of the house seemed to warrant. And lastly, he caught a glimpse of a heap of gold coins on a settee just inside the next room, and heard a sound from thence which could only be a woman's sobbing.

"The letter is mine, thank you," said the stranger, turning round in a way intended to convey the hint that the Baron had better go, and that at once.

Too inquisitive to know that he himself was being submitted to a thorough scrutiny, Auguste did not see the semi-magnetic glances, the devouring gaze which the stranger turned on him. If he had met those basilisk eyes, he would have seen his danger, but he was too violently in love to think of himself. He raised his hat, went downstairs, and back to his own home. What could a meeting of three such persons as Ida, Ferragus, and Mme. Jules mean? He might as well have taken up a Chinese puzzle, and tried to fit the odd-shaped bits of wood together without a clue.

But Mme. Jules had seen him; Mme. Jules went to the house; Mme. Jules had lied to him. Next day he would call upon her; she would not dare to refuse to see him; he was now her accomplice; he was hand and foot in this shady intrigue. Already he began to play the sultan, and thought how he would summon Mme. Jules to deliver up all her secrets.

Paris was afflicted in those days with a rage for building. If Paris is a monster, it is assuredly of all monsters the most subject to sudden rage. The city takes up with a thousand whimsies. Sometimes Paris begins to build like some great lord with a passion for bricks and mortar; then the trowel is dropped in an attack of military fever, every one turns out in a National Guard's uniform, and goes through the drill and smokes cigars, but the fit does not last; martial exercises are suddenly abandoned, and the cigar is thrown away. Then Paris begins to feel low, becomes insolvent, sells its effects in the Place du Châtelet, and files its petition; but in a few days all is straight again, and the city puts on festival array and dances. One day the city fills hands and mouth with barley sugar, yesterday it bought *Papier Weynen;* to-day the monster has the toothache, and plasters every wall with advertisements of *Alexipharmaques,* and to-morrow it will lay in a store of cough lozenges. Paris has the craze of the season or of the month as well as the rage of the day; and at this particular time everybody was building or pulling down something. What they built or pulled down no one knows to this day, but there was scarce a street in which you did not see erections of scaffolding, poles, planks, and cross bars lashed together at every story. The fragile structures, covered with white plaster dust, quivered under the tread of the Limousin bricklayers and shook with the vibrations of every passing carriage in spite of the protection of wooden hoardings, which people are bound to erect round the monumental buildings that never rise above their foundations. There is a nautical suggestion about the mast-like poles and ladders and rigging and the shouts of the bricklayers.

One of these temporary erections stood not a dozen paces away from the Hôtel Maulincour, in front of a house that was being built of blocks of free-stone. Next day, just as the Baron de Maulincour's cab passed by the scaffolding on the way to Mme. Jules, a block two feet square slipped from its rope cradle at the top of the pole, turned a somersault, fell, and killed the man-servant at the back of the vehicle. A cry of terror shook the scaffolding and the bricklayers. One of the two, in peril of his neck, could scarcely cling to the pole; it seemed that the block struck him in passing. A crowd quickly gathered. The men came down in a body, with shouts and oaths, declaring that M. de Maulincour's cab had shaken their crane. Two inches more, and the stone would have fallen on the Baron's head. It was an event in the quarter. It got into the newspapers.

M. de Maulincour, sure that he had touched nothing, brought an action for damages. The law stepped in. It turned out upon inquiry that a boy with a wooden lath had mounted guard to warn passengers to give the building a wide berth, and with that the affair came to an end. M. de Maulincour must even put up with the loss of his man-servant and the fright that he had had. He kept his bed for several days, for he had been bruised by the breakage of the cab, and he was feverish after the shock to his nerves. So there was no visit paid to Mme. Jules.

Ten days later, when he went out of doors for the first time, he drove to the Bois de Boulogne in the now repaired cab. He turned down the Rue de Bourgogne, and had reached the sewer just opposite the Chamber of Deputies, when the axle snapped in the middle. The Baron was driving so fast that the two wheels swerved and met with a shock that must have fractured his skull if it had not been for the hood of the vehicle, and, as it was, he sustained serious injury to the ribs. So for the second time in ten days he was brought home more dead than alive to the weeping dowager.

This second accident aroused his suspicions. He thought, vaguely, however, of Mme. Jules and Ferragus; and by way of clearing up his suspicions, he had the broken axle brought into his bedroom, and sent for his coachbuilder. The man inspected the fracture, and proved two things to M. Maulincour's mind. First, that the axle never came from his establishment, for he made a practice of cutting his initials roughly on every one that he supplied. How this axle had been exchanged for the previous one he was at a loss to explain. And secondly, he found that there was a very ingeniously contrived flaw in the iron bar, a kind of cavity made by a blowpipe while the metal was hot.

"Eh! M. le Baron, a man had need to be pretty clever to turn out an axle-bar on that pattern; you could swear it was natural——"

M. de Maulincour asked the man to keep his own counsel, and considered that he had had a sufficient warning. The two attempts on his life had been plotted with a skill which showed that his were no common enemies.

"It is a war of extermination," said he, turning restlessly on his bed, "a warfare of savages, ambushes, and treachery, a war declared in the name of Mme. Jules. In whose hands is she? And what power can this Ferragus wield?"

M. de Maulincour, brave man and soldier though he was, could not help shivering when all was done and said. Among the thoughts that beset him, there was one which found him defenceless and afraid. How if these mysterious enemies of his should resort next to poison? Terror, exaggerated by fever and low diet, got the better of him in his weak condition. He sent for an old attached servant of his grandmother's, a woman who loved him with that almost motherly affection through which an ordinary nature reaches the sublime. Without telling her all that was in his mind, he bade her buy all necessary articles of food for him, secretly, and every day at a fresh place; and at the same time, he warned her to keep everything under lock and key, and to allow no one whatsoever to be present while she prepared his meals. In short, he took the most minute precautions against this kind of death. He was lying ill in bed; he had therefore full leisure to consider his best way of defending himself, and love of life is the only craving sufficiently clairvoyant to allow human egoism to forget nothing. But the luckless patient had himself poisoned his own life with dread. Every hour was overshadowed by a gloomy suspicion that he could not throw off. Still, the two lessons in murder had taught him one qualification indispensable to a politic man; he understood how greatly dissimulation is needed in the complex action of the great interests of life. To keep a secret is nothing; but to be silent beforehand, to forget, if necessary, for thirty years, like Ali Pasha, the better to insure a revenge pondered during those thirty years,—this is a fine study in a country where few men can dissemble for thirty days together.

By this time Mme. Jules was Auguste de Maulincour's

whole life. His mind was always intently examining the means by which he might win a triumph in his mysterious duel with unknown antagonists. His desire for this woman grew the greater by every obstacle. Amid all his thoughts Mme. Jules was always present in his heart of hearts; there she stood more irresistible now in her imputed sin than she used to be with all the undoubted virtues for which he once had worshiped her.

The sick man, wishing to reconnoitre the enemy's position, thought there could be no danger in letting the old Vidame into the secret. The Vidame loved Auguste as a father loves his wife's children; he was shrewd and adroit, he was of a diplomatic turn of mind. So the Vidame came, heard the Baron's story, and shook his head, and the two held counsel. Auguste maintained that in the days in which they lived, the detective force and the powers that be were equal to finding out any mysteries, and that if there was absolutely no other way, the police would prove powerful auxiliaries. The Vidame did not share his young friend's confidence or his convictions.

"The police are the biggest bunglers on earth, dear boy, and the powers that be are the feeblest of all things where individuals are concerned. Neither the authorities nor the police can get to the bottom of people's minds. If they discover the causes of a fact, that is all that can reasonably be expected of them. Now the authorities and the police are eminently unsuited to a business of this kind; the personal interest which is not satisfied till everything is found out is essentially lacking in them. No human power can prevent a murderer or a poisoner from reaching a prince's heart or an honest man's stomach. It is passion that makes the complete detective."

With that the Vidame strongly advised his young friend the Baron to travel. Let him go to Italy, and from Italy to Greece, and from Greece to Syria and Asia, and come back only when his mysterious enemies should be convinced of his repentance. In this way he would conclude a tacit peace with them. Or, if he stayed, he had better keep to his house, and even to his room, since there he could secure himself against the attacks of this Ferragus, and never leave it except to crush the enemy once for all.

"A man should never touch his enemy except to smite off his head," the Vidame said gravely.

Nevertheless, the old man promised his favorite that he would bring all the astuteness with which Heaven had gifted him to bear on the case, and that, without committing any one, he would send a reconnoitring party into the enemy's camp, know all that went on there, and prepare a victory.

The Vidame had in his service a retired Figaro, as mischievous a monkey as ever took human shape. In former times the man had been diabolically clever, and a convict's physical frame could not have responded better to all demands made upon it; he was agile as a thief, and subtle as a woman, but he had fallen into the decadence of genius for want of practice. New social conditions in Paris have reformed away the old valets of comedy. This emeritus Scapin was attached to his master as to a being of superior order; but the crafty Vidame used to increase the annual wage of his sometime provost of gallantry by a tolerably substantial sum, in such sort that the natural ties of goodwill were strengthened by the bond of interest, and the old Vidame received in return such watchful attention as the tenderest of mistresses could scarcely devise in a lover's illness. In this relic of the eighteenth century, this pearl of old world stage servants, this minister incorruptible (since all his desires were gratified)—the Vidame and M. de Maulincour both put their trust.

"M. le Baron would spoil it all," said the great man in livery, summoned to the council. "Let monsieur eat and drink and sleep in peace. I will take it all upon myself."

And indeed, a week afterwards, when M. de Maulincour, now perfectly recovered, was breakfasting with his grandmother and the Vidame, Justin appeared to make his report. The dowager went back to her rooms, and he began with that false modesty which men of genius affect:

"Ferragus is not the real name of the enemy in pursuit of M. le Baron. The man, the devil rather, is called Gratien Henri Victor Jean Joseph Bourignard. The said Gratien Bourignard used to be a builder and contractor; he was a very rich man at one time; and most of all, he was one of the prettiest fellows in Paris, a Lovelace that might have led Grandison himself astray. My information goes no further. He once was a common workman; the journeymen of the order of Dévorants elected him as their head, with the name of Ferragus XXIII. The police should know that, if they are there to know anything. The man has moved, and at present is lodging in the Rue Joquelet. Mme. Jules Desmarets often goes to see him. Her husband pretty often sets her down in the Rue Vivienne on his way to the Bourse; or she leaves her husband at the Bourse, and comes back that way. M. le Vidame knows so much in these matters, that he will not expect me to tell him whether the husband rules the wife, or the wife rules her husband, but Mme. Jules is so pretty that I should bet on her. All this is absolutely certain. My Bourignard often goes to gamble at number 129. He is a gay dog, with a liking for women, saving your presence, and has his amours like a man of condition. As for the rest, he is frequently in luck, he makes up like an actor, and can make any grimace he likes; he just leads the queerest life you ever heard of. He has several addresses, I have no doubt, for he nearly always escapes what M. le Vidame calls 'parliamentary investigation.' If monsieur wishes, however, the man can be got rid of decently, leading such a life as he does. It is always easy to get rid of a man with a weakness for women. Still the capitalist is talking of moving again.—Now, have M. le Vidame and M. le Baron any orders to give?"

"I am pleased with you, Justin. Go no further in the affair without instructions, but keep an eye on everything here, so that M. le Baron shall have nothing to fear." He turned to Maulincour. "Live as before, dear boy," he said, "and forget Mme. Jules."

"No, no," said Auguste, "I will not give her up to Gratien Bourignard; I mean to have him bound hand and foot and Mme. Jules as well."

That evening Auguste de Maulincour, recently promoted to a higher rank in the Guards, went to a ball in Mme. la Duchesse de Berri's apartment at the Élysée-Bourbon. There, surely, there was no fear of the slightest danger; and yet, the Baron de Maulincour came away with an affair of honor on his hands, and no hope of arranging it. His antagonist, the Marquis de Ronquerolles, had the strongest reasons for complaining of him; the quarrel arose out of an old flirtation with M. de Ronquerolles' sister, the Comtesse de Sérizy. This lady, who could not endure high-flown German sentiment, was all the more particular with regard to every detail of the prude's costume in which she appeared in public. Some fatal inexplicable prompting moved Auguste to make a harmless joke, Mme. de Sérizy took it in very bad part, and her brother took offence. Explanations took place in whispers in a corner of the room. Both behaved like men of the world, there was no fuss of any kind; and not till next day did the Faubourg Saint-Honoré, the Faubourg Saint-Germain, and the Château hear what had happened. Mme. de Sérizy was warmly defended; all the blame was thrown on Maulincour. August persons intervened. Seconds of the highest rank were imposed on M. de Maulincour and M. de Ronquerolles; every precaution was taken on the ground to prevent a fatal termination.

Auguste's antagonist was a man of pleasure, not wanting, as every one admitted, in a sense of honor; it was impossible to think of the Marquis as a tool in the hands of Ferragus, Chef des Dévorants; and yet as Auguste de Maulincour stood up before his man, in his own mind he felt a wish to obey an unaccountable instinct, and to put a question to him.

"Gentlemen," he said, addressing his seconds, "I emphatically do not refuse to stand M. de Ronquerolles' fire; but, first, I own that I was in fault, I will make the apology which he is sure to require, and even in public if he wishes it; for when a lady is in the case, there is nothing, I think, dishonoring to a gentleman in such an apology. So I appeal to his common-sense and generosity, isn't there something rather senseless in fighting a duel when the better cause may happen to get the worst of it?"

But M. de Ronquerolles would not hear of such a way out of the affair. The Baron's suspicions were confirmed. He went across to his opponent.

"Well, M. le Marquis," he said, "will you pledge me your word as a noble, before these gentlemen, that you bear me no grudge save the one for which ostensibly we are to fight?"

"Monsieur, that is a question which ought not to be put to me."

M. de Maulincour returned to his place. It was agreed beforehand that only one shot should be fired on either side. The antagonists were so far apart, that a fatal end for M. de Maulincour seemed problematical, not to say impossible; but Auguste dropped. The bullet had passed through his ribs, missing the heart by two finger-breadths. Luckily, the extent of the injury was not great.

"This was no question of revenge for a dead passion; you aimed too well, monsieur, for that," said a Guardsman.

M. de Ronquerolles, thinking that he had killed his man, could not keep back a sardonic smile.

"Julius Cæsar's sister, monsieur, must be above suspicion."

"Mme. Jules again!" exclaimed Auguste, and he fainted away before he could finish the caustic sarcasm that died on his lips. He had lost a good deal of blood, but his wound was not dangerous. For a fortnight his grandmother and the Vidame nursed him with the lavish care which none but the old, wise with the experience of a lifetime, can give. Then one morning he received a rude shock. It came from his grandmother. She told him that her old age, the last days of her life, were filled with deadly anxiety. A letter addressed to her and signed "F." gave her the history of the espionage to which her grandson had stooped; it was given in full from

point to point. M. de Maulincour was accused of conduct
unworthy of a man of honor. He had posted an old woman
(so it was stated) near the cabstand in the Rue de Ménars.
Nominally his wrinkled spy supplied water to the cabmen,
but really she was stationed there to watch Mme. Jules Desmarets. He had deliberately set himself to play the detective
on one of the most harmless men in the world, and tried to
find out all about him when secrets which concerned the lives
of three persons were involved. Of his own accord he had
entered upon a pitiless struggle, in which he had been
wounded three times already, and must inevitably succumb at
last; for his death had been sworn; every human power
would be exerted to compass it. It was too late for M. de
Maulincour to escape his doom by a promise to respect the
mysterious life of these three persons; for it was impossible
to believe the word of a gentleman who could sink so low
as to make himself an agent of police. And for what reason?
To disturb, without cause, the existence of an innocent woman and a respectable old man.

The letter was as nothing to Auguste compared with the
Baronne de Maulincourt's loving reproaches. How could he
fail to trust and respect a woman? How could he play the
spy on her when he had no right to do so? Had any man a
right to spy on the woman who loved him? There followed a torrent of excellent reasoning which never proves
anything. It put the young man for the first time of his
life into one of those towering passions from which the most
decisive actions of life are apt to spring.

"If this is to be a duel to the death" (so he concluded),
"I am justified in using every means in my power to kill my
enemy."

Forthwith the Vidame, on behalf of M. de Maulincour,
waited on the superintendent of the detective force in Paris,
and gave him a full account of the adventure, without bringing Mme. Jules' name into the story, although she was the
secret knot of all the threads. He told him, in confidence,
of the fears of the Maulincour family, thus threatened by

some unknown person, an enemy daring enough to vow such vengeance on an officer in the Guards, in the teeth of the law and the police. He of the police was so much surprised, that he raised his green spectacles, blew his nose two or three times, and offered his mull to the Vidame, who said, to save his dignity, that he never took snuff, though his countenance was bedabbled with rappee. The head of the department took his notes, and promised that, with the help of Vidocq and his sleuth-hounds, the enemy of the Maulincour family should be accounted for in a very short time; there were no mysteries, so he was pleased to say, for the Paris police.

A few days afterwards, the superintendent came to the Hôtel Maulincour to see M. le Vidame, and found the Baron perfectly recovered from his last injuries. He thanked the family in formal style for the particulars which they had been so good as to communicate, and informed them that the man Bourignard was a convict sentenced to twenty years' penal servitude, and that in some miraculous way he made his escape from the gang on the way from Bicêtre to Toulon. The police had made fruitless efforts to catch him for the past fifteen years; they learned that he had very recklessly come back to live in Paris; and there, though he was constantly implicated in all sorts of shady affairs, hitherto he had eluded the most active search. To cut it short, the man, whose life presented a great many most curious details, was certain to be seized at one of his numerous addresses and given up to justice. This red-tape personage concluded his official report with the remark that if M. de Maulincour attached sufficient importance to the affair to care to be present at Bourignard's capture, he might repair to such and such a number in the Rue Sainte-Foi at eight o'clock next morning. M. de Maulincour, however, felt that he could dispense with this method of making certain; he shared the feeling of awe which the police inspires in Paris; he felt every confidence in the diligence of the local authorities.

Three days afterwards, as he saw nothing in the newspapers about an arrest which surely would have supplied ma-

terial for an interesting article, M. de Maulincour was beginning to feel uncomfortable, when the following letter relieved his mind:—

"MONSIEUR LE BARON,—I have the honor to announce that
you need no longer entertain any fears whatsoever with regard
to the matter in hand. The man Gratien Bourignard, alias
Ferragus, died yesterday at his address, number 7 Rue Joquelet. The suspicions which we were bound to raise as to his
identity were completely set at rest by facts. The doctor of
the prefecture was specially sent by us to act in concert
with the doctor of the mayor's office, and the superintendent
of the preventive police made all the necessary verifications,
so that the identity of the body might be established beyond
question. The personal character, moreover, of the witnesses
who signed the certificate of death, and the confirmatory evidence of those who were present at the time of the said Bourignard's death—including that of the curé of the Bonne-Nou-
velle, to whom he made a last confession (for he made a Christian end)—all these things taken together do not permit us
to retain the slightest doubt.

"Permit me, M. le Baron, to remain, etc."

M. de Maulincour, the dowager, and the Vidame drew a
breath of unspeakable relief. She, good woman, kissed her
grandson while a tear stole down her cheeks, and then crept
away to give thanks to God. The dear dowager had made a
nine days' prayer for Auguste's safety, and believed that she
had been heard.

"Well," said the Vidame, "now you can go to that ball that
you were speaking about; I have no more objections to make."

M. de Maulincour was the more eager to go to this ball
since Mme. Jules was sure to be there. It was an entertain-
ment given by the Prefect of the Seine in whose house the
two worlds of Paris society met as on a neutral ground.
Auguste de Maulincour went quickly through the rooms, but
the woman who exerted so great an influence on his life was

not to be seen. He went into a still empty card-room, where the tables awaited players, sat himself down on a sofa, and gave himself up to the most contradictory thoughts of Mme. Jules, when some one grasped him by the arm; and, to his utter amazement, he beheld the beggar of the Rue Coquillière, Ida's Ferragus, the man who lived in the Rue Soly, Justin's Bourignard, the convict that had died the day before.

"Not a sound, not a word, sir!" said Bourignard. Auguste knew that voice, though to any other it would surely have seemed unrecognizable.

The man was very well dressed; he wore the insignia of the Golden Fleece and the star of the Legion of Honor.

"Sir," he hissed out like a hyena, "you warrant all my attempts on your life by allying yourself with the police. You shall die, sir. There is no help for it. Are you in love with Mme. Jules? Did she once love you? What right have you to trouble her peace and smirch her reputation?"

Somebody else came up. Ferragus rose to go.

"Do you know this man?" asked M. de Maulincour, seizing Ferragus by the collar.

But Ferragus slipped briskly out of his grasp, caught M. de Maulincour by the hair, and shook him playfully several times.

"Is there absolutely nothing but a dose of lead that will bring you to your senses?" he replied.

"I am not personally acquainted with him," said de Marsay, who had witnessed this scene, "but I know that this gentleman is M. de Funcal, a very rich Portuguese."

M. de Funcal had vanished. The Baron went off in pursuit, he could not overtake him, but he reached the peristyle in time to see a splendid equipage and the sneer on Ferragus' face, before he was whirled away out of sight.

"For pity's sake, tell me where M. de Funcal lives," said Auguste, betaking himself to de Marsay, who happened to be an acquaintance.

"I do not know, but somebody here no doubt can tell you."

In answer to a question put to the Prefect, Auguste learned

that the Comte de Funcal's address was at the Portuguese
embassy. At that moment, while he fancied that he could
still feel those ice-cold fingers in his hair, he saw Mme.
Jules, in all the splendor of that beauty, fresh, graceful, unaffected, radiant with the sanctity of womanhood, which drew
him to her at the first. For him this creature was infernal;
Auguste felt nothing for her now but hate—hate that overflowed in murderous terrible glances. He watched for an opportunity of speaking to her alone.

"Madame," he said, "three times already your bravoes have
missed me——"

"What do you mean, sir?" she answered, reddening. "I
heard with much concern that several bad accidents had befallen you; but how can I have had anything to do with
them?"

"Then you know that the man in the Rue Soly has hired
ruffians on my track?"

"Sir!"

"Madame, henceforth I must call you to account not only
for my happiness, but also for my lifeblood——"

Jules Desmarets came up at that moment.

"What are you saying to my wife, sir?"

"Come to my house to inquire if you are curious to know."
And Maulincour went. Mme. Jules looked white and ready
to faint.

There are very few women who have not been called upon,
once in their lives, to face a definite, pointed, trenchant question with regard to some undeniable fact, one of those
questions which a husband puts in a pitiless way. The bare
thought of it sends a cold shiver through a woman; the first
word pierces her heart like a steel blade. Hence the axiom,
"All women are liars." They tell lies to spare the feelings
of others, white lies, heroic lies, hideous lies; but falsehood is
incumbent upon them. Once admit this, does it not follow
of necessity that the lies ought to be well told? Women tell
lies to admiration in France. Our manners are an excellent
school for dissimulation. And, after all, women are so art-

lessly insolent, so charming, so graceful, so true amid falsehood, so perfectly well aware of the value of insincerity as a
means of avoiding the rude shocks which put happiness in
peril, that falsehood is as indispensable to them as cotton
wool for their jewelry. Insincerity furnishes forth the staple
of their talk, and truth is only brought out occasionally.
They speak truth, as they are virtuous, from caprice or speculation. The methods vary with the individual character.
Some women laugh and lie, others weep, or grow grave, or put
themselves in a passion.

They begin life with a feigned indifference to the homage
which gratifies them most; they often end by insincerity with
themselves. Who has not admired their seeming loftiness
when they are trembling the while for the mysterious treasure of love? Who has not studied the ease, the ready wit,
the mental disengagement with which they confront the
greatest embarrassments of life? Everything is quite natural;
deceit flows out as snowflakes fall from the sky.

And yet what skill women have to discover the truth in another! How subtly they can use the hardest logic, in answer
to the passionately uttered question that never fails to yield
up some heart secret belonging to their interlocutor, if a
man is so guileless as to begin with questioning a woman.
If a man begins to question a woman, he delivers himself
into her hand. Will she not find out anything that he means
to hide, while she talks and says nothing?   And yet there are
men that have the audacity to enter upon a contest of wits
with a Parisienne—a woman who can put herself out of reach
of a thrust with "You are very inquisitive!"—"What does it
matter to you?"—"Oh! you are jealous!"—"And how if I
do not choose to answer you?"   A Parisienne, in short, has
a hundred and thirty-seven thousand ways of saying No, while
her variations on the word Yes surpass computation. Surely
one of the finest diplomatic, philosophic, logographic, and
moral performances which remain to be made would be a
treatise on No and Yes. But who save an androgynous being
could accomplish the diabolical feat? For which reason it

will never be attempted. Yet of all unpublished works, is
there one better known or more constantly in use among women?

Have you ever studied the conduct, the pose, the *disin-
voltura* of a lie? Look at it now. Mme. Jules was sitting in
the right-hand corner of her carriage, and her husband to her
left. She had contrived to repress her emotion as she left
the ballroom, and by this time her face was quite composed.
Her husband had said nothing to her then; he said nothing
now. Jules was staring out of the window at the dark walls
of the silent houses as they drove past; but suddenly, just
as they turned the corner of a street, he seemed to come to
some determination, he looked intently at his wife. She
seemed to feel cold in spite of the fur-lined pelisse in which
she was wrapped; she looked pensive, he thought, and perhaps
she really was pensive. Of all subtly communicable moods,
gravity and reflection are the most contagious.

"What can M. de Maulincour have said to move you so
deeply?" began Jules. "And what is this that he wishes me
to hear at his house?"

"Why, he can tell you nothing at his house that I cannot
tell you now," she replied.

And with that woman's subtlety, which is always slightly
dishonoring to virtue, Mme. Jules waited for another question. But her husband turned his head away and resumed
his study of arched gateways. Would it not mean suspicion
and distrust if he asked any more? It is a crime in love to
suspect a woman; and Jules had already killed a man, without a doubt of his wife. Clémence did not know how much
deep passion and reflection lay beneath her husband's silence; and little did Jules imagine the extraordinary drama
which locked his wife's heart from him. And the carriage went on and on through silent Paris, and the husband
and wife, two lovers who idolized each other, nestled softly
and closely together among the silken cushions, a deep gulf
yawning between them all the while.

How many strange scenes take place in the elegant broughams which pass through the streets between midnight and one o'clock in the morning after a ball! The carriages alluded to, be it understood, are fitted with transparent panes of glass, and lanterns that not merely light up the brougham itself, but the whole street as well on either side; they belong to law-sanctioned love, and the law gives a man the right to sulk and fall out with his wife, and kiss and make it up again, in a brougham or anywhere else. So married couples are at liberty to quarrel without fear of being seen by passers-by. And how many secrets are revealed to foot-passengers in the dark streets, to the young bachelors who drove to the ball and, for some reason or other, are walking home afterwards! For the first time in their lives, Jules and Clémence leaned back in their corners; usually Desmarets pressed close to his wife's side.

"It is very cold," said Mme. Jules. But her husband heard nothing; he was intent on reading all the dark signs above the shops.

"Clémence," he began at last, "forgive me for this question that I am about to ask?"

He came nearer, put his arm about her waist, and drew her towards him.

"Oh, dear! here it comes!" thought poor Clémence.

"Well," she said aloud, anticipating the question, "you wish to know what M. de Maulincour was saying to me? I will tell you, Jules; but, I am afraid. Ah, God! can we have secrets from each other? A moment ago I knew that you were struggling between the consciousness that we love each other and a vague dread; but that consciousness that we love each other is unclouded, is it not? and do not your debts seem very shadowy to you? Why not stay in the light that you love? When I have told you everything, you will wish to know more; and after all, I myself do not know what is lurking under that man's strange words. And then, perhaps, there would be a duel, ending in a death. I would far rather that we both put that unpleasant moment out of our minds. But in any case, give me your word to wait till this extraordinary adventure is cleared up in some natural way.

"M. de Maulincour declared that those three accidents of which you heard—the block of stone that killed his servant, the carriage accident, and the duel about Mme. de Sérizy— were all brought upon him by a plot which *I* had woven against him. And he threatened to explain my reasons for wishing to murder him to you.

"Can you make anything out of all this? It was his face that disturbed me; there was madness in it; his eyes were haggard; he was so excited that he could not bring out his words. I felt sure that he was mad. That was all. Now, I should not be a woman if I did not know that, for a year past, M. de Maulincour has been, as they say, quite wild about me. He has never met me except at dances; we have never exchanged any words but ballroom small talk. Perhaps he wants to separate us, so that I may be left defenceless and alone some day. You see how it is! You are frowning already. Oh, I detest the world with all my heart! We are so happy without it, why should we go in search of society?— Jules, I beg of you, promise me that you will forget all this! I expect we shall hear to-morrow that M. de Maulincour has gone out of his mind."

"What an extraordinary thing!" said Jules to himself, as he stepped out into the peristyle of his own abode.

And here, if this story is to be developed by giving it in all its truth of detail, by following its course through all its intricacies, there must be a revelation of some of the secrets of love—secrets learned by slipping under the canopy of a bed-chamber, not brazenly, but after the manner of Puck, without startling either Jeanie or Dougal, or anybody else. For this venture, one had needs be chaste as our noble French language consents to be, and daring as Gérard's brush in his picture of *Daphnis and Chloe*.

Mme. Jules' bedroom was a sacred place. No one but her husband and her maid was allowed to enter it. Wealth has great privileges, and the most enviable of them all is the power of carrying out thoughts and feelings to the uttermost; of quickening sensibility by fulfilling its myriad caprices; of encompassing that inner life with a splendor that exalts it, elegance that refines, and the subtle shades of expression that enhance the charm of love.

If you particularly detest picnic dinners and meals badly served; if you feel a certain pleasure at the sight of dazzling white damask, silver plate, exquisite porcelain, and richly carved and gilded tables lit up by translucent tapers; if you have a taste for miracles of the most refined culinary art beneath silver covers with armorial bearings;—then, if you have a mind to be consistent, you must come down from the heights of your garret, and you must leave the grisettes in the street. Garrets and grisettes, like umbrellas and hinged clogs, must be left to people who take tickets at the doors of restaurants to pay for their dinners; and you must think of love as something rudimentary, only to be developed in all its charm by a gilded fireside, in a room made deaf to all sound from without by drawn blinds and closed shutters and thick curtain folds, while the opal light of a Parian lamp falls over soft carpets from the Savonnerie and the silken hangings on the walls. You must have mirrors to reflect each other, to give you an infinite series of pictures of the woman in whom you would fain find many women, of her to whom Love gives so many forms. There should be long, low sofas, and a couch like a secret which you guess before it is revealed; and soft furs spread for bare feet on the floor of the dainty chamber, and wax tapers under glass shades, and white gauze draperies, so that you can see to read at any hour of the night; and flowers without too heavy-sweet a scent, and linen fine enough to satisfy Anne of Austria.

This delicious scheme had been carried out by Mme. Jules. But that is nothing; any woman of taste might do as much; though nevertheless, there is a certain touch of personality in the arrangement of these things, a something which stamps this ornament or that detail with a character of its own. The fanatical cult of individuality is more prevalent than ever in these days. Rich people in France are beginning to grow more and more exclusive in their tastes and belongings than they have been for the past thirty years. Mme. Jules knew that her programme must be carried out consistently; that everything about her must be part of a harmonious whole of luxury which made a fit setting for love.

"Fifteen hundred francs and my Sophie," or "Love in a Cottage," is the sort of talk to expect from famished creatures, and brown bread does very well at first; but if the pair are really in love, their palates grow nicer, and in the end they sigh for the riches of the kitchen. Love holds toil and want in abhorrence, and would rather die at once than live a miserable life of hand to mouth.

Most women after a ball are impatient for sleep. Their rooms are strewn with limp flowers, scentless bouquets, and ball gowns. Their little thick shoes are left under an armchair, they totter across the floor in their high-heeled slippers, take the combs out of their hair, and shake down their tresses without a thought of their appearance. Little do they care if they disclose to their husbands' eyes the clasps and pins and cunning contrivances which maintained the dainty fabric in erection. All mystery is laid aside, all pretence dropped for the husband—there is no make-up for him. The corset, fearfully and wonderfully made, is left lying about if the sleepy waiting-woman forgets to put it away. Whalebone stiffening, sleeves encased in buckram, delusive finery, hair supplied by the coiffeur, the whole factitious woman, in fact, lies scattered about. *Disjecta membra poetæ,* the artificial poetry so much admired by those for whose benefit the whole was conceived and elaborated, the remains of the pretty woman of an hour ago, encumber every corner, while the genuine woman in slatternly disorder, and the crumpled nightcap of yesterday, to-day, and to-morrow, presents herself yawning to the arms of a husband who yawns likewise.

"For, after all, monsieur, if you want a pretty nightcap to crumple every night, you must increase my allowance."

Such is life as it is. A woman is always old and unattractive to her husband; always smart, dainty, and dressed in her best for that Other, every husband's rival, the world that slanders women or picks them to pieces.

Mme. Jules did quite otherwise. Love, like all other beings, has its own instinct of self-preservation. Inspired by love, constantly rewarded by happiness, she never failed in the scrupulous performance of little duties in which no one can grow slack, for by such means love is kept unimpaired by time. Are not these pains, these tasks, imposed by a self-respect which becomes her passing well? What are they but sweet flatteries, a way of reverencing the beloved in one's own person?

So Mme. Jules had closed the door of her dressing-room on her husband; there she changed her ball gown and came out dressed for the night, mysteriously adorned for the mysterious festival of her heart. The chamber was always exquisite and dainty; Jules, when he entered it, found a woman coquettishly wrapped in a graceful loose gown, with her thick hair twisted simply about her head. She had nothing to fear from dishevelment; she robbed Love's sight and touch of nothing. This woman was always simpler and more beautiful for him than for the world—a woman revived by her toilet, a woman whose whole art consisted in being whiter than the cambrics that she wore, fresher than the freshest scent, more irresistible than the wiliest courtesan. In a word, she was always loving, and therefore always beloved. In this admirable skill in *le métier de femme*—in the art and mystery of being a woman—lay the great secret of Joséphine's charm for Napoleon, of Cesonia's influence over Caligula in older times, of the ascendency of Diane de Poitiers over Henri II. And if this secret is so potent in the hands of women who have counted seven or eight lustres, what a weapon is it for a young wife! The prescribed happiness of fidelity becomes rapture.

Mme. Jules had been particularly careful of her toilet for the night. After that conversation which froze the blood in her veins with terror, and still caused her the liveliest

anxiety, she meant to be exquisitely charming, and she succeeded. She fastened her cambric dressing-gown, leaving it
loose at the throat and let her dark hair fall loosely over her
shoulders. An intoxicating fragrance clung about her after
the scented bath, her bare feet were thrust into velvet slippers. Jules in his dressing-gown was standing meditatively
by the fire, with his elbow on the mantel-piece, and one foot
on the fender. Feeling strong on her vantage ground, she
tripped across to him and laid a hand over his eyes. Then
she whispered, close to his ear, so closely that he could feel
her warm breath on him and the tips of her teeth, "What are
you thinking about, monsieur?"

With quick tact, she held him closely to her and put her
arms about him to snatch him away from his gloomy thoughts.
A woman who loves knows well how to use her power; and
the better the woman, the more irresistible is her coquetry.

"Of you," said he.

"Only of me?"

"Yes!"

"Oh! that was a very venturesome 'Yes!'"

They went to bed. As Mme. Jules fell asleep she thought,
"Decidedly, M. de Maulincour will bring about some misfortune. Jules is preoccupied and absent-minded; he has
thoughts which he does not tell me."

Towards three o'clock in the morning Mme. Jules was
awakened by a foreboding that knocked at her heart while
she slept. She felt, physically and mentally, that her husband was not beside her. She missed Jules' arm, on which her
head had lain nightly for five years, while she slept happily
and peacefully, an arm that never wearied of the weight. A
voice cried, "Jules is in pain! Jules is weeping!" She lifted
her head, sat upright, felt that her husband's place was cold,
and saw him sitting by the fire, his feet on the fender, his
head leaned back in the great armchair. There were tears on
his cheeks. Poor Clémence was out of bed in a moment, and
sprang to her husband's knee.

"Jules, what is it? Are you not feeling well? Speak,
tell me; oh, speak to me, if you love me."

She poured out a hundred words of the deepest tenderness. Jules, at his wife's feet, kissed her knees, her hands. The tears flowed afresh as he answered:

"Clémence, dear, I am very wretched. It is not love if you cannot trust your mistress, and you are my mistress. I worship you, Clémence, even while I doubt you. . . . The things that man said last night went to my heart; and in spite of me, they stay there to trouble me. There is some mystery underneath this. Indeed, I blush to say it, but your explanation did not satisfy me. Common sense sheds a light on it which love bids me reject. It is a dreadful struggle. How could I lie there with your head on my shoulder and think that there were thoughts in your mind that I did not know?—Oh, I believe you, I believe you," he exclaimed, as she smiled sadly and seemed about to speak. "Say not a word, reproach me with nothing. The least little word from you would break my heart. And besides, could you say a single thing that I have not said to myself for the last three hours? Yes, for three hours I lay, watching you as you slept, so beautiful you were, your forehead looked so quiet and pure. —Ah! yes, you have always told me all your thoughts, have you not? I am alone in your inmost heart. When I look into the depths of your eyes, I read all that lies there. Your life is always as pure as those clear eyes. Ah! no, there is no secret beneath their transparent gaze."

He rose and kissed her eyelids.

"Let me confess it to you, beloved; all through these five years one thing has made me happier day by day, I have been glad that you should have none of the natural affections which always encroach a little upon love. You had neither sister nor father nor mother nor friend; I was neither above nor below any other in thy heart; I was there alone. Clémence, say over again for me all the intimate sweet words that you have spoken so often; do not scold me; comfort me, I am very wretched. I have a hateful suspicion to reproach myself with, while you have nothing burning in your heart. Tell me, my darling, may I stay by your side? How should two that are so truly one rest their heads on the same pillow, when one is at peace and the other in pain? . . . What can you be thinking of?" he cried abruptly, as Clémence looked meditative and confused, and could not keep back the tears.

"I am thinking of my mother," she said gravely. "You could not know, Jules, how it hurt your Clémence to recall her mother's last farewells, while your voice, the sweetest of all music, was sounding in her ears; to remember the solemn pressure of the chill hand of a dying woman, while I felt your caresses, and the overpowering sense of the sweetness of your love."

She made him rise, and held him tightly, with far more than man's strength, in her arms; she kissed his hair, her tears fell over him.

"Oh! I could be hewed into pieces for you! Tell me, beyond doubt, that I make you happy, that for you I am the fairest of women, that I am a thousand women for you. But you are loved as no other man can ever be loved. I do not know what the words 'duty,' 'virtue' mean. Jules, I love you for your own sake; it makes me happy to love you; I shall always love you; better and better, till my last sigh. I take a kind of pride in my love. I am sure that I am fated to know but the one great love in my life. Perhaps this that I am going to say is wicked, but I am glad to have no children, I wish for none. I feel that I am more a wife than a mother.—Have you any fears? Listen to me, my love; promise me to forget, not this hour of mingled love and doubt, but that madman's words. I ask it, Jules. Promise me not to see him again, to keep away from his house. I have a feeling that if you go a single step further in that labyrinth, we shall both sink into depths where I shall die, with your name still on my lips, your heart in my heart. Why do you put me so high in your inmost life, and so low in the outer? You can take so many men's fortunes on trust, and you cannot give me the alms of one doubt? And when, for the first time in your life, you can prove that your faith in me is unbounded,

would you dethrone me in your heart? Between a lunatic and
your wife, you believe the lunatic's word? Oh! Jules——"

She broke off, flung back the hair that fell over her forehead and throat, and in heartrending tones she added, "I
have said too much. A word should be enough. If there
is still a shadow across your mind and your forehead, however faint it may be, mind, it will kill me."

She shivered in spite of herself, and her face grew white.

"Oh! I will kill that man," said Jules to himself, as he
caught up his wife and carried her to the bed. "Let us sleep
in peace, dear angel," he said aloud; "I have put it all out
of my mind, I give you my word."

The loving words were repeated more lovingly, and Clémence slept. Jules, watching his sleeping wife, told himself—
"She is right. When love is so pure, a suspicion is like a
blight. Yes, and a blight on so innocent a soul, so delicate a
flower, is certain death."

If between two human creatures, each full of love for the
other, with a common life at every moment, there should arise
a cloud, the cloud will vanish away, but not without leaving
some trace of its passage behind. Perhaps their love grows
deeper, as earth is fairer after the rain; or perhaps the shock
reverberates like distant thunder in a blue sky; but, at any
rate, they cannot take up life where it was before, love must
increase or diminish. At breakfast, M. and Mme. Jules
showed each other an exaggerated attention. In their glances
there was an almost forced gaiety which might have been expected of people eager to be deceived. Jules had involuntary
suspicions; his wife, a definite dread. And yet, feeling sure
of each other, they had slept. Was the embarrassment due
to want of trust? to the recollection of the scene in the night?
They themselves could not tell. But they loved each other,
and were loved so sincerely, that the bitter-sweet impression
could not fail to leave its traces; and each, besides, was so
anxious to be the first to efface them, to be the first to return,
that they could not but remember the original cause of a first
discord. For those who love, vexation is out of the question,

and pain is still afar off, but the feeling is a kind of mourning difficult to describe. If there is a parallel between colors
and the moods of the mind; if, as Locke's blind man said,
scarlet produces the same effect on the eyes as the blast of a
trumpet on the ears, then this melancholy reaction may be
compared with sober gray tints. Yet saddened love, love conscious of its real happiness beneath the momentary trouble,
knows a wholly new luxurious blending of pain and pleasure.
Jules dwelt on the tones of his wife's voice, and watched for
her glances with the young passion that stirred him in the
early days of their love; and memories of five perfectly happy
years, Clémence's beauty, her artless love, soon effaced (for
the time) the last pangs of an intolerable ache.

It was Sunday. There was no Bourse and no business.
Husband and wife could spend the whole day together, and
each made more progress in the other's heart than ever before, as two children in a moment's terror cling closely and
tightly together, instinctively united against danger. Where
two have but one life, they know such hours of perfect happiness sent by chance, flowers of a day, which have nothing to
do with yesterday or to-morrow.

To Jules and Clémence it was a day of exquisite enjoyment. They might almost have felt a dim foreboding that
this was to be the last day of their life as lovers. What name
can be given to the mysterious impulse which hastens the
traveler's steps before the storm has given warning?—it
fills the dying with a glow of life and beauty a few days before
the end, and sets them making the most joyous plans; it counsels the learned man to raise the flame of the midnight lamp
when it burns most brightly; it wakens a mother's fears when
some keen-sighted observer looks too intently at her child.
We all feel this influence in great crises in our lives, yet we
have neither studied it nor found a name for it. It is something more than a presentiment, something less than. vision.

All went well till the next day. It was Monday, Jules
Desmarets was obliged to be at the Bourse at the usual time;
and, according to his custom, he asked his wife before he went
if she would take the opportunity of driving with him.

"No," she said; "the weather is too bad."

And, indeed, it was pouring with rain. It was about half-past two o'clock. M. Desmarets went on the market, and thence to the Treasury. At four o'clock, when he came out, he confronted M. de Maulincour, who was waiting for him with the pertinacity bred of hate and revenge.

"I have some important information to give you, sir," he said, taking Desmarets by the arm. "Listen to me. I am an honorable man; I do not wish to send anonymous letters which would trouble your peace of mind; I prefer to speak directly. In short, you may believe that if my life were not at stake, I should never interfere between husband and wife, even if I believed that I had a right to do so."

"If you are going to say anything that concerns Mme. Desmarets," answered Jules, "I beg you to be silent, sir."

"If I keep silence, sir, you may see Mme. Jules in the dock beside a convict before very long. Now, am I to be silent?"

Jules' handsome face grew white, but seemingly he was calm again in a moment. He drew Maulincour under one of the porches of the temporary building then frequented by stockbrokers, and spoke, his voice unsteady with deep emotion:

"I am listening, sir, but there will be a duel to the death between us if——"

"Oh! I am quite willing," exclaimed M. de Maulincour. "I have the greatest respect for you. Do you speak of death, sir? You are not aware, I expect, that your wife probably employed somebody to poison me on Saturday evening? Yes, sir, since the day before yesterday, some extraordinary change has taken place in me. All the hairs of my head distil a fever and mortal languor that pierces through the bone; and I know perfectly well what man it was that touched my head at the dance."

M. de Maulincour told the whole story of his Platonic love for Mme. Jules and the details of the adventure with which this Scene opens. Anybody would have listened to him as attentively as Desmarets, but Mme. Jules' husband might be expected to be more astonished than anybody else in the world. And here his character showed itself—he was more surprised than overwhelmed. Thus constituted a judge, and the judge of an adored wife, in his inmost mind he assumed a judicial directness and inflexibility of mind. He was a lover still; he thought less of his own broken life than of the woman; he heard, not his own grief, but a far-off voice crying to him, "Clémence could not lie! Why should she be false to you?"

"I felt certain that in M. de Funcal I recognized this Ferragus, whom the police believe to be dead," concluded M. de Maulincour, "so I put an intelligent man on his track at once. As I went home, I fortunately chanced to call to mind a Mme. Meynardie, mentioned in this Ida's letter, Ida being apparently my persecutor's mistress. With this one bit of information, my emissary speedily cleared up this ghastly adventure, for he is more skilled at finding out the truth than the police themselves."

"I am unable to thank you, sir, for your confidence," said Desmarets. "You speak of proof and witnesses; I am waiting for them. I shall not flinch from tracking down the truth in this extraordinary business; but you will permit me to suspend my judgment until the case is proved by circumstantial evidence. In any case, you shall have satisfaction, for you must understand that we both require it."

Jules went home.

"What is it?" asked his wife. "You look dreadfully pale."

"It is a cold day," he said, as he walked slowly away to the bedroom, where everything spoke of happiness and love, the so quiet chamber where a deadly storm was brewing.

"Have you been out to-day?" he asked, with seeming carelessness. The question, no doubt, was prompted by the last of a thousand thoughts, which had gathered unconsciously in his mind, till they took the shape of a single lucid reflection, which jealousy brought out on the spur of the moment.

"No," she answered, and her voice sounded frank.

Even as she spoke, Jules, glancing through the dressing-room door, noticed drops of rain on the bonnet which his wife used to wear in the morning. Jules was a violent tempered man, but he was likewise extremely sensitive; he shrank from confronting his wife with a lie. And yet those drops of water shed, as it were, a gleam of light which tortured his brain. He went downstairs to the porter's room.

"Fouquereau," he said, when he had made sure that they were alone, "three hundred francs per annum to you if you tell me the truth; if you deceive me, out you go; and if you mention my question and your answer to any one else, you will get nothing at all."

He stopped, looked steadily at the man, and then drawing him to the light of the window, he asked:

"Did your mistress go out this morning?"

"Madame went out at a quarter to three, and I think I saw her come in again half-an-hour ago."

"Is that true, upon your honor?"

"Yes, sir."

"You shall have the annual sum I promised you. But if you mention it, remember what I said; for if you do, you lose it all."

Jules went back to his wife.

"Clémence," he said, "I want to put my house accounts a bit straight, so do not be vexed if I ask you something. I have let you have forty thousand francs this year, have I not?"

"More than that," she answered. "Forty-seven."

"Could you tell me exactly how it was spent?"

"Why, yes. First of all, there were several outstanding bills from last year——"

"I shall find out nothing in this way," thought Jules. "I have gone the wrong way to work."

Just at that moment the man brought in a note. Jules opened it for the sake of appearances, but seeing the signature at the foot, he read it eagerly:—

"MONSIEUR,—To set your mind and our minds at rest, I take the step of writing to you, although I have not the privilege of being known to you; but my position, my age, and the fear that some misfortune may befall, compels me to beseech your forbearance in the distressing situation in which our af-

flicted family is placed. For some days past, M. Auguste de
Maulincour has shown unmistakable symptoms of mental de-
rangement; and we are afraid that he may disturb your happiness with the wild fancies of which he spoke to M. le Commandeur de Pamiers and to me, in the first fit of fever. We
desire to give you warning of a malady which is still curable,
no doubt; and as it might have very serious consequences for
the honor of the family and my grandson's future, I count
upon your discretion. If M. le Commandeur or I, monsieur,
had been able to make the journey to your house, we should
have dispensed with a written communication; but you will
comply, I do not doubt, with the request of a mother who be-
seeches you to burn this letter.

"Permit me to add that I am with the highest regard,
        "BARONNE DE MAULINCOURT *née* DE RIEUX."

"What tortures!" exclaimed Jules.

"What can be passing in your thoughts?" asked his wife,
with intense anxiety in her face.

"I have come to this!" cried Jules; "I ask myself whether
you have had this note sent to me to dispel my suspicions.
So judge what I am suffering," he added, tossing the letter
to her.

"The unhappy man," said Mme. Jules, letting the sheet
fall; "I am sorry for him, though he has given me a great
deal of pain."

"You know that he spoke to me "

"Oh! Did you go to see him when you had given your
word?" was her terror-stricken answer.

"Clémence, our love is in danger; we are outside all the
ordinary laws of life, so let us leave minor considerations in
great perils. Now, tell me, why did you go out this morning?
Women think they are privileged to tell us fibs now and again.
You often amuse yourselves with preparing pleasant surprises
for us, do you not? Just now you said one thing and meant
another no doubt; you said a 'No' for a 'Yes.'"

He brought her bonnet out of the dressing-room.

"Look here! Without meaning to play the Bartholo here, your bonnet has betrayed you. Are these not rain-drops? Then you must have gone out and caught the drops of rain as you looked about for a cab, or in coming in or out of the house to which you drove. Still, a woman can go out even if she has told her husband that she means to stay indoors; there is no harm in that. There are so many reasons for changing one's mind. A whim, a woman has a right to be whimsical, is that not so? You are not bound to be consistent with yourselves. Perhaps you forgot something; something to be done for somebody else, or a call, or a charitable errand? But there can be nothing to prevent a wife from telling her husband what she has done. How should one ever blush on a friend's breast? And it is not a jealous husband who speaks, my Clémence; it is the friend, the lover, the comrade."

He flung himself passionately at her feet.

"Speak, not to justify yourself, but to soothe an intolerable pain. I know for certain that you left the house. Well, what did you do? Where did you go?"

"Yes, Jules, I left the house," she said, and though her voice shook her face was composed. "But do not ask me anything more. Wait and trust me, or you may lay up lifelong regrets for yourself. Jules, my Jules, trust is love's great virtue. I confess it, I am too much troubled to answer you at this moment; I am a woman unapt at lying, and I love you, you know I love you."

"With all that shakes a man's belief and rouses his jealousy—for I am not the first in your heart, Clémence, it seems; I am not your very self?—well, with it all, I would still rather trust you, Clémence, trust your voice and those eyes of yours. If you are deceiving me, you would deserve——"

"Oh! a thousand deaths," she broke in.

"And I have not one thought hidden from you, while——"

"Hush," she cried, "our happiness depends upon silence between us."

"Ah! I will know all!" he shouted, with a burst of violent anger.

As he spoke a sound reached them, a shrill-tongued woman's voice raised to a scream in the ante-chamber.

"I will come in, I tell you! Yes, I will come in, I want to see her, I will see her!" somebody cried.

Jules and Clémence hurried into the drawing-room, and in another moment the door was flung open. A young woman suddenly appeared with two servants behind her.

"This woman would come in, sir, in spite of us. We told her once before that madame was not at home. She said she knew quite well that madame had gone out, but she had just seen her come in. She threatens to stop at the house door until she had spoken to madame."

"You can go," said M. Desmarets, addressing the servants.

"What do you want, mademoiselle?" he added, turning to the visitor.

The "young lady" was a feminine type known only in Paris; a type as much a product of the city as the mud or the curbstones in the streets, or the Seine water which is filtered through half a score of great reservoirs before it sparkles clear and pure in cut-glass decanters, all its muddy sediment left behind. She is, moreover, a truly characteristic product. Pencil and pen and charcoal, painter and caricaturist and draughtsman, have caught her likeness repeatedly; yet she eludes analysis, because you can no more grasp her in all her moods than you can grasp Nature, or the fantastic city herself. Her circle has but one point of contact with vice, from which the rest of its circumference is far removed. Yet the one flaw in her character is the only trait that reveals her; all her fine qualities lie out of sight while she flaunts her ingenuous shamelessness. The plays and books that bring her before the public, with all the illusion that clings about her, give but a very inadequate idea of her; she never is, and never will be, herself except in her garret; elsewhere she is either worse or better than she really is. Give her wealth, she degenerates; in poverty she is misconstrued. How should it be otherwise? She has so many faults and so many virtues; she lives too close to a tragic end in the river on the one hand, and a branding laugh upon the other; she is too fair and too foul; too much like a personification of that Paris which she provides with toothless old portresses, washerwomen, street-sweepers, and beggars; sometimes too with insolent comtesses and admired and applauded actress and opera singer. Twice in former times she even gave two queens, in all but name, to the Monarchy. Who could seize such a Protean woman-shape?

She is a very woman, less than a woman, and more than a woman. The painter of contemporary life can only give a few details, the general effect of so vast a subject, and some idea of its boundlessness.

This was a Paris grisette—a grisette, however, in her glory. She was the grisette that drives about in a cab; a happy, handsome, and fresh young person, but still a grisette, a grisette with claws and scissors; bold as a Spaniard, quarrelsome as an English prude instituting a suit for restitution of conjugal rights, coquettish as a great lady, and more outspoken; equal to all occasions, a typical "lioness," issuing from her little apartment.

Many and many a time had she dreamed of that establishment with its red cotton curtains and its furniture covered with Utrecht velvet, of the tea-table and the hand-painted china tea-service and the settee; the small square of velvet pile carpet, the alabaster timepiece and vases under glass shades, the yellow bedroom, the soft eiderdown quilt,—of all the joys of a grisette's life, in short. Now she had a servant, a superannuated member of her own profession, a veteran grisette with moustaches and good-conduct stripes. Now she went to the theatres and had as many sweetmeats as she liked; she had silk dresses and finery to soil and draggle, and all the joys of life from the point of view of the milliner's assistant, except a carriage of her own, a carriage being to the milliner's assistant's dreams what the marshal's baton is for the private soldier. Yes, all these things this particular grisette possessed in return for a real affection, or perhaps in spite of a real affection on her part; for others of her class will often exact as much for one hour in the day, a sort of toll carelessly paid for by a brief space in some old man's clutches.

The young person now confronting M. and Mme. Jules wore shoes, which displayed so much white stocking that they looked like an almost invisible black boundary line against the carpet. This kind of footgear, very neatly rendered by French comic drawings, is one of the Parisian grisette's peculiar charms of dress; but a still more unmistakable sign for observant eyes is the precision with which her gown is moulded to her figure, which is very clearly outlined. Moreover, the visitor was "turned out" in a green dress, to use the picturesque expression coined by the French soldier, a dress with a chemisette, which revealed a fine figure, fully displayed, for her Ternaux shawl would have slipped down to the floor if she had not held the two loosely-knotted ends in her grasp. She had a delicate face, a white skin and color in her cheeks, sparkling gray eyes, a very prominent rounded forehead, and carefully waved hair, which escaped from under a little bonnet, and fell in large curls about her neck.

"My name is Ida, sir. And if that is Mme. Jules whom I have the privilege of addressing, I have come to tell her all that I have against her on my mind. It is a shame, when she has made her bargain, and has such furniture as you have here, to try to take away the man to whom a poor girl is as good as married, and him talking of making it all right by marrying me at the registry office. There's quite plenty nice young men in the world—isn't there, sir?—for her to fancy without her coming and taking a man well on in years away from me when I am happy with him. *Quien,* I haven't a fine house, I haven't, I have my love! I detest your fine-looking men and money; I am all heart and——"

Mme. Jules turned to her husband:

"You will permit me, sir, to hear no more of this," said she, and went back to her room.

"If the lady is living with you, I have made a hash of it, as far as I can see; but so much the worser," continued Ida. "What business has she to come and see M. Ferragus every day?"

"You are mistaken, mademoiselle," said Jules, in dull amazement; "my wife could not possibly——"

"Oh! so you are married, are you, the two of you?" said the grisette, evidently rather surprised. "Then it's far worse, sir, is it not, when a woman has a lawful husband of her own to have anything to do with a man like Henri——"

"But what Henri?" said Jules, taking Ida aside into another room lest his wife should overhear anything further.

"Well, then, M. Ferragus."

"But he is dead," protested Jules.

"What stuff! I went to Franconi's yesterday evening, and he brought me home again, as he ought to do. Your lady too can give you news of him. Didn't she go to see him at three o'clock? That she did, I know, for I was waiting for her in the street; being as a very nice man, M. Justin—perhaps you know him? a little old fogy that wears stays and has seals on his watch-chain—it was he that told me that I had a Mme. Jules for my rival. That name, sir, is well known among fancy names; asking your pardon, since it's your own, but Mme. Jules might be a duchess at court, Henri is so rich he can afford all his whims. It is my business to look after my own, as I have a right to do; for I love Henri, I do. He was my first fancy, and my love and the rest of my life is at stake. I am afraid of nothing, sir; I am honest, and I never told a lie yet, nor took a thing belonging to anybody whatever. If I had an empress for my rival I should go right straight to her, and if she took my husband that is to be from me, I feel that I could kill her, was she never so much an empress, for one fine woman is as good as another, sir——"

"That will do, that will do!" interrupted Jules. "Where do you live?"

"Number 14 Rue de la Corderie du Temple, sir. Ida Gruget, corset-maker at your service, sir; for we make a good many corsets for gentlemen."

"And this man Ferragus, as you call him, where does he live?"

"Why, sir" (tightening her lips), "in the first place, he is not just 'a man'—he is a gentleman, and better off than you are, maybe. But what makes you ask me for his address, when your wife knows where he lives? He told me I was not to give it to anybody. Am I bound to give you an answer? I am not in the police court nor the confessional, the Lord be thanked, and I am not beholden to any one."

"And how if I offer you twenty, thirty, forty thousand francs to tell me his address?"

"Oh, not quite, my little dear; it's no go," said she, with a gesture learned in the streets, as accompaniment to her singular answer. "No amount of money would get that out of me. I have the honor to wish you good-evening.—Which way do you get out of this?"

Jules allowed her to go. He was stricken to earth. The whole world seemed to be crumbling away under him, the sky above had fallen with a crash.

"Dinner is ready, sir," said the footman.

For fifteen minutes the footman and Desmarets' man-servant waited in the dining-room, but no one appeared. The maid came in to say that "the mistress would not take dinner."

"Why, what is the matter, Joséphine?" asked the footman.

"I don't know. The mistress is crying, and she is going to bed. The master has a fancy somewhere else, I expect, and it has been found out at an awkward time; do you understand? I would not answer for the mistress' life. Men are all so clumsy, always making scenes without thinking in the least."

"Not a bit of it," said the man, lowering his voice; "on the contrary it is the mistress who—in short, you understand. What time could the master have for gadding about, when he hasn't spent a night out of five years, and goes down to his office at ten o'clock, and only comes up to lunch at twelve? In fact, his life is open and regular, while the mistress goes off pretty nearly every day at three o'clock, no one knows where."

"So does the master," said the maid, taking her mistress' part.

"But he goes to the Bourse, the master does.—This is the third time I have told him that dinner is ready," he added, after a pause; "you might as well talk to a statue."

Jules came in.

"Where is your mistress?" asked he.

"Madame has gone to bed, she has a sick headache," said the maid, assuming an important air.

"You can take the dinner away," said Jules, with much cool self-possession. "I shall keep madame company." And he went to his wife. She was crying, and stifling her sobs with her handkerchief.

"Why do you cry?" said Jules, using the formal *vous*. "You have no violence, no reproaches to expect from me. Why should I avenge myself? If you have not been faithful to my love, it is because you were not worthy of it——"

"Not worthy!"

The words repeated amid her sobs, and the tone in which they were spoken, would have softened any man but Jules.

"To kill you, a man must love more, perhaps, than I," he resumed; "but I have not the heart to do it, I would sooner make away with myself and leave you to your—your happiness—and to—whom—— ?"

He broke off.

"Make away with yourself!" cried Clémence. She flung herself at Jules' feet and clung about them; but he tried to shake her off, and dragged her to the bed.

"Leave me alone," said he.

"No, no, Jules! If you love me no longer, I shall die. Do you wish to know all?"

"Yes." He took her, held her forcibly in his grasp, sat down on the bedside, and held her between his knees; then he gazed dry-eyed at the fair face, now red as fire, and seamed with tear-stains. "Now, tell me," he said for the second time.

Clémence began to sob afresh.

"I cannot. It is a secret of life and death. If I told you, I . . . No, I *cannot*. Have pity, Jules!"

"You are deceiving me still," he said, but he replaced the formal *vous* by *tu*.

"Ah!" she cried, at this sign of relenting. "Yes, Jules, you may believe that I am deceiving you, now you shall know everything very soon."

"But this Ferragus, this convict that you go to see, this man enriched by crime, if he is not your lover, if you are not his——"

"Oh, Jules!"

"Well, is he your unknown benefactor, the man to whom we owe our success, as people have said before this?"

"Who said so?"

"A man whom I killed in a duel."

"Oh, God! one man dead already."

"If he is not your protector, if he does not give you money, and you take money to him, is he your brother?"

"Well," she said, "and if he were?"

M. Desmarets folded his arms.

"Why should this have been kept from my knowledge?" returned he. "Did you both deceive me—you and your mother? And do people go to see their brothers every day, or nearly every day, eh?"

But his wife fell swooning at his feet.

He pulled the bell ropes, summoned Joséphine, and laid Clémence on the bed.

"She is dead," he thought, "and how if I am wrong?"

"This will kill me," murmured Mme. Jules, as she came to herself.

"Joséphine," exclaimed M. Desmarets, "go for M. Desplein; and then go to my brother's house and ask him to come as soon as possible."

"Why your brother?" asked Clémence. But Jules had already left the room. For the first time in five years Mme. Jules slept alone in her bed, and was obliged to allow a doctor to enter the sanctuary, two troubles that she felt keenly.

Desplein found Mme. Jules very ill; never had violent emotion been worse timed. He postponed his decision on the case till the morrow, and left divers prescriptions which were not carried out, all physical suffering was forgotten in heart dis-

tress. Daylight was at hand, and still Clémence lay awake.
Her thoughts were busy with the murmur of conversation,
which lasted for several hours, between the brothers, but no
single word reached her through the thickness of the walls to
give a clue to the meaning of the prolonged conference. M.
Desmarets, the notary, went at length; and then, in the stillness of the night, with that strange stimulation of the senses
that comes with passion, Clémence could hear the squeaking
of a pen and the unconscious movements made by some one
busily writing. Those who are accustomed to sit up through
the night, and have noticed the effect of deep silence on the
laws of acoustics, know that a faint sound at intervals is easily
heard, when a continuous and even murmur is scarcely dis-
tinguishable.

Clémence rose, anxious and trembling. She forgot her
condition, forgot that she was damp with perspiration, and,
barefooted and without a dressing-gown, went across and
opened the door. Luckily it turned noiselessly on its hinges.
She saw her husband, pen in hand, sitting fast asleep in his
easy-chair. The candles were burning low in the sockets. She
crept forward, and on an envelope that lay sealed already,
she saw the words, "My Will."

She knelt down, as if at a graveside, and kissed her husband's hand. He woke at once.

"Jules, dear, even criminals condemned to death are given
a few days' respite," she said, looking at him with eyes shining with love and fever. "Your innocent wife asks for two
days—only two days. Leave me free for two days, and——
wait. After that I shall die happy; at any rate, you will be
sorry."

"You shall have the delay, Clémence."

And while she kissed her husband's hands in a pathetic
outpouring of her heart, Jules, fascinated by that cry of innocence, took her in his arms and kissed her on the forehead,
utterly ashamed that he should still submit to the power of
that noble beauty.

Next morning, after a few hours of sleep, Jules went to his wife's room, mechanically obedient to his custom of never leaving home without first seeing her. Clémence was asleep. A ray of light from a chink in the highest window fell on the face of a woman worn out with grief. Sorrow had left traces on her brow already, and faded the fresh red of her lips. A lover's eyes could not mistake the significance of the dark marbled streaks and the pallor of illness, which took the place of the even color in her cheeks and the white velvet of her skin, the transparent surface over which all the feelings that stirred that fair soul so unconsciously flitted.

"She is not well," thought Jules. "Poor Clémence, may God protect us!"

He kissed her very gently on the forehead; she awoke, looked into her husband's face, and understood. She could not speak, but she took his hand, and her eyes grew soft with tears.

"I am innocent," she said, finishing her dream.

"You will not go out to-day, will you?" said Jules.

"No; I feel too weak to get up."

"If you change your mind, wait till I come home," said Jules, and he went down to the porter's lodge.

"Fouquereau, you must keep a strict watch to-day," he said. "I wish to know every one who comes in or out."

With that, Jules sprang into a cab, bade the man drive to the Hôtel de Maulincour, and asked for the Baron.

"Monsieur is ill," was the reply.

Jules insisted, and sent in his name. If he could not see M. de Maulincour, he would see the Vidame or the dowager. He waited for some time in the old Baroness' drawing-room; she came at last, however, to say that her grandson was far too ill to see him.

"I know the nature of his illness, madame," said Jules, "from the letter which you did me the honor to send, and I entreat you to believe——"

"A letter, monsieur? I letter that I sent to you?" broke in the Baroness. "I have not written a word. And what am I supposed to say, monsieur, in this letter?"

"Madame, as I meant to call on M. de Maulincour this very day, and to return the note to you, I thought I need not destroy it in spite of the request at the end. Here it is."

The dowager rang for her double-strength spectacles, and glanced down the sheet with every sign of the greatest astonishment.

"The handwriting is so exactly like mine, monsieur, that if we were not speaking of a quite recent event, I should be deceived by it myself. My grandson certainly is ill, monsieur, but his mind has not been affected the least bit in the world. We are puppets in the hands of wicked people; still, I cannot guess the object of this piece of impertinence. . . . You shall see my grandson, monsieur, and you will admit that he is perfectly sane."

She rang the bell again to ask if it were possible for the Baron to receive a visit from M. Desmarets. The footman brought an answer in the affirmative. Jules went up to Auguste de Maulincour's room, and found that young officer seated in an armchair by the fireside. He was too weak to rise, and greeted his visitor with a melancholy inclination of the head. The Vidame de Pamiers was keeping him company.

"M. le Baron," began Jules, "I have something to say of so private a nature that I should wish to speak with you alone."

"Monsieur," said Auguste, "M. le Commandeur knows all about this affair; you need not fear to speak before him."

"M. le Baron, you have disturbed and almost destroyed my happiness; and you had no right to do so. Until we know which of us must ask, or give satisfaction to the other, you are bound to give me your assistance in the dark ways to which you have suddenly brought me. So I have come to inquire the present address of this mysterious being who exercises such an unlucky influence on our lives, and seems to have some supernatural power at his orders. I received this letter yesterday, just as I came in after hearing your account of yourself."

Jules handed the forged letter.

"This Ferragus or Bourignard or M. de Funcal is a fiend incarnate!" shouted Maulincour. "In what hideous labyrinth have I set foot? Whither am I going?—I was wrong, monsieur," he added, looking full at Jules, "but death surely is the greatest expiation of all, and I am dying. So you can ask me anything you wish; I am at your service."

"You should know where this strange man lives; I absolutely must get to the bottom of this mystery, if it costs me all that I have; and with such a cruelly ingenious enemy, every moment is precious."

"Justin will tell us all about it directly," replied the Baron. The Vidame fidgeted upon his chair. Auguste rang the bell.

"Justin is not in the house," exclaimed the Vidame in a hasty fashion, which said a good deal more than the words.

"Well," Auguste said quickly, "and if he is not, our servants here know where he is. A man on horseback shall go at once to find him. Your servant is in Paris, is he not? They will find him somewhere."

The old Vidame de Pamiers was visibly troubled.

"Justin will not come, dear fellow," he said. "I wanted to keep the accident from your knowledge, but——"

"Is he dead?" exclaimed M. de Maulincour. "And when? and how?"

"It happened yesterday night. He went out to supper with some old friends, and got drunk no doubt; his friends, being also the worse for wine, must have left him to lie in the street; a heavy carriage drove right over him——"

"The convict did not fail that time; he killed his man at the first attempt," said Auguste. "He was not so lucky with me; he had to try four times."

Jules grew moody and thoughtful.

"So I shall find out nothing, it seems," he exclaimed, after a long pause. "Perhaps your man was rightly served; he went beyond your orders when he slandered Mme. Desmarets to one 'Ida,' to stir up the girl's jealousy and let her loose upon us."

"Ah, monsieur, in my fury I gave over Mme. Jules to him."

"Sir!" exclaimed Mme. Jules' husband, stung to the quick; but Maulincour silenced him with a wave of the hand

"Oh! now I am prepared for all that may happen. What is done is done, and you will do no better; nor can you say anything that my own conscience has not told me already. I am expecting the most famous specialist in toxicology to know my fate. If the pain is likely to be intolerable, I have made up my mind; I shall blow my brains out."

"You are talking like a boy," cried the old Vidame, aghast at the Baron's coolness. "Your grandmother would die of grief!"

"And so, monsieur, there is no way of finding out in what part of Paris this extraordinary man lives?" asked Jules.

"I think, monsieur, that I heard this poor Justin say that M. de Funcal was to be found at the Portuguese or else the Brazilian Embassy," said the Vidame. "M. de Funcal is of a good family; he belongs to both countries. As for the convict, he is dead and buried. Your persecutor, whoever he may be, is so powerful, it seems to me, that you had better accept him in his new metamorphosis until you are in a position to overwhelm him with confusion and crush him; but set about it prudently, my dear sir. If M. de Maulincour had taken my advice, nothing of all this would have happened."

Jules withdrew, coolly but politely. He was at his wits' end to find Ferragus. As he came in, the porter came out to inform him that madame had gone out to put a letter into the box opposite the Rue de Ménars. Jules felt humiliated by the profound intelligence with which the man aided and abetted his scheme, and by the very skill with which he found means to serve him. The zeal and peculiar ingenuity which inferiors will show to compromise their betters, when their betters compromise themselves, were well known to Jules, and he appreciated the danger of having such accomplices in any affair whatsoever; but he had forgotten his personal dignity till he suddenly saw how far he had fallen. What a triumph for a serf, unable to rise to his master, to bring that master down to his own level.

Jules was stern and abrupt with the man. Another blunder. But he was so wretched! His life, till then so straight and clean, had grown crooked; and now there was nothing for it but to use craft and lies. And Clémence, too, was using lies and craft with him. It was a sickening moment. Lost in depths of bitter thought, he stood forgetful of himself and motionless on the doorstep. Sometimes he gave way to despair which counseled flight; he would leave France and carry with him his love and all the illusions of unproved guilt; and then again, never doubting but that Clémence's letter was addressed to Ferragus, he cast about for ways of intercepting the reply sent by that mysterious being. Again, examining into this singular success since his marriage, he asked himself whether that slander which he had avenged was not after all a truth. At length, returning to Ferragus' answer, he reasoned with himself on this wise:—

"But will this Ferragus, so profoundly astute as he is, so consequent in the least things that he does; this man who sees, and foresees, and calculates, and even guesses our thoughts, will he send an answer? Is he not sure to employ some means in keeping with his power? Can he not send a reply by some ingenious scoundrel, or, more likely still, in a jewel case brought by some unsuspecting, honest creature, or in a parcel with a pair of shoes which some working-girl, in all innocence, brings home for my wife? Suppose that there should be an understanding between him and Clémence?"

He could trust nothing and nobody. He made a hurried survey of the boundless field, the shoreless sea of conjecture; and after drifting hither and thither, and in every possible direction, it occurred to him that he was stronger in his own house than anywhere else; so he resolved to stay at home and watch like an ant-lion at the bottom of its funnel in the sand.

"Fouquereau," he said, "if any one asks for me, I am not at home. But if any one wishes to speak with madame, or brings anything for her, ring twice. And you must let me see every letter left here, no matter to whom it is addressed.— And so," he thought within himself, as he went into his office on the entresol, "and so I shall outwit Master Ferragus. And if his messenger is cunning enough to ask for me, so as to find out whether madame is alone, at any rate I shall not be gulled like a fool."

His office windows looked into the street. As he stood with his face pressed against the panes, jealousy inspired him with a final stratagem. He determined to send his head-clerk to the Bourse in his carriage; the clerk should take a letter to a friend of his, another stockbroker, to whom he would explain his business transactions—he would beg his friend to take his place. His most difficult business he put off till the morrow, regardless of the rise and fall of stocks, and all the funds of Europe. Fair prerogative of love! Love eclipses all things else. The rest of the world fades away before it; and altar, throne, and government securities are as though they were not. At half-past three o'clock, just when the Bourse is all agog with rates and premiums, rises and falls, current accounts, and the rest of it, Jules looked up and saw Fouquereau with a beaming countenance.

"An old woman has just been here, sir; she is as sharp as they make them. Oh! she is an artful one, I can tell you. She asked for you and seemed put out to find you were not at home; then she gave me this letter here for madame."

Jules broke the seal with feverish anguish, but he dropped exhausted into his chair. The letter was a string of meaningless words, and quite unintelligible without a key. It was written in cipher.

"You can go, Fouquereau."

The man went.

"This mystery is deeper than the unplumbed sea. Oh, this is love beyond a doubt. Love, and love only, could be as sagacious, as ingenious as the writer of this letter. Oh, God! I will kill Clémence."

Even at that moment a bright idea burst upon his brain, and struck him so forcibly, that it seemed almost like the breaking out of light. In the old days of poverty and hard work before his marriage, Jules had made a real friend. The excessive delicacy with which Jules spared the susceptibilities of a poor and shy comrade, the respect that he paid his friend, the tactful ingenuity with which he made that friend accept a share of his good fortune without a blush,—all these things had increased their friendship since those days. In spite of Desmarets' prosperity, Jacquet was faithful to him.

Jacquet, an honest man, and a toiler of austere life, had slowly made his way in that Department which of all others employs most rascality and most honesty. He was in the Foreign Office; the most delicate part of its archives was in his charge. He was a kind of departmental glow-worm, shedding light during his working hours on secret correspondence, deciphering and classifying despatches. Rather above the rank and file of the middle classes, he held the highest (subaltern) posts at the Foreign Office, and lived unrecognized; rejoicing in an obscurity which put him beyond reverses of fortune, and content to pay his debt to his fatherland in small coin. A born assistant-registrar, he enjoyed the respect that was due to him, in newspaper language. And, as an unknown patriot in a Government Department, he resigned himself to groan, by his fireside, over the aberrations of the Government that he served. His position, thanks to Jules, had been improved by a suitable marriage. In his own home, Jacquet was a debonair king, a "man with an umbrella"; his wife had a jobbed carriage which he never used himself; and as a final touch to this portrait of an unconscious philosopher, it should be added that he had never yet suspected, and never would suspect, how much he might make out of his position, with a stockbroker for his intimate friend, and a knowledge of State secrets. A hero after the manner of that unknown private soldier who died to save Napoleon with a cry of "Who goes there?" he was faithful to his department.

In another ten minutes Jules stood in Jacquet's private office. His friend brought forward a chair, laid his green silk eye-shade down methodically upon the table, rubbed his hands, took out his snuff-box, rose to his feet, threw out his chest with a crack of the shoulder-blades, and said:

"What chance brings you here, *Mosieur* Desmarets? What do you want with me?"

"I want you to find out a secret for me, Jacquet; it is a matter of life and death."

"It is not about politics?"

"You are not the man I should come to if I wanted to know anything of that kind," said Jules. "No, it is a private affair, and I must ask you to keep it as secret as possible."

"Claude Joseph Jacquet, professional mute. Why, don't you know me?" laughed he. "My line of business is discretion."

Jules put the letter before him.

"This is addressed to my wife; I must have it read to me," he said.

"The devil! the devil! a bad business," said Jacquet, scrutinizing the document as a money-lender examines a negotiable bill. "Aha! a stencil cipher. Wait."

He left Jules alone in the office, but came back pretty soon.

"Tomfoolery, my friend. It is written with an old stencil cipher which the Portuguese ambassador used in M. de Choiseul's time after the expulsion of the Jesuits. Stay, look here."

Jacquet took up a sheet of paper with holes cut in it at regular intervals; it looked rather like the lace paper which confectioners put over their sugar-plums. When this was set over the sheet below, Jules could easily make sense of the words left uncovered.

"My dear Clemence,—Do not trouble yourself any more; no one shall trouble our happiness again, and your husband will put his suspicions aside. I cannot go to see you. However ill you may be, you must gather up your courage to come to me; summon up your strength, love will give it you. I have been through a most cruel operation for your sake, and I cannot stir out of bed. Moxas were applied yesterday evening to the nape of the neck and across the shoulders; it was necessary to cauterize pretty deeply. Do you understand? But I thought of you, and found the pain not intolerable. I have

left the sheltering roof of the embassy to baffle Maulincour,
who shall not persecute us much longer; and here I am safe
from all search at number 12 Rue des Enfants-Rouges, with
an old woman, one Mme. Étienne Gruget, mother of that Ida,
who shall shortly pay dear for her silly prank. Come to-morrow at nine o'clock. My room can only be reached by an inner
staircase. Ask for M. Camuset. Good-bye till to-morrow. A kiss on thy forehead, my darling."

Jacquet gazed at Jules with a kind of shocked expression
with a very real sympathy in it, and brought out his favorite invocations, "The devil! the devil!" in two distinct intona-
tions.

"It seems clear to you, doesn't it?" said Jules. "Well, and
yet, in the bottom of my heart a voice pleads for my wife,
and that voice rises above all the pangs of jealousy. I shall
endure the most horrid torture until to-morrow; but at last,
to-morrow between nine and ten, I shall know all. I shall
either be wretched or happy for life. Think of me, Jacquet."

"I will be at your house at eight o'clock. We will go yonder together. I will wait outside in the street for you, if you
like. There may be risks to run; you ought to have some one
you can trust within call, a sure hand that can take a hint.
Count upon me."

"Even to help me to kill a man?"

"The devil! the devil!" Jacquet said quickly, repeating,
so to speak, the same musical note. "I have two children and
a wife——"

Jules squeezed Claude Jacquet's hand and went out. But
he came back in haste.

"I am forgetting the letter," said he. "And that is not
all; it must be sealed again."

"The devil! the devil! you opened it without taking an impression; but, luckily, the edge of the fracture is pretty clean.
There, let me have it, I will give it you back again *secundum
scripturam.*"

"When?"

"By half-past five——"

"If I am not in, simply give it to the porter, and tell him to send it up to madame."

"Do you want me to-morrow?"

"No. Good-bye."

Jules soon reached the Place de la Rotonde du Temple, dismissed his cabriolet, and walked down to the Rue des Enfants-Rouges, to take a look at Mme. Étienne Gruget's abode. The mystery on which so many lives hung was to be cleared up there. Ferragus was there, and Ferragus held all the ends of the threads in this obscure business.—Was not the connection between Mme. Jules, her husband, and this man the Gordian knot of a tragedy stained even now with blood? Nor should the sword be wanting to cut asunder the tightest of all bonds.

The house belonged to the class commonly known as *cabajoutis*—an expressive name given by working people in Paris to patchwork buildings, as they may be called. Several houses, originally separate, have sometimes been run into one, according to the fancy of the various proprietors who successively enlarged them; or they were begun and left unfinished for a time, and afterwards resumed and completed. Unlucky dwellings are they that have passed, like sundry nations, under the rule of several dynasties of capricious rulers. The various stories and windows do not belong to each other, to borrow one of the most picturesque of painter's words; every detail, even the decoration outside, clashes with the rest of the building. The *cabajoutis* is to Parisian street architecture what the *capharnaüm,* or lumber-room, is to the house—a regular rubbish-heap where the most unlikely things are shot down together pell-mell.

"Mme. Étienne?" Jules asked of the portress.

That functionary was installed in the great centre doorway in a sort of hencoop, a little wooden house on wheels, not unlike the cabins which the police authorities put up at every cabstand.

"Eh?" said the portress, laying down the stocking which

she was knitting. The living accessories which contribute
to the general effect of any portion of the great monster Paris,
fit in, as a rule, remarkably well with the character of their
surroundings. The porter, concierge, Swiss, or whatever you
may choose to call this indispensable muscle in the monster's
economy, is always in keeping with the quarter of which he is
an integral part; very often he is the Quarter incarnate. The
concierge of the Faubourg Saint-Germain, an idle being embroidered at every seam, speculates in stocks and shares; in
the Chaussée d'Antin, the porter is a comfortable personage;
in the neighborhood of the Bourse, he reads the newspaper;
in the Faubourg Montmartre, he carries on some industry or
other. In low neighborhoods the portress is a worn-out
prostitute; in the Marais she keeps herself respectable, she
is apt to be peevish, she has her "ways."

At sight of Jules, the portress of the Rue des Enfants-
Rouges stirred up the dying embers of block fuel in her foot-
warmer, taking a knife for the purpose. Then she said,
"You want Mme. Étienne; do you mean Mme. Étienne
Gruget?"

"Yes," said Jules Desmarets, with a touch of vexation.

"She that works at trimmings?"

"Yes."

"Very well, sir," and emerging from her cage, she laid a
hand on Jules' arm and drew him to the further end of a
long narrow passage, vaulted like a cellar; "you go up the
second staircase opposite, just across the yard. Do you see
the windows with the gilliflowers? That's where Mme.
Étienne lives."

"Thank you, madame. Is she alone, do you think?"

"Why shouldn't she be alone when she is a lone woman?"

Jules sprang noiselessly up a very dark staircase, every
step incrusted with dried lumps of mud deposited by the
lodgers' boots. He found three doors on the second floor, but
no sign of gilliflowers. Luckily for him, some words were
written in chalk on the grimiest and greasiest of the three—
Ida will be back at nine o'clock to-night.

"Here it is," said Jules to himself.

He tugged at an old blackened bell-pull, with a fawn's foot attached, and heard the smothered tinkle of a little cracked bell, and the yapping of an asthmatic little dog. He could tell by the sound that the bell made inside that the room was so lumbered up with things that there was no room for an echo—a characteristic trait of workmen's lodgings and little households generally, where there is neither space nor air. Jules looked about involuntarily for the gilliflowers, and found them at last on the window-sill, between two pestiferous sinks. Here were flowers, a garden two feet long and six inches wide, and a sprouting grain of wheat—all life condensed into that narrow space, and not one of life's miseries lacking! A ray of sunlight shone down, as if in pity on the sickly blossoms and the superb green column of wheat-stalk, bringing out the indescribable color peculiar to Paris slums; dust, grease, and inconceivable filth incrusted and corroded the rubbed, discolored, damp walls, the worm-eaten balusters, the gaping window-sashes, the doors that once had been painted red. In another moment he heard an old woman's cough and the sound of heavy feet dragging painfully along in list slippers. This must be Ida Gruget's mother. She opened the door, came out upon the landing, raised her face to his, and said:

"Ah! it's M. Bocquillon! Why, no it isn't. My word! how like you are to M. Bocquillon! You are a brother of his perhaps? What can I do for you, sir? Just step inside."

Jules followed her into the first room, and caught a general impression of bird-cages, pots and pans, stoves, furniture, little earthenware dishes full of broken meat, or milk for the dog and the cats; a wooden clock-case, blankets, Eisen's engravings, and a heap of old ironmongery piled up with the most curiously grotesque effect. It was a genuine Parisian *capharnaüm;* nothing was lacking, not even a few odd numbers of the *Constitutionnel.*

"Just come in here and warm yourself," said the Widow Gruget, but prudence prevailed. Jules was afraid that Fer-

ragus might overhear, and wondered whether the bargain
which he proposed to make had not better be concluded in
the outer room; just then, however, a hen came cackling down
a staircase and cut short his inward conference. He made up
his mind and followed Ida's mother into the next room, where
a fire was burning. A wheezy little pug-dog, a dumb spectator, followed them, and scrambled up on an old stool. Mme.
Gruget's request to come in and get warm was prompted by
the very coxcombry of poverty on the brink of destitution.
Her stock-pot completely hid a couple of smouldering sticks
which ostentatiously shunned each other. A skimmer lay on
the floor, with the handle among the ashes. On the wooden
ledge above the fireplace, amid a litter of wools, cottonreels,
and odds and ends, needed for the manufacture of trimmings,
stood a little waxen crucifix under a shade made of pieces of
glass joined together with strips of bluish paper. Jules looked
round at the furniture with a curiosity in which self-interest
was blended, and in spite of himself he showed his secret satisfaction.

"Well, sir, do you think you can do with my furniture?"
inquired the widow, sitting down in a yellow cane-seated
armchair, her headquarters apparently; for it contained her
pocket-handkerchief, her snuff-box, some half-peeled vegetables, her spectacles, an almanac, a length of galoon on which
she was at work, a pack of greasy playing-cards, and a couple
of novels. All this sounded hollow. The piece of furniture
on which the widow was "descending the river of life" was
something like the comprehensive bag which women take on
a journey, a sort of house in miniature, containing everything
from the husband's portrait to the drop of balm tea in case
she feels faint, from the sugar-plums for the little ones to
sticking-plaster for cut fingers.

Jules made a careful survey of it all. He looked very
closely at Mme. Gruget herself, with her gray eyes, denuded
of lashes and eyebrows, at her toothless mouth, at the dark
shades in her wrinkles, at her rusty net cap, with its yet more
rusty frill, at her tattered cotton petticoats, her worn slippers,

and charred foot-warmer, and then at the table covered with crockery, silks, and patterns of work in worsted and cotton, with the neck of a wine-bottle rising out of the middle of the litter, and said within himself, "This woman has some passion, some failing that she keeps quiet; she is in my power."—Aloud he said with a significant gesture, "I have come to order some galoon of you, madame;" then lowered his voice to add, "I know that you have a lodger here, a man that goes by the name of Camuset."

The old woman looked up at once, but there was not a sign of surprise in her countenance.

"Look here, can he overhear us? There is a fortune involved for you, mind you."

"You can speak, sir, there is nothing to be afraid of; there is nobody here. There is somebody upstairs, but it is quite impossible that he should hear you."

"Ah! cunning old thing! She can give you a Norman's answer," thought Jules. "We may come to terms.—You need not trouble yourself to tell a lie, madame. To begin with, bear in mind that I mean no harm whatever to you, nor to your invalid lodger with his blisters, nor to your daughter Ida the staymaker, Ferragus' sweetheart. You see, I know all about it. Never mind, I have nothing to do with the police, and I want nothing that is likely to hurt your conscience.

"A young lady will come here to-morrow between nine and ten to have some talk with your daughter's sweetheart. I want to be somewhere near, so that I can hear and see everything without being heard or seen. You must arrange this for me, and I will give you two thousand francs down, and an annuity of six hundred francs. My notary shall draw up the agreement this evening in your presence, and I will give the money into his hands to pay over to you to-morrow after this meeting at which I wish to be present, when I shall have proof of your good faith."

"It will not do any harm to my daughter, will it, my dear gentleman?" she returned, on the watch like a suspicious cat.

"None whatever, madame. But, at the same time, your daughter is behaving very badly to you, it seems to me. When a man as rich and powerful as Ferragus is fond of her, it ought to be easy to make you more comfortable than you appear to be."

"Ah, my dear gentleman, not so much as a miserable ticket for the Ambigu or the Gaieté, where she can go whenever she likes. It is shameful. And I that sold my silver spoons, and am eating now off German silver in my old age, all to apprentice that girl, and give her a business where she could coin gold if she chose. For as to that, she takes after her mother; she is as neat-fingered as a fairy, it must be said in justice to her. At any rate, she might as well hand over her old silk dresses to me, so fond as I am of wearing silk; but no, sir. She goes to the *Cadran bleu,* to dine at fifty francs a head, and rolls in her carriage like a princess, and doesn't care a rap for her mother. God Almighty! we bring these scatter-brained girls into the world, and it is not the best that could be said for us. A mother, sir, and a good mother too, for I have hidden her giddiness, and cosseted her to that degree that I took the bread out of my mouth to stuff her with all that I had! Well, and that is not enough, but she must come and coax you, and then wish you 'Good-day, mother!' That is the way they do their duty to them that brought them into the world! Just let them go their ways. But she will have children some day or other, and then she will know what it is for herself; bad bargains they are, but one loves them, all the same."

"What, does she do nothing for you?"

"Nothing? Oh, no, sir, I don't say that. If she did nothing at all for me, it would be rather too bad. She pays the rent, and gives me firewood and thirty-six francs a month. But is it right, sir, that I should have to go on working at my age? I am fifty-two, and my eyes are weak of an evening. And what is more, why won't she have me with her? If she is ashamed of me, she may as well say so at once. You had need to bury yourself, and that is the truth, for these beastly children that forget all about you before they have so much as shut the door."

She drew her handkerchief from her pocket, and a lottery ticket fell out, but she picked it up in a moment.

"*Quien!* that is the rate-collector's receipt."

Jules suddenly guessed the reason of the prudent parsimony of which the mother complained, and felt the more sure that the Widow Gruget would agree to his proposal.

"Very well, madame," he said, "in that case you will accept my offer."

"Two thousand francs down, did you say, sir? and six hundred francs a year?"

"I have changed my mind, madame. I will promise you only three hundred francs of annuity. The arrangement suits me better. But I will pay you five thousand francs down. You would rather have it so, would you not?"

"Lord, yes, sir."

"You will be more comfortable, you can go to the Ambigu Comique, or Franconi's, or anywhere else, and go comfortably in a cab."

"Oh, I do not care about Franconi's at all, being as you don't hear talk of it. And if I agree to take the money, sir, it is because it will be a fine thing for my child. And I shall not be living on her. Poor little thing, after all, I don't grudge her such pleasure as she gets. Young things must have amusement, sir. And so, if you will assure me that I shall be doing nobody any harm——"

"Nobody," repeated Jules. "But see now, how are you going to set about it?"

"Oh, well, sir, if M. Ferragus has just a little drink of poppy water to-night, he will sleep sound, the dear man! And much he stands in need of sleep, in such pain as he is, for he suffers so that it makes you sorry to see it. And by the by, just tell me what sort of a notion it is for a healthy man to have his back burned to cure the neuralgia that does not trouble him once in two years?—But to go back to our business, sir. My neighbor that lives just above has left her

key with me; her room is next door to M. Ferragus' bedroom. She has gone to the country for ten days. So if you
have a hole made to-night in the partition wall, you can look
in and hear at your ease. There is a locksmith, a great friend
of mine, a very nice man, that talks like an angel; he will
do that for me, and nobody any the wiser."

"Here are a hundred francs for him. You must come this
evening to M. Desmarets'; he is a notary; here is his address.
The paper will be ready at nine o'clock, but—mum!"

"Right; mum, as you say. Good-day, sir."

Jules went home again, almost soothed by the certainty
of knowing everything to-morrow. He found the letter,
sealed flawlessly again, in the porter's room.

"How are you?" he asked his wife, in spite of the coolness
between them, so difficult is it to break from the old habits
of affection.

"Rather better, Jules," she answered in winning tones;
"will you dine here with me?"

"Yes. Stay, here is something that Fouquereau gave me
for you," and he handed her the letter. At the sight of it
Clémence's white face flushed a deep red; the sudden crimson
sent an intolerable pang through her husband.

"Is that joy?" laughed he, "or relief from suspense?"

"Oh! many things," she said, as she looked at the seal.

"I will leave you, madame."

He went down to his office and wrote to his brother about
the annuity to the Widow Gruget. When he came back again,
dinner was ready on a little table by Clémence's bedside, and
Joséphine waited upon them.

"If I were not lying in bed, what a pleasure it would be
to me to serve you!" she said, when Joséphine had gone.
"Oh, and even on my knees," she went on, passing her white
fingers through Jules' hair. "Dear noble heart! you were very
merciful and good to me just now. You have done me more
good by your trust in me than all the doctors in the world
could do with their prescriptions. Your woman's delicacy—
for you can love as a woman can—shed balm in my soul; I feel

almost well again. There is a truce. Jules, come closer,
let me kiss you."

Jules could not forego the joy of Clémence's kiss, and yet
it was not without something like remorse in his heart. He
felt small before this woman, in whose innocence he was always tempted to believe. There was a sort of sorrowful
gladness about Clémence. A chastened hope shone through
the troubled expression of her face. They seemed both alike
unhappy that the deceit must be kept up; another kiss, and
they must tell each other all; they could endure their pain
no longer.

"To-morrow evening, Clémence?"

"No, monsieur, to-morrow at noon you shall know everything, and you will kneel before your wife. Ah! no, you
shall not humble yourself. No, all is forgiven you.—No, you
have done no wrong. Listen. Yesterday you shattered me
very ruthlessly, but life perhaps might not have been complete if I had not known that anguish; it is a dark shadow to
bring out the brightness of days like heaven."

"You are bewitching me," Jules exclaimed, "and you would
give me remorse."

"Poor love, fate overrules us, and I cannot help my destiny.
I am going out to-morrow."

"When?"

"At half-past nine."

"Clémence, you must be very careful. You must consult
Dr. Desplein and old Haudry."

"I shall consult my own heart and courage only."

"I will leave you free. I shall not come to see you till
noon."

"Will you not stay with me a little while to-night? I am
not ill now——"

Jules finished his work and came back to sit with her.
He could not keep away. Love was stronger in him than all
his griefs.

Next morning, at nine o'clock, Jules slipped out of the

house, hurried to the Rue des Enfants-Rouges, climbed the stairs, and rang the bell at the Widow Gruget's door.

"Ah! you are a man of your word, punctual as sunrise," was old Mme. Gruget's greeting. "Come in, sir.—I have a cup of coffee and cream ready for you in case——" she added, when the door was closed. "Oh! and genuine cream, a little jar that I saw them fill with my own eyes at the cowkeeper's near by in the Marché des Enfants-Rouges."

"Thank you, no, madame, nothing. Show me upstairs——"

"Very good, my dear gentleman. Step this way."

She showed Jules into a room just above her own, and pointed triumphantly to a hole about as large as a two-franc piece, cut during the night so as to correspond with a rose in the pattern of the paper in Ferragus' room. The opening had been made above a cupboard on either side the wall; the locksmith had left no trace of his handiwork; and from below it was very difficult to see this improvised loophole in a dark corner. If Jules meant to see or hear anything, he was obliged to stay there in a tolerably cramped position, perched on the top of a step which the Widow Gruget had thoughtfully placed for him.

"There's a gentleman with him," she said, as she went. And, in fact, Jules saw that someone was busy dressing a line of blisters raised on Ferragus' shoulders. He recognized Ferragus from M. de Maulincour's description of the man.

"When shall I be all right, do you think?" asked the patient.

"I do not know," said the other; "but from what the doctors say, seven or eight more dressings will be needed at least.

"Very well, see you again this evening," returned Ferragus, holding out a hand to the man as he adjusted the last bandage.

"This evening," returned the other, shaking Ferragus cordially by the hand. "I should be glad to see you out of your pain."

"At last M. de Funcal's papers are to be handed over to-morrow, and Henri Bourignard is really dead," continued

Ferragus. "Those two unlucky letters that cost us so dear have been destroyed, so I shall be somebody, socially speaking; a man among men again, and I am quite as good as the sailor whom the fishes have eaten. God knows whether it is for my own sake that I have taken a count's title."

"Poor Gratien! you are the best head among us, our beloved brother, the Benjamin of the band. You know that."

"Good-bye; take good care of my Maulincour."

"You can set your mind at rest on that score."

"Hey, Marquis!" cried the convict.

"What?"

"Ida is capable of anything after the scene yesterday evening. If she flings herself into the river, I certainly shall not fish her out; she will the better keep the secret of my name, the only secret she knows; but look after her, for, after all, she is a kind creature."

"Very well."

The stranger went. Ten minutes afterwards Jules heard the unmistakable rustle of silk, and almost knew the sound of his wife's footsteps, not without a fevered shiver.

"Well, father, poor father, how are you? How brave you are!" It was Clémence who spoke.

"Come here, child," said Ferragus, holding out his hand. And Clémence bent her forehead for his kiss.

"Let us see you, what is it, poor little girl? What new troubles?——"

"Troubles, father? It is killing me, killing the daughter who loves you so. As I wrote to tell you yesterday, you absolutely must use that fertile brain of yours to find some way of seeing poor Jules this very day. If you only knew how good he has been to me in spite of suspicions that seemed so well founded! Love is my life, father. Do you wish to see me die? Oh! I have been through so much as it is, and my life is in danger, I feel it."

"To lose you, my child! to lose you for a miserable Parisian's curiosity! I would set Paris on fire. Ah! you know what a lover is, but what a father is you do not know."

"You frighten me, father, when you look like that. Do not put two such different sentiments in the balance. I had my husband before I knew that my father was living——"

"If your husband was the first to set a kiss upon your forehead, I was the first to let tears fall there," said Ferragus. "Reassure yourself, Clémence, open your heart to me. I love you well enough to be happy in the knowledge that you are happy; although your father is almost nothing in your heart, while you fill his."

"Ah, God! such words make me too happy. You make me love you more than ever, and it seems to me that I am robbing Jules. But just think that he is in despair, my good father. What shall I tell him in two hours' time?"

"Child, do you think that I waited for your letter to save you from this threatened unhappiness? What came to those who took it into their heads to meddle with your happy life, or to come between us? Why, have you never recognized a second providence watching over you? And you do not know that twelve men, full of vigor in mind and body, are like an escort about your love and your life, always ready to do any deed to save you? And the father who used to risk his life to see you as you took your walks; or came at night to see you in your little cot in your mother's room; that father who, from the memory of your childish kisses, and from these alone, drew strength to live when a man of honor must take his own life to escape a shameful fate;—how should not he—how should not I, in short, that draw breath only through your lips—see only with your eyes, feel through your heart, how should not I defend you with a lion's claws and a father's soul, when you are all that I have, my life, my daughter? . . . Why, since the angel died, that was your mother once, I have dreamed only one dream—of the joy of calling you my daughter openly, of clasping you in my arms before heaven and earth, of killing the convict . . ."(he paused for a moment)—"of giving you a father," he continued; "I saw a time when I could grasp your husband's hand without a blush, and live

fearlessly in both your hearts, and say to the world, 'This is
my child!'—in short, I had visions of being a father at my
ease."

"Oh! father, father!"

"After many efforts, after searching the world over, my
friends have found me a man's shape to fill," continued Ferragus. "In a few day's time I shall be M. de Funcal, a Portuguese count. There, dear child, there are few men of my age
that would have patience to learn Portuguese and English,
with which that confounded naval officer was perfectly acquainted."

"My dear father!"

"Every contingency is provided for. In a few days His
Majesty, John VI., King of Portugal, will be my accomplice.
So you only need a little patience when your father had much.
But for me it was quite natural. What would I not do to
reward your devotion during these three years? To come so
dutifully to see your old father, risking your happiness as
you did."

"Father!" Clémence took Ferragus' hands and kissed them.

"Come! a little more courage, Clémence; let us keep the
fatal secret to the end. Jules is not an ordinary man; and
yet, do we know whether with his lofty character and great
love he will not feel something like disrespect for the daughter
of——"

"Ah! you have read your child's soul," cried Clémence;
"I have no fear but that," she added, in a heartrending tone.
"The thought freezes my blood. But remember, father, I
have promised him the truth in two hours."

"Well, my child, tell him to go to the Portuguese Embassy
to see the Comte de Funcal, your father; I will be there."

"And how about M. de Maulincour, who talked about Ferragus? Ah, dear! to tell lie upon lie, what torture, father!'"

"To whom are you speaking? Yet a few days, and no man
alive can give me the lie. And besides, M. de Maulincour is
in no condition to remember anything by this time——
There, there, silly child, dry your tears, and bear in mind
that——"

A dreadful cry rang through the next room, where Jules Desmarets was hiding.

"My girl, my poor girl!" The wail came through the loophole above the cupboard; Ferragus and Mme. Jules were terror-stricken by it.

"Go and see what it is, Clémence."

Clémence fled down the narrow staircase, found the door of Mme. Gruget's room standing wide open, and heard her voice ring out overhead. The sound of sobbing attracted her to the fatal room, and these words reached her ears as she entered:

"It is you, sir, with your notions, that have been the death of her!"

"Hush, wretched woman!" exclaimed Jules, trying to stop her cries with his pocket-handkerchief.

"Murder! Help!" cried the Widow Gruget. At that moment Clémence came in, saw her husband, shrieked aloud, and fled.

There was a long pause. "Who will save my daughter?" asked Mme. Gruget. "You have murdered her."

"And how?" asked Jules mechanically, stupefied by the thought that his wife had recognized him.

"Read that, sir," said she, bursting into tears. "Will any money comfort me for this?" and she held out a letter:—

"Good-bye, mother. I leave you all I have. I ask your pardon for my faults, and for this last grief I am bringing on you by making away with myself. Henry, that I love better than myself, said that I had done him harm, and he would have no more to do with me afterwards; I have lost all hopes of establishing myself, and I shall go and throw myself into the river. I am going down below Neuilly, so as they shall never put me in the Morgue. If Henry doesn't hate me after I have punished myself with death, ask him to bury a poor girl whose heart only beat for him, and to forgive me, for I did wrong to meddle with what was no concern of mine. Dress his blisters carefully. He has suffered a deal, the poor dear. But I shall have as much courage to drown myself as he had to have himself burned. There are some corsets ready; see that they are sent home. And pray God for your daughter. IDA."

"Take the letter to M. de Funcal, in the next room. He is the only man that can save my daughter, if it is not too late." And Jules vanished, flying like a criminal when the deed is done. His legs shook under him. His swelling heart was sending a hotter and fuller tide through his veins, with a mightier pulse than he had ever known before. The most conflicting thoughts filled his mind, and yet one idea prevailed above them all. He had been disloyal to the one whom he loved best in the world; he could not compound with his conscience, its voice grew in proportion to the extent of the wrong that he had done, till the clamor filled him, as passion had filled his inmost being during the bitterest hours of the suspense which had shaken him but a short while ago. He dared not go home, and spent most of the day in wandering about Paris. Upright as he was, he shrank from confronting the blameless brows of the wife he had not rightly valued. The sin is in proportion to the purity of the conscience; and an act which for some is scarcely a mistake will weigh like a crime upon a few white souls. Is there not, indeed, a divine significance in that word white? and does not the slightest spot on maiden garments degrade them at once to the level of the beggar's rags? Between the two there is but the difference between misfortune and error. Repentance is not proportioned to the sin; God makes no distinctions; it is as hard to wipe out one stain as to wash away the sins of a lifetime.

These thoughts lay heavily on Jules' soul. Justice is not more inexorable than passion, nor more ruthless in its reasoning; for passion has a conscience of its own, infallible as instinct. He went home again in despair, overwhelmed with a sense of the wrong he had done; but, in spite of himself, joy in his wife's innocence was visible in his pale face.

He went to her room with a fast-throbbing heart, and found her lying in bed. She was in a high fever. He sat down by the bedside, took her hand, and kissed it and covered it with tears.

"Dear angel, they are tears of repentance," he said, when they were alone.

"What is there to repent of?" she asked.

She bent her head down on the pillow as she spoke, and shut her eyes, and lay quite still, fearing, with a mother's, an angel's delicacy, to betray her pain and alarm her husband. The whole woman was summed up in those words. There was a long silence. Jules, fancying that Clémence was asleep, stole out to ask Joséphine about her mistress.

"Madame came in half dead, sir. We sent for M. Haudry."

"Has he been? What did he say?"

"Nothing, sir. He did not seem satisfied, he said that no one was to be allowed in the room except the nurse, and he would come again in the course of the evening."

Jules stole softly back to his wife, and sat down in an armchair by the bedside. He did not move; his eyes never left hers. Whenever Clémence looked up she met their gaze, and from under her lashes there escaped a tender, sorrowful, impassioned glance—a glance that fell like a fiery dart in the inmost soul of the man thus generously absolved, and loved through everything by her whom he had done to death. Forebodings of death lay between them; death was a presence felt alike by both. Their looks were blended in the same agony, as their two hearts had been made one through love equally felt and shared. There were no questions now, but a dreadful certainty. In the wife, a perfect generosity; in the husband, a hideous remorse; and in both their souls one vision of the End, and the same consciousness of the inevitable.

There was a moment when Jules, thinking that his wife was asleep, kissed her softly on the forehead, gazed long at her, and said to himself, "Ah, God! leave this angel with me yet a while longer, that I may expiate my sins by long adoration. . . . Heroic as a daughter; what word could describe her as a wife?"

Clémence opened her eyes; they were full of tears.

"You hurt me," she said in a weak voice.

It was growing late. Dr. Haudry came and asked Jules to leave the room while he saw his patient; and when he came out afterwards there was no need to ask any questions—a gesture told all.

"Send for any of my colleagues in whom you have most confidence," said the doctor; "I may be mistaken."

"But, doctor, tell me the truth. I am not a child, I can hear it; and besides, I have the strongest reasons for wishing to know it, there are accounts to settle——"

"Mme. Jules is death stricken," said the doctor. "There is something on her mind which complicates the physical illness; the situation was dangerous as it was, and repeated imprudence has made it worse——Getting out of bed in the night with bare feet; going out on foot yesterday, and in the carriage to-day, when I forbade it, she has done her best to kill nerself. Still my verdict is not final; there is youth, and astonishing nervous strength—it might be worth while to risk all to save all by some violent reagent; but I could not take it upon myself to prescribe the treatment, I should not even advise it. I should oppose it in consultation."

Jules went back to the room again. For eleven days he stayed night and day by his wife's bedside, sleeping only in the daytime, with his head on the bedfoot. Never did any man carry the ambition of devotion so far as Jules Desmarets. In a jealous anxiety to do everything himself, he would not allow any one else to perform the least service for his wife; he sat with her hand in his, as if in this way he could give of his own vitality to her. There were times of doubt and fallacious joy, good days, and an improvement, and crises, and the dreadful reverberations of the coming death, that hesitates while life hangs in the balance, but strikes at last. Mme. Jules was never too weak to smile; she was sorry for her husband, knowing that very soon he would be left alone. It was the twofold agony of life and love; but as life ebbed, love grew stronger.

Then came a dreadful night, when Clémence suffered from the delirium that always comes before death in young creatures. She talked aloud of her happy love, of her father, of her mother's deathbed revelations, and the charge she had laid upon her daughter. Clémence was struggling, not for life, but for the passionate love that she could not let go.

"God in Heaven!" she cried out, "do not let him know how I want to have him die with me."

Jules, unable to bear the sight, happened to be in the next room and so did not hear the wish that he would have fulfilled.

When the crisis was over, Mme. Jules found strength. Next day she looked lovely and peaceful once more; she talked, she began to hope, and made a pretty invalid's toilet. She wanted to be alone all day, and entreated her husband to leave her so earnestly, that he was fain to grant her wish, as a child's pleading is always granted. Jules, moreover, had need of the day. He went to M. de Maulincour to claim the duel to which both had agreed. He obtained an interview with the cause of his troubles, not without great difficulty; but the Vidame, informed that it was an affair of honor, gave way in obedience to the prejudices which had always ruled his life, and brought Jules up to the Baron de Maulincour.

"Oh, it really is he," said the Commander, indicating the figure in the armchair by the fireside.

"He? who? Jules?" asked the dying man, in a broken voice.

Auguste had lost the one central faculty by which we live—memory. At sight of him M. Desmarets shrank back in horror. He could not recognize the youthful, fine gentleman in this Thing, for which there was no name in any language, to quote Bossuet's saying. It was, in truth, a white-haired corpse, a skeleton scarcely covered by the wrinkled, shriveled, withered skin. The eyes were pale and fixed, the mouth gaped hideously, like the mouth of an imbecile, or of some debauchee dying of excess. Not the faintest spark of intelligence was left to the forehead, nor indeed to any other feature; nor was there any appearance of color or of circulating blood in the flabby flesh. These were the shrunken, dissolving remains of what had been a human being, a man reduced to the condition of the monstrosities preserved in spirits at the Muséum. Jules fancied he could see Ferragus' terrible head rising above that visage, and his hate shrank appalled at the completeness of the vengeance. Clémence's husband could find it in his heart to pity the unrecognizable wreck of what had been so lately a young man.

"The duel has taken place," said the Vidame.

"Monsieur de Maulincour has taken many lives," exclaimed Jules in distress.

"And the lives of his nearest and dearest," added the old noble. "His grandmother is dying of grief, and I perhaps shall follow her to the tomb."

Mme. Jules grew worse from hour to hour on the day after the visit. She took advantage of a momentary strength to draw a letter from her pillow, and gave it quickly to Jules with a sign which no one could mistake; she wished to spend her last breath of life in a kiss. He took it, and she died.

Jules dropped down half dead, and was taken away to his brother's house. There, as in the midst of tears and ravings he bewailed his absence of the day before, his brother told him how anxious Clémence had been that he should not be present during the Church's administration of the last sacrament to the dying, that rite so terribly impressive for a sensitive imagination.

"You could not have borne it," said his brother. "I myself could scarcely endure to see it, and every one broke out into weeping. Clémence looked like a saint. She summoned up her strength to bid us good-bye; it was heartrending to hear that voice for the last time. And when she asked pardon for any involuntary unkindness to those who had served her, a wail went up among the sobs, a wail——"

"Enough, that will do——"

He wanted to be alone to read his wife's last thoughts, now that she, the woman whom the world had admired, had faded away like a flower:—

"This is my will, my dearest. Why should not people dispose of their heart's treasures, as of everything else that is theirs? The love in my heart—was it not all that I had? And here I want to think of nothing but love; it was all that your Clémence brought you, it is all that she can leave you when she dies. Jules, I am loved again, I can die a happy woman. The doctors will have their theories of my death; but no one knows the real cause but I. I will tell you about it, in spite of the pain it may give you. I am dying because I kept a secret that could not be told, but I will not carry away a secret unsaid in the heart that is wholly yours.

"I was nurtured and brought up in complete solitude, far away from the vices and deceits of the world, by the amiable woman whom you knew, Jules. Society did justice to the conventional qualities by which a woman gains social popularity; but I, in secret, enjoyed communion with an angel's soul; I could love the mother who gave me a childhood of joy without bitterness, knowing well why I loved her. Which means, does it not, that she was twice loved? Yes. I loved and feared and respected her, yet neither the fear nor the respect oppressed my heart. I was all in all to her; she was all in all to me. Through nineteen years of happiness, known to the full, nineteen years without a care, my soul, lonely amid the world which murmured about me, mirrored nothing but the one most pure vision of my mother, and my heart beat for her alone. I was conscientiously devout. I was glad to lead a pure life in the sight of God. My mother cultivated all noble and lofty feelings and thoughts in me. Ah! it gladdens me to own it, Jules. I know now that my girlhood was complete, that I came to you with a maiden heart.

"When I came out of the profound solitude; when for

the first time I smoothed my hair beneath a wreath of almond blossom, and added a few knots of satin ribbon to my white gown, thinking how pretty they looked, and wondering about this world that I was to see, and felt curious to see; well, Jules, even then, that simple girlish coquetry was for you; at my first entrance into that new world I saw *you*—— I saw your face; it stood out from all the others; you were handsome, I thought; your voice and your manner prepossessed me in your favor; and when you came up and spoke to me, and your forehead flushed and your voice was tremulous—the memory of that moment sets my heart throbbing even now as I write to you to-day, when I think of it for the last time. Our love has been from the first the keenest of sympathies, and it was not long before we divined each other, and began to share, as we have shared ever since, the uncounted joys of love.

"From that day my mother had but the second place in my heart. I told her so, and she smiled, my adorable mother! And since then I have been yours—yours wholly. That is my life, my whole life, my dear husband.

"And this is what remains to be said.

"One evening, a few days before my mother died, she told me the secret of her life, not without hot tears. I loved her more, far more, when I heard in the presence of the priest who absolved her that there was such a thing as passion condemned by the world and the Church. Yet, surely, God must be merciful when love is the sin of souls as loving as hers, even though that angel could not bring herself to repent of it. She loved with all her heart, Jules, for her heart was love. And so I prayed for her every day, without judging her. From that time I knew why her mother's love had been so deep and tender; from that time I knew too that in Paris there was some one living for whom I was everything—life and love. I knew, besides, that your success was due to him, and that he liked you, and that he was an outlaw with a blighted name, and that these things troubled him less for his own sake than for mine—for both our sakes.—My mother had been his one comfort; I promised to take her place now that she was dead. With all the enthusiasm of an unsophisticated nature, I thought of nothing but the joy of sweetening the bitterness of her last moments, so I pledged myself to continue her work of secret charity—the charity of the heart.

"I saw my father for the first time by the bed on which my mother had just drawn her last breath. When he raised his tear-filled eyes, it was to find all his dead hopes once more in me. I vowed, not to lie, but to keep silence; and what woman could have broken that silence? Therein lay my mistake, a mistake expiated by death—I could not trust you, Jules. But fear is so natural to a woman, especially to a wife who knows all that she has to lose. I was afraid for my love. It seemed to me that my father's secret might cost me my happiness; and the more I loved, the more I dreaded the loss of love. I dared not confess this to my father; it would have hurt him, and in his position any wound smarts keenly. But while he said not a word to me, he felt my fears. The true father's heart trembled for my happiness, as I trembled for myself, and shrank from speaking of it with the same delicacy which kept me mute.

"Yes, Jules, I thought that some day you might not love Gratien's daughter as you loved your Clémence. But for that dread in the depths of my heart, could I have hidden anything from you—from you that filled even this inmost recess?

"When that odious, miserable officer spoke to you, I was forced to tell a lie. That day I knew sorrow for the second time in my life, and that sorrow has grown day by day till this last moment of converse with you. What does my father's position matter now? You know everything. With love to aid me, I might have wrestled with disease and borne any pain; but I cannot smother the voice of doubt. Is it not possible that the knowledge of my origin may take something from your love, Jules, and weaken it, and spoil its purity? And this fear nothing can extinguish in me. *This* is the cause of my death.

"I could not live in continual dread of a word or a look, one word which might never be uttered, one glance that would never be given; but, I cannot help it—*I am afraid!* I have your love till I die, that comforts me. I have known for four years past that father and his friends have all but turned the world upside down to act a lie to the world. They have bought a dead man, a reputation, and a fortune, and all to give a new life to a living man, and a social position to me— all this for your sake, for our sakes! We were to know nothing about it. Well, my death will probably save my father from the necessity of lying any longer, for he will die when I am dead.

"So, farewell, Jules. I have put my whole heart here in this letter. When I show you my love in the innocence of its dread, do I not leave you my very soul? I should not have had strength to tell you this, but I could write it for you.

"I have just made confession of the sins of my lifetime to God; I have promised, it is true, to think of nothing now but the Father in Heaven; but I could not resist the pleasure of confession to you, that are all to me upon earth. Alas! who would not forgive me this last sigh between the life that is no more and the life to come. So, farewell, Jules, my beloved; I am going to God, with whom there is love unclouded for evermore, to whom you also will come one day. There, at the foot of the Throne of God, together for evermore, we shall love through all the ages. That hope alone can comfort me. If I am worthy to go first, I shall follow you through your life, my spirit will be with you and around you, for you must live on here below awhile. Lead a holy life, to rejoin me the more surely. You can do so much good here on this earth! Is it not an angel's mission for a stricken soul to spread happiness around, to give that which he has not?

"I leave the unhappy to your care; how should I be jealous of their smiles, their tears? We shall find a great charm in these sweet charities. Cannot we be together still, if you will associate my name, your Clémence's name, with every kindly deed? When two have loved as we have loved, Jules, there is nothing left but God; God does not lie, God does not fail Give all your love to Him, I ask it of you. Cultivate good in those who suffer, comfort the afflicted among the Church on earth.

"Adieu, dear heart that I have filled. I know you, I know that you will not love twice; and I can die happy in a thought that would make any wife glad. Yes, I shall lie buried in your heart. Now that I have told you the story of my childhood, is not my whole life poured into your heart? I shall never be driven from it after I am dead. You have only known me in the flower of my youth; I shall leave nothing but regrets behind, and no disenchantment. Jules, that is a very happy death.

"May I ask one thing of you that have understood me so well, one thing needless to ask, no doubt—the fulfilment of a woman's fancy, of a wish prompted by a jealousy to which all women are subject. I beg of you to burn all that belonged to us, to destroy our room, and everything that may recall our love.

"Once again, farewell, a last farewell full of love, as my last thought will be, and my latest breath."

Jules finished the letter, and a frantic grief came upon his heart in terrible paroxysms which cannot be described. Every agony takes its own course, and obeys no fixed rule; some men stop their ears to hear no sound, and women sometimes close their eyes to shut out all sights; and here and there a great and powerful soul plunges into sorrow as into an abyss. Despair makes an end of all insincerities. Jules escaped from his brother's house, and returned to the Rue de Ménars, meaning to spend the night at his wife's side, and to keep that divine creature in sight till the last. As he went, with the recklessness of a man brought to the lowest depths of misery, he began to understand why Asiatic laws forbid widows to survive their husbands. He wanted to die. He was in the fever of sorrow; the collapse had not yet set in.

He reached the sacred chamber without hindrance, saw

Clémence lying on her deathbed, fair as a saint, her hair smoothed over her brows, her hands folded. She had been laid already in her shroud. The light of the tall candles fell upon a priest at his prayers, on Joséphine, who was crying in a corner, and on two men by the bed. One of these was Ferragus. He stood upright and motionless, gazing dry-eyed at his daughter, you might have taken his face for a bronze statue; he did not see Jules. The other was Jacquet—Jacquet to whom Mme. Jules had always been kind. He had felt for her the respectful friendship that brings warmth to the heart without troubling it, a softened passion, love without its longings, and its tumult, and now he had come religiously to pay his debt of tears, to bid a long adieu to his friend's wife, and set a first and last kiss on the forehead of the woman of whom he had tacitly made a sister.

All was silent there. This was not the Terrible Death of the Church, nor the pageantry of Death that passes through the streets; it was Death that glides in under the roof, Death in his pathetic aspects; this was a lying in state for the heart amid tears shed in secret.

Jules sat down beside Jacquet, squeezed his friend's hand, and thus without a word they stayed till the morning. When the candles burned faintly in the dawn, Jacquet thought of the painful scenes to come, and led Jules away into the next room. For a moment Clémence's husband looked full at her father, and Ferragus looked at Jules. Anguish questioned and sounded the depths of anguish, and both understood at a glance. A flash of rage glittered for an instant in Ferragus' eyes.

"It is your doing!" he thought.

"Why not have trusted me?" the other seemed to retort.

So might two tigers have seen the uselessness of a conflict, after eyeing each other during a moment of hesitation, without so much as a growl.

"Jacquet, did you see to everything?" asked Jules.

"Yes, to everything; and everywhere some one else had been before me and given orders and paid."

"He is snatching his daughter from me!" shouted Jules, in a paroxysm of despair.

He dashed into the bedroom. The father had gone. Clémence had been laid in her leaden coffin. One or two workmen were preparing to solder down the lid, and Jules retreated aghast. At the sound of the hammer he broke out into dull weeping.

"Jacquet," he said at length, "one idea stays with me after this dreadful night, just one thought, but I must realize it, cost what it may. Clémence shall not lie in a Paris cemetery. She shall be cremated, and I will keep her ashes beside me. Do not say a word about it to me, but just arrange to have it done. I shall shut myself up in *her* room and stay there till I am ready to go. No one shall come in but you to tell me what you have done. There, spare for nothing."

That morning Mme. Jules' coffin lay under the archway with lighted candles round it, and afterwards was removed to St. Roch. The whole church was hung with black. The kind of display made for the funeral service had attracted a great many people. Everything, even the most heartfelt anguish, is a theatrical spectacle in Paris. There are people who will stand at the windows to watch curiously while a son weeps in his mother's funeral procession, just as there are others who want good seats to see an execution. No people in the world have such voracious eyes. But the curious in St. Roch were particularly astonished to find the six side chapels in the church likewise draped with black, and two men in mourning attending a mass for the dead in each. In the choir there were but two persons present at the funeral—M. Desmarets the notary, and Jacquet—the servants were beyond the screen. The hangers-on of the church were puzzled by the splendor of the funeral and the insignificant number of mourners. Jules would have no indifferent persons.

High mass was celebrated with all the sombre grandeur of the funeral service. Thirteen priests from various parishes were there beside the officiating clergy of St. Roch. The sound of blended voices rose as the eight chanters, the priests, and the child-choristers sang alternately; and never perhaps was the *Dies iræ* more deeply impressive than at that moment, never did it strike an icier chill to the nerves of Christians by accident of birth, assembled there by chance, curiosity, and greed of sensation. From the side chapels children's voices, shrill with grief, rose wailing in the chorus. A dull note of dismay reverberated through the church; cries of anguish answered wails of terror on every side. That awful music spoke of agony unknown on earth, of secret friendship weeping for the dead. Never has any known religion given so powerful a rendering of the terrors of the soul, stripped violently of the body, and tossed as by tempest into the presence of the intolerable Majesty of God. Before that clamor of clamors, artists and their most impassioned work must shrink abashed. No, nothing can stand beside that music which gathers up all human passions, galvanizing them into a life beyond the grave, bringing them, yet palpitating, into the presence of the living God, the Avenger. Man's life, with all its developments, is embraced by that Canticle of Death; for the cries of children, mingled with the notes of deeper voices, recall the pains of cradled infancy, swelled by the sum of all the pain of life's later stages, by the full-toned bass, and the quavering notes of old men and of priests. Does not the volume of strident harmony, full of thunder and lightnings, speak to the most undaunted imagination, to the ice-bound heart, nay, to philosophists themselves? As you hear it, it seems that God thunders. The vaults of every church are cold no longer; they quiver, and find a voice, and pour forth fear with all the might of their echoes. You seem to see visions of the uncounted dead rising and holding up their hands. It is not a father, a wife or child, that lies beneath the black drapery; it is Humanity emerging from the dust. It is impossible to be just to the Apostolic and Roman Catholic Church until you have passed through a supreme sorrow, and wept for the beloved dead lying beneath the cenotaph; until you have heard all the emotion which fills your heart, interpreted by that hymn of despair, by those cries that overwhelm the soul, by the religious awe that rises from strophe to strophe, eddying up to heaven, appalling, diminishing, exalting the soul, till as the last verse comes to an end you are left with the sense of Eternity. You have been wrestling with the great idea of the Infinite; and now all is hushed in the church. Not a word is uttered there. Unbelievers themselves "know not what ails them." Spanish genius alone could invest unspeakable sorrow with such transcendent majesty.

When the supreme ceremony was over, twelve men in mourning emerged from the chapels, and stood grouped around the coffin to hear the chant of hope which the Church raises for the Christian's soul before the human form is committed to earth. Then each of them entered a mourning coach, Jacquet and M. Desmarets took the thirteenth, and the servants followed on foot.

An hour afterwards the twelve strangers were gathered about a grave, dug at the highest point of the cemetery familiarly known as Père-Lachaise; the coffin had just been lowered; a curious crowd had gathered from all parts of that public garden. The priest recited a short prayer, and flung a handful of earth over the mortal remains; and the sexton and his men having claimed their fee, hastily began to fill up the grave before going to another.

And here this story would seem to finish. Yet perhaps it would be incomplete if the practical effects of death should be forgotten at the close of a slight sketch of Parisian life, and its capricious undulations. Death in Paris is unlike death in any other great city; few people know what it is to bring a heartfelt sorrow into conflict with civilization in the shape of the municipal authorities of Paris. Perhaps, too, the reader may feel sufficient interest in Ferragus XXIII. and Jules Desmarets to care to know what became of them. And in any case, there are plenty of people who like to know all about everything; and, as the most ingenious of French critics once said, would find out the chemistry of the combustion of the oil in Aladdin's lamp if they could.

Jacquet, being a civil servant, naturally applied to the au-

thorities for permission to exhume and cremate Mme. Jules'
body. The dead sleep under the protection of the Prefect of
Police; to the Prefect of Police, therefore, Jacquet betook
himself. That functionary required a formal application. A
sheet of stamped paper must be purchased, sorrow must appear in the regulation form; and when a man is so overwhelmed with grief that words fail him, he must express himself in the peculiar idiom of red-tape, and translate his wishes
into business-like phrases with a marginal note.

*The petitioner prays permission to cremate
the body of his wife.*

The head of the department, whose duty it was to draw up a
report for the Prefect of Police, a member of the Council of
State, glanced over the apostille, in which the object of the
request was clearly stated by his own recommendation, and
said:

"But this is a serious question. It is impossible to draw up
a report in less than a week."

Jacquet was obliged to explain the delay, and Jules
thought of the words he had heard Ferragus utter, "Set Paris
on fire!" Nothing seemed more natural than a thorough destruction of that receptacle of monstrous things.

"Why, there is nothing for it but to apply to the Home
Office and set your Minister on to the Home Secretary," he
told Jacquet.

Jacquet accordingly applied to the Home Office, and asked
for an audience, which he obtained—for that day fortnight.
Jacquet was naturally persistent. He went, therefore, from
department to department, and succeeded in reaching the private secretary of the Minister of Foreign Affairs. With such
influence he received a promise of a private interview with
the Pasha of the Home Office, and a few lines written by the
Autocrat of Foreign Affairs by way of passport. Jacquet now
had hopes of carrying his point by storm. He was ready for
every emergency with arguments and categorical answers. All
ended in failure.

"This is no affair of mine," said the Minister. "The thing concerns the Prefect of Police. And what is more: no law gives a husband the custody of his wife's body, nor has a father a right to a child's corpse. It is a serious matter. It ought to be looked into, besides, in the interests of the public. The city of Paris might suffer. In short, if the matter were referred directly to me, I could not give a decision *hic et nunc;* a report would be required."

In the administrative system a "report" answers much the same ends as limbo in theology. Jacquet had met with the "report" craze before; nor had he neglected previous opportunities of groaning over the absurdities of red tape. He knew that since the administrative Revolution of 1804, when the report had carried all before it in Government departments, the Minister had not yet been found that would take it upon himself to have an opinion, or give a decision on any matter, however small, until the thing had been winnowed, sifted, and thoroughly scrutinized by the scribblers and scratchers and sublime official intelligences of his department.

Jacquet—the man deserved to have a Plutarch for his biographer—Jacquet saw that he had set off on the wrong track, and defeated his own ends by trying to proceed by the proper forms. He should simply have removed Mme. Jules' coffin after the service to one of the Desmarets' houses in the country. There the mayor of the village would have made no difficulty about gratifying the sorrowing widower's request. Constitutional and administrative legalism is sterile; it is a barren monster for nations and kings and the interests of private individuals; but the nations as yet have only learned to spell those principles that are written in blood; and as the evils of ruling by the letter of the law are never accompanied by strife and bloodshed, legalism reduces a nation to a dead level, and there is an end of it.

Jacquet, being a stickler for liberty, returned home, meditating by the way on the blessings of arbitrary government; for a man only criticises the law of the land by the light of his own passions. But when he came to talk to Jules, there was nothing for it but to deceive his friend; the unhappy man was in a high fever, and for a couple of days he stayed in bed.

That evening at dinner the Minister chanced to mention that the fancy had taken some one in Paris to have his wife's body cremated in the Roman fashion. And for a moment classical funeral rites were the talk of the clubs. As things ancient were coming into fashion, several people were of the opinion that it would be a fine thing to revive the funeral pyre for distinguished personages. Some were for, and others against, the idea. Some held that there were so many great men, that the practice would raise the price of fuel; they opined that with a nation so fond of the mental exercise of changing its opinions, it would be a ridiculous thing to see a whole Longchamp of ancestors trotted out in their urns at the expiration of a lease; while if the urns happened to be valuable, creditors (a race that never respect anything) would seize upon them, and they, with their contents of honorable dust, would be put up to public auction. Others retorted that it was scarcely possible for a man to insure a permanent residence for his grandparents in Père Lachaise; for that in time the city of Paris would be compelled to order a St. Bartholomew of its dead. The cemeteries were invading the open country, and threatened to encroach upon the corn land of Brie. In short, the question raised one of the futile and ingenious discussions which, in Paris, too often aggravates deepseated evils. Happily for Jules, he knew nothing of the conversation, jokes, and epigrams with which his sorrow supplied the town.

The Prefect of Police took offence because M. Jacquet had gone straight to the Minister to avoid the delays and matured wisdom of the Board of Works. The exhumation of Mme. Jules' body was a question within the jurisdiction of the municipal police. Wherefore the Police Department was elaborating a sharp answer to the petition. A single demand is enough, the administration has a tight hold, and a thing once in its grasp is like to go a long way. Any matter, moreover, may be referred to the Council of State, another piece of machinery very hard to set in motion. Another day went by, and Jacquet made his friend understand that the idea must be given up; that in a city where the number of "tears" embroidered on the black trappings are prescribed, where the law recognizes seven classes of funerals, where land in which to bury the dead is sold by its weight in silver, where grief is exploited on a system of double entry, and the prayers of the Church are sold dear, or the vestry puts in a claim for a few extra voices in the *Dies iræ*—any deviation from the beaten rut traced out for grief by the authorities was impossible.

"It would have been one joy in my misery," said Jules; "I meant to go somewhere, a long way off, to die, and I wished when I lay in the grave to have Clémence in my arms. I did not know that officialdom could put out its claws to reach us even in our coffins."

He would go to see whether there was a little room for him beside his wife. So the friends went together to Père Lachaise. At the gateway they found a crowd of ciceroni waiting to guide sight-seers through the labyrinth, as if Père Lachaise were a museum or the Cour des Diligences or some other sight. It was impossible that Jules or Jacquet should find Clémence's tomb. Terrible agony! They went to consult the gatekeeper.

The dead have a concierge, and there are hours at which the dead cannot receive visitors. Only by shaking all the rules and regulations from top to bottom can any one obtain the right to go thither in the darkness to weep in silence and solitude over the grave which holds his beloved dead. There are summer regulations and winter regulations. Of all the concierges of Paris, the gatekeeper of Père Lachaise is the best off. There is no cord to pull, to begin with. Instead of a single room, he has a house, an establishment that cannot exactly be described as a government department, although there is a considerable staff attached, and the jurisdiction is wide, and the governor of the dead draws a salary and wields an immense power over a population who cannot possibly

complain of him; he plays the despot at his ease. Neither is
his abode exactly a place of business, albeit there are offices
and books to be kept, and clerks to keep them, and receipts
and expenditure and profits. And the gatekeeper himself is
neither a Swiss nor a concierge nor a porter, for the door is
always yawning wide for the dead; and though there certainly
are monuments to be kept in order, he is not there to look
after them. He is, in short, an anomaly which cannot be defined; his office is akin in one way or another to every power
in existence, and yet he is a nobody, for his authority, like
Death, by which it lives, lies completely beyond the pale.
Nevertheless, exception as he is, he holds his tenure from the
City of Paris, a creature as chimerical as the emblematical
vessel on her coat-of-arms; an imaginary being swayed by
hundreds of paws and claws which seldom move in concert;
and as a result, her public servants are, to all intents and purposes, fixtures. The cemetery-keeper, therefore, is the concierge promoted to the rank of a public servant, a permanent
element amid dissolution.

His place, for that matter, is no sinecure. No one can be
buried till the gatekeeper has seen the permit; and he is
bound to give account of his dead. He can lay his finger on a
spot in that huge burying ground to point out the six feet of
earth in which some day you will lay all that you love, or hate,
as the case may be—the woman you love or your unloved
cousin. For, mind you, to this lodge all loves and hates must
come at the last, and are duly docketed and passed through
the office. The man keeps a register of sleeping-places for the
dead; they go down on his list when they go down into the
grave.

The gatekeeper has custodians under him, and gardeners
and grave-diggers and assistants. He is a personage.
Mourners are not brought into direct contact with him as a
rule; he only comes forward if something serious occurs, if
one dead man is mistaken for another, or if a body is exhumed
for a murder case, or a corpse comes to life again. The bust
of the reigning sovereign presides in his room. Possibly he

keeps other busts of departed monarchs, with various royal, imperial, or semi-royal persons, in a cupboard somewhere, a sort of miniature Père Lachaise for changes in the Government. In other respects, he is a public servant; an excellent man, a good husband and father, epitaphs apart; but—so much varied emotion has passed under his eyes in the shape of hearses! he has seen so many tears shed, both sham and real, and been acquainted with grief in so many shapes and in so many faces—with six millions of eternal sorrows, in short! For him, grief means a stone slab an inch thick, four feet high by twenty-two inches wide. As for regrets, they are one of the things to be put up with in his profession, and he never dines but he has witnessed torrents of tears shed by inconsolable affliction. Every other emotion finds him kindly and sympathetic; he too can shed tears over the tragic end of a stage hero like M. Germeuil in *L'Auberge des Adrets,* he is moved when the man in the butter-colored breeches is murdered by Robert Macaire; but when it comes to a real genuine death, his heart is ossified. Deaths mean rows of figures for him; it is his business to tabulate statistics of the dead. And, as a last word, twice, or perhaps thrice in a century, it may happen that he has a sublime part to play, and then he is a hero at every hour—in time of Pestilence.

When Jacquet went in search of this absolute monarch, his majesty's temper had suffered somewhat.

"I told you," he cried, "to water all the flowers from the Rue Masséna to the Place Regnault de Saint-Jean d'Angely! You fellows simply took not the least notice of what I told you. My patience! if the relatives take it into their heads to come, as it is a fine day, they will be throwing all the blame on me. They will call out as if they had been burned, and say frightful things about us up here, and our characters will be taken away——"

"Sir," put in Jacquet, "we should like to know where Mme. Jules was buried."

"Mme. Jules *who?* We have had three Jules this week. . . . Ah!" (interrupting himself as he glanced at the gate), "here comes Colonel de Maulincour's funeral, go out for the permit.—My word! it is a fine funeral," he added. "He has not been long about following his grandmother. Some families seem to drop off for a wager. They have such bad blood, have those Parisians!"

Jacquet tapped him on the arm.

"Sir, the person of whom I am speaking was Mme. Jules Desmarets, the stockbroker's wife."

"Oh, I know!" returned he, looking at Jacquet. "Thirteen mourning coaches at the funeral, weren't there? and only one relation apiece in the first dozen. It was so queer that we noticed it——"

"Take care, sir; M. Jules is with me, he might overhear you; and you ought not to talk like that."

"I beg your pardon, sir, you are right. Excuse me, I took you for the next-of-kin.—Mme. Jules is in the Rue du Maréchal Lefebvre, side walk Number 4," he continued, after consulting a plan of the ground; "she lies between Mlle. Raucourt of the Comédie Française and M. Moreau-Malvin, a butcher in a big way of business. There is a white marble monument on order for him; it will be one of the finest things in the cemetery here, and that's a fact."

"We are no nearer, sir," Jacquet broke in.

"And that is true," said the other, looking round.

"Jean!" he called, as a man came in sight. "Show these gentlemen the way to Mme. Jules' grave, the stockbroker's wife. You know! Next to Mlle. Raucourt's, where there is a bust."

And the friends set out with their conductor; but before they reached the steep path which leads to the higher part of the cemetery, they must run the gauntlet of a score or more of stone-cutters, carvers, and makers of wrought-iron work, who came up to insinuate in honeyed accents that "if monsieur would like to have something put up we could do it for him very reasonably——"

Jacquet was glad enough to be there to stand between his friend and words intolerable for bleeding hearts. They

reached the spot where she lay. At the sight of the rough
sods and the row of pegs driven in by the laborers to mark out
the space for the iron railings, Jules leaned upon Jacquet's
shoulder, raising his head at intervals to give a long look at
the little patch of clay where he must leave all that remained
of her for whom and through whom he still lived.

"How hard for her to lie there!"

"But she is not there!" protested Jacquet; "she lives in
your memory.   Come away; let us leave this horrid place,
where the dead are tricked out like women at a ball."

"How if we took her out of it?"

"Is it possible?"

"Anything is possible!" cried Jules.   Then, after a pause,
"So I shall come here some day; there is room for me."

Jacquet succeeded in getting him out of the inclosure. The
tombs inclosed in those sprucely-kept chessboard compartments marked out by iron railings are covered with inscrip-
tions and sculptured palms, and tears as cold as the marble
on which survivors record their regrets and their coats-of-
arms. You may read jests there, carved in black letters, epigrams at the expense of the curious, pompous biographies, and
ingeniously worded farewells.   Here some one bides tryst,
and, as usual in such cases, bides alone. Here you behold a
thyrsus, there a lance-head railing; further on there are
Egyptian vases and now and again cannon; while spangles,
tinsel, and trash meet your eyes wherever you turn them. You
see trade-signs in every direction.   Every style—Moorish,
Grecian, and Gothic—is represented, together with every
variety of decoration—friezes, egg-mouldings, paintings, urns,
genii, and temples, among any quantity of dead rose-bushes
and faded immortelles. It is a scandalous comedy! Here is
Paris over again—streets, trade-signs, industries, houses and
all complete; but it is a Paris seen through the wrong end of
the perspective glass, a microscopic city, a Paris diminished
to a shadow of itself, and shrunk to the measure of these
chrysalids of the dead, this human species that has dwindled
so much in everything save vanity.

A girl's body stranded that morning on the bank

Jules caught a glimpse of the view. At his feet, in the long valley of the Seine, between the low ridges of Vaugirard and Meudon, Belleville and Montmartre, lay the real Paris, in a blue haze of its own smoke, now sunlit and transparent. He glanced from under his eyelids over the forty thousand houses of the city, and waved his hand towards the space between the column of the Place Vendôme and the cupola of the Invalides.

"There she was taken from me," he cried, "by the fatal curiosity of a world which seeks bustle and excitement for the sake of excitement and bustle."

Eight or nine miles further away down the Seine valley, in a little village on one of the lower slopes of those ridges of hill, between which the great restless city lies, like a child in its cradle, another sad death scene was taking place; but here there was none of the funeral pomp of Paris—there were no torches, no tall candle, no mourning coaches hung with black, no prayers of the Church; this was death reduced to the bare fact. And this was the fact. A girl's body stranded that morning on the bank, among the reeds that grow in the Seine mud. Some dredgers on their way to work caught sight of it as they went up the river in their crazy boat.

"Hullo; fifty francs for us!" cried one.

"Right you are!" said the other.

They came close up to the dead body.

"She is a very fine girl."

"Let us go and give notice."

And the two dredgers, first covering the corpse with their jackets, went off to the mayor; and that worthy was not a little puzzled to know how to draw up an official report of the discovery.

The rumor spread with the telegraphic speed peculiar to neighborhoods where communications are uninterrupted; the gossip on which the world battens, and scandal, tittle-tattle, and slander rush in to fill the vacuum between any given points. In a very short time people came to the mayor's office to relieve that gentleman of any difficulty, and among them they converted the official report into an ordinary certi-

ficate of death. Through their assiduity the girl's body was
identified; she was proved to be Mlle. Ida Gruget, staymaker,
of No. 14 Rue de la Corderie du Temple. At this stage of the
proceedings the police intervened, and the Widow Gruget, the
girl's mother, appeared with her daughter's farewell letter.
While the mother sighed and groaned, a medical man ascertained that death had ensued from asphyxia and an access of
venous blood to the pulmonary organs. That was all.

The inquest being over, and particulars filled in, the authorities gave permission for the burial of the body. The curé of
the place declined to allow the procession to enter the church
or to pray for the repose of the dead.   So an old peasant
woman sewed Ida Gruget in her shroud, she was laid in a
rough coffin made of deal boards, and carried to the churchyard on four men's shoulders. Some few country women had
the curiosity to follow, telling the story of the death with
comments of pitying surprise. An old lady charitably kept
the widow, and would not allow her to join the sad little procession. A man, who fulfilled the threefold office of sexton,
beadle, and bell-ringer, dug a grave in the churchyard, a half
acre of ground at the back of the well-known church, a classical building with a square tower buttressed at the corners,
and a slate-covered spire. The churchyard, bounded by
crumbling walls, lies behind the round apse; there are no
marble headstones there, and no visitors; but not one, surely,
of all the mounds that furrow the space, lacked the tears and
heartfelt regrets which no one gave to Ida Gruget. They put
her down out of sight in a corner among the brambles and tall
grasses; the bier was lowered into its place in that field so
idyllic in its simplicity, and in another moment the grave-
digger was left alone to fill in the grave in the gathering dusk.
He stopped now and again to look over into the road below
the wall; once, with his hand on his pickaxe, he gazed intently
at the Seine which had brought this body for him to bury.

"Poor girl!" exclaimed a voice; and suddenly a man came
up.

"How you startled me, sir!" said the sexton.

"Was there any service for this woman that you are burying?"

"No, sir. M. le Curé would not allow it. She is the first person buried here that is not of this parish. Everybody knows everybody else hereabouts. Does monsieur——? Hullo! he is gone!"

Several days slipped by. A man in black came to the house in the Rue de Ménars; the stranger did not wish to speak to Jules; he went to Mme. Jules' room and left a large porphyry vase there, bearing the inscription:

INVITA LEGE,

CONJUGI MOERENTI

FILIOLÆ CINERES

RESTITUIT

AMICIS XIII JUVANTIBUS

MORIBUNDUS PATER

"What a man!" exclaimed Jules, bursting into tears.

In one week Jules had carried out all his wife's wishes, and set his own affairs in order. He sold his professional connection to a brother of Martin Falleix's, and left Paris behind him, while the municipality was still debating whether or no a citizen had any legal claim to his wife's dead body.

Who has not met on the Paris boulevards, at a street corner, under the arcades of the Palais Royal—anywhere, in short, as chance may determine—some stranger, man or woman, whose face sets a host of confused thoughts springing up in his brain? It grows suddenly interesting at sight, perhaps because some personal singularity suggests a stormy life; perhaps gestures, gait, air, and costume all combine to present a curious whole; perhaps because a searching glance or an indescribable something makes a sudden, strong impression before you can explain the cause very clearly to yourself. On the morrow, other thoughts, other pictures of Paris life sweep

away the passing dream. But if you happen to meet the same
person again; if he is always passing along the street at the
same hour (like a clerk at the registrar's office, for instance,
whose presence is required at marriages eight hours daily);
if he is one of those wandering mortals who seem to be a part
of the furniture of the streets of Paris, and you see him again
and again in public places, on first nights, or in those restaurants of which he is the fairest ornament—then that figure
becomes a tenant in your memory, and stays there like an odd
volume of a novel without a conclusion.

You are tempted to go up to the stranger and ask, "Who
are you?—Why are you sauntering about the streets?—What
right have you to wear a crumpled collar, a cane with an ivory
knob, and a seedy waistcoat?—Why those blue spectacles with
double glasses?" or "What makes you cling to that *muscadin's*
cravat?"

Some among these errant creatures belong to the progeny
of Terminus, god of boundaries; they say nothing to your
soul. There they are; that is all. Why are they there?
Nobody knows. They are conventional signs, like the hackneyed figures used by sculptors to represent the Four Sea-
sons, or Commerce, or Plenty. Others, again, retired attor-
neys, or shopkeepers, or antique generals, walk about, and
always appear to be much the same. They never seem to be a
part of the torrent of Paris, with its throng of young bustling
men; rather, they remind you of half-uprooted trees by a
river-side. It is impossible to say whether other people forgot to bury them, or whether they escaped out of their coffins.
They have reached a semi-fossil condition.

One of these Paris Melmoths had come for several days
past to make one of a sedate, self-contained little crowd which
never fails to fill the space between the southern gate of the
Luxembourg Gardens and the north gate of the Observatory,
whenever the weather is bright. It is a place by itself, a neutral space in Paris. It lies out of the city, as it were, and yet
the city is all about it. It partakes of the nature of a square, a
thoroughfare, a boulevard, a fortification, a garden, an avenue, and a highway; it is provincial and Parisian; it is every

one of these things, and not one of them; it is a desert. All about that nameless spot rise the walls of the Foundling Hospital, the Hôpital Cochin, the Capuchins, La Bourbe, the Hospice de la Rochefoucauld, the Deaf and Dumb Asylum, and the hospital of the Val-de-Grâce. All the sin and suffering of Paris, in fact, finds a refuge in its neighborhood; and that nothing may be wanting in so philanthropic a quarter, students of science repair thither to study the ebb and flow of the tides and latitude and longitude. M. de Chateaubriand too established the Infirmerie Marie Thérèse not very far away, and the Carmelites founded a convent near by. In that desert the sound of bells never ceases, every stroke represents one of the solemn moments in man's life; the mother in travail, the new-born babe, the dying laborer, the nun at prayer, perishing vice, shivering age, disappointed genius. Only a few paces away lies the Cimetière du Mont Parnasse, whither shabby funerals go all day long from the crowded Faubourg Saint-Marceau.

Players at bowls have monopolized this esplanade with its view of Paris,—gray-headed, homely, good-natured worthies are they, who continue the line of our ancestors, and can only be compared as to externals with their public, the moving gallery which follows them about. The man before alluded to as new to this deserted quarter was an assiduous spectator of the game, and certainly might be said to be the most striking figure in these groups; for if it is permissible to classify Parisians zoologically, the other bystanders unmistakably belonged to the mollusk species. The newcomer would walk sympathetically with the jack, the small ball at which the others are aimed, the centre of interest in the game; and when it came to a stand, he would lean against a tree, and watch as a dog watches his master, while the bowls flew or rolled past. You might have taken him for the fantastic tutelar spirit of the jack. He never uttered a word. The players themselves, as zealous fanatics as could be found in any religious sect, had never taken him to task for his persistent silence, though some free-thinkers among them held that the man was deaf and dumb. Whenever there was occasion to

measure the distance between the bowls and the jack, the
stranger's cane was taken as the standard of measurement.
The players used to take it from his ice-cold fingers without
a word, or even a friendly nod. The loan of the cane was a
kind of "easement" which he tacitly permitted. If a shower
came on he stayed beside the jack—the slave of the bowls, the
guardian of the unfinished game. He took rain and fine
weather equally as a matter of course; like the players, he was
a sort of intermediate species between the stupidest Parisian
and the most intelligent of brutes. In other respects he was
pale and withered-looking, absent-minded, and careless of his
dress. He often came without his hat. His square-shaped
head and bald, sallow cranium showed through his white hair,
like a beggar's knee thrust through a hole in his breeches. He
shambled uncertainly about with his mouth open; his vacant
eyes were never turned to the sky, he never raised them indeed,
and always seemed to be looking for something on the ground.
At four o'clock an old woman would come for him and take
him away somewhere or other, towing him after her as a girl
tugs a capricious goat which insists on browsing when it is
time to go back to the shed. It was something dreadful to see
the old man.

It was afternoon. Jules, sitting alone in his traveling carriage, was driven lightly along the Rue de l'Est, and came out
upon the Carrefour de l'Observatoire, just as the old man,
leaning against a tree, allowed himself to be despoiled of his
cane amid vociferous clamor of players, in pacific dispute over
their game. Jules, fancying that he knew the face, called to
the postilion to stop, and the carriage came to a stand there
and then. As a matter of fact, the postilion, wedged in
among heavy carts, was in nowise anxious to ask the in-
surgent players at bowls to allow him to pass; he had too
much respect for *émeutes,* had that postilion.

"It is he!" Jules exclaimed, finally recognizing Ferragus
XXIII., Chef des Dévorants, in that human wreck.—"How
he loved her!" he added after a pause.—"Go on postilion!"
he shouted.

PARIS, *February* 1833.

II.

THE DUCHESSE DE LANGEAIS

To Franz Liszt.

IN a Spanish city on an island in the Mediterranean, there
stands a convent of the Order of Barefoot Carmelites, where
the rule instituted by St. Theresa is still preserved with all
the first rigor of the reformation brought about by that illustrious woman. Extraordinary as this may seem, it is none
the less true. Almost every religious house in the Peninsula,
or in Europe for that matter, was either destroyed or disor-
ganized by the outbreak of the French Revolution and the
Napoleonic wars; but as this island was protected through
those times by the English fleet, its wealthy convent and
peaceable inhabitants were secure from the general trouble
and spoliation. The storms of many kinds which shook the
first fifteen years of the nineteenth century spent their force
before they reached those cliffs at so short a distance from the
coast of Andalusia.

If the rumor of the Emperor's name so much as reached the
shore of the island, it is doubtful whether the holy women
kneeling in the cloisters grasped the reality of his dream-like
progress of glory, or the majesty that blazed in flame across
kingdom after kingdom during his meteor life.

In the minds of the Roman Catholic world, the convent
stood out pre-eminent for a stern discipline which nothing
had changed; the purity of its rule had attracted unhappy
women from the furthest parts of Europe, women deprived
of all human ties, sighing after the long suicide accomplished
in the breast of God. No convent, indeed, was so well fitted
for that complete detachment of the soul from all earthly

things, which is demanded by the religious life, albeit on the continent of Europe there are many convents magnificently adapted to the purpose of their existence. Buried away in the loneliest valleys, hanging in mid-air on the steepest mountain sides, set down on the brink of precipices, in every place man has sought for the poetry of the Infinite, the solemn awe of Silence; in every place man has striven to draw closer to God, seeking Him on mountain peaks, in the depths below the crags, at the cliff's edge; and everywhere man has found God. But nowhere, save on this half-European, half-African ledge of rock could you find so many different harmonies, combining so to raise the soul, that the sharpest pain comes to be like other memories; the strongest impressions are dulled, till the sorrows of life are laid to rest in the depths.

The convent stands on the highest point of the crags at the uttermost end of the island. On the side towards the sea the rock was once rent sheer away in some globe-cataclysm; it rises up a straight wall from the base where the waves gnaw at the stone below highwater mark. Any assault is made impossible by the dangerous reefs that stretch far out to sea, with the sparkling waves of the Mediterranean playing over them. So, only from the sea can you discern the square mass of the convent built conformably to the minute rules laid down as to the shape, height, doors, and windows of monastic buildings. From the side of the town, the church completely hides the solid structure of the cloisters and their roofs, covered with broad slabs of stone impervious to sun or storm or gales of wind.

The church itself, built by the munificence of a Spanish family, is the crowning edifice of the town.   Its fine, bold front gives an imposing and picturesque look to the little city in the sea. The sight of such a city, with its close-huddled roofs, arranged for the most part amphitheatre-wise above a picturesque harbor, and crowned by a glorious cathedral front with triple-arched Gothic doorways, belfry towers and filigree spires, is a spectacle surely in every way the sublimest on earth. Religion towering above daily life, to put men con-

tinually in mind of the End and the way, is in truth a thoroughly Spanish conception. But now surround this picture
by the Mediterranean, and a burning sky, imagine a few
palms here and there, a few stunted evergreen trees
mingling their waving leaves with the motionless flowers
and foliage of carved stone; look out over the reef
with its white fringes of foam in contrast to the sap-
phire sea; and then turn to the city, with its galleries and
terraces whither the townsfolk come to take the air among
their flowers of an evening, above the houses and the tops of
the trees in their little gardens; add a few sails down in the
harbor; and lastly, in the stillness of falling night, listen to
the organ music, the chanting of the services, the wonderful
sound of bells pealing out over the open sea. There is sound
and silence everywhere; oftener still there is silence over all.

The church is divided within into a sombre mysterious nave
and narrow aisles.   For some reason, probably because the
winds are so high, the architect was unable to build the flying
buttresses and intervening chapels which adorn almost all
cathedrals, nor are there openings of any kind in the walls
which support the weight of the roof. Outside there is simply
the heavy wall structure, a solid mass of gray stone further
strengthened by huge piers placed at intervals. Inside, the
nave and its little side galleries are lighted entirely by the
great stained-glass rose-window suspended by a miracle of art
above the centre doorway; for upon that side the exposure
permits of the display of lacework in stone and of other
beauties peculiar to the style improperly called Gothic.

The larger part of the nave and aisles was left for the
townsfolk, who came and went and heard mass there. The
choir was shut off from the rest of the church by a grating
and thick folds of brown curtain, left slightly apart in the
middle in such a way that nothing of the choir could be seen
from the church except the high altar and the officiating
priest. The grating itself was divided up by the pillars which
supported the organ loft; and this part of the structure, with
its carved wooden columns, completed the line of the arcading

in the gallery carried by the shafts in the nave. If any inquisitive person, therefore, had been bold enough to climb
upon the narrow balustrade in the gallery to look down into
the choir, he could have seen nothing but the tall, eight-sided
windows of stained glass beyond the high altar.

At the time of the French expedition into Spain to establish
Ferdinand VII. once more on the throne, a French general
came to the island after the taking of Cadiz, ostensibly to require the recognition of the King's government, really to see
the convent and to find some means of entering it. The undertaking was certainly a delicate one; but a man of passionate
temper, whose life had been, as it were, but one series of poems
in action, a man who all his life long had lived romances instead of writing them, a man pre-eminently a Doer, was sure
to be tempted by a deed which seemed to be impossible.

To open the doors of a convent of nuns by lawful means!
The metropolitan or the Pope would scarcely have permitted
it! And as for force or stratagem—might not any indiscretion
cost him his position, his whole career as a soldier, and the end
in view to boot? The Duc d'Angoulême was still in Spain;
and of all the crimes which a man in favor with the Com-
mander-in-Chief might commit, this one alone was certain
to find him inexorable. The General had asked for the mission to gratify private motives of curiosity, though never was
curiosity more hopeless. This final attempt was a matter of
conscience. The Carmelite convent on the island was the
only nunnery in Spain which had baffled his search.

As he crossed from the mainland, scarcely an hour's distance, he felt a presentiment that his hopes were to be fulfilled; and afterwards, when as yet he had seen nothing of the
convent but its walls, and of the nuns not so much as their
robes; while he had merely heard the chanting of the service,
there were dim auguries under the walls and in the sound of
the voices to justify his frail hope. And, indeed, however faint
those so unaccountable presentiments might be, never was
human passion more vehemently excited than the General's
curiosity at that moment. There are no small events for the

heart; the heart exaggerates everything; the heart weighs the fall of a fourteen-year-old Empire and the dropping of a woman's glove in the same scales, and the glove is nearly always the heavier of the two. So here are the facts in all their prosaic simplicity. The facts first, the emotions will follow.

An hour after the General landed on the island, the royal authority was re-established there. Some few Constitutional Spaniards who had found their way thither after the fall of Cadiz were allowed to charter a vessel and sail for London. So there was neither resistance nor reaction. But the change of government could not be effected in the little town without a mass, at which the two divisions under the General's command were obliged to be present. Now, it was upon this mass that the General had built his hopes of gaining some information as to the sisters in the convent; he was quite unaware how absolutely the Carmelites were cut off from the world; but he knew that there might be among them one whom he held dearer than life, dearer than honor.

His hopes were cruelly dashed at once. Mass, it is true, was celebrated in state. In honor of such a solemnity, the curtains which always hid the choir were drawn back to display its riches, its valuable paintings and shrines so bright with gems that they eclipsed the glories of the ex-votos of gold and silver hung up by sailors of the port on the columns in the nave. But all the nuns had taken refuge in the organ-loft. And yet, in spite of this first check, during this very mass of thanksgiving, the most intimately thrilling drama that ever set a man's heart beating opened out widely before him.

The sister who played the organ aroused such intense enthusiasm, that not a single man regretted that he had come to the service. Even the men in the ranks were delighted, and the officers were in ecstasy. As for the General, he was seemingly calm and indifferent. The sensations stirred in him as the sister played one piece after another belong to the small number of things which it is not lawful to utter; words are powerless to express them; like Death, God, Eternity, they can only be realized through their one point of contact with humanity. Strangely enough, the organ music seemed to belong to the school of Rossini, the musician who brings most human passion into his art. Some day his works, by their number and extent, will receive the reverence due to the Homer of music. From among all the scores that we owe to his great genius, the nun seemed to have chosen *Moses in Egypt* for special study, doubtless because the spirit of sacred music finds therein its supreme expression. Perhaps the soul of the great musician, so gloriously known to Europe, and the soul of this unknown executant had met in the intuitive apprehension of the same poetry. So at least thought two dilettanti officers who must have missed the Théâtre Favart in Spain.

At last in the *Te Deum* no one could fail to discern a French soul in the sudden change that came over the music. Joy for the victory of the Most Christian King evidently stirred this nun's heart to the depths. She was a Frenchwoman beyond mistake. Soon the love of country shone out, breaking forth like shafts of light from the fugue, as the sister introduced variations with all a Parisienne's fastidious taste, and blended vague suggestions of our grandest national airs with her music. A Spaniard's fingers would not have brought this warmth into a graceful tribute paid to the victorious arms of France. The musician's nationality was revealed.

"We find France everywhere, it seems," said one of the men. The General had left the church during the *Te Deum;* he could not listen any longer. The nun's music had been a revelation of a woman loved to frenzy; a woman so carefully hidden from the world's eyes, so deeply buried in the bosom of the Church, that hitherto the most ingenious and persistent efforts made by men who brought great influence and unusual powers to bear upon the search had failed to find her. The suspicion aroused in the General's heart became all but a certainty with the vague reminiscence of a sad, delicious melody, the air of *Fleuve du Tage*. The woman he loved had played the prelude to the ballad in a boudoir in Paris, how often! and now this nun had chosen the song to express an exile's longing, amid the joy of those that triumphed. Terrible sensation! To hope for the resurrection of a lost love, to find her only to know that she was lost, to catch a mysterious glimpse of her after five years—five years, in which the pent-up passion, chafing in an empty life, had grown the mightier for every fruitless effort to satisfy it!

Who has not known, at least once in his life, what it is to lose some precious thing; and after hunting through his papers, ransacking his memory, and turning his house upside down; after one or two days spent in vain search, and hope, and despair; after a prodigious expenditure of the liveliest irritation of soul, who has not known the ineffable pleasure of finding that all-important nothing which had come to be a kind of monomania? Very good. Now, spread that fury of search over five years; put a woman, put a heart, put Love in the place of the trifle; transpose the monomania into the key of high passion; and, furthermore, let the seeker be a man of ardent temper, with a lion's heart and a leonine head and mane, a man to inspire awe and fear in those who come in contact with him—realize this, and you may, perhaps, understand why the General walked abruptly out of the church when the first notes of a ballad, which he used to hear with a rapture of delight in a gilt-paneled boudoir, began to vibrate along the aisles of the church in the sea.

The General walked away down the steep street which led to the port, and only stopped when he could not hear the deep notes of the organ. Unable to think of anything but the love which broke out in volcanic eruption, filling his heart with fire, he only knew that the *Te Deum* was over when the Spanish congregation came pouring out of the church. Feeling that his behavior and attitude might seem ridiculous, he went back to head the procession, telling the alcalde and the governor that, feeling suddenly faint, he had gone out into the air. Casting about for a plea for prolonging his stay, it at once occurred to him to make the most of this excuse, framed on the spur of the moment. He declined, on a plea

of increasing indisposition, to preside at the banquet given by
the town to the French officers, betook himself to his bed, and
sent a message to the Major-General, to the effect that temporary illness obliged him to leave the Colonel in command of
the troops for the time being. This commonplace but very
plausible stratagem relieved him of all responsibility for the
time necessary to carry out his plans. The General, nothing
if not "catholic and monarchical," took occasion to inform
himself of the hours of the services, and manifested the
greatest zeal for the performance of his religious duties, piety
which caused no remark in Spain.

The very next day, while the division was marching out of
the town, the General went to the convent to be present at
vespers. He found an empty church. The townsfolk, devout though they were, had all gone down to the quay to
watch the embarkation of the troops. He felt glad to be the
only man there. He tramped noisily up the nave, clanking
his spurs till the vaulted roof rang with the sound; he
coughed, he talked aloud to himself to let the nuns know, and
more particularly to let the organist know that if the troops
were gone, one Frenchman was left behind. Was this singular warning heard and understood? He thought so. It
seemed to him that in the *Magnificat* the organ made response
which was borne to him on the vibrating air. The nun's spirit
found wings in music and fled towards him, throbbing with
the rhythmical pulse of the sounds. Then, in all its might,
the music burst forth and filled the church with warmth. The
Song of Joy set apart in the sublime liturgy of Latin Christianity to express the exaltation of the soul in the presence
of the glory of the Ever-living God, became the utterance of
a heart almost terrified by its gladness in the presence of the
glory of a mortal love; a love that yet lived, a love that had
risen to trouble her even beyond the grave in which the nun
is laid, that she may rise again as the bride of Christ.

The organ is in truth the grandest, the most daring, the
most magnificent of all instruments invented by human
genius. It is a whole orchestra in itself. It can express any-

thing in response to a skilled touch. Surely it is in some sort a pedestal on which the soul poises for a flight forth into space, essaying on her course to draw picture after picture in an endless series, to paint human life, to cross the Infinite that separates heaven from earth? And the longer a dreamer listens to those giant harmonies, the better he realizes that nothing save this hundred-voiced choir on earth can fill all the space between kneeling men and a God hidden by the blinding light of the Sanctuary. The music is the one inter- preter strong enough to bear up the prayers of humanity to heaven, prayer in its omnipotent moods, prayer tinged by the melancholy of many different natures, colored by meditative ecstasy, upspringing with the impulse of repentance,— blended with the myriad fancies of every creed. Yes. In those long vaulted aisles, the melodies inspired by the sense of things divine are blended with a grandeur unknown before, are decked with new glory and might. Out of the dim day- light, and the deep silence broken by the chanting of the choir in response to the thunder of the organ, a veil is woven for God, and the brightness of His attributes shines through it.

And this wealth of holy things seemed to be flung down like a grain of incense upon the fragile altar raised to Love beneath the eternal throne of a jealous and avenging God. Indeed, in the joy of the nun there was little of that awe and gravity which should harmonize with the solemnities of the *Magnificat.* She had enriched the music with graceful varia- tions, earthly gladness throbbing through the rhythm of each. In such brilliant quivering notes some great singer might strive to find a voice for her love, her melodies fluttered as a bird flutters about her mate. There were moments when she seemed to leap back into the past, to dally there now with laughter, now with tears. Her changing moods, as it were, ran riot. She was like a woman excited and happy over her lover's return.

But at length, after the swaying fugues of delirium, after the marvelous rendering of a vision of the past, a revulsion

swept over the soul that thus found utterance for itself. With
a swift transition from the major to the minor, the organist
told her hearer of her present lot. She gave the story of long
melancholy broodings, of the slow course of her moral malady.
How day by day she deadened the senses, how every night cut
off one more thought, how her heart was slowly reduced to
ashes. The sadness deepened shade after shade through languid modulations, and in a little while the echoes were pouring out a torrent of grief. Then on a sudden, high notes rang
out like the voices of angels singing together, as if to tell the
lost but not forgotten lover that their spirits now could only
meet in heaven. Pathetic hope! Then followed the *Amen*.
No more joy, no more tears in the air, no sadness, no regrets.
The *Amen* was the return to God. The final chord was deep,
solemn, even terrible; for the last rumblings of the bass sent
a shiver through the audience that raised the hair on their
heads; the nun shook out her veiling of crape, and seemed to
sink again into the grave from which she had risen for a
moment. Slowly the reverberations died away; it seemed as
if the church, but now so full of light, had returned to thick
darkness.

The General had been caught up and borne swiftly away
by this strong-winged spirit; he had followed the course of
its flight from beginning to end. He understood to the fullest
extent the imagery of that burning symphony; for him the
chords reached deep and far. For him, as for the sister, the
poem meant future, present, and past. Is not music, and even
opera music, a sort of text, which a susceptible or poetic temper, or a sore and stricken heart, may expand as memories
shall determine? If a musician must needs have the heart
of a poet, must not the listener too be in a manner a poet
and a lover to hear all that lies in great music? Religion,
love, and music—what are they but a threefold expression of
the same fact, of that craving for expansion which stirs in
every noble soul. And these three forms of poetry ascend to
God, in whom all passion on earth finds its end. Wherefore
the holy human trinity finds a place amid the infinite

glories of God; of God, whom we always represent surrounded with the fires of love and seistrons of gold—music and light and harmony. Is not He the Cause and the End of all our strivings?

The French General guessed rightly that here in the desert, on this bare rock in the sea, the nun had seized upon music as an outpouring of the passion that still consumed her. Was this her manner of offering up her love as a sacrifice to God? Or was it Love exultant in triumph over God? The questions were hard to answer. But one thing at least the General could not mistake—in this heart, dead to the world, the fire of passion burned as fiercely as in his own.

Vespers over, he went back to the alcalde with whom he was staying. In the all-absorbing joy which comes in such full measure when a satisfaction sought long and painfully is attained at last, he could see nothing beyond this—he was still loved! In her heart love had grown in loneliness, even as his love had grown stronger as he surmounted one barrier after another which this woman had set between them! The glow of soul came to its natural end. There followed a longing to see her again, to contend with God for her, to snatch her away—a rash scheme, which appealed to a daring nature. He went to bed, when the meal was over, to avoid questions; to be alone and think at his ease; and he lay absorbed by deep thought till day broke.

He rose only to go to mass. He went to the church and knelt close to the screen, with his forehead touching the curtain; he would have torn a hole in it if he had been alone, but his host had come with him out of politeness, and the least imprudence might compromise the whole future of his love, and ruin the new hopes.

The organ sounded, but it was another player, and not the nun of the last two days whose hands touched the keys. It was all colorless and cold for the General. Was the woman he loved prostrated by emotion which well-nigh overcame a strong man's heart? Had she so fully realized and shared an unchanged, longed-for love, that now she lay dying on her bed in her cell? While innumerable thoughts of this kind perplexed his mind, the voice of the woman he worshiped rang out close beside him; he knew its clear resonant soprano. It was her voice, with that faint tremor in it which gave it all the charm that shyness and diffidence gives to a young girl; her voice, distinct from the mass of singing as a *prima donna's* in the chorus of a finale. It was like a gold or silver thread in dark frieze.

It was she! There could be no mistake. Parisienne now as ever, she had not laid coquetry aside when she threw off worldly adornments for the veil and the Carmelite's coarse serge. She who had affirmed her love last evening in the praise sent up to God, seemed now to say to her lover, "Yes, it is I. I am here. My love is unchanged, but I am beyond the reach of love. You will hear my voice, my soul shall enfold you, and I shall abide here under the brown shroud in the choir from which no power on earth can tear me. You shall never see me more!"

"It is she indeed!" the General said to himself, raising his head. He had leaned his face on his hands, unable at first to bear the intolerable emotion that surged like a whirlpool in his heart, when that well-known voice vibrated under the arcading, with the sound of the sea for accompaniment.

Storm was without, and calm within the sanctuary. Still that rich voice poured out all its caressing notes; it fell like balm on the lover's burning heart; it blossomed upon the air— the air that a man would fain breathe more deeply to receive the effluence of a soul breathed forth with love in the words of the prayer. The alcalde coming to join his guest found him in tears during the elevation, while the nun was singing, and brought him back to his house. Surprised to find so much piety in a French military man, the worthy magistrate invited the confessor of the convent to meet his guest. Never had news given the General more pleasure; he paid the ecclesiastic a good deal of attention at supper, and confirmed his Spanish hosts in the high opinion they had formed of his piety by a not wholly disinterested respect. He inquired with gravity how many sisters there were in the convent, and asked for particulars of its endowment and revenues, as if from courtesy he wished to hear the good priest discourse on the subject most interesting to him. He informed himself as to the manner of life led by the holy women. Were they allowed to go out of the convent, or to see visitors?

"Señor," replied the venerable churchman, "the rule is strict. A woman cannot enter a monastery of the order of St. Bruno without a special permission from His Holiness, and the rule here is equally stringent. No man may enter a convent of Barefoot Carmelites unless he is a priest specially attached to the services of the house by the Archbishop. None of the nuns may leave the convent; though the great Saint, St. Theresa, often left her cell. The Visitor or the Mothers Superior can alone give permission, subject to an authorization from the Archbishop, for a nun to see a visitor, and then especially in a case of illness. Now we are one of the principal houses, and consequently we have a Mother Superior here. Among other foreign sisters there is one Frenchwoman, Sister Theresa; she it is who directs the music in the chapel."

"Oh!" said the General, with feigned surprise. "She must have rejoiced over the victory of the House of Bourbon."

"I told them the reason of the mass; they are always a little bit inquisitive."

"But Sister Theresa may have interests in France. Perhaps she would like to send some message or to hear news."

"I do not think so. She would have come to ask me."

"As a fellow-countryman, I should be quite curious to see her," said the General. "If it is possible, if the Lady Superior consents, if——"

"Even at the grating and in the Reverend Mother's presence, an interview would be quite impossible for anybody whatsover; but, strict as the Mother is, for a deliverer of our holy religion and the throne of his Catholic Majesty, the rule might be relaxed for a moment," said the confessor, blinking. "I will speak about it."

"How old is Sister Theresa?" inquired the lover. He

dared not ask any questions of the priest as to the nun's beauty.

"She does not reckon years now," the good man answered, with a simplicity that made the General shudder.

Next day before siesta, the confessor came to inform the French General that Sister Theresa and the Mother consented to receive him at the grating in the parlor before vespers. The General spent the siesta in pacing to and fro along the quay in the noonday heat. Thither the priest came to find him, and brought him to the convent by way of the gallery round the cemetery. Fountains, green trees, and rows of arcading maintained a cool freshness in keeping with the place.

At the further end of the long gallery the priest led the way into a large room divided in two by a grating covered with a brown curtain. In the first, and in some sort public half of the apartment, where the confessor left the newcomer, a wooden bench ran round the wall, and two or three chairs, also of wood, were placed near the grating. The ceiling consisted of bare unornamented joists and cross-beams of ilex wood. As the two windows were both on the inner side of the grating, and the dark surface of the wood was a bad reflector, the light in the place was so dim that you could scarcely see the great black crucifix, the portrait of Saint Theresa, and a picture of the Madonna which adorned the gray parlor walls. Tumultuous as the General's feelings were, they took something of the melancholy of the place. He grew calm in that homely quiet. A sense of something vast as the tomb took possession of him beneath the chill unceiled roof. Here, as in the grave, was there not eternal silence, deep peace—the sense of the Infinite? And besides this there was the quiet and the fixed thought of the cloister—a thought which you felt like a subtle presence in the air, and in the dim dusk of the room; an all-pervasive thought nowhere definitely expressed, and looming the larger in the imagination; for in the cloister the great saying, "Peace in the Lord," enters the least religious soul as a living force.

The monk's life is scarcely comprehensible. A man seems

confessed a weakling in a monastery; he was born to act, to live out a life of work; he is evading a man's destiny in his cell. But what man's strength, blended with pathetic weakness, is implied by a woman's choice of the convent life! A man may have any number of motives for burying himself in a monastery; for him it is the leap over the precipice. A woman has but one motive—she is a woman still; she betrothes herself to a Heavenly Bridegroom. Of the monk you may ask, "Why did you not fight your battle?" But if a woman immures herself in the cloister, is there not always a sublime battle fought first?

At length it seemed to the General that that still room, and the lonely convent in the sea, were full of thoughts of him. Love seldom attains to solemnity; yet surely a love still faithful in the breast of God was something solemn, something more than a man had a right to look for as things are in this nineteenth century? The infinite grandeur of the situation might well produce an effect upon the General's mind; he had precisely enough elevation of soul to forget politics, honors, Spain, and society in Paris, and to rise to the height of this lofty climax. And what in truth could be more tragic? How much must pass in the souls of these two lovers, brought together in a place of strangers, on a ledge of granite in the sea; yet held apart by an intangible, unsurmountable barrier! Try to imagine the man saying within himself, "Shall I triumph over God in her heart?" when a faint rustling sound made him quiver, and the curtain was drawn aside.

Between him and the light stood a woman. Her face was hidden by the veil that drooped from the folds upon her head; she was dressed according to the rule of the order in a gown of the color become proverbial. Her bare feet were hidden; if the General could have seen them, he would have known how appallingly thin she had grown; and yet in spite of the thick folds of her coarse gown, a mere covering and no ornament, he could guess how tears, and prayer, and passion, and loneliness had wasted the woman before him.

An ice-cold hand, belonging, no doubt, to the Mother Superior, held back the curtain. The General gave the enforced witness of their interview a searching glance, and met the dark, inscrutable gaze of an aged recluse. The Mother might have been a century old, but the bright, youthful eyes belied the wrinkles that furrowed her pale face.

"Mme. la Duchesse," he began, his voice shaken with emotion, "does your companion understand French?" The veiled figure bowed her head at the sound of his voice.

"There is no duchess here," she replied. "It is Sister Theresa whom you see before you. She whom you call my companion is my mother in God, my superior here on earth."

The words were so meekly spoken by the voice that sounded in other years amid harmonious surroundings of refined luxury, the voice of a queen of fashion in Paris. Such words from the lips that once spoke so lightly and flippantly struck the General dumb with amazement.

"The Holy Mother only speaks Latin and Spanish," she added.

"I understand neither. Dear Antoinette, make my excuses to her."

The light fell full upon the nun's figure; a thrill of deep emotion betrayed itself in a faint quiver of her veil as she heard her name softly spoken by the man who had been so hard in the past.

"My brother," she said, drawing her sleeve under her veil, perhaps to brush tears away, "I am Sister Theresa."

Then, turning to the Superior, she spoke in Spanish; the General knew enough of the language to understand what she said perfectly well; possibly he could have spoken it had he chosen to do so.

"Dear mother, the gentleman presents his respect to you, and begs you to pardon him if he cannot pay them himself, but he knows neither of the languages which you speak——"

The aged nun bent her head slowly, with an expression of angelic sweetness, enhanced at the same time by the consciousness of her power and dignity.

"Do you know this gentleman?" she asked, with a keen glance.

"Yes, Mother."

"Go back to your cell, my daughter!" said the Mother imperiously.

The General slipped aside behind the curtain lest the dreadful tumult within him should appear in his face; even in the shadow it seemed to him that he could still see the Superior's piercing eyes. He was afraid of her; she held his little, frail, hardly-won happiness in her hands; and he, who had never quailed under a triple row of guns, now trembled before this nun. The Duchess went towards the door, but she turned back.

"Mother," she said, with dreadful calmness, "the Frenchman is one of my brothers."

"Then stay, my daughter," said the Superior, after a pause.

The piece of admirable Jesuitry told of such love and regret, that a man less strongly constituted might have broken down under the keen delight in the midst of a great and, for him, an entirely novel peril. Oh! how precious words, looks, and gestures became when love must baffle lynx eyes and tiger's claws! Sister Theresa came back.

"You see, my brother, what I have dared to do only to speak to you for a moment of your salvation and of the prayers that my soul puts up for your soul daily. I am committing mortal sin. I have told a lie. How many days of penance must expiate that lie! But I shall endure it for your sake. My brother, you do not know what happiness it is to love in heaven; to feel that you can confess love purified by religion, love transported into the highest heights of all, so that we are permitted to lose sight of all but the soul. If the doctrine and the spirit of the Saint to whom we owe this refuge had not raised me above earth's anguish, and caught me up and set me, far indeed beneath the Sphere wherein she dwells, yet truly above this world, I should not have seen you again. But now I can see you, and hear your voice, and remain calm——"

The General broke in, "But, Antoinette, let me see you, you whom I love passionately, desperately, as you could have wished me to love you."

"Do not call me Antoinette, I implore you. Memories of the past hurt me. You must see no one here but Sister Theresa, a creature who trusts in the Divine mercy." She paused for a little, and then added, "You must control yourself, my brother. Our Mother would separate us without pity if there is any worldly passion in your face, or if you allow the tears to fall from your eyes."

The General bowed his head to regain self-control; when he looked up again he saw her face beyond the grating—the thin, white, but still impassioned face of the nun. All the magic charm of youth that once bloomed there, all the fair contrast of velvet whiteness and the color of the Bengal rose, had given place to a burning glow, as of a porcelain jar with a faint light shining through it. The wonderful hair in which she took such pride had been shaven; there was a bandage round her forehead and about her face. An ascetic life had left dark traces about the eyes, which still sometimes shot out fevered glances; their ordinary calm expression was but a veil. In a few words, she was but the ghost of her former self.

"Ah! you that have come to be my life, you must come out of this tomb! You were mine; you had no right to give yourself, even to God. Did you not promise me to give up all at the least command from me? You may perhaps think me worthy of that promise now when you hear what I have done for you. I have sought you all through the world. You have been in my thoughts at every moment for five years; my life has been given to you. My friends, very powerful friends, as you know, have helped me with all their might to search every convent in France, Italy, Spain, Sicily, and America. Love burned more brightly for every vain search. Again and again I made long journeys with a false hope; I have wasted my life and the heaviest throbbings of my heart in vain under many a dark convent wall. I am not speaking of a faithfulness that knows no bounds, for what is it?—nothing compared with the infinite longings of my love. If your remorse long ago was sincere, you ought not to hesitate to follow me to-day."

"You forget that I am not free."

"The Duke is dead," he answered quickly.

Sister Theresa flushed red.

"May heaven be open to him!" she cried with a quick rush of feeling. "He was generous to me.—But I did not mean such ties; it was one of my sins that I was ready to break them all without scruple—for you."

"Are you speaking of your vows?" the General asked, frowning. "I did not think that anything weighed heavier with your heart than love. But do not think twice of it, Antoinette; the Holy Father himself shall absolve you of your oath. I will surely go to Rome, I will entreat all the powers of earth; if God could come down from heaven, I would——"

"Do not blaspheme."

"So do not fear the anger of God. Ah! I would far rather hear that you would leave your prison for me; that this very night you would let yourself down into a boat at the foot of the cliffs. And we would go away to be happy somewhere at the world's end, I know not where. And with me at your side, you should come back to life and health under the wings of love."

"You must not talk like this," said Sister Theresa; "you do not know what you are to me now. I love you far better than I ever loved you before. Every day I pray for you; I see you with other eyes. Armand, if you but knew the happiness of giving yourself up, without shame, to a pure friendship which God watches over! You do not know what joy it is to me to pray for heaven's blessing on you. I never pray for myself: God will do with me according to His will; but, at the price of my soul, I wish I could be sure that you are happy here on earth, and that you will he happy hereafter throughout all ages. My eternal life is all that trouble has left me to

offer up to you now. I am old now with weeping; I am neither
young nor fair; and in any case, you could not respect the
nun who became a wife; no love, not even motherhood, could
give me absolution. . . . What can you say to outweigh
the uncounted thoughts that have gathered in my heart during the past five years, thoughts that have changed, and
worn, and blighted it? I ought to have given a heart less
sorrowful to God."

"What can I say? Dear Antoinette, I will say this, that
I love you; that affection, love, a great love, the joy of living
in another heart that is ours, utterly and wholly ours, is so
rare a thing and so hard to find, that I doubted you, and put
you to sharp proof; but now, to-day, I love you, Antoinette,
with all my soul's strength. . . . If you will follow me
into solitude, I will hear no voice but yours, I will see no
other face."

"Hush, Armand! You are shortening the little time that
we may be together here on earth."

"Antoinette, will you come with me?"

"I am never away from you. My life is in your heart, not
through the selfish ties of earthly happiness, or vanity, or
enjoyment; pale and withered as I am, I live here for you, in
the breast of God. As God is just, you shall be happy——"

"Words, words all of it! Pale and withered? How if I
want you? How if I cannot be happy without you? Do you
still think of nothing but duty with your lover before you?
Is he never to come first and above all things else in your
heart? In times past you put social success, yourself, heaven
knows what, before him; now it is God, it is the welfare of
my soul! In Sister Theresa I find the Duchess over again,
ignorant of the happiness of love, insensible as ever, beneath
the semblance of sensibility. You do not love me; you have
never loved me——"

"Oh, my brother——!"

"You do not wish to leave this tomb. You love my soul,
do you say? Very well, through you it will be lost for ever!
I shall make away with myself——"

"Mother!" Sister Theresa called aloud in Spanish, "I have lied to you; this man is my lover!"

The curtain fell at once. The General, in his stupor, scarcely heard the doors within as they clanged.

"Ah! she loves me still!" he cried, understanding all the sublimity of that cry of hers. "She loves me still. She must be carried off. . . ."

The General left the island, returned to headquarters, pleaded ill-health, asked for leave of absence, and forthwith took his departure for France.

And now for the incidents which brought the two personages in this Scene into their present relation to each other.

The thing known in France as the Faubourg Saint-Germain is neither a Quarter, nor a sect, nor an institution, nor anything else that admits of a precise definition. There are great houses in the Place Royale, the Faubourg Saint-Honoré, and the Chaussée d'Antin, in any one of which you may breathe the same atmosphere of Faubourg Saint-Germain. So, to begin with, the whole Faubourg is not within the Faubourg. There are men and women born far enough away from its influences who respond to them and take their place in the circle; and again there are others, born within its limits, who may yet be driven forth for ever. For the last forty years the manners, and customs, and speech, in a word, the tradition of the Faubourg Saint-Germain, has been to Paris what the Court used to be in other times; it is what the Hôtel Saint-Paul was to the Fourteenth Century; the Louvre to the Fifteenth; the Palais, the Hôtel Rambouillet, and the Place Royale to the Sixteenth; and lastly, as Versailles was to the Seventeenth and the Eighteenth.

Just as the ordinary work-a-day Paris will always centre about some point; so, through all periods of history, the Paris of the nobles and the upper classes converges towards some particular spot. It is a periodically recurrent phenomenon which presents ample matter for reflection to those who are fain to observe or describe the various social zones; and possibly an inquiry into the causes that bring about this centralization may do more than merely justify the probability of this episode; it may be of service to serious interests which some day will be more deeply rooted in the commonwealth, unless, indeed, experience is as meaningless for political parties as it is for youth.

In every age the great nobles, and the rich who always ape the great nobles, build their houses as far as possible from crowded streets. When the Duc d'Uzés built his splendid hôtel in the Rue Montmartre in the reign of Louis XIV., and set the fountain at his gates—for which beneficent action, to say nothing of his other virtues, he was held in such veneration that the whole quarter turned out in a body to follow his funeral—when the Duke, I say, chose this site for his house, he did so because that part of Paris was almost deserted in those days. But when the fortifications were pulled down, and the market gardens beyond the line of the boulevards began to fill with houses, then the d'Uzés family left their fine mansion, and in our time it was occupied by a banker. Later still, the noblesse began to find themselves out of their element among shopkeepers, left the Place Royale and the centre of Paris for good, and crossed the river to breathe freely in the Faubourg Saint-Germain, where palaces were reared already about the great hôtel built by Louis XIV. for the Duc de Maine—the Benjamin among his legitimated offspring. And indeed, for people accustomed to a stately life, can there be more unseemly surroundings than the bustle, the mud, the street cries, the bad smells, and narrow thoroughfares of a populous quarter? The very habits of life in a mercantile or manufacturing district are completely at variance with the lives of nobles. The shopkeeper and artisan are just going to bed when the great world is thinking of dinner; and the noisy stir of life begins among the former when the latter have gone to rest. Their day's calculations never coincide; the one class represents the expenditure, the other the receipts. Consequently their manners and customs are diametrically opposed.

Nothing contemptuous is intended by this statement. An aristocracy is in a manner the intellect of the social system, as the middle classes and the proletariat may be said to be its organizing and working power. It naturally follows that these forces are differently situated; and of their antagonism there is bred a seeming antipathy produced by the performance of different functions, all of them, however, existing for one common end.

Such social dissonances are so inevitably the outcome of any charter of the constitution, that however much a Liberal may be disposed to complain of them, as of treason against those sublime ideas with which the ambitious plebeian is apt to cover his designs, he would none the less think it a preposterous notion that M. le Prince de Montmorency, for instance, should continue to live in the Rue Saint-Martin at the corner of the street which bears that nobleman's name; or that M. le Duc de Fitz-James, descendant of the royal house of Scotland, should have his hôtel at the angle of the Rue Marie Stuart and the Rue Montorgueil. *Sint ut sunt, aut non sint,* the grand words of the Jesuit, might be taken as a motto by the great of all countries. These social differences are patent in all ages; the fact is always accepted by the people; its "reasons of state" are self-evident; it is at once cause and effect, a principle and a law. The common sense of the masses never deserts them until demagogues stir them up to gain ends of their own; that common sense is based on the verities of social order; and the social order is the same everywhere, in Moscow as in London, in Geneva as in Calcutta. Given a certain number of families of unequal fortune in any given space, you will see an aristocracy forming under your eyes; there will be the patricians, the upper classes, and yet other ranks below them. Equality may be a *right,* but no power on earth can convert it into *fact.* It would be a good thing for France if this idea could be popularized. The benefits of political harmony are obvious to the least intelligent classes. Harmony is, as it were, the poetry of order, and order is a matter of vital importance to the working population. And what is order, reduced to its simplest expression, but the agreement of things among themselves—unity, in short? Architecture, music, and poetry, everything in France, and in France more than in any other country, is based upon this principle; it is written upon the very foundations of her clear accurate language, and a language must always be the most infallible index of national character. In the same way you may note that the French popular airs are those most calculated to strike the imagination, the best-modulated melodies are taken over by the people; clearness of thought, the intellectual simplicity of an idea attracts them; they like the incisive sayings that hold the greatest number of ideas. France is the one country in the world where a little phrase may bring about a great revolution. Whenever the masses have risen, it has been to bring men, affairs, and principles into agreement. No nation has a clearer conception of that idea of unity which should permeate the life of an aristocracy; possibly no other nation has so intelligent a comprehension of a political necessity; history will never find her behind the time. France has been led astray many a time, but she is deluded, woman-like, by generous ideas, by a glow of enthusiasm which at first outstrips sober reason.

So, to begin with, the most striking characteristic of the Faubourg is the splendor of its great mansions, its great gardens, and a surrounding quiet in keeping with princely revenues drawn from great estates. And what is this distance set between a class and a whole metropolis but the visible and outward expression of the widely different attitude of mind which must inevitably keep them apart? The position of the head is well defined in every organism. If by any chance a nation allows its head to fall at its feet, it is pretty sure sooner or later to discover that this is a suicidal measure; and since nations have no desire to perish, they set to work at once to grow a new head. If they lack the strength for this, they perish as Rome perished, and Venice, and so many other states.

This distinction between the upper and lower spheres of social activity, emphasized by differences in their manner of living, necessarily implies that in the highest aristocracy there is real worth and some distinguishing merit. In any State, no matter what form of "government" is affected, so soon as the patrician class fails to maintain that complete superiority which is the condition of its existence, it ceases to be a force, and is pulled down at once by the populace. The people always wish to see money, power, and initiative in their leaders'. hands, hearts, and heads; they must be the spokesmen, they must represent the intelligence and the glory of the nation. Nations, like women, love strength in those who rule them; they cannot give love without respect; they refuse utterly to obey those of whom they do not stand in awe. An aristocracy fallen into contempt is a *roi fainéant,* a husband in petticoats; first it ceases to be itself, and then it ceases to be.

And in this way the isolation of the great, the sharply marked distinction in their manner of life, or in a word, the general custom of the patrician caste is at once the sign of a real power, and their destruction so soon as that power is lost. The Faubourg Saint-Germain failed to recognize the conditions of its being, while it would still have been easy to perpetuate its existence, and therefore was brought low for a time. The Faubourg should have looked the facts fairly in the face, as the English aristocracy did before them; they should have seen that every institution has its climacteric periods, when words lose their old meanings, and ideas reappear in a new guise, and the whole conditions of politics wear a changed aspect, while the underlying realities undergo no essential alteration.

These ideas demand further developments which form an essential part of this episode; they are given here both as a succinct statement of the causes, and an explanation of the things which happen in the course of the story.

The stateliness of the castles and palaces where nobles dwell; the luxury of the details; the constantly maintained sumptuousness of the furniture; the "atmosphere" in which the fortunate owner of landed estates (a rich man before he was born) lives and moves easily and without friction; the habit of mind which never descends to calculate the petty work-a-day gains of existence; the leisure; the higher education attainable at a much earlier age; and lastly, the aristocratic condition that makes of him a social force, for which his opponents, by dint of study and a strong will and tenacity of vocation, are scarcely a match—all these things should contribute to form a lofty spirit in a man, possessed of such privileges from his youth up; they should stamp his character with that high self-respect, of which the least consequence is a nobleness of heart in harmony with the noble name that he bears. And in some few families all this is realized. There are noble characters here and there in the Faubourg, but they are marked exceptions to a general rule of egoism which has been the ruin of this world within a world. The privileges above enumerated are the birthright of the French noblesse, as of every patrician efflorescence ever formed on the surface of a nation; and will continue to be theirs so long as their existence is based upon real estate, or money; *domaine-sol* and *domaine-argent* alike, the only solid bases of an organized society; but such privileges are held upon the understanding that the patricians must continue to justify their existence. There is a sort of moral *fief* held on a tenure of service rendered to the sovereign, and here in France the people are undoubtedly the sovereigns nowadays. The times are changed, and so are the weapons. The knight-banneret of old wore a coat of chain armor and a hauberk; he could handle a lance well and display his pennon, and no more was required of him; to-day he is bound to give proof of his intelligence. A stout heart was enough in the days of old; in our days he is required to have a capacious brain-pan. Skill and knowledge and capital—these three points mark out a social triangle on which the scutcheon of power is blazoned; our modern aristocracy must take its stand on these.

A fine theorem is as good as a great name. The Roths-

childs, the Fuggers of the nineteenth century, are princes
de facto. A great artist is in reality an oligarch; he represents a whole century, and almost always he is a law to others.
And the art of words, the high pressure machinery of the
writer, the poet's genius, the merchant's steady endurance,
the strong will of the statesman who concentrates a thousand
dazzling qualities in himself, the general's sword,—all these
victories, in short, which a single individual will win, that he
may tower above the rest of the world, the patrician class is
now bound to win and keep exclusively. They must head
the new forces as they once headed the material forces; how
should they keep the position unless they are worthy of it?
How, unless they are the soul and brain of a nation, shall
they set its hands moving? How lead a people without the
power of command? And what is the marshal's bâton without the innate power of the captain in the man who wields
it? The Faubourg Saint-Germain took to playing with
bâtons, and fancied that all the power was in its hands.
It inverted the terms of the proposition which called it into
existence. And instead of flinging away the insignia which
offended the people, and quietly grasping the power, it allowed the bourgeoisie to seize the authority, clung with fatal
obstinacy to its shadow, and over and over again forgot the
laws which a minority must observe if it would live. When
an aristocracy is scarce a thousandth part of the body social,
it is bound to-day, as of old, to multiply its points of action,
so as to counterbalance the weight of the masses in a great
crisis. And in our days those means of action must be living
forces, and not historical memories.

In France, unluckily, the noblesse were still so puffed up
with the notion of their vanished power, that it was difficult
to contend against a kind of innate presumption in themselves. Perhaps this is a national defect. The Frenchman is
less given than any one else to undervalue himself; it comes
natural to him to go from his degree to the one above it; and
while it is a rare thing for him to pity the unfortunates over
whose heads he rises, he always groans in spirit to see so many

fortunate people above him. He is very far from heartless, but too often he prefers to listen to his intellect. The national instinct which brings the Frenchman to the front, the vanity that wastes his substance, is as much a dominant passion as thrift in the Dutch. For three centuries it swayed the noblesse, who, in this respect, were certainly pre-eminently French. The scion of the Faubourg Saint-Germain, beholding his material superiority, was fully persuaded of his intellectual superiority. And everything contributed to confirm him in his belief; for ever since the Faubourg Saint-Germain existed at all—which is to say, ever since Versailles ceased to be the royal residence—the Faubourg, with some few gaps in continuity, was always backed up by the central power, which in France seldom fails to support that side. Thence its downfall in 1830.

At that time the party of the Faubourg Saint-Germain was rather like an army without a base of operation. It had utterly failed to take advantage of the peace to plant itself in the heart of the nation. It sinned for want of learning its lesson, and through an utter incapability of regarding its interests as a whole. A future certainty was sacrificed to a doubtless present gain. This blunder in policy may perhaps be attributed to the following cause.

The class-isolation so strenuously kept up by the noblesse brought about fatal results during the last forty years; even caste-patriotism was extinguished by it, and rivalry fostered among themselves. When the French noblesse of other times were rich and powerful, the nobles (*gentilhommes*) could choose their chiefs and obey them in the hour of danger. As their power diminished, they grew less amenable to discipline; and as in the last days of the Byzantine Empire, every one wished to be emperor. They mistook their uniform weakness for uniform strength.

Each family ruined by the Revolution and the abolition of the law of primogeniture thought only of itself, and not at all of the great family of the noblesse. It seemed to them that as each individual grew rich, the party as a whole would gain in strength. And herein lay their mistake. Money, likewise, is only the outward and visible sign of power. All these families were made up of persons who preserved a high tradition of courtesy, of true graciousness of life, of refined speech, with a family pride, and a squeamish sense of *noblesse oblige* which suited well with the kind of life they led; a life wholly filled with occupations which become contemptible so soon as they cease to be accessories and take the chief place in existence. There was a certain intrinsic merit in all these people, but the merit was on the surface, and none of them were worth their face-value.

Not a single one among those families had courage to ask itself the question, "Are we strong enough for the responsibility of power?" They were cast on the top, like the lawyers of 1830; and instead of taking the patron's place, like a great man, the Faubourg Saint-Germain showed itself greedy as an upstart. The most intelligent nation in the world perceived clearly that the restored nobles were organizing everything for their own particular benefit. From that day the noblesse was doomed. The Faubourg Saint-Germain tried to be an aristocracy when it could only be an oligarchy—two very different systems, as any man may see for himself if he gives an intelligent perusal to the list of the patronymics of the House of Peers.

The King's Government certainly meant well; but the maxim that the people must be made to *will* everything, even their own welfare, was pretty constantly forgotten, nor did they bear in mind that La France is a woman and capricious, and must be happy or chastised at her own good pleasure. If there had been any dukes like the Duc de Laval, whose modesty made him worthy of the name he bore, the elder branch would have been as securely seated on the throne as the House of Hanover at this day.

In 1814 the noblesse of France were called upon to assert their superiority over the most aristocratic bourgeoisie in the most feminine of all countries, to take the lead in the most highly educated epoch the world had yet seen. And this was even more notably the case in 1820. The Faubourg Saint-Germain might very easily have led and amused the middle classes in days when people's heads were turned with distinctions, and art and science were all the rage. But the narrow-minded leaders of a time of great intellectual progress, all of them detested art and science. They had not even the wit to present religion in attractive colors, though they needed its support. While Lamartine, Lamennais, Montalembert, and other writers were putting new life and elevation into men's ideas of religion, and gilding it with poetry, these bunglers in the Government chose to make the harshness of their creed felt all over the country. Never was nation in a more tractable humor; La France, like a tired woman, was ready to agree to anything; never was mismanagement so clumsy; and La France, like a woman, would have forgiven wrongs more easily than bungling.

If the noblesse meant to reinstate themselves, the better to found a strong oligarchy, they should have honestly and diligently searched their houses for men of the stamp that Napoleon used; they should have turned themselves inside out to see if peradventure there was a Constitutionalist Richelieu lurking in the entrails of the Faubourg; and if that genius was not forthcoming from among them, they should have set out to find him, even in the fireless garret where he might happen to be perishing of cold; they should have assimilated him, as the English House of Lords continually assimilates aristocrats made by chance; and finally ordered him to be ruthless, to lop away the old wood, and cut the tree down to the living shoots. But, in the first place, the great system of English Toryism was far too large for narrow minds; the importation required time, and in France a tardy success is no better than a fiasco. So far, moreover, from adopting a policy of redemption, and looking for new forces where God puts them, these petty great folk took a dislike to any capacity that did not issue from their midst; and, lastly, instead of growing young again, the Faubourg Saint-Germain grew positively older.

Etiquette, not an institution of primary necessity, might have been maintained if it had appeared only on state occasions, but as it was, there was a daily wrangle over precedence; it ceased to be a matter of art or court ceremonial, it became a question of power. And if from the outset the Crown lacked an adviser equal to so great a crisis, the aristocracy was still more lacking in a sense of its wider interests, an instinct which might have supplied the deficiency. They stood nice about M. de Talleyrand's marriage, when M. de Talleyrand was the one man among them with the steel-encompassed brains that can forge a new political system and begin a new career of glory for a nation. The Faubourg scoffed at a minister if he was not gently born, and produced no one of gentle birth that was fit to be a minister. There were plenty of nobles fitted to serve their country by raising the dignity of justices of the peace, by improving the land, by opening out roads and canals, and taking an active and leading part as country gentlemen; but these had sold their estates to gamble on the Stock Exchange. Again the Faubourg might have absorbed the energetic men among the bourgeoisie, and opened their ranks to the ambition which was undermining authority; they preferred instead to fight, and to fight unarmed, for of all that they once possessed there was nothing left but tradition. For their misfortune there was just precisely enough of their former wealth left them as a class to keep up their bitter pride. They were content with their past. Not one of them seriously thought of bidding the son of the house take up arms from the pile of weapons which the Nineteenth Century flings down in the market-place. Young men, shut out from office, were dancing at Madame's balls, while they should have been doing the work done under the Republic and the Empire by young, conscientious, harmlessly employed energies. It was their place to carry out at Paris the programme which their seniors should have been following in the country. The heads of houses might have won back recognition of their titles by unremitting attention to local interests, by falling in with the spirit of the age, by recasting their order to suit the taste of the times.

But, pent up together in the Faubourg Saint-Germain, where the spirit of the ancient court and traditions of bygone feuds between the nobles and the Crown still lingered on, the aristocracy was not whole-hearted in its allegiance to the Tuileries, and so much the more easily defeated because it was concentrated in the Chamber of Peers, and badly organized even there. If the noblesse had woven themselves into a network over the country, they could have held their own; but cooped up in their Faubourg, with their backs against the Château, or spread at full length over the Budget, a single blow cut the thread of a fast-expiring life, and a petty, smug-faced lawyer came forward with the axe. In spite of M. Royer-Collard's admirable discourse, the hereditary peerage and law of entail fell before the lampoons of a man who made it a boast that he had adroitly argued some few heads out of the executioner's clutches, and now forsooth must clumsily proceed in the slaying of old institutions.

There are examples and lessons for the future in all this. For if there were not still a future before the French aristocracy, there would be no need to do more than find a suitable sarcophagus; it were something pitilessly cruel to burn the dead body of it with fire of Tophet. But though the surgeon's scalpel is ruthless, it sometimes gives back life to a dying man; and the Faubourg Saint-Germain may wax more powerful under persecution than in its day of triumph, if it but chooses to organize itself under a leader.

And now it is easy to give a summary of this semi-political survey. The wish to re-establish a large fortune was uppermost in every one's mind; a lack of broad views, and a mass of small defects, a real need of religion as a political factor, combined with a thirst for pleasure which damaged the cause of religion and necessitated a good deal of hypocrisy; a certain attitude of protest on the part of loftier and clearer-sighted men who set their faces against Court jealousies; and the disaffection of the provincial families, who often came

of purer descent than the nobles of the Court which alienated
them from itself,—all these things combined to bring about
a most discordant state of things in the Faubourg Saint-Germain. It was neither compact in its organization, nor consequent in its action; neither completely moral, nor frankly
dissolute; it did not corrupt, nor was it corrupted; it would
neither wholly abandon the disputed points which damaged
its cause, nor yet adopt the policy that might have saved it.
In short, however effete individuals might be, the party as
a whole was none the less armed with all the great principles
which lie at the roots of national existence. What was there
in the Faubourg that it should perish in its strength?

It was very hard to please in the choice of candidates; the
Faubourg had good taste, it was scornfully fastidious, yet
there was nothing very glorious nor chivalrous truly about
its fall.

In the Emigration of 1789 there were some traces of a
loftier feeling; but in the Emigration of 1830 from Paris
into the country there was nothing discernible but self-interest. A few famous men of letters, a few oratorical triumphs in the Chambers, M. de Talleyrand's attitude in the
Congress, the taking of Algiers, and not a few names that
found their way from the battlefield into the pages of history,
—all these things were so many examples set before the
French noblesse to show that it was still open to them to take
their part in the national existence, and to win recognition
of their claims, if, indeed, they could condescend thus far.
In every living organism the work of bringing the whole into
harmony within itself was going on. If a man is indolent,
the indolence shows itself in everything that he does; and,
in the same manner, the general spirit of a class is pretty
plainly manifested in the face it turns on the world, and the
soul informs the body.

The women of the Restoration displayed neither the proud
disregard of public opinion shown by the court ladies of olden
time in their wantonness, nor yet the simple grandeur of the
tardy virtues by which they expiated their sins and shed so

bright a glory about their names. There was nothing either very frivolous or very serious about the woman of the Restoration. She was hypocritical as a rule in her passion, and compounded, so to speak, with its pleasures. Some few families led the domestic life of the Duchesse d'Orléans, whose connubial couch was exhibited so absurdly to visitors at the Palais Royal. Two or three kept up the traditions of the Regency, filling cleverer women with something like disgust. The great lady of the new school exercised no influence at all over the manners of the time; and yet she might have done much. She might, at worst, have presented as dignified a spectacle as Englishwomen of the same rank. But she hesitated feebly among old precedents, became a bigot by force of circumstances, and allowed nothing of herself to appear, not even her better qualities.

Not one among the Frenchwomen of that day had the ability to create a salon whither leaders of fashion might come to take lessons in taste and elegance. Their voices, which once laid down the law to literature, that living expression of a time, now counted absolutely for nought. Now when a literature lacks a general system, it fails to shape a body for itself, and dies out with its period.

When in a nation at any time there is a people apart thus constituted, the historian is pretty certain to find some representative figure, some central personage who embodies the qualities and the defects of the whole party to which he belongs; there is Coligny, for instance, among the Huguenots, the Coadjuteur in the time of the Fronde, the Maréchal de Richelieu under Louis XV., Danton during the Terror. It is in the nature of things that the man should be identified with the company in which history finds him. How is it possible to lead a party without conforming to its ideas? or to shine in any epoch unless a man represents the ideas of his time? The wise and prudent head of a party is continually obliged to bow to the prejudices and follies of its rear; and this is the cause of actions for which he is afterwards criticised by this or that historian sitting at a safer distance from terrific popular explosions, coolly judging the passion and ferment without which the great struggles of the world could not be carried on at all.   And if this is true of the Historical Comedy of the Centuries, it is equally true in a more restricted sphere in the detached scenes of the national drama known as the *Manners of the Age*.

At the beginning of that ephemeral life led by the Faubourg Saint-Germain under the Restoration, to which, if there is any truth in the above reflections, they failed to give stability, the most perfect type of the aristocratic caste in its weakness and strength, its greatness and littleness, might have been found for a brief space in a young married woman who belonged to it.   This was a woman artificially educated, but in reality ignorant; a woman whose instincts and feelings were lofty, while the thought which should have controlled them was wanting.   She squandered the wealth of her nature in obedience to social conventions; she was ready to brave society, yet she hesitated till her scruples degenerated into artifice.   With more wilfulness than real force of character, impressionable rather than enthusiastic, gifted with more brain than heart; she was supremely a woman, supremely a coquette, and above all things a Parisienne, loving a brilliant life and gaiety, reflecting never, or too late; imprudent to the verge of poetry, and humble in the depths of her heart, in spite of her charming insolence.   Like some straight-growing reed, she made a show of independence; yet, like the reed, she was ready to bend to a strong hand.   She talked much of religion, and had it not at heart, though she was prepared to find in it a solution of her life.   How explain a creature so complex?   Capable of heroism, yet sinking unconsciously from heroic heights to utter a spiteful word; young and sweet-natured, not so much old at heart as aged by the maxims of those about her; versed in a selfish philosophy in which she was all unpractised, she had all the vices of a courtier, all the nobleness of developing womanhood.   She trusted nothing and no one, yet there were times when she quitted her sceptical attitude for a submissive credulity.

How should any portrait be anything but incomplete of her, in whom the play of swiftly-changing color made discord only to produce a poetic confusion? for in her there shone a divine brightness, a radiance of youth that blended all her bewildering characteristics in a certain completeness and unity informed by her charm. Nothing was feigned. The passion or semi-passion, the ineffectual high aspirations, the actual pettiness, the coolness of sentiment and warmth of impulse, were all spontaneous and unaffected and as much the outcome of her own position as of the position of the aristocracy to which she belonged. She was wholly self-constrained; she put herself proudly above the world and beneath the shelter of her name. There was something of the egoism of Medea in her life, as in the life of the aristocracy that lay a-dying, and would not so much as raise itself or stretch out a hand to any political physician; so well aware of its feebleness, or so conscious that it was already dust, that it refused to touch or be touched.

The Duchesse de Langeais (for that was her name) had been married about four years when the Restoration was finally consummated, which is to say, in 1816. By that time the revolution of the Hundred Days had let in the light on the mind of Louis XVIII. In spite of his surroundings, he comprehended the situation and the age in which he was living; and it was only later, when Louis XI., without the axe, lay stricken down by disease, that those about him got the upper hand. The Duchesse de Langeais, a Navarreins by birth, came of a ducal house which had made a point of never marrying below its rank since the reign of Louis XIV. Every daughter of the house must sooner or later take a *tabouret* at Court. So, Antoinette de Navarreins, at the age of eighteen, came out of the profound solitude in which her girlhood had been spent to marry the Duc de Langeais' eldest son. The two families at that time were living quite out of the world; but after the invasion of France, the return of the Bourbons seemed to every Royalist mind the only possible way of putting an end to the miseries of the war.

The Ducs de Navarreins and de Langeais had been faithful throughout to the exiled Princes, nobly resisting all the temptations of glory under the Empire. Under the circumstances they naturally followed out the old family policy; and Mlle. Antoinette, a beautiful and portionless girl, was married to M. le Marquis de Langeais only a few months before the death of the Duke his father.

After the return of the Bourbons, the families resumed their rank, offices, and dignity at Court; once more they entered public life, from which hitherto they held aloof, and took their place high on the sun-lit summits of the new political world. In that time of general baseness and sham political conversions, the public conscience was glad to recognize the unstained loyalty of the two houses, and a consistency in political and private life for which all parties involuntarily respected them. But, unfortunately, as so often happens in a time of transition, the most disinterested persons, the men whose loftiness of view and wise principles would have gained the confidence of the French nation and led them to believe in the generosity of a novel and spirited policy;—these men, to repeat, were taken out of affairs, and public business was allowed to fall into the hands of others, who found it to their interest to push principles to their extreme consequences by way of proving their devotion.

The families of Langeais and Navarreins remained about the Court, condemned to perform the duties required by Court ceremonial amid the reproaches and sneers of the Liberal party. They were accused of gorging themselves with riches and honors, and all the while their family estates were no larger than before, and liberal allowances from the civil list were wholly expended in keeping up the state necessary for any European Government, even if it be a Republic.

In 1818, M. le Duc de Langeais commanded a division of the army, and the Duchess held a post about one of the Princesses, in virtue of which she was free to live in Paris and apart from her husband without scandal. The Duke, moreover, besides his military duties, had a place at Court, to which he came during his term of waiting, leaving his major-general in command. The Duke and Duchess were leading lives entirely apart, the world none the wiser. Their marriage of convention shared the fate of nearly all family arrangements of the kind. Two more antipathetic dispositions could not well have been found; they were brought together; they jarred upon each other; there was soreness on either side; then they were divided once for all. Then they went their separate ways, with a due regard for appearances. The Duc de Langeais, by nature as methodical as the Chevalier de Folard himself, gave himself up methodically to his own tastes and amusements, and left his wife at liberty to do as she pleased so soon as he felt sure of her character. He recognized in her a spirit pre-eminently proud, a cold heart, a profound submissiveness to the usages of the world, and a youthful loyalty. Under the eyes of great relations, with the light of a prudish and bigoted Court turned full upon the Duchess, his honor was safe.

So the Duke calmly did as the *grands seigneurs* of the eighteenth century did before him, and left a young wife of two-and-twenty to her own devices. He had deeply offended that wife, and in her nature there was one appalling characteristic—she would never forgive an offence when woman's vanity and self-love, with all that was best in her nature, perhaps, had been slighted, wounded in secret. Insult and injury in the face of the world a woman loves to forget; there is a way open to her of showing herself great; she is a woman in her forgiveness; but a secret offence woman never pardon; for secret baseness, as for hidden virtues and hidden love, they have no kindness.

This was Mme. la Duchesse de Langeais' real position, unknown to the world. She herself did not reflect upon it. It was the time of the rejoicings over the Duc de Berri's marriage. The Court and the Faubourg roused itself from its listlessness and reserve. This was the real beginning of that unheard-of splendor which the Government of the Restoration carried too far. At that time the Duchess, whether for reasons of her own, or from vanity, never appeared in public without a following of women equally distinguished by name and fortune. As queen of fashion she had her *dames d'atours,* her ladies, who modeled their manner and their wit on hers. They had been cleverly chosen. None of her satellites belonged to the inmost Court circle, nor to the highest level of the Faubourg Saint-Germain; but they had set their minds upon admission to those inner sanctuaries. Being as yet simple denominations, they wished to rise to the neighborhood of the throne, and mingle with the seraphic powers in the high sphere known as *le petit château.* Thus surrounded, the Duchess' position was stronger and more commanding and secure. Her "ladies" defended her character and helped her to play her detestable part of a woman of fashion. She could laugh at men at her ease, play with fire, receive the homage on which the feminine nature is nourished, and remain mistress of herself.

At Paris, in the highest society of all, a woman is a woman still; she lives on incense, adulation, and honors. No beauty, however undoubted, no face, however fair, is anything without admiration. Flattery and a lover are proofs of power. And what is power without recognition? Nothing. If the prettiest of women were left alone in a corner of a drawing-room, she would droop. Put her in the very centre and summit of social grandeur, she will at once aspire to reign over all hearts—often because it is out of her power to be the happy queen of one. Dress and manner and coquetry are all meant to please one of the poorest creatures extant—the brainless coxcomb, whose handsome face is his sole merit; it was for such as these that women threw themselves away. The gilded wooden idols of the Restoration, for they were neither more nor less, had neither the antecedents of the *petits maîtres* of the time of the Fronde, nor the rough sterling worth of Napoleon's heroes, nor the wit and fine manners of their grandsires; but something of all three they meant to be without any trouble to themselves. Brave they were, like all young Frenchmen; ability they possessed, no doubt, if they had had a chance of proving it, but their places were filled up by the old worn-out men, who kept them in leading strings. It was a day of small things, a cold prosaic era. Perhaps it takes a long time for a Restoration to become a Monarchy.

For the past eighteen months the Duchesse de Langeais had been leading this empty life, filled with balls and subsequent visits, objectless triumphs, and the transient loves that spring up and die in an evening's space. All eyes were turned on her when she entered a room; she reaped her harvest of flatteries and some few words of warmer admiration, which she encouraged by a gesture or a glance, but never suffered to penetrate deeper than the skin. Her tone and bearing and everything else about her imposed her will upon others. Her life was a sort of fever of vanity and perpetual enjoyment, which turned her head. She was daring enough n conversation; she would listen to anything, corrupting the surface, as it were, of her heart. Yet when she returned home, she often blushed at the story that had made her laugh; at the scandalous tale that supplied the details, on the strength of which she analyzed the love that she had never known, and marked the subtle distinctions of modern passion, not with comment on the part of complacent hypocrites. For women know how to say everything among themselves, and more of them are ruined by each other than corrupted by men.

There came a moment when she discerned that not until a woman is loved will the world fully recognize her beauty and her wit. What does a husband prove? Simply that a girl or woman was endowed with wealth, or well brought up; that her mother managed cleverly; that in some way she satisfied a man's ambitions. A lover constantly bears witness to her personal perfections. Then followed the discovery, still in Mme. de Langeais' early womanhood, that it was possible to be loved without committing herself, without permission, without vouchsafing any satisfaction beyond the most meagre dues. There was more than one demure feminine hypocrite to instruct her in the art of playing such dangerous comedies.

So the Duchess had her court, and the number of her
adorers and courtiers guaranteed her virtue. She was amiable
and fascinating; she flirted till the ball or the evening's gaiety
was at an end. Then the curtain dropped. She was cold,
indifferent, self-contained again, till the next day brought its
renewed sensations, superficial as before. Two or three men
were completely deceived, and fell in love in earnest. She
laughed at them, she was utterly insensible. "I am loved!"
she told herself. "He loves me!" The certainty sufficed her.
It is enough for the miser to know that his every whim might
be fulfilled if he chose; so it was with the Duchess, and perhaps she did not even go as far as to form a wish.

One evening she chanced to be at the house of an intimate
friend, Mme. la Vicomtesse de Fontaine, one of the humble
rivals who cordially detested her, and went with her everywhere. In a "friendship" of this sort both sides are on their
guard, and never lay their armor aside; confidences are ingeniously indiscreet, and not unfrequently treacherous. Mme.
de Langeais had distributed her little patronizing, friendly,
or freezing bows, with the air natural to a woman who knows
the worth of her smiles, when her eyes fell upon a total
stranger. Something in the man's large gravity of aspect
startled her, and, with a feeling almost like dread, she turned
to Mme. de Maufrigneuse with, "Who is the newcomer,
dear?"

"Some one that you have heard of, no doubt. The Marquis de Montriveau."

"Oh! is it he?"

She took up her eyeglass and submitted him to a very insolent scrutiny, as if he had been a picture meant to receive glances, not to return them.

"Do introduce him; he ought to be interesting."

"Nobody more tiresome and dull, dear. But he is the
fashion."

M. Armand de Montriveau, at that moment all unwittingly
the object of general curiosity, better deserved attention than
any of the idols that Paris needs must set up to worship for

a brief space, for the city is vexed by periodical fits of craving, a passion for *engouement* and sham enthusiasm, which
must be satisfied. The Marquis was the only son of General
de Montriveau, one of the *ci-devants* who served the Republic
nobly, and fell by Joubert's side at Novi. Bonaparte had
placed his son at the school at Châlons, with the orphans of
other generals who fell on the battlefield, leaving their children under the protection of the Republic. Armand de
Montriveau left school with his way to make, entered the
artillery, and had only reached a major's rank at the time of
the Fontainebleau disaster. In this section of the service
the chances of advancement were not many. There are fewer
officers, in the first place, among the gunners than in any
other corps; and in the second place, the feeling in the artillery was decidedly Liberal, not to say Republican; and the
Emperor, feeling little confidence in a body of highly educated men who were apt to think for themselves, gave
promotion grudgingly in the service. In the artillery, accordingly, the general rule of the army did not apply; the
commanding officers were not invariably the most remarkable
men in their department, because there was less to be feared
from mediocrities. The artillery was a separate corps in those
days, and only came under Napoleon in action.

Besides these general causes, other reasons, inherent in
Armand de Montriveau's character, were sufficient in themselves to account for his tardy promotion. He was alone in
the world. He had been thrown at the age of twenty into
the whirlwind of men directed by Napoleon; his interests
were bounded by himself, any day he might lose his life; it
became a habit of mind with him to live by his own self-respect and the consciousness that he had done his duty. Like
all shy men, he was habitually silent; but his shyness sprang
by no means from timidity; it was a kind of modesty in him;
he found any demonstration of vanity intolerable. There was
no sort of swagger about his fearlessness in action; nothing escaped his eyes; he could give sensible advice to his chums with
unshaken coolness; he could go under fire, and duck upon oc-

casion to avoid bullets. He was kindly; but his expression was haughty and stern, and his face gained him this character. In everything he was rigorous as arithmetic; he never permitted the slightest deviation from duty on any plausible pretext, nor blinked the consequences of a fact. He would lend himself to nothing of which he was ashamed; he never asked anything for himself; in short, Armand de Montriveau was one of many great men unknown to fame, and philosophical enough to despise it; living without attaching themselves to life, because they have not found their opportunity of developing to the full their power to do and feel.

People were afraid of Montriveau; they respected him, but he was not very popular. Men may indeed allow you to rise above them, but to decline to descend as low as they can do is the one unpardonable sin. In their feeling towards loftier natures, there is a trace of hate and fear. Too much honor with them implies censure of themselves, a thing forgiven neither to the living nor to the dead.

After the Emperor's farewells at Fontainebleau, Montriveau, noble though he was, was put on half-pay. Perhaps the heads of the War Office took fright at uncompromising uprightness worthy of antiquity, or perhaps it was known that he felt bound by his oath to the Imperial Eagle. During the Hundred Days he was made a Colonel of the Guard, and left on the field of Waterloo. His wounds kept him in Belgium; he was not present at the disbanding of the Army of the Loire, but the King's government declined to recognize promotion made during the Hundred Days, and Armand de Montriveau left France.

An adventurous spirit, a loftiness of thought hitherto satisfied by the hazards of war, drove him on an exploring expedition through Upper Egypt; his sanity of impulse directed his enthusiasm to a project of great importance, he turned his attention to that unexplored Central Africa which occupies the learned of to-day. The scientific expedition was long and unfortunate. He had made a valuable collection of notes bearing on various geographical and commercial problems, of which solutions are still eagerly sought; and succeeded, after surmounting many difficulties, in reaching the heart of the continent, when he was betrayed into the hands of a hostile native tribe. Then, stripped of all that he had, for two years he led a wandering life in the desert, the slave of savages, threatened with death at every moment, and more cruelly treated than a dumb animal in the power of pitiless children. Physical strength, and a mind braced by endurance, enabled him to survive the horrors of that captivity; but his miraculous escape well-nigh exhausted his energies. When he reached the French colony at Senegal, a half-dead fugitive covered with rags, his memories of his former life were dim and shapeless. The great sacrifices made in his travels were all forgotten like his studies of African dialects, his discoveries, and observations. One story will give an idea of all that he passed through. Once for several days the children of the sheikh of the tribe amused themselves by putting him up for a mark and flinging horses' knuckle-bones at his head.

Montriveau came back to Paris in 1818 a ruined man. He had no interest, and wished for none. He would have died twenty times over sooner than ask a favor of any one; he would not even press the recognition of his claims. Adversity and hardship had developed his energy even in trifles, while the habit of preserving his self-respect before that spiritual self which we call conscience led him to attach consequence to the most apparently trivial actions. His merits and adventures became known, however, through his acquaintances, among the principal men of science in Paris, and some few well-read military men. The incidents of his slavery and subsequent escape bore witness to a courage, intelligence, and coolness which won him celebrity without his knowledge, and that transient fame of which Paris salons are lavish, though the artist that fain would keep it must make untold efforts.

Montriveau's position suddenly changed towards the end of that year. He had been a poor man, he was now rich; or, externally at any rate, he had all the advantages of wealth.

The King's government, trying to attach capable men to itself and to strengthen the army, made concessions about that time to Napoleon's old officers if their known loyalty and character offered guarantees of fidelity. M. de Montriveau's name once more appeared in the army list with the rank of colonel; he received his arrears of pay and passed into the Guards. All these favors, one after another, came to seek the Marquis de Montriveau; he had asked for nothing however small. Friends had taken the steps for him which he would have refused to take for himself.

After this, his habits were modified all at once; contrary to his custom, he went into society. He was well received, everywhere he met with great deference and respect. He seemed to have found some end in life; but everything passed within the man; there was no external signs; in society he was silent, cold, and wore a grave, reserved face. His social success was great, precisely because he stood out in such strong contrast to the conventional faces which line the walls of Paris salons. He was, indeed, something quite new there. Terse of speech, like a hermit or a savage, his shyness was thought to be haughtiness, and people were greatly taken with it. He was something strange and great. Women generally were so much the more smitten with this original person because he was not to be caught by their flatteries, however adroit, nor by the wiles with which they circumvent the strongest men and corrode the steel temper. Their Parisian grimaces were lost on M. de Montriveau; his nature only responded to the sonorous vibration of lofty thought and feeling. And he would very promptly have been dropped but for the romance that hung about his adventures and his life; but for the men who cried him up behind his back; but for a woman who looked for a triumph for her vanity, the woman who was to fill his thoughts.

For these reasons the Duchesse de Langeais' curiosity was no less lively than natural. Chance had so ordered it that her interest in the man before her had been aroused only the day before, when she heard the story of one of M. de Montriveau's adventures, a story calculated to make the strongest impression upon a woman's ever-changing fancy.

During M. de Montriveau's voyage of discovery to the sources of the Nile, he had had an argument with one of his guides, surely the most extraordinary debate in the annals of travel. The district that he wished to explore could only be reached on foot across a tract of desert. Only one of his guides knew the way; no traveler had penetrated before into that part of the country, where the undaunted officer hoped to find a solution of several scientific problems. In spite of the representations made to him by the guide and the older men of the place, he started upon the formidable journey. Summoning up courage, already highly strung by the prospect of dreadful difficulties, he set out in the morning.

The loose sand shifted under his feet at every step; and when, at the end of a long day's march, he lay down to sleep on the ground, he had never been so tired in his life. He knew, however, that he must be up and on his way before dawn next day, and his guide assured him that they should reach the end of their journey towards noon. That promise kept up his courage and gave him new strength. In spite of his sufferings, he continued his march, with some blasphemings against science; he was ashamed to complain to his guide, and kept his pain to himself. After marching for a third of the day, he felt his strength failing, his feet were bleeding, he asked if they should reach the place soon. "In an hour's time," said the guide. Armand braced himself for another hour's march, and they went on.

The hour slipped by; he could not so much as see against the sky the palm-trees and crests of hill that should tell of the end of the journey near at hand; the horizon line of sand was vast as the circle of the open sea.

He came to a stand, and refused to go further, and threatened the guide—he had deceived him, murdered him; tears of rage and weariness flowed over his fevered cheeks; he was bowed down with fatigue upon fatigue, his throat seemed to be glued by the desert thirst. The guide mean-

" Sound yourself ; if you have not courage enough, here is my dagger "

while stood motionless, listening to these complaints with an ironical expression, studying the while, with the apparent indifference of an Oriental, the scarcely perceptible indications in the lie of the sands, which looked almost black, like burnished gold.

"I have made a mistake," he remarked coolly. "I could not make out the track, it is so long since I came this way; we are surely on it now, but we must push on for two hours."

"The man is right," thought M. de Montriveau.

So he went on again, struggling to follow the pitiless native. It seemed as if he were bound to his guide by some thread like the invisible tie between the condemned man and the headsman. But the two hours went by, Montriveau had spent his last drops of energy, and the sky-line was a blank, there were no palm-trees, no hills. He could neither cry out nor groan, he lay down on the sand to die, but his eyes would have frightened the boldest; something in his face seemed to say that he would not die alone. His guide, like a very fiend, gave him back a cool glance like a man that knows his power, left him to lie there, and kept at a safe distance out of reach of his desperate victim. At last M. de Montriveau recovered strength enough for a last curse. The guide came nearer, silenced him with a steady look, and said, "Was it not your own will to go where I am taking you, in spite of us all? You say that I have lied to you. If I had not, you would not be even here. Do you want the truth? Here it is. *We have still another five hours' march before us, and we cannot go back*. Sound yourself; if you have not courage enough, here is my dagger."

Startled by this dreadful knowledge of pain and human strength, M. de Montriveau would not be behind a savage; he drew a fresh stock of courage from his pride as a European, rose to his feet, and followed his guide. The five hours were at an end, and still M. de Montriveau saw nothing, he turned his failing eyes upon his guide; but the Nubian hoisted him on his shoulders, and showed him a wide pool of water with greenness all about it, and a noble forest lighted up by the sunset. It lay only a hundred paces away; a vast ledge of granite hid the glorious landscape. It seemed to Armand that he had taken a new lease of life. His guide, that giant in courage and intelligence, finished his work of devotion by carrying him across the hot, slippery, scarcely discernible track on the granite. Behind him lay the hell of burning sand, before him the earthly paradise of the most beautiful oasis in the desert.

The Duchess, struck from the first by the appearance of this romantic figure, was even more impressed when she learned that this was that Marquis de Montriveau of whom she had dreamed during the night. She had been with him among the hot desert sands, he had been the companion of her nightmare wanderings; for such a woman was not this a delightful presage of a new interest in her life? And never was a man's exterior a better exponent of his character; never were curious glances so well justified. The principal characteristic of his great, square-hewn head was the thick, luxuriant black hair which framed his face, and gave him a strikingly close resemblance to General Kléber; and the likeness still held good in the vigorous forehead, in the outlines of his face, the quiet fearlessness of his eyes, and a kind of fiery vehemence expressed by strongly marked features. He was short, deep-chested, and muscular as a lion. There was something of the despot about him, and an indescribable suggestion of the security of strength in his gait, bearing, and slightest movements. He seemed to know that his will was irresistible, perhaps because he wished for nothing unjust. And yet, like all really strong men, he was mild of speech, simple in his manners, and kindly natured; although it seemed as if, in the stress of a great crisis, all these finer qualities must disappear, and the man would show himself implacable, unshaken in his resolve, terrific in action. There was a certain drawing in of the inner line of the lips which, to a close observer, indicated an ironical bent.

The Duchesse de Langeais, realizing that a fleeting glory was to be won by such a conquest, made up her mind to gain a lover in Armand de Montriveau during the brief interval before the Duchesse de Maufrigneuse brought him to be introduced. She would prefer him above the others; she would attach him to herself, display all her powers of coquetry for him. It was a fancy, such a merest Duchess' whim as furnished a Lope or a Calderon with the plot of the *Dog in the Manger*. She would not suffer another woman to engross him; but she had not the remotest intention of being his.

Nature had given the Duchess every qualification for the part of coquette, and education had perfected her. Women envied her, and men fell in love with her, not without reason. Nothing that can inspire love, justify it, and give it lasting empire was wanting in her. Her style of beauty, her manner, her voice, her bearing, all combined to give her that instinctive coquetry which seems to be the consciousness of power. Her shape was graceful; perhaps there was a trace of self-consciousness in her changes of movement, the one affectation that could be laid to her charge; but everything about her was a part of her personality, from her least little gesture to the peculiar turn of her phrases, the demure glance of her eyes. Her great lady's grace, her most striking characteristic, had not destroyed the very French quick mobility of her person. There was an extraordinary fascination in her swift, incessant changes of attitude. She seemed as if she surely would be a most delicious mistress when her corset and the encumbering costume of her part was laid aside. All the rapture of love surely was latent in the freedom of her expressive glances, in her caressing tones, in the charm of her words. She gave glimpses of the high-born courtesan within her, vainly protesting against the creeds of the duchess.

You might sit near her through an evening, she would be gay and melancholy in turn, and her gaiety, like her sadness, seemed spontaneous. She would be gracious, disdainful, insolent, or confiding at will. Her apparent good nature was real; she had no temptation to descend to malignity. But at each moment her mood changed; she was full of confidence or craft; her moving tenderness would give place to a heartbreaking hardness and insensibility. Yet how paint her as she was, without bringing together all the extremes of feminine nature? In a word, the Duchess was anything that she wished to be or to seem. Her face was slightly too long. There was a grace in it, and a certain thinness and fineness that recalled the portraits of the Middle Ages. Her skin was white, with a faint rose tint. Everything about her erred, as it were, by an excess of delicacy.

M. de Montriveau willingly consented to be introduced to the Duchesse de Langeais; and she, after the manner of persons whose sensitive taste leads them to avoid banalities, refrained from overwhelming him with questions and compliments. She received him with a gracious deference which could not fail to flatter a man of more than ordinary powers, for the fact that a man rises above the ordinary level implies that he possesses something of that tact which makes women quick to read feeling. If the Duchess showed any curiosity, it was by her glances; her compliments were conveyed in her manner; there was a winning grace displayed in her words, a subtle suggestion of a desire to please which she of all women knew the art of manifesting. Yet her whole conversation was but, in a manner, the body of the letter; the postscript with the principal thought in it was still to come. After half an hour spent in ordinary talk, in which the words gained all their value from her tone and smiles, M. de Montriveau was about to retire discreetly, when the Duchess stopped him with an expressive gesture.

"I do not know, monsieur, whether these few minutes during which I have had the pleasure of talking to you proved so sufficiently attractive, that I may venture to ask you to call upon me; I am afraid that it may be very selfish of me to wish to have you all to myself. If I should be so fortunate as to find that my house is agreeable to you, you will always find me at home in the evening until ten o'clock."

The invitation was given with such irresistible grace, that M. de Montriveau could not refuse to accept it. When he fell back again among the groups of men gathered at a distance from the women, his friends congratulated him, half laugh-ingly, half in earnest, on the extraordinary reception vouch-safed him by the Duchesse de Langeais. The difficult and brilliant conquest had been made beyond a doubt, and the glory of it was reserved for the Artillery of the Guard. It is easy to imagine the jests, good and bad, when this topic had once been started; the world of Paris salons is so eager for amusement, and a joke lasts for such a short time, that every one is eager to make the most of it while it is fresh.

All unconsciously, the General felt flattered by this non-sense. From his place where he had taken his stand, his eyes were drawn again and again to the Duchess by countless wav-ering reflections. He could not help admitting to himself that of all the women whose beauty had captivated his eyes, not one had seemed to be a more exquisite embodiment of faults and fair qualities blended in a completeness that might realize the dreams of earliest manhood. Is there a man in any rank of life that has not felt indefinable rapture in his secret soul over the woman singled out (if only in his dreams) to be his own; when she, in body, soul, and social aspects, satisfies his every requirement, a thrice perfect woman? And if this threefold perfection that flatters his pride is no argument for loving her, it is beyond cavil one of the great inducements to the sentiment. Love would soon be convalescent, as the eighteenth century moralist remarked, were it not for vanity. And it is certainly true that for every one, man or woman, there is a wealth of pleasure in the superiority of the beloved. Is she set so high by birth that a contemptuous glance can never wound her? is she wealthy enough to surround herself with state which falls nothing short of royalty of kings of finance during their short reign of splendor? is she so ready-witted that a keen-edged jest never brings her into confusion? beautiful enough to rival any woman?—Is it such a small thing to know that your self-love will never suffer through her? A man makes these reflections in the twinkling of an eye. And how if, in the future opened out by early ripened passion, he catches glimpses of the changeful delight of her charm, the frank innocence of a maiden soul, the perils of love's voyage, the thousand folds of the veil of coquetry? Is not this enough to move the coldest man's heart?

This, therefore, was M. de Montriveau's position with regard to woman; his past life in some measure explaining the extraordinary fact. He had been thrown, when little more than a boy, into the hurricane of Napoleon's wars; his life had been spent on fields of battle. Of women he knew just so much as a traveler knows of a country when he travels across it in haste from one inn to another. The verdict which Voltaire passed upon his eighty years of life might, perhaps, have been applied by Montriveau to his own thirty-seven years of existence; had he not thirty-seven follies with which to reproach himself? At his age he was as much a novice in love as the lad that has just been furtively reading *Faublas*. Of women he had nothing to learn; of love he knew nothing; and thus, desires, quite unknown before, sprang from this virginity of feeling.

There are men here and there as much engrossed in the work demanded of them by poverty or ambition, art or science, as M. de Montriveau by war and a life of adventure,—these know what it is to be in this unusual position if they very seldom confess to it. Every man in Paris is supposed to have been in love. No woman in Paris cares to take what other women have passed over. The dread of being taken for a fool is the source of the coxcomb's bragging so common in France; for in France to have the reputation of a fool is to be a foreigner in one's own country. Vehement desire seized on M. de Montriveau, desire that had gathered strength from the heat of the desert and the first stirrings of a heart unknown as yet in its suppressed turbulence. A strong man, and violent as he was strong, he could keep mastery over himself; but as he talked of indifferent things, he retired within himself, and swore to possess this woman, for through that thought lay the only way to love for him. Desire became a solemn compact made with himself, an oath after the manner of the Arabs among whom he had lived; for among them a vow is a kind of contract made with Destiny, a man's whole future is solemnly pledged to fulfil it, and everything, even his own death, is regarded simply as a means to the one end.

A younger man would have said to himself, "I should very much like to have the Duchess for my mistress!" or, "If the Duchesse de Langeais cared for a man, he would be a very lucky rascal!" But the General said, "I will have Mme. de Langeais for my mistress." And if a man takes such an idea into his head when his heart has never been touched before, and love begins to be a kind of religion with him, he little knows in what a hell he has set his foot.

Armand de Montriveau suddenly took flight and went home in the first hot fever-fit of the first love that he had known. When a man has kept all his boyish beliefs, illusions, frankness, and impetuosity into middle age, his first impulse is, as it were, to stretch out a hand to take the thing that he desires; a little later he realizes that there is a gulf set between them, and that it is all but impossible to cross it. A sort of childish impatience seizes him, he wants the thing the more, and trembles or cries. Wherefore, the next day, after the stormiest reflections that had yet perturbed his mind, Armand de Montriveau discovered that he was under the yoke of the senses, and his bondage made the heavier by his love.

The woman so cavalierly treated in his thoughts of yesterday had become a most sacred and dreadful power. She was to be his world, his life, from this time forth. The greatest joy, the keenest anguish, that he had yet known grew colorless before the bare recollection of the least sensation stirred in him by her. The swiftest revolutions in a man's outward life only touch his interests, while passion brings a complete revulsion of feeling. And so in those who live by feeling, rather than by self-interest, the doers rather than the reasoners, the sanguine rather than the lymphatic temperaments, love works a complete revolution. In a flash, with one single reflection, Armand de Montriveau wiped out his whole past life.

A score of times he asked himself, like a boy, "Shall I go,

or shall I not?" and then at last he dressed, came to the
Hôtel de Langeais towards eight o'clock that evening, and was
admitted. He was to see the woman—ah! not the woman—
the idol that he had seen yesterday, among lights, a fresh innocent girl in gauze and silken lace and veiling. He burst
in upon her to declare his love, as if it were a question of
firing the first shot on a field of battle.

Poor novice! He found his ethereal sylphide shrouded in a
brown cashmere dressing-gown ingeniously befrilled, lying
languidly stretched out upon a sofa in a dimly lighted boudoir. Mme. de Langeais did not so much as rise, nothing was
visible of her but her face, her hair was loose but confined
by a scarf. A hand indicated a seat, a hand that seemed
white as marble to Montriveau by the flickering light of a
single candle at the further side of the room, and a voice as
soft as the light said:

"If it had been any one else, M. le Marquis, a friend with
whom I could dispense with ceremony, or a mere acquaintance in whom I felt but slight interest, I should have closed
my door. I am exceedingly unwell."

"I will go," Armand said to himself.

"But I do not know how it is," she continued (and the simple warrior attributed the shining of her eyes to fever), "perhaps it was a presentiment of your kind visit (and no one
can be more sensible of the prompt attention than I), but
the vapors have left my head."

"Then may I stay?"

"Oh, I should be very sorry to allow you to go. I told myself this morning that it was impossible that I should have
made the slightest impression on your mind, and that in all
probability you took my request for one of the commonplaces
of which Parisians are lavish on every occasion. And I forgave your ingratitude in advance. An explorer from the
deserts is not supposed to know how exclusive we are in our
friendships in the Faubourg."

The gracious, half-murmured words dropped one by one,
as if they had been weighted with the gladness that appar-

ently brought them to her lips. The Duchess meant to have
the full benefit of her headache, and her speculation was fully
successful. The General, poor man, was really distressed by
the lady's simulated distress. Like Crillon listening to the
story of the Crucifixion, he was ready to draw his sword
against the vapors. How could a man dare to speak just then
to this suffering woman of the love that she inspired? Armand had already felt that it would be absurd to fire off a declaration of love point-blank at one so far above other women.
With a single thought came understanding of the delicacies
of feeling, of the soul's requirements. To love: what was that
but to know how to plead, to beg for alms, to wait? And as
for the love that he felt, must he not prove it? His tongue
was mute, it was frozen by the conventions of the noble Faubourg, the majesty of a sick headache, the bashfulness of love.
But no power on earth could veil his glances; the heat and
the Infinite of the Desert blazed in eyes, calm as a panther's,
beneath the lids that fell so seldom. The Duchess enjoyed
the steady gaze that enveloped her in light and warmth.

"Mme. la Duchesse," he answered, "I am afraid I express
my gratitude for your goodness very badly. At this moment
I have but one desire—I wish it were in my power to cure the
pain."

"Permit me to throw this off, I feel too warm now," she
said, gracefully tossing aside a cushion that covered her feet.

"Madame, in Asia your feet would be worth some ten thousand sequins."

"A traveler's compliment!" smiled she.

It pleased the sprightly lady to involve a rough soldier in
a labyrinth of nonsense, commonplaces, and meaningless talk,
in which he manœuvred, in military language, as Prince
Charles might have done at close quarters with Napoleon.
She took a mischievous amusement in reconnoitring the extent of his infatuation by the number of foolish speeches extracted from a novice whom she led step by step into a hopeless
maze, meaning to leave him there in confusion. She began
by laughing at him, but nevertheless it pleased her to make
him forget how time went.

The length of a first visit is frequently a compliment, but Armand was innocent of any such intent. The famous explorer spent an hour in chat on all sorts of subjects, said nothing that he meant to say, and was feeling that he was only an instrument on whom this woman played, when she rose, sat upright, drew the scarf from her hair, and wrapped it about her throat, leaned her elbow on the cushions, did him the honor of a complete cure, and rang for lights. The most graceful movement succeeded to complete repose. She turned to M. de Montriveau, from whom she had just extracted a confidence which seemed to interest her deeply, and said:

"You wish to make game of me by trying to make me believe that you have never loved. It is a man's great pretension with us. And we always believe it! Out of pure politeness. Do we not know what to expect from it for ourselves? Where is the man that has found but a single opportunity of losing his heart? But you love to deceive us, and we submit to be deceived, poor foolish creatures that we are; for your hypocrisy is, after all, a homage paid to the superiority of our sentiments, which are all purity."

The last words were spoken with a disdainful pride that made the novice in love feel like a worthless bale flung into the deep, while the Duchess was an angel soaring back to her particular heaven.

"Confound it!" thought Armand de Montriveau, "how am I to tell this wild thing that I love her?"

He had told her already a score of times; or rather, the Duchess had a score of times read his secret in his eyes; and the passion in this unmistakably great man promised her amusement, and an interest in her empty life. So she prepared with no little dexterity to raise a certain number of redoubts for him to carry by storm before he should gain an entrance into her heart. Montriveau should overleap one difficulty after another; he should be a plaything for her caprice, just as an insect teased by children is made to jump from one finger to another, and in spite of all its pains is kept in the same place by its mischievous tormentor. And yet it gave the Duchess inexpressible happiness to see that this strong man had told her the truth. Armand had never loved, as he had said. He was about to go, in a bad humor with himself, and still more out of humor with her; but it delighted her to see a sullenness that she could conjure away with a word, a glance, or a gesture.

"Will you come to-morrow evening?" she asked. "I am going to a ball, but I shall stay at home for you until ten o'clock.

Montriveau spent most of the next day in smoking an indeterminate quantity of cigars in his study window, and so got through the hours till he could dress and go to the Hôtel de Langeais. To any one who had known the magnificent worth of the man, it would have been grievous to see him grown so small, so distrustful of himself; the mind that might have shed light over undiscovered worlds shrunk to the proportions of a she-coxcomb's boudoir. Even he himself felt that he had fallen so low already in his happiness that to save his life he could not have told his love to one of his closest friends. Is there not always a trace of shame in the lover's bashfulness, and perhaps in woman a certain exultation over diminished masculine stature? Indeed, but for a host of motives of this kind, how explain why women are nearly always the first to betray the secret?—a secret of which, perhaps, they soon weary.

"Mme. la Duchesse cannot see visitors, monsieur," said the man; "she is dressing, she begs you to wait for her here."

Armand walked up and down the drawing-room, studying her taste in the least details. He admired Mme. de Langeais herself in the objects of her choosing; they revealed her life before he could grasp her personality and ideas. About an hour later the Duchess came noiselessly out of her chamber. Montriveau turned, saw her flit like a shadow across the room, and trembled. She came up to him, not with a bourgeoise's inquiry, "How do I look?" She was sure of herself; her steady eyes said plainly, "I am adorned to please you."

No one, surely, save the old fairy godmother of some
princess in disguise, could have wound a cloud of gauze about
the dainty throat, so that the dazzling satin skin beneath
should gleam through the gleaming folds. The Duchess was
dazzling. The pale blue color of her gown, repeated in the
flowers in her hair, appeared by the richness of its hue to lend
substance to a fragile form grown too wholly ethereal; for as
she glided towards Armand, the loose ends of her scarf floated
about her, putting that valiant warrior in mind of the bright
damosel flies that hover now over water, now over the flowers
with which they seem to mingle and blend.

"I have kept you waiting," she said, with the tone that a
woman can always bring into her voice for the man whom she
wishes to please.

"I would wait patiently through an eternity," said he, "if
I were sure of finding a divinity so fair; but it is no compliment to speak of your beauty to you; nothing save worship
could touch you. Suffer me only to kiss your scarf."

"Oh, fie!" she said, with a commanding gesture, "I esteem
you enough to give you my hand."

She held it out for his kiss. A woman's hand, still moist
from the scented bath, has a soft freshness, a velvet smooth-
ness that sends a tingling thrill from the lips to the soul. And
if a man is attracted to a woman, and his senses are as quick
to feel pleasure as his heart is full of love, such a kiss, though
chaste in appearance, may conjure up a terrific storm.

"Will you always give it me like this?" the General asked
humbly, when he had pressed that dangerous hand respectfully to his lips.

"Yes, but there we must stop," she said, smiling. She sat
down, and seemed very slow over putting on her gloves, trying to slip the unstretched kid over all her fingers at once,
while she watched M. de Montriveau; and he was lost in admiration of the Duchess and those repeated graceful movements of hers.

"Ah! you were punctual," she said; "that is right. I like
punctuality. It is the courtesy of kings, His Majesty says;

but to my thinking, from you men it is the most respectful
flattery of all.   Now, is it not?   Just tell me."

Again she gave him a side glance to express her insidious
friendship, for he was dumb with happiness—sheer happiness through such nothings as these!   Oh, the Duchess
understood *son métier de femme*—the art and mystery of being a woman—most marvelously well; she knew, to admiration, how to raise a man in his own esteem as he humbled himself to her; how to reward every step of the descent to sentimental folly with hollow flatteries.

"You will never forget to come at nine o'clock."

"No; but are you going to a ball every night?"

"Do I know?" she answered, with a little childlike shrug
of the shoulders; the gesture was meant to say that she was
nothing if not capricious, and that a lover must take her as
she was.—"Besides," she added, "what is that to you?   You
shall be my escort."

"That would be difficult to-night," he objected; "I am not
properly dressed."

"It seems to me," she returned loftily, "that if any one has
a right to complain of your costume, it is I.   Know, therefore, *monsieur le voyageur,* that if I accept a man's arm, he is
forthwith above the laws of fashion, nobody would venture
to criticise him.   You do not know the world, I see; I like
you the better for it."

And even as she spoke she swept him into the pettiness of
that world by the attempt to initiate him into the vanities of
a woman of fashion.

"If she chooses to do a foolish thing for me, I should be a
simpleton to prevent her," said Armand to himself.   "She has
a liking for me beyond a doubt; and as for the world, she
cannot despise it more than I do.   So, now for the ball if she
likes."

The Duchess probably thought that if the General came
with her and appeared in a ballroom in boots and a black tie,
nobody would hesitate to believe that he was violently in love
with her.   And the General was well pleased that the queen

of fashion should think of compromising herself for him; hope gave him wit. He had gained confidence, he brought out his thoughts and views; he felt nothing of the restraint that weighed on his spirits yesterday. His talk was interesting and animated, and full of those first confidences so sweet to make and to receive.

Was Mme. de Langeais really carried away by his talk, or had she devised this charming piece of coquetry? At any rate, she looked up mischievously as the clock struck twelve.

"Ah! you have made me too late for the ball!" she exclaimed, surprised and vexed that she had forgotten how time was going.

The next moment she approved the exchange of pleasures with a smile that made Armand's heart give a sudden leap.

"I certainly promised Mme. de Beauséant," she added. "They are all expecting me."

"Very well—go."

"No—go on. I will stay. Your Eastern adventures fascinate me. Tell me the whole story of your life. I love to share in a brave man's hardships, and I feel them all, indeed I do!"

She was playing with her scarf, twisting it and pulling it to pieces, with jerky, impatient movements that seemed to tell of inward dissatisfaction and deep reflection.

"*We* are fit for nothing," she went on. "Ah! we are contemptible, selfish, frivolous creatures. We can bore ourselves with amusements, and that is all we can do. Not one of us that understands that she has a part to play in life. In old days in France, women were beneficent lights; they lived to comfort those that mourned, to encourage high virtues, to reward artists and stir new life with noble thoughts. If the world has grown so petty, ours is the fault. You make me loathe the ball and this world in which I live. No, I am not giving up much for you."

She had plucked her scarf to pieces, as a child plays with a flower, pulling away all the petals one by one; and now she crushed it into a ball, and flung it away. She could show her swan's neck.

She rang the bell. "I shall not go out to-night," she told the footman. Her long, blue eyes turned timidly to Armand; and by the look of misgiving in them, he knew that he was meant to take the order for a confession, for a first and great favor. There was a pause, filled with many thoughts, before she spoke with that tenderness which is often in women's voices, and not so often in their hearts. "You have had a hard life," she said.

"No," returned Armand. "Until to-day I did not know what happiness was."

"Then you know it now?" she asked, looking at him with a demure, keen glance.

"What is happiness for me henceforth but this—to see you, to hear you? . . . Until now I have only known privation; now I know that I can be unhappy——"

"That will do, that will do," she said. "You must go; it is past midnight. Let us regard appearances. People must not talk about us. I do not know quite what I shall say; but the headache is a good-natured friend, and tells no tales."

"Is there to be a ball to-morrow night?"

"You would grow accustomed to the life, I think. Very well. Yes, we will go again to-morrow night."

There was not a happier man in the world than Armand when he went out from her. Every evening he came to Mme. de Langeais' at the hour kept for him by a tacit understanding.

It would be tedious, and, for the many young men who carry a redundance of such sweet memories in their hearts, it were superfluous to follow the story step by step—the progress of a romance growing in those hours spent together, a romance controlled entirely by a woman's will. If sentiment went too fast, she would raise a quarrel over a word, or when words flagged behind her thoughts, she appealed to the feelings. Perhaps the only way of following such Penelope's progress is by marking its outward and visible signs.

As, for instance, within a few days of their first meeting, the assiduous General had won and kept the right to kiss his lady's insatiable hands. Wherever Mme. de Langeais went, M. de Montriveau was certain to be seen, till people jokingly called him "Her Grace's orderly." And already he had made enemies; others were jealous, and envied him his position. Mme. de Langeais had attained her end. The Marquis de Montriveau was among her numerous train of adorers, and a means of humiliating those who boasted of their progress in her good graces, for she publicly gave him preference over them all.

"Decidedly, M. de Montriveau is the man for whom the Duchess shows a preference," pronounced Mme. de Sérizy.

And who in Paris does not know what it means when a woman "shows a preference"? All went on therefore according to prescribed rule. The anecdotes which people were pleased to circulate concerning the General put that warrior in so formidable a light, that the more adroit quietly dropped their pretensions to the Duchess, and remained in her train merely to turn the position to account, and to use her name and personality to make better terms for themselves with certain stars of the second magnitude. And those lesser powers were delighted to take a lover away from Mme. de Langeais. The Duchess was keen-sighted enough to see these desertions and treaties with the enemy; and her pride would not suffer her to be the dupe of them. As M. de Talleyrand, one of her great admirers, said, she knew how to take a second edition of revenge, laying the two-edged blade of a sarcasm between the pairs in these "morganatic" unions. Her mocking disdain contributed not a little to increase her reputation as an extremely clever woman and a person to be feared. Her character for virtue was consolidated while she amused herself with other people's secrets, and kept her own to herself. Yet, after two months of assiduities, she saw with a vague dread in the depths of her soul that M. de Montriveau understood nothing of the subtleties of flirtation after the manner of the Faubourg Saint-Germain; he was taking a Parisienne's coquetry in earnest.

"You will not tame *him,* dear Duchess," the old Vidame

de Pamiers had said. " 'Tis a first cousin to the eagle; he will
carry you off to his eyrie if you do not take care."

Then Mme. de Langeais felt afraid. The shrewd old
noble's words sounded like a prophecy. The next day she
tried to turn love to hate. She was harsh, exacting, irritable,
unbearable; Montriveau disarmed her with angelic sweetness.
She so little knew the great generosity of a large nature, that
the kindly jests with which her first complaints were met went
to her heart. She sought a quarrel, and found proofs of affection. She persisted.

"When a man idolizes you, how can he have vexed you?"
asked Armand.

"You do not vex me," she answered, suddenly grown gentle
and submissive. "But why do you wish to compromise me?
For me you ought to be nothing but a *friend*. Do you not
know it? I wish I could see that you had the instincts, the
delicacy of real friendship, so that I might lose neither your
respect nor the pleasure that your presence gives me."

"Nothing but your *friend!*" he cried out. The terrible
word sent an electric shock through his brain. "On the faith
of these happy hours that you grant me, I sleep and wake in
your heart. And now to-day, for no reason, you are pleased
to destroy all the secret hopes by which I live. You have required promises of such constancy in me, you have said so
much of your horror of women made up of nothing but caprice; and now do you wish me to understand that, like other
women here in Paris, you have passions, and know nothing of
love? If so, why did you ask my life of me? why did you
accept it?"

"I was wrong, my friend. Oh, it is wrong of a woman to
yield to such intoxication when she must not and cannot make
any return."

"I understand. You have merely been coquetting with me,
and——"

"Coquetting?" she repeated. "I detest coquetry. A coquette, Armand, makes promises to many, and gives herself
to none; and a woman who keeps such promises is a libertine.

This much I believed I had grasped of our code. But to be melancholy with humorists, gay with the frivolous, and politic with ambitious souls; to listen to a babbler with every appearance of admiration, to talk of war with a soldier, wax enthusiastic with philanthropists over the good of the nation, and to give to each one his little dole of flattery,—it seems to me that this is as much a matter of necessity as dress, diamonds, and gloves, or flowers in one's hair. Such talk is the moral counterpart of the toilette. You take it up and lay it aside with the plumed head-dress. Do you call this coquetry? Why, I have never treated you as I treat every one else. With you, my friend, I am sincere. Have I not always shared your views, and when you convinced me after a discussion was I not always perfectly glad? In short, I love you, but only as a devout and pure woman may love. I have thought it over. I am a married woman, Armand. My way of life with M. de Langeais gives me liberty to bestow my heart; but law and custom leave me no right to dispose of my person. If a woman loses her honor, she is an outcast in any rank of life; and I have yet to meet with a single example of a man that realizes all that our sacrifices demand of him in such a case. Quite otherwise. Any one can foresee the rupture between Mme. de Beauséant and M. d'Ajuda (for he is going to marry Mlle. de Rochefide, it seems), that affair made it clear to my mind that these very sacrifices on the woman's part are almost always the cause of the man's desertion. If you had loved me sincerely, you would have kept away for a time.—Now, I will lay aside all vanity for you; is not that something? What will not people say of a woman to whom no man attaches himself? Oh, she is heartless, brainless, soulless; and what is more, devoid of charm! Coquettes will not spare me. They will rob me of the very qualities that mortify them. So long as my reputation is safe, what do I care if my rivals deny my merits? They certainly will not inherit them. Come, my friend; give up something for her who sacrifices so much for you. Do not come quite so often; I shall love you none the less."

"Ah!" said Armand, with the profound irony of a wounded heart in his words and tone. "Love, so the scribblers say, only feeds on illusions. Nothing could be truer, I see; I am expected to imagine that I am loved. But, there!—there are some thoughts like wounds, from which there is no recovery. My belief in you was one of the last left to me, and now I see that there is nothing left to believe in this earth."

She began to smile.

"Yes," Montriveau went on in an unsteady voice, "this Catholic faith to which you wish to convert me is a lie that men make for themselves; hope is a lie at the expense of the future; pride, a lie between us and our fellows; and pity, and prudence, and terror are cunning lies. And now my happiness is to be one more lying delusion; I am expected to delude myself, to be willing to give gold coin for silver to the end. If you can so easily dispense with my visits; if you can confess me neither as your friend nor your lover, you do not care for me! And I, poor fool that I am, tell myself this, and know it, and love you!"

"But, dear me, poor Armand, you are flying into a passion!"

"I flying into a passion?"

"Yes. You think that the whole question is opened because I ask you to be careful."

In her heart of hearts she was delighted with the anger that leaped out in her lover's eyes. Even as she tortured him, she was criticising him, watching every slightest change that passed over his face. If the General had been so unluckily inspired as to show himself generous without discussion (as happens occasionally with some artless souls), he would have been a banished man for ever, accused and convicted of not knowing how to love. Most women are not displeased to have their code of right and wrong broken through. Do they not flatter themselves that they never yield except to force? But Armand was not learned enough in this kind of lore to see the snare ingeniously spread for him by the Duchess. So much of the child was there in the strong man in love.

"If all you want is to preserve appearances," he began in his simplicity, "I am willing to——"

"Simply to preserve appearances!" the lady broke in; "why, what idea can you have of me? Have I given you the slightest reason to suppose that I can be yours?"

"Why, what else are we talking about?" demanded Montriveau.

"Monsieur, you frighten me! . . . No, pardon me. Thank you," she added, coldly; "thank you, Armand. You have given me timely warning of imprudence; committed quite unconsciously, believe it, my friend. You know how to endure, you say. I also know how to endure. We will not see each other for a time; and then, when both of us have contrived to recover calmness to some extent, we will think about arrangements for a happiness sanctioned by the world. I am young, Armand; a man with no delicacy might tempt a woman of four-and-twenty to do many foolish, wild things for his sake. But *you!* You will be my friend, promise me that you will?"

"The woman of four-and-twenty," returned he, "knows what she is about."

He sat down on the sofa in the boudoir, and leaned his head on his hands.

"Do you love me, madame?" he asked at length, raising his head, and turning a face full of resolution upon her. "Say it straight out; Yes or No!"

His direct question dismayed the Duchess more than a threat of suicide could have done; indeed, the woman of the nineteenth century is not to be frightened by that stale stratagem, the sword has ceased to be a part of the masculine costume. But in the effect of eyelids and lashes, in the contraction of the gaze, in the twitching of the lips, is there not some influence that communicates the terror which they express with such vivid magnetic power?

"Ah, if I were free, if——"

"Oh! is it only your husband that stands in the way?" the General exclaimed joyfully, as he strode to and fro in the boudoir. "Dear Antoinette, I wield a more absolute power than the Autocrat of all the Russias. I have a compact with Fate; I can advance or retard destiny, so far as men are concerned, at my fancy, as you alter the hands of a watch. If you can direct the course of fate in our political machinery, it simply means (does it not?) that you understand the ins and outs of it. You shall be free before very long, and then you must remember your promise."

"Armand!" she cried. "What do you mean? Great heavens! Can you imagine that I am to be the prize of a crime? Do you want to kill me? Why! you cannot have any religion in you! For my own part, I fear God. M. de Langeais may have given me reason to hate him, but I wish him no manner of harm."

M. de Montriveau beat a tattoo on the marble chimney-piece, and only looked composedly at the lady.

"Dear," continued she, "respect him. He does not love me, he is not kind to me, but I have duties to fulfil with regard to him. What would I not do to avert the calamities with which you threaten him?—Listen," she continued after a pause, "I will not say another word about separation; you shall come here as in the past, and I will still give you my forehead to kiss. If I refused once or twice, it was pure coquetry, indeed it was. But let us understand each other," she added as he came closer. "You will permit me to add to the number of my satellites; to receive even more visitors in the morning than heretofore; I mean to be twice as frivolous; I mean to use you to all appearance very badly; to feign a rupture; you must come not quite so often, and then, afterwards——"

While she spoke, she had allowed him to put an arm about her waist, Montriveau was holding her tightly to him, and she seemed to feel the exceeding pleasure that women usually feel in that close contact, an earnest of the bliss of a closer union. And then, doubtless she meant to elicit some confidence, for she raised herself on tiptoe, and laid her forehead against Armand's burning lips.

"And then," Montriveau finished her sentence for her, "you shall not speak to me of your husband. You ought not to think of him again."

Mme. de Langeais was silent awhile.

"At least," she said, after a significant pause, "at least you will do all that I wish without grumbling, you will not be naughty; tell me so, my friend? You wanted to frighten me, did you not? Come, now, confess it? . . . You are too good ever to think of crimes. But is it possible that you can have secrets that I do not know? How can you control Fate?"

"Now, when you confirm the gift of the heart that you have already given me, I am far too happy to know exactly how to answer you. I can trust you, Antoinette; I shall have no suspicion, no unfounded jealousy of you. But if accident should set you free, we shall be one——"

"Accident, Armand?" (with that little dainty turn of the head that seems to say so many things, a gesture that such women as the Duchess can use on light occasions, as a great singer can act with her voice). "Pure accident," she repeated. "Mind that. If anything should happen to M. de Langeais by your fault, I should never be yours."

And so they parted, mutually content. The Duchess had made a pact that left her free to prove to the world by words and deeds that M. de Montriveau was no lover of hers. And as for him, the wily Duchess vowed to tire him out. He should have nothing of her beyond the little concessions snatched in the course of contests that she could stop at her pleasure. She had so pretty an art of revoking the grant of yesterday, she was so much in earnest in her purpose to remain technically virtuous, that she felt that there was not the slightest danger for her in preliminaries fraught with peril for a woman less sure of her self-command. After all, the Duchess was practically separated from her husband; a marriage long since annulled was no great sacrifice to make to her love.

Montriveau on his side was quite happy to win the vaguest promise, glad once for all to sweep aside, with all scruples

of conjugal fidelity, her stock of excuses for refusing herself
to his love. He had gained ground a little, and congratulated himself. And so for a time he took unfair advantage of
the rights so hardly won. More a boy than he had ever been
in his life, he gave himself up to all the childishness that
makes first love the flower of life. He was a child again as
he poured out all his soul, all the thwarted forces that passion
had given him, upon her hands, upon the dazzling forehead
that looked so pure to his eyes; upon her fair hair; on the
tufted curls where his lips were pressed. And the Duchess, on
whom his love was poured like a flood, was vanquished by the
magnetic influence of her lover's warmth; she hesitated to
begin the quarrel that must part them for ever. She was
more a woman than she thought, this slight creature, in her
effort to reconcile the demands of religion with the ever-new
sensations of vanity, the semblance of pleasure which turns a
Parisienne's head. Every Sunday she went to Mass; she
never missed a service; then, when evening came, she was
steeped in the intoxicating bliss of repressed desire. Armand
and Mme. de Langeais, like Hindoo fakirs, found the reward
of their continence in the temptations to which it gave rise.
Possibly, the Duchess had ended by resolving love into fra-
ternal caresses, harmless enough, as it might have seemed to
the rest of the world, while they borrowed extremes of degradation from the license of her thoughts. How else explain the
incomprehensible mystery of her continual fluctuations?
Every morning she proposed to herself to shut her door on
the Marquis de Montriveau; every evening, at the appointed
hour, she fell under the charm of his presence. There was a
languid defence; then she grew less unkind. Her words were
sweet and soothing. They were lovers—lovers only could have
been thus. For him the Duchess would display her most
sparkling wit, her most captivating wiles; and when at last
she had wrought upon his senses and his soul, she might submit herself passively to his fierce caresses, but she had her *nec
plus ultra* of passion; and when once it was reached, she grew
angry if he lost the mastery of himself and made as though

he would pass beyond. No woman on earth can brave the consequences of refusal without some motive; nothing is more natural than to yield to love; wherefore Mme. de Langeais promptly raised a second line of fortification, a stronghold less easy to carry than the first. She evoked the terrors of religion. Never did Father of the Church, however eloquent, plead the cause of God better than the Duchess. Never was the wrath of the Most High better justified than by her voice. She used no preacher's commonplaces, no rhetorical amplifications. No. She had a "pulpit-tremor" of her own. To Armand's most passionate entreaty, she replied with a tearful gaze, and a gesture in which a terrible plenitude of emotion found expression. She stopped his mouth with an appeal for mercy. She would not hear another word; if she did, she must succumb; and better death than criminal happiness.

"Is it nothing to disobey God?" she asked him, recovering a voice grown faint in the crises of inward struggles, through which the fair actress appeared to find it hard to preserve her self-control. "I would sacrifice society, I would give up the whole world for you, gladly; but it is very selfish of you to ask my whole after-life of me for a moment of pleasure. Come, now! are you not happy?" she added, holding out her hand; and certainly in her careless toilette the sight of her afforded consolations to her lover, who made the most of them.

Sometimes from policy, to keep her hold on a man whose ardent passion gave her emotions unknown before, sometimes in weakness, she suffered him to snatch a swift kiss; and immediately in feigned terror, she flushed red and exiled Armand from the sofa so soon as the sofa became dangerous ground.

"Your joys are sins for me to expiate, Armand; they are paid for by penitence and remorse," she cried.

And Montriveau, now at two chairs' distance from that aristocratic petticoat, betook himself to blasphemy and railed against Providence. The Duchess grew angry at such times.

"My friend," she said drily, "I do not understand why you

decline to believe in God, for it is impossible to believe in man. Hush, do not talk like that. You have too great a nature to take up their Liberal nonsense with its pretension to abolish God."

Theological and political disputes acted like a cold douche on Montriveau; he calmed down; he could not return to love when the Duchess stirred up his wrath by suddenly setting him down a thousand miles away from the boudoir, discussing theories of absolute monarchy, which she defended to admiration. Few women venture to be democrats; the attitude of democratic champion is scarcely compatible with tyrannous feminine sway. But often, on the other hand, the General shook out his mane, dropped politics with a leonine growling and lashing of the flanks, and sprang upon his prey; he was no longer capable of carrying a heart and brain at such variance for very far; he came back, terrible with love, to his mistress. And she, if she felt the prick of fancy stimulated to a dangerous point, knew that it was time to leave her boudoir; she came out of the atmosphere surcharged with desires that she drew in with her breath, sat down to the piano and sang the most exquisite songs of modern music, and so baffled the physical attraction which at times showed her no mercy, though she was strong enough to fight it down.

At such times she was something sublime in Armand's eyes; she was not acting; she was genuine; the unhappy lover was convinced that she loved him. Her egoistic resistance deluded him into a belief that she was a pure and sainted woman; he resigned himself; he talked of Platonic love, did this artillery officer.

When Mme. de Langeais had played with religion sufficiently to suit her own purposes, she played with it again for Armand's benefit. She wanted to bring him back to a Christian frame of mind; she brought out her edition of *Le Génie du Christianisme,* adapted for the use of military men. Montriveau chafed; his yoke was heavy. Oh! at that, possessed by the spirit of contradiction, she dinned religion into his ears, to see whether God might not rid her of this suitor,

for the man's persistence was beginning to frighten her. And
in any case she was glad to prolong any quarrel, if it bade
fair to keep the dispute on moral grounds for an indefinite
period; the material struggle which followed it was more
dangerous.

But if the time of her opposition on the ground of the
marriage law might be said to be the *époque civile* of this
sentimental warfare, the ensuing phase which might be taken
to constitute the *époque religieuse* had also its crisis and consequent decline of severity.

Armand, happening to come in very early one evening,
found M. l'Abbé Gondrand, the Duchess' spiritual director,
established in an armchair by the fireside, looking as a spiritual director might be expected to look while digesting his
dinner and the charming sins of his penitent. In the ecclesiastic's bearing there was a stateliness befitting a dignitary
of the Church; and the episcopal violet hue already appeared
in his dress. At sight of his fresh, well-preserved complexion,
smooth forehead, and ascetic's mouth, Montriveau's countenance grew uncommonly dark; he said not a word under the
malicious scrutiny of the other's gaze, and greeted neither
the lady nor the priest. The lover apart, Montriveau was
not wanting in tact; so a few glances exchanged with the
bishop-designate told him that here was the real forger of
the Duchess' armory of scruples.

That an ambitious abbé should control the happiness of a
man of Montriveau's temper, and by underhand ways! The
thought burst in a furious tide over his face, clenched his fists,
and set him chafing and pacing to and fro; but when he came
back to his place intending to make a scene, a single look
from the Duchess was enough. He was quiet.

Any other woman would have been put out by her lover's
gloomy silence; it was quite otherwise with Mme. de Langeais.
She continued her conversation with M. de Gondrand on the
necessity of re-establishing the Church in its ancient splendor.
And she talked brilliantly. The Church, she maintained,
ought to be a temporal as well as a spiritual power, stating

her case better than the Abbé had done, and regretting that
the Chamber of Peers, unlike the English House of Lords,
had no bench of bishops. Nevertheless, the Abbé rose,
yielded his place to the General, and took his leave, knowing
that in Lent he could play a return game. As for the
Duchess, Montriveau's behavior had excited her curiosity to
such a pitch that she scarcely rose to return her director's low
bow.

"What is the matter with you, my friend?"

"Why, I cannot stomach that Abbé of yours."

"Why did you not take a book?" she asked, careless whether
the Abbé, then closing the door, heard her or no.

The General paused, for the gesture which accompanied
the Duchess' speech further increased the exceeding insolence
of her words.

"My dear Antoinette, thank you for giving love precedence
of the Church; but, for pity's sake, allow me to ask one question."

"Oh! you are questioning me! I am quite willing. You
are my friend, are you not? I certainly can open the bottom
of my heart to you; you will see only one image there."

"Do you talk about our love to that man?"

"He is my confessor."

"Does he know that I love you?"

"M. de Montriveau, you cannot claim, I think, to penetrate
the secrets of the confessional?"

"Does that man know all about our quarrels and my love
for you?——"

"That man, monsieur; say God!"

"God again! *I* ought to be alone in your heart. But leave
God alone where He is, for the love of God and me. Madame, you *shall not* go to confession again, or——"

"Or?" she repeated sweetly.

"Or I will never come back here."

"Then go, Armand. Good-bye, good-bye for ever."

She rose and went to her boudoir without so much as a
glance at Armand, as he stood with his hand on the back of

a chair. How long he stood there motionless he himself
never knew. The soul within has the mysterious power of
expanding as of contracting space.

He opened the door of the boudoir. It was dark within.
A faint voice raised to say sharply:

"I did not ring. What made you come in without orders?
Go away, Suzette."

"Then you are ill," exclaimed Montriveau.

"Stand up, monsieur, and go out of the room for a minute
at any rate," she said, ringing the bell.

"Mme. la Duchesse rang for lights?" said the footman,
coming in with the candles. When the lovers were alone
together, Mme. de Langeais still lay on the couch; she was
just as silent and motionless as if Montriveau had not been
there.

"Dear, I was wrong," he began, a note of pain and a sublime kindness in his voice. "Indeed, I would not have you
without religion——"

"It is fortunate that you can recognize the necessity of a
conscience," she said in a hard voice, without looking at
him. "I thank you in God's name."

The General was broken down by her harshness; this
woman seemed as if she could be at will a sister or a stranger
to him. He made one despairing stride towards the door.
He would leave her for ever without another word. He was
wretched; and the Duchess was laughing within herself over
mental anguish far more cruel than the old judicial torture.
But as for going away, it was not in his power to do it. In
any sort of crisis, a woman is, as it were, bursting with a
certain quantity of things to say; so long as she has not delivered herself of them, she experiences the sensation which we
are apt to feel at the sight of something incomplete. Mme.
de Langeais had not said all that was on her mind. She
took up her parable and said:

"We have not the same convictions, General, I am pained
to think. It would be dreadful if a woman could not believe
in a religion which permits us to love beyond the grave. I

set Christian sentiments aside; you cannot understand them. Let me simply speak to you of expediency. Would you forbid a woman at court the table of the Lord when it is customary to take the sacrament at Easter? People must certainly do something for their party. The Liberals, whatever they may wish to do, will never destroy the religious instinct. Religion will always be a political necessity. Would you undertake to govern a nation of logic-choppers? Napoleon was afraid to try; he persecuted ideologists. If you want to keep people from reasoning, you must give them something to feel. So let us accept the Roman Catholic Church with all its consequences. And if we would have France go to mass, ought we not to begin by going ourselves? Religion, you see, Armand, is a bond uniting all the conservative principles which enable the rich to live in tranquillity. Religion and the rights of property are intimately connected. It is certainly a finer thing to lead a nation by ideas of morality than by fear of the scaffold, as in the time of the Terror—the one method by which your odious Revolution could enforce obedience. The priest and the king—that means you, and me, and the Princess my neighbor; and, in a word, the interests of all honest people personified. There, my friend, just be so good as to belong to your party, you that might be its Scylla if you had the slightest ambition that way. I know nothing about politics myself; I argue from my own feelings; but still I know enough to guess that society would be overturned if people were always calling its foundations in question——"

"If that is how your Court and your Government think, I am sorry for you," broke in Montriveau. "The Restoration, madame, ought to say, like Catherine de Medici, when she heard that the battle of Dreux was lost, 'Very well; now we will go to the meeting-house.' Now 1815 was your battle of Dreux. Like the royal power of those days, you won in fact, while you lost in right. Political Protestantism has gained an ascendency over people's minds. If you have no mind to issue your Edict of Nantes; or if, when it is issued, you publish a Revocation; if you should one day be accused

and convicted of repudiating the Charter, which is simply a
pledge given to maintain the interests established under the
Republic, then the Revolution will rise again, terrible in her
strength, and strike but a single blow. It will not be the
Revolution that will go into exile; she is the very soil of
France. Men die, but people's interests do not die. . . .
Eh, great Heavens! what are France and the crown and rightful sovereigns, and the whole world besides, to us? Idle
words compared with my happiness. Let them reign or be
hurled from the throne, little do I care. Where am I now?"

"In the Duchesse de Langeais' boudoir, my friend."

"No, no. No more of the Duchess, no more of Langeais;
I am with my dear Antoinette."

"Will you do me the pleasure to stay where you are," she
said, laughing and pushing him back, gently however.

"So you have never loved me," he retorted, and anger
flashed in lightning from his eyes.

"No, dear;" but the "No" was equivalent to "Yes."

"I am a great ass," he said, kissing her hands. The terrible
queen was a woman once more.—"Antoinette," he went on,
laying his head on her feet, "you are too chastely tender to
speak of our happiness to any one in this world."

"Oh!" she cried, rising to her feet with a swift, graceful
spring, "you are a great simpleton." And without another
word she fled into the drawing-room.

"What is it now?" wondered the General, little knowing
that the touch of his burning forehead had sent a swift electric thrill through her from foot to head.

In hot wrath he followed her to the drawing-room, only
to hear divinely sweet chords. The Duchess was at the piano.
If the man of science or the poet can at once enjoy and comprehend, bringing his intelligence to bear upon his enjoyment
without loss of delight, he is conscious that the alphabet and
phraseology of music are but cunning instruments for the
composer, like the wood and copper wire under the hands of
the executant. For the poet and the man of science there is
a music existing apart, underlying the double expression of

this language of the spirit and senses. *Andiamo mio ben* can
draw tears of joy or pitying laughter at the will of the singer;
and not unfrequently one here and there in the world, some
girl unable to live and bear the heavy burden of an unguessed
pain, some man whose soul vibrates with the throb of passion,
may take up a musical theme, and lo! heaven is opened for
them, or they find a language for themselves in some sublime
melody, some song lost to the world.

The General was listening now to such a song; a mysterious
music unknown to all other ears, as the solitary plaint of some
mateless bird dying alone in a virgin forest.

"Great Heavens! what are you playing there?" he asked
in an unsteady voice.

"The prelude of a ballad, called, I believe, *Fleuve du Tage.*"

"I did not know that there was such music in a piano,"
he returned.

"Ah!" she said, and for the first time she looked at him
as a woman looks at the man she loves, "nor do you know,
my friend, that I love you, and that you cause me horrible
suffering; and that I feel that I must utter my cry of pain
without putting it too plainly into words. If I did not, I
should yield—— But you see nothing."

"And you will not make me happy?"

"Armand, I should die of sorrow the next day."

The General turned abruptly from her and went. But out
in the streets he brushed away the tears that he would not let
fall.

The religious phase lasted for three months. At the end
of that time the Duchess grew weary of vain repetitions; the
Deity, bound hand and foot, was delivered up to her lover.
Possibly she may have feared that by sheer dint of talking
of eternity she might perpetuate his love in this world and
the next. For her own sake, it must be believed that no man
had touched her heart, or her conduct would be inexcusable.
She was young; the time when men and women feel that they
cannot afford to lose time or to quibble over their joys was
still far off. She, no doubt, was on the verge not of first

love, but of her firs xperience of the bliss of love. And from
inexperience, for want of the painful lessons which would
have taught her the value of the treasure poured out at her
feet, she was playing with it. Knowing nothing of the glory
and rapture of the light, she was fain to stay in the shadow.

Armand was just beginning to understand this strange
situation; he put his hope in the first word spoken by nature.
Every evening, as he came away from Mme. de Langeais', he
told himself that no woman would accept the tenderest, most
delicate proofs of a man's love during seven months, nor yield
passively to the slighter demands of passion, only to cheat love
at the last. He was waiting patiently for the sun to gain power,
not doubting but that he should receive the earliest fruits.
The married woman's hesitations and the religious scruples
he could quite well understand. He even rejoiced over those
battles. He mistook the Duchess' heartless coquetry for modesty; and he would not have had her otherwise. So he had
loved to see her devising obstacles; was he not gradually triumphing over them? Did not every victory won swell the
meagre sum of lovers' intimacies long denied, and at last
conceded with every sign of love? Still, he had had such
leisure to taste the full sweetness of every small successive
conquest on which a lover feeds his love, that these had come
to be matters of use and wont. So far as obstacles went,
there were none now save his own awe of her; nothing else
left between him and his desire save the whims of her who allowed him to call her Antoinette. So he made up his mind
to demand more, to demand all. Embarrassed like a young
lover who cannot dare to believe that his idol can stoop so
low, he hesitated for a long time. He passed through the
experience of terrible reactions within himself. A set purpose
was annihilated by a word and definite resolves died within
him on the threshold. He despised himself for his weakness,
and still his desire remained unuttered. Nevertheless, one
evening, after sitting in gloomy melancholy, he brought out
a fierce demand for his illegally legitimate rights. The
Duchess had not to wait for her bond-slave's request to guess

his desire. When was a man's desire a secret? And have not women an intuitive knowledge of the meaning of certain changes of countenance?

"What! you wish to be my friend no longer?" she broke in at the first words, and a divine red surging like new blood under the transparent skin, lent brightness to her eyes. "As a reward for my generosity, you would dishonor me? Just reflect a little. I myself have thought much over this; and I think always for us *both*. There is such a thing as a woman's loyalty, and we can no more fail in it than you can fail in honor. *I* cannot blind myself. If I am yours, how, in any sense, can I be M. de Langeais' wife? Can you require the sacrifice of my position, my rank, my whole life in return for a doubtful love that could not wait patiently for seven months? What! already you would rob me of the right to dispose of myself? No, no; you must not talk like this again. No, not another word. I will not, I cannot listen to you."

Mme. de Langeais raised both hands to her head to push back the tufted curls from her hot forehead; she seemed very much excited.

"You come to a weak woman with your purpose definitely planned out. You say—'For a certain length of time she will talk to me of her husband, then of God, and then of the inevitable consequences. But I will use and abuse the ascendency I shall gain over her; I will make myself indispensable; all the bonds of habit, all the misconstructions of outsiders, will make for me; and at length, when our *liaison* is taken for granted by all the world, I shall be this woman's master.'—Now, be frank; these are your thoughts! Oh! you calculate, and you say that you love. Shame on you! You are enamored? Ah! that I well believe! You wish to possess me, to have me for your mistress, that is all! Very well then, No! The *Duchesse de Langeais* will not descend so far. Simple *bourgeoises* may be the victims of your treachery—I, never! Nothing gives me assurance of your love. You speak of my beauty; I may lose every trace of it in six months, like

the dear Princess, my neighbor. You are captivated by my
wit, my grace. Great Heavens! you would soon grow used to
them and to the pleasures of possession. Have not the little
concessions that I was weak enough to make come to be a
matter of course in the last few months? Some day, when
ruin comes, you will give me no reason for the change in you
beyond a curt, 'I have ceased to care for you.'—Then, rank
and fortune and honor and all that was the Duchesse de
Langeais will be swallowed up in one disappointed hope. I
shall have children to bear witness to my shame, and——"
With an involuntary gesture she interrupted herself, and
continued: "But I am too good-natured to explain all this
to you when you know it better than I. Come! let us stay
as we are. I am only too fortunate in that I can still break
these bonds which you think so strong. Is there anything so
very heroic in coming to the Hôtel de Langeais to spend an
evening with a woman whose prattle amuses you?—a woman
whom you take for a plaything? Why, half-a-dozen young
coxcombs come here just as regularly every afternoon between three and five. They, too, are very generous, I am to
suppose? I make fun of them; they stand my petulance and
insolence pretty quietly, and make me laugh; but as for you,
I give all the treasures of my soul to you, and you wish to
ruin me, you try my patience in endless ways. Hush, that
will do, that will do," she continued, seeing that he was about
to speak, "you have no heart, no soul, no delicacy. I know
what you want to tell me. Very well, then—yes. I would
rather you should take me for a cold, insensible woman, with
no devotion in her composition, no heart even, than be taken
by everybody else for a vulgar person, and be condemned to
your so-called pleasures, of which you would most certainly
tire, and to everlasting punishment for it afterwards. Your
selfish love is not worth so many sacrifices . . ."

The words give but a very inadequate idea of the discourse
which the Duchess trilled out with the quick volubility of a
bird-organ. Nor, truly, was there anything to prevent her
from talking on for some time to come, for poor Armand's

only reply to the torrent of flute notes was a silence filled with cruelly painful thoughts. He was just beginning to see that this woman was playing with him; he divined instinctively that a devoted love, a responsive love, does not reason and count the consequences in this way. Then, as he heard her reproach him with detestable motives, he felt something like shame as he remembered that unconsciously he had made those very calculations. With angelic honesty of purpose, he looked within, and self-examination found nothing but selfishness in all his thoughts and motives, in the answers which he framed and could not utter. He was self-convicted. In his despair he longed to fling himself from the window. The egoism of it was intolerable.

What indeed can a man say when a woman will not believe in love?—Let me prove how much I love you?—The *I* is always there.

The heroes of the boudoir, in such circumstances, can follow the example of the primitive logician who preceded the Pyrrhonists and denied movement. Montriveau was not equal to this feat. With all his audacity, he lacked this precise kind which never deserts an adept in the formulas of feminine algebra. If so many women, and even the best of women, fall a prey to a kind of expert to whom the vulgar give a grosser name, it is perhaps because the said experts are great *provers,* and love, in spite of its delicious poetry of sentiment, requires a little more geometry than people are wont to think.

Now the Duchess and Montriveau were alike in this— they were both equally unversed in love lore. The lady's knowledge of theory was but scanty; in practice she knew nothing whatever; she felt nothing, and reflected over everything. Montriveau had had but little experience, was absolutely ignorant of theory, and felt too much to reflect at all. Both therefore were enduring the consequences of the singular situation. At that supreme moment the myriad thoughts in his mind might have been reduced to the formula—"Submit to be mine——" words which seem horribly selfish to a

woman for whom they awaken no memories, recall no ideas.
Something nevertheless he must say. And what was more,
though her barbed shafts had set his blood tingling, though
the short phrases that she discharged at him one by one were
very keen and sharp and cold, he must control himself lest he
should lose all by an outbreak of anger.

"Mme. la Duchesse, I am in despair that God should have
invented no way for a woman to confirm the gift of her heart
save by adding the gift of her person. The high value which
you yourself put upon the gift teaches me that I cannot attach less impörtance to it. If you have given me your utmost self and your whole heart, as you tell me, what can the
rest matter? And besides, if my happiness means so painful
a sacrifice, let us say no more about it. But you must pardon a man of spirit if he feels humiliated at being taken for
a spaniel."

The tone in which the last remark was uttered might perhaps have frightened another woman; but when the wearer
of a petticoat has allowed herself to be addressed as a Divinity, and thereby set herself above all other mortals, no
power on earth can be so haughty.

"M. le Marquis, I am in despair that God should not have
invented some nobler way for a man to confirm the gift of his
heart than by the manifestation of prodigiously vulgar desires. We become bond-slaves when we give ourselves body
and soul, but a man is bound to nothing by accepting the gift.
Who will assure me that love will last? The very love that
I might show for you at every moment, the better to keep
your love, might serve you as a reason for deserting me. I
have no wish to be a second edition of Mme. de Beauséant.
Who can ever know what it is that keeps you beside us? Our
persistent coldness of heart is the cause of an unfailing passion in some of you; other men ask for an untiring devotion,
to be idolized at every moment; some for gentleness, others
for tyranny. No woman in this world as yet has really read
the riddle of man's heart."

There was a pause. When she spoke again it was in a different tone.

"After all, my friend, you cannot prevent a woman from trembling at the question, 'Will this love last always?' Hard though my words may be, the dread of losing you puts them into my mouth. Oh, me! it is not I who speak, dear, it is reason; and how should any one so mad as I be reasonable? In truth, I am nothing of the sort."

The poignant irony of her answer had changed before the end into the most musical accents in which a woman could find utterance for ingenuous love. To listen to her words was to pass in a moment from martyrdom to heaven. Montriveau grew pale; and for the first time in his life, he fell on his knees before a woman. He kissed the Duchess' skirt hem, her knees, her feet; but for the credit of the Faubourg Saint-Germain it is necessary to respect the mysteries of its boudoirs, where many are fain to take the utmost that Love can give without giving proof of love in return.

The Duchess thought herself generous when she suffered herself to be adored. But Montriveau was in a wild frenzy of joy over her complete surrender of the position.

"Dear Antoinette," he cried. "Yes, you are right; I will not have you doubt any longer. I too am trembling at this moment—lest the angel of my life should leave me; I wish I could invent some tie that might bind us to each other irrevocably."

"Ah!" she said, under her breath, "so I was right, you see."

"Let me say all that I have to say; I will scatter all your fears with a word. Listen! if I deserted you, I should deserve to die a thousand deaths. Be wholly mine, and I will give you the right to kill me if I am false. I myself will write a letter explaining certain reasons for taking my own life; I will make my final arrangements, in short. You shall have the letter in your keeping; in the eye of the law it will be a sufficient explanation of my death. You can avenge yourself, and fear nothing from God or men."

"What good would the letter be to me? What would life be if I had lost your love? If I wished to kill you, should I not be ready to follow? No; thank you for the thought, but I do not want the letter. Should I not begin to dread that you were faithful to me through fear? And if a man knows that he must risk his life for a stolen pleasure, might it not seem more tempting? Armand, the thing I ask of you is the one thing hard to do."

"Then what is it that you wish?"

"Your obedience and my liberty."

"Ah, God!" cried he, "I am a child."

"A wayward, much spoilt child," she said, stroking the thick hair, for his head still lay on her knee. "Ah! and loved far more than he believes, and yet he is very disobedient. Why not stay as we are? Why not sacrifice to me the desires that hurt me? Why not take what I can give, when it is all that I can honestly grant? Are you not happy?"

"Oh yes, I am happy when I have not a doubt left. Antoinette, doubt in love is a kind of death, is it not?"

In a moment he showed himself as he was, as all men are under the influence of that hot fever; he grew eloquent, insinuating. And the Duchess tasted the pleasures which she reconciled with her conscience by some private, Jesuitical ukase of her own; Armand's love gave her a thrill of cerebral excitement which custom made as necessary to her as society, or the Opera. To feel that she was adored by this man, who rose above other men, whose character frightened her; to treat him like a child; to play with him as Poppæa played with Nero—many women, like the wives of King Henry VIII., have paid for such a perilous delight with all the blood in their veins. Grim presentiment! Even as she surrendered the delicate, pale, gold curls to his touch, and felt the close pressure of his hand, the little hand of a man whose greatness she could not mistake; even as she herself played with his dark, thick locks, in that boudoir where she reigned a queen, the Duchess would say to herself:

"This man is capable of killing me if he once finds out that I am playing with him."

Armand de Montriveau stayed with her till two o'clock in

the morning. From that moment this woman, whom he loved, was neither a duchess nor a Navarreins; Antoinette, in her disguises, had gone so far as to appear to be a woman. On that most blissful evening, the sweetest prelude ever played by a Parisienne to what the world calls "a slip"; in spite of all her affectations of a coyness which she did not feel, the General saw all maidenly beauty in her. He had some excuse for believing that so many storms of caprice had been but clouds covering a heavenly soul; that these must be lifted one by one like the veils that hid her divine loveliness. The Duchess became, for him, the most simple and girlish mistress; she was the one woman in the world for him; and he went away quite happy in that at last he had brought her to give him such pledges of love, that it seemed to him impossible but that he should be but her husband henceforth in secret, her choice sanctioned by Heaven.

Armand went slowly home, turning this thought in his mind with the impartiality of a man who is conscious of all the responsibilities that love lays on him while he tastes the sweetness of its joys. He went along the Quais to see the widest possible space of sky; his heart had grown in him; he would fain have had the bounds of the firmament and of earth enlarged. It seemed to him that his lungs drew an ampler breath. In the course of his self-examination, as he walked, he vowed to love this woman so devoutly, that every day of her life she should find absolution for her sins against society in unfailing happiness. Sweet stirrings of life when life is at the full! The man that is strong enough to steep his soul in the color of one emotion, feels infinite joy as glimpses open out for him of an ardent lifetime that knows no diminution of passion to the end; even so it is permitted to certain mystics, in ecstasy, to behold the Light of God. Love would be naught without the belief that it would last for ever; love grows great through constancy. It was thus that, wholly absorbed by his happiness, Montriveau understood passion.

"We belong to each other for ever!"

The thought was like a talisman fulfilling the wishes of
his life. He did not ask whether the Duchess might not
change, whether her love might not last. No, for he had
faith. Without that virtue there is no future for Christianity,
and perhaps it is even more necessary to society. A conception of life as feeling occurred to him for the first time;
hitherto he had lived by action, the most strenuous exertion
of human energies, the physical devotion, as it may be called,
of the soldier.

Next day M. de Montriveau went early in the direction
of the Faubourg Saint-Germain. He had made an appointment at a house not far from the Hôtel de Langeais; and the
business over, he went thither as if to his own home. The
General's companion chanced to be a man for whom he felt
a kind of repulsion whenever he met him in other houses.
This was the Marquis de Ronquerolles, whose reputation had
grown so great in Paris boudoirs. He was witty, clever, and
what was more—courageous; he set the fashion to all the
young men in Paris. As a man of gallantry, his success and
experience were equally matters of envy; and neither fortune
nor birth was wanting in his case, qualifications which add
such lustre in Paris to a reputation as a leader of fashion.

"Where are you going?" asked M. de Ronquerolles.

"To Mme. de Langeais'."

"Ah, true. I forgot that you had allowed her to lime you.
You are wasting your affections on her when they might be
much better employed elsewhere. I could have told you of
half-a-score of women in the financial world, any one of them
a thousand times better worth your while than that titled
courtesan, who does with her brains what less artificial women
do with——"

"What is this, my dear fellow?" Armand broke in. "The
Duchess is an angel of innocence."

Ronquerolles began to laugh.

"Things being thus, dear boy," said he, "it is my duty
to enlighten you. Just a word; there is no harm in it between ourselves. Has the Duchess surrendered? If so, I

have nothing more to say. Come, give me your confidence.
There is no occasion to waste your time in grafting your great
nature on that unthankful stock, when all your hopes and
cultivation will come to nothing."

Armand ingenuously made a kind of general report of
his position, enumerating with much minuteness the slender
rights so hardly won. Ronquerolles burst into a peal of laughter so heartless, that it would have cost any other man his
life. But from their manner of speaking and looking at each
other during their colloquy beneath the wall, in a corner almost as remote from intrusion as the desert itself, it was easy
to imagine the friendship between the two men knew
no bounds, and that no power on earth could estrange them.

"My dear Armand, why did you not tell me that the
Duchess was a puzzle to you? I would have given you a little
advice which might have brought your flirtation properly
through. You must know, to begin with, that the women of
our Faubourg, like any other women, love to steep themselves
in love; but they have a mind to possess and not to be possessed. They have made a sort of compromise with human
nature. The code of their parish gives them a pretty wide
latitude short of the last transgression. The sweets enjoyed
by this fair Duchess of yours are so many venial sins to be
washed away in the waters of penitence. But if you had the
impertinence to ask in earnest for the mortal sin to which
naturally you are sure to attach the highest importance, you
would see the deep disdain with which the door of the boudoir
and the house would be incontinently shut upon you. The
tender Antoinette would dismiss everything from her memory; you would be less than a cipher for her. She would
wipe away your kisses, my dear friend, as indifferently as she
would perform her ablutions. She would sponge love from
her cheeks as she washes off rouge. We know women of that
sort—the thoroughbred Parisienne. Have you ever noticed
a grisette tripping along the street? Her face is as good as
a picture. A pretty cap, fresh cheeks, trim hair, a guileful
smile, and the rest of her almost neglected. Is not this true

to the life? Well, that is the Parisienne. She knows that her face is all that will be seen, so she devotes all her care, finery, and vanity to her head The Duchess is the same; the head is everything with her. She can only feel through her intellect, her heart lies in her brain, she is a sort of intellectual epicure, she has a head-voice. We call that kind of poor creature a Laïs of the intellect. You have been taken in like a boy. If you doubt it, you can have proof of it to-night, this morning, this instant. Go up to her, try the demand as an experiment, insist peremptorily if it is refused. You might set about it like the late Maréchal de Richelieu, and get nothing for your pains."

Armand was dumb with amazement.

"Has your desire reached the point of infatuation?"

"I want her at any cost!" Montriveau cried out despairingly.

"Very well. Now, look here. Be as inexorable as she is herself. Try to humiliate her, to sting her vanity. Do *not* try to move her heart, nor her soul, but the woman's nerves and temperament, for she is both nervous and lymphatic. If you can once awaken desire in her, you are safe. But you must drop these romantic boyish notions of yours. If when once you have her in your eagle talons you yield a point or draw back, if you so much as stir an eyelid, if she thinks that she can regain her ascendency over you, she will slip out of your clutches like a fish, and you will never catch her again. Be as inflexible as law. Show no more charity than the headsman. Hit hard, and then hit again. Strike, and keep on striking as if you were giving her the knout. Duchesses are made of hard stuff, my dear Armand; there is a sort of feminine nature that is only softened by repeated blows; and as suffering develops a heart in women of that sort, so it is a work of charity not to spare the rod. Do you persevere. Ah! when pain has thoroughly relaxed those nerves and softened the fibres that you take to be so pliant and yielding; when a shriveled heart has learned to expand and contract and to beat under this discipline; when the brain has capitulated—then, perhaps, passion may enter among the steel springs of this machinery that turns out tears and affectations and languors and melting phrases; then you shall see a most magnificent conflagration (always supposing that the chimney takes fire). The steel feminine system will glow red-hot like iron in the forge; that kind of heat lasts longer than any other, and the glow of it may possibly turn to love.

"Still," he continued, "I have my doubts. And, after all, is it worth while to take so much trouble with the Duchess? Between ourselves, a man of my stamp ought first to take her in hand and break her in; I would make a charming woman of her; she is a thoroughbred; whereas, you two left to yourselves will never get beyond the A B C. But you are in love with her, and just now you might not perhaps share my views on this subject—— A pleasant time to you, my children," added Ronquerolles, after a pause. Then with a laugh: "I have decided myself for facile beauties; they are tender, at any rate, the natural woman appears in their love without any of your social seasonings. A woman that haggles over herself, my poor boy, and only means to inspire love! Well, have her like an extra horse—for show. The match between the sofa and confessional, black and white, queen and knight, conscientious scruples and pleasure, is an uncommonly amusing game of chess. And if a man knows the game, let him be never so little of a rake, he wins in three moves. Now, if I undertook a woman of that sort, I should start with the deliberate purpose of——" His voice sank to a whisper over the last words in Armand's ear, and he went before there was time to reply.

As for Montriveau, he sprang at a bound across the courtyard of the Hôtel de Langeais, went unannounced up the stairs straight to the Duchess' bedroom.

"This is an unheard-of thing," she said, hastily wrapping her dressing gown about her. "Armand! this is abominable of you! Come, leave the room, I beg. Just go out of the room, and go at once. Wait for me in the drawing-room.— Come now!"

"Dear angel, has a plighted lover no privilege whatsoever?"

"But, monsieur, it is in the worst possible taste of a plighted lover or a wedded husband to break in like this upon his wife."

He came up to the Duchess, took her in his arms, and held her tightly to him.

"Forgive, dear Antoinette; but a host of horrid doubts are fermenting in my heart."

"*Doubts?* Fie!—Oh, fie on you!"

"Doubts all but justified. If you loved me, would you make this quarrel? Would you not be glad to see me? Would you not have felt a something stir in your heart? For I, that am not a woman, feel a thrill in my inmost self at the mere sound of your voice. Often in a ballroom a longing has come upon me to spring to your side and put my arms about your neck."

"Oh! if you have doubts of me so long as I am not ready to spring to your arms before all the world, I shall be doubted all my life long, I suppose. Why, Othello was a mere child compared with you!"

"Ah!" he cried despairingly, "you have no love for me——"

"Admit, at any rate, that at this moment you are not lovable."

"Then I have still to find favor in your sight?"

"Oh, I should think so. Come," added she, with a little imperious air, "go out of the room, leave me. I am not like you; I wish always to find favor in your eyes."

Never woman better understood the art of putting charm into insolence, and does not the charm double the effect? is it not enough to infuriate the coolest of men? There was a sort of untrammeled freedom about Mme. de Langeais; a something in her eyes, her voice, her attitude, which is never seen in a woman who loves when she stands face to face with him at the mere sight of whom her heart must needs begin to beat. The Marquis de Ronquerolles' counsels had cured

Armand of sheepishness; and further, there came to his aid
that rapid power of intuition which passion will develop at
moments in the least wise among mortals, while a great man
at such a time possesses it to the full. He guessed the terrible truth revealed by the Duchess' nonchalance, and his
heart swelled with the storm like a lake rising in flood.

"If you told me the truth yesterday, be mine, dear Antoinette," he cried; "you shall——"

"In the first place," said she composedly, thrusting him
back as he came nearer—"in the first place, you are not to
compromise me. My woman might overhear you. Respect
me, I beg of you. Your familiarity is all very well in my
boudoir in an evening; here it is quite different. Besides,
what may your 'you shall' mean? 'You shall.' No one as
yet has ever used that word to me. It is quite ridiculous,
it seems to me, absolutely ridiculous."

"Will you surrender nothing to me on this point?"

"Oh! do you call a woman's right to dispose of herself a
'point'? A capital point indeed; you will permit me to be
entirely my own mistress on that 'point.' "

"And how if, believing in your promises to me, I should
absolutely require it?"

"Oh! then you would prove that I made the greatest possible mistake when I made you a promise of any kind; and I
should beg you to leave me in peace."

The General's face grew white; he was about to spring
to her side, when Mme. de Langeais rang the bell, the maid
appeared, and, smiling with a mocking grace, the Duchess
added, "Be so good as to return when I am visible."

Then Montriveau felt the hardness of a woman as cold
and keen as a steel blade; she was crushing in her scorn. In
one moment she had snapped the bonds which held firm only
for her lover. She had read Armand's intention in his face,
and held that the moment had come for teaching the Imperial
soldier his lesson. He was to be made to feel that though
duchesses may lend themselves to love, they do not give themselves, and that the conquest of one of them would prove a
harder matter than the conquest of Europe.

"Madame," returned Armand, "I have not time to wait. I am a spoilt child, as you told me yourself. When I seriously resolve to have that of which we have been speaking, I shall have it."

"You will have it?" queried she, and there was a trace of surprise in her loftiness.

"I shall have it."

"Oh! you would do me a great pleasure by 'resolving' to have it. For curiosity's sake, I should be delighted to know how you would set about it——"

"I am delighted to put a new interest into your life," interrupted Montriveau, breaking into a laugh which dismayed the Duchess. "Will you permit me to take you to the ball to-night?"

"A thousand thanks. M. de Marsay has been beforehand with you. I gave him my promise."

Montriveau bowed gravely and went.

"So Ronquerolles was right," thought he, "and now for a game of chess."

Thenceforward he hid his agitation by complete composure. No man is strong enough to bear such sudden alternations from the height of happiness to the depths of wretchedness. So he had caught a glimpse of happy life the better to feel the emptiness of his previous existence? There was a terrible storm within him; but he had learned to endure, and bore the shock of tumultuous thoughts as a granite cliff stands out against the surge of an angry sea.

"I could say nothing. When I am with her my wits desert me. She does not know how vile and contemptible she is. Nobody has ventured to bring her face to face with herself. She has played with many a man, no doubt; I will avenge them all."

For the first time, it may be, in a man's heart, revenge and love were blended so equally that Montriveau himself could not know whether love or revenge would carry all before it. That very evening he went to the ball at which he was sure of seeing the Duchesse de Langeais, and almost despaired of

reaching her heart. He inclined to think that there was something diabolical about this woman, who was gracious to him
and radiant with charming smiles; probably because she had
no wish to allow the world to think that she had compromised herself with M. de Montriveau. Coolness on both sides
is a sign of love; but so long as the Duchess was the same as
ever, while the Marquis looked sullen and morose, was it not
plain that she had conceded nothing? Onlookers know the
rejected lover by various signs and tokens; they never mistake
the genuine symptoms for a coolness such as some women
command their adorers to feign, in the hope of concealing
their love. Every one laughed at Montriveau; and he, having omitted to consult his cornac, was abstracted and ill at
ease. M. de Ronquerolles would very likely have bidden him
compromise the Duchess by responding to her show of friend-
liness by passionate demonstrations; but as it was, Armand
de Montriveau came away from the ball, loathing human nature, and even then scarcely ready to believe in such complete depravity.

"If there is no executioner for such crimes," he said, as
he looked up at the lighted windows of the ballroom where
the most enchanting women in Paris were dancing, laughing,
and chatting, "I will take you by the nape of the neck, Mme.
la Duchesse, and make you feel something that bites more
deeply than the knife in the Place de la Grève. Steel against
steel; we shall see which heart will leave the deeper mark."

For a week or so Mme. de Langeais hoped to see the Marquis de Montriveau again; but he contented himself with
sending his card every morning to the Hôtel de Langeais.
The Duchess could not help shuddering each time that the
card was brought in, and a dim foreboding crossed her mind,
but the thought was vague as a presentiment of disaster.
When her eye fell on the name, it seemed to her that she felt
the touch of the implacable man's strong hand in her hair;
sometimes the words seemed like a prognostication of vengeance which her lively intellect invented in the most shocking forms. She had studied him too well not to dread him.

Would he murder her, she wondered? Would that bull-necked man dash out her vitals by flinging her over his head? Would he trample her body under his feet? When, where, and how would he get her into his power? Would he make her suffer very much, and what kind of pain would he in-flict? She repented of her conduct. There were hours when, if he had come, she would have gone to his arms in complete self-surrender.

Every night before she slept she saw Montriveau's face; every night it wore a different aspect. Sometimes she saw his bitter smile, sometimes the Jovelike knitting of the brows; or his leonine look, or some disdainful movement of the shoul-ders made him terrible for her. Next day the card seemed stained with blood. The name of Montriveau stirred her now as the presence of the fiery, stubborn, exacting lover had never done. Her apprehensions gathered strength in the silence. She was forced, without aid from without, to face the thought of a hideous duel of which she could not speak. Her proud hard nature was more responsive to thrills of hate than it had ever been to the caresses of love. Ah! if the General could but have seen her as she sat with her forehead drawn into folds between her brows; immersed in bitter thoughts in that boudoir where he had enjoyed such happy moments, he might perhaps have conceived high hopes. Of all human passions, is not pride alone incapable of engendering anything base? Mme. de Langeais kept her thoughts to herself, but is it not permissible to suppose that M. de Montriveau was no longer indifferent to her? And has not a man gained ground immensely when a woman thinks about him? He is bound to make progress with her either one way or the other afterwards.

Put any feminine creature under the feet of a furious horse or other fearsome beast; she will certainly drop on her knees and look for death: but if the brute shows a milder mood and does not utterly slay her, she will love the horse, lion, bull, or what not, and will speak of him quite at her ease. The Duchess felt that she was under the lion's paws; she quaked, but she did not hate him.

The man and woman thus singularly placed with regard to each other, met three times in society during the course of that week. Each time, in reply to coquettish questioning glances, the Duchess received a respectful bow, and smiles tinged with such savage irony, that all her apprehensions over the card in the morning were revived at night. Our lives are simply such as our feelings shape them for us; and the feelings of these two had hollowed out a great gulf between them.

The Comtesse de Sérizy, the Marquis de Ronquerolles' sister, gave a great ball at the beginning of the following week, and Mme. de Langeais was sure to go to it. Armand was the first person whom the Duchess saw when she came into the room, and this time Armand was looking out for her, or so she thought at least. The two exchanged a look, and suddenly the woman felt a cold perspiration break from every pore. She had thought all along that Montriveau was capable of taking reprisals in some unheard-of way proportioned to their conditions; and now the revenge had been discovered, it was ready, heated, and boiling. Lightnings flashed from the foiled lover's eyes, his face was radiant with exultant vengeance. And the Duchess? Her eyes were haggard in spite of her resolution to be cool and insolent. She went to take her place beside the Comtesse de Sérizy, who could not help exclaiming, "Dear Antoinette! what is the matter with you? You are enough to frighten one."

"I shall be all right after a quadrille," she answered, giving a hand to the young man who came up at that moment.

Mme. de Langeais waltzed that evening with a sort of excitement and transport which redoubled Montriveau's lowering looks. He stood in front of the line of spectators, who were amusing themselves by looking on. Every time that *she* came past him, his eyes darted down upon her eddying face; he might have been a tiger with the prey in his grasp. The waltz came to an end, Mme. de Langeais went back to her place beside the Countess, and Montriveau never took his eyes off her, talking all the while with a stranger.

"One of the things that struck me most on the journey," he was saying (and the Duchess listened with all her ears), "was the remark which the man makes at Westminster when you are shown the axe with which a man in a mask cut off Charles the First's head, so they tell you. The King made it first of all to some inquisitive person, and they repeat it still in memory of him."

"What does the man say?" asked Mme. de Sérizy.

"Do not touch the axe!" replied Montriveau, and there was menace in the sound of his voice.

"Really, my Lord Marquis," said Mme. de Langeais, "you tell this old story that everybody knows if they have been to London, and look at my neck in such a melodramatic way that you seem to me to have an axe in your hand."

The Duchess was in a cold sweat, but nevertheless she laughed as she spoke the last words.

"But circumstances give the story a quite new application," returned he.

"How so; pray tell me, for pity's sake?"

"In this way, madame—you have touched the axe," said Montriveau, lowering his voice.

"What an enchanting prophecy!" returned she, smiling with assumed grace. "And when is my head to fall?"

"I have no wish to see that pretty head of yours cut off. I only fear some great misfortune for you. If your head were clipped close, would you feel no regrets for the dainty golden hair that you turn to such good account?"

"There are those for whom a woman would love to make such a sacrifice; even if, as often happens, it is for the sake of a man who cannot make allowances for an outbreak of temper."

"Quite so. Well, and if some wag were to spoil your beauty on a sudden by some chemical process, and you, who are but eighteen for us, were to be a hundred years old?"

"Why, the small-pox is our battle of Waterloo, monsieur," she interrupted. "After it is over we find out those who love us sincerely."

"Would you not regret the lovely face that——?"

"Oh! indeed I should, but less for my own sake than for the sake of some one else whose delight it might have been. And, after all, if I were loved, always loved, and truly loved, what would my beauty matter to me?—What do you say, Clara?"

"It is a dangerous speculation," replied Mme. de Sérizy.

"Is it permissible to ask His Majesty the King of Sorcerers when I made the mistake of touching the axe, since I have not been to London as yet?——"

"*Not so,*" he answered in English, with a burst of ironical laughter.

"And when will the punishment begin?"

At this Montriveau coolly took out his watch, and ascertained the hour with a truly appalling air of conviction.

"A dreadful misfortune will befall you before this day is out."

"I am not a child to be easily frightened, or rather, I am a child ignorant of danger," said the Duchess. "I shall dance now without fear on the edge of the precipice."

"I am delighted to know that you have so much strength of character," he answered, as he watched her go to take her place in a square dance.

But the Duchess, in spite of her apparent contempt for Armand's dark prophecies, was really frightened. Her late lover's presence weighed upon her morally and physically with a sense of oppression that scarcely ceased when he left the ballroom. And yet when she had drawn freer breath, and enjoyed the relief for a moment, she found herself regretting the sensation of dread, so greedy of extreme sensations is the feminine nature. The regret was not love, but it was certainly akin to other feelings which prepare the way for love. And then—as if the impression which Montriveau had made upon her were suddenly revived—she recollected his air of conviction as he took out his watch, and in a sudden spasm of dread she went out.

By this time it was about midnight. One of her servants,

waiting with her pelisse, went down to order her carriage. On her way home she fell naturally enough to musing over M. de Montriveau's prediction. Arrived in her own court-yard, as she supposed, she entered a vestibule almost like that of her own hotel, and suddenly saw that the staircase was different. She was in a strange house. Turning to call her servants, she was attacked by several men, who rapidly flung a handkerchief over her mouth, bound her hand and foot, and carried her off. She shrieked aloud.

"Madame, our orders are to kill you if you scream," a voice said in her ear.

So great was the Duchess' terror, that she could never recollect how nor by whom she was transported. When she came to herself, she was lying on a couch in a bachelor's lodging, her hands and feet tied with silken cords. In spite of herself, she shrieked aloud as she looked round and met Armand de Montriveau's eyes. He was sitting in his dressing-gown, quietly smoking a cigar in his armchair.

"Do not cry out, Mme. la Duchesse," he said, coolly taking the cigar out of his mouth; "I have a headache. Besides, I will untie you. But listen attentively to what I have the honor to say to you."

Very carefully he untied the knots that bound her feet.

"What would be the use of calling out? Nobody can hear your cries. You are too well bred to make any unnecessary fuss. If you do not stay quietly, if you insist upon a struggle with me, I shall tie your hands and feet again. All things considered, I think that you have self-respect enough to stay on this sofa as if you were lying on your own at home; cold as ever, if you will. You have made me shed many tears on this couch, tears that I hid from all other eyes."

While Montriveau was speaking, the Duchess glanced about her; it was a woman's glance, a stolen look that saw all things and seemed to see nothing. She was much pleased with the room. It was rather like a monk's cell. The man's character and thoughts seemed to pervade it. No decoration of any kind broke the gray painted surface of the walls. A green

carpet covered the floor. A black sofa, a table littered with
papers, two big easy-chairs, a chest of drawers with an
alarm clock by way of ornament, a very low bedstead with a
coverlet flung over it—a red cloth with a black key border,—
all these things made part of a whole that told of a life reduced to its simplest terms. A triple candle sconce of
Egyptian design on the chimney-piece recalled the vast spaces
of the desert and Montriveau's long wanderings; a huge
sphinx-claw stood out beneath the folds of stuff at the bedfoot; and just beyond, a green curtain with a black and scarlet border was suspended by large rings from a spear handle
above a door near one corner of the room. The other door
by which the band had entered was likewise curtained, but
the drapery hung from an ordinary curtain-rod. As the
Duchess finally noted that the pattern was the same on both,
she saw that the door at the bedfoot stood open; gleams of
ruddy light from the room beyond flickered below the fringed
border. Naturally, the ominous light roused her curiosity;
she fancied she could distinguish strange shapes in the
shadows; but as it did not occur to her at the time that danger could come from that quarter, she tried to gratify a more
ardent curiosity.

"Monsieur, if it is not indiscreet, may I ask what you mean
to do with me?" The insolence and irony of the tone stung
through the words. The Duchess quite believed that she read
extravagant love in Montriveau's speech. He had carried her
off; was not that in itself an acknowledgment of her power?

"Nothing whatever, madame," he returned, gracefully puff-
ing the last whiff of cigar smoke. "You will remain here for
a short time. First of all, I should like to explain to you what
you are, and what I am. I cannot put my thoughts into words
whilst you are twisting on the sofa in your boudoir; and besides, in your own house you take offence at the slightest hint,
you ring the bell, make an outcry, and turn your lover out at
the door as if he were the basest of wretches. Here my mind
is unfettered. Here nobody can turn me out. Here you shall
be my victim for a few seconds, and you are going to be so

exceedingly kind as to listen to me. You need fear nothing.
I did not carry you off to insult you, nor yet to take by force
what you refused to grant of your own will to my unworthi-
ness. I could not stoop so low. You possibly think of out-
rage; for myself, I have no such thoughts."

He flung his cigar coolly into the fire.

"The smoke is unpleasant to you, no doubt, madame?" he
said, and rising at once, he took a chafing-dish from the
hearth, burned perfumes, and purified the air. The Duchess'
astonishment was only equaled by her humiliation. She was
in this man's power; and he would not abuse his power. The
eyes in which love had once blazed like flame were now quiet
and steady as stars. She trembled. Her dread of Armand
was increased by a nightmare sensation of restlessness and
utter inability to move; she felt as if she were turned to stone.
She lay passive in the grip of fear. She thought she saw the
light behind the curtains grow to a blaze, as if blown up by a
pair of bellows; in another moment the gleams of flame grew
brighter, and she fancied that three masked figures suddenly
flashed out; but the terrible vision disappeared so swiftly that
she took it for an optical illusion.

"Madame," Armand continued with cold contempt, "one
minute, just one minute is enough for me, and you shall feel
it afterwards at every moment throughout your lifetime, the
one eternity over which I have power. I am not God. Listen
carefully to me," he continued, pausing to add solemnity to
his words. "Love will always come at your call. You have
boundless power over men; but remember that once you called
love, and love came to you; love as pure and true-hearted as
may be on earth, and as reverent as it was passionate; fond as
a devoted woman's, as a mother's love; a love so great indeed,
that it was past the bounds of reason. You played with it,
and you committed a crime. Every woman has a right to
refuse herself to love which she feels she cannot share; and if
a man loves and cannot win love in return, he is not to be
pitied, he has no right to complain. But with a semblance of
love to attract an unfortunate creature cut off from all affec-

tion; to teach him to understand happiness to the full, only to snatch it from him; to rob him of his future of felicity; to slay his happiness not merely to-day, but as long as his life lasts, by poisoning every hour of it, and every thought—this I call a fearful crime!"

"Monsieur——"

"I cannot allow you to answer me yet. So listen to me still. In any case I have rights over you; but I only choose to exercise one—the right of the judge over the criminal, so that I may arouse your conscience. If you had no conscience left, I should not reproach you at all; but you are so young! You must feel some life still in your heart; or so I like to believe. While I think of you as depraved enough to do a wrong which the law does not punish, I do not think you so degraded that you cannot comprehend the full meaning of my words. I resume."

As he spoke the Duchess heard the smothered sound of a pair of bellows. Those mysterious figures which she had just seen were blowing up the fire, no doubt; the glow shone through the curtain. But Montriveau's lurid face was turned upon her; she could not choose but wait with a fast-beating heart and eyes fixed in a stare. However curious she felt, the heat in Armand's words interested her even more than the crackling of the mysterious flames.

"Madame," he went on after a pause, "if some poor wretch commits a murder in Paris, it is the executioner's duty, you know, to lay hands on him and stretch him on the plank, where murderers pay for their crimes with their heads. Then the newspapers inform every one, rich and poor, so that the former are assured that they may sleep in peace, and the latter are warned that they must be on the watch if they would live. Well, you that are religious, and even a little of a bigot, may have masses said for such a man's soul. You both belong to the same family, but yours is the elder branch; and the elder branch may occupy high places in peace and live happily and without cares. Want or anger may drive your brother the convict to take a man's life; you have taken more, you

have taken the joy out of a man's life, you have killed all that
was best in his life—his dearest beliefs. The murderer simply lay in wait for his victim, and killed him reluctantly, and
in fear of the scaffold; but *you* . . .! You heaped up
every sin that weakness can commit against strength that suspected no evil; you tamed a passive victim, the better to gnaw
his heart out; you lured him with caresses; you left nothing
undone that could set him dreaming, imagining, longing for
the bliss of love. You asked innumerable sacrifices of him,
only to refuse to make any in return He should see the light
indeed before you put out his eyes! It is wonderful how you
found the heart to do it! Such villainies demand a display
of resource quite above the comprehension of those bourgeoises
whom you laugh at and despise. They can give and forgive;
they know how to love and suffer. The grandeur of their devotion dwarfs us. Rising higher in the social scale, one finds
just as much mud as at the lower end; but with this difference, at the upper end it is hard and gilded over.

"Yes, to find baseness in perfection, you must look for a
noble bringing up, a great name, a fair woman, a Duchess.
You cannot fall lower than the lowest unless you are set high
above the rest of the world.—I express my thoughts badly;
the wounds you dealt me are too painful as yet, but do not
think that I complain. My words are not the expression of
any hope for myself; there is no trace of bitterness in them.
Know this, madame, for a certainty—I forgive you. My forgiveness is so complete that you need not feel in the least sorry
that you came hither to find it against your will. . . .
But you might take advantage of other hearts as childlike as
my own, and it is my duty to spare them anguish. So you
have inspired the thought of justice. Expiate your sin here
on earth; God may perhaps forgive you; I wish that He may,
but He is inexorable, and will strike."

The broken-spirited, broken-hearted woman looked up, her
eyes filled with tears.

"Why do you cry? Be true to your nature. You could
look on indifferently at the torture of a heart as you broke it.

That will do, madame, do not cry. I cannot bear it any longer. Other men will tell you that you have given them life; as for myself, I tell you, with rapture, that you have given me blank extinction. Perhaps you guess that I am not my own, that I am bound to live for my friends, that from this time forth I must endure the cold chill of death, as well as the burden of life? Is it possible that there can be so much kindness in you? Are you like the desert tigress that licks the wounds she has inflicted?"

The Duchess burst out sobbing.

"Pray, spare your tears, madame. If I believed in them at all, it would merely set me on my guard. Is this another of your artifices? or is it not? You have used so many with me; how can one think that there is any truth in you? Nothing that you do or say has any power now to move me. That is all I have to say."

Mme. de Langeais rose to her feet, with a great dignity and humility in her bearing.

"You are right to treat me very hardly," she said, holding out a hand to the man, who did not take it; "you have not spoken hardly enough; and I deserve this punishment."

"*I* punish you, madame! A man must love still, to punish, must he not? From me you must expect no feeling, nothing resembling it. If I chose, I might be accuser and judge in my cause, and pronounce and carry out the sentence. But I am about to fulfil a duty, not a desire of vengeance of any kind. The cruelest revenge of all, I think, is scorn of revenge when it is in our power to take it. Perhaps I shall be the minister of your pleasures; who knows? Perhaps from this time forth, as you gracefully wear the tokens of disgrace by which society marks out the criminal, you may perforce learn something of the convict's sense of honor. And then, you will love!"

The Duchess sat listening; her meekness was unfeigned; it was no coquettish device. When she spoke at last, it was after a silence.

"Armand," she began, "it seems to me that when I resisted

love, I was obeying all the instincts of woman's modesty; I should not have looked for such reproaches from *you*. I was weak; you have turned all my weaknesses against me, and made so many crimes of them. How could you fail to understand that the curiosity of love might have carried me further than I ought to go; and that next morning I might be angry with myself, and wretched because I had gone too far? Alas! I sinned in ignorance. I was as sincere in my wrongdoing, I swear to you, as in my remorse. There was far more love for you in my severity than in my concessions. And besides, of what do you complain? I gave you my heart; that was not enough; you demanded, brutally, that I should give my person——"

"Brutally?" repeated Montriveau. But to himself he said, "If I once allow her to dispute over words, I am lost."

"Yes. You came to me as if I were one of those women. You showed none of the respect, none of the attentions of love. Had I not reason to reflect? Very well, I reflected. The unseemliness of your conduct is not inexcusable; love lay at the source of it; let me think so, and justify you to myself. —Well, Armand, this evening, even while you were prophesying evil, I felt convinced that there was happiness in store for us both. Yes, I put my faith in the noble, proud nature so often tested and proved." She bent lower. "And I was yours wholly," she murmured in his ear. "I felt a longing that I cannot express to give happiness to a man so violently tried by adversity. If I must have a master, my master should be a great man. As I felt conscious of my height, the less I cared to descend. I felt I could trust you, I saw a whole lifetime of love, while you were pointing to death. . . . Strength and kindness always go together. My friend, you are so strong, you will not be unkind to a helpless woman who loves you. If I was wrong, is there no way of obtaining forgiveness? No way of making reparation? Repentance is the charm of love; I should like to be very charming for you. How could I, alone among women, fail to know a woman's doubts and fears, the timidity that it is so natural to feel when you bind yourself for life, and know how easily a man snaps such ties? The bourgeoises, with whom you compared me just now, give themselves, but they struggle first. Very well—I struggled; but here I am!—Ah! God, he does not hear me!" she broke off, and wringing her hands, she cried out, "But I love you! I am yours!" and fell at Armand's feet.

"Yours! yours! my one and only master!"

Armand tried to raise her.

"Madame, it is too late! Antoinette cannot save the Duchesse de Langeais. I cannot believe in either. To-day you may give yourself; to-morrow, you may refuse. No power in earth or heaven can insure me the sweet constancy of love. All love's pledges lay in the past; and now nothing of that past exists."

The light behind the curtain blazed up so brightly, that the Duchess could not help turning her head; this time she distinctly saw the three masked figures.

"Armand," she said, "I would not wish to think ill of you. Why are those men there? What are you going to do to me?"

"Those men will be as silent as I myself with regard to the thing which is about to be done. Think of them simply as my hands and my heart. One of them is a surgeon——"

"A surgeon! Armand, my friend, of all things, suspense is the hardest to bear. Just speak; tell me if you wish for my life; I will give it to you, you shall not take it——"

"Then you did not understand me? Did I not speak just now of justice? To put an end to your misapprehensions," continued he, taking up a small steel object from the table, "I will now explain what I have decided with regard to you."

He held out a Lorraine cross, fastened to the tip of a steel rod.

"Two of my friends at this very moment are heating another cross, made on this pattern, red-hot. We are going to stamp it upon your forehead, here between the eyes, so that there will be no possibility of hiding the mark with diamonds, and so avoiding people's questions. In short, you shall bear

on your forehead the brand of infamy which your brothers
the convicts wear on their shoulders. The pain is a mere
trifle, but I feared a nervous crisis of some kind, of resistance——"

"Resistance?" she cried, clapping her hands for joy. "Oh
no, no! I would have the whole world here to see. Ah, my
Armand, brand her quickly, this creature of yours; brand her
with your mark as a poor little trifle belonging to you. You
asked for pledges of my love; here they are all in one. Ah!
for me there is nothing but mercy and forgiveness and eternal
happiness in this revenge of yours. When you have marked
this woman with your mark, when you set your crimson brand
on her, your slave in soul, you can never afterwards abandon
her, you will be mine for evermore! When you cut me off
from my kind, you make yourself responsible for my happiness, or you prove yourself base; and I know that you are
noble and great! Why, when a woman loves, the brand of
love is burned into her soul by her own will.—Come in, gentlemen! come in and brand her, this Duchesse de Langeais. She
is M. de Montriveau's for ever! Ah! come quickly, all of you,
my forehead burns hotter than your fire!"

Armand turned his head sharply away lest he should see the
Duchess kneeling, quivering with the throbbings of her heart.
He said some word, and his three friends vanished.

The women of Paris salons know how one mirror reflects
another. The Duchess, with every motive for reading the
depths of Armand's heart, was all eyes; and Armand, all unsuspicious of the mirror, brushed away two tears as they fell.
Her whole future lay in those two tears. When he turned
round again to help her to rise, she was standing before him,
sure of love. Her pulses must have throbbed fast when he
spoke with the firmness she had known so well how to use of
old while she played with him.

"I spare you, madame. All that has taken place shall be as
if it had never been, you may believe me. But now, let us bid
each other good-bye. I like to think that you were sincere in
your coquetries on your sofa, sincere again in this outpouring

of your heart. Good-bye. I feel that there is no faith in you
left in me. You would torment me again; you would always
be the Duchess, and—— But there, good-bye, we shall never
understand each other.

"Now, what do you wish?" he continued, taking the tone of
a master of the ceremonies—"to return home, or to go back
to Mme. de Sérizy's ball? I have done all in my power to
prevent any scandal. Neither your servants nor any one else
can possibly know what has passed between us in the last quarter of an hour. Your servants have no idea that you have left
the ballroom; your carriage never left Mme. de Sérizy's
courtyard; your brougham may likewise be found in the court
of your own hôtel. Where do you wish to be?"

"What do you counsel, Armand?"

"There is no Armand now, Mme. la Duchesse. We are
strangers to each other."

"Then take me to the ball," she said, still curious to put
Armand's power to the test. "Thrust a soul that suffered in
the world, and must always suffer there, if there is no happiness for her now, down into hell again. And yet, oh my
friend, I love you as your bourgeoises love; I love you so that
I could come to you and fling my arms about your neck before
all the world if you asked it of me. The hateful world has
not corrupted me. I am young at least, and I have grown
younger still. I am a child, yes, your child, your new creature. Ah! do not drive me forth out of my Eden!"

Armand shook his head.

"Ah! let me take something with me, if I go, some little
thing to wear to-night on my heart," she said, taking possession of Armand's glove, which she twisted into her handkerchief

"No, I am *not* like all those depraved women. You do not
know the world, and so you cannot know my worth. You
shall know it now! There are women who sell themselves for
money; there are others to be gained by gifts, it is a vile
world! Oh, I wish I were a simple bourgeoise, a working girl,
if you would rather have a woman beneath you than a woman

whose devotion is accompanied by high rank, as men count it. Oh, my Armand, there are noble, high, and chaste and pure natures among us; and then they are lovely indeed. I would have all nobleness that I might offer it all up to you. Misfortune willed that I should be a duchess; I would I were a royal princess, that my offering might be complete. I would be a grisette for you, and a queen for every one besides."

He listened, damping his cigar with his lips.

"You will let me know when you'wish to go," he said.

"But I should like to stay——"

"That is another matter!"

"Stay, that was badly rolled," she cried, seizing on a cigar and devouring all that Armand's lips had touched.

"Do you smoke?"

"Oh, what would I not do to please you?"

"Very well. Go, madame."

"I will obey you," she answered, with tears in her eyes.

"You must be blindfolded; you must not see a glimpse of the way."

"I am ready, Armand," she said, bandaging her eyes.

"Can you see?"

"No."

Noiselessly he knelt before her.

"Ah! I can hear you!" she cried, with a little fond gesture, thinking that the pretence of harshness was over.

He made as if he would kiss her lips; she held up her face.

"You can see, madame."

"I am just a little bit curious."

"So you always deceive me?"

"Ah! take off this handkerchief, sir," she cried out, with the passion of a great generosity repelled with scorn, "lead me; I will not open my eyes."

Armand felt sure of her after that cry. He led the way; the Duchess, nobly true to her word, was blind. But while Montriveau held her hand as a father might, and led her up and down flights of stairs, he was studying the throbbing pulses of this woman's heart so suddenly invaded by Love.

Mme. de Langeais, rejoicing in this power of speech, was glad to let him know all; but he was inflexible; his hand was passive in reply to the questionings of her hand.

At length, after some journey made together, Armand bade her go forward; the opening was doubtless narrow, for as she went she felt that his hand protected her dress. His care touched her; it was a revelation surely that there was a little love still left; yet it was in some sort a farewell, for Montriveau left her without a word. The air was warm; the Duchess, feeling the heat, opened her eyes, and found herself standing by the fire in the Comtesse de Sérizy's boudoir. She was alone. Her first thought was for her disordered toilette; in a moment she had adjusted her dress and restored her picturesque coiffure.

"Well, dear Antoinette, we have been looking for you everywhere." It was the Comtesse de Sérizy who spoke as she opened the door.

"I came here to breathe," said the Duchess; "it is unbearably hot in the rooms."

"People thought that you had gone; but my brother Ronquerolles told me that your servants were waiting for you."

"I am tired out, dear, let me stay and rest here for a minute," and the Duchess sat down on the sofa.

"Why, what is the matter with you? You are shaking from head to foot!"

The Marquis de Ronquerolles came in.

"Mme. la Duchesse, I was afraid that something might have happened. I have just come across your coachman, the man is as tipsy as all the Swiss in Switzerland."

The Duchess made no answer; she was looking round the room, at the chimney-piece and the tall mirrors, seeking the trace of an opening. Then with an extraordinary sensation she recollected that she was again in the midst of the gaiety of the ballroom after that terrific scene which had changed the whole course of her life. She began to shiver violently.

"M. de Montriveau's prophecy has shaken my nerves," she said. "It was a joke, but still I will see whether his axe from

London will haunt me even in my sleep. So good-bye, dear.—
Good-bye, M. le Marquis."

As she went through the rooms she was beset with inquiries
and regrets. Her world seemed to have dwindled now that
she, its queen, had fallen so low, was so diminished. And
what, moreover, were these men compared with him whom she
loved with all her heart; with the man grown great by all that
she had lost in stature? The giant had regained the height
that he had lost for a while, and she exaggerated it perhaps
beyond measure. She looked, in spite of herself, at the servant who had attended her to the ball. He was fast asleep.

"Have you been here all the time?" she asked.

"Yes, madame."

As she took her seat in her carriage she saw, in fact, that
her coachman was drunk—so drunk, that at any other time
she would have been afraid; but after a great crisis in life,
fear loses its appetite for common food. She reached home,
at any rate, without accident; but even there she felt a change
in herself, a new feeling that she could not shake off. For
her, there was now but one man in the world; which is to say,
that henceforth she cared to shine for his sake alone.

While the physiologist can define love promptly by following out natural laws, the moralist finds a far more perplexing
problem before him if he attempts to consider love in all its
developments due to social conditions. Still, in spite of the
heresies of the endless sects that divide the church of Love,
there is one broad and trenchant line of difference in doctrine,
a line that all the discussion in the world can never deflect. A
rigid application of this line explains the nature of the crisis
through which the Duchess, like most women, was to pass.
Passion she knew, but she did not love as yet.

Love and passion are two different conditions which poets
and men of the world, philosophers and fools, alike continually confound. Love implies a give and take, a certainty of
bliss that nothing can change; it means so close a clinging
of the heart, and an exchange of happiness so constant, that
there is no room left for jealousy. Then possession is a means

and not an end; unfaithfulness may give pain, but the bond
is not less close; the soul is neither more nor less ardent or
troubled, but happy at every moment; in short, the divine
breath of desire spreading from end to end of the immensity
of Time steeps it all for us in the selfsame hue; life takes the
tint of the unclouded heaven. But Passion is the foreshadow-
ing of Love, and of that Infinite to which all suffering souls
aspire. Passion is a hope that may be cheated. Passion
means both suffering and transition. Passion dies out when
hope is dead. Men and women may pass through this experience many times without dishonor, for it is so natural to
spring towards happiness; but there is only one love in a lifetime. All discussions of sentiment ever conducted on paper
or by word of mouth may therefore be resumed by two questions—"Is it passion? Is it love?" So, since love comes into
existence only through the intimate experience of the bliss
which gives it lasting life, the Duchess was beneath the yoke of
passion as yet; and as she knew the fierce tumult, the unconscious calculations, the fevered cravings, and all that is meant
by that word *passion*—she suffered. Through all the trouble
of her soul there rose eddying gusts of tempest, raised by vanity or self-love, or pride or a high spirit; for all these forms
of egoism make common cause together.

She had said to this man, "I love you; I am yours!" Was
it possible that the Duchesse de Langeais should have uttered
those words—in vain? She must either be loved now or play
her part of queen no longer. And then she felt the loneliness
of the luxurious couch where pleasure had never yet set his
glowing feet; and over and over again, while she tossed and
writhed there, she said, "I want to be loved."

But the belief that she still had in herself gave her hope of
success. The Duchess might be piqued, the vain Parisienne
might be humiliated; but the woman saw glimpses of wedded
happiness, and imagination, avenging the time lost for nature, took a delight in kindling the inextinguishable fire in her
veins. She all but attained to the sensations of love; for
amid her poignant doubt whether she was loved in return, she

felt glad at heart to say to herself, "I love him!" As for her scruples, religion, and the world she could trample them under foot! Montriveau was her religion now. She spent the next day in a state of moral torpor, troubled by a physical unrest, which no words could express. She wrote letters and tore them all up, and invented a thousand impossible fancies.

When M. de Montriveau's usual hour arrived, she tried to think that he would come, and enjoyed the feeling of expectation. Her whole life was concentrated in the single sense of hearing. Sometimes she shut her eyes, straining her ears to listen through space, wishing that she could annihilate everything that lay between her and her lover, and so establish that perfect silence which sounds may traverse from afar. In her tense self-concentration, the ticking of the clock grew hateful to her; she stopped its ill-omened garrulity. The twelve strokes of midnight sounded from the drawing-room.

"Ah, God!" she cried, "to see him here would be happiness. And yet, it is not so very long since he came here, brought by desire, and tones of his voice filled this boudoir. And now there is nothing."

She remembered the times that she had played the coquette with him, and how that her coquetry had cost her her lover, and the despairing tears flowed for long.

Her woman came at length with, "Mme. la Duchesse does not know, perhaps, that it is two o'clock in the morning; I thought that madame was not feeling well."

"Yes, I am going to bed," said the Duchess, drying her eyes. "But remember, Suzanne, never to come in again without orders; I tell you this for the last time."

For a week, Mme. de Langeais went to every house where there was a hope of meeting M. de Montriveau. Contrary to her usual habits, she came early and went late; gave up dancing, and went to the card-tables. Her experiments were fruitless. She did not succeed in getting a glimpse of Armand. She did not dare to utter his name now. One evening, however, in a fit of despair, she spoke to Mme. de Sérizy, and asked as carelessly as she could, "You must have quarreled with M. de Montriveau? He is not to be seen at your house now."

The Countess laughed. "So he does not come here either?" she returned. "He is not to be seen anywhere, for that matter. He is interested in some woman, no doubt."

"I used to think that the Marquis de Ronquerolles was one of his friends——" the Duchess began sweetly.

"I have never heard my brother say that he was acquainted with him."

Mme. de Langeais did not reply. Mme. de Sérizy concluded from the Duchess' silence that she might apply the scourge with impunity to a discreet friendship which she had seen, with bitterness of soul, for a long time past.

"So you miss that melancholy personage, do you? I have heard most extraordinary things of him. Wound his feelings, he never comes back, he forgives nothing; and, if you love him, he keeps you in chains. To everything that I said of him, one of those that praise him sky-high would always answer, 'He knows how to love!' People are always telling me that Montriveau would give up all for his friend; that his is a great nature. Pooh! society does not want such tremendous natures. Men of that stamp are all very well at home; let them stay there and leave us to our pleasant littlenesses. What do you say, Antoinette?"

Woman of the world though she was, the Duchess seemed agitated, yet she replied in a natural voice that deceived her fair friend:

"I am sorry to miss him. I took a great interest in him, and promised to myself to be his sincere friend. I like great natures, dear friend, ridiculous though you may think it. To give oneself to a fool is a clear confession, is it not, that one is governed wholly by one's senses?"

Mme. de Sérizy's "preferences" had always been for commonplace men; her lover at the moment, the Marquis d'Aiglemont, was a fine, tall man.

After this, the Countess soon took her departure, you may be sure. Mme. de Langeais saw hope in Armand's withdrawal from the world; she wrote to him at once; it was a humble, gentle letter, surely it would bring him if he loved her still. She sent her footman with it next day. On the servant's return, she asked whether he had given the letter to M. de Montriveau himself, and could not restrain the movement of joy at the affirmative answer. Armand was in Paris! He stayed alone in his house; he did not go out into society! So she was loved! All day long she waited for an answer that never came. Again and again, when impatience grew unbearable, Antoinette found reasons for his delay. Armand felt embarrassed; the reply would come by post; but night came, and she could not deceive herself any longer. It was a dreadful day, a day of pain grown sweet, of intolerable heart-throbs, a day when the heart squanders the very forces of life in riot.

Next day she sent for an answer.

"M. le Marquis sent word that he would call on Mme. la Duchesse," reported Julien.

She fled lest her happiness should be seen in her face, and flung herself on her couch to devour her first sensations.

"He is coming!"

The thought rent her soul. And, in truth, woe unto those for whom suspense is not the most horrible time of tempest, while it increases and multiplies the sweetest joys; for they have nothing in them of that flame which quickens the images of things, giving to them a second existence, so that we cling as closely to the pure essence as to its outward and visible manifestation. What is suspense in love but a constant drawing upon an unfailing hope?—a submission to the terrible scourging of passion, while passion is yet happy, and disenchantment of reality has not set in. The constant putting forth of strength and longing, called suspense, is surely, to the human soul, as fragrance to the flower that breathes it forth. We soon leave the brilliant, unsatisfying colors of tulips and coreopsis, but we turn again and again to drink in the sweetness of orange-blossoms or volkameria—flowers compared separately, each in its own land, to a betrothed bride, full of love, made fair by the past and future.

The Duchess learned the joys of this new life of hers through the rapture with which she received the scourgings of love. As this change wrought in her, she saw other destinies before her, and a better meaning in the things of life. As she hurried to her dressing-room, she understood what studied adornment and the most minute attention to her toilet mean when these are undertaken for love's sake and not for vanity. Even now this making ready helped her to bear the long time of waiting. A relapse of intense agitation set in when she was dressed; she passed through nervous paroxysms brought on by the dreadful power which sets the whole mind in ferment. Perhaps that power is only a disease, though the pain of it is sweet. The Duchess was dressed and waiting at two o'clock in the afternoon. At half-past eleven that night M. de Montriveau had not arrived. To try to give an idea of the anguish endured by a woman who might be said to be the spoiled child of civilization, would be to attempt to say how many imaginings the heart can condense into one thought. As well endeavor to measure the forces expended by the soul in a sigh whenever the bell rang; to estimate the drain of life when a carriage rolled past without stopping, and left her prostrate.

"Can he be playing with me?" she said, as the clocks struck midnight.

She grew white; her teeth chattered; she struck her hands together and leaped up and crossed the boudoir, recollecting as she did so how often he had come thither without a summons. But she resigned herself. Had she not seen him grow pale, and start up under the stinging barbs of her irony? Then Mme. de Langeais felt the horror of the woman's appointed lot; a man's is the active part, a woman must wait passively when she loves. If a woman goes beyond her beloved, she makes a mistake which few men can forgive; almost every man would feel that a woman lowers herself by this piece of angelic flattery. But Armand's was a great nature; he surely must be one of the very few who can repay such exceeding love by love that lasts for ever.

"Well, I will make the advance," she told herself, as she tossed on her bed and found no sleep there; "I will go to him. I will not weary myself with holding out a hand to him, but I will hold it out. A man of a thousand will see a promise of love and constancy in every step that a woman takes towards him. Yes, the angels must come down from heaven to reach men; and I wish to be an angel for him."

Next day she wrote. It was a billet of the kind in which the intellects of the ten thousand Sévignés that Paris now can number particularly excel. And yet only a Duchesse de Langeais, brought up by Mme. la Princesse de Blamont-Chauvry, could have written that delicious note; no other woman could complain without lowering herself; could spread wings in such a flight without draggling her pinions in humiliation; rise gracefully in revolt; scold without giving offence; and pardon without compromising her personal dignity.

Julien went with the note. Julien, like his kind, was the victim of love's marches and countermarches.

"What did M. de Montriveau reply?" she asked, as indifferently as she could, when the man came back to report himself.

"M. le Marquis requested me to tell Mme. la Duchesse that it was all right."

Oh the dreadful reaction of the soul upon herself! To have her heart stretched on the rack before curious witnesses; yet not to utter a sound, to be forced to keep silence! One of the countless miseries of the rich!

More than three weeks went by. Mme. de Langeais wrote again and again, and no answer came from Montriveau. At last she gave out that she was ill, to gain a dispensation from attendance on the Princess and from social duties. She was only at home to her father the Duc de Navarreins, her aunt the Princesse de Blamont-Chauvry, the old Vidame de Pamiers (her maternal great-uncle), and to her husband's uncle, the Duc de Grandlieu. These persons found no difficulty in believing that the Duchess was ill, seeing that she grew thinner and paler and more dejected every day. The vague ardor of love, the smart of wounded pride, the continual prick of the only scorn that could touch her, the yearnings towards joy that she craved with a vain continual longing—all these things told upon her, mind and body; all the forces of her nature were stimulated to no purpose. She was paying the arrears of her life of make-believe.

She went out at last to a review. M. de Montriveau was to be there. For the Duchess, on the balcony of the Tuileries with the Royal Family, it was one of those festival days that are long remembered. She looked supremely beautiful in her languor; she was greeted with admiration in all eyes. It was Montriveau's presence that made her so fair. Once or twice they exchanged glances. The General came almost to her feet in all the glory of that soldier's uniform, which produces an effect upon the feminine imagination to which the most prudish will confess. When a woman is very much in love, and has not seen her lover for two months, such a swift moment must be something like the phase of a dream when the eyes embrace a world that stretches away for ever. Only women or young men can imagine the dull, frenzied hunger in the Duchess' eyes. As for older men, if during the paroxysms of early passion in youth they had experience of such phenomena of nervous power; at a later day it is so completely forgotten that they deny the very existence of the luxuriant ecstasy—the only name that can be given to these wonderful intuitions. Religious ecstasy is the aberration of a soul that has shaken off its bonds of flesh; whereas in amorous ecstasy all the forces of soul and body are embraced and blended in one. If a woman falls a victim to the tyrannous frenzy before which Mme. de Langeais was forced to bend, she will take one decisive resolution after another so swiftly that it is impossible to give account of them. Thought after thought rises and flits across her brain, as clouds are whirled by the wind across the gray veil of mist that shuts out the sun. Thenceforth the facts reveal all. And the facts are these.

The day after the review, Mme. de Langeais sent her carriage and liveried servants to wait at the Marquis de Montri-

veau's door from eight o'clock in the morning till three in the
afternoon. Armand lived in the Rue de Tournon, a few steps
away from the Chamber of Peers, and that very day the
House was sitting; but long before the peers returned to their
palaces, several people had recognized the Duchess' carriage
and liveries. The first of these was the Baron de Maulincour.
That young officer had met with disdain from Mme. de
Langeais and a better reception from Mme. de Sérizy; he betook himself at once therefore to his mistress, and under seal
of secrecy told her of this strange freak.

In a moment the news was spread with telegraphic speed
through all the coteries in the Faubourg Saint-Germain; it
reached the Tuileries and the Élysée-Bourbon; it was the
sensation of the day, the matter of all the talk from noon till
night. Almost everywhere the women denied the facts, but
in such a manner that the report was confirmed; the men one
and all believed it, and manifested a most indulgent interest
in Mme. de Langeais. Some among them threw the blame on
Armand.

"That savage of a Montriveau is a man of bronze," said
they; "he insisted on making this scandal, no doubt."

"Very well, then," others replied, "Mme. de Langeais has
been guilty of a most generous piece of imprudence. To renounce the world, and rank, and fortune, and consideration
for her lover's sake, and that in the face of all Paris, is as fine
a *coup d'état* for a woman as that barber's knife-thrust, which
so affected Canning in a court of assize. Not one of the women who blame the Duchess would make a declaration worthy
of ancient times. It is heroic of Mme. de Langeais to proclaim herself so frankly. Now there is nothing left to her
but to love Montriveau. There must be something great about
a woman if she says, 'I will have but one passion.'"

"But what is to become of society, monsieur, if you honor
vice in this way without respect for virtue?" asked the Comtesse de Granville, the attorney-general's wife.

While the Château, the Faubourg, and the Chausée d'Antin
were discussing the shipwreck of aristocratic virtue; while ex-

cited young men rushed about on horseback to make sure that
the carriage was standing in the Rue de Tournon, and the
Duchess in consequence was beyond a doubt in M. de Montriveau's rooms, Mme. de Langeais, with heavy throbbing
pulses, was lying hidden away in her boudoir. And Armand?
—he had been out all night, and at that moment was walking with M. de Marsay in the Gardens of the Tuileries. The
elder members of Mme. de Langeais' family were engaged in
calling upon one another, arranging to read her a homily
and to hold a consultation as to the best way of putting a stop
to the scandal.

At three o'clock, therefore, M. le Duc de Navarreins, the
Vidame de Pamiers, the old Princesse de Blamont-Chauvry,
and the Duc de Grandlieu were assembled in Mme. la
Duchesse de Langeais' drawing-room.   To them, as to all
curious inquirers, the servants said that their mistress was
not at home; the Duchess had made no exceptions to her orders.   But these four personages shone conspicuous in that
lofty sphere, of which the revolutions and hereditary pretensions are solemnly recorded year by year in the *Almanach de
Gotha,* wherefore without some slight sketch of each of them
this picture of society were incomplete.

The Princesse de Blamont-Chauvry, in the feminine world,
was a most poetic wreck of the reign of Louis Quinze.   In
her beautiful prime, so it was said, she had done her part to
win for that monarch his appellation of *le Bien-aimé.*   Of her
past charms of feature, little remained save a remarkably
prominent slender nose, curved like a Turkish scimitar, now
the principal ornament of a countenance that put you in mind
of an old white glove.   Add a few powdered curls, high-heeled
pantoufles, a cap with upstanding loops of lace, black mit-
tens, and a decided taste for *ombre.*   But to do full justice to
the lady, it must be said that she appeared in low-necked
gowns of an evening (so high an opinion of her ruins had
she), wore long gloves, and raddled her cheeks with Martin's
classic rouge.   An appalling amiability in her wrinkles, a
prodigious brightness in the old lady's eyes, a profound dig-

nity in her whole person, together with the triple barbed wit of her tongue, and an infallible memory in her head, made of her a real power in the land. The whole Cabinet des Chartes was entered in duplicate on the parchment of her brain. She knew all the genealogies of every noble house in Europe—princes, dukes, and counts—and could put her hand on the last descendants of Charlemagne in the direct line. No usurpation of title could escape the Princesse de Blamont-Chauvry.

Young men who wished to stand well at Court, ambitious men, and young married women paid her assiduous homage. Her salon set the tone of the Faubourg Saint-Germain. The words of this Talleyrand in petticoats were taken as final decrees. People came to consult her on questions of etiquette or usages, or to take lessons in good taste. And, in truth, no other old woman could put back her snuff-box in her pocket as the Princess could; while there was a precision and a grace about the movements of her skirts, when she sat down or crossed her feet, which drove the finest ladies of the young generation to despair. Her voice had remained in her head during one-third of her lifetime; but she could not prevent a descent into the membranes of the nose, which lent to it a peculiar expressiveness. She still retained a hundred and fifty thousand livres of her great fortune, for Napoleon had generously returned her woods to her; so that personally and in the matter of possessions she was a woman of no little consequence.

This curious antique, seated in a low chair by the fireside, was chatting with the Vidame de Pamiers, a contemporary ruin. The Vidame was a big, tall, and spare man, a *seigneur* of the old school, and had been a Commander of the Order of Malta. His neck had always been so tightly compressed by a strangulation stock, that his cheeks pouched over it a little, and he held his head high; to many people this would have given an air of self-sufficiency, but in the Vidame it was justified by a Voltairean wit. His wide prominent eyes seemed to see everything, and as a matter of fact there was not much

that they had not seen. Altogether, his person was a perfect
model of aristocratic outline, slim and slender, supple and
agreeable. He seemed as if he could be pliant or rigid at will,
and twist and bend, or rear his head like a snake.

The Duc de Navarreins was pacing up and down the room
with the Duc de Grandlieu. Both were men of fifty-six or
thereabouts, and still hale; both were short, corpulent, flour-
ishing, somewhat florid-complexioned men with jaded eyes,
and lower lips that had begun to hang already. But for an exquisite refinement of accent, an urbane courtesy, and an ease
of manner that could change in a moment to insolence, a
superficial observer might have taken them for a couple of
bankers. Any such mistake would have been impossible, however, if the listener could have heard them converse, and seen
them on their guard with men whom they feared, vapid and
commonplace with their equals, slippery with the inferiors
whom courtiers and statesmen know how to tame by a tactful
word, or to humiliate with an unexpected phrase.

Such were the representatives of the great noblesse that determined to perish rather than submit to any change. It was
a noblesse that deserved praise and blame in equal measure;
a noblesse that will never be judged impartially until some
poet shall rise to tell how joyfully the nobles obeyed the King
though their heads fell under a Richelieu's axe, and how
deeply they scorned the guillotine of '89 as a foul revenge.

Another noticeable trait in all the four was a thin voice that
agreed peculiarly well with their ideas and bearing. Among
themselves, at any rate, they were on terms of perfect equality. None of them betrayed any sign of annoyance over the
Duchess' escapade, but all of them had learned at Court to
hide their feelings.

And here, lest critics should condemn the puerility of the
opening of the forthcoming scene, it is perhaps as well to remind the reader that Locke, once happening to be in the company of several great lords, renowned no less for their wit than
for their breeding and political consistency, wickedly amused
himself by taking down their conversation by some shorthand

process of his own; and afterwards, when he read it over to them to see what they could make of it, they all burst out laughing. And, in truth, the tinsel jargon which circulates among the upper ranks in every country yields mighty little gold to the crucible when washed in the ashes of literature or philosophy. In every rank of society (some few Parisian salons excepted) the curious observer finds folly a constant quantity beneath a more or less transparent varnish. Conversation with any substance in it is a rare exception, and bœotianism is current coin in every zone. In the higher regions they must perforce talk more, but to make up for it they think the less. Thinking is a tiring exercise, and the rich like their lives to flow by easily and without effort. It is by comparing the fundamental matter of jests, as you rise in the social scale from the street-boy to the peer of France, that the observer arrives at a true comprehension of M. de Talleyrand's maxim, "The manner is everything;" an elegant rendering of the legal axiom, "The form is of more consequence than the matter." In the eyes of the poet the advantage rests with the lower classes, for they seldom fail to give a certain character of rude poetry to their thoughts. Perhaps also this same observation may explain the sterility of the salons, their emptiness, their shallowness, and the repugnance felt by men of ability for bartering their ideas for such pitiful small change.

The Duke suddenly stopped as if some bright idea occurred to him, and remarked to his neighbor:

"So you have sold Tornthon?"

"No, he is ill. I am very much afraid I shall lose him, and I should be uncommonly sorry. He is a very good hunter. Do you know how the Duchesse de Marigny is?"

"No. I did not go this morning. I was just going out to call when you came in to speak about Antoinette. But yesterday she was very ill indeed; they had given her up, she took the sacrament."

"Her death will make a change in your cousin's position."

"Not at all. She gave away her property in her lifetime,

only keeping an annuity. She made over the Guébriant estate
to her niece, Mme. de Soulanges, subject to a yearly charge."

"It will be a great loss for society. She was a kind woman.
Her family will miss her; her experience and advice carried
weight. Her son Marigny is an amiable man; he has a sharp
wit, he can talk. He is pleasant, very pleasant. Pleasant? oh,
that no one can deny, but—ill regulated to the last degree.
Well, and yet it is an extraordinary thing, he is very acute.
He was dining at the club the other day with that moneyed
Chaussée-d'Antin set. Your uncle (he always goes there for
his game of cards) found him there to his astonishment, and
asked if he was a member. 'Yes,' said he, 'I don't go into
society now; I am living among the bankers.'—You know
why," added the Marquis, with a meaning smile.

"No," said the Duke.

"He is smitten with that little Mme. Keller, Gondreville's
daughter; she is only lately married, and has a great vogue,
they say, in that set."

"Well, Antoinette does not find time heavy on her hands,
it seems," remarked the Vidame.

"My affection for that little woman has driven me to find
a singular pastime," replied the Princess, as she returned her
snuff-box to her pocket.

"Dear aunt, I am extremely vexed," said the Duke, stopping short in his walk. "Nobody but one of Bonaparte's men
could ask such an indecorous thing of a woman of fashion.
Between ourselves, Antoinette might have made a better
choice."

"The Montriveaus are a very old family and very well connected, my dear," replied the Princess; "they are related to all
the noblest houses of Burgundy. If the Dulmen branch of
the Arschoot Rivaudoults should come to an end in Galicia,
the Montriveaus would succeed to the Arschoot title and estates. They inherit through their great-grandfather."

"Are you sure?"

"I know it better than this Montriveau's father did. I
told him about it, I used to see a good deal of him; and, Chev-

alier of several orders though he was, he only laughed; he was
an encyclopædist. But his brother turned the relationship
to good account during the emigration. I have heard it said
that his northern kinsfolk were most kind in every way——"

"Yes, to be sure The Comte de Montriveau died at St.
Petersburg," said the Vidame. "I met him there. He was a
big man with an incredible passion for oysters."

"How ever many did he eat?" asked the Duc de Grandlieu.

"Ten dozen every day."

"And did they not disagree with him?"

"Not the least bit in the world."

"Why, that is extraordinary! Had he neither the stone nor
gout, nor any other complaint, in consequence?"

"No; his health was perfectly good, and he died through
an accident."

"By accident! Nature prompted him to eat oysters, so
probably he required them; for up to a certain point our pre-
dominant tastes are conditions of our existence."

"I am of your opinion," said the Princess, with a smile.

"Madame, you always put a malicious construction on
things," returned the Marquis.

"I only want you to understand that these remarks might
leave a wrong impression on a young woman's mind," said
she, and interrupted herself to exclaim, "But this niece, this
niece of mine!"

"Dear aunt, I still refuse to believe that she can have gone
to M. de Montriveau," said the Duc de Navarreins.

"Bah!" returned the Princess.

"What do you think, Vidame?" asked the Marquis.

"If the Duchess were an artless simpleton, I should think
that——"

"But when a woman is in love she becomes an artless simpleton," retorted the Princess. "Really, my poor Vidame,
you must be getting older."

"After all, what is to be done?" asked the Duke.

"If my dear niece is wise," said the Princess, "she will go
to Court this evening—fortunately, to-day is Monday, and re-

ception day—and you must see that we all rally round her and give the lie to this absurd rumor. There are hundreds of ways of explaining things; and if the Marquis de Montriveau is a gentleman, he will come to our assistance. We will bring these children to listen to reason——"

"But, dear aunt, it is not easy to tell M. de Montriveau the truth to his face. He is one of Bonaparte's pupils, and he has a position. Why, he is one of the great men of the day; he is high up in the Guards, and very useful there. He has not a spark of ambition. He is just the man to say, 'Here is my commission, leave me in peace,' if the King should say a word that he did not like."

"Then, pray, what are his opinions?"

"Very unsound."

"Really," sighed the Princess, "the King is, as he always has been, a Jacobin under the Lilies of France."

"Oh! not quite so bad," said the Vidame.

"Yes; I have known him for a long while. The man that pointed out the Court to his wife on the occasion of her first state dinner in public with, 'These are our people,' could only be a black-hearted scoundrel. I can see Monsieur exactly the same as ever in the King. The bad brother who voted so wrongly in his department of the Constituent Assembly was sure to compound with the Liberals and allow them to argue and talk. This philosophical cant will be just as dangerous now for the younger brother as it used to be for the elder; this fat man with the little mind is amusing himself by creating difficulties, and how his successor is to get out of them I do not know; he holds his younger brother in abhorrence; he would be glad to think as he lay dying, 'He will not reign very long——' "

"Aunt, he is the King, and I have the honor to be in his service——"

"But does your post take away your right of free speech, my dear? You come of quite as good a house as the Bourbons. If the Guises had shown a little more resolution, His Majesty would be a nobody at this day. It is time I went out of this world, the noblesse is dead. Yes, it is all over with you, my children," she continued, looking as she spoke at the Vidame. "What has my niece done that the whole town should be talking about her? She is in the wrong; I disapprove of her conduct, a useless scandal is a blunder; that is why I still have my doubts about this want of regard for appearances; I brought her up, and I know that——"

Just at that moment the Duchess came out of her boudoir. She had recognized her aunt's voice and heard the name of Montriveau. She was still in her loose morning-gown; and even as she came in, M. de Grandlieu, looking carelessly out of the window, saw his niece's carriage driving back along the street. The Duke took his daughter's face in both hands and kissed her on the forehead. "So, dear girl," he said, "you do not know what is going on?"

"Has anything extraordinary happened, father dear?"

"Why, all Paris believes that you are with M. de Montriveau.

"My dear Antoinette, you were at home all the time, were you not?" said the Princess, holding out a hand, which the Duchess kissed with affectionate respect.

"Yes, dear mother; I was at home all the time. And," she added, as she turned to greet the Vidame and the Marquis, "I wished that all Paris should think that I was with M. de Montriveau."

The Duke flung up his hands, struck them together in despair, and folded his arms.

"Then, cannot you see what will come of this mad freak?" he asked at last.

But the aged Princess had suddenly risen, and stood looking steadily at the Duchess; the younger woman flushed, and her eyes fell. Mme. de Chauvry gently drew her closer, and said, "My little angel, let me kiss you!"

She kissed her niece very affectionately on the forehead, and continued smiling, while she held her hand in a tight clasp.

"We are not under the Valois now, dear child. You have

compromised your husband and your position. Still, we will arrange to make everything right."

"But, dear aunt, I do not wish to make it right at all. It is my wish that all Paris should say that I was with M. de Montriveau this morning. If you destroy that belief, however ill grounded it may be, you will do me a singular disservice."

"Do you really wish to ruin yourself, child, and to grieve your family?"

"My family, father, unintentionally condemned me to irreparable misfortune when they sacrificed me to family considerations. You may, perhaps, blame me for seeking alleviations, but you will certainly feel for me."

"After all the endless pains you take to settle your daughters suitably!" muttered M. de Navarreins, addressing the Vidame.

The Princess shook a stray grain of snuff from her skirts. "My dear little girl," she said, "be happy, if you can. We are not talking of troubling your felicity, but of reconciling it with social usages. We all of us here assembled know that marriage is a defective institution tempered by love. But when you take a lover, is there any need to make your bed in the Place du Carrousel? See now, just be a bit reasonable, and hear what we have to say."

"I am listening."

"Mme. la Duchesse," began the **Duc** de Grandlieu, "if it were any part of an uncle's duty to look after his nieces, he ought to have a position; society would owe him honors and rewards and a salary, exactly as if he were in the King's service. So I am not here to talk about my nephew, but of your own interests. Let us look ahead a little. If you persist in making a scandal—I have seen the animal before, and I own that I have no great liking for him—Langeais is stingy enough, and he does not care a rap for any one but himself; he will have a separation; he will stick to your money, and leave you poor, and consequently you will be a nobody. The income of a hundred thousand livres that you have just inherited from your

maternal great-aunt will go to pay for his mistress' amusements. You will be bound and gagged by the law; you will
have to say Amen to all these arrangements. Suppose M. de
Montriveau leaves you—dear me! do not let us put ourselves
in a passion, my dear niece; a man does not leave a woman
while she is young and pretty; still, we have seen so many
pretty women left disconsolate, even among princesses, that
you will permit the supposition, an all but impossible supposition I quite wish to believe—— Well, suppose that he goes,
what will become of you without a husband? Keep well with
your husband as you take care of your beauty; for beauty,
after all, is a woman's parachute, and a husband also stands
between you and worse. I am supposing that you are happy
and loved to the end, and I am leaving unpleasant or unfortunate events altogether out of the reckoning. This being so,
fortunately or unfortunately, you may have children. What
are they to be? Montriveaus? Very well; they certainly will
not succeed to their father's whole fortune. You will want to
give them all that you have; he will wish to do the same.
Nothing more natural, dear me! And you will find the law
against you. How many times have we seen heirs-at-law
bringing a lawsuit to recover the property from illegitimate
children? Every court of law rings with such actions all over
the world. You will create a *fidei commissum* perhaps; and
if the trustee betrays your confidence, your children have no
remedy against him; and they are ruined. So choose
carefully. You see the perplexities of the position.
In every possible way your children will be sacrificed
of necessity to the fancies of your heart; they will have
no recognized status. While they are little they will be
charming; but, Lord! some day they will reproach you for
thinking of no one but your two selves. We old gentlemen
know all about it. Little boys grow up into men, and men
are ungrateful beings. When I was in Germany, did I not
hear young de Horn say, after supper, 'If my mother had been
an honest woman, I should be prince-regnant!' 'If?' We
have spent our lives in hearing plebeians say *if*. *If* brought

about the Revolution. When a man cannot lay the blame on his father or mother, he holds God responsible for his hard lot. In short, dear child, we are here to open your eyes. I will say all I have to say in a few words, on which you had better meditate: A woman ought never to put her husband in the right."

"Uncle, so long as I cared for nobody, I could calculate; I looked at interests then, as you do; now, I can only feel."

"But, my dear little girl," remonstrated the Vidame, "life is simply a complication of interests and feelings; to be happy, more particularly in your position, one must try to reconcile one's feelings with one's interests. A grisette may love according to her fancy, that is intelligible enough, but you have a pretty fortune, a family, a name and a place at Court, and you ought not to fling them out of the window. And what have we been asking you to do to keep them all?—To manœuvre carefully instead of falling foul of social conventions. Lord! I shall very soon be eighty years old, and I cannot recollect, under any régime, a love worth the price that you are willing to pay for the love of this lucky young man."

The Duchess silenced the Vidame with a look; if Montriveau could have seen that glance, he would have forgiven all.

"It would be very effective on the stage," remarked the Duc de Grandlieu, "but it all amounts to nothing when your jointure and position and independence is concerned. You are not grateful, my dear niece. You will not find many families where the relatives have courage enough to teach the wisdom gained by experience, and to make rash young heads listen to reason. Renounce your salvation in two minutes, if it pleases you to damn yourself; well and good; but reflect well beforehand when it comes to renouncing your income. I know of no confessor who remits the pains of poverty. I have a right, I think, to speak in this way to you; for if you are ruined, I am the one person who can offer you a refuge. I am almost an uncle to Langeais, and I alone have a right to put him in the wrong."

The Duc de Navarreins roused himself from painful reflections.

"Since you speak of feeling, my child," he said, "let me remind you that a woman who bears your name ought to be moved by sentiments which do not touch ordinary people. Can you wish to give an advantage to the Liberals, to those Jesuits of Robespierre's that are doing all they can to vilify the noblesse? Some things a Navarreins cannot do without failing in duty to his house. You would not be alone in your dishonor——"

"Come, come!" said the Princess. "Dishonor? Do not make such a fuss about the journey of an empty carriage, children, and leave me alone with Antoinette. All three of you come and dine with me. I will undertake to arrange matters suitably. You men understand nothing; you are beginning to talk sourly already, and I have no wish to see a quarrel between you and my dear child. Do me the pleasure to go."

The three gentlemen probably guessed the Princess' intentions; they took their leave. M. de Navarreins kissed his daughter on the forehead with, "Come, be good, dear child. It is not too late yet if you choose."

"Couldn't we find some good fellow in the family to pick a quarrel with this Montriveau?" said the Vidame, as they went downstairs.

When the two women were alone, the Princess beckoned her niece to a little low chair by her side.

"My pearl," said she, "in this world below, I know nothing worse calumniated than God and the Eighteenth Century; for as I look back over my own young days, I do not recollect that a single duchess trampled the proprieties under foot as you have just done. Novelists and scribblers brought the reign of Louis XV. into disrepute. Do not believe them. The du Barry, my dear, was quite as good as the Widow Scarron, and the more agreeable woman of the two. In my time a woman could keep her dignity among her gallantries. Indiscretion was the ruin of us, and the beginning of all the mis-

chief. The philosophists—the nobodies whom we admitted
into our salons—had no more gratitude or sense of decency
than to make an inventory of our hearts, to traduce us one
and all, and to rail against the age by way of a return for our
kindness. The people are not in a position to judge of anything whatsoever; they looked at the facts, not at the form.
But the men and women of those times, my heart, were quite
as remarkable as at any other period of the Monarchy. Not
one of your Werthers, none of your notabilities, as they are
called, never a one of your men in yellow kid gloves and trousers that disguise the poverty of their legs, would cross
Europe in the dress of a traveling hawker to brave the daggers of a Duke of Modena, and to shut himself up in the dressing-room of the Regent's daughter at the risk of his life. Not
one of your little consumptive patients with their tortoise-
shell eyeglasses would hide himself in a closet for six weeks,
like Lauzun, to keep up his mistress' courage while she was
lying in of her child. There was more passion in M. de Jau-
court's little finger than in your whole race of higglers that
leave a woman to better themselves elsewhere! Just tell me
where to find the page that would be cut in pieces and buried
under the floor boards for one kiss on the Königsmark's
gloved finger!

"Really, it would seem to-day that the rôles are exchanged,
and women are expected to show their devotion for men.
These modern gentlemen are worth less, and think more of
themselves. Believe me, my dear, all these adventures that
have been made public, and now are turned against our good
Louis XV., were kept quite secret at first. If it had not been
for a pack of poetasters, scribblers, and moralists, who hung
about our waiting-women, and took down their slanders, our
epoch would have appeared in literature as a well-conducted
age. I am justifying the century and not its fringe. Perhaps a hundred women of quality were lost; but for every one,
the rogues set down ten, like the gazettes after a battle when
they count up the losses of the beaten side. And in any case
I do not know that the Revolution and the Empire can re-

proach us; they were coarse, dull, licentious times. Faugh!
it is revolting. Those are the brothels of French history.

"This preamble, my dear child," she continued after a
pause, "brings me to the thing that I have to say. If you
care for Montriveau, you are quite at liberty to love him at
your ease, and as much as you can. I know by experience that,
unless you are locked up (but locking people up is out of
fashion now), you will do as you please; I should have done
the same at your age. Only, sweetheart, I should not have
given up my right to be the mother of future Ducs de Langeais. So mind appearances. The Vidame is right. No man is
worth a single one of the sacrifices which we are foolish
enough to make for their love. Put yourself in such a position that you may still be M. de Langeais' wife, in case you
should have the misfortune to repent. When you are an old
woman, you will be very glad to hear mass said at Court, and
not in some provincial convent. Therein lies the whole question. A single imprudence means an allowance and a wandering life; it means that you are at the mercy of your lover; it
means that you must put up with insolence from women that
are not so honest, precisely because they have been very vul-
garly sharp-witted. It would be a hundred times better to go
to Montriveau's at night in a cab, and disguised, instead of
sending your carriage in broad daylight. You are a little
fool, my dear child! Your carriage flattered his vanity; your
person would have ensnared his heart. All this that I have
said is just and true; but, for my own part, I do not blame
you. You are two centuries behind the times with your false
ideas of greatness. There, leave us to arrange your affairs,
and say that Montriveau made your servants drunk to gratify
his vanity and to compromise you——"

The Duchess rose to her feet with a spring. "In Heaven's
name, aunt, do not slander him!"

The old Princess' eyes flashed.

"Dear child," she said, "I should have liked to spare such
of your illusions as were not fatal. But there must be an end
of all illusions now. You would soften me if I were not so

old. Come, now, do not vex him, or us, or any one else. I will undertake to satisfy everybody; but promise me not to permit yourself a single step henceforth until you have consulted me. Tell me all, and perhaps I may bring it all right again."

"Aunt, I promise——"

"To tell me everything?"

"Yes, everything. Everything that can be told."

"But, my sweetheart, it is precisely what cannot be told that I want to know. Let us understand each other thoroughly. Come, let me put my withered old lips on your beautiful forehead. No; let me do as I wish. I forbid you to kiss my bones. Old people have a courtesy of their own. . . . There, take me down to my carriage," she added, when she had kissed her niece.

"Then may I go to him in disguise, dear aunt?"

"Why—yes. The story can always be denied," said the old Princess.

This was the one idea which the Duchess had clearly grasped in the sermon. When Mme. de Chauvry was seated in the corner of her carriage, Mme. de Langeais bade her a graceful adieu and went up to her room. She was quite happy again.

"My person would have snared his heart; my aunt is right; a man cannot surely refuse a pretty woman when she understands how to offer herself."

That evening, at the Élysée-Bourbon, the Duc de Navarreins, M. de Pamiers, M. de Marsay, M. de Grandlieu, and the Duc de Maufrigneuse triumphantly refuted the scandals that were circulating with regard to the Duchesse de Langeais. So many officers and other persons had seen Montriveau walking in the Tuileries that morning, that the silly story was set down to chance, which takes all that is offered. And so, in spite of the fact that the Duchess' carriage had waited before Montriveau's door, her character became as clear and as spotless as Membrino's sword after Sancho had polished it up.

But, at two o'clock, M. de Ronquerolles passed Montriveau in a deserted alley, and said with a smile, "She is coming on, is your Duchess. Go on, keep it up!" he added, and gave a significant cut of the riding whip to his mare, who sped off like a bullet down the avenue.

Two days after the fruitless scandal, Mme. de Langeais wrote to M. de Montriveau. That letter, like the preceding ones, remained unanswered. This time she took her own measures, and bribed M. de Montriveau's man, Auguste. And so at eight o'clock that evening she was introduced into Armand's apartment. It was not the room in which that secret scene had passed; it was entirely different. The Duchess was told that the General would not be at home that night. Had he two houses? The man would give no answer. Mme. de Langeais had bought the key of the room, but not the man's whole loyalty.

When she was left alone she saw her fourteen letters lying on an old-fashioned stand, all of them uncreased and unopened. He had not read them. She sank into an easy-chair, and for a while she lost consciousness. When she came to herself, Auguste was holding vinegar for her to inhale.

"A carriage; quick!" she ordered.

The carriage came. She hastened downstairs with convulsive speed, and left orders that no one was to be admitted. For twenty-four hours she lay in bed, and would have no one near her but her woman, who brought her a cup of orange-flower water from time to time. Suzette heard her mistress moan once or twice, and caught a glimpse of tears in the brilliant eyes, now circled with dark shadows.

The next day, amid despairing tears, Mme. de Langeais took her resolution. Her man of business came for an interview, and no doubt received instructions of some kind. Afterwards she sent for the Vidame de Pamiers; and while she waited, she wrote a letter to M. de Montriveau. The Vidame punctually came towards two o'clock that afternoon, to find his young cousin looking white and worn, but resigned; never had her divine loveliness been more poetic than now in the languor of her agony.

"You owe this assignation to your eighty-four years, dear

cousin," she said. "Ah! do not smile, I beg of you, when an unhappy woman has reached the lowest depths of wretchedness. You are a gentleman, and after the adventures of your youth you must feel some indulgence for women."

"None whatever," said he

"Indeed!"

"Everything is in their favor."

"Ah! Well, you are one of the inner family circle; possibly you will be the last relative, the last friend whose hand I shall press, so I can ask your good offices. Will you, dear Vidame, do me a service which I could not ask of my own father, nor of my uncle Grandlieu, nor of any woman? You cannot fail to understand. I beg of you to do my bidding, and then to forget what you have done, whatever may come of it. It is this: Will you take this letter and go to M. de Montriveau? will you see him yourself, give it into his hands, and ask him, as you men can ask things between yourselves— for you have a code of honor between man and man which you do not use with us, and a different way of regarding things between yourselves—ask him if he will read this letter? Not in your presence. Certain feelings men hide from each other. I give you authority to say, if you think it necessary to bring him, that it is a question of life or death for me. If he deigns——"

"*Deigns!*" repeated the Vidame.

"If he deigns to read it," the Duchess continued with dignity, "say one thing more. You will go to see him about five o'clock, for I know that he will dine at home to-day at that time. Very good. By way of answer he must come to see me. If, three hours afterwards, by eight o'clock, he does not leave his house, all will be over. The Duchesse de Langeais will have vanished from the world. I shall not be dead, dear friend, no, but no human power will ever find me again on this earth. Come and dine with me; I shall at least have one friend with me in the last agony. Yes, dear cousin, to-night will decide my fate; and whatever happens to me, I pass through an ordeal by fire. There! not a word. I will hear

nothing of the nature of comment or advice—— Let us
chat and laugh together," she added, holding out a hand,
which he kissed. "We will be like two gray-headed philosophers who have learned how to enjoy life to the last moment.
I will look my best; I will be very enchanting for you. You
perhaps will be the last man to set eyes on the Duchesse de
Langeais."

The Vicomte bowed, took the letter, and went without a
word. At five o'clock he returned. His cousin had studied
to please him, and she looked lovely indeed. The room was
gay with flowers as if for a festivity; the dinner was exquisite. For the gray-headed Vidame the Duchess displayed
all the brilliancy of her wit; she was more charming than
she had ever been before. At first the Vidame tried to look
on all the preparations as a young woman's jest; but now and
again the attempted illusion faded, the spell of his fair
cousin's charm was broken. He detected a shudder caused by
some kind of sudden dread, and once she seemed to listen
during a pause.

"What is the matter?" he asked.

"Hush!" she said.

At seven o'clock the Duchess left him for a few minutes.
When she came back again she was dressed as her maid might
have dressed for a journey. She asked her guest to be her
escort, took his arm, sprang into a hackney coach, and by a
quarter to eight they stood outside M. de Montriveau's door.

Armand meantime had been reading the following letter:

"MY FRIEND,—I went to your room for a few minutes
without your knowledge; I found my letters there, and took
them away. This cannot be indifference, Armand, between
us; and hatred would show itself quite differently. If you
love me, make an end of this cruel play, or you will kill me,
and afterwards, learning how much you were loved, you
might be in despair. If I have not rightly understood you,
if you have no feeling towards me but aversion, which implies
both contempt and disgust, then I give up all hope. A man

never recovers from those feelings. You will have no regrets. Dreadful though that thought may be, it will comfort me in my long sorrow. Regrets? Oh! my Armand, may I never know of them; if I thought that I had caused you a single regret—— But, no, I will not tell you what desolation I should feel. I should be living still, and I could not be your wife; it would be too late!

"Now that I have given myself wholly to you in thought, to whom else should I give myself?—to God. The eyes that you loved for a little while shall never look on another man's face; and may the glory of God blind them to all besides. I shall never hear human voices more since I heard yours—so gentle at the first, so terrible yesterday; for it seems to me that I am still only on the morrow of your vengeance. And now may the will of God consume me. Between His wrath and yours, my friend, there will be nothing left for me but a little space for tears and prayers.

"Perhaps you wonder why I write to you? Ah! do not think ill of me if I keep a gleam of hope, and give one last sigh to happy life before I take leave of it for ever. I am in a hideous position. I feel all the inward serenity that comes when a great resolution has been taken, even while I hear the last growlings of the storm. When you went out on that terrible adventure which so drew me to you Armand, you went from the desert to the oasis with a good guide to show you the way. Well, I am going out of the oasis into the desert, and you are a pitiless guide to me. And yet you only, my friend, can understand how melancholy it is to look back for the last time on happiness—to you, and you only, I can make moan without a blush. If you grant my entreaty, I shall be happy; if you are inexorable, I shall expiate the wrong that I have done. After all, it is natural, is it not, that a woman should wish to live, invested with all noble feelings, in her friend's memory? Oh! my one and only love, let her to whom you gave life go down into the tomb in the belief that she is great in your eyes. Your harshness led me to reflect; and now that I love you so, it seems to me that I am less

guilty than you think. Listen to my justification, I owe it to
you; and you that are all the world to me, owe me at least a
moment's justice.

"I have learned by my own anguish all that I made you
suffer by my coquetry; but in those days I was utterly ignorant of love. *You* know what the torture is, and you mete
it out to me! During those first eight months that you gave
me you never roused any feeling of love in me. Do you ask
why this was so, my friend? I can no more explain it than I
can tell you why I love you now. Oh! certainly it flattered
my vanity that I should be the subject of your passionate
talk, and receive those burning glances of yours; but you left
me cold. No, I was not a woman; I had no conception of
womanly devotion and happiness. Who was to blame? You
would have despised me, would you not, if I had given myself without the impulse of passion? Perhaps it is the highest
height to which we can rise—to give all and receive no joy;
perhaps there is no merit in yielding oneself to bliss that is
foreseen and ardently desired. Alas, my friend, I can say
this now; these thoughts came to me when I played with you;
and you seemed to me so great even then that I would not
have you owe the gift to pity—— What is this that I have
written?

"I have taken back all my letters; I am flinging them one
by one on the fire; they are burning. You will never know
what they confessed—all the love and the passion and the
madness——

"I will say no more, Armand; I will stop. I will not say
another word of my feelings. If my prayers have not echoed
from my soul through yours, I also, woman that I am, decline to owe your love to your pity. It is my wish to be loved,
because you cannot choose but love me, or else to be left without mercy. If you refuse to read this letter, it shall be
burned. If, after you have read it, you do not come to me
within three hours, to be henceforth for ever my husband,
the one man in the world for me; then I shall never blush
to know that this letter is in your hands, the pride of my de-

spair will protect my memory from all insult, and my end shall be worthy of my love. When you see me no more on earth, albeit I shall still be alive, you yourself will not think without a shudder of the woman who, in three hours' time, will live only to overwhelm you with her tenderness; a woman consumed by a hopeless love, and faithful—not to memories of past joys—but to a love that was slighted.

"The Duchesse de la Vallière wept for lost happiness and vanished power; but the Duchesse de Langeais will be happy that she may weep and be a power for you still. Yes, you will regret me. I see clearly that I was not of this world, and I thank you for making it clear to me.

"Farewell; you will never touch *my* axe. Yours was the executioner's axe, mine is God's; yours kills, mine saves. Your love was but mortal, it could not endure disdain or ridicule; mine can endure all things without growing weaker, it will last eternally. Ah! I feel a sombre joy in crushing you that believe yourself so great; in humbling you with the calm, indulgent smile of one of the least among the angels that lie at the feet of God, for to them is given the right and the power to protect and watch over men in His name. You have but felt fleeting desires, and while the poor nun will shed the light of her ceaseless and ardent prayer about you, she will shelter you all your life long beneath the wings of a love that has nothing of earth in it.

"I have a presentiment of your answer; our trysting place shall be—in heaven. Strength and weakness can both enter there, dear Armand; the strong and the weak are bound to suffer. This thought soothes the anguish of my final ordeal. So calm am I that I should fear that I had ceased to love you if I were not about to leave the world for your sake.

"ANTOINETTE."

"Dear Vidame," said the Duchess as they reached Montriveau's house, "do me the kindness to ask at the door whether he is at home."

The Vidame, obedient after the manner of the eighteenth

century to a woman's wish, got out, and came back to bring his cousin an affirmative answer that sent a shudder through her. She grasped his hand tightly in hers, suffered him to kiss her on either cheek, and begged him to go at once. He must not watch her movements nor try to protect her.

"But the people passing in the street," he objected.

"No one can fail in respect to me," she said. It was the last word spoken by the Duchess and the woman of fashion.

The Vidame went. Mme. de Langeais wrapped herself about in her cloak, and stood on the doorstep until the clocks struck eight. The last stroke died away. The unhappy woman waited ten, fifteen minutes; to the last she tried to see a fresh humiliation in the delay, then her faith ebbed. She turned to leave the fatal threshold.

"Oh, God!" the cry broke from her in spite of herself; it was the first word spoken by the Carmelite.

Montriveau and some of his friends were talking together. He tried to hasten them to a conclusion, but his clock was slow, and by the time he started out for the Hôtel de Langeais the Duchess was hurrying on foot through the streets of Paris, goaded by the dull rage in her heart. She had reached the Boulevard d'Enfer, and looked out for the last time through the falling tears in the noisy, smoky city that lay below in a red mist, lighted up by its own lamps. Then she hailed a cab and drove away, never to return

When the Marquis de Montriveau reached the Hôtel de Langeais, and found no trace of his mistress, he thought that he had been duped. He hurried away at once to the Vidame, and found that worthy gentleman in the act of slipping on his flowered dressing-gown, thinking the while of his fair cousin's happiness. Montriveau gave him one of the terrific glances that produced the effect of an electric shock on men and women alike.

"Is it possible that you have lent yourself to some cruel hoax, monsieur?" Montriveau exclaimed. "I have just come from Mme. de Langeais' house; the servants say that she is out."

"Then a great misfortune has happened, no doubt," returned the Vidame, "and through your fault. I left the
Duchess at your door——"

"When?"

"At a quarter to eight."

"Good-evening," returned Montriveau, and he hurried home
to ask the porter whether he had seen a lady standing on the
doorstep that evening.

"Yes, my Lord Marquis, a handsome woman, who seemed
very much put out. She was crying like a Magdalen, but
she never made a sound, and stood as upright as a post.
Then at last she went, and my wife and I that were watching
her while she could not hear us, heard her say, 'Oh, God!'
so that it went to our hearts, asking your pardon, to hear
her say it."

Montriveau, in spite of all his firmness, turned pale at
those few words. He wrote a few lines to Ronquerolles, sent
off the message at once, and went up to his rooms. Ronquerolles came just about midnight.

Armand gave him the Duchess' letter to read.

"Well?" asked Ronquerolles.

"She was here at my door at eight o'clock; at a quarter-
past eight she had gone. I have lost her, and I love her. Oh!
if my life were my own, I could blow my brains out."

"Pooh, pooh! Keep cool," said Ronquerolles. "Duchesses
do not fly off like wagtails. She cannot travel faster than
three leagues an hour, and to-morrow we will ride six.—Confound it! Mme. de Langeais is no ordinary woman," he continued. "To-morrow we will all of us mount and ride. The
police will put us on her track during the day. She must have
a carriage; angels of that sort have no wings. We shall find
her whether she is on the road or hidden in Paris. There
is the semaphore. We can stop her. You shall be happy.
But, my dear fellow, you have made a blunder, of which men
of your energy are very often guilty. They judge others by
themselves, and do not know the point when human nature
gives way if you strain the cords too tightly. Why did you

not say a word to me sooner? I would have told you to be
punctual. Good-bye till to-morrow," he added, as Montriveau
said nothing. "Sleep if you can," he added, with a grasp of
the hand.

But the greatest resources which society has ever placed at
the disposal of statesmen, kings, ministers, bankers, or any
human power, in fact, were all exhausted in vain. Neither
Montriveau nor his friends could find any trace of the
Duchess. It was clear that she had entered a convent. Montriveau determined to search, or to institute a search, for her
through every convent in the world. He must have her, even
at the cost of all the lives in a town. And in justice to this
extraordinary man, it must be said that his frenzied passion
awoke to the same ardor daily and lasted through five years.
Only in 1829 did the Duke de Navarreins hear by chance that
his daughter had traveled to Spain as Lady Julia Hopwood's
maid, that she had left her service at Cadiz, and that Lady
Julia never discovered that Mlle. Caroline was the illustrious
duchess whose sudden disappearance filled the minds of the
highest society of Paris.

The feelings of the two lovers when they met again on either
side of the grating in the Carmelite convent should now be
comprehended to the full, and the violence of the passion
awakened in either soul will doubtless explain the catastrophe
of the story.

In 1823 the Duc de Langeais was dead, and his wife was
free. Antoinette de Navarreins was living, consumed by love,
on a ledge of rock in the Mediterranean; but it was in the
Pope's power to dissolve Sister Theresa's vows. The happiness bought by so much love might yet bloom for the two
lovers. These thoughts sent Montriveau flying from Cadiz to
Marseilles, and from Marseilles to Paris.

A few months after his return to France, a merchant brig,
fitted out and munitioned for active service, set sail from the
port of Marseilles for Spain. The vessel had been chartered
by several distinguished men, most of them Frenchmen, who

smitten with a romantic passion for the East, wished to make a journey to those lands. Montriveau's familiar knowledge of Eastern customs made him an invaluable traveling companion, and at the entreaty of the rest he had joined the expedition; the Minister of War appointed him lieutenant-general, and put him on the Artillery Commission to facilitate his departure.

Twenty-four hours later the brig lay to off the northwest shore of an island within sight of the Spanish coast. She had been specially chosen for her shallow keel and light mastage, so that she might lie at anchor in safety half a league away from the reefs that secure the island from approach in this direction. If fishing vessels or the people on the island caught sight of the brig, they were scarcely likely to feel suspicious of her at once; and besides, it was easy to give a reason for her presence without delay. Montriveau hoisted the flag of the United States before they came in sight of the island, and the crew of the vessel were all American sailors, who spoke nothing but English. One of M. de Montriveau's companions took the men ashore in the ship's long boat, and made them so drunk at an inn in the little town that they could not talk. Then he gave out that the brig was manned by treasure-seekers, a gang of men whose hobby was well known in the United States; indeed, some Spanish writer had written a history of them. The presence of the brig among the reefs was now sufficiently explained. The owners of the vessel, according to the self-styled boatswain's mate, were looking for the wreck of a galleon which foundered thereabouts in 1778 with a cargo of treasure from Mexico. The people at the inn and the authorities asked no more questions.

Armand, and the devoted friends who were helping him in his difficult enterprise, were all from the first of the opinion that there was no hope of rescuing or carrying off Sister Theresa by force or stratagem from the side of the little town. Wherefore these bold spirits, with one accord, determined to take the bull by the horns. They would make a way

to the convent at the most seeming inaccessible point; like
General Lamarque, at the storming of Capri, they would con-
quer Nature. The cliff at the end of the island, a sheer block
of granite, afforded even less hold than the rock of Capri.
So it seemed at least to Montriveau, who had taken part in
that incredible exploit, while the nuns in his eyes were much
more redoubtable than Sir Hudson Lowe. To raise a hubbub
over carrying off the Duchess would cover them with confusion. They might as well set siege to the town and convent, like pirates, and leave not a single soul to tell of their
victory. So for them their expedition wore but two aspects.
There should be a conflagration and a feat of arms that should
dismay all Europe, while the motives of the crime remained
unknown; or, on the other hand, a mysterious aerial descent
which should persuade the nuns that the Devil himself had
paid them a visit. They had decided upon the latter course
in the secret council held before they left Paris, and subsequently everything had been done to insure the success of an
expedition which promised some real excitement to jaded
spirits weary of Paris and its pleasures.

An extremely light pirogue, made at Marseilles on a Ma-
layan model, enabled them to cross the reef, until the rocks
rose from out of the water. Then two cables of iron were
fastened several feet apart between one rock and another.
These wire ropes slanted upwards and downwards in opposite
directions, so that baskets of iron wire could travel to and
fro along them; and in this manner the rocks were covered
with a system of baskets and wire-cables, not unlike the fila-
ments which a certain species of spider weaves about a tree.
The Chinese, an essentially imitative people, were the first
to take a lesson from the work of instinct. Fragile as these
bridges were, they were always ready for use; high waves
and the caprices of the sea could not throw them out of
working order. The ropes hung just sufficiently slack, so as
to present to the breakers that particular curve discovered
by Cachin, the immortal creator of the harbor at Cherbourg.
Against this cunningly devised line the angry surge is power-

less; the law of that curve was a secret wrested from Nature by that faculty of observation in which nearly all human genius consists.

M. de Montriveau's companions were alone on board the vessel, and out of sight of every human eye. No one from the deck of a passing vessel could have discovered either the brig hidden among the reefs, or the men at work among the rocks; they lay below the ordinary range of the most powerful telescope. Eleven days were spent in preparation, before the Thirteen, with all their infernal power, could reach the foot of the cliffs. The body of the rock rose up straight from the sea to a height of thirty fathoms. Any attempt to climb the sheer wall of granite seemed impossible; a mouse might as well try to creep up the slippery sides of a plain china vase. Still there was a cleft, a straight line of fissure so fortunately placed that large blocks of wood could be wedged firmly into it at a distance of about a foot apart. Into these blocks the daring workers drove iron cramps, specially made for the purpose, with a broad iron bracket at the outer end, through which a hole had been drilled. Each bracket carried a light deal board which corresponded with a notch made in a pole that reached to the top of the cliffs, and was firmly planted in the beach at their feet. With ingenuity worthy of these men who found nothing impossible, one of their number, a skilled mathematician, had calculated the angle from which the steps must start; so that from the middle they rose gradually, like the sticks of a fan, to the top of the cliff, and descended in the same fashion to its base. That miraculously light, yet perfectly firm, staircase cost them twenty-two days of toil. A little tinder and the surf of the sea would destroy all trace of it for ever in a single night. A betrayal of the secret was impossible; and all search for the violators of the convent was doomed to failure.

At the top of the rock there was a platform with sheer precipice on all sides. The Thirteen, reconnoitering the ground with their glasses from the masthead, made certain that though the ascent was steep and rough, there would be no difficulty in gaining the convent garden, where the trees were thick enough for a hiding-place. After such great efforts they would not risk the success of their enterprise, and were compelled to wait till the moon passed out of her last quarter.

For two nights Montriveau, wrapped in his cloak, lay out on the rock platform. The singing at vespers and matins filled him with unutterable joy. He stood under the wall to hear the music of the organ, listening intently for one voice among the rest. But in spite of the silence, the confused effect of music was all that reached his ears. In those sweet harmonies defects of execution are lost; the pure spirit of art comes into direct communication with the spirit of the hearer, making no demand on the attention, no strain on the power of listening. Intolerable memories awoke. All the love within him seemed to break into blossom again at the breath of that music; he tried to find auguries of happiness in the air. During the last night he sat with his eyes fixed upon an ungrated window, for bars were not needed on the side of the precipice. A light shone there all through the hours; and that instinct of the heart, which is sometimes true, and as often false, cried within him, "She is there!"

"She is certainly there! To-morrow she will be mine," he said to himself, and joy blended with the slow tinkling of a bell that began to ring.

Strange unaccountable workings of the heart! The nun, wasted by yearning love, worn out with tears and fasting, prayer and vigils; the woman of nine-and-twenty, who had passed through heavy trials, was loved more passionately than the light-hearted woman of four-and-twenty, the sylphide, had ever been. But is there not for men of vigorous character, something attractive in the sublime expression engraven on women's faces by the impetuous stirrings of thought and misfortunes of no ignoble kind? Is there not a beauty of suffering which is the most interesting of all beauty to those men who feel that within them there is an inexhaustible wealth of tenderness and consoling pity for a creature so gracious in weakness, so strong with love? It is the ordinary nature that is attracted by young, smooth, pink-and-white beauty, or, in one word, by prettiness. In some faces love awakens amid the wrinkles carved by sorrow and the ruin made by melancholy; Montriveau could not but feel drawn to these. For cannot a lover, with the voice of a great longing, call forth a wholly new creature? a creature athrob with the life but just begun breaks forth for him alone, from the outward form that is fair for him, and faded for all the world besides. Does he not love two women?—One of them, as others see her, is pale and wan and sad; but the other, the unseen love that his heart knows, is an angel who understands life through feeling, and is adorned in all her glory only for love's high festivals.

The General left his post before sunrise, but not before he had heard voices singing together, sweet voices full of tenderness sounding faintly from the cell. When he came down to the foot of the cliffs where his friends were waiting, he told them that never in his life had he felt such enthralling bliss, and in the few words there was that unmistakable thrill of repressed strong feeling, that magnificent utterance which all men respect.

That night eleven of his devoted comrades made the ascent in the darkness. Each man carried a poniard, a provision of chocolate, and a set of house-breaking tools. They climbed the outer walls with scaling ladders, and crossed the cemetery of the convent. Montriveau recognized the long, vaulted gallery through which he went to the parlor, and remembered the windows of the room His plans were made and adopted in a moment. They would effect an entrance through one of the windows in the Carmelite's half of the parlor, find their way along the corridors, ascertain whether the sisters' names were written on the doors, find Sister Theresa's cell, surprise her as she slept, and carry her off, bound and gagged. The programme presented no difficulties to men who combined boldness and a convict's dexterity with the knowledge peculiar to men of the world, especially as they would not scruple to give a stab to insure silence.

In two hours the bars were sawn through. Three men stood on guard outside, and two inside the parlor. The rest, barefooted, took up their posts along the corridor. Young Henri de Marsay, the most dexterous man among them, disguised by way of precaution in a Carmelite's robe, exactly like the costume of the convent, led the way, and Montriveau came immediately behind him. The clock struck three just as the two men reached the dormitory cells. They soon saw the position. Everything was perfectly quiet. With the help of a dark lantern they read the names luckily written on every door, together with the picture of a saint or saints and the mystical words which every nun takes as a kind of motto for the beginning of her new life and the revelation of her last thought. Montriveau reached Sister Theresa's door and read the inscription, *Sub invocatione sanctæ matris Theresæ,* and her motto, *Adoremus in æternum.* Suddenly his companion laid a hand on his shoulder. A bright light was streaming through the chinks of the door. M. de Ronquerolles came up at that moment.

"All the nuns are in the church," he said; "they are beginning the Office for the Dead."

"I will stay here," said Montriveau. "Go back into the parlor, and shut the door at the end of the passage."

He threw open the door and rushed in, preceded by his disguised companion, who let down the veil over his face.

There before them lay the dead Duchess; her plank bed had been laid on the floor of the outer room of her cell, between two lighted candles. Neither Montriveau nor de Marsay spoke a word or uttered a cry; but they looked into each other's faces. The General's dumb gesture tried to say, "Let us carry her away!"

"Quick!" shouted Ronquerolles, "the procession of nuns is leaving the church. You will be caught!"

With magical swiftness of movement, prompted by an intense desire, the dead woman was carried into the convent parlor, passed through the window, and lowered from the walls before the Abbess, followed by the nuns, returned to take up Sister Theresa's body. The sister left in charge had imprudently left her post; there were secrets that she longed to know; and so busy was she ransacking the inner room, that she heard nothing, and was horrified when she came back to find that the body was gone. Before the women, in their blank amazement, could think of making a search, the Duchess had been lowered by a cord to the foot of the crags, and Montriveau's companions had destroyed all traces of their work. By nine that morning there was not a sign to show that either staircase or wire-cables had ever existed, and Sister Theresa's body had been taken on board. The brig came into the port to ship her crew, and sailed that day.

Montriveau, down in the cabin, was left alone with Antoinette de Navarreins. For some hours it seemed as if her dead face was transfigured for him by that unearthly beauty which the calm of death gives to the body before it perishes.

"Look here!" said Ronquerolles when Montriveau reappeared on deck, "*that* was a woman once, now it is nothing. Let us tie a cannon-ball to both feet and throw the body overboard; and if ever you think of her again, think of her as of some book that you read as a boy."

"Yes," assented Montriveau, "it is nothing now but a dream."

"That is sensible of you. Now, after this, have passions; but as for love, a man ought to know how to place it wisely; it is only a woman's last love that can satisfy a man's first love."

PRE-LEVEQUE, GENEVA, *January* 26, 1834.

III.

THE GIRL WITH THE GOLDEN EYES

To Eugène Delacroix, Painter.

ONE of those sights in which most horror is to be encountered is, surely, the general aspect of the Parisian populace—a people fearful to behold, gaunt, yellow, tawny. Is not Paris a vast field in perpetual turmoil from a storm of interests beneath which are whirled along a crop of human beings, who are, more often than not, reaped by death, only to be born again as pinched as ever, men whose twisted and contorted faces give out at every pore the instinct, the desire, the poisons with which their brains are pregnant; not faces so much as masks; masks of weakness, masks of strength, masks of misery, masks of joy, masks of hypocrisy; all alike worn and stamped with the indelible signs of a panting cupidity? What is it they want? Gold or pleasure? A few observations upon the soul of Paris may explain the causes of its cadaverous physiognomy, which has but two ages—youth and decay: youth, wan and colorless; decay, painted to seem young. In looking at this excavated people, foreigners, who are not prone to reflection, experience at first a movement of disgust towards the capital, that vast workshop of delights, from which, in a short time, they cannot even extricate themselves, and where they stay willingly to be corrupted. A few words will suffice to justify physiologically the almost infernal hue of Parisian faces, for it is not in mere sport that Paris has been called a hell. Take the phrase for truth. There all is smoke and fire, everything gleams, crackles, flames, evaporates, dies out, then lights up again, with shoot-

ing sparks, and is consumed. In no other country has life
ever been more ardent or acute. The social nature, even in
fusion, seems to say after each completed work: "Pass on
to another!" just as Nature says herself. Like Nature herself, this social nature is busied with insects and flowers of
a day—ephemeral trifles; and so, too, it throws up fire and
flame from its eternal crater. Perhaps, before analyzing the
causes which lend a special physiognomy to each tribe of this
intelligent and mobile nation, the general cause should be
pointed out which bleaches and discolors, tints with blue or
brown individuals in more or less degree.

By dint of taking interest in everything, the Parisian ends
by being interested in nothing. No emotion dominating his
face, which friction has rubbed away, it turns gray like the
faces of those houses upon which all kinds of dust and smoke
have blown. In effect, the Parisian, with his indifference on
the day for what the morrow will bring forth, lives like a
child, whatever may be his age. He grumbles at everything,
consoles himself for everything, jests at everything, forgets,
desires, and tastes everything, seizes all with passion, quits all
with indifference—his kings, his conquests, his glory, his idols
of bronze or glass—as he throws away his stockings, his hats,
and his fortune. In Paris no sentiment can withstand the drift
of things, and their current compels a struggle in which the
passions are relaxed: there love is a desire, and hatred a
whim; there's no true kinsman but the thousand-franc note,
no better friend than the pawnbroker. This universal tolera-
tion bears its fruits, and in the salon, as in the street, there
is no one *de trop,* there is no one absolutely useful, or absolutely harmful—knaves or fools, men of wit or integrity.
There everything is tolerated: the government and the guillotine, religion and the cholera. You are always acceptable
to this world, you will never be missed by it. What, then, is
the dominating impulse in this country without morals, without faith, without any sentiment, wherein, however, every
sentiment, belief, and moral has its origin and end? It is

gold and pleasure. Take those two words for a lantern, and
explore that great stucco cage, that hive with its black gutters, and follow the windings of that thought which agitates,
sustains, and occupies it! Consider! And, in the first place,
examine the world which possesses nothing.

The artisan, the man of the proletariat, who uses his hands,
his tongue, his back, his right arm, his five fingers, to live
—well, this very man, who should be the first to economize
his vital principle, outruns his strength, yokes his wife to
some machine, wears out his child, and ties him to the wheel.
The manufacturer—or I know not what secondary thread
which sets in motion all these folk who with their foul hands
mould and gild porcelain, sew coats and dresses, beat out
iron, turn wood and steel, weave hemp, festoon crystal, imitate flowers, work woolen things, break in horses, dress harness, carve in copper, paint carriages, blow glass, corrode the
diamond, polish metals, turn marble into leaves, labor on
pebbles, deck out thought, tinge, bleach, or blacken everything—well, this middleman has come to that world of sweat
and good-will, of study and patience, with promises of lavish
wages, either in the names of the town's caprices or with the
voice of the monster dubbed speculation. Thus, these *quadru-
manes* set themselves to watch, work, and suffer, to fast, sweat,
and bestir them. Then, careless of the future, greedy of
pleasure, counting on their right arm as the painter on his
palette, lords for one day, they throw their money on Mon-
days to the *cabarets* which gird the town like a belt of mud,
haunts of the most shameless of the daughters of Venus, in
which the periodical money of this people, as ferocious in
their pleasures as they are calm at work, is squandered as
it had been at play. For five days, then, there is no repose
for this laborious portion of Paris! It is given up to actions
which make it warped and rough, lean and pale, gush forth
with a thousand fits of creative energy. And then its pleasure, its repose, are an exhausting debauch, swarthy and black
with blows, white with intoxication, or yellow with indigestion. It lasts but two days, but it steals to-morrow's bread,

the week's soup, the wife's dress, the child's wretched rags. Men, born doubtless to be beautiful—for all creatures have a relative beauty—are enrolled from their childhood beneath the yoke of force, beneath the rule of the hammer, the chisel, the loom, and have been promptly vulcanized. Is not Vulcan, with his hideousness and his strength, the emblem of this strong and hideous nation—sublime in its mechanical intelligence, patient in its season, and once in a century terrible, inflammable as gunpowder, and ripe with brandy for the madness of revolution, with wits enough, in fine, to take fire at a captious word, which signifies to it always: Gold and Pleasure! If we comprise in it all those who hold out their hands for an alms, for lawful wages, or the five francs that are granted to every kind of Parisian prostitution, in short, for all money well or ill earned, this people numbers three hundred thousand individuals. Were it not for the *cabarets,* would not the Government be overturned every Tuesday? Happily, by Tuesday, this people is glutted, sleeps off its pleasure, is penniless, and returns to its labor, to dry bread, stimulated by a need of material procreation, which has become a habit to it. None the less, this people has its phenomenal virtues, its complete men, unknown Napoleons, who are the type of its strength carried to its highest expression, and sum up its social capacity in an existence wherein thought and movement combine less to bring joy into it than to neutralize the action of sorrow.

Chance has made an artisan economical, chance has favored him with forethought, he has been able to look forward, has met with a wife and found himself a father, and, after some years of hard privation, he embarks in some little draper's business, hires a shop. If neither sickness nor vice blocks his way—if he has prospered—there is the sketch of this normal life.

And, in the first place, hail to that king of Parisian activity, to whom time and space give way. Yes, hail to that being, composed of saltpetre and gas, who makes children for France during his laborious nights, and in the day mul-

tiplies his personality for the service, glory, and pleasure of
his fellow-citizens.   This man solves the problem of suffic-
ing at once to his amiable wife, to his hearth, to the *Constitutionnel,* to his office, to the National Guard, to the opera,
and to God; but, only in order that the *Constitutionnel,* his
office, the National Guard, the opera, his wife, and God
may be changed into coin.   In fine, hail to an irreproachable pluralist.   Up every day at five o'clock, he traverses like
a bird the space which separates his dwelling from the Rue
Montmartre.   Let it blow or thunder, rain or snow, he is at
the *Constitutionnel,* and waits there for the load of newspapers which he has undertaken to distribute.   He receives
this political bread with eagerness, takes it, bears it away.
At nine o'clock he is in the bosom of his family, flings a
jest to his wife, snatches a loud kiss from her, gulps down a
cup of coffee, or scolds his children.   At a quarter to ten
he puts in an appearance at the *Mairie.*   There, stuck upon
a stool, like a parrot on its perch, warmed by Paris town, he
registers until four o'clock, with never a tear or a smile, the
deaths and births of an entire district.   The sorrow, the
happiness, of the parish flow beneath his pen—as the essence of the *Constitutionnel* traveled before upon his shoulders.   Nothing weighs upon him!   He goes always straight
before him, takes his patriotism ready made from the newspaper, contradicts no one, shouts or applauds with the world,
and lives like a bird.   Two yards from his parish, in the
event of an important ceremony, he can yield his place to an
assistant, and betake himself to chant a requiem from a stall
in the church of which on Sundays he is the fairest ornament,
where his is the most imposing voice, where he distorts his
huge mouth with energy to thunder out a joyous *Amen.*   So
is he chorister.   At four o'clock, freed from his official
servitude, he reappears to shed joy and gaiety upon the most
famous shop in the city.   Happy is his wife, he has no time
to be jealous: he is a man of action rather than of sentiment.   His mere arrival spurs the young ladies at the
counter; their bright eyes storm the customers; he expands

in the midst of all the finery, the lace and muslin kerchiefs, that their cunning hands have wrought. Or, again, more often still, before his dinner he waits on a client, copies the page of a newspaper, or carries to the doorkeeper some goods that have been delayed. Every other day, at six, he is faithful to his post. A permanent bass for the chorus, he betakes himself to the opera, prepared to become a soldier or an arab, prisoner, savage, peasant, spirit, camel's leg or lion, a devil or a genie, a slave or a eunuch, black or white; always ready to feign joy or sorrow, pity or astonishment, to utter cries that never vary, to hold his tongue, to hunt, or fight for Rome or Egypt, but always at heart—a huckster still.

At midnight he returns—a man, the good husband, the tender father; he slips into the conjugal bed, his imagination still afire with the illusive forms of the operatic nymphs, and so turns to the profit of conjugal love the world's depravities, the voluptuous curves of Taglioni's leg. And, finally, if he sleeps, he sleeps apace, and hurries through his slumber as he does his life.

This man sums up all things—history, literature, politics, government, religion, military science. Is he not a living encyclopædia, a grotesque Atlas; ceaselessly in motion, like Paris itself, and knowing not repose? He is all legs. No physiognomy could preserve its purity amid such toils. Perhaps the artisan who dies at thirty, an old man, his stomach tanned by repeated doses of brandy, will be held, according to certain leisured philosophers, to be happier than the huckster is. The one perishes in a breath, and the other by degrees. From his eight industries, from the labor of his shoulders, his throat, his hands, from his wife and his business, the one derives—as from so many farms—children, some thousands of francs, and the most laborious happiness that has ever diverted the heart of man. This fortune and these children, or the children who sum up everything for him, become the prey of the world above, to which he brings his ducats and his daughter or his son, reared at college, who, with more education than his father, raises higher his ambi-

tious gaze. Often the son of a retail tradesman would fain
be something in the State.

Ambition of that sort carries on our thought to the second Parisian sphere. Go up one story, then, and descend to
the *entresol:* or climb down from the attic and remain on the
fourth floor; in fine, penetrate into the world which has possessions: the same result! Wholesale merchants, and their
men—people with small banking accounts and much integrity—rogues and catspaws, clerks old and young, sheriffs'
clerks, barristers' clerks, solicitors' clerks; in fine, all the
working, thinking, and speculating members of that lower
middle class which honeycombs the interests of Paris and
watches over its granary, accumulates the coin, stores the
products that the proletariat have made, preserves the fruits
of the South, the fishes, the wine from every sun-favored
hill; which stretches its hands over the Orient, and takes from
it the shawls that the Russ and the Turk despise; which har-
vests even from the Indies; crouches down in expectation of
a sale, greedy of profit; which discounts bills, turns over and
collects all kinds of securities, holds all Paris in its hand,
watches over the fantasies of children, spies out the caprices
and the vices of mature age, sucks money out of disease.
Even so, if they drink no brandy, like the artisan, nor wallow
in the mire of debauch, all equally abuse their strength, im-
measurably strain their bodies and their minds alike, are
burned away with desires, devastated with the swiftness of
the pace. In their case the physical distortion is accomplished beneath the whip of interests, beneath the scourge
of ambitions which torture the educated portion of this monstrous city, just as in the case of the proletariat it is brought
about by the cruel see-saw of the material elaborations perpetually required from the despotism of the aristocratic
"I will." Here, too, then, in order to obey that universal
master, pleasure or gold, they must devour time, hasten time,
find more than four-and-twenty hours in the day and night,
waste themselves, slay themselves, and purchase two years
of unhealthy repose with thirty years of old age. Only, the

working-man dies in hospital when the last term of his
stunted growth expires; whereas the man of the middle class
is set upon living, and lives on, but in a state of idiocy. You
will meet him, with his worn, flat old face, with no light in
his eyes, with no strength in his limbs, dragging himself
with a dazed air along the boulevard—the belt of his Venus,
of his beloved city. What was his want? The sabre of the
National Guard, a permanent stock-pot, a decent plot in Père
Lachaise, and, for his old age, a little gold honestly earned.
His Monday is on Sunday, his rest a drive in a hired carriage
—a country excursion during which his wife and children
glut themselves merrily with dust or bask in the sun; his dissipation is at the restaurateur's, whose poisonous dinner has
won renown, or at some family ball, where he suffocates till
midnight. Some fools are surprised at the phantasmagoria of
the monads which they see with the aid of the microscope in a
drop of water; but what would Rabelais' Gargantua,—that
misunderstood figure of an audacity so sublime,—what would
that giant say, fallen from the celestial spheres, if he amused
himself by contemplating the motions of this secondary life
of Paris, of which here is one of the formulæ? Have you
seen one of those little constructions—cold in summer, and
with no other warmth than a small stove in winter—placed
beneath the vast copper dome which crowns the Halle-au-
blé? Madame is there by morning. She is engaged at the
markets, and makes by this occupation twelve thousand francs
a year, people say. Monsieur, when Madame is up, passes into
a gloomy office, where he lends money till the week-end to
the tradesmen of his district. By nine o'clock he is at the
passport office, of which he is one of the minor officials. By
evening he is at the box-office of the Théâtre Italien, or of
any other theatre you like. The children are put out to
nurse, and only return to be sent to college or to boarding-
school. Monsieur and Madame live on the third floor, have
but one cook, give dances in a salon twelve foot by eight, lit
by argand lamps; but they give a hundred and fifty thousand francs to their daughter, and retire at the age of fifty,

an age when they begin to show themselves on the balcony
of the opera, in a *fiacre* at Longchamps; or, on sunny days,
in faded clothes on the boulevards—the fruit of all this sow-
ing. Respected by their neighbors, in good odor with the
government, connected with the upper middle classes, Monsieur obtains at sixty-five the Cross of the Legion of Honor,
and his daughter's father-in-law, a parochial mayor, in-
vites him to his evenings. These life-long labors, then, are
for the good of the children, whom these lower middle classes
are inevitably driven to exalt. Thus each sphere directs all
its efforts towards the sphere above it. The son of the rich
grocer becomes a notary, the son of the timber merchant becomes a magistrate. No link is wanting in the chain, and
everything stimulates the upward march of money.

Thus we are brought to the third circle of this hell, which,
perhaps, will some day find its Dante. In this third social
circle, a sort of Parisian belly, in which the interests of the
town are digested, and where they are condensed into the
form known as *business,* there moves and agitates, as by
some acrid and bitter intestinal process, the crowd of lawyers,
doctors, notaries, councillors, business men, bankers, big
merchants, speculators, and magistrates. Here are to be
found even more causes of moral and physical destruction
than elsewhere. These people—almost all of them—live
in unhealthy offices, in fetid ante-chambers, in little barred
dens, and spend their days bowed down beneath the weight
of affairs; they rise at dawn to be in time, not to be left behind, to gain all or not to lose, to overreach a man or his
money, to open or wind up some business, to take advantage
of some fleeting opportunity, to get a man hanged or set
him free. They infect their horses, they overdrive and age
and break them, like their own legs, before their time. Time
is their tyrant: it fails them, it escapes them; they can neither
expand it nor cut it short. What soul can remain great, pure,
moral, and generous, and, consequently, what face retain
its beauty in this depraving practice of a calling which compels one to bear the weight of the public sorrows, to analyze

them, to weigh them, estimate them, and mark them out by
rule?   Where do these folk put aside their hearts? . . .
I do not know; but they leave them somewhere or other, when
they have any, before they descend each morning into the
abyss of the misery which puts families on the rack.   For
them there is no such thing as mystery; they see the reverse
side of society, whose confessors they are, and despise it
Then, whatever they do, owing to their contact with corruption, they either are horrified at it and grow gloomy, or
else, out of lassitude, or some secret compromise, espouse it.
In fine, they necessarily become callous to every sentiment,
since man, his laws and his institutions, make them steal,
like jackals, from corpses that are still warm.   At all hours
the financier is trampling on the living, the attorney on the
dead, the pleader on the conscience.   Forced to be speaking
without a rest, they all substitute words for ideas, phrases
for feelings, and their soul becomes a larynx.   Neither the
great merchant, nor the judge, nor the pleader preserves his
sense of right; they feel no more, they apply set rules that
leave cases out of count.   Borne along by their headlong
course, they are neither husbands nor fathers nor lovers; they
glide on sledges over the facts of life, and live at all times
at the high pressure conduced by business and the vast city.
When they return to their homes they are required to go to
a ball, to the opera, into society, where they can make clients,
acquaintances, protectors.   They all eat to excess, play and
keep vigil, and their faces become bloated, flushed, and
emaciated.

   To this terrific expenditure of intellectual strength, to such
multifold moral contradictions, they oppose—not, indeed,
pleasure, it would be too pale a contrast—but debauchery, a
debauchery both secret and alarming, for they have all means
at their disposal, and fix the morality of society.   Their genuine stupidity lies hid beneath their specialism.   They know
their business, but are ignorant of everything which is outside
it.   So that to preserve their self-conceit they question everything, are crudely and crookedly critical.   They appear to be

sceptics and are in reality simpletons; they swamp their wits
in interminable arguments. Almost all conveniently adopt
social, literary, or political prejudices, to do away with the
need of having opinions, just as they adapt their conscience
to the standard of the Code or the Tribunal of Commerce.
Having started early to become men of note, they turn into
mediocrities, and crawl over the high places of the world.
So, too, their faces present the harsh pallor, the deceitful
coloring, those dull, tarnished eyes, and garrulous, sensual
mouths, in which the observer recognizes the symptoms of the
degeneracy of the thought and its rotation in the circle of a
special idea which destroys the creative faculties of the brain
and the gift of seeing in large, of generalizing and deducing.
No man who has allowed himself to be caught in the revolutions of the gear of these huge machines can ever become
great. If he is a doctor, either he has practised little or he
is an exception—a Bichat who dies young. If a great merchant, something remains—he is almost Jacques Cœur. Did
Robespierre practise? Danton was an idler who waited. But
who, moreover, has ever felt envious of the figures of Danton
and Robespierre, however lofty they were? These men of affairs, *par excellence,* attract money to them, and hoard it in
order to ally themselves with aristocratic families. If the
ambition of the working-man is that of the small tradesman,
here, too, are the same passions. In Paris vanity sums up
all the passions. The type of this class might be either
an ambitious *bourgeois,* who, after a life of privation and continual scheming, passes into the Council of State as an ant
passes through a chink; or some newspaper editor, jaded with
intrigue, whom the king makes a peer of France—perhaps to
revenge himself on the nobility; or some notary become
mayor of his parish: all people crushed with business, who,
if they attain their end, are literally *killed* in its attain-
ment. In France the usage is to glorify wigs. Napoleon,
Louis XVI., the great rulers, alone have always wished for
young men to fulfil their projects.

Above this sphere the artist world exists. But here, too,

the faces stamped with the seal of originality are worn, nobly indeed, but worn, fatigued, nervous. Harassed by a need of production, outrun by their costly fantasies, worn out by devouring genius, hungry for pleasure, the artists of Paris would all regain by excessive labor what they have lost by idleness, and vainly seek to reconcile the world and glory, money and art. To begin with, the artist is ceaselessly panting under his creditors; his necessities beget his debts, and his debts require of him his nights. After his labor, his pleasure. The comedian plays till midnight, studies in the morning, rehearses at noon; the sculptor is bent before his statue; the journalist is a marching thought, like the soldier when at war; the painter who is the fashion is crushed with work, the painter with no occupation, if he feels himself to be a man of genius, gnaws his entrails. Competition, rivalry, calumny assail talent. Some, in desperation, plunge into the abyss of vice, others die young and unknown because they have discounted their future too soon. Few of these figures, originally sublime, remain beautiful. On the other hand, the flagrant beauty of their heads is not understood. An artist's face is always exorbitant, it is always above or below the conventional lines of what fools call the *beau-idéal*. What power is it that destroys them? Passion. Every passion in Paris resolves into two terms: gold and pleasure. Now, do you not breathe again? Do you not feel air and space purified? Here is neither labor nor suffering. The soaring arch of gold has reached the summit. From the lowest gutters, where its stream commences, from the little shops where it is stopped by puny coffer-dams, from the heart of the counting-houses and great workshops, where its volume is that of ingots—gold, in the shape of dowries and inheritances, guided by the hands of young girls or the bony fingers of age, courses towards the aristocracy, where it will become a blazing, expansive stream. But, before leaving the four territories upon which the utmost wealth of Paris is based, it is fitting, having cited the moral causes, to deduce those which are physical, and to call attention to a pestilence, latent, as it were, which incessantly acts upon the faces of the porter, the artisan, the small shopkeeper; to point out a deleterious influence the corruption of which equals that of the Parisian administrators who allow it so complacently to exist!

If the air of the houses in which the greater proportion of the middle classes live is noxious, if the atmosphere of the streets belches out cruel miasmas into stuffy back-kitchens where there is little air, realize that, apart from this pestilence, the forty thousand houses of this great city have their foundations in filth, which the powers that be have not yet seriously attempted to enclose with mortar walls solid enough to prevent even the most fetid mud from filtering through the soil, poisoning the wells, and maintaining subterraneously to Lutetia the tradition of her celebrated name. Half of Paris sleeps amidst the putrid exhalations of courts and streets and sewers. But let us turn to the vast saloons, gilded and airy; the hotels in their gardens, the rich, indolent, happy, moneyed world. There the faces are lined and scarred with vanity. There nothing is real. To seek for pleasure is it not to find *ennui?* People in society have at an early age warped their nature. Having no occupation other than to wallow in pleasure, they have speedily misused their sense, as the artisan has misused brandy. Pleasure is of the nature of certain medical substances: in order to obtain constantly the same effects the doses must be doubled, and death or degradation is contained in the last. All the lower classes are on their knees before the wealthy, and watch their tastes in order to turn them into vices and exploit them. Thus you see in these folk at an early age tastes instead of passions, romantic fantasies and lukewarm loves. There impotence reigns; there ideas have ceased—they have evaporated together with energy amongst the affectations of the boudoir and the cajolements of women. There are fledglings of forty, old doctors of sixty years. The wealthy obtain in Paris ready-made wit and science—formulated opinions which save them from the need of having wit, science, or opinion of their own. The irrationality of this world is

equaled by its weakness and its licentiousness It is greedy
of time to the point of wasting it. Seek in it for affection
as little as for ideas. Its kisses conceal a profound indifference, its urbanity a perpetual contempt. It has no other
fashion of love. Flashes of wit without profundity, a wealth
of indiscretion, scandal, and, above all, commonplace. Such
is the sum of its speech; but these happy fortunates pretend
that they do not meet to make and repeat maxims in the
manner of La Rochefoucauld as though there did not exist
a mean, invented by the eighteenth century, between a
superfluity and absolute blank. If a few men of character
indulge in witticism, at once subtle and refined, they are
misunderstood; soon, tired of giving without receiving, they
remain at home, and leave fools to reign over their territory.
This hollow life, this perpetual expectation of a pleasure
which never comes, this permanent *ennui* and emptiness of
soul, heart, and mind, the lassitude of the upper Parisian
world, is reproduced on its features, and stamps its parchment faces, its premature wrinkles, that physiognomy of the
wealthy upon which impotence has set its grimace, in which
gold is mirrored, and whence intelligence has fled.

Such a view of moral Paris proves that physical Paris could
not be other than it is. This coroneted town is like a queen,
who, being always with child, has desires of irresistible fury.
Paris is the crown of the world, a brain which perishes of
genius and leads human civilization; it is a great man, a
perpetually creative artist, a politician with second-sight
who must of necessity have wrinkles on his forehead, the vices
of the great man, the fantasies of the artist, and the politician's disillusions. Its physiognomy suggests the evolution
of good and evil, battle and victory; the moral combat of
'89, the clarion calls of which still re-echo in every corner of
the world; and also the downfall of 1814. Thus this city
can no more be moral, or cordial, or clean, than the engines which impel those proud leviathans which you admire
when they cleave the waves! Is not Paris a sublime vessel
laden with intelligence? Yes, her arms are one of those

oracles which fatality sometimes allows. The *City of Paris* has her great mast, all of bronze, carved with victories, and for watchman—Napoleon. The barque may roll and pitch, but she cleaves the world, illuminates it through the hundred mouths of her tribunes, ploughs the seas of science, rides with full sail, cries from the height of her tops, with the voice of her scientists and artists: "Onward, advance! Follow me!" She carries a huge crew, which delights in adorning her with fresh streamers. Boys and urchins laughing in the rigging; ballast of heavy *bourgeoisie;* working-men and sailor-men touched with tar; in her cabins the lucky passengers; elegant midshipmen smoke their cigars leaning over the bulwarks; then, on the deck, her soldiers, innovators or ambitious, would accost every fresh shore, and shooting out their bright lights upon it, ask for glory which is pleasure, or for love which needs gold.

Thus the exorbitant movement of the proletariat, the corrupting influence of the interests which consume the two middle classes, the cruelties of the artist's thought, and the excessive pleasure which is sought for incessantly by the great, explain the normal ugliness of the Parisian physiognomy. It is only in the Orient that the human race presents a magnificent figure, but that is an effect of the constant calm affected by those profound philosophers with their long pipes, their short legs, their square contour, who despise and hold activity in horror, whilst in Paris the little and the great and the mediocre run and leap and drive, whipped on by an inexorable goddess, Necessity—the necessity for money, glory, and amusement. Thus, any face which is fresh and graceful and reposeful, any really young face, is in Paris the most extraordinary of exceptions; it is met with rarely. Should you see one there, be sure it belongs either to a young and ardent ecclesiastic or to some good abbé of forty with three chins; to a young girl of pure life such as is brought up in certain middle-class families; to a mother of twenty, still full of illusions, as she suckles her first-born; to a young man newly embarked from the provinces, and intrusted

to the care of some devout dowager who keeps him without a
sou; or, perhaps, to some shop assistant who goes to bed
at midnight wearied out with folding and unfolding calico,
and rises at seven o'clock to arrange the window; often again
to some man of science or poetry, who lives monastically in
the embrace of a fine idea, who remains sober, patient, and
chaste; else to some self-contented fool, feeding himself on
folly, reeking of health, in a perpetual state of absorption
with his own smile; or to the soft and happy race of loungers,
the only folk really happy in Paris, which unfolds for them
hour by hour its moving poetry.

Nevertheless, there is in Paris a proportion of privileged
beings to whom this excessive movement of industries, interests, affairs, arts, and gold is profitable. These beings are
women. Although they also have a thousand secret causes
which, here more than elsewhere, destroy their physiognomy,
there are to be found in the feminine world little happy
colonies, who live in Oriental fashion and can preserve their
beauty; but these women rarely show themselves on foot in
the streets, they lie hid like rare plants who only unfold their
petals at certain hours, and constitute veritable exotic exceptions. However, Paris is essentially the country of contrasts.
If true sentiments are rare there, there also are to be
found, as elsewhere, noble friendships and unlimited devotion. On this battlefield of interests and passions, just as in
the midst of those marching societies where egoism triumphs,
where every one is obliged to defend himself, and which we
call *armies,* it seems as though sentiments liked to be complete
when they showed themselves, and are sublime by juxtaposi-
tion. So it is with faces. In Paris one sometimes sees in
the aristocracy, set like stars, the ravishing faces of young
people, the fruit of quite exceptional manners and education.
To the youthful beauty of the English stock they unite the
firmness of Southern traits. The fire of their eyes, a delicious bloom on their lips, the lustrous black of their soft
locks, a white complexion, a distinguished caste of features,
render them the flowers of the human race, magnificent to

behold against the mass of other faces, worn, old, wrinkled, and grimacing. So women, too, admire such young people with that eager pleasure which men take in watching a pretty girl, elegant, gracious, and embellished with all the virginal charms with which our imagination pleases to adorn the perfect woman. If this hurried glance at the population of Paris has enabled us to conceive the rarity of a Raphaelesque face, and the passionate admiration which such an one must inspire at the first sight, the prime interest of our history will have been justified. *Quod erat demonstrandum*—if one may be permitted to apply scholastic formulæ to the science of manners.

Upon one of those fine spring mornings, when the leaves, although unfolded, are not yet green, when the sun begins to gild the roofs, and the sky is blue, when the population of Paris issues from its cells to swarm along the boulevards, glides like a serpent of a thousand coils through the Rue de la Paix towards the Tuileries, saluting the hymeneal magnificence which the country puts on; on one of these joyous days, then, a young man as beautiful as the day itself, dressed with taste, easy of manner—to let out the secret he was a love-child, the natural son of Lord Dudley and the famous Marquise de Vordac—was walking in the great avenue of the Tuileries. This Adonis, by name Henri de Marsay, was born in France, when Lord Dudley had just married the young lady, already Henri's mother, to an old gentleman called M. de Marsay. This faded and almost extinguished butterfly recognized the child as his own in consideration of the life interest in a fund of a hundred thousand francs definitively assigned to his putative son; a generosity which did not cost Lord Dudley too dear. French funds were worth at that time seventeen francs, fifty centimes. The old gentleman died without having ever known his wife. Madame de Marsay subsequently married the Marquis de Vordac, but before becoming a marquise she showed very little anxiety as to her son and Lord Dudley. To begin with, the declaration of war between France and England had separated the two lovers, and fidelity at all costs was not, and never will be, the fashion of Paris. Then the successes of the woman, elegant, pretty, universally adored, crushed in the Parisienne the maternal sentiment. Lord Dudley was no more troubled about his offspring than was the mother,—the speedy infidelity of a young girl he had ardently loved gave him, perhaps, a sort of aversion for all that issued from her. Moreover, fathers can, perhaps, only love the children with whom they are fully acquainted, a social belief of the utmost importance for the peace of families, which should be held by all the celibate, proving as it does that paternity is a sentiment nourished artificially by woman, custom, and the law.

Poor Henri de Marsay knew no other father than that one of the two who was not compelled to be one. The paternity of M. de Marsay was naturally most incomplete. In the natural order, it is but for a few fleeting instants that children have a father, and M. de Marsay imitated nature. The worthy man would not have sold his name had he been free from vices. Thus he squandered without remorse in gambling hells, and drank elsewhere, the few dividends which the National Treasury paid to its bondholders. Then he handed over the child to an aged sister, a Demoiselle de Marsay, who took much care of him, and provided him, out of the meagre sum allowed by her brother, with a tutor, an abbé without a farthing, who took the measure of the youth's future, and determined to pay himself out of the hundred thousand livres for the care given to his pupil, for whom he conceived an affection. As chance had it, this tutor was a true priest, one of those ecclesiastics cut out to become cardinals in France, or Borgias beneath the tiara. He taught the child in three years what he might have learned at college in ten. Then the great man, by name the Abbé de Maronis, completed the education of his pupil by making him study civilization under all its aspects: he nourished him on his experience, led him little into churches, which at that time were closed; introduced him sometimes behind the scenes of theatres, more often into the houses of courtesans;

he exhibited human emotions to him one by one; taught him politics in the drawing-rooms, where they simmered at the time, explained to him the machinery of government, and endeavored out of attraction towards a fine nature, deserted, yet rich in promise, virilely to replace a mother: is not the Church the mother of orphans? The pupil was responsive to so much care. The worthy priest died in 1812, a bishop, with the satisfaction of having left in this world a child whose heart and mind were so well moulded that he could outwit a man of forty. Who would have expected to have found a heart of bronze, a brain of steel, beneath external traits as seductive as ever the old painters, those naïve artists, had given to the serpent in the terrestrial paradise? Nor was that all. In addition, the good-natured prelate had procured for the child of his choice certain acquaintances in the best Parisian society, which might equal in value, in the young man's hand, another hundred thousand invested livres. In fine, this priest, vicious but politic, sceptical yet learned, treacherous yet amiable, weak in appearance yet as vigorous physically as intellectually, was so genuinely useful to his pupil, so complacent to his vices, so fine a calculator of all kinds of strength, so profound when it was needful to make some human reckoning, so youthful at table, at Frascati, at— I know not where, that the grateful Henri de Marsay was hardly moved at aught in 1814, except when he looked at the portrait of his beloved bishop, the only personal possession which the prelate had been able to bequeath him (admirable type of the men whose genius will preserve the Catholic, Apostolic, and Roman Church, compromised for the moment by the feebleness of its recruits and the decrepit age of its pontiffs; but if the church likes!).

The continental war prevented young De Marsay from knowing his real father. It is doubtful whether he was aware of his name. A deserted child, he was equally ignorant of Madame de Marsay. Naturally, he had little regret for his putative father. As for Mademoiselle de Marsay, his only mother, he built for her a handsome little monument in Père

Lachaise when she died. Monseigneur de Maronis had guaranteed to this old lady one of the best places in the skies, so that when he saw her die happy, Henri gave her some egotistical tears; he began to weep on his own account. Observing this grief, the abbé dried his pupil's tears, bidding him observe that the good woman took her snuff most offensively, and was becoming so ugly and deaf and tedious that he ought to return thanks for her death. The bishop had emancipated his pupil in 1811. Then, when the mother of M. de Marsay remarried, the priest chose, in a family council, one of those honest dullards, picked out by him through the windows of his confessional, and charged him with the administration of the fortune, the revenues of which he was willing to apply to the needs of the community, but of which he wished to preserve the capital.

Towards the end of 1814, then, Henri de Marsay had no sentiment of obligation in the world, and was as free as an unmated bird. Although he had lived twenty-two years he appeared to be barely seventeen. As a rule the most fastidious of his rivals considered him to be the prettiest youth in Paris. From his father, Lord Dudley, he had derived a pair of the most amorously deceiving blue eyes; from his mother the bushiest of black hair; from both pure blood, the skin of a young girl, a gentle and modest expression, a refined and aristocratic figure, and beautiful hands. For a woman, to see him was to lose her head for him; do you understand? to conceive one of those desires which eat the heart, which are forgotten because of the impossibility of satisfying them, because women in Paris are commonly without tenacity. Few of them say to themselves, after the fashion of men, the *"Je Maintiendrai,"* of the House of Orange.

Underneath this fresh young life, and in spite of the limpid springs in his eyes, Henri had a lion's courage, a monkey's agility. He could cut a ball in half at ten paces on the blade of a knife; he rode his horse in a way that made you realize the fable of the Centaur; drove a four-in-hand with grace; was as light as a cherub and quiet as a lamb, but knew how to beat a townsman at the terrible game of *savate* or cudgels; moreover, he played the piano in a fashion which would have enabled him to become an artist should he fall on calamity, and owned a voice which would have been worth to Barbaja fifty thousand francs a season. Alas, that all these fine qualities, these pretty faults, were tarnished by one abominable vice: he believed neither in man nor woman, God nor Devil. Capricious nature had commenced by endowing him, a priest had completed the work.

To render this adventure comprehensible, it is necessary to add here that Lord Dudley naturally found many women disposed to reproduce samples of such a delicious pattern. His second masterpiece of this kind was a young girl named Euphémie, born of a Spanish lady, reared in Havana, and brought to Madrid with a young Creole woman of the Antilles, and with all the ruinous tastes of the Colonies, but fortunately married to an old and extremely rich Spanish noble, Don Hijos, Marquis de San-Réal, who, since the occupation of Spain by French troops, had taken up his abode in Paris, and lived in the Rue St. Lazare. As much from indifference as from any respect for the innocence of youth, Lord Dudley was not in the habit of keeping his children informed of the relations he created for them in all parts. That is a slightly inconvenient form of civilization; it has so many advantages that we must overlook its drawbacks in consideration of its benefits. Lord Dudley, to make no more words of it, came to Paris in 1816 to take refuge from the pursuit of English justice, which protects nothing Oriental except commerce. The exiled lord, when he saw Henri, asked who that handsome young man might be. Then, upon hearing the name, "Ah, it is my son. . . . What a pity!" he said.

Such was the story of the young man who, about the middle of the month of April, 1815, was walking indolently up the broad avenue of the Tuileries, after the fashion of all those animals who, knowing their strength, pass along in majesty and peace. Middle-class matrons turned back naïvely to look at him again; other women, without turning round, waited for him to pass again, and engraved him in their minds that they might remember in due season that fragrant face, which would not have disadorned the body of the fairest among themselves.

"What are you doing here on Sunday?" said the Marquis de Ronquerolles to Henri, as he passed.

"There's a fish in the net," answered the young man.

This exchange of thoughts was accomplished by means of two significant glances, without it appearing that either De Ronquerolles or De Marsay had any knowledge of the other. The young man was taking note of the passers-by with that promptitude of eye and ear which is peculiar to the Parisian, who seems, at first sight, to see and hear nothing, but who sees and hears all.

At that moment a young man came up to him and took him familiarly by the arm, saying to him: "How are you, my dear De Marsay?"

"Extremely well," De Marsay answered, with that air of apparent affection which amongst the young men of Paris proves nothing, either for the present or the future.

In effect, the youth of Paris resemble the youth of no other town. They may be divided into two classes: the young man who has something, and the young man who has nothing; or the young man who thinks and he who spends. But, be it well understood, this applies only to those natives of the soil who maintain in Paris the delicious course of the elegant life. There exist, as well, plenty of other young men, but they are children who are late in conceiving Parisian life, and who remain its dupes. They do not speculate, they study; they *fag,* as the others say. Finally there are to be found, besides, certain young people, rich or poor, who embrace careers and follow them with a single heart; they are somewhat like the Émile of Rousseau, of the flesh of citizens, and they never appear in society. The diplomatic impolitely dub them fools. Be they that or no, they augment the num-

ber of those mediocrities beneath the yoke of which France is
bowed down.   They are always there, always ready to bungle
public or private concerns with the dull trowel of their mediocrity, bragging of their impotence, which they count for conduct and integrity.   This sort of social *prizemen* infests the
administration, the army, the magistracy, the chambers, the
courts.   They diminish and level down the country and constitute, in some manner, in the body politic, a lymph which
infects it and renders it flabby.   These honest folk call men
of talent immoral or rogues.   If such rogues require to be
paid for their services, at least their services are there;
whereas the other sort do harm and are respected by the mob;
but, happily for France, elegant youth stigmatizes them ceaselessly under the name of louts.

At the first glance, then, it is natural to consider as very
distinct the two sorts of young men who lead the life of elegance, the amiable corporation to which Henri de Marsay belonged.   But the observer, who goes beyond the superficial
aspect of things, is soon convinced that the difference is purely
moral, and that nothing is so deceptive as this pretty outside.
Nevertheless, all alike take precedence over everybody else;
speak rightly or wrongly of things, of men, literature, and
the fine arts; have ever in their mouth the Pitt and Coburg
of each year; interrupt a conversation with a pun; turn into
ridicule science and the *savant;* despise all things which they
do not know or which they fear; set themselves above all by
constituting themselves the supreme judges of all.   They
would all hoax their fathers, and be ready to shed crocodile
tears upon their mothers' breasts; but generally they believe
in nothing, blaspheme women, or play at modesty, and in
reality are led by some old woman or an evil courtesan.   They
are all equally eaten to the bone with calculation, with depravity, with a brutal lust to succeed, and if you plumbed
for their hearts you would find in all a stone.   In their normal state they have the prettiest exterior, stake their friendship at every turn, are captivating alike.   The same badinage
dominates their ever-changing jargon; they seek for oddity

in their toilette, glory in repeating the stupidities of such and such actor who is in fashion, and commence operations, it matters not with whom, with contempt and impertinence, in order to have, as it were, the first move in the game; but, woe betide him who does not know how to take a blow on one cheek for the sake of rendering two. They resemble, in fine, that pretty white spray which crests the stormy waves. They dress and dance, dine and take their pleasure, on the day of Waterloo, in the time of cholera or revolution. Finally, their expenses are all the same, but here the contrast comes in. Of this fluctuating fortune, so agreeably flung away, some possess the capital for which the others wait; they have the same tailors, but the bills of the latter are still to pay. Next, if the first, like sieves, take in ideas of all kinds without retaining any, the latter compare them and assimilate all the good. If the first believe they know something, know nothing and understand everything, lend all to those who need nothing and offer nothing to those who are in need; the latter study secretly others' thoughts and place out their money, like their follies, at big interest. The one class have no more faithful impressions, because their soul, like a mirror, worn from use, no longer reflects any image; the others economize their senses and life, even while they seem, like the first, to be flinging them away broadcast. The first, on the faith of a hope, devote themselves without conviction to a system which has wind and tide against it, but they leap upon another political craft when the first goes adrift; the second take the measure of the future, sound it, and see in political fidelity what the English see in commercial integrity, an element of success. Where the young man of possessions makes a pun or an epigram upon the restoration of the throne, he who has nothing makes a public calculation or a secret reservation, and obtains everything by giving a handshake to his friends. The one deny every faculty to others, look upon all their ideas as new, as though the world had been made yesterday, they have unlimited confidence in themselves, and no crueler enemy than those same selves. But the others are

armed with an incessant distrust of men, whom they estimate
at their value, and are sufficiently profound to have one
thought beyond their friends, whom they exploit; then of
evenings, when they lay their heads on their pillows, they
weigh men as a miser weighs his golden pieces. The one are
vexed at an aimless impertinence, and allow themselves to be
ridiculed by the diplomatic, who make them dance for them
by pulling what is the main string of these puppets—their
vanity. Thus, a day comes when those who had nothing have
something, and those who had something have nothing. The
latter look at their comrades who have achieved positions as
cunning fellows; their hearts may be bad, but their heads
are strong. "He is very strong!" is the supreme praise accorded to those who have attained *quibuscumque viis,* political rank, a woman, or a fortune. Amongst them are to be
found certain young men who play this *rôle* by commencing
with having debts. Naturally, these are more dangerous than
those who play it without a farthing.

The young man who called himself a friend of Henri de
Marsay was a rattle-head who had come from the provinces,
and whom the young men then in the fashion were teaching
the art of running through an inheritance; but he had one
last leg to stand on in his province, in the shape of a secure
establishment. He was simply an heir who had passed without any transition from his pittance of a hundred francs a
month to the entire paternal fortune, and who, if he had not
wit enough to perceive that he was laughed at, was sufficiently
cautious to stop short at two-thirds of his capital. He had
learned at Paris, for a consideration of some thousands of
francs, the exact value of harness, the art of not being too
respectful to his gloves, learned to make skilful meditations
upon the right wages to give people, and to seek out what
bargain was the best to close with them. He set store on his
capacity to speak in good terms of his horses, of his Pyrenean
hound; to tell by her dress, her walk, her shoes, to what class
a woman belonged; to study *écarté,* remember a few fashionable catchwords, and win by his sojourn in Parisian society

the necessary authority to import later into his province a
taste for tea and silver of an English fashion, and to obtain
the right of despising everything around him for the rest of
his days.

De Marsay had admitted him to his society in order to
make use of him in the world, just as a bold speculator employs a confidential clerk. The friendship, real or feigned,
of De Marsay was a social position for Paul de Manerville,
who, on his side, thought himself astute in exploiting, after
his fashion, his intimate friend. He lived in the reflecting
lustre of his friend, walked constantly under his umbrella,
wore his boots, gilded himself with his rays. When he posed
in Henri's company or walked at his side, he had the air of
saying: "Don't insult us, we are real dogs." He often permitted himself to remark fatuously: "If I were to ask Henri
for such and such a thing, he is a good enough friend of mine
to do it." But he was careful never to ask anything of him.
He feared him, and his fear, although imperceptible, reacted
upon the others, and was of use to De Marsay.

"De Marsay is a man of a thousand," said Paul. "Ah,
you will see, he will be what he likes. I should not be surprised to find him one of these days Minister of Foreign Affairs. Nothing can withstand him."

He made of De Marsay what Corporal Trim made of his
cap, a perpetual instance.

"Ask De Marsay and you will see!"

Or again:

"The other day we were hunting, De Marsay and I, he
would not believe me, but I jumped a hedge without moving
on my horse!"

Or again:

"We were with some women, De Marsay and I, and upon
my word of honor, I was——" etc.

Thus Paul de Manerville could not be classed amongst the
great, illustrious, and powerful family of fools who succeed.
He would one day be a deputy. For the time he was not even
a young man. His friend, De Marsay, defined him thus:

"You ask me what is Paul? Paul? Why, Paul de Manerville!"

"I am surprised, my dear fellow," he said to De Marsay,
"to see you here on a Sunday."

"I was going to ask you the same question."

"Is it an intrigue?"

"An intrigue."

"Bah!"

"I can mention it to you without compromising my passion. Besides, a woman who comes to the Tuileries on Sundays is of no account, aristocratically speaking."

"Ah! ah!"

"Hold your tongue then, or I shall tell you nothing. Your
laugh is too loud, you will make people think that we have
lunched too well. Last Thursday, here on the Terrasse des
Feuillants, I was walking along, thinking of nothing at all,
but when I got to the gate of the Rue de Castiglione, by
which I intended to leave, I came face to face with a woman,
or rather with a young girl; who, if she did not throw herself at my head, stopped short, less I think, from human respect, than from one of those movements of profound surprise which affect the limbs, creep down the length of the
spine, and cease only in the sole of the feet, to nail you to
the ground. I have often produced effects of this nature, a
sort of animal magnetism which becomes enormously powerful when the relations are reciprocally precise. But, my dear
fellow, this was not stupefaction, nor was she a common girl.
Morally speaking, her face seemed to say: 'What, is it you,
my ideal! The creation of my thoughts, of my morning and
evening dreams! What, are you there? Why this morning?
Why not yesterday? Take me, I am thine, *et cetera!*' Good,
I said to myself, another one! Then I scrutinize her. Ah,
my dear fellow, speaking physically, my incognita is the most
adorable feminine person whom I ever met. She belongs to
that feminine variety which the Romans call *fulva, flava*—
the woman of fire. And in chief, what struck me the most,
what I am still taken with, are her two yellow eyes, like a

tiger's, a golden yellow that gleams, living gold, gold which thinks, gold which loves, and is determined to take refuge in your pocket."

"My dear fellow, we are full of her!" cried Paul. "She comes here sometimes—*the girl with the golden eyes!* That is the name we have given her. She is a young creature—not more than twenty-two, and I have seen her here in the time of the Bourbons, but with a woman who was worth a hundred thousand of her."

"Silence, Paul! It is impossible for any woman to surpass this girl; she is like the cat who rubs herself against your legs; a white girl with ash-colored hair, delicate in appearance, but who must have downy threads on the third phalanx of her fingers, and all along her cheeks a white down whose line, luminous on fine days, begins at her ears and loses itself on her neck."

"Ah, the other, my dear De Marsay! She has black eyes which have never wept, but which burn; black eyebrows which meet and give her an air of hardness contradicted by the compact curve of her lips, on which the kisses do not stay, lips burning and fresh; a Moorish color that warms a man like the sun. But—upon my word of honor, she is like you!"

"You flatter her!"

"A firm figure, the tapering figure of a corvette built for speed, which rushes down upon the merchant vessel with French impetuosity, which grapples with her and sinks her at the same time."

"After all, my dear fellow," answered De Marsay, "what has that got to do with me, since I have never seen her? Ever since I have studied women, my incognita is the only one whose virginal bosom, whose ardent and voluptuous forms, have realized for me the only woman of my dreams— of my dreams! She is the original of that ravishing picture called *La Femme Caressant sa Chimère,* the warmest, the most infernal inspiration of the genius of antiquity; a holy poem prostituted by those who have copied it for frescoes and mosaics; for a heap of bourgeois who see in this gem nothing

more than a gew-gaw and hang it on their watch-chains—
whereas, it is the whole woman, an abyss of pleasure into
which one plunges and finds no end; whereas, it is the ideal
woman, to be seen sometimes in reality in Spain or Italy, almost never in France. Well, I have again seen this girl of the
gold eyes, this woman caressing her chimera. I saw her on Fri-
day. I had a presentiment that on the following day she would
be here at the same hour; I was not mistaken. I have taken a
pleasure in following her without being observed, in studying her indolent walk, the walk of the woman without occupation, but in the movements of which one divines all the
pleasure that lies asleep. Well, she turned back again, she
saw me, once more she adored me, once more trembled, shivered. It was then I noticed the genuine Spanish duenna who
looked after her, a hyena upon whom some jealous man has
put a dress, a she-devil well paid, no doubt, to guard this delicious creature. . . . Ah, then the duenna made me
deeper in love. I grew curious. On Saturday, nobody. And
here I am to-day waiting for this girl whose chimera I am,
asking nothing better than to pose as the monster in the
fresco."

"There she is," said Paul. "Every one is turning round
to look at her."

The unknown blushed, her eyes shone; as she saw Henri,
she shut them and passed by.

"You say that she notices you?" cried Paul, facetiously.

The duenna looked fixedly and attentively at the two young
men. When the unknown and Henri passed each other again,
the young girl touched him, and with her hand pressed the
hand of the young man. Then she turned her head and
smiled with passion, but the duenna led her away very quickly
to the gate of the Rue de Castiglione.

The two friends followed the young girl, admiring the magnificent grace of the neck which met her head in a harmony
of vigorous lines, and upon which a few coils of hair were
tightly wound. The girl with the golden eyes had that well-
knitted, arched, slender foot which presents so many attrac-

tions to the dainty imagination. Moreover, she was shod with elegance, and wore a short skirt. During her course she turned from time to time to look at Henri, and appeared to follow the old woman regretfully, seeming to be at once her mistress and her slave; she could break her with blows, but could not dismiss her. All that was perceptible. The two friends reached the gate. Two men in livery let down the step of a tasteful *coupé* emblazoned with armorial bearings. The girl with the golden eyes was the first to enter it, took her seat at the side where she could be best seen when the carriage turned, put her hand on the door, and waved her handkerchief in the duenna's despite. In contempt of what might be said by the curious, her handkerchief cried to Henri openly: "Follow me!"

"Have you ever seen the handkerchief better thrown?" said Henri to Paul de Manerville.

Then, observing a fiacre on the point of departure, having just set down a fare, he made a sign to the driver to wait.

"Follow that carriage, notice the house and the street where it stops—you shall have ten francs. . . . Paul, adieu."

The cab followed the *coupé*. The *coupé* stopped in the Rue Saint Lazare before one of the finest houses of the neighborhood.

De Marsay was not impulsive. Any other young man would have obeyed his impulse to obtain at once some information about a girl who realized so fully the most luminous ideas ever expressed upon women in the poetry of the East; but, too experienced to compromise his good fortune, he had told his coachman to continue along the Rue Saint Lazare and carry him back to his house. The next day, his confidential valet, Laurent by name, as cunning a fellow as the Frontin of the old comedy, waited in the vicinity of the house inhabited by the unknown for the hour at which letters were distributed. In order to be able to spy at his ease and hang about the house, he had followed the example of those police officers who seek a good disguise, and bought up cast-off clothes of an Auvergnat, the appearance of whom he sought to imitate. When the postman, who went the round of the Rue Saint Lazare that morning, passed by, Laurent feigned to be a porter unable to remember the name of a person to whom he had to deliver a parcel, and consulted the postman. Deceived at first by appearances, this personage, so picturesque in the midst of Parisian civilization, informed him that the house in which the girl with the golden eyes dwelt belonged to Don Hijos, Marquis de San-Réal, grandee of Spain. Naturally, it was not with the Marquis that the Auvergnat was concerned.

"My parcel," he said, "is for the marquise."

"She is away," replied the postman. "Her letters are forwarded to London."

"Then the marquise is not a young girl who . . . ?"

"Ah!" said the postman, interrupting the *valet de chambre* and observing him attentively, "you are as much a porter as I'm . . ."

Laurent chinked some pieces of gold before the functionary, who began to smile.

"Come, here's the name of your quarry," he said, taking from his leather wallet a letter bearing a London stamp, upon which the address, "To Mademoiselle Paquita Valdès, Rue Saint Lazare, Hotel San-Réal, Paris," was written in long, fine characters, which spoke of a woman's hand.

"Could you tap a bottle of Chablis, with a few dozen oysters, and a *filet sauté* with mushrooms to follow it?" said Laurent, who wished to win the postman's valuable friendship.

"At half-past nine, when my round is finished——Where?"

"At the corner of the Rue de la Chaussée-d'Antin and the Rue Neuve-des-Mathurins, at the *Puits sans Vin*," said Laurent.

"Hark ye, my friend," said the postman, when he rejoined the valet an hour after this encounter, "if your master is in love with the girl, he is in for a famous task. I doubt you'll not succeed in seeing her. In the ten years that I've been postman in Paris, I have seen plenty of different kinds of doors! But I can tell you, and no fear of being called a liar by any of my comrades, there never was a door so mysterious as M. de San-Réal's. No one can get into the house without the Lord knows what counter-word; and, notice, it has been selected on purpose between a courtyard and a garden to avoid any communication with other houses. The porter is an old Spaniard, who never speaks a word of French, but peers at people, as Vidocq might, to see if they are not thieves. If a lover, a thief, or you—I make no comparisons—could get the better of this first wicket, well, in the first hall, which is shut by a glazed door, you would run across a butler surrounded by lackeys, an old joker more savage and surly even than the porter. If any one gets past the porter's lodge, my butler comes out, waits for you at the entrance, and puts you through a cross-examination like a criminal. That has happened to me, a mere postman. He took me for an eavesdropper in disguise, he said, laughing at his nonsense. As for the servants, don't hope to get aught out of them; I think they are mutes, no one in the neighborhood knows the color of their speech; I don't know what wages they can pay them to keep them from talk and drink; the fact is, they are not to be got at, whether because they are afraid of being shot, or that they have some enormous sum to lose in the case of an indiscretion. If your master is fond enough of Mademoiselle Paquita Valdès to surmount all these obstacles, he certainly won't triumph over Doña Concha Marialva, the duenna who accompanies her and would put her under her petticoats sooner than leave her. The two women look as if they were sewn to one another."

"All that you say, worthy postman," went on Laurent, after having drunk off his wine, "confirms me in what I have learned before. Upon my word, I thought they were making fun of me! The fruiterer opposite told me that of nights they let loose dogs whose food is hung up on stakes just out of their reach. These cursed animals think, therefore, that any one likely to come in has designs on their victuals, and would tear one to pieces. You will tell me one might throw

them down pieces, but it seems they have been trained to
touch nothing except from the hand of the porter."

"The porter of the Baron de Nucingen, whose garden joins
at the top that of the Hotel San-Réal, told me the same
thing," replied the postman.

"Good! my master knows him," said Laurent, to himself.
"Do you know," he went on, leering at the postman, "I serve
a master who is a rare man, and if he took it into his head to
kiss the sole of the foot of an empress, she would have to give
in to him. If he had need of you, which is what I wish for
you, for he is generous, could one count on you?"

"Lord, Monsieur Laurent, my name is Moinot. My name
is written exactly like *Moineau,* magpie: M-o-i-n-o-t, Moinot."

"Exactly," said Laurent.

"I live at No. 11, Rue des Trois Frères, on the fifth floor,"
went on Moinot; "I have a wife and four children. If what
you want of me doesn't transgress the limits of my conscience
and my official duties, you understand! I am your man."

"You are an honest fellow," said Laurent, shaking his
hand. . . .

"Paquita Valdès is, no doubt, the mistress of the Marquis
de San-Réal, the friend of King Ferdinand. Only an old
Spanish mummy of eighty years is capable of taking such
precautions," said Henri, when his *valet de chambre* had related the result of his researches.

"Monsieur," said Laurent, "unless he takes a balloon no
one can get into that hotel."

"You are a fool! Is it necessary to get into the hotel to
have Paquita, when Paquita can get out of it?"

"But, sir, the duenna?"

"We will shut her up for a day or two, your duenna."

"So, we shall have Paquita!" said Laurent, rubbing his
hands.

"Rascal!" answered Henri, "I shall condemn you to the
Concha, if you carry your impudence so far as to speak so of
a woman before she has become mine. . . . Turn your
thoughts to dressing me, I am going out."

Henri remained for a moment plunged in joyous reflections. Let us say it to the praise of women, he obtained all those whom he deigned to desire. And what could one think of a woman, having no lover, who should have known how to resist a young man armed with beauty which is the intelligence of the body, with intelligence which is a grace of the soul, armed with moral force and fortune, which are the only two real powers? Yet, in triumphing with such ease, De Marsay was bound to grow weary of his triumphs; thus, for about two years he had grown very weary indeed. And diving deep into the sea of pleasures he brought back more grit than pearls. Thus had he come, like potentates, to implore of Chance some obstacle to surmount, some enterprise which should ask the employment of his dormant moral and physical strength. Although Paquita Valdès presented him with a marvelous concentration of perfections which he had only yet enjoyed in detail, the attraction of passion was almost *nil* with him. Constant satiety had weakened in his heart the sentiment of love. Like old men and people disillusioned, he had no longer anything but extravagant caprices, ruinous tastes, fantasies, which, once satisfied, left no pleasant memory in his heart. Amongst young people love is the finest of the emotions, it makes the life of the soul blossom, it nourishes by its solar power the finest inspirations and their great thoughts; the first fruits in all things have a delicious savor. Amongst men love becomes a passion; strength leads to abuse. Amongst old men it turns to vice; impotence tends to extremes. Henri was at once an old man, a man, and a youth. To afford him the feelings of a real love, he needed, like Lovelace, a Clarissa Harlowe. Without the magic lustre of that unattainable pearl he could only have either passions rendered acute by some Parisian vanity, or set determinations with himself to bring such and such a woman to such and such a point of corruption, or else adventures which stimulated his curiosity.

The report of Laurent, his *valet de chambre,* had just given an enormous value to the girl with the golden eyes. It was a question of doing battle with some secret enemy who seemed as dangerous as he was cunning; and to carry off the victory, all the forces which Henri could dispose of would be useful. He was about to play in that eternal old comedy which will be always fresh, and the characters in which are an old man, a young girl, and a lover: Don Hijos, Paquita, De Marsay. If Laurent was the equal of Figaro, the duenna seemed incorruptible. Thus, the living play was supplied by Chance with a stronger plot than it had ever been by dramatic author! But then is not Chance, too, a man of genius?

"It must be a cautious game," said Henri, to himself.

"Well," said Paul de Manerville, as he entered the room. "How are we getting on? I have come to breakfast with you."

"So be it" said Henri. "You won't be shocked if I make my toilette before you?"

"How absurd!"

"We take so many things from the English just now that we might well become as great prudes and hypocrites as themselves," said Henri.

Laurent had set before his master such a quantity of utensils, so many different articles of such elegance, that Paul could not refrain from saying:

"But you will take a couple of hours over that?"

"No!" said Henri, "two hours and a half."

"Well, then, since we are by ourselves, and can say what we like, explain to me why a man as superior as yourself— for you are superior—should affect to exaggerate a foppery which cannot be natural. Why spend two hours and a half in adorning yourself, when it is sufficient to spend a quarter of an hour in your bath, to do your hair in two minutes, and to dress! There, tell me your system."

"I must be very fond of you, my good dunce, to confide such high thoughts to you," said the young man, who was at that moment having his feet rubbed with a soft brush lathered with English soap.

"Have I not the most devoted attachment to you," replied

Paul de Manerville, "and do I not like you because I know your superiority? . . ."

"You must have noticed, if you are in the least capable of observing any moral fact, that women love fops," went on De Marsay, without replying in any way to Paul's declaration except by a look. "Do you know why women love fops? My friend, fops are the only men who take care of themselves. Now, to take excessive care of oneself, does it not imply that one takes care in oneself of what belongs to another? The man who does not belong to himself is precisely the man on whom women are keen. Love is essentially a thief. I say nothing about that excess of niceness to which they are so devoted. Do you know of any woman who has had a passion for a sloven, even if he were a remarkable man? If such a fact has occurred, we must put it to the account of those morbid affections of the breeding woman, mad fancies which float through the minds of everybody. On the other hand, I have seen most remarkable people left in the lurch because of their carelessness. A fop, who is concerned about his person, is concerned with folly, with petty things. And what is a woman? A petty thing, a bundle of follies. With two words said to the winds, can you not make her busy for four hours? She is sure that the fop will be occupied with her, seeing that he has no mind for great things. She will never be neglected for glory, ambition, politics, art—those prostitutes who for her are rivals. Then fops have the courage to cover themselves with ridicule in order to please a woman, and her heart is full of gratitude towards the man who is ridiculous for love. In fine, a fop can be no fop unless he is right in being one. It is women who bestow that rank. The fop is love's colonel; he has his victories, his regiment of women at his command. My dear fellow, in Paris everything is known, and a man cannot be a fop there *gratis*. You, who have only one woman, and who, perhaps, are right to have but one, try to act the fop! . . . You will not even become ridiculous, you will be dead. You will become a foregone conclusion, one of those men condemned inevitably to do one and the same thing.

You will come to signify *folly* as inseparably as M. de La
Fayette signifies *America;* M. de Talleyrand, *diplomacy;*
Désaugiers, *song;* M. de Ségur, *romance.* If they once forsake their own line people no longer attach any value to what
they do. So, foppery, my friend Paul, is the sign of an in-
contestable power over the female folk. A man who is loved
by many women passes for having superior qualities, and then,
poor fellow, it is a question who shall have him! But do
you think it is nothing to have the right of going into a
drawing-room, of looking down at people from over your
cravat, or through your eye-glass, and of despising the most
superior of men should he wear an old-fashioned waistcoat?
. . . Laurent, you are hurting me! After breakfast,
Paul, we will go to the Tuileries and see the adorable girl
with the golden eyes."

When, after making an excellent meal, the two young men
had traversed the Terrasse des Feuillants and the broad
walk of the Tuileries, they nowhere discovered the sublime
Paquita Valdès, on whose account some fifty of the most elegant young men in Paris were to be seen, all scented, with
their high scarfs, spurred and booted, riding, walking, talking, laughing, and damning themselves mightily.

"It's a white Mass," said Henri; "but I have the most excellent idea in the world. This girl receives letters from
London. The postman must be bought or made drunk, a letter opened, read of course, and a love-letter slipped in before
it is sealed up again. The old tyrant, *crudel tirano,* is certain
to know the person who writes the letters from London, and
has ceased to be suspicious of them."

The day after, De Marsay came again to walk on the Terrasse des Feuillants, and saw Paquita Valdès; already passion had embellished her for him. Seriously, he was wild
for those eyes, whose rays seemed akin to those which the sun
emits, and whose ardor set the seal upon that of her perfect
body, in which all was delight. De Marsay was on fire to
brush the dress of this enchanting girl as they passed one
another in their walk; but his attempts were always vain.

But at one moment, when he had repassed Paquita and the duenna, in order to find himself on the same side as the girl of the golden eyes, when he returned, Paquita, no less impatient, came forward hurriedly, and De Marsay felt his hand pressed by her in a fashion at once so swift and so passionately significant that it was as though he had received the shock of an electric current. In an instant all his youthful emotions surged up in his heart. When the two lovers glanced at one another, Paquita seemed ashamed, she dropped her eyes lest she should meet the eyes of Henri, but her gaze sank lower to fasten on the feet and form of him whom women, before the Revolution, called *their conqueror*.

"I am determined to make this girl my mistress," said Henri to himself.

As he followed her along the terrace, in the direction of the Place Louis XV., he caught sight of the aged Marquis de San-Réal, who was walking on the arm of his valet, stepping with all the precautions due to gout and decrepitude. Doña Concha, who distrusted Henri, made Paquita pass between herself and the old man.

"Oh, for you," said De Marsay to himself, casting a glance of disdain upon the duenna, "if one cannot make you capitulate, with a little opium one can make you sleep. We know mythology and the fable of Argus."

Before entering the carriage, the golden-eyed girl exchanged certain glances with her lover, of which the meaning was unmistakable and which enchanted Henri, but one of them was surprised by the duenna; she said a few rapid words to Paquita, who threw herself into the *coupé* with an air of desperation. For some days Paquita did not appear in the Tuileries. Laurent, who by his master's orders was on watch by the hotel, learned from the neighbors that neither the two women nor the aged marquis had been abroad since the day upon which the duenna had surprised a glance between the young girl in her charge and Henri. The bond, so flimsy withal, which united the two lovers was already severed.

Some days later, none knew by what means, De Marsay had attained his end; he had a seal and wax, exactly resembling the seal and the wax affixed to the letters sent to Mademoiselle Valdès from London; paper similar to that which her correspondent used; moreover, all the implements and stamps necessary to affix the French and English postmarks.

He wrote the following letter, to which he gave all the appearances of a letter sent from London:—

"My dear Paquita,—I shall not try to paint to you in words the passion with which you have inspired me. If, to my happiness, you reciprocate it, understand that I have found a means of corresponding with you. My name is Adolphe de Gouges, and I live at No. 54 Rue de l'Université. If you are too closely watched to be able to write to me, if you have neither pen nor paper, I shall understand it by your silence. If then, to-morrow, you have not, between eight o'clock in the morning and ten o'clock in the evening, thrown a letter over the wall of your garden into that of the Baron de Nucingen, where it will be waited for during the whole of the day, a man, who is entirely devoted to me, will let down two flasks by a string over your wall at ten o'clock the next morning. Be walking there at that hour. One of the two flasks will contain opium to send your Argus to sleep; it will be sufficient to employ six drops; the other will contain ink. The flask of ink is of cut glass; the other is plain. Both are of such a size as can easily be concealed within your bosom. All that I have already done, in order to be able to correspond with you, should tell you how greatly I love you. Should you have any doubt of it, I will confess to you, that to obtain an interview of one hour with you I would give my life."

"At least they believe that, poor creatures!" said De Marsay; "but they are right. What should we think of a woman who refused to be beguiled by a love-letter accompanied by such convincing accessories?"

This letter was delivered by Master Moinot, postman, on the following day, about eight o'clock in the morning, to the porter of the Hotel San-Réal.

In order to be nearer to the field of action, De Marsay went and breakfasted with Paul, who lived in the Rue de la Pépinière. At two o'clock, just as the two friends were laughingly discussing the discomfiture of a young man who had attempted to lead the life of fashion without a settled income, and were devising an end for him, Henri's coachman came to seek his master at Paul's house, and presented to him a mysterious personage who insisted on speaking himself with his master.

This individual was a mulatto, who would assuredly have given Talma a model for the part of Othello, if he had come across him. Never did any African face better express the grand vengefulness, the ready suspicion, the promptitude in the execution of a thought, the strength of the Moor, and his childish lack of reflection. His black eyes had the fixity of the eyes of a bird of prey, and they were framed, like a vulture's, by a bluish membrane devoid of lashes. His forehead, low and narrow, had something menacing. Evidently, this man was under the yoke of some single and unique thought. His sinewy arm did not belong to him.

He was followed by a man whom the imaginations of all folk, from those who shiver in Greenland to those who sweat in the tropics, would paint in the single phrase: *He was an unfortunate man*. From this phrase, everybody will conceive him according to the special ideas of each country. But who can best imagine his face—white and wrinkled, red at the extremities, and his long beard. Who will see his lean and yellow scarf, his greasy shirt-collar, his battered hat, his green frock coat, his deplorable trousers, his dilapidated waistcoat, his imitation gold pin, and battered shoes, the strings of which were plastered in mud? Who will see all that but the Parisian? The unfortunate man of Paris is the unfortunate man *in toto,* for he has still enough mirth to know the extent of his misfortune. The mulatto was like an executioner of Louis XI. leading a man to the gallows.

"Who has hunted us out these two extraordinary creatures?" said Henri.

"Faith! there is one of them who makes me shudder," replied Paul.

"Who are you—you fellow who look the most like a Christian of the two?" said Henri, looking at the unfortunate man.

The mulatto stood with his eyes fixed upon the two young men, like a man who understood nothing, and who sought no less to divine something from the gestures and movements of the lips.

"I am a public scribe and interpreter; I live at the Palais de Justice, and am named Poincet."

"Good! . . . and this one?" said Henri to Poincet, looking towards the mulatto.

"I do not know; he only speaks a sort of Spanish *patois,* and he has brought me here to make himself understood by you."

The mulatto drew from his pocket the letter which Henri had written to Paquita and handed it to him. Henri threw it in the fire.

"Ah—so—the game is beginning," said Henri to himself. "Paul, leave us alone for a moment."

"I translated this letter for him," went on the interpreter, when they were alone. "When it was translated, he was in some place which I don't remember. Then he came back to look for me, and promised me two *louis* to fetch him here."

"What have you got to say to me, nigger?" asked Henri.

"I did not translate *nigger,*" said the interpreter, waiting for the mulatto's reply. . . .

"He said, sir," went on the interpreter, after having listened to the unknown, "that you must be at half-past ten tomorrow night on the Boulevard Montmartre, near the café. You will see a carriage there, in which you must take your place, saying to the man, who will wait to open the door for you, the word *cortejo*—a Spanish word, which means *lover,*" added Poincet, casting a glance of congratulation upon Henri.

"Good."

The mulatto was about to bestow the two *louis,* but De Marsay would not permit it, and himself rewarded the interpreter. As he was paying him, the mulatto began to speak.

"What is he saying?"

"He is warning me," replied the unfortunate, "that if I commit a single indiscretion he will strangle me. He speaks fair and he looks remarkably as if he were capable of carrying out his threat."

"I am sure of it," answered Henri; "he would keep his word."

"He says, as well," replied the interpreter, "that the person from whom he is sent implores you, for your sake and for hers, to act with the greatest prudence, because the daggers which are raised above your head would strike your heart before any human power could save you from them."

"He said that? So much the better, it will be more amusing. You can come in now, Paul," he cried to his friend.

The mulatto, who had not ceased to gaze at the lover of Paquita Valdès with magnetic attention, went away, followed by the interpreter.

"Well, at last I have an adventure which is entirely romantic," said Henri, when Paul returned. "After having shared in a certain number I have finished by finding in Paris an intrigue accompanied by serious accidents, by grave perils. The deuce! what courage danger gives a woman! To torment a woman, to try and contradict her—doesn't it give her the right and the courage to scale in one moment obstacles which it would take her years to surmount of herself? Pretty creature, jump then! To die? Poor child! Daggers? Oh, imagination of women! They cannot help trying to find authority for their little jests. Besides, can one think of it, Paquita? Can one think of it, my child? The devil take me, now that I know this beautiful girl, this masterpiece of nature, is mine, the adventure has lost its charm."

For all his light words, the youth in Henri had reappeared.

In order to live until the morrow without too much pain, he had recourse to exorbitant pleasure; he played, dined, supped with his friends; he drank like a fish, ate like a German, and won ten or twelve thousand francs. He left the Rocher de Cancale at two o'clock in the morning, slept like a child, awoke the next morning fresh and rosy, and dressed to go to the Tuileries, with the intention of taking a ride, after having seen Paquita, in order to get himself an appetite and dine the better, and so kill the time.

At the hour mentioned Henri was on the boulevard, saw the carriage, and gave the counter-word to a man who looked to him like the mulatto. Hearing the word, the man opened the door and quickly let down the step. Henri was so rapidly carried through Paris, and his thoughts left him so little capacity to pay attention to the streets through which he passed, that he did not know where the carriage stopped. The mulatto let him into a house, the staircase of which was quite close to the entrance. This staircase was dark, as was also the landing upon which Henri was obliged to wait while the mulatto was opening the door of a damp apartment, fetid and unlit, the chambers of which, barely illuminated by the candle which his guide found in the ante-chamber, seemed to him empty and ill furnished, like those of a house the inhabitants of which are away. He recognized the sensation which he had experienced from the perusal of one of those romances of Anne Radcliffe, in which the hero traverses the cold, sombre, and uninhabited saloons of some sad and desert spot.

At last the mulatto opened the door of a *salon*. The condition of the old furniture and the dilapidated curtains with which the room was adorned gave it the air of the reception-room of a house of ill fame. There was the same pretension to elegance, and the same collection of things in bad taste, of dust and dirt. Upon a sofa covered with red Utrecht velvet, by the side of a smoking hearth, the fire of which was buried in ashes, sat an old, poorly dressed woman, her head capped by one of those turbans which English women of a certain age have invented and which would have a mighty success in China, where the artist's ideal is the monstrous.

The room, the old woman, the cold hearth, all would have chilled love to death had not Paquita been there, upon an ottoman, in a loose voluptuous wrapper, free to scatter her gaze of gold and flame, free to show her arched foot, free of her luminous movements. This first interview was what every *rendezvous* must be between persons of passionate disposition, who have stepped over a wide distance quickly, who desire each other ardently, and who, nevertheless, do not know each other. It is impossible that at first there should not occur certain discordant notes in the situation, which is embarrassing until the moment when two souls find themselves in unison.

If desire gives a man boldness and disposes him to lay restraint aside, the mistress, under pain of ceasing to be woman, however great may be her love, is afraid of arriving at the end so promptly, and face to face with the necessity of giving herself, which to many women is equivalent to a fall into an abyss, at the bottom of which they know not what they shall find. The involuntary coldness of the woman contrasts with her confessed passion, and necessarily reacts upon the most passionate lover. Thus ideas, which often float around souls like vapors, determine in them a sort of temporary malady. In the sweet journey which two beings undertake through the fair domains of love, this moment is like a waste land to be traversed, a land without a tree, alternatively damp and warm, full of scorching sand, traversed by marshes, which leads to smiling groves clad with roses, where Love and his retinue of pleasures disport themselves on carpets of soft verdure. Often the witty man finds himself afflicted with a foolish laugh which is his only answer to everything; his wit is, as it were, suffocated beneath the icy pressure of his desires. It would not be impossible for two beings of equal beauty, intelligence, and passion to utter at first nothing but the most silly commonplaces, until chance, a word, the tremor of a certain glance, the communication of a spark, should

have brought them to the happy transition which leads to that
flowery way in which one does not walk, but where one sways
and at the same time does not lapse.

Such a state of mind is always in proportion with the violence of the feeling. Two creatures who love one another
weakly feel nothing similar. The effect of this crisis can
even be compared with that which is produced by the glow of
a clear sky. Nature, at the first view, appears to be covered
with a gauze veil, the azure of the firmament seems black,
the intensity of light is like darkness. With Henri, as with
the Spanish girl, there was an equal intensity of feeling; and
that law of statics, in virtue of which two identical forces
cancel each other, might have been true also in the moral order. And the embarrassment of that moment was singularly
increased by the presence of the old hag. Love takes pleasure or fright at all, all has a meaning for it, everything is
an omen of happiness or sorrow for it.

This decrepit woman was there like a suggestion of catastrophe, and represented the horrid fish's tail with which the
allegorical geniuses of Greece have terminated their chime-
ras and sirens, whose figures, like all passions, are so seductive, so deceptive.

Although Henri was not a free-thinker—the phrase is always a mockery—but a man of extraordinary power, a man
as great as a man can be without faith, the conjunction struck
him. Moreover, the strongest men are naturally the most
impressionable, and consequently the most superstitious, if,
indeed, one may call superstition the prejudice of first
thoughts, which, without doubt, is the appreciation of the
result in causes hidden to other eyes but perceptible to their
own.

The Spanish girl profited by this moment of stupefaction
to let herself fall into the ecstasy of that infinite adoration
which seizes the heart of a woman, when she truly loves and
finds herself in the presence of an idol for whom she has
vainly longed. Her eyes were all joy, all happiness, and
sparks flew from them. She was under the charm, and fear-

lessly intoxicated herself with a felicity of which she had dreamed long. She seemed then so marvelously beautiful to Henri, that all this phantasmagoria of rags and old age, of worn red drapery and of the green mats in front of the armchairs, the ill-washed red tiles, all this sick and dilapidated luxury, disappeared.

The room seemed lit up; and it was only through a cloud that one could see the fearful harpy fixed and dumb on her red sofa, her yellow eyes betraying the servile sentiments, inspired by misfortune, or caused by some vice beneath whose servitude one has fallen as beneath a tyrant who brutalizes one with the flagellations of his despotism. Her eyes had the cold glitter of a caged tiger, knowing his impotence and being compelled to swallow his rage of destruction.

"Who is that woman?" said Henri to Paquita.

But Paquita did not answer. She made a sign that she understood no French, and asked Henri if he spoke English.

De Marsay repeated his question in English.

"She is the only woman in whom I can confide, although she has sold me already," said Paquita, tranquilly. "My dear Adolphe, she is my mother, a slave bought in Georgia for her rare beauty, little enough of which remains to-day. She only speaks her native tongue."

The attitude of this woman and her eagerness to guess from the gestures of her daughter and Henri what was passing between them, were suddenly explained to the young man; and this explanation put him at his ease.

"Paquita," he said, "are we never to be free then?"

"Never," she said, with an air of sadness. "Even now we have but a few days before us."

She lowered her eyes, looked at and counted with her right hand on the fingers of her left, revealing so the most beautiful hands which Henri had ever seen.

"One, two, three——"

She counted up to twelve.

"Yes," she said, "we have twelve days."

"And after?"

"After," she said, showing the absorption of a weak woman before the executioner's axe, and slain in advance, as it were, by a fear which stripped her of that magnificent energy which Nature seemed to have bestowed upon her only to aggrandize pleasure and convert the most vulgar delights into endless poems. "After——" she repeated. Her eyes took a fixed stare; she seemed to contemplate a threatening object far away.

"I do not know," she said.

"This girl is mad," said Henri to himself, falling into strange reflections.

Paquita appeared to him occupied by something which was not himself, like a woman constrained equally by remorse and passion. Perhaps she had in her heart another love which she alternately remembered and forgot. In a moment Henri was assailed by a thousand contradictory thoughts. This girl became a mystery for him; but as he contemplated her with the scientific attention of the *blasé* man, famished for new pleasures, like that Eastern king who asked that a pleasure should be created for him,—a horrible thirst with which great souls are seized,—Henri recognized in Paquita the richest organization that Nature had ever deigned to compose for love. The presumptive play of this machinery, setting aside the soul, would have frightened any other man than Henri; but he was fascinated by that rich harvest of promised pleasures, by that constant variety in happiness, the dream of every man, and the desire of every loving woman too. He was infuriated by the infinite rendered palpable, and transported into the most excessive raptures of which the creature is capable. All that he saw in this girl more distinctly than he had yet seen it, for she let herself be viewed complacently, happy to be admired. The admiration of De Marsay became a secret fury, and he unveiled her completely, throwing a glance at her which the Spaniard understood as though she had been used to receive such.

"If you are not to be mine, mine only, I will kill you!" he cried.

Hearing this speech, Paquita covered her face in her hands, and cried naïvely:

"Holy Virgin! What have I brought upon myself?"

She rose, flung herself down upon the red sofa, and buried her head in the rags which covered the bosom of her mother, and wept there. The old woman received her daughter without issuing from her state of immobility, or displaying any emotion. The mother possessed in the highest degree that gravity of savage races, the impassiveness of a statue upon which all remarks are lost. Did she or did she not love her daughter? Beneath that mask every human emotion might brood—good and evil; and from this creature all might be expected. Her gaze passed slowly from her daughter's beautiful hair, which covered her like a mantle, to the face of Henri, which she considered with an indescribable curiosity.

She seemed to ask by what fatality he was there, from what caprice Nature had made so seductive a man.

"These women are making sport of me," said Henri to himself.

At that moment Paquita raised her head, cast at him one of those looks which reach the very soul and consume it. So beautiful seemed she that he swore he would possess such a treasure of beauty.

"My Paquita! Be mine!"

"Wouldst thou kill me?" she said fearfully, palpitating and anxious, but drawn towards him by an inexplicable force.

"Kill thee—I!" he said, smiling.

Paquita uttered a cry of alarm, said a word to the old woman, who authoritatively seized Henri's hand and that of her daughter. She gazed at them for a long time, and then released them, wagging her head in a fashion horribly significant.

"Be mine—this evening, this moment; follow me, do not leave me! It must be, Paquita! Dost thou love me? Come!"

In a moment he had poured out a thousand foolish words to her, with the rapidity of a torrent coursing between the rocks,

and repeating the same sound in a thousand different forms.
"It is the same voice!" said Paquita, in a melancholy voice,
which De Marsay could not overhear, "and the same ardor,"
she added. "So be it—yes," she said, with an abandonment
of passion which no words can describe. "Yes; but not to-
night. To-night, Adolphe, I gave too little opium to La
Concha. She might wake up, and I should be lost. At this
moment the whole household believes me to be asleep in my
room. In two days be at the same spot, say the same word
to the same man. That man is my foster-father. Cristemio
worships me, and would die in torments for me before they
could extract one word against me from him. Farewell," she
said, seizing Henri by the waist and twining round him like
a serpent.

She pressed him on every side at once, lifted her head to
his, and offered him her lips, then snatched a kiss which filled
them both with such a dizziness that it seemed to Henri as
though the earth opened; and Paquita cried: "Enough, depart!" in a voice which told how little she was mistress of
herself. But she clung to him still, still crying "Depart!"
and brought him slowly to the staircase. There the mulatto,
whose white eyes lit up at the sight of Paquita, took the torch
from the hands of his idol, and conducted Henri to the street.
He left the light under the arch, opened the door, put Henri
into the carriage, and set him down on the Boulevard des
Italiens with marvelous rapidity. It was as though the
horses had hell-fire in their veins.

The scene was like a dream to De Marsay, but one of those
dreams which, even when they fade away, leave a feeling of
supernatural voluptuousness, which a man runs after for the
remainder of his life. A single kiss had been enough. Never
had *rendezvous* been spent in a manner more decorous or
chaste, or, perhaps, more coldly, in a spot of which the surroundings were more gruesome, in presence of a more hideous
divinity; for the mother had remained in Henri's imagination like some infernal, cowering thing, cadaverous, monstrous,
savagely ferocious, which the imagination of poets and

painters had not yet conceived. In effect, no *rendezvous* had ever irritated his senses more, revealed more audacious pleasures, or better aroused love from its centre to shed itself round him like an atmosphere. There was something sombre, mysterious, sweet, tender, constrained, and expansive, an intermingling of the awful and the celestial, of paradise and hell, which made De Marsay like a drunken man.

He was no longer himself, and he was, withal, great enough to be able to resist the intoxication of pleasure.

In order to render his conduct intelligible in the catastrophe of this story, it is needful to explain how his soul had broadened at an age when young men generally belittle themselves in their relations with women, or in too much occupation with them. Its growth was due to a concurrence of secret circumstances, which invested him with a vast and unsuspected power.*

This young man held in his hand a sceptre more powerful than that of modern kings, almost all of whom are curbed in their least wishes by the laws. De Marsay exercised the autocratic power of an Oriental despot. But this power, so stupidly put into execution in Asia by brutish men, was increased tenfold by its conjunction with European intelligence, with French wit—the most subtle, the keenest of all intellectual instruments. Henri could do what he would in the interest of his pleasures and vanities. This invisible action upon the social world had invested him with a real, but secret, majesty, without emphasis and deriving from himself. He had not the opinion which Louis XIV. could have of himself, but that which the proudest of the Caliphs, the Pharaohs, the Xerxes, who held themselves to be of divine origin, had of themselves when they imitated God, and veiled themselves from their subjects under the pretext that their looks dealt forth death. Thus, without any remorse at being at once the judge and the accuser, De Marsay coldly condemned to death the man or the woman who had seriously offended him. Although often pronounced almost lightly, the verdict was irrev-

* *Vid.* Translator's Preface.

ocable. An error was a misfortune similar to that which a thunderbolt causes when it falls upon a smiling Parisienne in some hackney coach, instead of crushing the old coachman who is driving her to a *rendezvous*. Thus the bitter and profound sarcasm which distinguished the young man's conversation usually tended to frighten people; no one was anxious to put him out. Women are prodigiously fond of those persons who call themselves pashas, and who are, as it were, accompanied by lions and executioners, and who walk in a panoply of terror. The result, in the case of such men, is a security of action, a certitude of power, a pride of gaze, a leonine consciousness, which makes women realize the type of strength of which they all dream. Such was De Marsay.

Happy, for the moment, with his future, he grew young and pliable, and thought of nothing but love as he went to bed. He dreamed of the girl with the golden eyes, as the young and passionate can dream. His dreams were monstrous images, unattainable extravagances—full of light, revealing invisible worlds, yet in a manner always incomplete, for an intervening veil changes the conditions of vision.

For the next and succeeding day Henri disappeared, and no one knew what had become of him. His power only belonged to him under certain conditions, and, happily for him, during those two days he was a private soldier in the service of the demon to whom he owed his talismanic existence. But at the appointed time, in the evening, he was waiting—and he had not long to wait—for the carriage. The mulatto approached Henri, in order to repeat to him in French a phrase which he seemed to have learned by heart.

"If you wish to come, she told me, you must consent to have your eyes bandaged."

And Cristemio produced a white silk handkerchief.

"No!" said Henri, whose omnipotence revolted suddenly.

He tried to leap in. The mulatto made a sign, and the carriage drove off.

"Yes!" cried De Marsay, furious at the thought of losing a piece of good fortune which had been promised him.

He saw, moreover, the impossibility of making terms with a slave whose obedience was as blind as the hangman's. Nor was it this passive instrument upon whom his anger could fall.

The mulatto whistled, the carriage returned. Henri got in hastily. Already a few curious onlookers had assembled like sheep on the boulevard. Henri was strong; he tried to play the mulatto. When the carriage started at a gallop he seized his hands, in order to master him, and retain, by subduing his attendant, the possession of his faculties, so that he might know whither he was going. It was a vain attempt. The eyes of the mulatto flashed from the darkness. The fellow uttered a cry which his fury stifled in his throat, released himself, threw back De Marsay with a hand like iron, and nailed him, so to speak, to the bottom of the carriage; then with his free hand, he drew a triangular dagger, and whistled. The coachman heard the whistle and stopped. Henri was un-armed, he was forced to yield. He moved his head towards the handkerchief. The gesture of submission calmed Criste-mio, and he bound his eyes with a respect and care which manifested a sort of veneration for the person of the man whom his idol loved. But, before taking this course, he had placed his dagger distrustfully in his side pocket, and but-toned himself up to the chin.

"That nigger would have killed me!" said De Marsay to himself.

Once more the carriage moved on rapidly. There was one resource still open to a young man who knew Paris as well as Henri. To know whither he was going, he had but to collect himself and count, by the number of gutters crossed, the streets leading from the boulevards by which the carriage passed, so long as it continued straight along. He could thus discover into which lateral street it would turn, either towards the Seine or towards the heights of Montmartre, and guess the name or position of the street in which his guide should bring him to a halt. But the violent emotion which his struggle had caused him, the rage into which his compromised dignity had thrown him, the ideas of vengeance to which he abandoned himself, the suppositions suggested to him by the circumstantial care which this girl had taken in order to bring him to her, all hindered him from that attention, which the blind have, necessary for the concentration of his intelligence and the perfect lucidity of his recollection. The journey lasted half an hour. When the carriage stopped, it was no longer on the street. The mulatto and the coachman took Henri in their arms, lifted him out, and, putting him into a sort of litter, conveyed him across a garden. He could smell its flowers and the perfume peculiar to trees and grass.

The silence which reigned there was so profound that he could distinguish the noise made by the drops of water falling from the moist leaves. The two men took him to a staircase, set him on his feet, led him by his hands through several apartments, and left him in a room whose atmosphere was perfumed, and the thick carpet of which he could feel beneath his feet.

A woman's hand pushed him on to a divan, and untied the handkerchief for him. Henri saw Paquita before him, but Paquita in all her womanly and voluptuous glory. The section of the boudoir in which Henri found himself described a circular line, softly gracious, which was faced opposite by the other perfectly square half, in the midst of which a chimney-piece shone of gold and white marble. He had entered by a door on one side, hidden by a rich tapestried screen, opposite which was a window. The semicircular portion was adorned with a real Turkish divan, that is to say, a mattress thrown on the ground, but a mattress as broad as a bed, a divan fifty feet in circumference, made of white cashmere, relieved by bows of black and scarlet silk, arranged in panels. The top of this huge bed was raised several inches by numerous cushions, which further enriched it by their tasteful comfort. The boudoir was lined with some red stuff, over which an Indian muslin was stretched, fluted after the fashion of Corinthian columns, in plaits going in and out, and bound at the top and bottom by bands of poppy-colored stuff, on which were designs in black arabesque.

Below the muslin the poppy turned to rose, that amorous color, which was matched by window-curtains, which were of Indian muslin lined with rose-colored taffeta, and set off with a fringe of poppy-color and black. Six silver-gilt arms, each supporting two candles, were attached to the tapestry at an equal distance, to illuminate the divan. The ceiling, from the middle of which a lustre of unpolished silver hung, was of a brilliant whiteness, and the cornice was gilded. The carpet was like an Oriental shawl; it had the designs and recalled the poetry of Persia, where the hands of slaves had worked on it. The furniture was covered in white cashmere, relieved by black and poppy-colored ornaments. The clock, the candelabra, all were in white marble and gold. The only table there had a cloth of cashmere. Elegant flower-pots held roses of every kind, flowers white or red. In fine, the least detail seemed to have been the object of loving thought. Never had richness hidden itself more coquettishly to become elegance, to express grace, to inspire pleasure. Everything there would have warmed the coldest of beings. The caresses of the tapestry, of which the color changed according to the direction of one's gaze, becoming either all white or all rose, harmonized with the effects of the light shed upon the diaphanous tissues of the muslin, which produced an appearance of mistiness. The soul has I know not what attraction towards white, love delights in red, and the passions are flattered by gold, which has the power of realizing their caprices. Thus all that man possesses within him of vague and mysterious, all his inexplicable affinities, were caressed in their involuntary sympathies. There was in this perfect harmony a concert of color to which the soul responded with vague and voluptuous and fluctuating ideas.

It was out of a misty atmosphere, laden with exquisite perfumes, that Paquita, clad in a white wrapper, her feet bare, orange blossoms in her black hair, appeared to Henri, knelt before him, adoring him as the god of this temple, whither he had deigned to come. Although De Marsay was accustomed to seeing the utmost efforts of Parisian luxury, he was surprised at the aspect of this shell, like that from which Venus rose out of the sea. Whether from an effect of contrast between the darkness from which he issued and the light which bathed his soul, whether from a comparison which he swiftly made between this scene and that of their first interview, he experienced one of those delicate sensations which true poetry gives. Perceiving in the midst of this retreat, which had been opened to him as by a fairy's magic wand, the masterpiece of creation, this girl, whose warmly colored tints, whose soft skin—soft, but slightly gilded by the shadows, by I know not what vaporous effusion of love—gleamed as though it reflected the rays of color and light, his anger, his desire for vengeance, his wounded vanity, all were lost.

Like an eagle darting on his prey, he took her utterly to him, set her on his knees, and felt with an indescribable intoxication the voluptuous pressure of this girl, whose richly developed beauties softly enveloped him.

"Come to me, Paquita!" he said, in a low voice,

"Speak, speak without fear!" she said. "This retreat was built for love. No sound can escape from it, so greatly was it desired to guard avariciously the accents and music of the beloved voice. However loud should be the cries, they would not be heard outside these walls. A person might be murdered, and his moans would be as vain as if he were in the midst of the great desert.

"Who has understood jealousy and its needs so well?"

"Never question me as to that," she answered, untying with a gesture of wonderful sweetness the young man's scarf, doubtless in order the better to behold his neck.

"Yes, there is the neck I love so well!" she said. "Wouldst thou please me?"

This interrogation, rendered by the accent almost lascivious, drew De Marsay from the reverie in which he had been plunged by Paquita's authoritative refusal to allow him any research as to the unknown being who hovered like a shadow about them.

"And if I wished to know who reigns here?"

Paquita looked at him trembling.

"It is not I, then?" he said, rising and freeing himself from the girl, whose head fell backwards. "Where I am, I would be alone."

"Strike, strike! . . ." said the poor slave, a prey to terror.

"For what do you take me, then? . . . Will you answer?"

Paquita got up gently, her eyes full of tears, took a poniard from one of the two ebony pieces of furniture, and presented it to Henri with a gesture of submission which would have moved a tiger.

"Give me a feast such as men give when they love," she said, "and whilst I sleep, slay me, for I know not how to answer thee. Hearken! I am bound like some poor beast to a stake; I am amazed that I have been able to throw a bridge over the abyss which divides us. Intoxicate me, then kill me! Ah, no, no!" she cried, joining her hands, "do not kill me! I love life! Life is fair to me! If I am a slave, I am a queen too. I could beguile you with words, tell you that I love you alone, prove it to you, profit by my momentary empire to say to you: 'Take me as one tastes the perfume of a flower when one passes it in a king's garden.' Then, after having used the cunning eloquence of woman and soared on the wings of pleasure, after having quenched my thirst, I could have you cast into a pit, where none could find you, which has been made to gratify vengeance without having to fear that of the law, a pit full of lime which would kindle and consume you, until no particle of you were left. You would stay in my heart, mine forever."

Henri looked at the girl without trembling, and this fearless gaze filled her with joy.

"No, I shall not do it! You have fallen into no trap here,

but upon the heart of a woman who adores you, and it is I who will be cast into the pit."

"All this appears to me prodigiously strange," said De Marsay, considering her. "But you seem to me a good girl, a strange nature; you are, upon my word of honor, a living riddle, the answer to which is very difficult to find."

Paquita understood nothing of what the young man said; she looked at him gently, opening wide eyes which could never be stupid, so much was pleasure written in them.

"Come, then, my love," she said, returning to her first idea, "wouldst thou please me?"

"I would do all that thou wouldst, and even that thou wouldst not," answered De Marsay, with a laugh. He had recovered his foppish ease, as he took the resolve to let himself go to the climax of his good fortune, looking neither before nor after. Perhaps he counted, moreover, on his power and his capacity of a man used to adventures, to dominate this girl a few hours later and learn all her secrets.

"Well," said she, "let me arrange you as I would like."

Paquita went joyously and took from one of the two chests a robe of red velvet, in which she dressed De Marsay, then adorned his head with a woman's bonnet and wrapped a shawl round him. Abandoning herself to these follies with a child's innocence, she laughed a convulsive laugh, and resembled some bird flapping its wings; but he saw nothing beyond.

If it be impossible to paint the unheard-of delights which these two creatures—made by heaven in a joyous moment—found, it is perhaps necessary to translate metaphysically the extraordinary and almost fantastic impressions of the young man. That which persons in the social position of De Marsay, living as he lived, are best able to recognize is a girl's innocence. But, strange phenomenon! The girl of the golden eyes might be virgin, but innocent she was certainly not. The fantastic union of the mysterious and the real, of darkness and light, horror and beauty, pleasure and danger, paradise and hell, which had already been met with in this adventure, was resumed in the capricious and sublime being with which De Marsay dallied. All the utmost science of the most refined pleasure, all that Henri could know of that poetry of the senses which is called love, was excelled by the treasures poured forth by this girl, whose radiant eyes gave the lie to none of the promises which they made.

She was an Oriental poem, in which shone the sun that Saadi, that Hafiz, have set in their pulsing strophes. Only, neither the rhythm of Saadi, nor that of Pindar, could have expressed the ecstasy—full of confusion and stupefaction—which seized the delicious girl when the error in which an iron hand had caused her to live was at an end.

"Dead!" she said, "I am dead, Adolphe! Take me away to the world's end, to an island where no one knows us. Let there be no traces of our flight! We should be followed to the gates of hell. God! here is the day! Escape! Shall I ever see you again? Yes, to-morrow I will see you, if I have to deal death to all my warders to have that joy. Till to-morrow."

She pressed him in her arms with an embrace in which the terror of death mingled. Then she touched a spring, which must have been in connection with a bell, and implored De Marsay to permit his eyes to be bandaged.

"And if I would not—and if I wished to stay here?"

"You would be the death of me more speedily," she said, "for now I know I am certain to die on your account."

Henri submitted. In the man who had just gorged himself with pleasure there occurs a propensity to forgetfulness, I know not what ingratitude, a desire for liberty, a whim to go elsewhere, a tinge of contempt and, perhaps, of disgust for his idol; in fine, indescribable sentiments which render him ignoble and ashamed. The certainty of this confused, but real, feeling in souls who are not illuminated by that celestial light, nor perfumed with that holy essence from which the performance of sentiment springs, doubtless suggested to Rousseau the adventures of Lord Edward, which conclude the letters of the *Nouvelle Héloïse*. If Rousseau is obviously inspired by the work of Richardson, he departs from it in a thousand details, which leave his achievement magnificently original; he has recommended it to posterity by great ideas which it is difficult to liberate by analysis, when, in one's youth, one reads this work with the object of finding in it the lurid representation of the most physical of our feelings, whereas serious and philosophical writers never employ its images except as the consequence or the corollary of a vast thought; and the adventures of Lord Edward are one of the most Europeanly delicate ideas of the whole work.

Henri, therefore, found himself beneath the domination of that confused sentiment which is unknown to true love. There was needful, in some sort, the persuasive grip of comparisons, and the irresistible attraction of memories to lead him back to a woman. True love rules above all through recollection. A woman who is not engraven upon the soul by excess of pleasure or by strength of emotion, how can she ever be loved? In Henri's case, Paquita had established herself by both of these reasons. But at this moment, seized as he was by the satiety of his happiness, that delicious melancholy of the body, he could hardly analyze his heart, even by recalling to his lips the taste of the liveliest gratifications that he had ever grasped.

He found himself on the Boulevard Montmartre at the break of day, gazed stupidly at the retreating carriage, produced two cigars from his pocket, lit one from the lantern of a good woman who sold brandy and coffee to workmen and street arabs and chestnut venders—to all the Parisian populace which begins its work before daybreak; then he went off, smoking his cigar, and putting his hands in his trousers' pockets with a devil-may-care air which did him small honor.

"What a good thing a cigar is! That's one thing a man will never tire of," he said to himself.

Of the girl with the golden eyes, over whom at that time all the elegant youth of Paris was mad, he hardly thought. The idea of death, expressed in the midst of their pleasure, and the fear of which had more than once darkened the brow of that beautiful creature, who held to the houris of Asia by her mother, to Europe by her education, to the tropics by her birth, seemed to him merely one of those deceptions by which women seek to make themselves interesting.

"She is from Havana—the most Spanish region to be found in the New World. So she preferred to feign terror rather than cast in my teeth indisposition or difficulty, coquetry or duty, like a Parisian woman. By her golden eyes, how glad I shall be to sleep."

He saw a hackney coach standing at the corner of Frascati's waiting for some gambler; he awoke the driver, was driven home, went to bed, and slept the sleep of the dissipated, which, for some queer reason—of which no rhymer has yet taken advantage—is as profound as that of innocence. Perhaps it is an instance of the proverbial axiom, *extremes meet.*

About noon De Marsay awoke and stretched himself; he felt the grip of that sort of voracious hunger which old soldiers can remember having experienced on the morrow of victory. He was delighted, therefore, to see Paul de Manerville standing in front of him, for at such a time nothing is more agreeable than to eat in company.

"Well," his friend remarked, "we all imagined that you had been shut up for the last ten days with the girl of the golden eyes."

"The girl of the golden eyes! I have forgotten her. Faith! I have other fish to fry!"

"Ah! you are playing at discretion."

"Why not?" asked De Marsay, with a laugh. "My dear fellow, discretion is the best form of calculation. Listen—however, no! I will not say a word. You never teach me anything; I am not disposed to make you a gratuitous present of the treasures of my policy. Life is a river which is of use for the promotion of commerce. In the name of all that is most sacred in life—of cigars! I am no professor of social economy for the instruction of fools. Let us breakfast! It costs less to give you a tunny omelette than to lavish the resources of my brain on you."

"Do you bargain with your friends?"

"My dear fellow," said Henri, who rarely denied himself a sarcasm, "since, all the same, you may some day need, like anybody else, to use discretion, and since I have much love for you—yes, I like you! Upon my word, if you only wanted a thousand-franc note to keep you from blowing your brains out, you would find it here, for we haven't yet done any business of that sort, eh, Paul? If you had to fight to-morrow, I would measure the ground and load the pistols, so that you might be killed according to rule. In short, if anybody besides myself took it into his head to say ill of you in your absence, he would have to deal with the somewhat nasty gentleman who walks in my shoes—there's what I call a friendship beyond question. Well, my good fellow, if you should ever have need of discretion, understand that there are two sorts of discretion—the active and the negative. Negative discretion is that of fools who make use of silence, negation, an air of refusal, the discretion of locked doors— mere impotence! Active discretion proceeds by affirmation. Suppose at the club this evening I were to say: 'Upon my word of honor the golden-eyed was not worth all she cost me!' Everybody would exclaim when I was gone: 'Did you hear that fop De Marsay, who tried to make us believe that he has already had the girl of the golden eyes? It's his way of trying to disembarrass himself of his rivals; he's no simpleton.' But such a ruse is vulgar and dangerous. However gross a folly one utters, there are always idiots to be found who will believe it. The best form of discretion is that of women when they want to take the change out of their husbands. It consists in compromising a woman with whom we are not concerned, or whom we do not love, in order to save the honor of the one whom we love well enough to respect. It is what is called the *woman-screen*. . . . Ah! here is Laurent. What have you got for us?"

"Some Ostend oysters, Monsieur le Comte."

"You will know some day, Paul, how amusing it is to make a fool of the world by depriving it of the secret of one's affections. I derive an immense pleasure in escaping from the

stupid jurisdiction of the crowd, which knows neither what it
wants, nor what one wants of it, which takes the means for
the end, and by turns curses and adores, elevates and destroys! What a delight to impose emotions on it and receive none from it, to tame it, never to obey it. If one may
ever be proud of anything, is it not of a self-acquired power,
of which one is at once the cause and effect, the principle
and the result? Well, no man knows what I love, nor what I
wish. Perhaps what I have loved, or what I may have wished
will be known, as a drama which is accomplished is known;
but to let my game be seen—weakness, mistake! I know
nothing more despicable than strength outwitted by cunning. Can I initiate myself with a laugh into the ambassador's part, if indeed diplomacy is as difficult as life? I doubt
it. Have you any ambition? Would you like to become something?"

"But, Henri, you are laughing at me—as though I were
not sufficiently mediocre to arrive at anything."

"Good, Paul! If you go on laughing at yourself, you will
soon be able to laugh at everybody else."

At breakfast, by the time he had started his cigars, De
Marsay began to see the events of the night in a singular
light. Like many men of great intelligence, his perspicuity
was not spontaneous, as it did not at once penetrate to the
heart of things. As with all natures endowed with the
faculty of living greatly in the present, of extracting, so to
speak, the essence of it and assimilating it, his second-sight
had need of a sort of slumber before it could identify itself
with causes. Cardinal de Richelieu was so constituted, and
it did not debar in him the gift of foresight necessary to the
conception of great designs.

De Marsay's conditions were alike, but at first he only
used his weapons for the benefit of his pleasures, and only
became one of the most profound politicians of his day when
he had saturated himself with those pleasures to which a
young man's thoughts—when he has money and power—
are primarily directed. Man hardens himself thus: he uses
woman in order that she may not make use of him.

At this moment, then, De Marsay perceived that he had been fooled by the girl of the golden eyes, seeing, as he did, in perspective, all that night of which the delights had been poured upon him by degrees until they had ended by flooding him in torrents. He could read, at last, that page in effect so brilliant, divine its hidden meaning. The purely physical innocence of Paquita, the bewilderment of her joy, certain words, obscure at first, but now clear, which had escaped her in the midst of that joy, all proved to him that he had posed for another person. As no social corruption was unknown to him, as he professed a complete indifference towards all perversities, and believed them to be justified on the simple ground that they were capable of satisfaction, he was not startled at vice, he knew it as one knows a friend, but he was wounded at having served as sustenance for it. If his presumption was right, he had been outraged in the most sensitive part of him. The mere suspicion filled him with fury, he broke out with the roar of a tiger who has been the sport of a deer, the cry of a tiger which united a brute's strength with the intelligence of the demon.

"I say, what is the matter with you?" asked Paul.

"Nothing!"

"I should be sorry, if you were to be asked whether you had anything against me and were to reply with a *nothing* like that! It would be a sure case of fighting the next day."

"I fight no more duels," said De Marsay.

"That seems to me even more tragical. Do you assassinate, then?"

"You travesty words. I execute."

"My dear friend," said Paul, "your jokes are of a very sombre color this morning."

"What would you have? Pleasure ends in cruelty. Why? I don't know, and am not sufficiently curious to try and find out. . . . These cigars are excellent. Give your friend some tea. Do you know, Paul, I live a brute's life? It should be time to choose oneself a destiny, to employ one's powers on something which makes life worth living. Life is a

singular comedy. I am frightened, I laugh at the inconse-
quence of our social order. The Government cuts off the heads
of poor devils who have killed a man and licenses creatures
who despatch, medically speaking, a dozen young folks in a
season. Morality is powerless against a dozen vices which
destroy society and which nothing can punish.—Another
cup!—Upon my word of honor! man is a jester dancing upon
a precipice. They talk to us about the immorality of the
Liaisons Dangereuses, and any other book you like with a
vulgar reputation; but there exists a book, horrible, filthy,
fearful, corrupting, which is always open and will never be
shut, the great book of the world; not to mention another
book, a thousand times more dangerous, which is composed
of all that men whisper into each other's ears, or women murmur behind their fans, of an evening in society."

"Henri, there is certainly something extraordinary the matter with you; that is obvious in spite of your active discretion."

"Yes! . . . Come, I must kill the time until this
evening. Let's to the tables. . . . Perhaps I shall have
the good luck to lose."

De Marsay rose, took a handful of banknotes and folded
them into his cigar-case, dressed himself, and took advantage of Paul's carriage to repair to the Salon des Étrangers,
where until dinner he consumed the time in those exciting
alternations of loss and gain which are the last resource of
powerful organizations when they are compelled to exercise
themselves in the void. In the evening he repaired to the
trysting-place and submitted complacently to having his eyes
bandaged. Then, with that firm will which only really strong
men have the faculty of concentrating, he devoted his attention and applied his intelligence to the task of divining
through what streets the carriage passed. He had a sort of
certitude of being taken to the Rue Saint-Lazare, and being
brought to a halt at the little gate in the garden of the
Hôtel San-Réal. When he passed, as on the first occasion,
through this gate, and was put in a litter, carried, doubtless,

by the mulatto and the coachman, he understood, as he heard
the gravel grate beneath their feet, why they took such
minute precautions. He would have been able, had he been
free, or if he had walked, to pluck a twig of laurel, to observe the nature of the soil which clung to his boots; whereas,
transported, so to speak, ethereally into an inaccessible mansion, his good fortune must remain what it had been hitherto, a dream. But it is man's despair that all his work, whether
for good or evil, is imperfect. All his labors, physical or
intellectual, are sealed with the mark of destruction. There
had been a gentle rain, the earth was moist. At night-time
certain vegetable perfumes are far stronger than during the
day; Henri could smell, therefore, the scent of the mignonette
which lined the avenue along which he was conveyed. This
indication was enough to light him in the researches which
he promised himself to make in order to recognize the hotel
which contained Paquita's boudoir. He studied in the same
way the turnings which his bearers took within the house,
and believed himself able to recall them.

As on the previous night, he found himself on the ottoman
before Paquita, who was undoing his bandage; but he saw
her pale and altered. She had wept. On her knees like an
angel in prayer, but like an angel profoundly sad and melancholy, the poor girl no longer resembled the curious, impatient, and impetuous creature who had carried De Marsay
on her wings to transport him to the seventh heaven of love.
There was something so true in this despair veiled by pleasure, that the terrible De Marsay felt within him an admiration for this new masterpiece of nature, and forgot, for the
moment, the chief interest of his assignation.

"What is the matter with thee, my Paquita?"

"My friend," she said, "carry me away this very night.
Bear me to some place where no one can say who sees me:
'That is Paquita,' where no one can answer: 'There is a girl
with a golden gaze here, who has long hair.' Yonder I will
give thee as many pleasures as thou wouldst have of me.
Then when you love me no longer, you shall leave me, I shall

not complain, I shall say nothing; and your desertion need cause you no remorse, for one day passed with you, only one day, in which I have had you before my eyes, will be worth all my life to me. But if I stay here, I am lost."

"I cannot leave Paris, little one!" replied Henri. "I do not belong to myself, I am bound by a vow to the fortune of several persons who stand to me, as I do to them. But I can place you in a refuge in Paris, where no human power can reach you."

"No," she said, "you forget the power of woman."

Never did phrase uttered by human voice express terror more absolutely.

"What could reach you, then, if I put myself between you and the world?"

"Poison!" she said. "Doña Concha suspects you already . . . and," she resumed, letting the tears fall and glisten on her cheeks, "it is easy enough to see I am no longer the same. Well, if you abandon me to the fury of the monster who will destroy me, your holy will be done! But come, let there be all the pleasures of life in our love. Besides, I will implore, I will weep and cry out and defend myself; perhaps I shall be saved."

"Whom will you implore?" he asked.

"Silence!" said Paquita. "If I obtain mercy it will perhaps be on account of my discretion."

"Give me my robe," said Henri, insidiously.

"No, no!" she answered quickly, "be what you are, one of those angels whom I have been taught to hate, and in whom I only saw ogres, whilst you are what is fairest under the skies," she said, caressing Henri's hair. "You do not know how silly I am. I have learned nothing. Since I was twelve years old I have been shut up without ever seeing any one. I can neither read nor write, I can only speak English and Spanish."

"How is it, then, that you receive letters from London?"

"My letters? . . . See, here they are!" she said, proceeding to take some papers out of a tall Japanese vase.

She offered De Marsay some letters, in which the young man saw, with surprise, strange figures, similar to those of a rebus, traced in blood, and illustrating phrases full of passion.

"But," he cried, marveling at these hieroglyphics created by the alertness of jealousy, "you are in the power of an infernal genius?"

"Infernal," she repeated.

"But how, then, were you able to get out?"

"Ah!" she said, "that was my ruin. I drove Doña Concha to choose between the fear of immediate death and anger to be. I had the curiosity of a demon, I wished to break the bronze circle which they had described between creation and me, I wished to see what young people were like, for I knew nothing of man except the Marquis and Cristemio. Our coachman and the lackey who accompanies us are old men. . . ."

"But you were not always thus shut up? Your health . . . ?"

"Ah," she answered, "we used to walk, but it was at night and in the country, by the side of the Seine, away from people."

"Are you not proud of being loved like that?"

"No," she said, "no longer. However full it be, this hidden life is but darkness in comparison with the light."

"What do you call the light?"

"Thee, my lovely Adolphe! Thee, for whom I would give my life. All the passionate things that have been told me, and that I have inspired, I feel for thee! For a certain time I understood nothing of existence, but now I know what love is, and hitherto I have been the loved one only; for myself, I did not love. I would give up everything for you, take me away. If you like, take me as a toy, but let me be near you until you break me."

"You will have no regrets?"

"Not one!" she said, letting him read her eyes, whose golden tint was pure and clear.

"Am I the favored one?" said Henri to himself. If he suspected the truth, he was ready at that time to pardon the offence in view of a love so single minded. "I shall soon see," he thought.

If Paquita owed him no account of the past, yet the least recollection of it became in his eyes a crime. He had therefore the sombre strength to withhold a portion of his thought, to study her, even while abandoning himself to the most enticing pleasures that ever peri descended from the skies had devised for her beloved.

Paquita seemed to have been created for love by a particular effort of nature. In a night her feminine genius had made the most rapid progress. Whatever might be the power of this young man, and his indifference in the matter of pleasures, in spite of his satiety of the previous night, he found in the girl with the golden eyes that seraglio which a loving woman knows how to create and which a man never refuses. Paquita responded to that passion which is felt by all really great men for the infinite—that mysterious passion so dramatically expressed in Faust, so poetically translated in Manfred, and which urged Don Juan to search the heart of women, in his hope to find there that limitless thought in pursuit of which so many hunters after spectres have started, which wise men think to discover in science, and which mystics find in God alone. The hope of possessing at last the ideal being with whom the struggle could be constant and tireless ravished De Marsay, who, for the first time for long, opened his heart. His nerves expanded, his coldness was dissipated in the atmosphere of that ardent soul, his hard and fast theories melted away, and happiness colored his existence to the tint of the rose and white boudoir. Experiencing the sting of a higher pleasure, he was carried beyond the limits within which he had hitherto confined passion. He would not be surpassed by this girl, whom a somewhat artificial love had formed all ready for the needs of his soul, and then he found in that vanity which urges a man to be in all things a victor, strength enough to tame the girl; but, at the same time, urged beyond that line where the soul is mistress over herself, he lost himself in those delicious limboes, which the vulgar call so foolishly "the imaginary regions." He was tender, kind, and confidential. He affected Paquita almost to madness.

"Why should not we go to Sorrento, to Nice, to Chiavari, and pass all our life so? Will you?" he asked of Paquita, in a penetrating voice.

"Was there need to say to me: 'Will you'?" she cried. "Have I a will? I am nothing apart from you, except in so far as I am a pleasure for you. If you would choose a retreat worthy of us, Asia is the only country where love can unfold his wings. . . ."

"You are right," answered Henri. "Let us go to the Indies, there where spring is eternal, where the earth grows only flowers, where man can display the magnificence of kings and none shall say him nay, as in the foolish lands where they would realize the dull chimera of equality. Let us go to the country where one lives in the midst of a nation of slaves, where the sun shines ever on a palace which is always white, where the air sheds perfumes, the birds sing of love, and where, when one can love no more, one dies. . . ."

"And where one dies together!" said Paquita. "But do not let us start to-morrow, let us start this moment . . . take Cristemio."

"Faith! pleasure is the fairest climax of life. Let us go to Asia; but to start, my child, one needs much gold, and to have gold one must set one's affairs in order."

She understood no part of these ideas.

"Gold! There is a pile of it here—as high as that," she said, holding up her hand.

"It is not mine."

"What does that matter?" she went on; "if we have need of it let us take it."

"It does not belong to you."

"Belong!" she repeated. "Have you not taken me? When we have taken it, it will belong to us."

He gave a laugh.

"Poor innocent! You know nothing of the world."

"Nay, but this is what I know," she cried, clasping Henri to her.

At the very moment when De Marsay was forgetting all, and conceiving the desire to appropriate this creature forever, he received in the midst of his joy a dagger-thrust, which smote through his heart and mortified it for the first time. Paquita, who had lifted him vigorously in the air, as though to contemplate him, exclaimed: "Oh, Margarita!"

"Margarita!" cried the young man, with a roar; "now I know all that I still tried to disbelieve."

He leaped upon the cabinet in which the long poniard was kept. Happily for Paquita and for himself, the cupboard was shut. His fury waxed at this impediment, but he recovered his tranquillity, went and found his cravat, and advanced towards her with an air of such ferocious meaning that, without knowing of what crime she had been guilty, Paquita understood, none the less, that her life was in question. With one bound she rushed to the other end of the room to escape the fatal knot which De Marsay tried to pass round her neck. There was a struggle. On either side there was an equality of strength, agility, and suppleness. To end the combat Paquita threw between the legs of her lover a cushion which made him fall, and profited by the respite which this advantage gave her, to push the button of the spring which caused the bell to ring. Promptly the mulatto arrived. In a second Cristemio leaped on De Marsay and held him down with one foot on his chest, his heel turned towards the throat. De Marsay realized that, if he struggled, at a single sign from Paquita he would be instantly crushed.

"Why did you want to kill me, my beloved?" she said. De Marsay made no reply.

"In what have I angered you?" she asked. "Speak, let us understand each other."

Henri maintained the phlegmatic attitude of a strong man who feels himself vanquished; his countenance, cold, silent, entirely English, revealed the consciousness of his dignity in a momentary resignation. Moreover, he had already thought, in spite of the vehemence of his anger, that it was scarcely prudent to compromise himself with the law by killing this girl on the spur of the moment, before he had arranged the murder in such a manner as should insure his impunity.

"My beloved," went on Paquita, "speak to me; do not leave me without one loving farewell! I would not keep in my heart the terror which you have just inspired in it. . . . Will you speak?" she said, stamping her foot with anger.

De Marsay, for all reply, gave her a glance, which signified so plainly, *"You must die!"* that Paquita threw herself upon him.

"Ah, well, you want to kill me! . . . If my death can give you any pleasure—kill me!"

She made a sign to Cristemio, who withdrew his foot from the body of the young man, and retired without letting his face show that he had formed any opinion, good or bad, with regard to Paquita.

"That is a man," said De Marsay, pointing to the mulatto, with a sombre gesture. "There is no devotion like the devotion which obeys in friendship, and does not stop to weigh motives. In that man you possess a true friend."

"I will give him you, if you like," she answered; "he will serve you with the same devotion that he has for me, if I so instruct him."

She waited for a word of recognition, and went on with an accent replete with tenderness:

"Adolphe, give me then one kind word! . . . It is nearly day."

Henri did not answer. The young man had one sorry quality, for one considers as something great everything which resembles strength, and often men invent extravagances. Henri knew not how to pardon. That *returning upon itself* which is one of the soul's graces, was a non-existent sense for him. The ferocity of the Northern man, with which the English blood is deeply tainted, had been transmitted to him

by his father.   He was inexorable both in his good and evil
impulses.   Paquita's exclamation had been all the more horrible to him, in that it had dethroned him from the sweetest
triumph which had ever flattered his man's vanity.   Hope,
love, and every emotion had been exalted with him, all had lit
up within his heart and his intelligence, then these torches
illuminating his life had been extinguished by a cold wind.
Paquita, in her stupefaction of grief, had only strength
enough to give the signal for departure.

"What is the use of that!" she said, throwing away the
bandage.   "If he does not love me, if he hates me, it is all
over."

She waited for one look, did not obtain it, and fell, half
dead.   The mulatto cast a glance at Henri, so horribly significant, that, for the first time in his life, the young man, to
whom no one denied the gift of rare courage, trembled.   *"If
you do not love her well, if you give her the least pain, I will
kill you."*   Such was the sense of that brief gaze.   De Marsay
was escorted, with a care almost obsequious, along the dimly-
lit corridor, at the end of which he issued by a secret door
into the garden of the Hotel San-Réal.   The mulatto made
him walk cautiously through an avenue of lime trees, which
led to a little gate opening upon a street which was at that
hour deserted.   De Marsay took a keen notice of everything.
The carriage awaited him.   This time the mulatto did not
accompany him, and at the moment when Henri put his head
out of the window to look once more at the gardens of the
hotel, he encountered the white eyes of Cristemio, with whom
he exchanged a glance.   On either side there was a provoca-
tion, a challenge, the declaration of a savage war, of a duel
in which ordinary laws were invalid, where treason and treachery were admitted means.   Cristemio knew that Henri had
sworn Paquita's death.   Henri knew that Cristemio would
like to kill him before he killed Paquita.   Both understood
each other to perfection.

"The adventure is growing complicated in a most interesting way," said Henri.

"Where is the gentleman going to?" asked the coachman.

De Marsay was driven to the house of Paul de Manerville. For more than a week Henri was away from home, and no one could discover either what he did during this period, nor where he stayed. This retreat saved him from the fury of the mulatto and caused the ruin of the charming creature who had placed all her hope in him whom she loved as never human heart had loved on this earth before. On the last day of the week, about eleven o'clock at night, Henri drove up in a carriage to the little gate in the garden of the Hotel San-Réal. Four men accompanied him. The driver was evidently one of his friends, for he stood up on his box, like a man who was to listen, an attentive sentinel, for the least sound. One of the other three took his stand outside the gate in the street; the second waited in the garden, leaning against the wall; the last, who carried in his hand a bunch of keys, accompanied De Marsay.

"Henri," said his companion to him, "we are betrayed."

"By whom, my good Ferragus?"*

"They are not all asleep," replied the chief of the Devourers; "it is absolutely certain that some one in the house has neither eaten nor drunk. . . . Look! see that light!"

"We have a plan of the house; from where does it come?"

"I need no plan to know," replied Ferragus; "it comes from the room of the Marquise."

"Ah," cried De Marsay, "no doubt she arrived from London to-day. The woman has robbed me even of my revenge! But if she has anticipated me, my good Gratien, we will give her up to the law."

"Listen, listen! . . . The thing is settled," said Ferragus to Henri.

The two friends listened intently, and heard some feeble cries which might have aroused pity in the breast of a tiger.

"Your marquise did not think the sound would escape by the chimney," said the chief of the Devourers, with the laugh of a critic, enchanted to detect a fault in a work of merit.

* *Vid.* Translator's Preface.

"We alone, we know how to provide for every contingency," said Henri. "Wait for me. I want to see what is going on upstairs—I want to know how their domestic quarrels are managed. By God! I believe she is roasting her at a slow fire."

De Marsay lightly scaled the stairs, with which he was familiar, and recognized the passage leading to the boudoir. When he opened the door he experienced the involuntary shudder which the sight of bloodshed gives to the most determined of men. The spectacle which was offered to his view was, moreover, in more than one respect astonishing to him. The Marquise was a woman; she had calculated her vengeance with that perfection of perfidy which distinguishes the weaker animals. She had dissimulated her anger in order to assure herself of the crime before she punished it.

"Too late, my beloved!" said Paquita, in her death agony, casting her pale eyes upon De Marsay.

The girl of the golden eyes expired in a bath of blood. The great illumination of candles, a delicate perfume which was perceptible, a certain disorder, in which the eye of a man accustomed to amorous adventures could not but discern the madness which is common to all the passions, revealed how cunningly the Marquise had interrogated the guilty one. The white room, where the blood showed so well, betrayed a long struggle. The prints of Paquita's hands were on the cushions. Here she had clung to her life, here she had defended herself, here she had been struck. Long strips of the tapestry had been torn down by her bleeding hands, which, without a doubt, had struggled long. Paquita must have tried to reach the window; her bare feet had left their imprints on the edge of the divan, along which she must have run. Her body, mutilated by the dagger-thrusts of her executioner, told of the fury with which she had disputed a life which Henri had made precious to her. She lay stretched on the floor, and in her death-throes had bitten the ankles of Madame de San-Réal, who still held in her hand her dagger, dripping blood. The hair of the Marquise had been torn out, she was covered with bites, many of which were bleeding, and her torn dress revealed her in a state of semi-nudity, with the scratches on her breasts. She was sublime so. Her head, eager and maddened, exhaled the odor of blood. Her panting mouth was open, and her nostrils were not sufficient for her breath. There are certain animals who fall upon their enemy in their rage, do it to death, and seem in the tranquillity of victory to have forgotten it. There are others who prowl around their victim, who guard it in fear lest it should be taken away from them, and who, like the Achilles of Homer, drag their enemy by the feet nine times round the walls of Troy. The Marquise was like that. She did not see Henri. In the first place, she was too secure of her solitude to be afraid of witnesses; and, secondly, she was too intoxicated with warm blood, too excited with the fray, too exalted, to take notice of the whole of Paris, if Paris had formed a circle round her. A thunderbolt would not have disturbed her. She had not even heard Paquita's last sigh, and believed that the dead girl could still hear her.

"Die without confessing!" she said. "Go down to hell, monster of ingratitude; belong to no one but the fiend. For the blood you gave him you owe me all your own! Die, die, suffer a thousand deaths! I have been too kind—I was only a moment killing you. I should have made you experience all the tortures that you have bequeathed to me. I—I shall live! I shall live in misery. I have no one left to love but God!"

She gazed at her.

"She is dead!" she said to herself, after a pause, in a violent reaction. "Dead! Oh, I shall die of grief!"

The Marquise was throwing herself upon the divan, stricken with a despair which deprived her of speech, when this movement brought her in view of Henri de Marsay.

"Who are you?" she asked, rushing at him with her dagger raised.

Henri caught her arm, and thus they could contemplate each other face to face. A horrible surprise froze the blood in their veins, and their limbs quivered like those of frightened horses. In effect, the two Menœchmi had not been more alike. With one accord they uttered the same phrase:

"Lord Dudley must have been your father!"

The head of each was drooped in affirmation.

"She was true to the blood," said Henri, pointing to Paquita.

"She was as little guilty as it is possible to be," replied Margarita Euphémia Porrabéril, and she threw herself upon the body of Paquita, giving vent to a cry of despair. "Poor child! Oh, if I could bring thee to life again! I was wrong —forgive me, Paquita! Dead! and I live! I—I am the most unhappy."

At that moment the horrible face of the mother of Paquita appeared.

"You are come to tell me that you never sold her to me to kill," cried the Marquise. "I know why you have left your lair. I will pay you twice over. Hold your peace."

She took a bag of gold from the ebony cabinet, and threw it contemptuously at the old woman's feet. The chink of the gold was potent enough to excite a smile on the Georgian's impassive face.

"I come at the right moment for you, my sister," said Henri. "The law will ask of you——"

"Nothing," replied the Marquise. "One person alone might ask a reckoning for the death of this girl. Cristemio is dead."

"And the mother," said Henri, pointing to the old woman. "Will you not be always in her power?"

"She comes from a country where women are not beings, but things—chattels, with which one does as one wills, which one buys, sells, and slays; in short, which one uses for one's caprices as you, here, use a piece of furniture. Besides, she has one passion which dominates all the others, and which would have stifled her maternal love, even if she had loved her daughter, a passion——"

"What?" Henri asked quickly, interrupting his sister.

"Play! God keep you from it," answered the Marquise.

"But whom have you," said Henri, looking at the girl of the golden eyes, "who will help you to remove the traces of this fantasy which the law would not overlook?"

"I have her mother," replied the Marquise, designating the Georgian, to whom she made a sign to remain.

"We shall meet again," said Henri, who was thinking anxiously of his friends and felt that it was time to leave.

"No, brother," she said, "we shall not meet again. I am going back to Spain to enter the Convent of *los Dolores.*"

"You are too young yet, too lovely," said Henri, taking her in his arms and giving her a kiss.

"Good-bye," she said; "there is no consolation when you have lost that which has seemed to you the infinite."

A week later Paul de Manerville met De Marsay in the Tuileries, on the Terrasse des Feuillants.

"Well, what has become of our beautiful girl of the golden eyes, you rascal?"

"She is dead."

"What of?"

"Consumption."

PARIS, *March* 1834—*April* 1835.

FATHER GORIOT

AND OTHER STORIES

INTRODUCTION

Le Père Goriot perhaps deserves to be ranked as that one of
Balzac's novels which has united the greatest number of
suffrages, and which exhibits his peculiar merits, not
indeed without any of his faults, but with the merits in
eminent, and the faults not in glaring, degree. It was written (the preface is dated 1834) at the time when his genius
was at its very height, when it had completely burst the
strange shell which had so long enveloped and cramped it,
when the scheme of the *Comédie Humaine* was not quite
finally settled (it never was that), but elaborated to a very
considerable extent, when the author had already acquired
most of the knowledge of the actual world which he possessed, and when his physical powers were as yet unimpaired
by his enormous labor and his reckless disregard of "burning
the candle at both ends." Although it exhibits, like nearly
all his work, the complication of interest and scheme which
was almost a necessity to him, that complication is kept
within reasonable bounds, and managed with wonderful address. The history of Goriot and his daughters, the fortunes
of Eugène de Rastignac, and the mysterious personality and
operations of Vautrin, not only all receive due and unper-
plexed development, but work upon each other with that
correspondence and interdependence which form the rarest gift
of the novelist, and which, when present, too commonly have
attached to them the curse of over-minuteness and com-
plexity. No piece of Balzac's Dutch painting is worked out

with such marvelous minuteness as the Pension Vauquer, and hardly any book of his has more lifelike studies of character.

It would, however, not be difficult to find books with an almost, if not quite, equal accumulation of attractions, which have somehow failed to make the mark that has been made by *Le Père Goriot*. And the practised critic of novels knows perfectly well why this is. It is almost invariably, and perhaps quite invariably, because there is no sufficiently central interest, or because that interest is not of the broadly human kind. Had Goriot had no daughters, he would undoubtedly have been a happier man (or a less happy, for it is possible to take it both ways) ; but the history of his decadence and death never could have been such a good novel. It is because this history of the daughters—not exactly unnatural, not wholly without excuse, but as surely murderesses of their father as Goneril and Regan—at once unites and over-shadows the whole, because of its intensity, its simple and suasive appeal, that *Le Père Goriot* holds the place it does hold. That it owes something in point of suggestion to *Lear* does not in the least impair its claims. The circumstances and treatment have that entire difference which, when genius is indebted to genius, pays all the score there is at once. And besides, *Lear* has offered its motive for three hundred years to thousands and millions of people who have been writing plays and novels, and yet there is only one *Père Goriot*.

It is, however, a fair subject of debate for those who like critical argument of the nicer kind, whether Balzac has or has not made a mistake in representing the ex-dealer in floury compounds as a sort of idiot outside his trade abilities and his love for his daughters. That in doing so he was guided by a sense of poetical justice and consistency—the same sense which made Shakespeare dwell on the ungovernable temper and the undignified haste to get rid of the cares of sovereignty that bring on and justify the woes of Lear— is undeniable. But it would perhaps not have been unnatural, and it would have been even more tragic, if the *ci-devant* manufacturer had been represented as more intellectually capable, and as ruining himself in spite of his better judgment. On this point, however, both sides may be held with equal ease and cogency, and I do not decide either way. Of the force and pathos of the actual representation, no two opinions are possible. There is hardly a touch of the one fault which can be urged against Balzac very often with some, and sometimes with very great, justice—the fault of exaggeration and phantasmagoric excess. Here at least the possibilities of actual life, as translatable into literature, are not one whit exceeded; and the artist has his full reward for being true to art.

Almost equally free from the abnormal and the gigantic is the portraiture of Rastignac. Even those who demur to the description of Balzac as an impeccable chronicler of society must admit the extraordinary felicity of the pictures of the young man's introduction to the drawing-rooms of Mesdames de Restaud and de Beauséant. Neither Fielding nor Thackeray—that is to say, no one else in the world of letters—could have drawn with more absolute vividness and more absolute veracity a young man, not a *parvenu* in point of birth, not devoid of native cleverness and "star," but hampered by the consciousness of poverty and by utter ignorance of the actual ways and current social fashions of the great world when he is first thrown, to sink or swim, into this

great world itself. We may pass from the certain to the
dubious, or at least the debatable, when we pass from Rastignac's first appearance to his later experiences. Here comes
in what has been said in the general introduction as to the
somewhat fantastic and imaginary, the conventional and
artificial character of Balzac's world. But it must be remembered that for centuries the whole structure of Parisian
society has been to a very great extent fantastic and imaginary, conventional and artificial. Men and women have always played parts there as they have played them nowhere
else. And it must be confessed that some of the parts here, if
planned to the stage, are played to the life—that of Madame
de Beauséant especially.

It is Vautrin on whom Balzac's decriers, if they are so
hardy as to attack this most unattackable book of his at all,
must chiefly fasten. It was long ago noticed—indeed, sober
eyes both in France and elsewhere noticed it at the time—
that the criminal, more or less virtuous, more or less terrible,
more or less superhuman, exercised a kind of sorcery over
minds in France from the greatest to the least at this particular time, and even later. Not merely Balzac, but Victor
Hugo and George Sand, succumbed to his fascinations; and
after these three names it is quite unnecessary to mention
any others. And Balzac's proneness to the enormous and
gigantesque made the fascination peculiarly dangerous in
his case. Undoubtedly the Vautrin who talks to Rastignac
in the arbor is neither quite a real man nor quite the same
man who is somewhat ignominiously caught by the treachery
of his boarding-house fellows; undoubtedly we feel that with
him we have left Shakespeare a long way behind, and are
getting rather into the society of Bouchardy or Eugène Sue.

But the genius is here likewise, and, as usual, it saves everything.

How it extends to the minutest and even the least savory details of Madame Vauquer's establishment, how it irradiates the meannesses and the sordidnesses of the inhabitants thereof, those who have read know, and those who are about to read this new presentation in English will find. Let it only be repeated, that if the rarest and strangest charms which Balzac can produce are elsewhere, nowhere else is his charm presented in a more pervading and satisfactory manner.

Le Père Goriot originally appeared as a book in 1835, published by Werdet and Spahmann in two volumes. It had, however, appeared serially in the *Revue de Paris* during the previous winter. The first and some subsequent editions had seven chapter-divisions, six of them headed. These, according to Balzac's usual practice, were swept away when the book became, in 1843, part of the *Scènes de la Vie Parisienne* and the *Comédie* itself. The transference to the *Vie Privée* which is accomplished in the *édition définitive* was only executed in accordance with notes found after Balzac's death, and is far from happy, the book being essentially Parisian.

———

Les Comédiens sans le savoir seems to me one of the best and most amusing of what may be called (though it might also be called by a dozen other names) the Bixiou cycle of stories, in which journalism, art, provincials in Paris, young persons of the other sex with more beauty than morals, and so forth, play a somewhat artificial but often amusing series of scenes and characters. In this particular division of the

series the satire is happy, the adventures are agreeably
Arabian-Nightish with a modern adjustment, the central
figure of the Southern Gazonal is good in itself, and an excellent rallying-point for the others, and the good-natured
mystification played off on him is a pleasant dream. I think,
indeed, that there is little doubt that the late Mr. Stevenson
took his idea of "New Arabian Nights" from Balzac, of
whom he was an unwearied student, and I do not know that
Balzac was ever happier in his "Parisian Nights," as we may
call them, than here. The artists and the actresses, the corn-
cutters and the fortune-tellers, the politicians, the money-
lenders, the furnishers of garments, and all the rest, appear
and disappear in an easy phantasmagoric fashion which Balzac's expression does not always achieve except when his imagination is at a white heat not easily excited by such slight
matter as this. The way in which the excellent Gazonal is
forced to recognize the majesty of the capital may not be in
exact accordance with the views of the grave and precise, but it
is a pleasant fairy tale, and there is nothing so good as a fairy
tale.

Les Comédiens sans le savoir appeared in the *Courrier
Français* during April 1846, and shortly thereafter found its
way into the *Comédie*. But in 1848 it did outpost duty, with
some other short stories, as *Le Provincial à Paris*. There are
some interesting minor details as its variants which must be
sought in M. de Lovenjoul.

I have sometimes wondered whether it was accident or intention which made Balzac so frequently combine early and
late work in the same volume. The question is certainly in-

soluble, and perhaps not worth solving, but it presents itself once more in the present instance. *L'Illustre Gaudissart* is a story of 1832, the very heyday of Balzac's creative period, when even his pen could hardly keep up with the abundance of his fancy and the gathered stores of his minute observation. *La Muse du Département** dates ten years and more later, when, though there was plenty of both left, both sacks had been deeply dipped into.

L'Illustre Gaudissart is, of course, slight, not merely in bulk, but in conception. Balzac's Tourangeau patriotism may have amused itself by the idea of the villagers "rolling" the great Gaudissart; but the ending of the tale can hardly be thought to be quite so good as the beginning. Still, that beginning is altogether excellent. The sketch of the *commis-voyageur* generally smacks of that *physiologie* style of which Balzac was so fond; but it is good, and Gaudissart himself, as well as the whole scene with his *épouse libre,* is delightful. The Illustrious One was evidently a favorite character with his creator. He nowhere plays a very great part; but it is everywhere a rather favorable and, except in this little mishap with Margaritis (which, it must be observed, does not turn entirely to his discomfiture), a rather successful part. We have him in *César Birotteau* superintending the early efforts of Popinot to launch the Huile Céphalique. He was present at the great ball. He served as intermediary to M. de Bauvan in the merciful scheme of buying at fancy prices the handiwork of the Count's faithful spouse, and so providing her with a livelihood; and later as a theatrical manager, a little spoilt by his profession, we find him in *Le Cousin Pons*.

---

* The second and final section of *Les Parisiens en Province;* but since the two ~~ries~~ are unconnected, *La Muse du Département* has been reserved for another ~~ime~~.

But he is always with the French called a "good devil," and here he is a very good devil indeed.

The history of *L'Illustre Gaudissart* is, for a story of Balzac's, almost null. It was inserted without any previous newspaper appearance in the first edition of *Scènes de la Vie de Province* in 1833, and entered with the rest of them into the first edition also of the *Comédie,* when the joint title, which it has kept since and shared with *La Muse du Département,* of *Les Parisiens en Province* was given to it.

G. S.

FATHER GORIOT

To the great and illustrious Geoffroy Saint-Hilaire, a token of
admiration for his works and genius.

DE BALZAC.

MME. VAUQUER (*née* de Conflans) is an elderly person, who
for the past forty years has kept a lodging-house in the Rue
Neuve-Sainte-Geneviève, in the district that lies between the
Latin Quarter and the Faubourg Saint-Marcel. Her house
(known in the neighborhood as the *Maison Vauquer*) receives men and women, old and young, and no word has ever
been breathed against her respectable establishment; but, at
the same time, it must be said that as a matter of fact no
young woman has been under her roof for thirty years, and
that if a young man stays there for any length of time it
is a sure sign that his allowance must be of the slenderest.
In 1819, however, the time when this drama opens, there
was an almost penniless young girl among Mme. Vauquer's
boarders.

That word drama has been somewhat discredited of late;
it has been overworked and twisted to strange uses in these
days of dolorous literature; but it must do service again
here, not because this story is dramatic in the restricted
sense of the word, but because some tears may perhaps be
shed *intra et extra muros* before it is over.

Will any one without the walls of Paris understand it?
It is open to doubt. The only audience who could appreciate the results of close observation, the careful reproduction of minute detail and local color, are dwellers between
the heights of Montrouge and Montmartre, in a vale of

crumbling stucco watered by streams of black mud, a vale
of sorrows which are real and of joys too often hollow; but
this audience is so accustomed to terrible sensations, that
only some unimaginable and well-nigh impossible woe could
produce any lasting impression there. Now and again there
are tragedies so awful and so grand by reason of the complication of virtues and vices that bring them about, that ego-
tism and selfishness are forced to pause and are moved to
pity; but the impression that they receive is like a luscious
fruit, soon consumed. Civilization, like the car of Jugger-
naut, is scarcely stayed perceptibly in its progress by a heart
less easy to break than the others that lie in its course; this
also is broken, and Civilization continues on her course triumphant. And you, too, will do the like; you who with this
book in your white hand will sink back among the cushions
of your armchair, and say to yourself, "Perhaps this may
amuse me." You will read the story of Father Goriot's secret
woes, and, dining thereafter with an unspoiled appetite, will
lay the blame of your insensibility upon the writer, and accuse him of exaggeration, of writing romances. Ah! once
for all, this drama is neither a fiction nor a romance! *All
is true,*—so true, that every one can discern the elements of
the tragedy in his own house, perhaps in his own heart.

The lodging-house is Mme. Vauquer's own property. It is
still standing at the lower end of the Rue Neuve-Sainte-Geneviève, just where the road slopes so sharply down to the Rue
de l'Arbalète, that wheeled traffic seldom passes that way,
because it is so stony and steep. This position is sufficient
to account for the silence prevalent in the streets shut in between the dome of the Panthéon and the dome of the Val-de-
Grâce, two conspicuous public buildings which give a yellowish tone to the landscape and darken the whole district
that lies beneath the shadow of their leaden-hued cupolas.

In that district the pavements are clean and dry, there is
neither mud nor water in the gutters, grass grows in the
chinks of the walls. The most heedless passer-by feels the
depressing influences of a place where the sound of wheels

creates a sensation; there is a grim look about the houses, a suggestion of a jail about those high garden walls. A Parisian straying into a suburb apparently composed of lodging-houses and public institutions would see poverty and dulness, old age lying down to die, and joyous youth condemned to drudgery. It is the ugliest quarter of Paris, and, it may be added, the least known. But, before all things, the Rue Neuve-Sainte-Geneviève is like a bronze frame for a picture for which the mind cannot be too well prepared by the contemplation of sad hues and sober images. Even so, step by step the daylight decreases, and the cicerone's droning voice grows hollower as the traveler descends into the Catacombs. The comparison holds good! Who shall say which is more ghastly, the sight of the bleached skulls or of dried-up human hearts?

The front of the lodging-house is at right angles to the road, and looks out upon a little garden, so that you see the side of the house in section, as it were, from the Rue Neuve-Sainte-Geneviève. Beneath the wall of the house front there lies a channel, a fathom wide, paved with cobble-stones, and beside it runs a graveled walk bordered by geraniums and oleanders and pomegranates set in great blue and white glazed earthenware pots. Access into the graveled walk is afforded by a door, above which the words MAISON VAUQUER may be read, and beneath, in rather smaller letters, *"Lodgings for both sexes, etc."*

During the day a glimpse into the garden is easily obtained through a wicket to which a bell is attached. On the opposite wall, at the further end of the graveled walk, a green marble arch was painted once upon a time by a local artist, and in this semblance of a shrine a statue representing Cupid is installed; a Parisian Cupid, so blistered and disfigured that he looks like a candidate for one of the adjacent hospitals, and might suggest an allegory to lovers of symbolism. The half-obliterated inscription on the pedestal beneath determines the date of this work of art, for it bears witness to the widespread enthusiasm felt for Voltaire on his return to Paris in 1777:

> "Whoe'er thou art, thy master see;
> He is, or was, or ought to be."

At night the wicket gate is replaced by a solid door. The little garden is no wider than the front of the house; it is shut in between the wall of the street and the partition wall of the neighboring house. A mantle of ivy conceals the bricks and attracts the eyes of passers-by to an effect which is picturesque in Paris, for each of the walls is covered with trellised vines that yield a scanty dusty crop of fruit, and furnish besides a subject of conversation for Mme. Vauquer and her lodgers; every year the widow trembles for her vintage.

A straight path beneath the walls on either side of the garden leads to a clump of lime-trees at the further end of it; *line*-trees, as Mme. Vauquer persists in calling them, in spite of the fact that she was a de Conflans, and regardless of repeated corrections from her lodgers.

The central space between the walls is filled with artichokes and rows of pyramid fruit-trees, and surrounded by a border of lettuce, pot-herbs, and parsley. Under the lime-trees there are a few green-painted garden seats and a wooden table, and hither, during the dog-days, such of the lodgers as are rich enough to indulge in a cup of coffee come to take their pleasure, though it is hot enough to roast eggs even in the shade.

The house itself is three stories high, without counting the attics under the roof. It is built of rough stone, and covered with the yellowish stucco that gives a mean appearance to almost every house in Paris. There are five windows in each story in the front of the house; all the blinds visible through the small square panes are drawn up awry, so that the lines are all at cross purposes. At the side of the house there are but two windows on each floor, and the lowest of all are adorned with a heavy iron grating.

Behind the house a yard extends for some twenty feet, a space inhabited by a happy family of pigs, poultry, and rabbits; the wood-shed is situated on the further side, and on the wall between the wood-shed and the kitchen window hangs the meat-safe, just above the place where the sink discharges its greasy streams. The cook sweeps all the refuse out through a little door into the Rue Neuve-Sainte-Geneviève, and frequently cleanses the yard with copious supplies of water, under pain of pestilence.

The house might have been built on purpose for its present uses. Access is given by a French window to the first room on the ground floor, a sitting-room which looks out upon the street through the two barred windows already mentioned. Another door opens out of it into the dining-room, which is separated from the kitchen by the well of the staircase, the steps being constructed partly of wood, partly of tiles, which are colored and beeswaxed. Nothing can be more depressing than the sight of that sitting-room. The furniture is covered with horse hair woven in alternate dull and glossy stripes. There is a round table in the middle, with a purplish-red marble top, on which there stands, by way of ornament, the inevitable white china tea-service, covered with a half-effaced gilt network. The floor is sufficiently uneven, the wainscot rises to elbow height, and the rest of the wall space is decorated with a varnished paper, on which the principal scenes from *Télémaque* are depicted, the various classical personages being colored. The subject between the two windows is the banquet given by Calypso to the son of Ulysses, displayed thereon for the admiration of the boarders, and has furnished jokes these forty years to the young men who show themselves superior to their position by making fun of the dinners to which poverty condemns them. The hearth is always so clean and neat that it is evident that a fire is only kindled there on great occasions; the stone chimney-piece is adorned by a couple of vases filled with faded artificial flowers imprisoned under glass shades, on either side of a bluish marble clock in the very worst taste.

The first room exhales an odor for which there is no name in the language, and which should be called the *odeur de pension*. The damp atmosphere sends a chill through you as you breathe it; it has a stuffy, musty, and rancid quality; it permeates your clothing; after-dinner scents seem to be mingled in it with smells from the kitchen and scullery and the reek of a hospital. It might be possible to describe it if some one should discover a process by which to distil from the atmosphere all the nauseating elements with which it is charged by the catarrhal exhalations of every individual lodger, young or old. Yet, in spite of these stale horrors, the sitting-room is as charming and as delicately perfumed as a boudoir, when compared with the adjoining dining-room.

The paneled walls of that apartment were once painted some color, now a matter of conjecture, for the surface is incrusted with accumulated layers of grimy deposit, which cover it with fantastic outlines. A collection of dim-ribbed glass decanters, metal discs with a satin sheen on them, and piles of blue-edged earthenware plates of Touraine ware cover the sticky surfaces of the sideboards that line the room. In a corner stands a box containing a set of numbered pigeon-holes, in which the lodgers' table napkins, more or less soiled and stained with wine, are kept. Here you see that inde-structible furniture never met with elsewhere, which finds its way into lodging-houses much as the wrecks of our civiliza-tion drift into hospitals for incurables. You expect in such places as these to find the weather-house whence a Capuchin issues on wet days; you look to find the execrable engravings which spoil your appetite, framed every one in a black var-nished frame, with a gilt beading round it; you know the sort of tortoise-shell clock-case, inlaid with brass; the green stove, the Argand lamps, covered with oil and dust, have met your eyes before. The oilcloth which covers the long table is so greasy that a waggish *externe* will write his name on the surface, using his thumb-nail as a style. The chairs are broken-down invalids; the wretched little hempen mats slip away from under your feet without slipping away for good; and finally, the foot-warmers are miserable wrecks, hingeless, charred, broken away about the holes. It would be impossible to give an idea of the old, rotten, shaky, cranky, worm-eaten, halt, maimed, one-eyed, rickety, and ramshackle condition of the furniture without an exhaustive description, which would delay the progress of the story to an extent that impatient people would not pardon. The red tiles of the floor are full of depressions brought about by scouring and periodical renewings of color. In short, there is no illusory grace left to the poverty that reigns here; it is dire, parsimonious, concentrated, threadbare poverty; as yet it has not sunk into the mire, it is only splashed by it, and though not in rags as yet, its clothing is ready to drop to pieces.

This apartment is in all its glory at seven o'clock in the morning, when Mme. Vauquer's cat appears, announcing the near approach of his mistress, and jumps upon the sideboards to sniff at the milk in the bowls, each protected by a plate, while he purrs his morning greeting to the world. A moment later the widow shows her face; she is tricked out in a net cap attached to a false front set on awry, and shuffles into the room in her slipshod fashion. She is an oldish woman, with a bloated countenance, and a nose like a parrot's beak set in the middle of it; her fat little hands (she is as sleek as a church rat) and her shapeless, slouching figure are in keeping with the room that reeks of misfortune, where hope is reduced to speculate for the meanest stakes. Mme. Vauquer alone can breathe that tainted air without being disheartened by it. Her face is as fresh as a frosty morning in autumn; there are wrinkles about the eyes that vary in their expression from the set smile of a ballet-dancer to the dark, suspicious scowl of a discounter of bills; in short, she is at once the embodiment and interpretation of her lodging-house, as surely as her lodging-house implies the existence of its mistress. You can no more imagine the one without the other, than you can think of a jail without a turnkey. The unwholesome corpulence of the little woman is produced by the life she leads, just as typhus fever is bred in the tainted air of a hospital. The very knitted woolen petticoat that she wears beneath a skirt made of an old gown, with the wadding protruding through the rents in the material, is a sort of epitome of the sitting-room, the dining-room, and the little garden; it discovers the cook; it foreshadows the lodgers —the picture of the house is completed by the portrait of its mistress.

Mme. Vauquer at the age of fifty is like all women who "have seen a deal of trouble." She has the glassy eyes and innocent air of a trafficker in flesh and blood, who will wax virtuously indignant to obtain a higher price for her services, but who is quite ready to betray a Georges or a Pichegru, if a Georges or a Pichegru were in hiding and still to be betrayed, or for any other expedient that may alleviate her lot. Still, "she is a good woman at bottom," said the lodgers, who believed that the widow was wholly dependent upon the money that they paid her, and sympathized when they heard her cough and groan like one of themselves.

What had M. Vauquer been? The lady was never very explicit on this head. How had she lost her money? "Through trouble," was her answer. He had treated her badly, had left her nothing but her eyes to cry over his cruelty, the house she lived in, and the privilege of pitying nobody, because, so she was wont to say, she herself had been through every possible misfortune.

Sylvie, the stout cook, hearing her mistress' shuffling footsteps, hastened to serve the lodgers' breakfasts. Beside those who lived in the house, Mme. Vauquer took boarders who came for their meals; but these *externes* usually only came to dinner, for which they paid thirty francs a month.

At the time when this story begins, the lodging-house contained seven inmates. The best rooms in the house were on the first story, Mme. Vauquer herself occupying the least important, while the rest were let to a Mme. Couture, the widow of a commissary-general in the service of the Republic. With her lived Victorine Taillefer, a schoolgirl, to whom she filled the place of mother. These two ladies paid eighteen hundred francs a year.

The two sets of rooms on the second floor were respectively occupied by an old man named Poiret and a man of forty or thereabouts, the wearer of a black wig and dyed whiskers, who gave out that he was a retired merchant, and was addressed as M. Vautrin. Two of the four rooms on the third floor were also let—one to an elderly spinster, a Mlle. Michonneau, and the other to a retired manufacturer of vermicelli, Italian paste and starch, who allowed the others to address him as "Father Goriot." The remaining rooms were allotted to various birds of passage, to impecunious students, who, like "Father Goriot" and Mlle. Michonneau, could only muster forty-five francs a month to pay for their board and lodging. Mme. Vauquer had little desire for lodgers of this sort; they ate too much bread, and she only took them in default of better.

At that time one of the rooms was tenanted by a law student, a young man from the neighborhood of Angoulême, one of a large family who pinched and starved themselves to spare twelve hundred francs a year for him. Misfortune had accustomed Eugène de Rastignac, for that was his name, to work. He belonged to the number of young men who know as children that their parents' hopes are centered on them, and deliberately prepare themselves for a great career, subordinating their studies from the first to this end, carefully watching the indications of the course of events, calculating the probable turn that affairs will take, that they may be the first to profit by them. But for his observant curiosity, and the skill with which he managed to introduce himself into the salons of Paris, this story would not have been colored by the tones of truth which it certainly owes to him, for they are entirely due to his penetrating sagacity and desire to fathom the mysteries of an appalling condition of things, which was concealed as carefully by the victim as by those who had brought it to pass.

Above the third story there was a garret where the linen was hung to dry, and a couple of attics. Christophe, the man-of-all-work, slept in one, and Sylvie, the stout cook, in the other. Beside the seven inmates thus enumerated, taking one year with another, some eight law or medical students dined in the house, as well as two or three regular comers who lived in the neighborhood. There were usually eighteen people at dinner, and there was room, if need be, for twenty at Mme. Vauquer's table; at breakfast, however, only the seven lodgers appeared. It was almost like a family party. Every one came down in dressing-gown and slippers, and the conversation usually turned on anything that had happened the evening before; comments on the dress or appearance of the dinner contingent were exchanged in friendly confidence.

These seven lodgers were Mme. Vauquer's spoiled children. Among them she distributed, with astronomical precision, the exact proportion of respect and attention due to the varying amounts they paid for their board. One single consideration influenced all these human beings thrown together by chance. The two second-floor lodgers only paid seventy-two francs a month. Such prices as these are confined to the Faubourg Saint-Marcel and the district between La Bourbe and the Salpêtrière; and, as might be expected, poverty, more or less apparent, weighed upon them all, Mme. Couture being the sole exception to the rule.

The dreary surroundings were reflected in the costumes of the inmates of the house; all were alike threadbare. The color of the men's coats was problematical; such shoes, in more fashionable quarters, are only to be seen lying in the gutter; the cuffs and collars were worn and frayed at the edges; every limp article of clothing looked like the ghost of its former self. The women's dresses were faded, old-fashioned, dyed and re-dyed; they wore gloves that were glazed with hard wear, much-mended lace, dingy ruffles, crumpled muslin fichus. So much for their clothing; but, for the most part, their frames were solid enough; their constitutions had weathered the storms of life; their cold, hard faces were worn like coins that have been withdrawn from circulation, but there were greedy teeth behind the withered lips. Dramas brought to a close or still in progress are foreshadowed by the sight of such actors as these, not the dramas that are played before the footlights and against a background of painted canvas, but dumb dramas of life, frost-bound dramas that sere hearts like fire, dramas that do not end with the actors' lives.

Mlle. Michonneau, that elderly young lady, screened her weak eyes from the daylight by a soiled green silk shade with a rim of brass, an object fit to scare away the Angel of Pity himself. Her shawl, with its scanty, draggled fringe, might have covered a skeleton, so meagre and angular was the form beneath it. Yet she must have been pretty and shapely once. What corrosive had destroyed the feminine outlines? Was it trouble, or vice, or greed? Had she loved too well? Had she been a second-hand clothes dealer, a frequenter of the backstairs of great houses, or had she been merely a courtesan? Was she expiating the flaunting triumphs of a youth over-crowded with pleasures by an old age in which she was shunned by every passer-by? Her vacant gaze sent a chill through you; her shriveled face seemed like a menace. Her voice was like the shrill, thin note of the grasshopper sounding from the thicket when winter is at hand. She said that she had nursed an old gentleman, ill of catarrh of the bladder, and left to die by his children, who thought that he had nothing left. His bequest to her, a life annuity of a thousand francs, was periodically disputed by his heirs, who mingled slander with their persecutions. In spite of the ravages of conflicting passions, her face retained some traces of its former fairness and fineness of tissue, some vestiges of the physical charms of her youth still survived.

M. Poiret was a sort of automaton. He might be seen any day sailing like a gray shadow along the walks of the Jardin des Plantes, on his head a shabby cap, a cane with an old yellow ivory handle in the tips of his thin fingers; the outspread skirts of his threadbare overcoat failed to conceal his meagre figure; his breeches hung loosely on his shrunken limbs; the thin, blue-stockinged legs trembled like those of a drunken man; there was a notable breach of continuity between the dingy white waistcoat and crumpled shirt frills and the cravat twisted about a throat like a turkey gobbler's; altogether, his appearance set people wondering whether this outlandish ghost belonged to the audacious race of the sons of Japhet who flutter about on the Boulevard Italien. What kind of toil could have so shriveled him? What devouring passions had darkened that bulbous countenance, which would have seemed outrageous as a caricature? What had he been? Well, perhaps he had been part of the machinery of justice, a clerk in the office to which the executioner sends in his accounts,—so much for providing black veils for parricides, so much for sawdust, so much for pulleys and cord for the knife. Or he might have been a receiver at the door of a public slaughter-house, or a sub-inspector of nuisances. Indeed, the man appeared to have been one of the beasts of burden in our great social mill; one of those Parisian Ratons whom their Bertrands do not even know by sight; a pivot in the obscure machinery that disposes of misery and things unclean; one of those men, in short, at sight of whom we are prompted to remark that, "After all, we cannot do without them."

Stately Paris ignores the existence of these faces bleached by moral or physical suffering; but, then, Paris is in truth an ocean that no line can plumb. You may survey its surface and describe it; but no matter what pains you take with your investigations and recognizances, no matter how numerous and painstaking the toilers in this sea, there will always be lonely and unexplored regions in its depths, caverns unknown, flowers and pearls and monsters of the deep overlooked or forgotten by the divers of literature. The Maison Vauquer is one of these curious monstrosities.

Two, however, of Mme. Vauquer's boarders formed a striking contrast to the rest. There was a sickly pallor, such as is often seen in anæmic girls, in Mlle. Victorine Taillefer's face; and her unvarying expression of sadness, like her embarrassed manner and pinched look, was in keeping with the general wretchedness of the establishment in the Rue Neuve-

Sainte-Geneviève, which forms a background to this picture; but her face was young, there was youthfulness in her voice and elasticity in her movements. This young misfortune was not unlike a shrub, newly planted in an uncongenial soil, where its leaves have already begun to wither. The outlines of her figure, revealed by her dress of the simplest and cheapest materials, were also youthful. There was the same kind of charm about her too slender form, her faintly colored face and light-brown hair, that modern poets find in mediæval statuettes; and a sweet expression, a look of Christian resignation in the dark gray eyes. She was pretty by force of contrast; if she had been happy, she would have been charming. Happiness is the poetry of woman, as the toilette is her tinsel. If the delightful excitement of a ball had made the pale face glow with color; if the delights of a luxurious life had brought the color to the wan cheeks that were slightly hollowed already; if love had put light into the sad eyes, then Victorine might have ranked among the fairest; but she lacked the two things which create woman a second time—pretty dresses and love-letters.

A book might have been made of her story. Her father was persuaded that he had sufficient reason for declining to acknowledge her, and allowed her a bare six hundred francs a year; he had further taken measures to disinherit his daughter, and had converted all his real estate into personalty, that he might leave it undivided to his son. Victorine's mother had died broken-hearted in Mme. Couture's house; and the latter, who was a near relation, had taken charge of the little orphan. Unluckily, the widow of the commissary-general to the armies of the Republic had nothing in the world but her jointure and her widow's pension, and some day she might be obliged to leave the helpless, inexperienced girl to the mercy of the world. The good soul, therefore, took Victorine to mass every Sunday, and to confession once a fortnight, thinking that, in any case, she would bring up her ward to be devout. She was right; religion offered a solution of the problem of the young girl's future. The poor

child loved the father who refused to acknowledge her. Once
every year she tried to see him to deliver her mother's message of forgiveness, but every year hitherto she had knocked
at that door in vain; her father was inexorable. Her brother,
her only means of communication, had not come to see her for
four years, and had sent her no assistance; yet she prayed to
God to unseal her father's eyes and to soften her brother's
heart, and no accusations mingled with her prayers. Mme.
Couture and Mme. Vauquer exhausted the vocabulary of
abuse, and failed to find words that did justice to the banker's
iniquitous conduct; but while they heaped execrations on the
millionaire, Victorine's words were as gentle as the moan of
the wounded dove, and affection found expression even in the
cry drawn from her by pain.

Eugène de Rastignac was a thoroughly southern type; he
had a fair complexion, blue eyes, black hair. In his figure,
manner, and his whole bearing it was easy to see that he either
came of a noble family, or that, from his earliest childhood,
he had been gently bred. If he was careful of his wardrobe,
only taking last year's clothes into daily wear, still upon occasion he could issue forth as a young man of fashion. Ordi-
narily he wore a shabby coat and waistcoat, the limp black
cravat, untidily knotted, that students affect, trousers that
matched the rest of his costume, and boots that had been re-
soled.

Vautrin (the man of forty with the dyed whiskers) marked
a transition stage between these two young people and the
others. He was the kind of man that calls forth the remark:
"He looks a jovial sort!" He had broad shoulders, a well-
developed chest, muscular arms, and strong square-fisted
hands; the joints of his fingers were covered with tufts of
fiery red hair. His face was furrowed by premature wrinkles; there was a certain hardness about it in spite of his
bland and insinuating manner. His bass voice was by no
means unpleasant, and was in keeping with his boisterous
laughter. He was always obliging, always in good spirits; if
anything went wrong with one of the locks, he would soon

unscrew it, take it to pieces, file it, oil and clean and set it in
order, and put it back in its place again: "I am an old hand
at it," he used to say. Not only so, he knew all about ships,
the sea, France, foreign countries, men, business, law, great
houses and prisons,—there was nothing that he did not know.
If any one complained rather more than usual, he would
offer his services at once. He had several times lent money
to Mme. Vauquer, or to the boarders; but, somehow, those
whom he obliged felt that they would sooner face death than
fail to repay him; a certain resolute look, sometimes seen on
his face, inspired fear of him, for all his appearance of easy
good-nature. In the way he spat there was an imperturbable
coolness which seemed to indicate that this was a man who
would not stick at a crime to extricate himself from a false
position. His eyes, like those of a pitiless judge, seemed to
go to the very bottom of all questions, to read all natures.
all feelings and thoughts. His habit of life was very regular;
he usually went out after breakfast, returning in time for
dinner, and disappeared for the rest of the evening, letting
himself in about midnight with a latch key, a privilege that
Mme. Vauquer accorded to no other boarder. But then he
was on very good terms with the widow; he used to call her
"mamma," and put his arm round her waist, a piece of flattery perhaps not appreciated to the full! The worthy woman
might imagine this to be an easy feat; but, as a matter of
fact, no arm but Vautrin's was long enough to encircle her.

It was a characteristic trait of his generously to pay fifteen
francs a month for the cup of coffee with a dash of brandy
in it, which he took after dinner. Less superficial observers
than young men engulfed by the whirlpool of Parisian life,
or old men, who took no interest in anything that did not
directly concern them, would not have stopped short at the
vaguely unsatisfactory impression that Vautrin made upon
them. He knew or guessed the concerns of every one about
him; but none of them had been able to penetrate his
thoughts, or to discover his occupation. He had deliberately
made his apparent good-nature, his unfailing readiness to

oblige, and his high spirits into a barrier between himself and the rest of them, but not seldom he gave glimpses of appalling depths of character. He seemed to delight in scourging the upper classes of society with the lash of his tongue, to take pleasure in convicting it of inconsistency, in mocking at law and order with some grim jest worthy of Juvenal, as if some grudge against the social system rankled in him, as if there were some mystery carefully hidden away in his life.

Mlle. Taillefer felt attracted, perhaps unconsciously, by the strength of the one man, and the good looks of the other; her stolen glances and secret thoughts were divided between them; but neither of them seemed to take any notice of her, although some day a chance might alter her position, and she would be a wealthy heiress. For that matter, there was not a soul in the house who took any trouble to investigate the various chronicles of misfortunes, real or imaginary, related by the rest. Each one regarded the others with indifference, tempered by suspicion; it was a natural result of their relative positions. Practical assistance not one of them could give, this they all knew, and they had long since exhausted their stock of condolence over previous discussions of their grievances. They were in something the same position as an elderly couple who have nothing left to say to each other. The routine of existence kept them in contact, but they were parts of a mechanism which wanted oil. There was not one of them but would have passed a blind man begging in the street, not one that felt moved to pity by a tale of misfortune, not one who did not see in death the solution of the all-absorbing problem of misery which left them cold to the most terrible anguish in others.

The happiest of these hapless beings was certainly Mme. Vauquer, who reigned supreme over this hospital supported by voluntary contributions. For her, the little garden, which silence, and cold, and rain, and drought combined to make as dreary as an Asian *steppe,* was a pleasant shaded nook; the gaunt yellow house, the musty odors of a back shop had charms for her, and for her alone. Those cells belonged to her. She fed those convicts condemned to penal servitude for life, and her authority was recognized among them. Where else in Paris would they have found wholesome food in sufficient quantity at the prices she charged them, and rooms which they were at liberty to make, if not exactly elegant or comfortable, at any rate clean and healthy? If she had committed some flagrant act of injustice, the victim would have borne it in silence.

Such a gathering contained, as might have been expected, the elements out of which a complete society might be constructed. And, as in a school, as in the world itself, there was among the eighteen men and women who met round the dinner table a poor creature, despised by all the others, condemned to be the butt of all their jokes. At the beginning of Eugène de Rastignac's second twelvemonth, this figure suddenly started out into bold relief against the background of human forms and faces among which the law student was yet to live for another two years to come. This laughingstock was the retired vermicelli-merchant, Father Goriot, upon whose face a painter, like the historian, would have concentrated all the light in his picture.

How had it come about that the boarders regarded him with a half-malignant contempt? Why did they subject the oldest among their number to a kind of persecution, in which there was mingled some pity, but no respect for his misfortunes? Had he brought it upon himself by some eccentricity or absurdity, which is less easily forgiven or forgotten than more serious defects? The question strikes at the root of many a social injustice. Perhaps it is only human nature to inflict suffering on anything that will endure suffering, whether by reason of its genuine humility, or indifference, or sheer helplessness. Do we not, one and all, like to feel our strength even at the expense of some one or of something? The poorest sample of humanity, the street arab, will pull the bell handle at every street door in bitter weather, and scramble up to write his name on the unsullied marble of a monument.

In the year 1813, at the age of sixty-nine or thereabouts,
"Father Goriot" had sold his business and retired—to Mme.
Vauquer's boarding-house.   When he first came there he
had taken the rooms now occupied by Mme. Couture; he had
paid twelve hundred francs a year like a man to whom five
louis more or less was a mere trifle.   For him Mme. Vauquer
had made various improvements in the three rooms destined
for his use, in consideration of a certain sum paid in advance,
so it was said, for the miserable furniture, that is to say, for
some yellow cotton curtains, a few chairs of stained wood
covered with Utrecht velvet, several wretched colored prints
in frames, and wall papers that a little suburban tavern
would have disdained.   Possibly it was the careless generosity
with which Father Goriot allowed himself to be overreached at
this period of his life (they called him Monsieur Goriot very
respectfully then) that gave Mme. Vauquer the meanest
opinion of his business abilities; she looked on him as an
imbecile where money was concerned.

Goriot had brought with him a considerable wardrobe, the
gorgeous outfit of a retired tradesman who denies himself
nothing.   Mme. Vauquer's astonished eyes beheld no less than
eighteen cambric-fronted shirts, the splendor of their fineness being enhanced by a pair of pins each bearing a large
diamond, and connected by a short chain, an ornament which
adorned the vermicelli-maker's shirt front.   He usually wore
a coat of corn-flower blue; his rotund and portly person was
still further set off by a clean white waistcoat, and a gold
chain and seals which dangled over that broad expanse.
When his hostess accused him of being "a bit of a beau," he
smiled with the vanity of a citizen whose foible is gratified.
His cupboards (*ormoires,* as he called them in the popular
dialect) were filled with a quantity of plate that he brought
with him.   The widow's eyes gleamed as she obligingly helped
him to unpack the soup ladles, table-spoons, forks, cruet-
stands, tureens, dishes, and breakfast services—all of silver,
which were duly arranged upon the shelves, besides a few
more or less handsome pieces of plate, all weighing no incon-

siderable number of ounces; he could not bring himself to
part with these gifts that reminded him of past domestic
festivals.

"This was my wife's present to me on the first anniversary
of our wedding day," he said to Mme. Vauquer, as he put
away a little silver posset dish, with two turtle-doves billing
on the cover. "Poor dear! she spent on it all the money she
had saved before we married. Do you know, I would sooner
scratch the earth with my nails for a living, madame, than
part with that. But I shall be able to take my coffee out of
it every morning for the rest of my days, thank the Lord! I
am not to be pitied. There's not much fear of my starving
for some time to come."

Finally, Mme. Vauquer's magpie's eye had discovered and
read certain entries in the list of shareholders in the funds,
and, after a rough calculation, was disposed to credit Goriot
(worthy man) with something like ten thousand francs a
year. From that day forward Mme. Vauquer (*née* De Conflans), who, as a matter of fact, had seen forty-eight sum-
mers, though she would only own to thirty-nine of them—
Mme. Vauquer had her own ideas. Though Goriot's eyes
seemed to have shrunk in their sockets, though they were
weak and watery, owing to some glandular affection which
compelled him to wipe them continually, she considered him
to be a very gentlemanly and pleasant-looking man. Moreover, the widow saw favorable indications of character in the
well-developed calves of his legs and in his square-shaped
nose, indications still further borne out by the worthy man's
full-moon countenance and look of stupid good-nature. This,
in all probability, was a strongly-built animal, whose brains
mostly consisted in a capacity for affection. His hair, worn
in *ailes de pigeon,* and duly powdered every morning by the
barber from the École Polytechnique, described five points
on his low forehead, and made an elegant setting to his face.
Though his manners were somewhat boorish, he was always
as neat as a new pin and he took his snuff in a lordly way,
like a man who knows that his snuff-box is always likely to

be filled with maccaboy; so that when Mme. Vauquer lay
down to rest on the day of M. Goriot's installation, her heart,
like a larded partridge, sweltered before the fire of a burning
desire to shake off the shroud of Vauquer and rise again as
Goriot. She would marry again, sell her boarding-house, give
her hand to this fine flower of citizenship, become a lady of
consequence in the quarter, and ask for subscriptions for
charitable purposes; she would make little Sunday excursions
to Choisy, Soisy, Gentilly; she would have a box at the theatre when she liked, instead of waiting for the author's tickets
that one of her boarders sometimes gave her, in July; the
whole Eldorado of a little Parisian household rose up before
Mme. Vauquer in her dreams. Nobody knew that she herself
possessed forty thousand francs, accumulated *sou* by *sou,* that
was her secret; surely as far as money was concerned she was
a very tolerable match. "And in other respects, I am quite
his equal," she said to herself, turning as if to assure herself
of the charms of a form that the portly Sylvie found moulded
in down feathers every morning.

For three months from that day Mme. Veuve Vauquer
availed herself of the services of M. Goriot's coiffeur, and
went to some expense over her toilette, expense justifiable
on the ground that she owed it to herself and her establishment to pay some attention to appearances when such highly-
respectable persons honored her house with their presence.
She expended no small amount of ingenuity in a sort of
weeding process of her lodgers, announcing her intention of
receiving henceforward none but people who were in every
way select. If a stranger presented himself, she let him
know that M. Goriot, one of the best known and most highly-
respected merchants in Paris, had singled out her boarding-
house for a residence. She drew up a prospectus headed
MAISON VAUQUER, in which it was asserted that hers was
*"one of the oldest and most highly recommended boarding-
houses in the Latin Quarter."* "From the windows of the
house," thus ran the prospectus, "there is a charming view
of the Vallée des Gobelins (so there is—from the third floor),

and a *beautiful* garden, *extending* down to *an avenue of lin-dens* at the further end." Mention was made of the bracing air of the place and its quiet situation.

It was this prospectus that attracted Mme. la Comtesse de l'Ambermesnil, a widow of six-and-thirty, who was awaiting the final settlement of her husband's affairs, and of another matter regarding a pension due to her as the wife of a gen-eral who had died "on the field of battle." On this Mme. Vauquer saw to her table, lighted a fire baily in the sitting-room for nearly six months, and kept the promise of her prospectus, even going to some expense to do so. And the Countess, on her side, addressed Mme. Vauquer as "my dear," and promised her two more boarders, the Baronne de Vau-merland and the widow of a colonel, the late Comte de Pic-quoisie, who were about to leave a boarding-house in the Marais, where the terms were higher than at the Maison Vauquer. Both these ladies, moreover, would be very well to do when the people at the War Office had come to an end of their formalities. "But Government departments are al-ways so dilatory," the lady added.

After dinner the two widows went together up to Mme. Vauquer's room, and had a snug little chat over some cordial and various delicacies reserved for the mistress of the house. Mme. Vauquer's ideas as to Goriot were cordially approved by Mme. de l'Ambermesnil; it was a capital notion, which for that matter she had guessed from the very first; in her opinion the vermicelli maker was an excellent man.

"Ah! my dear lady, such a well-preserved man of his age, as sound as my eyesight—a man who might make a woman happy!" said the widow.

The good-natured Countess turned to the subject of Mme. Vauquer's dress, which was not in harmony with her proj-ects. "You must put yourself on a war footing," said she.

After much serious consideration the two widows went shopping together—they purchased a hat adorned with ostrich feathers and a cap at the Palais Royal, and the Countess took her friend to the Magasin de la Petite Jean-

nette, where they chose a dress and a scarf. Thus equipped
for the campaign, the widow looked exactly like the prize
animal hung out for a sign above an à la mode beef shop;
but she herself was so much pleased with the improvement,
as she considered it, in her appearance, that she felt that she
lay under some obligation to the Countess; and, though by
no means open-handed, she begged that lady to accept a hat
that cost twenty francs. The fact was that she needed the
Countess' services on the delicate mission of sounding Goriot;
the Countess must sing her praises in his ears. Mme. de
l'Ambermesnil lent herself very good-naturedly to this manœuvre, began her operations, and succeeded in obtaining a
private interview; but the overtures that she made, with a
view to securing him for herself, were received with embarrassment, not to say a repulse. She left him, revolted by his
coarseness.

"My angel," said she to her dear friend, "you will make
nothing of that man yonder. He is absurdly suspicious, and
he is a mean curmudgeon, an idiot, a fool; you would never
be happy with him."

After what had passed between M. Goriot and Mme. de
l'Ambermesnil, the Countess would no longer live under the
same roof. She left the next day, forgot to pay for six
months' board, and left behind her her wardrobe, cast-off
clothing to the value of five francs. Eagerly and persistently
as Mme. Vauquer sought her quondam lodger, the Comtesse
de l'Ambermesnil was never heard of again in Paris. The
widow often talked of this deplorable business, and regretted
her own too confiding disposition. As a matter of fact, she
was as suspicious as a cat; but she was like many other people,
who cannot trust their own kin and put themselves at the
mercy of the next chance comer—an odd but common phenomenon, whose causes may readily be traced to the depths
of the human heart.

Perhaps there are people who know that they have nothing
more to look for from those with whom they live; they have
shown the emptiness of their hearts to their housemates,

and in their secret selves they are conscious that they are severely judged, and that they deserve to be judged severely; but still they feel an unconquerable craving for praises that they do not hear, or they are consumed by a desire to appear to possess, in the eyes of a new audience, the qualities which they have not, hoping to win the admiration or affection of strangers at the risk of forfeiting it again some day. Or, once more, there are other mercenary natures who never do a kindness to a friend or a relation simply because these have a claim upon them, while a service done to a stranger brings its reward to self-love. Such natures feel but little affection for those who are nearest to them; they keep their kindness for remoter circles of acquaintance, and show most to those who dwell on its utmost limits. Mme. Vauquer belonged to both these essentially mean, false, and execrable classes.

"If I had been here at the time," Vautrin would say at the end of the story, "I would have shown her up, and that misfortune would not have befallen you. I know that kind of phiz!"

Like all narrow natures, Mme. Vauquer was wont to confine her attention to events, and did not go very deeply into the causes that brought them about; she likewise preferred to throw the blame of her own mistakes on other people, so she chose to consider that the honest vermicelli maker was responsible for her misfortune. It had opened her eyes, so she said, with regard to him. As soon as she saw that her blandishments were in vain, and that her outlay on her toilette was money thrown away, she was not slow to discover the reason of his indifference. It became plain to her at once that there was *some other attraction,* to use her own expression. In short, it was evident that the hope she had so fondly cherished was a baseless delusion, and that she would "never make anything out of that man yonder," in the Countess' forcible phrase. The Countess seemed to have been a judge of character. Mme. Vauquer's aversion was naturally more energetic than her friendship, for her hatred was not in proportion to her love, but to her disappointed expectations. The human heart may find here and there a resting-place short of the highest height of affection, but we seldom stop in the steep, downward slope of hatred. Still, M. Goriot was a lodger, and the widow's wounded self-love could not vent itself in an explosion of wrath; like a monk harassed by the prior of his convent, she was forced to stifle her sighs of disappointment, and to gulp down her craving for revenge. Little minds find gratification for their feelings, benevolent or otherwise, by a constant exercise of petty ingenuity. The widow employed her woman's malice to devise a system of covert persecution. She began by a course of retrenchment—various luxuries which had found their way to the table appeared there no more.

"No more gherkins, no more anchovies; they have made a fool of me!" she said to Sylvie one morning, and they returned to the old bill of fare.

The thrifty frugality necessary to those who mean to make their way in the world had become an inveterate habit of life with M. Goriot. Soup, boiled beef, and a dish of vegetables had been, and always would be, the dinner he liked best, so Mme. Vauquer found it very difficult to annoy a boarder whose tastes were so simple. He was proof against her malice, and in desperation she spoke to him and of him slightingly before the other lodgers, who began to amuse themselves at his expense, and so gratified her desire for revenge.

Towards the end of the first year the widow's suspicions had reached such a pitch that she began to wonder how it was that a retired merchant with a secure income of seven or eight thousand livres, the owner of such magnificent plate and jewelry handsome enough for a kept mistress, should be living in her house. Why should he devote so small a proportion of his money to his expenses? Until the first year was nearly at an end, Goriot had dined out once or twice every week, but these occasions came less frequently, and at last he was scarcely absent from the dinner-table twice a month.

It was hardly to be expected that Mme. Vauquer should regard the increased regularity of her boarder's habits with complacency, when those little excursions of his had been so much to her interest. She attributed the change not so much to a gradual diminution of fortune as to a spiteful wish to annoy his hostess. It is one of the most detestable habits of a Liliputian mind to credit other people with its own malignant pettiness.

Unluckily, towards the end of the second year, M. Goriot's conduct gave some color to the idle talk about him. He asked Mme. Vauquer to give him a room on the second floor, and to make a corresponding reduction in her charges. Apparently, such strict economy was called for, that he did without a fire all through the winter. Mme. Vauquer asked to be paid in advance, an arrangement to which M. Goriot consented, and thenceforward she spoke of him as "Father Goriot."

What had brought about this decline and fall? Conjecture was keen, but investigation was difficult. Father Goriot was not communicative; in the sham countess' phrase, he was "a curmudgeon." Empty-headed people who babble about their own affairs because they have nothing else to occupy them, naturally conclude that if people say nothing of their doings it is because their doings will not bear being talked about; so the highly respectable merchant became a scoundrel, and the late beau was an old rogue. Opinion fluctuated. Sometimes, according to Vautrin, who came about this time to live in the Maison Vauquer, Father Goriot was a man who went on 'Change and *dabbled* (to use the sufficiently expressive language of the Stock Exchange) in stocks and shares after he had ruined himself by heavy speculation. Sometimes it was held that he was one of those petty gamblers who nightly play for small stakes until they win a few francs. A theory that he was a detective in the employ of the Home Office found favor at one time, but Vautrin urged that "Goriot was not sharp enough for one of that sort." There were yet other solutions; Father Goriot was a skinflint, a shark of a money-lender, a man who lived by selling lottery tickets. He was by turns all the most mysterious brood of vice and shame and misery; yet, however vile his life might be, the feeling of repulsion which he aroused in others was not so strong that he must be banished from their society— he paid his way. Besides, Goriot had his uses, every one vented his spleen or sharpened his wit on him; he was pelted with jokes and belabored with hard words. The general consensus of opinion was in favor of a theory which seemed the most likely; this was Mme. Vauquer's view. According to her, the man so well preserved at his time of life, as sound as her eyesight, with whom a woman might be very happy, was a libertine who had strange tastes. These are the facts upon which Mme. Vauquer's slanders were based.

Early one morning, some few months after the departure of the unlucky Countess who had managed to live for six months at the widow's expense, Mme. Vauquer (not yet dressed) heard the rustle of a silk dress and a young woman's light footstep on the stair; some one was going to Goriot's room. He seemed to expect the visit, for his door stood ajar. The portly Sylvie presently came up to tell her mistress that a girl too pretty to be honest, "dressed like a goddess," and not a speck of mud on her laced cashmere boots, had glided in from the street like a snake, had found the kitchen, and asked for M. Goriot's room. Mme. Vauquer and the cook, listening, overheard several words affectionately spoken during the visit, which lasted for some time. When M. Goriot went downstairs with the lady, the stout Sylvie forthwith took her basket and followed the lover-like couple, under pretext of going to do her marketing.

"M. Goriot must be awfully rich, all the same, madame," she reported on her return, "to keep her in such style. Just imagine it! There was a splendid carriage waiting at the corner of the Place de l'Estrapade, and *she* got into it."

While they were at dinner that evening, Mme. Vauquer went to the window and drew the curtain, as the sun was shining into Goriot's eyes.

"You are beloved of fair ladies, M. Goriot—the sun seeks you out," she said, alluding to his visitor. *"Peste!* you have good taste; she was very pretty."

"That was my daughter," he said, with a kind of pride in his voice, and the rest chose to consider this as the fatuity of an old man who wishes to save appearances.

A month after this visit M. Goriot received another. The same daughter who had come to see him that morning came again after dinner, this time in evening dress. The boarders, in deep discussion in the dining-room, caught a glimpse of a lovely, fair-haired woman, slender, graceful, and much too distinguished-looking to be a daughter of Father Goriot's.

"Two of them!" cried the portly Sylvie, who did not recognize the lady of the first visit.

A few days later, and another young lady—a tall, well-moulded brunette, with dark hair and bright eyes—came to ask for M. Goriot.

"Three of them!" said Sylvie.

Then the second daughter, who had first come in the morning to see her father, came shortly afterwards in the evening. She wore a ball dress, and came in a carriage.

"Four of them!" commented Mme. Vauquer and her plump handmaid. Sylvie saw not a trace of resemblance between this great lady and the girl in her simple morning dress who had entered her kitchen on the occasion of her first visit.

At that time Goriot was paying twelve hundred francs a year to his landlady, and Mme. Vauquer saw nothing out of the common in the fact that a rich man had four or five mistresses; nay, she thought it very knowing of him to pass them off as his daughters. She was not at all inclined to draw a hard-and-fast line, or to take umbrage at his sending for them to the Maison Vauquer; yet, inasmuch as these visits explained her boarder's indifference to her, she went so far (at the end of the second year) as to speak of him as an "ugly old wretch." When at length her boarder declined to nine hundred francs a year, she asked him very insolently what he took her house to be, after meeting one of these

ladies on the stairs. Father Goriot answered that the lady
was his eldest daughter.

"So you have two or three dozen daughters, have you?"
said Mme. Vauquer sharply.

"I have only two," her boarder answered meekly, like a
ruined man who is broken in to all the cruel usage of misfortune.

Towards the end of the third year Father Goriot reduced his
expenses still further; he went up to the third story, and now
paid forty-five francs a month. He did without snuff, told
his hairdresser that he no longer required his services, and
gave up wearing powder. When Goriot appeared for the
first time in this condition, an exclamation of astonishment
broke from his hostess at the color of his hair—a dingy olive
gray. He had grown sadder day by day under the influence
of some hidden trouble; among all the faces round the table,
his was the most woe-begone. There was no longer any
doubt. Goriot was an elderly libertine, whose eyes had only
been preserved by the skill of the physician from the malign
influence of the remedies necessitated by the state of his
health. The disgusting color of his hair was a result of his
excesses and of the drugs which he had taken that he might
continue his career. The poor old man's mental and physical condition afforded some grounds for the absurd rubbish
talked about him. When his outfit was worn out, he replaced the fine linen by calico at fourteen *sous* the ell. His
diamonds, his gold snuff-box, watch-chain and trinkets, disappeared one by one. He had left off wearing the corn-
flower blue coat, and was sumptuously arrayed, summer as
winter, in a coarse chestnut-brown coat, a plush waistcoat,
and doeskin breeches. He grew thinner and thinner; his
legs were shrunken, his cheeks, once so puffed out by contented bourgeois prosperity, were covered with wrinkles, and
the outlines of the jawbones were distinctly visible; there
were deep furrows in his forehead. In the fourth year of
his residence in the Rue Neuve-Sainte-Geneviève he was no

longer like his former self. The hale vermicelli manufacturer, sixty-two years of age, who had looked scarce forty,
the stout, comfortable, prosperous tradesman, with an almost
bucolic air, and such a brisk demeanor that it did you good
to look at him; the man with something boyish in his smile,
had suddenly sunk into his dotage, and had become a feeble,
vacillating septuagenarian.

The keen, bright blue eyes had grown dull, and faded to a
steel-gray color; the red inflamed rims looked as though
they had shed tears of blood. He excited feelings of repulsion in some, and of pity in others. The young medical students who came to the house noticed the drooping of his
lower lip and the conformation of the facial angle; and,
after teasing him for some time to no purpose, they declared
that cretinism was setting in.

One evening after dinner Mme. Vauquer said half banteringly to him, "So those daughters of yours don't come to
see you any more, eh?" meaning to imply her doubts as to
his paternity; but Father Goriot shrank as if his hostess had
touched him with a sword-point.

"They come sometimes," he said in a tremulous voice.

"Aha! you still see them sometimes?" cried the students.
"Bravo, Father Goriot!"

The old man scarcely seemed to hear the witticisms at his
expense that followed on the words; he had relapsed into
the dreamy state of mind that these superficial observers
took for senile torpor, due to his lack of intelligence. If
they had only known, they might have been deeply interested
by the problem of his condition; but few problems were more
obscure. It was easy, of course, to find out whether Goriot
had really been a vermicelli manufacturer; the amount of
his fortune was readily discoverable; but the old people, who
were most inquisitive as to his concerns, never went beyond
the limits of the Quarter, and lived in the lodging-house
much as oysters cling to a rock. As for the rest, the current
of life in Paris daily awaited them, and swept them away
with it; so soon as they left the Rue Neuve-Sainte-Gene-

viève, they forgot the existence of the old man, their butt
at dinner. For those narrow souls, or for careless youth, the
misery in Father Goriot's withered face and its dull apathy
were quite incompatible with wealth or any sort of intelligence.
As for the creatures whom he called his daughters, all Mme.
Vauquer's boarders were of her opinion. With the faculty
for severe logic sedulously cultivated by elderly women during long evenings of gossip till they can always find an hy-
pothesis to fit all circumstances, she was wont to reason
thus:

"If Father Goriot had daughters of his own as rich as those
ladies who came here seemed to be, he would not be lodging
in my house, on the third floor, at forty-five francs a month;
and he would not go about dressed like a poor man."

No objection could be raised to these inferences. So by
the end of the month of November 1819, at the time when
the curtain rises on this drama, every one in the house had
come to have a very decided opinion as to the poor old man.
He had never had either wife or daughter; excesses had reduced him to this sluggish condition; he was a sort of
human mollusk who should be classed among the cap*ulidæ*,
so said one of the dinner contingent, an employé at the Muséum, who had a pretty wit of his own. Poiret was an eagle,
a gentleman, compared with Goriot. Poiret would join the
talk, argue, answer when he was spoken to; as a matter of
fact, his talk, arguments, and responses contributed nothing
to the conversation, for Poiret had a habit of repeating what
the others said in different words; still, he did join in the
talk; he was alive, and seemed capable of feeling; while
Father Goriot (to quote the Muséum official again) was invariably at zero—Réaumur.

Eugène de Rastignac had just returned to Paris in a state
of mind not unknown to young men who are conscious of
unusual powers, and to those whose faculties are so stimulated by a difficult position, that for the time being they rise
above the ordinary level.

Rastignac's first year of study for the preliminary examinations in law had left him free to see the sights of Paris and to enjoy some of its amusements. A student has not much time on his hands if he sets himself to learn the repertory of every theatre, and to study the ins and outs of the labyrinth of Paris. To know its customs; to learn the language, and become familiar with the amusements of the capital, he must explore its recesses, good and bad, follow the studies that please him best, and form some idea of the treasures contained in galleries and museums.

At this stage of his career a student grows eager and excited about all sorts of follies that seem to him to be of immense importance. He has his hero, his great man, a professor at the Collège de France, paid to talk down to the level of his audience. He adjusts his cravat, and strikes various attitudes for the benefit of the women in the first galleries at the Opéra-Comique. As he passes through all these successive initiations, and breaks out of his sheath, the horizons of life widen around him, and at length he grasps the plan of society with the different human strata of which it is composed.

If he begins by admiring the procession of carriages on sunny afternoons in the Champs-Élysées, he soon reaches the further stage of envying their owners. Unconsciously, Eugène had served his apprenticeship before he went back to Angoulême for the long vacation after taking his degrees as bachelor of arts and bachelor of law. The illusions of childhood had vanished, so also had the ideas he brought with him from the provinces; he had returned thither with an intelligence developed, with loftier ambitions, and saw things as they were at home in the old manor house. His father and mother, his two brothers and two sisters, with an aged aunt, whose whole fortune consisted in annuities, lived on the little estate of Rastignac. The whole property brought in about three thousand francs; and though the amount varied with the season (as must always be the case in a vine-growing district), they were obliged to spare an unvarying twelve hundred francs out of their income for him. He saw

how constantly the poverty, which they had generously
hidden from him, weighed upon them; he could not help comparing the sisters, who had seemed so beautiful to his boyish
eyes, with women in Paris, who had realized the beauty of his
dreams. The uncertain future of the whole family depended
upon him. It did not escape his eyes that not a crumb was
wasted in the house, nor that the wine they drank was made
from the second pressing; a multitude of small things, which
it is useless to speak of in detail here, made him burn to distinguish himself, and his ambition to succeed increased tenfold.

He meant, like all great souls, that his success should be
owing entirely to his merits; but his was pre-eminently a
southern temperament, the execution of his plans was sure
to be marred by the vertigo that seizes on youth when youth
sees itself alone in a wide sea, uncertain how to spend its
energies, whither to steer its course, how to adapt its sails to
the winds. At first he determined to fling himself heart and
soul into his work, but he was diverted from this purpose
by the need of society and connections; then he saw how great
an influence women exert in social life, and suddenly made
up his mind to go out into this world to seek a protectress
there. Surely a clever and high-spirited young man, whose
wit and courage were set off to advantage by a graceful figure,
and the vigorous kind of beauty that readily strikes a woman's
imagination, need not despair of finding a protectress. These
ideas occurred to him in his country walks with his sisters,
whom he had once joined so gaily. The girls thought him
very much changed.

His aunt, Mme. de Marcillac, had been presented at court,
and had moved among the brightest heights of that lofty
region. Suddenly the young man's ambition discerned in
those recollections of hers, which had been like nursery fairy
tales to her nephews and nieces, the elements of a social success at least as important as the success which he had
achieved at the École de Droit. He began to ask his aunt
about those relations; some of the old ties might still hold

good. After much shaking of the branches of the family tree, the old lady came to the conclusion that of all persons who could be useful to her nephew among the selfish genus of rich relations, the Vicomtesse de Beauséant was the least likely to refuse. To this lady, therefore, she wrote in the old-fashioned style, recommending Eugène to her; pointing out to her nephew that if he succeeded in pleasing Mme. de Beauséant, the Vicomtesse would introduce him to other relations. A few days after his return to Paris, therefore, Rastignac sent his aunt's letter to Mme. de Beauséant. The Vicomtesse replied by an invitation to a ball for the following evening. This was the position of affairs at the Maison Vauquer at the end of November 1819.

A few days later, after Mme. de Beauséant's ball, Eugène came in at two o'clock in the morning. The persevering student meant to make up for the lost time by working until daylight. It was the first time that he had attempted to spend the night in this way in that silent quarter. The spell of a factitious energy was upon him; he had beheld the pomp and splendor of the world. He had not dined at the Maison Vauquer; the boarders probably would think that he would walk home at daybreak from the dance, as he had done sometimes on former occasions, after a fête at the Prado, or a ball at the Odéon, splashing his silk stockings thereby, and ruining his pumps.

It so happened that Christophe took a look into the street before drawing the bolts of the door; and Rastignac, coming in at that moment, could go up to his room without making any noise, followed by Christophe, who made a great deal. Eugène exchanged his dress suit for a shabby overcoat and slippers, kindled a fire with some blocks of patent fuel, and prepared for his night's work in such a sort that the faint sounds he made were drowned by Christophe's heavy tramp on the stairs.

Eugène sat absorbed in thought for a few moments before plunging into his law books. He had just become aware of the fact that the Vicomtesse de Beauséant was one of the

queens of fashion, that her house was thought to be the
pleasantest in the Faubourg Saint-Germain. And not only
so, she was, by right of her fortune, and the name she bore,
one of the most conspicuous figures in that aristocratic world.
Thanks to the aunt, thanks to Mme. de Marcillac's letter
of introduction, the poor student had been kindly received
in that house before he knew the extent of the favor thus
shown to him. It was almost like a patent of nobility to
be admitted to those gilded salons; he had appeared in the
most exclusive circle in Paris, and now all doors were open
for him. Eugène had been dazzled at first by the brilliant
assembly, and had scarcely exchanged a few words with the
Vicomtesse; he had been content to single out a goddess
among this throng of Parisian divinities, one of those women
who are sure to attract a young man's fancy.

The Comtesse Anastasie de Restaud was tall and gracefully made; she had one of the prettiest figures in Paris.
Imagine a pair of great dark eyes, a magnificently moulded
hand, a shapely foot. There was a fiery energy in her movements; the Marquis de Ronquerolles had called her "a thoroughbred," but this fineness of nervous organization had
brought no accompanying defect; the outlines of her form
were full and rounded, without any tendency to stoutness.
"A thoroughbred," "a pure pedigree," these figures of speech
have replaced the "heavenly angel" and Ossianic nomencla-
ture; the old mythology of love is extinct, doomed to perish
by modern dandyism. But for Rastignac, Mme. Anastasie de
Restaud was the woman for whom he had sighed. He had
contrived to write his name twice upon the list of partners
upon her fan, and had snatched a few words with her during
the first quadrille.

"Where shall I meet you again, madame?" he asked abruptly, and the tones of his voice were full of the vehement
energy that women like so well.

"Oh, everywhere!" said she, "in the Bois, at the Bouffons,
in my own house."

With the impetuosity of his adventurous southern temper,

he did all he could to cultivate an acquaintance with this
lovely countess, making the best of his opportunities in
the quadrille and during a waltz that she gave him. When
he had told her that he was a cousin of Mme. de Beauséant's,
the Countess, whom he took for a great lady, asked him to
call at her house, and after her parting smile, Rastignac felt
convinced that he must make this visit. He was so lucky as
to light upon some one who did not laugh at his ignorance,
a fatal defect among the gilded and insolent youth of that
period; the coterie of Maulincourts, Maximes de Trailles,
de Marsays, Ronquerolles, Ajuda-Pintos, and Vandenesses
who shone there in all the glory of coxcombry among the
best-dressed women of fashion in Paris—Lady Brandon, the
Duchesse de Langeais, the Comtesse de Kergarouët, Mme.
de Sérizy, the Duchesse de Carigliano, the Comtesse Ferraud,
Mme. de Lanty, the Marquise d'Aiglemont, Mme. Firmiani,
the Marquise de Listomère and the Marquise d'Espard, the
Duchesse de Maufrigneuse and the Grandlieus. Luckily,
therefore, for him, the novice happened upon the Marquis
de Montriveau, the lover of the Duchesse de Langeais, a general as simple as a child; from him Rastignac learned that
the Comtesse lived in the Rue du Helder.

Ah, what it is to be young, eager to see the world, greedily
on the watch for any chance that brings you nearer the
woman of your dreams, and behold two houses open their
doors to you! To set foot in the Vicomtesse de Beauséant's
house in the Faubourg Saint-Germain; to fall on your knees
before a Comtesse de Restaud in the Chaussée d'Antin; to
look at one glance across a vista of Paris drawing-rooms,
conscious that, possessing sufficient good looks, you may hope
to find aid and protection there in a feminine heart! To
feel ambitious enough to spurn the tight-rope on which you
must walk with the steady head of an acrobat for whom a
fall is impossible, and to find in a charming woman the best
of all balancing poles.

He sat there with his thoughts for a while, Law on the one
hand, and Poverty on the other, beholding a radiant vision

of a woman rise above the dull, smouldering fire. Who would not have paused and questioned the future as Eugène was doing? who would not have pictured it full of success? His wandering thoughts took wings; he was transported out of the present into that blissful future; he was sitting by Mme. de Restaud's side, when a sort of sigh, like the grunt of an overburdened St. Joseph, broke the silence of the night. It vibrated through the student, who took the sound for a death-groan. He opened his door noiselessly, went out upon the landing, and saw a thin streak of light under Father Goriot's door. Eugène feared that his neighbor had been taken ill; he went over and looked through the keyhole; the old man was busily engaged in an occupation so singular and so sus-picious that Rastignac thought he was only doing a piece of necessary service to society to watch the self-styled vermicelli maker's nocturnal industries.

The table was upturned, and Goriot had doubtless in some way secured a silver plate and cup to the bar before knotting a thick rope round them; he was pulling at this rope with such enormous force that they were being crushed and twisted out of shape; to all appearance he meant to convert the richly wrought metal into ingots.

"*Peste!* what a man!" said Rastignac, as he watched Goriot's muscular arms; there was not a sound in the room while the old man, with the aid of the rope, was kneading the silver like dough. "Was he then, indeed, a thief, or a re-ceiver of stolen goods, who affected imbecility and de-crepitude, and lived like a beggar that he might carry on his pursuits the more securely?" Eugène stood for a moment revolving these questions, then he looked again through the keyhole.

Father Goriot had unwound his coil of rope; he had cov-ered the table with a blanket, and was now employed in roll-ing the flattened mass of silver into a bar, an operation which he performed with marvelous dexterity.

"Why, he must be as strong as Augustus, King of Poland!" said Eugène to himself when the bar was nearly finished.

Father Goriot looked sadly at his handiwork, tears fell from his eyes, he blew out the dip which had served him for a light while he manipulated the silver, and Eugène heard him sigh as he lay down again.

"He is mad," thought the student.

"*Poor child!*" Father Goriot said aloud. Rastignac, hearing those words, concluded to keep silence; he would not hastily condemn his neighbor. He was just in the doorway of his room when a strange sound from the staircase below reached his ears; it might have been made by two men coming up in list slippers. Eugène listened; two men there certainly were, he could hear their breathing. Yet there had been no sound of opening the street door, no footsteps in the passage. Suddenly, too, he saw a faint gleam of light on the second story; it came from M. Vautrin's room.

"There are a good many mysteries here for a lodging-house!" he said to himself.

He went part of the way downstairs and listened again. The rattle of gold reached his ears. In another moment the light was put out, and again he distinctly heard the breathing of two men, but no sound of a door being opened or shut. The two men went downstairs, the faint sounds growing fainter as they went.

"Who is there?" cried Mme. Vauquer out of her bedroom window.

"I, Mme. Vauquer," answered Vautrin's deep bass voice. "I am coming in."

"That is odd! Christophe drew the bolts," said Eugène, going back to his room. "You have to sit up at night, it seems, if you really mean to know all that is going on about you in Paris."

These incidents turned his thought from his ambitious dreams; he betook himself to his work, but his thought wandered back to Father Goriot's suspicious occupation; Mme. de Restaud's face swam again and again before his eyes like a vision of a brilliant future, and at last he lay down and slept with clenched fists. When a young man makes up his mind that he will work all night, the chances are that seven times out of ten he will sleep till morning. Such vigils do not begin before we are turned twenty.

The next morning Paris was wrapped in one of the dense fogs that throw the most punctual people out in their calculations as to the time; even the most business-like folk fail to keep their appointments in such weather, and ordinary mortals wake up at noon and fancy it is eight o'clock. On this morning it was half-past nine, and Mme. Vauquer still lay abed. Christophe was late, Sylvie was late, but the two sat comfortably taking their coffee as usual. It was Sylvie's custom to take the cream off the milk destined for the boarders' breakfast for her own, and to boil the remainder for some time, so that madame should not discover this illegal exaction.

"Sylvie," said Christophe, as he dipped a piece of toast into the coffee, "M. Vautrin, who is not such a bad sort, all the same, had two people come to see him again last night. If madame says anything, mind you say nothing about it."

"Has he given you something?"

"He gave me a five-franc piece this month, which is as good as saying, 'Hold your tongue.'"

"Except him and Mme. Couture, who don't look twice at every penny, there's no one in the house that doesn't try to get back with the left hand all that they give with the right at New Year," said Sylvie.

"And, after all," said Christophe, "what do they give you? A miserable five-franc piece. There is Father Goriot, who has cleaned his shoes himself these two years past. There is that old beggar Poiret, who goes without blacking altogether; he would sooner drink it than put it on his boots. Then there is that whipper-snapper of a student, who gives me a couple of francs. Two francs will not pay for my brushes, and he sells his old clothes, and gets more for them than they are worth. Oh! they're a shabby lot!"

"Pooh!" said Sylvie, sipping her coffee, "our places are the best in the Quarter, that I know. But about that great big chap Vautrin, Christophe; has any one told you anything about him?"

"Yes. I met a gentleman in the street a few days ago; he said to me, 'There's a gentleman in your place, isn't there? a tall man that dyes his whiskers?' I told him, 'No, sir; they aren't dyed. A gay fellow like him hasn't the time to do it.' And when I told M. Vautrin about it afterwards, he said, 'Quite right, my boy. That is the way to answer them. There is nothing more unpleasant than to have your little weaknesses known; it might spoil many a match.'"

"Well, and for my part," said Sylvie, "a man tried to humbug me at the market wanting to know if I had seen him put on his shirt. Such bosh! There," she cried, interrupting herself, "that's a quarter to ten striking at the Val-de-Grâce, and not a soul stirring!"

"Pooh! they are all gone out. Mme. Couture and the girl went out at eight o'clock to take the wafer at Saint-Étienne. Father Goriot started off somewhere with a parcel, and the student won't be back from his lecture till ten o'clock. I saw them go while I was sweeping the stairs; Father Goriot knocked up against me, and his parcel was as hard as iron. What is the old fellow up to, I wonder? He is as good as a plaything for the rest of them; they can never let him alone; but he is a good man, all the same, and worth more than all of them put together. He doesn't give you much himself, but he sometimes sends you with a message to ladies who fork out famous tips; they are dressed grandly, too."

"His daughters, as he calls them, eh? There are a dozen of them."

"I have never been to more than two—the two who came here."

"There is madame moving overhead; I shall have to go, or she will raise a fine racket. Just keep an eye on the milk, Christophe; don't let the cat get at it."

Sylvie went up to her mistress' room.

"Sylvie! How is this? It's nearly ten o'clock, and you let me sleep on like a dormouse! Such a thing has never happened before."

"It's the fog; it is that thick, you could cut it with a knife."

"But how about breakfast?"

"Bah! the boarders are possessed, I'm sure. They all cleared out before there was a wink of daylight."

"Do speak properly, Sylvie," Mme. Vauquer retorted; "say a blink of daylight."

"Ah, well, madame, whichever you please. Anyhow, you can have breakfast at ten o'clock. La Michonnette and Poiret have neither of them stirred. There are only those two upstairs, and they are sleeping like the logs they are."

"But, Sylvie, you put their names together as if——"

"As if what?" said Sylvie, bursting into a guffaw. "The two of them make a pair."

"It is a strange thing, isn't it, Sylvie, how M. Vautrin got in last night after Christophe had bolted the door?"

"Not at all, madame. Christophe heard M. Vautrin, and went down and undid the door. And here are you imagining that——"

"Give me my bodice, and be quick and get breakfast ready. Dish up the rest of the mutton with the potatoes, and you can put the stewed pears on the table, those at five a penny."

A few moments later Mme. Vauquer came down, just in time to see the cat knock down a plate that covered a bowl of milk, and begin to lap in all haste.

"Mistigris!" she cried

The cat fled, but promptly returned to rub against her ankles.

"Oh! yes, you can wheedle, you old hypocrite!" she said. "Sylvie! Sylvie!"

"Yes, madame; what is it?"

"Just see what the cat has done!"

"It is all that stupid Christophe's fault. I told him to stop and lay the table. What has become of him? Don't you worry, madame; Father Goriot shall have it. I will fill it up with water, and he won't know the difference; he never notices anything, not even what he eats."

"I wonder where the old heathen can have gone?" said Mme. Vauquer, setting the plates round the table.

"Who knows? He is up to all sorts of tricks."

"I have overslept myself," said Mme. Vauquer.

"But madame looks as fresh as a rose, all the same."

The door bell rang at that moment, and Vautrin came through the sitting-room, singing loudly:

> " 'Tis the same old story everywhere,
> A roving heart and a roving glance . .

"Oh! Mamma Vauquer! good-morning!" he cried at the sight of his hostess, and he put his arm gaily round her waist.

"There! have done——"

" 'Impertinence!' Say it!" he answered. "Come, say it! Now, isn't that what you really mean? Stop a bit, I will help you to set the table. Ah! I am a nice man, am I not?

> "For the locks of brown and the golden hair
> A sighing lover . . .

"Oh! I have just seen something so funny——

> . . . . led by chance."

"What?" asked the widow.

"Father Goriot in the goldsmith's shop in the Rue Dauphine at half-past eight this morning. They buy old spoons and forks and gold lace there, and Goriot sold a piece of silver plate for a good round sum. It had been twisted out of shape very neatly for a man that's not used to the trade."

"Really? You don't say so?"

"Yes. One of my friends is expatriating himself; I had been to see him off on board the Royal Mail steamer, and was coming back here. I waited after that to see what Father Goriot would do; it is a comical affair. He came back to this quarter of the world, to the Rue des Grès, and went into a money-lender's house; everybody knows him, Gobseck, a stuck-up rascal, that would make dominoes out of his father's bones; a Turk, a heathen, an old Jew, a Greek; it would be

a difficult matter to rob *him,* for he puts all his coin into
the Bank."

"Then what was Father Goriot doing there?"

"Doing?" said Vautrin. "Nothing; he was bent on his
own undoing. He is a simpleton, stupid enough to ruin
himself by running after——"

"There he is!" cried Sylvie.

"Christophe," cried Father Goriot's voice, "come upstairs
with me."

Christophe went up, and shortly afterwards came down
again.

"Where are you going?" Mme. Vauquer asked of her servant.

"Out on an errand for M. Goriot."

"What may that be?" said Vautrin, pouncing on a letter
in Christophe's hand. *"Mme. la Comtesse Anastasie de
Restaud,"* he read. "Where are you going with it?" he added,
as he gave the letter back to Christophe.

"To the Rue du Helder. I have orders to give this into
her hands myself."

"What is there inside it?" said Vautrin, holding the letter
up to the light. "A banknote? No." He peered into the
envelope. "A receipted account!" he cried. "My word! 'tis
a gallant old dotard. Off with you, old chap," he said, bringing down a hand on Christophe's head, and spinning the man
round like a thimble; "you will have a famous tip."

By this time the table was set. Sylvie was boiling the milk,
Mme. Vauquer was lighting a fire in the stove with some assistance from Vautrin, who kept on humming to himself:

> "The same old story everywhere,
>   A roving heart and a roving glance."

When everything was ready, Mme. Couture and Mlle.
Taillefer came in.

"Where have you been this morning, fair lady?" said Mme.
Vauquer, turning to Mme. Couture.

"We have just been to say our prayers at Saint-Étienne du Mont. To-day is the day when we must go to see M. Taillefer. Poor little thing! She is trembling like a leaf," Mme. Couture went on, as she seated herself before the fire and held the steaming soles of her boots to the blaze.

"Warm yourself, Victorine," said Mme. Vauquer.

"It is quite right and proper, mademoiselle, to pray to Heaven to soften your father's heart," said Vautrin, as he drew a chair nearer to the orphan girl; "but that is not enough. What you want is a friend who will give the monster a piece of his mind; a barbarian that has three millions (so they say), and will not give you a dowry; and a pretty girl needs a dowry nowadays."

"Poor child!" said Mme. Vauquer. "Never mind, my pet, your wretch of a father is going just the way to bring trouble upon himself."

Victorine's eyes filled with tears at the words, and the widow checked herself at a sign from Mme. Couture.

"If we could only see him!" said the Commissary-General's widow; "if I could speak to him myself and give him his wife's last letter! I have never dared to run the risk of sending it by post; he knew my handwriting——"

"'Oh woman, persecuted and injured innocent!'" exclaimed Vautrin, breaking in upon her. "So that is how you are, is it? In a few days' time I will look into your affairs, and it will be all right, you shall see."

"Oh! sir," said Victorine, with a tearful but eager glance at Vautrin, who showed no sign of being touched by it, "if you know of any way of communicating with my father, please be sure and tell him that his affection and my mother's honor are more to me than all the money in the world. If you can induce him to relent a little towards me, I will pray to God for you. You may be sure of my gratitude——"

"*The same old story everywhere*," sang Vautrin, with a satirical intonation. At this juncture, Goriot, Mlle. Michonneau, and Poiret came downstairs together; possibly the scent of the gravy which Sylvie was making to serve with the mutton had announced breakfast. The seven people thus assembled bade each other good-morning, and took their places at the table; the clock struck ten, and the student's footstep was heard outside.

"Ah! here you are, M. Eugène," said Sylvie; "every one is breakfasting at home to-day."

The student exchanged greetings with the lodgers, and sat down beside Goriot.

"I have just met with a queer adventure," he said, as he helped himself abundantly to the mutton, and cut a slice of bread, which Mme. Vauquer's eyes gauged as usual.

"An adventure?" queried Poiret.

"Well, and what is there to astonish you in that, old boy?" Vautrin asked of Poiret. "M. Eugène is cut out for that kind of thing."

Mlle. Taillefer stole a timid glance at the young student.

"Tell us about your adventure!" demanded M. Vautrin.

"Yesterday evening I went to a ball given by a cousin of mine, the Vicomtesse de Beauséant. She has a magnificent house; the rooms were hung with silk—in short, it was a splendid affair, and I was as happy as a king——"

"Fisher," put in Vautrin, interrupting.

"What do you mean, sir?" said Eugène sharply.

"I said 'fisher,' because kingfishers see a good deal more fun than kings."

"Quite true; I would much rather be the little careless bird than a king," said Poiret the ditto-ist, "because——"

"In fact"—the law-student cut him short—"I danced with one of the handsomest women in the room, a charming countess, the most exquisite creature I have ever seen. There was peach blossom in her hair, and she had the loveliest bouquet of flowers—real flowers, that scented the air——but there! it is no use trying to describe a woman glowing with the dance. You ought to have seen her! Well, and this morning I met this divine countess about nine o'clock, on foot in the Rue des Grès. Oh! how my heart beat! I began to think——"

"That she was coming here," said Vautrin, with a keen look at the student. "I expect that she was going to call on old Gobseck, a money-lender. If ever you explore a Parisian woman's heart, you will find the money-lender first, and the lover afterwards. Your countess is called Anastasie de Restaud, and she lives in the Rue du Helder."

The student stared hard at Vautrin. Father Goriot raised his head at the words, and gave the two speakers a glance so full of intelligence and uneasiness that the lodgers beheld him with astonishment.

"Then Christophe was too late, and she must have gone to him!" cried Goriot, with anguish in his voice.

"It is just as I guessed," said Vautrin, leaning over to whisper in Mme. Vauquer's ear.

Goriot went on with his breakfast, but seemed unconscious of what he was doing. He had never looked more stupid nor more taken up with his own thoughts than he did at that moment.

"Who the devil could have told you her name, M. Vautrin?" asked Eugène.

"Aha! there you are!" answered Vautrin. "Old Father Goriot there knew it quite well! and why should not I know it too?"

"M. Goriot?" the student cried.

"What is it?" said the old man. "So she was very beautiful, was she, yesterday night?"

"Who?"

"Mme. de Restaud."

"Look at the old wretch," said Mme. Vauquer, speaking to Vautrin; "how his eyes light up!"

"Then does he really keep her?" said Mlle. Michonneau, in a whisper to the student.

"Oh! yes, she was tremendously pretty," Eugène answered. Father Goriot watched him with eager eyes. "If Mme. de Beauséant had not been there, my divine countess would have been the queen of the ball; none of the younger men had eyes for any one else. I was the twelfth on her list, and she danced every quadrille. The other women were furious. She must have enjoyed herself, if ever creature did! It is a true saying that there is no more beautiful sight than a frigate in full sail, a galloping horse, or a woman dancing."

"So the wheel turns," said Vautrin; "yesterday night at a duchess' ball, this morning in a money-lender's office, on the lowest rung of the ladder—just like a Parisienne! If their husbands cannot afford to pay for their frantic extravagance, they will sell themselves. Or if they cannot do that, they will tear out their mothers' hearts to find something to pay for their splendor. They will turn the world upside down. Just a Parisienne through and through!"

Father Goriot's face, which had shone at the student's words like the sun on a bright day, clouded over all at once at this cruel speech of Vautrin's.

"Well," said Mme. Vauquer, "but where is your adventure? Did you speak to her? Did you ask her if she wanted to study law?"

"She did not see me," said Eugène. "But only think of meeting one of the prettiest women in Paris in the Rue des Grès at nine o'clock! She could not have reached home after the ball till two o'clock this morning. Wasn't it queer? There is no place like Paris for this sort of adventures."

"Pshaw! much funnier things than *that* happen here!" exclaimed Vautrin.

Mlle. Taillefer had scarcely heeded the talk, she was so absorbed by the thought of the new attempt that she was about to make. Mme. Couture made a sign that it was time to go upstairs and dress; the two ladies went out, and Father Goriot followed their example.

"Well, did you see?" said Mme. Vauquer, addressing Vautrin and the rest of the circle. "He is ruining himself for those women, that is plain."

"Nothing will ever make me believe that that beautiful Comtesse de Restaud is anything to Father Goriot," cried the student.

"Well, and if you don't," broke in Vautrin, "we are not

set on convincing you. You are too young to know Paris thoroughly yet; later on you will find out that there are what we call men with a passion——"

Mlle. Michonneau gave Vautrin a quick glance at these words. They seemed to be like the sound of a trumpet to a trooper's horse. "Aha!" said Vautrin, stopping in his speech to give her a searching glance, "so we have had our little experiences, have we?"

The old maid lowered her eyes like a nun who sees a statue.

"Well," he went on, "when folk of that kind get a notion into their heads, they cannot drop it. They must drink the water from some particular spring—it is stagnant as often as not; but they will sell their wives and families, they will sell their own souls to the devil to get it. For some this spring is play, or the stock-exchange, or music, or a collection of pictures or insects; for others it is some woman who can give them the dainties they like. You might offer these last all the women on earth—they would turn up their noses; they will have the only one who can gratify their passion. It often happens that the woman does not care for them at all, and treats them cruelly; they buy their morsels of satisfaction very dear; but no matter, the fools are never tired of it; they will take their last blanket to the pawnbroker's to give their last five-franc piece to her. Father Goriot here is one of that sort. He is discreet, so the Countess exploits him—just the way of the gay world. The poor old fellow thinks of her and of nothing else. In all other respects you see he is a stupid animal; but get him on that subject, and his eyes sparkle like diamonds. That secret is not difficult to guess. He took some plate himself this morning to the melting-pot, and I saw him at Daddy Gobseck's in the Rue des Grès. And now, mark what follows—he came back here, and gave a letter for the Comtesse de Restaud to that noodle of a Christophe, who showed us the address; there was a receipted bill inside it. It is clear that it was an urgent matter if the Countess also went herself to the old money lender. Father Goriot has financed her handsomely. There is no need to tack a tale together; the thing is self-evident. So that shows you, sir student, that all the time your Countess was smiling, dancing, flirting, swaying her peach-flower crowned head, with her gown gathered into her hand, her slippers were pinching her, as they say; she was thinking of her protested bills, or her lover's protested bills."

"You have made me wild to know the truth," cried Eugène; "I will go to call on Mme. de Restaud to-morrow."

"Yes," echoed Poiret; "you must go and call on Mme. de Restaud."

"And perhaps you will find Father Goriot there, who will take payment for the assistance he politely rendered."

Engène looked disgusted. "Why, then, this Paris of yours is a slough."

"And an uncommonly queer slough, too," replied Vautrin. "The mud splashes you as you drive through in your carriage—you are a respectable person; you go afoot and are splashed—you are a scoundrel. You are so unlucky as to walk off with something or other belonging to somebody else, and they exhibit you as a curiosity in the Place du Palais-de-Justice; you steal a million, and you are pointed out in every salon as a model of virtue. And you pay thirty millions for the police and the courts of justice, for the maintenance of law and order! A pretty state of things it is!"

"What," cried Mme. Vauquer, "has Father Goriot really melted down his silver posset-dish?"

"There were two turtle-doves on the lid, were there not?" asked Eugène.

"Yes, that there were."

"Then, was he fond of it?" said Eugène. "He cried while he was breaking up the cup and plate. I happened to see him by accident."

"It was dear to him as his own life," answered the widow.

"There! you see how infatuated the old fellow is!" cried Vautrin. "The woman yonder can coax the soul out of him."

The student went up to his room. Vautrin went out, and

a few moments later Mme. Couture and Victorine drove away in a cab which Sylvie had called for them. Poiret gave his arm to Mlle. Michonneau, and they went together to spend the two sunniest hours of the day in the Jardin des Plantes.

"Well, those two are as good as married," was the portly Sylvie's comment. "They are going out together to-day for the first time. They are such a couple of dry sticks that if they happen to strike against each other they will draw sparks like flint and steel."

"Keep clear of Mlle. Michonneau's shawl, then," said Mme. Vauquer, laughing; "it would flare up like tinder."

At four o'clock that evening, when Goriot came in, he saw, by the light of two smoky lamps, that Victorine's eyes were red. Mme. Vauquer was listening to the history of the visit made that morning to M. Taillefer; it had been made in vain. Taillefer was tired of the annual application made by his daughter and her elderly friend; he gave them a personal interview in order to arrive at an understanding with them.

"My dear lady," said Mme. Couture, addressing Mme. Vauquer, "just imagine it; he did not even ask Victorine to sit down, she was standing the whole time. He said to me quite coolly, without putting himself in a passion, that we might spare ourselves the trouble of going there; that the young lady (he would not call her his daughter) was injuring her cause by importuning him (*importuning!* once a year, the wretch!); that as Victorine's mother had nothing when he married her, Victorine ought not to expect anything from him; in fact, he said the most cruel things, that made the poor child burst out crying. The little thing threw herself at her father's feet and spoke up bravely; she said that she only persevered in her visits for her mother's sake; that she would obey him without a murmur, but that she begged him to read her poor dead mother's farewell letter. She took it up and gave it to him, saying the most beautiful things in the world, most beautifully expressed; I do not know where she learned them; God must have put them into her head, for the poor child was inspired to speak so nicely that it made me cry like a fool to hear her talk. And what do you think the monster was doing all the time? Cutting his nails! He took the letter that poor Mme. Taillefer had soaked with tears, and flung it on to the chimney-piece. 'That is all right,' he said. He held out his hands to raise his daughter, but she covered them with kisses, and he drew them away again. Scandalous, isn't it? And his great booby of a son came in and took no notice of his sister."

"What inhuman wretches they must be!" said Father Goriot.

"And then they both went out of the room," Mme. Couture went on, without heeding the worthy vermicelli maker's exclamation; "father and son bowed to me, and asked me to excuse them on account of urgent business! That is the history of our call. Well, he has seen his daughter at any rate. How he can refuse to acknowledge her I cannot think, for they are as like as two peas."

The boarders dropped in one after another, interchanging greetings and the empty jokes that certain classes of Parisians regard as humorous and witty. Dulness is their prevailing ingredient, and the whole point consists in mispronouncing a word or in a gesture. This kind of argot is always changing. The essence of the jest consists in some catchword suggested by a political event, an incident in the police courts, a street song, or a bit of burlesque at some theatre, and forgotten in a month. Anything and everything serves to keep up a game of battledore and shuttlecock with words and ideas. The diorama, a recent invention, which carried an optical illusion a degree further than panoramas, had given rise to a mania among art students for ending every word with *rama*. The Maison Vauquer had caught the infection from a young artist among the boarders.

"Well, Monsieur-r-r Poiret," said the employé from the Museum, "how is your health-orama?" Then, without waiting for an answer, he turned to Mme. Couture and Victorine with a "Ladies, you seem melancholy."

"Is dinner ready?" cried Horace Bianchon, a medical student, and a friend of Rastignac's; "my stomach is sinking *usque ad talones.*"

"There is an uncommon *frozerama* outside," said Vautrin. "Make room there, Father Goriot! Confound it, your foot covers the whole front of the stove."

"Illustrious M. Vautrin," put in Bianchon, "why do you say *frozerama?* It is incorrect; it should be *frozenrama.*"

"No, it shouldn't," said the official from the Muséum; "*frozerama* is right by the same rule that you say 'My feet are *froze.*'"

"Ah! ah!"

"Here is his Excellency the Marquis de Rastignac, Doctor of the Law of Contraries," cried Bianchon, seizing Eugène by the throat, and almost throttling him.

"Hallo there! hallo!"

Mlle. Michonneau came noiselessly in, bowed to the rest of the party, and took her place beside the three women without saying a word.

"That old bat always makes me shudder," said Bianchon in a low voice, indicating Mlle. Michonneau to Vautrin. "I have studied Gall's system, and I am sure she has the bump of Judas."

"Then you have seen a case before?" said Vautrin.

"Who has not?" answered Bianchon. "Upon my word, that ghastly old maid looks just like one of the long worms that will gnaw a beam through, give them time enough."

"That is the way, young man," returned he of the forty years and the dyed whiskers:

> "The rose has lived the life of a rose—
> A morning's space."

"Aha! here is a magnificent *soupe-au-rama,*" cried Poiret as Christophe came in bearing the soup with cautious heed.

"I beg your pardon, sir," said Mme. Vauquer; "it is *soupe aux choux.*"

All the young men roared with laughter.

"Had you there, Poiret!"

"Poir-r-r-rette! she had you there!"

"Score two points to Mamma Vauquer," said Vautrin.

"Did any one notice the fog this morning?" asked the official.

"It was a frantic fog," said Bianchon, "a fog unparalleled, doleful, melancholy, sea-green, asthmatical—a Goriot of a fog!"

"A Goriorama," said the art student, "because you couldn't see a thing in it."

"Hey! Milord Gâôriotte, they air talking about yoo-o-ou!"

Father Goriot, seated at the lower end of the table, close to the door through which the servant entered, raised his face; he had smelt at a scrap of bread that lay under his table napkin, an old trick acquired in his commercial capacity, that still showed itself at times.

"Well," Madame Vauquer cried in sharp tones, that rang above the rattle of spoons and plates and the sound of other voices, "and is there anything the matter with the bread?"

"Nothing whatever, madame," he answered; "on the contrary, it is made of the best quality of corn; flour from Étampes."

"How could you tell?" asked Eugène.

"By the color, by the flavor."

"You knew the flavor by the smell, I suppose," said Mme. Vauquer. "You have grown so economical, you will find out how to live on the smell of cooking at last."

"Take out a patent for it, then," cried the Muséum official; "you would make a handsome fortune."

"Never mind him," said the artist; "he does that sort of thing to delude us into thinking that he was a vermicelli maker."

"Your nose is a corn-sampler, it appears?" inquired the official.

"Corn *what?*" asked Bianchon.

"Corn-el."

"Corn-et."

"Corn-elian."

"Corn-ice."

"Corn-ucopia."

"Corn-crake."

"Corn-cockle."

"Corn-orama."

The eight responses came like a rolling fire from every part of the room, and the laughter that followed was the more uproarious because poor Father Goriot stared at the others with a puzzled look, like a foreigner trying to catch the meaning of words in a language which he does not understand.

"Corn? . . ." he said, turning to Vautrin, his next neighbor.

"Corn on your foot, old man!" said Vautrin, and he drove Father Goriot's cap down over his eyes by a blow on the crown.

The poor old man thus suddenly attacked was for a moment too bewildered to do anything. Christophe carried off his plate, thinking that he had finished his soup, so that when Goriot had pushed back his cap from his eyes his spoon encountered the table. Every one burst out laughing. "You are a disagreeable joker, sir," said the old man, "and if you take any further liberties with me——"

"Well, what then, old boy?" Vautrin interrupted.

"Well, then, you shall pay dearly for it some day——"

"Down below, eh?" said the artist, "in the little dark corner where they put naughty boys."

"Well, mademoiselle," Vautrin said, turning to Victorine, "you are eating nothing. So papa was refractory, was he?"

"A monster!" said Mme. Couture.

"Mademoiselle might make application for aliment pending her suit; she is not eating anything. Eh! eh! just see how Father Goriot is staring at Mlle. Victorine."

The old man had forgotten his dinner, he was so absorbed in gazing at the poor girl; the sorrow in her face was unmistakable,—the slighted love of a child whose father would not recognize her.

"We are mistaken about Father Goriot, my dear boy," said Eugène in a low voice. "He is not an idiot, nor wanting in energy. Try your Gall system on him, and let me know what you think. I saw him crush a silver dish last night as if it had been made of wax; there seems to be something extraordinary going on in his mind just now, to judge by his face. His life is so mysterious that it must be worth studying. Oh! you may laugh, Bianchon; I am not joking."

"The man is a subject, is he?" said Bianchon; "all right! I will dissect him, if he will give me a chance."

"No; feel his bumps."

"Hm!—his stupidity might perhaps be contagious."

The next day Rastignac dressed himself very elegantly, and about three o'clock in the afternoon went to call on Mme. de Restaud. On the way thither he indulged in the wild intoxicating dreams which fill a young head so full of delicious excitement. Young men at his age take no account of obstacles nor of dangers; they see success in every direction; imagination has free play, and turns their lives into a romance; they are saddened or discouraged by the collapse of one of the wild visionary schemes that have no existence save in their heated fancy. If youth were not ignorant and timid, civilization would be impossible.

Eugène took unheard-of pains to keep himself in a spotless condition, but on his way through the streets he began to think about Mme. de Restaud and what he should say to her. He equipped himself with wit, rehearsed repartees in the course of an imaginary conversation, and prepared certain neat speeches à la Talleyrand, conjuring up a series of small events which should prepare the way for the declaration on which he had based his future; and during these musings the law student was bespattered with mud, and by the time he reached the Palais Royal he was obliged to have his boots blacked and his trousers brushed.

"If I were rich," he said, as he changed the five-franc piece he had brought with him in case anything might happen, "I would take a cab, then I could think at my ease."

At last he reached the Rue du Helder, and asked for the Comtesse de Restaud. He bore the contemptuous glances of the servants, who had seen him cross the court on foot, with the cold fury of a man who knows that he will succeed some day. He understood the meaning of their glances at once, for he had felt his inferiority as soon as he entered the court, where a smart cab was waiting. All the delights of life in Paris seemed to be implied by this visible and manifest sign of luxury and extravagance. A fine horse, in magnificent harness, was pawing the ground, and all at once the law student felt out of humor with himself. Every compartment in his brain which he had thought to find so full of wit was bolted fast; he grew positively stupid. He sent up his name to the Countess, and waited in the ante-chamber, standing on one foot before a window that looked out upon the court; mechanically he leaned his elbow against the sash, and stared before him. The time seemed long; he would have left the house but for the southern tenacity of purpose which works miracles when it is single-minded.

"Madame is in her boudoir, and cannot see any one at present, sir," said the servant. "She gave me no answer; but if you will go into the dining-room, there is some one already there."

Rastignac was impressed with a sense of the formidable power of the lackey who can accuse or condemn his masters by a word; he coolly opened the door by which the man had just entered the ante-chamber, meaning, no doubt, to show these insolent flunkeys that he was familiar with the house; but he found that he had thoughtlessly precipitated himself into a small room full of dressers, where lamps were standing, and hot-water pipes, on which towels were being dried; a dark passage and a back staircase lay beyond it. Stifled laughter from the ante-chamber added to his confusion.

"This way to the drawing-room, sir," said the servant, with

the exaggerated respect which seemed to be one more jest at his expense.

Eugène turned so quickly that he stumbled against a bath. By good luck, he managed to keep his hat on his head, and saved it from immersion in the water; but just as he turned, a door opened at the further end of the dark passage, dimly lighted by a small lamp. Rastignac heard voices and the sound of a kiss; one of the speakers was Mme. de Restaud, the other was Father Goriot. Eugène followed the servant through the dining-room into the drawing-room; he went to a window that looked out into the courtyard, and stood there for a while. He meant to know whether this Goriot was really the Goriot that he knew. His heart beat unwontedly fast; he remembered Vautrin's hideous insinuations. A well-dressed young man suddenly emerged from the room almost as Eugène entered it, saying impatiently to the servant who stood at the door: "I am going, Maurice. Tell Madame la Comtesse that I waited more than half an hour for her."

Whereupon this insolent being, who, doubtless, had a right to be insolent, sang an Italian trill, and went towards the window where Eugène was standing, moved thereto quite as much by a desire to see the student's face as by a wish to look out into the courtyard.

"But M. le Comte had better wait a moment longer; madame is disengaged," said Maurice, as he returned to the ante-chamber.

Just at that moment Father Goriot appeared close to the gate; he had emerged from a door at the foot of the back staircase. The worthy soul was preparing to open his umbrella regardless of the fact that the great gate had opened to admit a tilbury, in which a young man with a ribbon at his button-hole was seated. Father Goriot had scarcely time to start back and save himself. The horse took fright at the umbrella, swerved, and dashed forward towards the flight of steps. The young man looked round in annoyance, saw Father Goriot, and greeted him as he went out with constrained courtesy, such as people usually show to a money-lender so long as they require his services, or the sort of respect they feel it necessary to show for some one whose reputation has been blown upon, so that they blush to acknowledge his acquaintance. Father Goriot gave him a little friendly nod and a good-natured smile. All this happened with lightning speed. Eugène was so deeply interested that he forgot that he was not alone till he suddenly heard the Countess' voice.

"Oh! Maxime, were you going away?" she said reproachfully, with a shade of pique in her manner. The Countess had not seen the incident nor the entrance of the tilbury. Rastignac turned abruptly and saw her standing before him, coquettishly dressed in a loose white cashmere gown with knots of rose-colored ribbon here and there; her hair was carelessly coiled about her head, as is the wont of Parisian women in the morning; there was a soft fragrance about her —doubtless she was fresh from a bath;—her graceful form seemed more flexible, her beauty more luxuriant. Her eyes glistened. A young man can see everything at a glance; he feels the radiant influence of woman as a plant discerns and absorbs its nutriment from the air; he did not need to touch her hands to feel their cool freshness. He saw faint rose tints through the cashmere of the dressing gown; it had fallen slightly open, giving glimpses of a bare throat, on which the student's eyes rested. The Countess had no need of the adventitious aid of corsets; her girdle defined the outlines of her slender waist; her throat was a challenge to love; her feet, thrust into slippers, were daintily small. As Maxime took her hand and kissed it, Eugène became aware of Maxime's existence, and the Countess saw Eugène.

"Oh! is that you, M. de Rastignac? I am very glad to see you," she said, but there was something in her manner that a shrewd observer would have taken as a hint to depart.

Maxime, as the Countess Anastasie had called the young man with the haughty insolence of bearing, looked from Eugène to the lady, and from the lady to Eugène; it was sufficiently evident that he wished to be rid of the latter. An exact and faithful rendering of the glance might be given in the words: "Look here, my dear; I hope you intend to send this little whipper-snapper about his business."

The Countess consulted the young man's face with an intent submissiveness that betrays all the secrets of a woman's heart, and Rastignac all at once began to hate him violently. To begin with, the sight of the fair carefully arranged curls on the other's comely head had convinced him that his own crop was hideous; Maxime's boots, moreover, were elegant and spotless, while his own, in spite of all his care, bore some traces of his recent walk; and, finally, Maxime's overcoat fitted the outline of his figure gracefully, he looked like a pretty woman, while Eugène was wearing a black coat at half-past two. The quick-witted child of the Charente felt the disadvantage at which he was placed beside this tall, slender dandy, with the clear gaze and the pale face, one of those men who would ruin orphan children without scruple. Mme. de Restaud fled into the next room without waiting for Eugène to speak; shaking out the skirts of her dressing-gown in her flight, so that she looked like a white butterfly, and Maxime hurried after her. Eugène, in a fury, followed Maxime and the Countess, and the three stood once more face to face by the hearth in the large drawing-room. The law student felt quite sure that the odious Maxime found him in the way, and even at the risk of displeasing Mme. de Restaud, he meant to annoy the dandy. It had struck him all at once that he had seen the young man before at Mme. de Beauséant's ball; he guessed the relation between Maxime and Mme. de Restaud; and with the youthful audacity that commits prodigious blunders or achieves signal success, he said to himself, "This is my rival; I mean to cut him out."

Rash resolve! He did not know that M. le Comte Maxime de Trailles would wait till he was insulted, so as to fire first and kill his man. Eugène was a sportsman and a good shot, but he had not yet hit the bull's eye twenty times out of twenty-two. The young Count dropped into a low chair by the hearth, took up the tongs, and made up the fire so vio-

lently and so sulkily, that Anastasie's fair face suddenly
clouded over. She turned to Eugène, with a cool, questioning
glance that asked plainly, "Why do you not go?" a glance
which well-bred people regard as a cue to make their exit.

Eugène assumed an amiable expression.

"Madame," he began, "I hastened to call upon you——"

He stopped short. The door opened, and the owner of the
tilbury suddenly appeared. He had left his hat outside, and
did not greet the Countess; he looked meditatively at Rastignac, and held out his hand to Maxime with a cordial "Good
morning," that astonished Eugène not a little. The young
provincial did not understand the amenities of a triple
alliance.

"M. de Restaud," said the Countess, introducing her husband to the law student.

Eugène bowed profoundly.

"This gentleman," she continued, presenting Eugène to her
husband, "is M. de Rastignac; he is related to Mme. la
Vicomtesse de Beauséant through the Marcillacs; I had the
pleasure of meeting him at her last ball."

*Related to Mme. la Vicomtesse de Beauséant through the
Marcillacs!* These words, on which the countess threw ever
so slight an emphasis, by reason of the pride that the mistress
of a house takes in showing that she only receives people of
distinction as visitors in her house, produced a magical effect.
The Count's stiff manner relaxed at once as he returned the
student's bow.

"Delighted to have an opportunity of making your
acquaintance," he said.

Maxime de Trailles himself gave Eugène an uneasy glance,
and suddenly dropped his insolent manner. The mighty
name had all the power of a fairy's wand; those closed compartments in the southern brain flew open again; Rastignac's
carefully drilled faculties returned. It was as if a sudden
light had pierced the obscurity of this upper world of Paris,
and he began to see, though everything was indistinct as yet.
Mme. Vauquer's lodging-house and Father Goriot were very
far remote from his thoughts.

"I thought that the Marcillacs were extinct," the Comte de Restaud said, addressing Eugène.

"Yes, they are extinct," answered the law student. "My great-uncle, the Chevalier de Rastignac, married the heiress of the Marcillac family. They had only one daughter, who married the Maréchal de Clarimbault, Mme. de Beauséant's grandfather on the mother's side. We are the younger branch of the family, and the younger branch is all the poorer because my great-uncle, the Vice-Admiral, lost all that he had in the King's service. The Government during the Revolution refused to admit our claims when the Compagnie des Indes was liquidated."

"Was not your great-uncle in command of the *Vengeur* before 1789?"

"Yes."

"Then he would be acquainted with my grandfather, who commanded the *Warwick*."

Maxime looked at Mme. de Restaud and shrugged his shoulders, as who should say, "If he is going to discuss nautical matters with that fellow, it is all over with us." Anastasie undertood the glance that M. de Trailles gave her. With a woman's admirable tact, she began to smile, and said:

"Come with me, Maxime; I have something to say to you. We will leave you two gentlemen to sail in company on board the *Warwick* and the *Vengeur*."

She rose to her feet and signed to Maxime to follow her, mirth and mischief in her whole attitude, and the two went in the direction of the boudoir. The *morganatic* couple (to use a convenient German expression which has no exact equivalent) had reached the door, when the Count interrupted himself in his talk with Eugène.

"Anastasie!" he cried pettishly, "just stay a moment, dear; you know very well that——"

"I am coming back in a minute," she interrupted; "I have a commission for Maxime to execute, and I want to tell him about it."

She came back almost immediately. She had noticed the

inflection in her husband's voice, and knew that it would not be safe to retire to the boudoir; like all women who are compelled to study their husbands' characters in order to have their own way, and whose business it is to know exactly how far they can go without endangering a good understanding, she was very careful to avoid petty collisions in domestic life. It was Eugène who had brought about this untoward incident; so the Countess looked at Maxime and indicated the law student with an air of exasperation. M. de Trailles addressed the Count, the Countess, and Eugène with the pointed remark, "You are busy, I do not want to interrupt you; good-day," and he went.

"Just wait a moment, Maxime!" the Count called after him.

"Come and dine with us," said the Countess, leaving Eugène and her husband together once more. She followed Maxime into the little drawing-room, where they sat together sufficiently long to feel sure that Rastignac had taken his leave.

The law student heard their laughter, and their voices, and the pauses in their talk; he grew malicious, exerted his conversational powers for M. de Restaud, flattered him, and drew him into discussions, to the end that he might see the Countess again and discover the nature of her relations with Father Goriot. This Countess with a husband and a lover, for Maxime clearly was her lover, was a mystery. What was the secret tie that bound her to the old tradesman? This mystery he meant to penetrate, hoping by its means to gain a sovereign ascendency over this fair typical Parisian.

"Anastasie!" the Count called again to his wife.

"Poor Maxime!" she said, addressing the young man. "Come, we must resign ourselves. This evening——"

"I hope, Nasie," he said in her ear, "that you will give orders not to admit that youngster, whose eyes light up like live coals when he looks at you. He will make you a declaration, and compromise you, and then you will compel me to kill him."

"Are you mad, Maxime?" she said. "A young lad of a student is, on the contrary, a capital lightning-conductor; is not that so? Of course, I mean to make Restaud furiously jealous of him."

Maxime burst out laughing, and went out, followed by the Countess, who stood at the window to watch him into his carriage; he shook his whip, and made his horse prance. She only returned when the great gate had been closed after him.

"What do you think, dear?" cried the Count, her husband, "this gentleman's family estate is not far from Verteuil, on the Charente; his great-uncle and my grandfather were acquainted."

"Delighted to find that we have acquaintances in common," said the Countess, with a preoccupied manner.

"More than you think," said Eugène, in a low voice.

"What do you mean?" she asked quickly.

"Why, only just now," said the student, "I saw a gentleman go out at the gate, Father Goriot, my next door neighbor in the house where I am lodging."

At the sound of this name, and the prefix that embellished it, the Count, who was stirring the fire, let the tongs fall as though they had burned his fingers, and rose to his feet.

"Sir," he cried, "you might have called him 'Monsieur Goriot'!"

The Countess turned pale at first at the sight of her husband's vexation, then she reddened; clearly she was embarrassed, her answer was made in a tone that she tried to make natural, and with an air of assumed carelessness:

"You could not know any one who is dearer to us both . . ."

She broke off, glanced at the piano as if some fancy had crossed her mind, and asked, "Are you fond of music, M. de Rastignac?"

"Exceedingly," answered Eugène, flushing, and disconcerted by a dim suspicion that he had somehow been guilty of a clumsy piece of folly.

"Do you sing?" she cried, going to the piano, and, sitting

down before it, she swept her fingers over the keyboard from end to end. R-r-r-r-ah!

"No, madame."

The Comte de Restaud walked to and fro.

"That is a pity; you are without one great means of success.—*Ca-ro, ca-a-ro, ca-a-a-ro, non du-bi-ta-re*," sang the Countess.

Eugène had a second time waved a magic wand when he uttered Goriot's name, but the effect seemed to be entirely opposite to that produced by the formula "related to Mme. de Beauséant." His position was not unlike that of some visitor permitted as a favor to inspect a private collection of curiosities, when by inadvertence he comes into collision with a glass case full of sculptured figures, and three or four heads, imperfectly secured, fall at the shock. He wished the earth would open and swallow him. Mme. de Restaud's expression was reserved and chilly, her eyes had grown indifferent, and sedulously avoided meeting those of the unlucky student of law.

"Madame," he said, "you wish to talk with M. de Restaud; permit me to wish you good-day——"

The Countess interrupted him by a gesture, saying hastily, "Whenever you come to see us, both M. de Restaud and I shall be delighted to see you."

Eugène made a profound bow and took his leave, followed by M. de Restaud, who insisted, in spite of his remonstrances, on accompanying him into the hall.

"Neither your mistress nor I are at home to that gentleman when he calls," the Count said to Maurice.

As Eugène set foot on the steps, he saw that it was raining.

"Come," said he to himself, "somehow I have just made a mess of it, I do not know how. And now I am going to spoil my hat and coat into the bargain. I ought to stop in my corner, grind away at law, and never look to be anything but a boorish country magistrate. How can I go into society, when to manage properly you want a lot of cabs, varnished boots, gold watch chains, and all sorts of things; you have to wear white doeskin gloves that cost six francs in the morning, and primrose kid gloves every evening? A fig for that old humbug of a Goriot!"

When he reached the street door, the driver of a hackney coach, who had probably just deposited a wedding party at their door, and asked nothing better than a chance of making a little money for himself without his employer's knowledge, saw that Eugène had no umbrella, remarked his black coat, white waistcoat, yellow gloves, and varnished boots, and stopped and looked at him inquiringly. Eugène, in the blind desperation that drives a young man to plunge deeper and deeper into an abyss, as if he might hope to find a fortunate issue in its lowest depths, nodded in reply to the driver's signal, and stepped into the cab; a few stray petals of orange blossom and scraps of wire bore witness to its recent occupation by a wedding party.

"Where am I to drive, sir?" demanded the man, who, by this time, had taken off his white gloves.

"Confound it!" Eugène said to himself, "I am in for it now, and at least I will not spend cab-hire for nothing!—Drive to the Hôtel Beauséant," he said aloud.

"Which?" asked the man, a portentous word that reduced Eugène to confusion. This young man of fashion, *species incerta,* did not know that there were two Hôtels Beauséant; he was not aware how rich he was in relations who did not care about him.

"The Vicomte de Beauséant, Rue——"

"De Grenelle," interrupted the driver, with a jerk of his head. "You see, there are the hôtels of the Marquis and Comte de Beauséant in the Rue Saint-Dominique," he added, drawing up the step.

"I know all about that," said Eugène, severely.—"Everybody is laughing at me to-day, it seems!" he said to himself, as he deposited his hat on the opposite seat. "This escapade will cost me a king's ransom, but, at any rate, I shall call on my so-called cousin in a thoroughly aristocratic fashion. Goriot has cost me ten francs already, the old scoundrel. My word! I will tell Mme. de Beauséant about my adventure; perhaps it may amuse her. Doubtless she will know the secret of the criminal relation between that handsome woman and the old rat without a tail. It would be better to find favor in my cousin's eyes than to come in contact with that shameless woman, who seems to me to have very expensive tastes. Surely the beautiful Vicomtesse's personal interest would turn the scale for me, when the mere mention of her name produces such an effect. Let us look higher. If you set yourself to carry the heights of heaven, you must face God."

The innumerable thoughts that surged through his brain might be summed up in these phrases. He grew calmer, and recovered something of his assurance as he watched the falling rain. He told himself that though he was about to squander two of the precious five-franc pieces that remained to him, the money was well laid out in preserving his coat, boots, and hat; and his cabman's cry of "Gate, if you please," almost put him in spirits. A Swiss, in scarlet and gold, appeared, the great door groaned on its hinges, and Rastignac, with sweet satisfaction, beheld his equipage pass under the archway and stop before the flight of steps beneath the awning. The driver, in a blue-and-red greatcoat, dismounted and let down the step. As Eugène stepped out of the cab, he heard smothered laughter from the peristyle. Three or four lackeys were making merry over the festal appearance of the vehicle. In another moment the law student was enlightened as to the cause of their hilarity; he felt the full force of the contrast between his equipage and one of the smartest broughams in Paris; a coachman, with powdered hair, seemed to find it difficult to hold a pair of spirited horses, who stood chafing the bit. In Mme. de Restaud's courtyard, in the Chaussée d'Antin, he had seen the neat turn-out of a young man of six-and-twenty; in the Faubourg Saint-Germain he found the luxurious equipage of a man of rank; thirty thousand francs would not have purchased it.

"Who can be here?" said Eugène to himself. He began to understand, though somewhat tardily, that he must not expect to find many women in Paris who were not already appropriated, and that the capture of one of these queens would be likely to cost something more than bloodshed. "Confound it all! I expect my cousin also has her Maxime."

He went up the steps, feeling that he was a blighted being. The glass door was opened for him; the servants were as solemn as jackasses under the curry comb. So far, Eugène had only been in the ballroom on the ground floor of the Hôtel Beauséant; the fête had followed so closely on the invitation, that he had not had time to call on his cousin, and had therefore never seen Mme. de Beauséant's apartments; he was about to behold for the first time a great lady among the wonderful and elegant surroundings that reveal her character and reflect her daily life. He was the more curious, because Mme. de Restaud's drawing-room had provided him with a standard of comparison.

At half-past four the Vicomtesse de Beauséant was visible. Five minutes earlier she would not have received her cousin, but Eugène knew nothing of the recognized routine of various houses in Paris. He was conducted up the wide, white-painted, crimson-carpeted staircase, between the gilded balusters and masses of flowering plants, to Mme. de Beauséant's apartments. He did not know the rumor current about Mme. de Beauséant, one of the biographies told, with variations, in whispers, every evening in the salons of Paris.

For three years past her name had been spoken of in connection with that of one of the most wealthy and distinguished Portuguese nobles, the Marquis d'Ajuda-Pinto. It was one of those innocent *liaisons* which possess so much charm for the two thus attached to each other that they find the presence of a third person intolerable. The Vicomte de Beauséant, therefore, had himself set an example to the rest of the world by respecting, with as good a grace as might be, this morganatic union. Any one who came to call on the Vicomtesse in the early days of this friendship was sure to find the Marquis d'Ajuda-Pinto there. As, under the circumstances, Mme. de Beauséant could not very well shut her door against these visitors, she gave them such a cold reception, and showed so much interest in the study of the ceiling, that no one could fail to understand how much he bored her; and when it became known in Paris that Mme. de Beauséant was bored by callers between two and four o'clock, she was left in perfect solitude during that interval. She went to the Bouffons or to the Opéra with M. de Beauséant and M. d'Ajuda-Pinto; and M. de Beauséant, like a well-bred man of the world, always left his wife and the Portuguese as soon as he had installed them. But M. d'Ajuda-Pinto must marry, and a Mlle. de Rochefide was the young lady. In the whole fashionable world there was but one person who as yet knew nothing of the arrangement, and that was Mme. de Beauséant. Some of her friends had hinted at the possibility, and she had laughed at them, believing that envy had prompted those ladies to try to make mischief. And now, though the bans were about to be published, and although the handsome Portuguese had come that day to break the news to the Vicomtesse, he had not found courage as yet to say one word about his treachery. How was it? Nothing is doubtless more difficult than the notification of an *ultimatum* of this kind. There are men who feel more at their ease when they stand up before another man who threatens their lives with sword or pistol than in the presence of a woman who, after two hours of lamentations and reproaches, falls into a dead swoon and requires salts. At this moment, therefore, M. d'Ajuda-Pinto was on thorns, and anxious to take his leave. He told himself that in some way or other the news would reach Mme. de Beauséant; he would write, it would be much better to do it by letter, and not to utter the words that should stab her to the heart.

So when the servant announced M. Eugène de Rastignac, the Marquis d'Ajuda-Pinto trembled with joy. To be sure, a loving woman shows even more ingenuity in inventing doubts of her lover than in varying the monotony of his happiness; and when she is about to be forsaken, she instinctively interprets every gesture as rapidly as Virgil's courser detected the presence of his companion by snuffing the breeze. It was impossible, therefore, that Mme. de Beauséant should not detect that involuntary thrill of satisfaction; slight though it was, it was appalling in its artlessness.

Eugène had yet to learn that no one in Paris should present himself in any house without first making himself acquainted with the whole history of its owner, and of its owner's wife and family, so that he may avoid making any of the terrible blunders which in Poland draw forth the picturesque exclamation, "Harness five bullocks to your cart!" probably because you will need them all to pull you out of the quagmire into which a false step has plunged you. If, down to the present day, our language has no name for these conversational disasters, it is probably because they are believed to be impossible, the publicity given in Paris to every scandal is so prodigious. After the awkward incident at Mme. de Restaud's, no one but Eugène could have reappeared in his character of bullock-driver in Mme. de Beauséant's drawing-room. But if Mme. de Restaud and M. de Trailles had found him horribly in the way, M. d'Ajuda hailed his coming with relief.

"Good-bye," said the Portuguese, hurrying to the door, as Eugène made his entrance into a dainty little pink-and-gray drawing-room, where luxury seemed nothing more than good taste.

"Until this evening," said Mme. de Beauséant, turning her head to give the Marquis a glance. "We are going to the Bouffons, are we not?"

"I cannot go," he said, with his fingers on the door handle.

Mme. de Beauséant rose and beckoned to him to return. She did not pay the slightest attention to Eugène, who stood there dazzled by the sparkling marvels around him; he began to think that this was some story out of the *Arabian Nights* made real, and did not know where to hide himself, when the woman before him seemed to be unconscious of his existence. The Vicomtesse had raised the forefinger of her right hand, and gracefully signed to the Marquis to seat himself beside her. The Marquis felt the imperious sway of passion in her gesture; he came back towards her. Eugène watched him, not without a feeling of envy.

"That is the owner of the brougham!" he said to himself. "But is it necessary to have a pair of spirited horses, servants in livery, and torrents of gold to draw a glance from a woman here in Paris?"

The demon of luxury gnawed at his heart, greed burned in his veins, his throat was parched with the thirst of gold.

He had a hundred and thirty francs every quarter. His father, mother, brothers, sisters, and aunt did not spend two hundred francs a month among them. This swift comparison between his present condition and the aims he had in view helped to benumb his faculties.

"Why not?" the Vicomtesse was saying, as she smiled at the Portuguese. "Why cannot you come to the Italiens?"

"Affairs! I am to dine with the English Ambassador."

"Throw him over."

When a man once enters on a course of deception, he is compelled to add lie to lie. M. d'Ajuda therefore said, smiling, "Do you lay your commands on me?"

"Yes, certainly."

"That was what I wanted to have you say to me," he answered, dissembling his feelings in a glance which would have reassured any other woman.

He took the Vicomtesse's hand, kissed it, and went.

Eugène ran his fingers through his hair, and constrained himself to bow. He thought that now Mme. de Beauséant would give him her attention; but suddenly she sprang forward, rushed to a window in the gallery, and watched M. d'Ajuda step into his carriage; she listened to the order that he gave, and heard the Swiss repeat it to the coachman:

"To M. de Rochefide's house."

Those words, and the way in which M. d'Ajuda flung himself back in the carriage, were like a lightning flash and a thunderbolt for her; she walked back again with a deadly fear gnawing at her heart. The most terrible catastrophes only happen among the heights. The Vicomtesse went to her own room, sat down at a table, and took up a sheet of dainty notepaper.

"When, instead of dining with the English Ambassador," she wrote, "you go to the Rochefides, you owe me an explanation, which I am waiting to hear."

She retraced several of the letters, for her hand was trembling so that they were indistinct; then she signed the note with an initial C for "Claire de Bourgogne," and rang the bell.

"Jacques," she said to the servant, who appeared immediately, "take this note to M. de Rochefide's house at half-past seven and ask for the Marquis d'Ajuda. If M. d'Ajuda is there, leave the note without waiting for an answer; if he is not there, bring the note back to me."

"Madame la Vicomtesse, there is a visitor in the drawing-room."

"Ah! yes, of course," she said, opening the door.

Eugène was beginning to feel very uncomfortable, but at last the Vicomtesse appeared; she spoke to him, and the tremulous tones of her voice vibrated through his heart.

"Pardon me, monsieur," she said; "I had a letter to write. Now I am quite at liberty."

She scarcely knew what she was saying, for even as she spoke she thought, "Ah! he means to marry Mlle. de Rochefide? But is he still free? This evening the marriage shall be broken off, or else . . . But before to-morrow I shall know."

"Cousin . . ." the student replied.

"Eh?" said the Countess, with an insolent glance that sent a cold shudder through Eugène; he understood what that "Eh?" meant; he had learned a great deal in three hours, and his wits were on the alert. He reddened:

"Madame . . ." he began; he hesitated a moment, and then went on. "Pardon me; I am in such need of protection that the merest scrap of relationship could do me no harm."

Mme. de Beauséant smiled, but there was sadness in her smile; even now she felt forebodings of the coming pain, the air she breathed was heavy with the storm that was about to burst.

"If you knew how my family are situated," he went on, "you would love to play the part of a beneficent fairy god-mother who graciously clears the obstacles from the path of her protégé."

"Well, cousin," she said, laughing, "and how can I be of service to you?"

"But do I know even that? I am distantly related to you, and this obscure and remote relationship is even now a perfect godsend to me. You have confused my ideas; I cannot re-member the things that I meant to say to you. I know no one else here in Paris. . . . Ah! if I could only ask you to counsel me, ask you to look upon me as a poor child who would fain cling to the hem of your dress, who would lay down his life for you."

"Would you kill a man for me?"

"Two," said Eugène.

"You, child. Yes, you are a child," she said, keeping back the tears that came to her eyes; "you would love sincerely."

"Oh!" he cried, flinging up his head.

The audacity of the student's answer interested the Vicomtesse in him. The southern brain was beginning to scheme for the first time. Between Mme. de Restaud's blue boudoir and Mme. de Beauséant's rose-colored drawing-room he had made a three years' advance in a kind of law which is not a recognized study in Paris, although it is a sort of higher jurisprudence, and, when well understood, is a highroad to success of every kind.

"Ah! this is what I meant to say!" said Eugène. "I met Mme. de Restaud at your ball, and this morning I went to see her."

"You must have been very much in the way," said Mme. de Beauséant, smiling as she spoke.

"Yes, indeed. I am a novice, and my blunders will set

every one against me, if you do not give me your counsel. I believe that in Paris it is very difficult to meet with a young, beautiful, and wealthy woman of fashion who would be willing to teach me, what you women can explain so well—life. I shall find a M. de Trailles everywhere. So I have come to you to ask you to give me a key to a puzzle, to entreat you to tell me what sort of blunder I made this morning. I mentioned an old man——"

"Madame la Duchesse de Langeais," Jacques cut the student short; Eugène gave expression to his intense annoyance by a gesture.

"If you mean to succeed," said the Vicomtesse in a low voice, "in the first place you must not be so demonstrative."

"Ah! good morning, dear," she continued, and rising and crossing the room, she grasped the Duchess' hands as affectionately as if they had been sisters; the Duchess responded in the prettiest and most gracious way.

"Two intimate friends!" said Rastignac to himself. "Henceforward I shall have two protectresses; those two women are great friends, no doubt, and this newcomer will doubtless interest herself in her friend's cousin."

"To what happy inspiration do I owe this piece of good fortune, dear Antoinette?" asked Mme. de Beauséant.

"Well, I saw M. d'Ajuda-Pinto at M. de Rochefide's door, so I thought that if I came I should find you alone."

Mme. de Beauséant's mouth did not tighten, her color did not rise, her expression did not alter, or rather, her brow seemed to clear as the Duchess uttered those deadly words.

"If I had known that you were engaged——" the speaker added, glancing at Eugène.

"This gentleman is M. Eugène de Rastignac, one of my cousins," said the Vicomtesse. "Have you any news of General de Montriveau?" she continued. "Sérizy told me yesterday that he never goes anywhere now; has he been to see you to-day?"

It was believed that the Duchess was desperately in love with M. de Montriveau, and that he was a faithless lover; she felt the question in her very heart, and her face flushed as she answered:

"He was at the Élysée yesterday."

"In attendance?"

"Claire," returned the Duchess, and hatred overflowed in the glances she threw at Mme. de Beauséant; "of course you know that M. d'Ajuda-Pinto is going to marry Mlle. de Rochefide; the bans will be published to-morrow."

This thrust was too cruel; the Vicomtesse's face grew white, but she answered, laughing, "One of those rumors that fools amuse themselves with. What should induce M. d'Ajuda to take one of the noblest names in Portugal to the Rochefides? The Rochefides were only ennobled yesterday."

"But Bertha will have two hundred thousand livres a year, they say."

"M. d'Ajuda is too wealthy to marry for money."

"But, my dear, Mlle. de Rochefide is a charming girl."

"Indeed?"

"And, as a matter of fact, he is dining with them to-day; the thing is settled. It is very surprising to me that you should know so little about it."

Mme. de Beauséant turned to Rastignac. "What was the blunder that you made, monsieur?" she asked. "The poor boy is only just launched into the world, Antoinette, so that he understands nothing of all this that we are speaking of. Be merciful to him, and let us finish our talk to-morrow. Everything will be announced to-morrow, you know, and your kind informal communication can be accompanied by official confirmation."

The Duchess gave Eugène one of those insolent glances that measure a man from head to foot, and leave him crushed and annihilated.

"Madame, I have unwittingly plunged a dagger into Mme. de Restaud's heart; unwittingly—therein lies my offence," said the student of law, whose keen brain had served him sufficiently well, for he had detected the biting epigrams that lurked beneath this friendly talk. "You continue to receive, possibly you fear, those who know the amount of pain that they deliberately inflict; but a clumsy blunderer who has no idea how deeply he wounds is looked upon as a fool who does not know how to make use of his opportunities, and every one despises him."

Mme. de Beauséant gave the student a glance, one of those glances in which a great soul can mingle dignity and gratitude. It was like balm to the law student, who was still smarting under the Duchess' insolent scrutiny; she had looked at him as an auctioneer might look at some article to appraise its value.

"Imagine, too, that I had just made some progress with the Comte de Restaud; for I should tell you, madame," he went on, turning to the Duchess with a mixture of humility and malice in his manner, "that as yet I am only a poor devil of a student, very much alone in the world, and very poor——"

"You should not tell us that, M. de Rastignac. We women never care about anything that no one else will take."

"Bah!" said Eugène. "I am only two-and-twenty, and I must make up my mind to the drawbacks of my time of life. Besides, I am confessing my sins, and it would be impossible to kneel in a more charming confessional; you commit your sins in one drawing-room, and receive absolution for them in another."

The Duchess' expression grew colder; she did not like the flippant tone of these remarks, and showed that she considered them to be in bad taste by turning to the Vicomtesse with —"This gentleman has only just come——"

Mme. de Beauséant began to laugh outright at her cousin and at the Duchess both.

"He has only just come to Paris, dear, and is in search of some one who will give him lessons in good taste."

"Mme. la Duchesse," said Eugène, "is it not natural to wish to be initiated into the mysteries which charm us?" ("Come, now," he said to himself, "my language is superfinely elegant, I'm sure.")

"But Mme. de Restaud is herself, I believe, M. de Trailles' pupil," said the Duchess.

"Of that I had no idea, madame," answered the law student, "so I rashly came between them. In fact, I got on very well with the lady's husband, and his wife tolerated me for a time until I took it into my head to tell them that I knew some one of whom I had just caught a glimpse as he went out by a back staircase, a man who had given the Countess a kiss at the end of a passage."

"Who was it?" both women asked together.

"An old man who lives at the rate of two louis a month in the Faubourg Saint-Marceau, where I, a poor student, lodge likewise. He is a truly unfortunate creature, everybody laughs at him—we all call him 'Father Goriot.'"

"Why, child that you are," cried the Vicomtesse, "Mme. de Restaud was a Mlle. Goriot!"

"The daughter of a vermicelli manufacturer," the Duchess added; "and when the little creature went to Court, the daughter of a pastry-cook was presented on the same day. Do you remember, Claire? The King began to laugh, and made some joke in Latin about flour. People—what was it?—people——"

"*Ejusdem farinœ*," said Eugène.

"Yes, that was it," said the Duchess.

"Oh! is that her father?" the law student continued, aghast.

"Yes, certainly; the old man had two daughters; he dotes on them, so to speak, though they will scarcely acknowledge him."

"Didn't the second daughter marry a banker with a German name?" the Vicomtesse asked, turning to Mme. de Langeais, "a Baron de Nucingen? And her name is Delphine, is it not? Isn't she a fair-haired woman who has a side-box at the Opéra? She comes sometimes to the Bouffons, and laughs loudly to attract attention."

The Duchess smiled, and said:

"I wonder at you, dear. Why do you take so much interest in people of that kind? One must have been as madly in love as Restaud was, to be infatuated with Mlle. Anastasie and her flour sacks. Oh! he will not find her a good bargain! She is in M. de Trailles' hands, and he will ruin her."

"And they do not acknowledge their father!" Eugène repeated.

"Oh! well, yes, their father, the father, a father," replied the Vicomtesse, "a kind father who gave them each five or six hundred thousand francs, it is said, to secure their happiness by marrying them well; while he only kept eight or ten thousand livres a year for himself, thinking that his daughters would always be his daughters, thinking that in them he would live his life twice over again, that in their houses he should find two homes, where he would be loved and looked up to, and made much of. And in two years' time both his sons-in-law had turned him out of their houses as if he were one of the lowest outcasts."

Tears came into Eugène's eyes. He was still under the spell of youthful beliefs, he had just left home, pure and sacred feelings had been stirred within him, and this was his first day on the battlefield of civilization in Paris. Genuine feeling is so infectious that for a moment the three looked at each other in silence.

"*Eh, mon Dieu!*" said Mme. de Langeais; "yes, it seems very horrible, and yet we see such things every day. Is there not a reason for it? Tell me, dear, have you ever really thought what a son-in-law is? A son-in-law is the man for whom we bring up, you and I, a dear little one, bound to us very closely in innumerable ways; for seventeen years she will be the joy of her family, its 'white soul,' as Lamartine says, and suddenly she will become its scourge. When *he* comes and takes her from us, his love from the very beginning is like an axe laid to the root of all the old affection in our darling's heart, and all the ties that bound her to her family are severed. But yesterday our little daughter thought of no one but her mother and father, as we had no thought that was not for her; by to-morrow she will have become a hostile stranger. The tragedy is always going on under our eyes. On the one hand you see a father who has sacrificed himself to his son, and his daughter-in-law shows him the last degree of insolence. On the other hand, it is the son-in-law who turns his wife's mother out of the house. I sometimes hear it said that there is nothing dramatic about society in these days; but the Drama of the Son-in-law is appalling, to say nothing of our marriages, which have come to be very poor farces. I can explain how it all came about in the old vermicelli maker's case. I think I recollect that Foriot——"

"Goriot, madame."

"Yes, that Moriot was once President of his Section during the Revolution. He was in the secret of the famous scarcity of grain, and laid the foundation of his fortune in those days by selling flour for ten times its cost. He had as much flour as he wanted. My grandmother's steward sold him immense quantities. No doubt Noriot shared the plunder with the Committee of Public Salvation, as that sort of person always did. I recollect the steward telling my grandmother that she might live at Grandvilliers in complete security, because her corn was as good as a certificate of civism. Well, then, this Loriot, who sold corn to those butchers, has never had but one passion, they say—he idolizes his daughters. He settled one of them under Restaud's roof, and grafted the other into the Nucingen family tree, the Baron de Nucingen being a rich banker who had turned Royalist. You can quite understand that so long as Bonaparte was Emperor, the two sons-in-law could manage to put up with the old Ninety-three; but after the restoration of the Bourbons, M. de Restaud felt bored by the old man's society, and the banker was still more tired of it. His daughters were still fond of him; they wanted 'to keep the goat and the cabbage,' so they used to see the Joriot whenever there was no one there, under pretence of affection. 'Come to-day, papa, we shall have you all to ourselves, and that will be much nicer!' and all that sort of thing. As for me, dear, I believe that love has second-sight: poor Ninety-three; his heart must have bled. He saw that his daughters were ashamed of him, that if they loved their husbands his visits must make mischief. So he immolated himself. He made the sacrifice because he was a father; he went into voluntary exile. His daughters were satisfied, so he thought that he had done the best thing he could; but it was a family crime, and father and daughters were accomplices. You see this sort of thing everywhere. What could this old Doriot have been but a splash of mud in his daughters' drawing-rooms? He would only have been in the way, and bored other people, besides being bored himself. And this that happened between father and daughters may happen to the prettiest woman in Paris and the man she loves the best; if her love grows tiresome, he will go; he will descend to the basest trickery to leave her. It is the same with all love and friendship. Our heart is a treasury; if you pour out all its wealth at once, you are bankrupt. We show no more mercy to the affection that reveals its utmost extent than we do to another kind of prodigal who has not a penny left. Their father had given them all he had. For twenty years he had given his whole heart to them; then, one day, he gave them all his fortune too. The lemon was squeezed; the girls left the rest in the gutter."

"The world is very base," said the Vicomtesse, plucking at the threads of her shawl. She did not raise her head as she spoke; the words that Mme. de Langeais had meant for her in the course of her story had cut her to the quick.

"Base? Oh, no," answered the Duchess; "the world goes its own way, that is all. If I speak in this way, it is only to show that I am not duped by it. I think as you do," she said, pressing the Vicomtesse's hand. "The world is a slough; let us try to live on the heights above it."

She rose to her feet and kissed Mme. de Beauséant on the forehead as she said: "You look very charming to-day, dear. I have never seen such a lovely color in your cheeks before."

Then she went out with a slight inclination of the head to the cousin.

"Father Goriot is sublime!" said Eugène to himself, as he remembered how he had watched his neighbor work the silver vessel into a shapeless mass that night.

Mme. de Beauséant did not hear him; she was absorbed in her own thoughts. For several minutes the silence remained unbroken till the law student became almost paralyzed with embarrassment, and was equally afraid to go or stay or speak a word.

"The world is basely ungrateful and ill-natured," said the Vicomtesse at last. "No sooner does a trouble befall you than a friend is ready to bring the tidings and to probe your heart with the point of a dagger while calling on you to admire the handle. Epigrams and sarcasms already! Ah! I will defend myself!"

She raised her head like the great lady that she was, and lightnings flashed from her proud eyes.

"Ah!" she said, as she saw Eugène, "are you there?"

"Still," he said piteously.

"Well, then, M. de Rastignac, deal with the world as it deserves. You are determined to succeed? I will help you. You shall sound the depths of corruption in woman; you shall measure the extent of man's pitiful vanity. Deeply as I am versed in such learning, there were pages in the book of life that I had not read. Now I know all. The more cold-blooded your calculations, the further you will go. Strike ruthlessly; you will be feared. Men and women for you must be nothing more than post-horses; take a fresh relay, and leave the last to drop by the roadside; in this way you will reach the goal of your ambition. You will be nothing here, you see, unless a woman interests herself in you; and she must be young and wealthy, and a woman of the world. Yet, if you have a heart, lock it carefully away like a treasure; do not let any one suspect it, or you will be lost; you would cease to be the executioner, you would take the victim's place. And if ever you should love, never let your secret escape you! trust no one until you are very sure of the heart to which you open your heart. Learn to mistrust every one; take every precaution for the sake of the love which does not exist as yet. Listen, Miguel"—the name slipped from her so naturally that she did not notice her mistake—"there is something still more appalling than the ingratitude of daughters who have cast off their old father and wish that he were dead, and that is a rivalry between two sisters. Restaud comes of a good family; his wife has been received into their circle; she has been presented at court; and her sister, her wealthy sister, Mme. Delphine de Nucingen, the wife of a great capitalist, is consumed with envy, and ready to die of spleen. There is a gulf set between the sisters—indeed, they are sisters no longer—the two women who refuse to acknowledge their father do not acknowledge each other. So Mme. de Nucingen would lap all the mud that lies between the Rue Saint-Lazare and the Rue de Grenelle to gain admittance to my salon. She fancied that she should gain her end through de Marsay; she has made herself de Marsay's slave, and she bores him. De Marsay cares very little about her. If you will introduce her to me, you will be her darling, her Benjamin; she will idolize you. If, after that, you can love her, do so; if not, make her useful. I will ask her to come once or twice to one of my great crushes, but I will never receive her here in the morning. I will bow to her when I see her, and that will be quite sufficient. You have shut the Comtesse de Restaud's door against you by mentioning Father Goriot's name. Yes, my good friend, you may call at her house twenty times, and every time out of the twenty you will find that she is not at home. The servants have their orders, and will not admit you. Very well, then, now let Father Goriot gain the right of entry into her sister's house for you. The beautiful Mme. de Nucingen will give the signal for a battle. As soon as she singles you out, other women will begin to lose their heads about you, and her enemies and rivals and intimate friends will all try to take you from her. There are women who will fall in love with a man because another woman has chosen him; like the city madams, poor things, who copy our millinery, and hope thereby to acquire our manners. You will have a success, and in Paris success is everything; it is the key of power. If the women credit you with wit and talent, the men will follow suit so long as you do not undeceive them yourself. There will be nothing you may not aspire to; you will go everywhere, and you will find out what the world is—an assemblage of fools and knaves. But you must be neither the one nor the other. I am giving you my name like Ariadne's clue of thread to take with you into this labyrinth; make no unworthy use of it," she said, with a queenly glance and curve of her throat; "give it back to me unsullied. And now, go; leave me. We women also have our battles to fight."

"And if you should ever need some one who would gladly set a match to a train for you——"

"Well?" she asked.

He tapped his heart, smiled in answer to his cousin's smile, and went.

It was five o'clock, and Eugène was hungry; he was afraid lest he should not be in time for dinner, a misgiving which made him feel that it was pleasant to be borne so quickly across Paris. This sensation of physical comfort left his mind free to grapple with the thoughts that assailed him. A mortification usually sends a young man of his age into a furious rage; he shakes his fist at society, and vows vengeance when his belief in himself is shaken. Just then Rastignac was overwhelmed by the words, "You have shut the Countess' door against you."

"I shall call!" he said to himself, "and if Mme. de Beauséant is right, if I never find her at home—I . . . well, Mme. de Restaud shall meet me in every salon in Paris. I will learn to fence, and have some pistol practice, and kill that Maxime of hers!"

"And money?" cried an inward monitor. "How about money, where is that to come from?" And all at once the wealth displayed in the Countess de Restaud's drawing-room rose before his eyes. That was the luxury which Goriot's daughter had loved too well; the gilding, the ostentatious splendor, the unintelligent luxury of the parvenu, the riotous extravagance of a courtesan. Then the attractive vision suddenly went under an eclipse as he remembered the stately grandeur of the Hôtel de Beauséant. As his fancy wandered among these lofty regions in the great world of Paris, innumerable dark thoughts gathered in his heart; his ideas widened, and his conscience grew more elastic. He saw the world as it is; saw how the rich lived beyond the jurisdiction of law and public opinion, and found in success the *ultima ratio mundi*.

"Vautrin is right, success is virtue!" he said to himself.

Arrived in the Rue Neuve-Sainte-Geneviève, he rushed up to his room for ten francs wherewith to satisfy the demands of the cabman, and went in to dinner. He glanced round the squalid room, saw the eighteen poverty-stricken creatures about to feed like cattle in their stalls, and the sight filled him with loathing. The transition was too sudden, and the contrast was so violent that it could not but act as a powerful stimulant; his ambition developed and grew beyond all bounds. On the one hand, he beheld a vision of social life in its most charming and refined forms, of quick-pulsed youth, of fair, impassioned faces invested with all the charm of poetry, framed in a marvelous setting of luxury or art; and, on the other hand, he saw a sombre picture, the miry verge beyond these faces, in which passion was extinct and nothing was left of the drama but the cords and pulleys and bare mechanism. Mme. de Beauséant's counsels, the words uttered in anger by the forsaken lady, her petulant offer, came to his mind, and poverty was a ready expositor. Rastignac determined to open two parallel trenches, so as to insure success; he would be a learned doctor of law and a man of fashion. Clearly he was still a child! Those two lines are asymptotes, and will never meet.

"You are very dull, my lord Marquis," said Vautrin, with one of the shrewd glances that seem to read the innermost secrets of another mind.

"I am not in the humor to stand jokes from people who call me 'my lord Marquis,'" answered Eugène. "A marquis here in Paris, if he is not the veriest sham, ought to have a hundred thousand livres a year at least; and a lodger in the Maison Vauquer is not exactly Fortune's favorite."

Vautrin's glance at Rastignac was half-paternal, half-contemptuous. "Puppy!" it seemed to say; "I should make one mouthful of him!" Then he answered:

"You are in a bad humor; perhaps your visit to the beautiful Comtesse de Restaud was not a success."

"She has shut her door against me because I told her that her father dined at our table," cried Rastignac.

Glances were exchanged all round the room; Father Goriot looked down.

"You have sent some snuff into my eye," he said to his neighbor, turning a little aside to rub his hand over his face.

"Any one who molests Father Goriot will have henceforward to reckon with me," said Eugène, looking at the old man's neighbor; "he is worth all the rest of us put together.—I am not speaking of the ladies," he added, turning in the direction of Mlle. Taillefer.

Eugène's remarks produced a sensation, and his tone silenced the dinner-table. Vautrin alone spoke. "If you are going to champion Father Goriot, and set up for his responsible editor into the bargain, you had need be a crack shot and know how to handle the foils," he said, banteringly.

"So I intend," said Eugène.

"Then you are taking the field to-day?"

"Perhaps," Rastignac answered. "But I owe no account of myself to any one, especially as I do not try to find out what other people do of a night."

Vautrin looked askance at Rastignac.

"If you do not mean to be deceived by the puppets, my boy, you must go behind and see the whole show, and not peep through holes in the curtain. That is enough," he added, seeing that Eugène was about to fly into a passion. "We can have a little talk whenever you like."

There was a general feeling of gloom and constraint. Father Goriot was so deeply dejected by the student's remark that he did not notice the change in the disposition of his fellow-lodgers, nor know that he had met with a champion capable of putting an end to the persecution.

"Then, M. Goriot sitting there is the father of a countess," said Mme. Vauquer in a low voice.

"And of a baroness," answered Rastignac.

"That is about all he is capable of," said Bianchon to Rastignac; "I have taken a look at his head; there is only one bump—the bump of Paternity; he must be an *eternal father.*"

Eugène was too intent on his thoughts to laugh at Bianchon's joke. He determined to profit by Mme. de Beauséant's counsels, and was asking himself how he could obtain the necessary money. He grew grave. The wide savannas of the world stretched before his eyes; all things lay before him, nothing was his. Dinner came to an end, the others went, and he was left in the dining-room.

"So you have seen my daughter?" Goriot spoke tremulously, and the sound of his voice broke in upon Eugène's dreams. The young man took the elder's hand, and looked at him with something like kindness in her eyes.

"You are a good and noble man," he said. "We will have some talk about your daughters by and by."

He rose without waiting for Goriot's answer, and went to his room. There he wrote the following letter to his mother:—

"MY DEAR MOTHER,—Can you nourish your child from your breast again? I am in a position to make a rapid fortune, but I want twelve hundred francs—I must have them at all costs. Say nothing about this to my father; perhaps he might make objections, and unless I have the money, I may be led to put an end to myself, and so escape the clutches of despair. I will tell you everything when I see you. I will not begin to try to describe my present situation; it would take volumes to put the whole story clearly and fully. I have not been gambling, my kind mother, I owe no one a penny; but if you would preserve the life that you gave me, you must send me the sum I mention. As a matter of fact,

I go to see the Vicomtesse de Beauséant; she is using her influence for me; I am obliged to go into society, and I have not a penny to lay out on clean gloves. I can manage to exist on bread and water, or go without food, if need be, but I cannot do without the tools with which they cultivate the vineyards in this country. I must resolutely make up my mind at once to make my way, or stick in the mire for the rest of my days. I know that all your hopes are set on me, and I want to realize them quickly. Sell some of your old jewelry, my kind mother; I will give you other jewels very soon. I know enough of our affairs at home to know all that such a sacrifice means, and you must not think that I would lightly ask you to make it; I should be a monster if I could. You must think of my entreaty as a cry forced from me by imperative necessity. Our whole future lies in the subsidy with which I must begin my first campaign, for life in Paris is one continual battle. If you cannot otherwise procure the whole of the money, and are forced to sell our aunt's lace, tell her that I will send her some still handsomer," and so forth.

He wrote to ask each of his sisters for their savings— would they despoil themselves for him, and keep the sacrifice a secret from the family? To his request he knew that they would not fail to respond gladly, and he added to it an appeal to their delicacy by touching the chord of honor that vibrates so loudly in young and highly-strung natures.

Yet when he had written the letters, he could not help feeling misgivings in spite of his youthful ambition; his heart beat fast, and he trembled. He knew the spotless nobleness of the lives buried away in the lonely manor house; he knew what trouble and what joy his request would cause his sisters, and how happy they would be as they talked at the bottom of the orchard of that dear brother of theirs in Paris. Visions rose before his eyes; a sudden strong light revealed his sisters secretly counting over their little store, devising some girlish stratagem by which the money could be sent to him *incognito,* essaying, for the first time in their lives, a piece of deceit that reached the sublime in its unselfishness.

"A sister's heart is a diamond for purity, a deep sea of tenderness!" he said to himself. He felt ashamed of those letters.

What power there must be in the petitions put up by such hearts; how pure the fervor that bears their souls to Heaven in prayer! What exquisite joy they would find in self-sacrifice! What a pang for his mother's heart if she could not send him all that he asked for! And this noble affection, these sacrifices made at such terrible cost, were to serve as the ladder by which he meant to climb to Delphine de Nucingen. A few tears, like the last grains of incense flung upon the sacred altar fire of the hearth, fell from his eyes. He walked up and down, and despair mingled with his emotion. Father Goriot saw him through the half-open door.

"What is the matter, sir?" he asked from the threshold.

"Ah! my good neighbor, I am as much a son and brother as you are a father. You do well to fear for the Comtesse Anastasie; there is one M. Maxime de Trailles, who will be her ruin."

Father Goriot withdrew, stammering some words, but Eugène failed to catch their meaning.

The next morning Rastignac went out to post his letters. Up to the last moment he wavered and doubted, but he ended by flinging them into the box. "I shall succeed!" he said to himself. So says the gambler; so says the great captain; but the three words that have been the salvation of some few, have been the ruin of many more.

A few days after this Eugène called at Mme. de Restaud's house; she was not at home. Three times he tried the experiment, and three times he found her doors closed against him, though he was careful to choose an hour when M. de Trailles was not there. The Vicomtesse was right.

The student studied no longer. He put in an appearance at lectures simply to answer to his name, and after thus attesting his presence, departed forthwith. He had been through a reasoning process familiar to most students. He had seen the advisability of deferring his studies to the last moment before going up for his examinations; he made up his mind to cram his second and third years' work into the third year, when he meant to begin to work in earnest, and to complete his studies in law with one great effort. In the meantime he had fifteen months in which to navigate the ocean of Paris, to spread the nets and set the lines that should bring him a protectress and a fortune. Twice during that week he saw Mme. de Beauséant; he did not go to her house until he had seen the Marquis d'Ajuda drive away.

Victory for yet a few more days was with the great lady, the most poetic figure in the Faubourg Saint-Germain; and the marriage of the Marquis d'Ajuda-Pinto with Mlle. de Rochefide was postponed. The dread of losing her happiness filled those days with a fever of joy unknown before, but the end was only so much the nearer. The Marquis d'Ajuda and the Rochefides agreed that this quarrel and reconciliation was a very fortunate thing; Mme. de Beauséant (so they hoped) would gradually become reconciled to the idea of the marriage, and in the end would be brought to sacrifice d'Ajuda's morning visits to the exigencies of a man's career, exigencies which she must have foreseen. In spite of the most solemn promises, daily renewed, M. d'Ajuda was playing a part, and the Vicomtesse was eager to be deceived. "Instead of taking the leap heroically from the window, she is falling headlong down the staircase," said her most intimate friend, the Duchesse de Langeais. Yet this after-glow of happiness lasted long enough for the Vicomtesse to be of service to her young cousin. She had a half-superstitious affection for him. Eugène had shown her sympathy and devotion at a crisis when a woman sees no pity, no real comfort in any eyes; when if a man is ready with soothing flatteries, it is because he has an interested motive.

Rastignac made up his mind that he must learn the whole of Goriot's previous history; he would come to his bearings before attempting to board the Maison de Nucingen. The results of his inquiries may be given briefly as follows:—

In the days before the Revolution, Jean-Joachim Goriot was simply a workman in the employ of a vermicelli maker. He was a skilful, thrifty workman, sufficiently enterprising to buy his master's business when the latter fell a chance victim to the disturbances of 1789. Goriot established himself in the Rue de la Jussienne, close to the Corn Exchange. His plain good sense led him to accept the position of President of the Section, so as to secure for his business the protection of those in power at that dangerous epoch. This prudent step had led to success; the foundations of his fortune were laid in the time of the Scarcity (real or artificial), when the price of grain of all kinds rose enormously in Paris. People used to fight for bread at the bakers' doors; while other persons went to the grocers' shops and bought Italian paste foods without brawling over it. It was during this year that Goriot made the money, which, at a later time, was to give him all the advantage of the great capitalist over the small buyer; he had, moreover, the usual luck of average ability; his mediocrity was the salvation of him. He excited no one's envy; it was not even suspected that he was rich till the peril of being rich was over, and all his intelligence was concentrated, not on political, but on commercial speculations. Goriot was an authority second to none on all questions relating to corn, flour, and "middlings"; and the production, storage, and quality of grain. He could estimate the yield of the harvest, and foresee market prices; he bought his cereals in Sicily, and imported Russian wheat. Any one who had heard him hold forth on the regulations that control the importation and exportation of grain, who had seen his grasp of the subject, his clear insight into the principles involved, his appreciation of weak points in the way that the system worked, would have thought that here was the stuff of which a minister is made. Patient, active, and persevering, energetic and prompt in action, he surveyed his business horizon with an eagle eye. Nothing there took him by surprise; he foresaw all things, knew all that was happening, and kept his own counsel; he was a diplomatist in his quick comprehension of a situation; and in the routine of business he was as patient and plodding as a soldier on the march. But beyond this business horizon he could not see. He used to spend his hours of leisure on the threshold of his shop, leaning against the framework of the door. Take him from his dark little counting-house, and he became once more the rough, slow-witted workman, a man who cannot understand a piece of reasoning, who is indifferent to all intellectual pleasures, and falls asleep at the play, a Parisian Dolibom in short, against whose stupidity other minds are powerless.

Natures of this kind are nearly all alike; in almost all of them you will find some hidden depth of sublime affection. Two all-absorbing affections filled the vermicelli maker's heart to the exclusion of every other feeling; into them he seemed to put all the forces of his nature, as he put the whole power of his brain into the corn trade. He had regarded his wife, the only daughter of a rich farmer of La Brie, with a devout admiration; his love for her had been boundless. Goriot had felt the charm of a lovely and sensitive nature, which, in its delicate strength, was the very opposite of his own. Is there any instinct more deeply implanted in the heart of man than the pride of protection, a protection which is constantly exerted for a fragile and defenceless creature? Join love thereto, the warmth of gratitude that all generous souls feel for the source of their pleasures, and you have the explanation of many strange incongruities in human nature.

After seven years of unclouded happiness, Goriot lost his wife. It was very unfortunate for him. She was beginning to gain an ascendency over him in other ways; possibly she might have brought that barren soil under cultivation, she might have widened his ideas and given other directions to his thoughts. But when she was dead, the instinct of fatherhood developed in him till it almost became a mania. All the affection balked by death seemed to turn to his daughters, and he found full satisfaction for his heart in loving them. More or less brilliant proposals were made to him from time to time; wealthy merchants or farmers with daughters vied with each other in offering inducements to him to marry again; but he determined to remain a widower. His father-in-law, the only man for whom he felt a decided friendship, gave out that Goriot had made a vow to be faithful to his wife's memory. The frequenters of the Corn Exchange, who could not comprehend this sublime piece of folly, joked about it among themselves, and found a ridiculous nickname for him. One of them ventured (after a glass over a bargain) to call him by it, and a blow from the vermicelli maker's fist sent him headlong into a gutter in the Rue Oblin. He could think of nothing else when his children were concerned; his love for them made him fidgety and anxious; and this was so well known, that one day a competitor, who wished to get rid of him to secure the field to himself, told Goriot that Delphine had just been knocked down by a cab. The vermicelli maker turned ghastly pale, left the Exchange at once, and did not return for several days afterwards; he was ill in consequence of the shock and the subsequent relief on discovering that it was a false alarm. This time, however, the offender did not escape with a bruised shoulder; at a critical moment in the man's affairs, Goriot drove him into bankruptcy, and forced him to disappear from the Corn Exchange.

As might have been expected, the two girls were spoiled. With an income of sixty thousand francs, Goriot scarcely spent twelve hundred on himself, and found all his happiness in satisfying the whims of the two girls. The best masters were engaged, that Anastasie and Delphine might be endowed with all the accomplishments which distinguish a good education. They had a chaperon—luckily for them, she was a woman who had good sense and good taste;—they learned to ride; they had a carriage for their use; they lived as the mistress of a rich old lord might live; they had only to express a wish, their father would hasten to give them their most extravagant desires, and asked nothing of them in return but a kiss. Goriot had raised the two girls to the level of the angels; and, quite naturally, he himself was left beneath them. Poor man! he loved them even for the pain that they gave him.

When the girls were old enough to be married, they were left free to choose for themselves. Each had half her father's fortune as her dowry; and when the Comte de Restaud came to woo Anastasie for her beauty, her social aspirations led her to leave her father's house for a more exalted sphere. Delphine wished for money; she married Nucingen, a banker of German extraction, who became a Baron of the Holy Roman Empire. Goriot remained a vermicelli maker as before. His daughters and his sons-in-law began to demur; they did not like to see him still engaged in trade, though his whole life was bound up with his business. For five years he stood out against their entreaties, then he yielded, and consented to retire on the amount realized by the sale of his business and the savings of the last few years. It was this capital that Mme. Vauquer, in the early days of his residence with her, had calculated would bring in eight or ten thousand livres in a year. He had taken refuge in her lodging-house, driven there by despair when he knew that his daughters were compelled by their husbands not only to refuse to receive him as an inmate in their houses, but even to see him no more except in private.

This was all the information which Rastignac gained from a M. Muret who had purchased Goriot's business, information which confirmed the Duchesse de Langeais' suppositions, and herewith the preliminary explanation of this obscure but terrible Parisian tragedy comes to an end.

Towards the end of the first week in December Rastignac received two letters—one from his mother, and one from his eldest sister. His heart beat fast, half with happiness, half with fear, at the sight of the familiar handwriting. Those two little scraps of paper contained life or death for his hopes. But while he felt a shiver of dread as he remembered their dire poverty at home, he knew their love for him so well that he could not help fearing that he was draining their very life-blood. His mother's letter ran as follows:—

"MY DEAR CHILD,—I am sending you the money that you asked for. Make a good use of it. Even to save your life I could not raise so large a sum a second time without your father's knowledge, and there would be trouble about it. We should be obliged to mortgage the land. It is impossible to judge of the merits of schemes of which I am ignorant; but what sort of schemes can they be, that you should fear to tell me about them? Volumes of explanation would not have been needed; we mothers can understand at a word, and that word would have spared me the anguish of uncertainty. I do not know how to hide the painful impression that your letter has made upon me, my dear son. What can you have felt when you were moved to send this chill of dread through my heart? It must have been very painful to you to write the letter that gave me so much pain as I read it. To what courses are you committed? You are going to appear to be something that you are not, and your whole life and success depends upon this? You are about to see a society into which you cannot enter without rushing into expense that you cannot afford, without losing precious time that is needed for your studies. Ah! my dear Eugène, believe your mother, crooked ways cannot lead to great ends. Patience and endurance are the two qualities most needed in your position. I am not scolding you; I do not want any tinge of bitterness to spoil our offering. I am only talking like a mother whose trust in you is as great as her foresight for you. You know the steps that you must take, and I, for my part, know your purity of heart, and how good your intentions are; so I can say to you without a doubt, 'Go forward, beloved!' If I tremble, it is because I am a mother, but my prayers and blessings will be with you at every step. Be very careful, dear boy. You must have a man's prudence, for it lies with you to shape the destinies of five others who are dear to you, and must look to you. Yes, our fortunes depend upon you, and your success is ours. We all pray to God to be with you in all that you do. Your aunt Marcillac has been most generous beyond words in this matter; she saw at once how

it was, even down to your gloves. 'But I have a weakness for
the eldest!' she said gaily. You must love your aunt very
much, dear Eugène. I shall wait till you have succeeded
before telling you all that she has done for you, or her money
would burn your fingers. You, who are young, do not know
what it is to part with something that is a piece of your past!
But what would we not sacrifice for your sakes? Your aunt
says that I am to send you a kiss on the forehead from her,
and that kiss is to bring you luck again and again, she says.
She would have written you herself, the dear kind-hearted
woman, but she is troubled with the gout in her fingers just
now. Your father is very well. The vintage of 1819 has
turned out better than we expected. Good-bye, dear boy; I
will say nothing about your sisters, because Laure is writing
to you, and I must let her have the pleasure of giving you
all the home news. Heaven send that you may succeed! Oh!
yes, dear Eugène, you must succeed. I have come, through
you, to a knowledge of a pain so sharp that I do not think
I could endure it a second time. I have come to know what
it is to be poor, and to long for money for my children's sake.
There, good-bye! Do not leave us for long without news of
you; and here, at the last, take a kiss from your mother."

By the time Eugène had finished the letter he was in tears.
He thought of Father Goriot crushing his silver keepsake into
a shapeless mass before he sold it to meet his daughter's bill
of exchange.

"Your mother has broken up her jewels for you," he said
to himself; "your aunt shed tears over those relics of hers
before she sold them for your sake. What right have you
to heap execrations on Anastasie? You have followed her
example; you have selfishly sacrificed others to your own future, and she sacrifices her father to her lover; and of you
two, which is the worse?"

He was ready to renounce his attempts; he could not bear
to take that money. The fires of remorse burned in his heart,
and gave him intolerable pain, the generous secret remorse
which men seldom take into account when they sit in judg-

ment upon their fellow-men; but perhaps the angels in heaven, beholding it, pardon the criminal whom our justice condemns. Rastignac opened his sister's letter; its simplicity and kindness revived his heart.

"Your letter came just at the right time, dear brother. Agathe and I had thought of so many different ways of spending our money, that we did not know what to buy with it; and now you have come 'in, and, like the servant who upset all the watches that belonged to the King of Spain, you have restored harmony; for, really and truly, we did not know which of all the things we wanted we wanted most, and we were always quarreling about it, never thinking, dear Eugène, of a way of spending our money which would satisfy us completely. Agathe jumped for joy. Indeed, we have been like two mad things all day, 'to such a prodigious degree' (as aunt would say), that mother said, with her severe expression, 'Whatever can be the matter with you, mesdemoiselles?' I think if we had been scolded a little, we should have been still better pleased. A woman ought to be very glad to suffer for one she loves! I, however, in my inmost soul, was doleful and cross in the midst of all my joy. I shall make a bad wife, I am afraid, I am too fond of spending. I had bougnt two sashes and a nice little stiletto for piercing eyelet-holes in my stays, trifles that I really did not want, so that I have less than that slow-coach Agathe, who is so economical, and hoards her money like a magpie. She had two hundred francs! And I have only one hundred and fifty! I am nicely punished; I could throw my sash down the well; it will be painful to me to wear it now. Poor dear, I have robbed you. And Agathe was so nice about it. She said, 'Let us send the three hundred and fifty francs in our two names!' But I could not help telling you everything just as it happened.

"Do you know how we managed to keep your commandments? We took our glittering hoard, we went out for a walk, and when once fairly on the highway we ran all the

way to Ruffec, where we handed over the coin, without more
ado, to M. Grimbert, of the Messageries Royales. We came
back again like swallows on the wing. 'Don't you think that
happiness has made us lighter?' Agathe said. We said all
sorts of things, which I shall not tell you, Monsieur le
Parisien, because they were all about you. Oh, we love you
dearly, dear brother; it was all summed up in those few
words. As for keeping the secret, little masqueraders like
us are capable of anything (according to our aunt), even of
holding our tongues. Our mother has been on a mysterious
journey to Angoulême, and the aunt went with her, not
without solemn councils, from which we were shut out, and
M. le Baron likewise. They are silent as to the weighty
political considerations that prompted their mission, and conjectures are rife in the State of Rastignac. The Infantas are
embroidering a muslin robe with open-work sprigs for her Majesty the Queen; the work progresses in the most profound secrecy. There be but two more breadths to finish. A decree has
gone forth that no wall shall be built on the side of Verteuil,
but that a hedge shall be planted instead thereof. Our subjects
may sustain some disappointment of fruit and espaliers, but
strangers will enjoy a fair prospect. Should the heir-pre-
sumptive lack pocket-handkerchiefs, be it known unto him
that the dowager Lady of Marcillac, exploring the recesses of
her drawers and boxes (known respectively as Pompeii and
Herculaneum), having brought to light a fair piece of cambric whereof she wotted not, the Princesses Agathe and Laure
place at their brother's disposal their thread, their needles,
and hands somewhat of the reddest. The two young Princes,
Don Henri and Don Gabriel, retain their fatal habits of stuff-
ing themselves with grape-jelly, of teasing their sisters, of
taking their pleasure by going a-bird-nesting, and of cutting
switches for themselves from the osier-beds, maugre the laws
of the realm. Moreover, they list not to learn naught, wherefore the Papal Nuncio (called of the commonalty, M. le
Curé) threateneth them with excommunication, since that
they neglect the sacred canons of grammatical construction

for the construction of other canon, deadly engines made of the stems of elder.

"Farewell, dear brother, never did letter carry so many wishes for your success, so much love fully satisfied. You will have a great deal to tell us when you come home! You will tell me everything, won't you? I am the oldest. From something the aunt let fall, we think you must have had some success.

"Something was said of a lady, but nothing more was said ...

"Of course not, in our family! Oh, by-the-by, Eugène, would you rather that we made that piece of cambric into shirts for you instead of pocket-handkerchiefs? If you want some really nice shirts at once, we ought to lose no time in beginning upon them; and if the fashion is different now in Paris, send us one for a pattern; we want more particularly to know about the cuffs. Good-bye! Good-bye! Take my kiss on the left side of your forehead, on the temple that belongs to me, and to no one else in the world. I am leaving the other side of the sheet for Agathe, who has solemnly promised not to read a word that I have written; but, all the same, I mean to sit by her while she writes, so as to be quite sure that she keeps her word.—Your loving sister,

"LAURE DE RASTIGNAC."

"Yes!" said Eugène to himself. "Yes! Success at all costs now! Riches could not repay such devotion as this. I wish I could give them every sort of happiness! Fifteen hundred and fifty francs," he went on after a pause. "Every shot must go to the mark! Laure is right. Trust a woman! I have only calico shirts. Where some one else's welfare is concerned, a young girl becomes as ingenious as a thief. Guileless where she herself is in question, and full of foresight for me,—she is like a heavenly angel forgiving the strange incomprehensible sins of earth."

The world lay before him. His tailor had been summoned

and sounded, and had finally surrendered. When Rastignac met M. de Trailles, he had seen at once how great a part the tailor plays in a young man's career; a tailor is either a deadly enemy or a staunch friend, with an invoice for a bond of friendship; between these two extremes there is, alack! no middle term. In this representative of his craft Eugène discovered a man who understood that his was a sort of paternal function for young men at their entrance into life, who regarded himself as a stepping-stone between a young man's present and future. And Rastignac in gratitude made the man's fortune by an epigram of a kind in which he excelled at a later period of his life.

"I have twice known a pair of trousers turned out by him make a match of twenty thousand livres a year!"

Fifteen hundred francs, and as many suits of clothes as he chose to order! At that moment the poor child of the South felt no more doubts of any kind. The young man went down to breakfast with the indefinable air which the consciousness of the possession of money gives to youth. No sooner are the coins slipped into a student's pocket than his wealth, in imagination at least, is piled into a fantastic column, which affords him a moral support. He begins to hold up his head as he walks; he is conscious that he has a means of bringing his powers to bear on a given point; he looks you straight in the face; his gestures are quick and decided; only yesterday he was diffident and shy, any one might have pushed him aside; to-morrow, he will take the wall of a prime minister. A miracle has been wrought in him. Nothing is beyond the reach of his ambition, and his ambition soars at random; he is light-hearted, generous, and enthusiastic; in short, the fledgling bird has discovered that he has wings. A poor student snatches at every chance pleasure much as a dog runs all sorts of risks to steal a bone, cracking it and sucking the marrow as he flies from pursuit; but a young man who can rattle a few runaway gold coins in his pocket can take his pleasure deliberately, can taste the whole of the sweets of secure possession; he soars far above earth; he has forgotten

what the word *poverty* means; all Paris is his. Those are
days when the whole world shines radiant with light, when
everything glows and sparkles before the eyes of youth, days
that bring joyous energy that is never brought into harness,
days of debts and of painful fears that go hand in hand with
every delight. Those who do not know the left bank of the
Seine between the Rue Saint-Jacques and the Rue des Saints-
Pères know nothing of life.

"Ah! if the women of Paris but knew," said Rastignac, as
he devoured Mme. Vauquer's stewed pears (at five for a
penny), "they would come here in search of a lover."

Just then a porter from the Messageries Royales appeared
at the door of the room; they had previously heard the bell
ring as the wicket opened to admit him. The man asked for
M. Eugène de Rastignac, holding out two bags for him to
take, and a form of receipt for his signature. Vautrin's keen
glance cut Eugène like a lash.

"Now you will be able to pay for those fencing lessons and
go to the shooting gallery," he said.

"Your ship has come in," said Mme. Vauquer, eyeing the
bags.

Mlle. Michonneau did not dare to look at the money, for
fear her eyes should betray her cupidity.

"You have a kind mother," said Mme. Couture.

"You have a kind mother, sir," echoed Poiret.

"Yes, mamma has been drained dry," said Vautrin, "and
now you can have your fling, go into society, and fish for
heiresses, and dance with countesses who have peach blossom
in their hair. But take my advice, young man, and don't
neglect your pistol practice."

Vautrin struck an attitude, as if he were facing an antagonist. Rastignac, meaning to give the porter a tip, felt in
his pockets and found nothing. Vautrin flung down a franc
piece on the table.

"Your credit is good," he remarked, eyeing the student, and
Rastignac was forced to thank him, though, since the sharp

encounter of wits at dinner that day, after Eugène came in from calling on Mme. de Beauséant, he had made up his mind that Vautrin was insufferable. For a week, in fact, they had both kept silence in each other's presence, and watched each other. The student tried in vain to account to himself for this attitude.

An idea, of course, gains in force by the energy with which it is expressed; it strikes where the brain sends it, by a law as mathematically exact as the law that determines the course of a shell from a mortar. The amount of impression it makes is not to be determined so exactly. Sometimes, in an impressible nature, the idea works havoc, but there are, no less, natures so robustly protected, that this sort of projectile falls flat and harmless on skulls of triple brass, as cannon-shot against solid masonry; then there are flaccid and spongy-fibred natures into which ideas from without sink like spent bullets into the earthworks of a redoubt. Rastignac's head was something of the powder-magazine order; the least shock sufficed to bring about an explosion. He was too quick, too young, not to be readily accessible to ideas; and open to that subtle influence of thought and feeling in others which causes so many strange phenomena that make an impression upon us of which we are all unconscious at the time. Nothing escaped his mental vision; he was lynx-eyed; in him the mental powers of perception, which seem like duplicates of the senses, had the mysterious power of swift projection that astonishes us in intellects of a high order—slingers who are quick to detect the weak spot in any armor.

In the past month Eugène's good qualities and defects had rapidly developed with his character. Intercourse with the world and the endeavor to satisfy his growing desires had brought out his defects. But Rastignac came from the South side of the Loire, and had the good qualities of his countrymen. He had the impetuous courage of the South, that rushes to the attack of a difficulty, as well as the southern impatience of delay or suspense. These traits are held to be defects in the North; they made the fortune of Murat, but they likewise cut short his career. The moral would appear to be that when the dash and boldness of the South side of the Loire meets, in a southern temperament, with the guile of the North, the character is complete, and such a man will gain (and keep) the crown of Sweden.

Rastignac, therefore, could not stand the fire from Vautrin's batteries for long without discovering whether this was a friend or a foe. He felt as if this strange being was reading his inmost soul, and dissecting his feelings, while Vautrin himself was so close and secretive that he seemed to have something of the profound and unmoved serenity of a sphinx, seeing and hearing all things and saying nothing. Eugène, conscious of that money in his pocket, grew rebellious.

"Be so good as to wait a moment," he said to Vautrin, as the latter rose, after slowly emptying his coffee-cup, sip by sip.

"What for?" inquired the older man, as he put on his large-brimmed hat and took up the sword-cane that he was wont to twirl like a man who will face three or four footpads without flinching.

"I will repay you in a minute," returned Eugène. He unsealed one of the bags as he spoke, counted out a hundred and forty francs, and pushed them towards Mme. Vauquer. "Short reckonings make good friends" he added, turning to the widow; "that clears our accounts till the end of the year. Can you give me change for a five-franc piece?"

"Good friends make short reckonings," echoed Poiret, with a glance at Vautrin.

"Here is your franc," said Rastignac, holding out the coin to the sphinx in the black wig.

"Any one might think that you were afraid to owe me a trifle," exclaimed this latter, with a searching glance that seemed to read the young man's inmost thoughts; there was a satirical and cynical smile on Vautrin's face such as Eugène had seen scores of times already; every time he saw it, it exasperated him almost beyond endurance.

"Well . . . so I am," he answered. He held both the bags in his hand, and had risen to go up to his room.

Vautrin made as if he were going out through the sitting-room, and the student turned to go through the second door that opened into the square lobby at the foot of the staircase.

"Do you know, Monsieur le Marquis de Rastignacorama, that what you were saying just now was not exactly polite?" Vautrin remarked, as he rattled his sword-cane across the panels of the sitting-room door, and came up to the student.

Rastignac looked coolly at Vautrin, drew him to the foot of the staircase, and shut the dining-room door. They were standing in the little square lobby between the kitchen and the dining-room; the place was lighted by an iron-barred fanlight above a door that gave access into the garden. Sylvie came out of her kitchen, and Eugène chose that moment to say:

"*Monsieur* Vautrin, I am not a marquis, and my name is not Rastignacorama."

"They will fight," said Mlle. Michonneau, in an indifferent tone.

"Fight!" echoed Poiret.

"Not they," replied Mme. Vauquer, lovingly fingering her pile of coins.

"But there they are under the lime-trees," cried Mlle. Victorine, who had risen so that she might see out into the garden. "Poor young man! he was in the right, after all."

"We must go upstairs, my pet," said Mme. Couture; "it is no business of ours."

At the door, however, Mme. Couture and Victorine found their progress barred by the portly form of Sylvie the cook.

"What ever can have happened?" she said. "M. Vautrin said to M. Eugène, 'Let us have an explanation!' then he took him by the arm, and there they are, out among the artichokes."

Vautrin came in while she was speaking. "Mamma Vauquer," he said smiling, "don't frighten yourself at all. I am only going to try my pistols under the lime-trees."

"Oh! monsieur," cried Victorine, clasping her hands as she spoke, "why do you want to kill M. Eugène?"

Vautrin stepped back a pace or two, and gazed at Victorine.

"Oh! this is something fresh!" he exclaimed in a bantering tone, that brought the color into the poor girl's face. "That young fellow yonder is very nice, isn't he?" he went on. "You have given me a notion, my pretty child; I will make you both happy."

Mme. Couture laid her hand on the arm of her ward, and drew the girl away, as she said in her ear:

"Why, Victorine, I cannot imagine what has come over you this morning."

"I don't want any shots fired in my garden," said Mme. Vauquer. "You will frighten the neighborhood and bring the police up here all in a moment."

"Come, keep cool, Mamma Vauquer," answered Vautrin. "There, there; it's all right; we will go to the shooting-gallery."

He went back to Rastignac, laying his hand familiarly on the young man's arm.

"When I have given you ocular demonstration of the fact that I can put a bullet through the ace on a card five times running at thirty-five paces," he said, "that won't take away your appetite, I suppose? You look to me to be inclined to be a trifle quarrelsome this morning, and as if you would rush on your death like a blockhead."

"Do you draw back?" asked Eugène.

"Don't try to raise my temperature," answered Vautrin; "it is not cold this morning. Let us go and sit over there," he added, pointing to the green-painted garden seats; "no one can overhear us. I want a little talk with you. You are not a bad sort of youngster, and I have no quarrel with you. I like you, take Trump—(confound it!)—take Vautrin's word for it. What makes me like you? I will tell you by-and-by. Meantime, I can tell you that I know you as well as if I had made you myself, as I will prove to you in a minute. Put down your bags," he continued, pointing to the round table.

Rastignac deposited his money on the table, and sat down. He was consumed with curiosity, which the sudden change in the manner of the man before him had excited to the highest pitch. Here was a strange being who, a moment ago, had talked of killing him, and now posed as his protector.

"You would like to know who I really am, what I was, and what I do now," Vautrin went on. "You want to know too much, youngster. Come! come! keep cool! You will hear more astonishing things than that. I have had my misfortunes. Just hear me out first, and you shall have your turn afterwards. Here is my past in three words. Who am I? Vautrin. What do I do? Just what I please. Let us change the subject. You want to know my character. I am good-natured to those who do me a good turn, or to those whose hearts speak to mine. These last may do anything they like with me; they may bruise my shins, and I shall not tell them to 'mind what they are about'; but, *nom d'une pipe,* the devil himself is not an uglier customer than I can be if people annoy me, or if I don't happen to take to them; and you may just as well know at once that I think no more of killing a man than of that," and he spat before him as he spoke. "Only when it is absolutely necessary to do so, I do my best to kill him properly. I am what you call an artist. I have read Benvenuto Cellini's *Memoirs,* such as you see me; and, what is more, in Italian! A fine-spirited fellow he was! From him I learned to follow the example set us by Providence, who strikes us down at random, and to admire the beautiful whenever and wherever it is found. And, setting other questions aside, is it not a glorious part to play, when you pit yourself against mankind, and the luck is on your side? I have thought a good deal about the constitution of your present social Dis-order. A duel is downright childish, my boy! utter nonsense and folly! When one of two living men must be got out of the way, none but an idiot would leave chance to decide which it is to be; and in a duel it is a toss-up—heads or tails—and there you are! Now I, for instance, can hit the ace in the middle of a card five times running, send one bullet after another through the same hole, and at thirty-five paces, moreover! With that little accomplishment you might think yourself certain of killing your man, mightn't you? Well, I have fired, at twenty paces, and missed, and the rogue who had never handled a pistol in his life—look here!"—(he unbottoned his waistcoat and exposed his chest, covered, like a bear's back, with a shaggy fell; the student gave a startled shudder)—"he was a raw lad, but he made his mark on me," the extraordinary man went on, drawing Rastignac's fingers over a deep scar on his breast. "But that happened when I myself was a mere boy; I was one-and-twenty then (your age), and I had some beliefs left—in a woman's love, and in a pack of rubbish that you will be over head and ears in directly. You and I were to have fought just now, weren't we? You might have killed me. Suppose that I were put under the earth, where would you be? You would have to clear out of this, go to Switzerland, draw on papa's purse—and he has none too much in it as it is. I mean to open your eyes to your real position, that is what I am going to do; but I shall do it from the point of view of a man who, after studying the world very closely, sees that there are but two alternatives—stupid obedience or revolt. I obey nobody; is that clear? Now, do you know how much you will want at the pace you are going? A million; and promptly, too, or that little head of ours will be swaying to and fro in the drag-nets at Saint-Cloud, while we are gone to find out whether or no there is a Supreme Being. I will put you in the way of that million."

He stopped for a moment and looked at Eugène.

"Aha! you do not look so sourly at papa Vautrin now! At the mention of the million you look like a young girl when somebody has said, 'I will come for you this evening!' and she betakes herself to her toilette as a cat licks its whiskers over a saucer of milk. All right. Come, now, let us go into the question, young man; all between ourselves, you know. We have a papa and mamma down yonder, a great-aunt, two sisters (aged eighteen and seventeen), two young brothers (one fifteen, and the other ten), that is about the roll-call of the crew. The aunt brings up the two sisters; the curé comes and teaches the boys Latin. Boiled chestnuts are oftener on the table than white bread. Papa makes a suit of clothes last a long while; if mamma has a different dress winter and summer, it is about as much as she has; the sisters manage as best they can. I know all about it; I have lived in the south.

"That is how things are at home. They send you twelve hundred francs a year, and the whole property only brings in three thousand francs all told. We have a cook and a man-servant; papa is a baron, and we must keep up appearances. Then we have our ambitions; we are connected with the Beauséants, and we go afoot through the streets; we want to be rich, and we have not a penny; we eat Mme. Vauquer's messes, and we like grand dinners in the Faubourg Saint-Germain; we sleep on a truckle-bed, and dream of a mansion! I do not blame you for wanting these things. It is not given to every one to have ambition, my little trump. What sort of men do the women run after? Men of ambition. Men of ambition have stronger frames, their blood is richer in iron, their hearts are warmer than those of ordinary men. Women feel that when their power is greatest they look their best, and that those are their happiest hours; they like power in men, and prefer the strongest even if it is a power that may be their own destruction. I am going to make an inventory of your desires in order to put the question at issue before you. Here it is:—

"We are as hungry as a wolf, and those newly-cut teeth of ours are sharp; what are we to do to keep the pot boiling? In the first place, we have the Code to browse upon; it is not amusing, and we are none the wiser for it, but that cannot be helped. So far so good. We mean to make an advocate of ourselves with a prospect of one day being made President of a Court of Assize, when we shall send poor devils, our betters, to the galleys with a T.F.* on their shoulders, so that the rich may be convinced that they can sleep in peace. There

* *Travaux forcés.*

is no fun in that; and you are a long while coming to it; for, to begin with, there are two years of nauseous drudgery in Paris, we see all the lollipops that we long for out of our reach. It is tiresome to want thing and never to have them. If you were a pallid creature of the mollusk order, you would have nothing to fear, but it is different when you have the hot blood of a lion and are ready to get into a score of scrapes every day of your life. This is the ghastliest form of torture known in this inferno of God's making, and you will give in to it. Or suppose that you are a good boy, drink nothing stronger than milk, and bemoan your hard lot; you, with your generous nature, will endure hardships that would drive a dog mad, and make a start, after long waiting, as deputy to some rascal or other in a hole of a place where the Government will fling you a thousand francs a year like the scraps that are thrown to the butcher's dog. Bark at thieves, plead the cause of the rich, send men of heart to the guillotine, that is your work! Many thanks! If you have no influence, you may rot in your provincial tribunal. At thirty you will be a Justice with twelve hundred francs a year (if you have not flung off the gown for good before then). By the time you are forty you may look to marry a miller's daughter, an heiress with some six thousand livres a year. Much obliged! If you have influence, you may possibly be Public Prosecutor by the time you are thirty; with a salary of a thousand crowns, you could look to marry the mayor's daughter. Some petty piece of political trickery, such as mistaking Villèle for Manuel in a bulletin (the names rhyme, and that quiets your conscience), and you will probably be Procureur Général by the time you are forty, with a chance of becoming a deputy. Please to observe, my dear boy, that our conscience will have been a little damaged in the process, and that we shall endure twenty years of drudgery and hidden poverty, and that our sisters are wearing Dian's livery. I have the honor to call your attention to another fact: to wit, that there are but twenty Procureurs Généraux at a time in all France, while there are some twenty thousand of you young men who aspire to that elevated position; that there are some mountebanks among you who would sell their family to screw their fortunes a peg higher. If this sort of thing sickens you, try another course. The Baron de Rastignac thinks of becoming an advocate, does he? There's a nice prospect for you! Ten years of drudgery straight away. You are obliged to live at the rate of a thousand francs a month; you must have a library of law books, live in chambers, go into society, go down on your knees to ask a solicitor for briefs, lick the dust off the floor of the Palais de Justice. If this kind of business led to anything, I should not say no; but just give me the names of five advocates here in Paris who by the time that they are fifty are making fifty thousand francs a year! Bah! I would sooner turn pirate on the high seas than have my soul shrivel up inside me like that. How will you find the capital? There is but one way, marry a woman who has money. There is no fun in it. Have you a mind to marry? You hang a stone round your neck; for if you marry for money, what becomes of our exalted notions of honor and so forth? You might as well fly in the face of social conventions at once. Is it nothing to crawl like a serpent before your wife, to lick her mother's feet, to descend to dirty actions that would sicken swine—faugh!—never mind if you at least make your fortune. But you will be as doleful as a dripstone if you marry for money. It is better to wrestle with men than to wrangle at home with your wife. You are at the crossway of the roads of life, my boy; choose your way.

"But you have chosen already. You have gone to see your cousin of Beauséant, and you have had an inkling of luxury; you have been to Mme. de Restaud's house, and in Father Goriot's daughter you have seen a glimpse of the Parisienne for the first time. That day you came back with a word written upon your forehead. I knew it, I could read it—'Success!' Yes, success at any price. 'Bravo,' said I to myself, 'here is the sort of fellow for me.' You wanted money. Where was it to come from? You have drained your sisters' little hoard (all brothers sponge more or less on their sisters).

Those fifteen hundred francs of yours (got together, God knows how! in a country where there are more chestnuts than five-franc pieces) will slip away like soldiers after pillage. And, then, what will you do? Shall you begin to work? Work, or what you understand by work at this moment, means, for a man of Poiret's calibre, an old age in Mamma Vauquer's lodging-house. There are fifty thousand young men in your position at this moment, all bent as you are on solving one and the same problem—how to acquire a fortune rapidly. You are but a unit in that aggregate. You can guess, therefore, what efforts you must make, how desperate the struggle is. There are not fifty thousand good positions for you; you must fight and devour one another like spiders in a pot. Do you know how a man makes his way here? By brilliant genius or by skilful corruption. You must either cut your way through these masses of men like a cannon ball, or steal among them like a plague. Honesty is nothing to the purpose. Men bow before the power of genius; they hate it, and try to slander it, because genius does not divide the spoil; but if genius persists, they bow before it. To sum it all up in a phrase, if they fail to smother genius in the mud, they fall on their knees and worship it. Corruption is a great power in the world, and talent is scarce. So corruption is the weapon of superfluous mediocrity; you will be made to feel the point of it everywhere. You will see women who spend more than ten thousand francs a year on dress, while their husband's salary (his whole income) is six thousand francs. You will see officials buying estates on twelve hundred francs a year. You will see women who sell themselves body and soul to drive in a carriage belonging to the son of a peer of France, who has a right to drive in the middle rank at Longchamp. You have seen that poor simpleton of a Goriot obliged to meet a bill with his daughter's name at the back of it, though her husband has fifty thousand francs a year. I defy you to walk a couple of yards anywhere in Paris without stumbling on some infernal complication. I'll bet my head to a head of that salad that you will stir up a hornet's nest by taking

a fancy to the first young, rich, and pretty woman you meet.
They are all dodging the law, all at loggerheads with their
husbands. If I were to begin to tell you all that vanity or
necessity (virtue is not often mixed up in it, you may be sure),
all that vanity and necessity drive them to do for lovers,
finery, housekeeping, or children, I should never come to an
end. So an honest man is the common enemy.

"But do you know what an honest man is? Here, in Paris,
an honest man is the man who keeps his own counsel, and
will not divide the plunder. I am not speaking now of those
poor bond-slaves who do the work of the world without a reward for their toil—God Almighty's outcasts, I call them.
Among them, I grant you, is virtue in all the flower of its
stupidity, but poverty is no less their portion. At this moment, I think I see the long faces those good folk would
pull if God played a practical joke on them and stayed away
at the Last Judgment.

"Well, then, if you mean to make a fortune quickly, you
must either be rich to begin with, or make people believe that
you are rich. It is no use playing here except for high stakes;
once take to low play, it is all up with you. If in the scores
of professions that are open to you, there are ten men who
rise very rapidly, people are sure to call them thieves. You
can draw your own conclusions. Such is life. It is no cleaner
than a kitchen; it reeks like a kitchen; and if you mean to
cook your dinner, you must expect to soil your hands; the
real art is in getting them clean again, and therein lies the
whole morality of our epoch. If I take this tone in speaking
of the world to you, I have the right to do so; I know it well.
Do you think that I am blaming it? Far from it; the world
has always been as it is now. Moralists' strictures will never
change it. Mankind are not perfect, but one age is more
or less hypocritical than another, and then simpletons say
that its morality is high or low. I do not think that the rich
are any worse than the poor; man is much the same, high or
low, or wherever he is. In a million of these human cattle
there may be half a score of bold spirits who rise above the

rest, above the laws; I am one of them. And you, if you are
cleverer than your fellows, make straight to your end, and
hold your head high. But you must lay your account with
envy and slander and mediocrity, and every man's hand will
be against you. Napoleon met with a Minister of War,
Aubry by name, who all but sent him to the colonies.

"Feel your pulse. Think whether you can get up morning after morning, strengthened in yesterday's purpose. In
that case I will make you an offer that no one would decline.
Listen attentively. You see, I have an idea of my own. My
idea is to live a patriarchal life on a vast estate, say a hundred thousand acres, somewhere in the Southern States of
America. I mean to be a planter, to have slaves, to make a
few snug millions by selling my cattle, timber, and tobacco;
I want to live an absolute monarch, and to do just as I please;
to lead such a life as no one here in these squalid dens of lath
and plaster ever imagines. I am a great poet; I do not write
my poems, I feel them, and act them. At this moment I
have fifty thousand francs, which might possibly buy forty
negroes. I want two hundred thousand francs, because I
want to have two hundred negroes to carry out my notions of
the patriarchal life properly. Negroes, you see, are like a sort
of family ready grown, and there are no inquisitive public
prosecutors out there to interfere with you. That investment in ebony ought to mean three or four million francs
in ten years' time. If I am successful, no one will ask me
who I am. I shall be Mr. Four Millions, an American citizen.
I shall be fifty years old by then, and sound and hearty still;
I shall enjoy life after my own fashion. In two words, if I
find you an heiress with a million, will you give me two
hundred thousand francs? Twenty per cent commission,
eh? Is that too much? Your little wife will be very much
in love with you. Once married, you will show signs of uneasiness and remorse; for a couple of weeks you will be depressed. Then, some night after sundry grimacings, comes
the confession, between two kisses, 'Two hundred thousand
francs of debts, my darling!' This sort of farce is played

every day in Paris, and by young men of the highest fashion.
When a young wife has given her heart, she will not refuse
her purse. Perhaps you are thinking that you will lose the
money for good? Not you. You will make two hundred
thousand francs again by some stroke of business. With
your capital and your brains you should be able to accumu-
late as large a fortune as you could wish. *Ergo,* in six
months you will have made your own fortune, and your old
friend Vautrin's, and made an amiable woman very happy,
to say nothing of your people at home, who must blow on
their fingers to warm them, in the winter, for lack of firewood.
You need not be surprised at my proposal, nor at the demand
I make. Forty-seven out of every sixty great matches here
in Paris are made after just such a bargain as this. The
Chamber of Notaries compels my gentleman to——"

"What must I do?" said Rastignac, eagerly interrupting
Vautrin's speech.

"Next to nothing," returned the other, with a slight involuntary movement, the suppressed exultation of the angler
when he feels a bite at the end of his line. "Follow me carefully! The heart of a girl whose life is wretched and unhappy is a sponge that will thirstily absorb love; a dry sponge
that swells at the first drop of sentiment. If you pay court
to a young girl whose existence is a compound of loneliness,
despair, and poverty, and who has no suspicion that she will
come into a fortune, good Lord! it is quint and quatorze
at piquet; it is knowing the numbers of the lottery beforehand; it is speculating in the funds when you have news from
a sure source; it is building up a marriage on an indestructi-
ble foundation. The girl may come in for millions, and she
will fling them, as if they were so many pebbles, at your feet.
'Take it, my beloved! Take it, Alfred, Adolphe, Eugène!'
or whoever it was that showed his sense by sacrificing
himself for her. And as for sacrificing himself, this is
how I understand it. You sell a coat that is getting
shabby, so that you can take her to the *Cadran bleu,*
treat her to mushrooms on toast, and then go to the Ambigu-

Comique in the evening; you pawn your watch to buy her a shawl. I need not remind you of the fiddle-faddle sentimentality that goes down so well with all women; you spill a few drops of water on your stationery, for instance; those are the tears you shed while far away from her. You look to me as if you were perfectly acquainted with the argot of the heart. Paris, you see, is like a forest in the New World, where you have to deal with a score of varieties of savages— Illinois and Hurons, who live on the proceeds of their social hunting. You are a hunter of millions; you set your snares; you use lures and nets; there are many ways of hunting. Some hunt heiresses, others a legacy; some fish for souls, yet others sell their clients, bound hand and foot. Every one who comes back from the chase with his game-bag well filled meets with a warm welcome in good society. In justice to this hospitable part of the world, it must be said that you have to do with the most easy and good-natured of great cities. If the proud aristocracies of the rest of Europe refuse admittance among their ranks to a disreputable millionaire, Paris stretches out a hand to him, goes to his banquets, eats his dinners, and hobnobs with his infamy."

"But where is such a girl to be found?" asked Eugène.

"Under your eyes; she is yours already."

"Mlle. Victorine?"

"Precisely."

"And what was that you said?"

"She is in love with you already, your little Baronne de Rastignac!"

"She has not a penny," Eugène continued, much mystified.

"Ah! now we are coming to it! Just another word or two, and it will all be clear enough. Her father, Taillefer, is an old scoundrel; it is said that he murdered one of his friends at the time of the Revolution. He is one of your comedians that sets up to have opinions of his own. He is a banker—senior partner in the house of Frédéric Taillefer and Company. He has one son, and means to leave all he has to the boy, to the prejudice of Victorine. For my part, I don't like to see injustice of this sort. I am like Don Quixote, I have a fancy for defending the weak against the strong. If it should please God to take that youth away from him, Taillefer would have only his daughter left; he would want to leave his money to some one or other; an absurd notion, but it is only human nature, and he is not likely to have any more children, as I know. Victorine is gentle and amiable; she will soon twist her father round her fingers, and set his head spinning like a German top by plying him with sentiment! She will be too much touched by your devotion to forget you; you will marry her. I mean to play Providence for you, and Providence is to do my will. I have a friend whom I have attached closely to myself, a colonel in the Army of the Loire, who has just been transferred into the *garde royale*. He has taken my advice and turned ultra-royalist; he is not one of those fools who never change their opinions. Of all pieces of advice, my cherub, I would give you this—don't stick to your opinions any more than to your words. If any one asks you for them, let him have them— at a price. A man who prides himself on going in a straight line through life is an idiot who believes in infallibility. There are no such things as principles; there are only events, and there are no laws but those of expediency: a man of talent accepts events and the circumstances in which he finds himself, and turns everything to his own ends. If laws and principles were fixed and invariable, nations would not change them as readily as we change our shirts. The individual is not obliged to be more particular than the nation. A man whose services to France have been of the very slightest is a fetich looked on with superstitious awe because he has always seen everything in red; but he is good, at the most, to be put into the Museum of Arts and Crafts, among the automatic machines, and labeled La Fayette; while the prince at whom everybody flings a stone, the man who despises humanity so much that he spits as many oaths as he is asked for in the face of humanity, saved France from being torn in pieces at the Congress of Vienna; and they who should have

given him laurels fling mud at him. Oh! I know something
of affairs, I can tell you; I have the secrets of many men!
Enough. When I find three minds in agreement as to the
application of a principle, I shall have a fixed and immovable
opinion—I shall have to wait a long while first. In the
Tribunals you will not find three judges of the same opinion
on a single point of law. To return to the man I was telling
you of. He would crucify Jesus Christ again, if I bade him.
At a word from his old chum Vautrin he will pick a quarrel
with a scamp that will not send so much as five francs to his
sister, poor girl, and" (here Vautrin rose to his feet and stood
like a fencing-master about to lunge)—"turn him off into
the dark!" he added.

"How frightful!" said Eugène. "You do not really mean
it? M. Vautrin, you are joking!"

"There! there! Keep cool!" said the other. "Don't behave
like a baby. But if you find any amusement in it, be indignant, flare up! Say that I am a scoundrel, a rascal, a
rogue, a bandit; but do not call me a blackleg nor a spy!
There, out with it, fire away! I forgive you; it is quite
natural at your age. I was like that myself once. Only remember this, you will do worse things yourself some day. You
will flirt with some pretty woman and take her money. You
have thought of that, of course," said Vautrin, "for how are
you to succeed unless love is laid under contribution? There
are no two ways about virtue, my dear student; it either is,
or it is not. Talk of doing penance for your sins! It is a
nice system of business, when you pay for your crime by
an act of contrition! You seduce a woman that you may
set your foot on such and such a rung of the social ladder; you sow dissension among the children of a family; you
descend, in short, to every base action that can be committed
at home or abroad, to gain your own ends for your own pleasure or your profit; and can you imagine that these are acts
of faith, hope, or charity? How is it that a dandy, who in
a night has robbed a boy of half his fortune, gets only a
couple of months in prison; while a poor devil who steals a

banknote for a thousand francs, with aggravating circumstances, is condemned to penal servitude? Those are your
laws. Not a single provision but lands you in some absurdity.
That man with yellow gloves and a golden tongue commits
many a murder; he sheds no blood, but he drains his victim's
veins as surely; a desperado forces open a door with a crow-
bar, dark deeds both of them! You yourself will do every
one of the things that I suggest to you to-day, bar the bloodshed. Do you believe that there is any absolute standard in
this world? Despise mankind and find out the meshes that
you can slip through in the net of the Code. The secret of a
great success for which you are at a loss to account is a crime
that has never been found out, because it was properly executed."

"Silence, sir! I will not hear any more; you make me doubt
myself. At this moment my sentiments are all my science."

"Just as you please, my fine fellow; I did not think you
were so weak-minded," said Vautrin, "I shall say no more
about it. One last word, however," and he looked hard at the
student—"you have my secret," he said.

"A young man who refuses your offer knows that he must
forget it."

"Quite right, quite right; I am glad to hear you say so.
Somebody else might not be so scrupulous, you see. Keep in
mind what I want to do for you. I will give you a fortnight. The offer is still open."

"What a head of iron the man has!" said Eugène to himself, as he watched Vautrin walk unconcernedly away with
his cane under his arm. "Yet Mme. de Beauséant said as
much more gracefully; he has only stated the case in cruder
language. He would tear my heart with claws of steel. What
made me think of going to Mme. de Nucingen? He guessed
my motives before I knew them myself. To sum it up, that
outlaw has told me more about virtue than all I have learned
from men and books. If virtue admits of no compromises,
I have certainly robbed my sisters," he said, throwing down
the bags on the table.

He sat down again and fell, unconscious of his surroundings, into deep thought.

"To be faithful to an ideal of virtue! A heroic martyrdom! Pshaw! every one believes in virtue, but who is virtuous? Nations have made an idol of Liberty, but what nation on the face of the earth is free? My youth is still like a blue and cloudless sky. If I set myself to obtain wealth or power, does it mean that I must make up my mind to lie, and fawn, and cringe, and swagger, and flatter, and dissemble? To consent to be the servant of others who have likewise fawned, and lied, and flattered? Must I cringe to them before I can hope to be their accomplice? Well, then, I decline. I mean to work nobly and with a single heart. I will work day and night; I will owe my fortune to nothing but my own exertions. It may be the slowest of all roads to success, but I shall lay my head on the pillow at night untroubled by evil thoughts. Is there a greater or a better thing than this—to look back over your life and know that it is stainless as a lily? I and my life are like a young man and his betrothed. Vautrin has put before me all that comes after ten years of marriage. The devil! my head is swimming. I do not want to think at all; the heart is a sure guide."

Eugène was roused from his musings by the voice of the stout Sylvie, who announced that the tailor had come, and Eugène therefore made his appearance before the man with the two money bags, and was not ill pleased that it should be so. When he had tried on his dress suit, he put on his new morning costume, which completely metamorphosed him.

"I am quite equal to M. de Trailles," he said to himself. "In short, I look like a gentleman."

"You asked me, sir, if I knew the houses where Mme. de Nucingen goes," Father Goriot's voice spoke from the doorway of Eugène's room.

"Yes."

"Very well then, she is going to the Maréchale Carigliano's ball on Monday. If you can manage to be there, I shall hear from you whether my two girls enjoyed themselves, and how they were dressed, and all about it in fact."

"How did you find that out, my good Goriot?" said Eugène, putting a chair by the fire for his visitor.

"Her maid told me. I hear all about their doings from Thérèse and Constance," he added gleefully.

The old man looked like a lover who is still young enough to be made happy by the discovery of some little stratagem which brings him information of his lady-love without her knowledge.

"*You* will see them both!" he said, giving artless expression to a pang of jealousy.

"I do not know," answered Eugène. "I will go to Mme. de Beauséant and ask her for an introduction to the Maréchale."

Eugène felt a thrill of pleasure at the thought of appearing before the Vicomtesse, dressed as henceforward he always meant to be. The "abysses of the human heart," in the moralists' phrase, are only insidious thoughts, involuntary promptings of personal interest. The instinct of enjoyment turns the scale; those rapid changes of purpose which have furnished the text for so much rhetoric are calculations prompted by the hope of pleasure. Rastignac beholding himself well dressed and impeccable as to gloves and boots, forgot his virtuous resolutions. Youth, moreover, when bent upon wrongdoing does not dare to behold himself in the mirror of consciousness; mature age has seen itself; and therein lies the whole difference between these two phases of life.

A friendship between Eugène and his neighbor, Father Goriot, had been growing up for several days past. This secret friendship and the antipathy that the student had begun to entertain for Vautrin arose from the same psychological causes. The bold philosopher who shall investigate the effects of mental action upon the physical world will doubtless find more than one proof of the material nature of our sentiments in the relations which they create between human beings and other animals. What physiognomist is as quick to discern character as a dog is to discover from a stranger's face whether this is a friend or no? Those by-words—"atoms," "affinities"—are facts surviving in modern languages for the confusion of philosophic wiseacres who amuse themselves by winnowing the chaff of language to find its grammatical roots. We *feel* that we are loved. Our sentiments make themselves felt in everything, even at a great distance. A letter is a living soul, and so faithful an echo of the voice that speaks in it, that finer natures look upon a letter as one of love's most precious treasures. Father Goriot's affection was of the instinctive order, a canine affection raised to a sublime pitch; he had scented compassion in the air, and the kindly respect and youthful sympathy in the student's heart. This friendship had, however, scarcely reached the stage at which confidences are made. Though Eugène had spoken of his wish to meet Mme. de Nucingen, it was not because he counted on the old man to introduce him to her house, for he hoped that his own audacity might stand him in good stead. All that Father Goriot had said as yet about his daughters had referred to the remarks that the student had made so freely in public on that day of the two visits.

"How could you think that Mme. de Restaud bore you a grudge for mentioning my name?" he had said on the day following that scene at dinner. "My daughters are very fond of me; I am a happy father; but my sons-in-law have behaved badly to me, and rather than make trouble between my darlings and their husbands, I choose to see my daughters secretly. Fathers who can see their daughters at any time have no idea of all the pleasure that all this mystery gives me; I cannot always see mine when I wish, do you understand? So when it is fine I walk out in the Champs-Élysées, after finding out from their waiting-maids whether my daughters mean to go out. I wait near the entrance; my heart beats fast when the carriages begin to come; I admire them in their dresses, and as they pass they give me a little smile, and it seems as if everything was lighted up for me by a ray of bright sunlight. I wait, for they always go back the same way, and then I see them again; the fresh air has done them good and brought color into their cheeks; all about me people say, 'What a beautiful woman that is!' and it does my heart good to hear them.

"Are they not my own flesh and blood? I love the very horses that draw them; I envy the little lap-dog on their knees. Their happiness is my life. Every one loves after his own fashion, and mine does no one any harm; why should people trouble their heads about me? I am happy in my own way. Is there any law against going to see my girls in the evening when they are going out to a ball? And what a disappointment it is when I get there too late, and am told that 'Madame has gone out!' Once I waited till three o'clock in the morning for Nasie; I had not seen her for two whole days. I was so pleased, that it was almost too much for me! Please do not speak of me unless it is to say how good my daughters are to me. They are always wanting to heap presents upon me, but I will not have it. 'Just keep your money,' I tell them. 'What should I do with it? I want nothing.' And what am I, sir, after all? An old carcase, whose soul is always where my daughters are. When you have seen Mme. de Nucingen, tell me which you like the most," said the old man after a moment's pause, while Eugène put the last touches to his toilette. The student was about to go out to walk in the Garden of the Tuileries until the hour when he could venture to appear in Mme. de Beauséant's drawing-room.

That walk was a turning-point in Eugène's career. Several women noticed him; he looked so handsome, so young, and so well dressed. This almost admiring attention gave a new turn to his thoughts. He forgot his sisters and the aunt who had robbed herself for him; he no longer remembered his own virtuous scruples. He had seen hovering above his head the fiend so easy to mistake for an angel, the Devil with rainbow wings, who scatters rubies, and aims his golden shafts at palace fronts, who invests women with purple, and thrones with a glory that dazzles the eyes of fools till they forget the simple origins of royal dominion; he had heard the rustle of that Vanity whose tinsel seems to us to be the symbol of power. However cynical Vautrin's words had been, they had made an impression on his mind, as the sordid features of the old crone who whispers, "A lover, and gold in torrents," remain engraven on a young girl's memory.

Eugène lounged about the walks till it was nearly five o'clock, then he went to Mme. de Beauséant, and received one of the terrible blows against which young hearts are defenceless. Hitherto the Vicomtesse had received him with the kindly urbanity, the bland grace of manner that is the result of fine breeding, but is only complete when it comes from the heart.

To-day Mme. de Beauséant bowed constrainedly, and spoke curtly:

"M. de Rastignac, I cannot possibly see you, at least not at this moment. I am engaged . . ."

An observer, and Rastignac instantly became an observer, could read the whole history, the character and customs of caste, in the phrase, in the tones of her voice, in her glance and bearing. He caught a glimpse of the iron hand beneath the velvet glove—the personality, the egoism beneath the manner, the wood beneath the varnish. In short, he heard that unmistakable I THE KING that issues from the plumed canopy of the throne, and finds its last echo under the crest of the simplest gentleman.

Eugène had trusted too implicitly to the generosity of a woman; he could not believe in her haughtiness. Like all the unfortunate, he had subscribed, in all good faith, the generous compact which should bind the benefactor to the recipient, and the first article in that bond, between two large-hearted natures, is a perfect equality. The kindness which knits two souls together is as rare, as divine, and as little understood as the passion of love, for both love and kindness are the lavish generosity of noble natures. Rastignac was set upon going to the Duchesse de Carigliano's ball, so he swallowed down this rebuff.

"Madame," he faltered out, "I would not have come to trouble you about a trifling matter; be so kind as to permit me to see you later, I can wait."

"Very well, come and dine with me," she said, a little confused by the harsh way in which she had spoken, for this lady was as genuinely kind-hearted as she was high-born.

Eugène was touched by this sudden relenting, but none the less he said to himself as he went away, "Crawl in the dust, put up with every kind of treatment. What must the rest of the world be like when one of the kindest of women forgets all her promises of befriending me in a moment, and tosses me aside like an old shoe? So it is every one for himself? It is true that her house is not a shop, and I have put myself in the wrong by needing her help. You should cut your way through the world like a cannon ball, as Vautrin said."

But the student's bitter thoughts were soon dissipated by the pleasure which he promised himself in this dinner with the Vicomtesse. Fate seemed to determine that the smallest accidents in his life should combine to urge him into a career, which the terrible sphinx of the Maison Vauquer had described as a field of battle where you must either slay or be slain, and cheat to avoid being cheated. You leave your conscience and your heart at the barriers, and wear a mask on entering into this game of grim earnest, where, as in ancient Sparta, you must snatch your prize without being detected if you would deserve the crown.

On his return he found the Vicomtesse gracious and kindly, as she had always been to him. They went together to the dining-room, where the Vicomte was waiting for his wife. In the time of the Restoration the luxury of the table was carried, as is well known, to the highest degree, and M. de Beauséant, like many jaded men of the world, had few pleasures left but those of good cheer; in this matter, in fact, he was a gourmand of the schools of Louis XVIII. and of the Duc d'Escars, and luxury was supplemented by splendor. Eugène, dining for the first time in a house where the traditions of grandeur had descended through many generations, had never seen any spectacle like this that now met his eyes. In the time of the Empire, balls had always ended with a supper, because the officers who took part in them must be fortified for immediate service, and even in Paris might be called upon to leave the ballroom for the battlefield. This arrangement had gone out of fashion under the Monarchy, and Eugène had so far only been asked to dances. The self-possession which pre-eminently distinguished him in later life already stood him in good stead, and he did not betray his amazement. Yet as he saw for the first time the finely wrought silver plate, the completeness of every detail, the sumptuous dinner, noiselessly served, it was difficult for such an ardent imagination not to prefer this life of studied and refined luxury to the hardships of the life which he had chosen only that morning.

His thoughts went back for a moment to the lodging-house, and with a feeling of profound loathing, he vowed to himself that at New Year he would go; prompted at least as much by a desire to live among cleaner surroundings as by a wish to shake off Vautrin, whose huge hand he seemed to feel on his shoulder at that moment. When you consider the numberless forms, clamorous or mute, that corruption takes in Paris, common-sense begins to wonder what mental aberration prompted the State to establish great colleges and schools there, and assemble young men in the capital; how it is that pretty women are respected, or that the gold coin displayed in the money-changer's wooden saucers does not take to itself wings in the twinkling of an eye; and when you come to think further, how comparatively few cases of crime there are, and to count up the misdemeanors committed by youth, is there not a certain amount of respect due to these patient Tantaluses who wrestle with themselves and nearly always come off victorious? The struggles of the poor student in Paris, if skilfully drawn, would furnish a most dramatic picture of modern civilization.

In vain Mme. de Beauséant looked at Eugène as if asking him to speak; the student was tongue-tied in the Vicomte's presence.

"Are you going to take me to the Italiens this evening?" the Vicomtesse asked her husband.

"You cannot doubt that I should obey you with pleasure," he answered, and there was a sarcastic tinge in his politeness which Eugène did not detect, "but I ought to go to meet some one at the Variétés."

"His mistress," said she to herself.

"Then, is not Ajuda coming for you this evening?" inquired the Vicomte.

"No," she answered, petulantly.

"Very well, then, if you really must have an arm, take that of M. de Rastignac."

The Vicomtesse turned to Eugène with a smile.

"That would be a very compromising step for you," she said.

" 'A Frenchman loves danger, because in danger there is glory,' to quote M. de Chateaubriand," said Rastignac, with a bow.

A few moments later he was sitting beside Mme. de Beauséant in a brougham, that whirled them through the streets of Paris to a fashionable theatre. It seemed to him that some fairy magic had suddenly transported him into a box facing the stage. All the lorgnettes of the house were pointed at him as he entered, and at the Vicomtesse in her charming toilette. He went from enchantment to enchantment.

"You must talk to me, you know," said Mme. de Beauséant. "Ah! look! There is Mme. de Nucingen in the third box from ours. Her sister and M. de Trailles are on the other side."

The Vicomtesse glanced as she spoke at the box where Mlle. de Rochefide should have been; M. d'Ajuda was not there, and Mme. de Beauséant's face lighted up in a marvelous way.

"She is charming," said Eugène, after looking at Mme. de Nucingen.

"She has white eyelashes."

"Yes, but she has such a pretty slender figure!"

"Her hands are large."

"Such beautiful eyes!"

"Her face is long."

"Yes, but length gives distinction."

"It is lucky for her that she has some distinction in her face. Just see how she fidgets with her opera-glass! The Goriot blood shows itself in every movement," said the Vicomtesse, much to Eugène's astonishment.

Indeed, Mme. de Beauséant seemed to be engaged in making a survey of the house, and to be unconscious of Mme. Nucingen's existence; but no movement made by the latter was lost upon the Vicomtesse. The house was full of the loveliest women in Paris, so that Delphine de Nucingen was not a little flattered to receive the undivided attention of Mme. de Beauséant's young, handsome, and well-dressed cousin, who seemed to have no eyes for any one else.

"If you look at her so persistently, you will make people talk, M. de Rastignac. You will never succeed if you fling yourself at any one's head like that."

"My dear cousin," said Eugène, "you have protected me indeed so far, and now if you would complete your work, I only ask of you a favor which will cost you but little, and be of very great service to me. I have lost my heart."

"Already!"

"Yes."

"And to that woman!"

"How could I aspire to find any one else to listen to me?" he asked, with a keen glance at his cousin. "Her Grace the Duchesse de Carigliano is a friend of the Duchesse de Berri," he went on, after a pause; "you are sure to see her, will you be so kind as to present me to her, and to take me with you to her ball on Monday? I shall meet Mme. de Nucingen there, and enter upon my first skirmish."

"Willingly," she said. "If you have a liking for her already, your affairs of the heart are like to prosper. That is de Marsay over there in the Princesse Galathionne's box. Mme. de Nucingen is racked with jealousy. There is no better time for approaching a woman, especially if she happens to be a banker's wife. All those ladies of the Chaussée-d'Antin love revenge."

"Then, what would you do yourself in such a case?"

"I should suffer in silence."

At this point the Marquis d'Ajuda appeared in Mme. de Beauséant's box.

"I have made a muddle of my affairs to come to you," he said, "and I am telling you about it, so that it may not be a sacrifice."

Eugène saw the glow of joy on the Vicomtesse's face, and knew that this was love, and learned the difference between love and the affectations of Parisian coquetry. He admired his cousin, grew mute, and yielded his place to M. d'Ajuda with a sigh.

"How noble, how sublime a woman is when she loves like that!" he said to himself. "And *he* could forsake her for a doll! Oh! how could any one forsake her?"

There was a boy's passionate indignation in his heart. He could have flung himself at Mme. de Beauséant's feet; he longed for the power of the devil if he could snatch her away and hide her in his heart, as an eagle snatches up some white yeanling from the plains and bears it to its eyrie. It was humiliating to him to think that in all this gallery of fair pictures he had not one picture of his own. "To have a mistress and an almost royal position is a sign of power," he said to himself. And he looked at Mme. de Nucingen as a man measures another who has insulted him.

The Vicomtesse turned to him, and the expression of her eyes thanked him a thousand times for his discretion. The first act came to an end just then.

"Do you know Mme. de Nucingen well enough to present M. de Rastignac to her?" she asked of the Marquis d'Ajuda.

"She will be delighted," said the Marquis. The handsome Portuguese rose as he spoke and took the student's arm, and in another moment Eugène found himself in Mme. de Nucingen's box.

"Madame," said the Marquis, "I have the honor of presenting to you the Chevalier Eugène de Rastignac; he is a cousin of Mme de Beauséant's. You have made so deep an impression upon him, that I thought I would fill up the measure of his happiness by bringing him nearer to his divinity."

Words spoken half jestingly to cover their somewhat disrespectful import; but such an implication, if carefully disguised, never gives offence to a woman. Mme. de Nucingen smiled, and offered Eugène the place which her husband had just left.

"I do not venture to suggest that you should stay with me, monsieur," she said. "Those who are so fortunate as to be in Mme. de Beauséant's company do not desire to leave it."

"Madame," Eugène said, lowering his voice, "I think that to please my cousin I should remain with you. Before my lord Marquis came we were speaking of you and of your exceedingly distinguished appearance," he added aloud.

M. d'Ajuda turned and left them.

"Are you really going to stay with me, monsieur?" asked the Baroness. "Then we shall make each other's acquaintance. Mme. de Restaud told me about you, and has made me anxious to meet you."

"She must be very insincere, then, for she has shut her door on me."

"What?"

"Madame, I will tell you honestly the reason why; but I must crave your indulgence before confiding such a secret to you. I am your father's neighbor; I had no idea that Mme. de Restaud was his daughter. I was rash enough to mention his name; I meant no harm, but I annoyed your sister and her husband very much. You cannot think how severely the Duchesse de Langeais and my cousin blamed this apostasy on a daughter's part, as a piece of bad taste. I told them all about it, and they both burst out laughing. Then Mme. de Beauséant made some comparison between you and your sister, speaking in high terms of you, and saying how very fond you were of my neighbor, M. Goriot. And, indeed, how could you help loving him? He adores you so passionately that I am jealous already. We talked about you this morning for two hours. So this evening I was quite full of all that your father had told me, and while I was dining with my cousin I said that you could not be as beautiful as affectionate. Mme. de Beauséant meant to gratify such warm admiration, I think, when she brought me here, telling me, in her gracious way, that I should see you."

"Then, even now, I owe you a debt of gratitude, monsieur," said the banker's wife. "We shall be quite old friends in a little while."

"Although a friendship with you could not be like an ordinary friendship," said Rastignac; "I should never wish to be your friend."

Such stereotyped phrases as these, in the mouths of beginners, possess an unfailing charm for women, and are insipid only when read coldly; for a young man's tone, glance, and attitude give a surpassing eloquence to the banal phrases. Mme. de Nucingen thought that Rastignac was adorable. Then, woman-like, being at a loss how to reply to the student's outspoken admiration, she answered a previous remark.

"Yes, it is very wrong of my sister to treat our poor father as she does," she said; "he has been a Providence to us. It was not until M. de Nucingen positively ordered me only to receive him in the mornings that I yielded the point. But I have been unhappy about it for a long while; I have shed many tears over it. This violence to my feelings, with my husband's brutal treatment, have been the two causes of my unhappy married life. There is certainly no woman in Paris whose lot seems more enviable than mine, and yet, in reality, there is not one so much to be pitied. You will think I must be out of my senses to talk to you like this; but you know my father, and I cannot regard you as a stranger."

"You will find no one," said Eugène, "who longs as eagerly as I do to be yours. What do all women seek? Happiness." (He answered his own question in low, vibrating tones.) "And if happiness for a woman means that she is to be loved and adored, to have a friend to whom she can pour out her wishes, her fancies, her sorrows and joys; to whom she can lay

bare her heart and soul, and all her fair defects and her gracious virtues, without fear of a betrayal; believe me, the devotion and the warmth that never fails can only be found in
the heart of a young man who, at a bare sign from you, would
go to his death, who neither knows nor cares to know anything as yet of the world, because you will be all the world to
him. I myself, you see (you will laugh at my simplicity),
have just come from a remote country district; I am quite
new to this world of Paris; I have only known true and loving
hearts; and I made up my mind that here I should find no
love. Then I chanced to meet my cousin, and to see my cousin's
heart from very near; I have divined the inexhaustible treasures of passion, and, like Cherubino, I am the lover of all
women, until the day comes when I find *the* woman to whom
I may devote myself. As soon as I saw you, as soon as I
came into the theatre this evening, I felt myself borne towards you as if by the current of a stream. I had so often
thought of you already, but I had never dreamed that you
would be so beautiful! Mme. de Beauséant told me that I
must not look so much at you. She does not know the charm
of your red lips, your fair face, nor see how soft your eyes
are. . . . I also am beginning to talk nonsense; but let
me talk."

Nothing pleases women better than to listen to such whispered words as these; the most puritanical among them listens
even when she ought not to reply to them; and Rastignac,
having once begun, continued to pour out his story, dropping
his voice, that she might lean and listen; and Mme. de Nucingen, smiling, glanced from time to time at de Marsay, who
still sat in the Princesse Galathionne's box.

Rastignac did not leave Mme. de Nucingen till her husband came to take her home.

"Madame," Eugène said, "I shall have the pleasure of calling upon you before the Duchesse de Carigliano's ball."

"If Matame infites you to come," said the Baron, a thick-
set Alsatian, with indications of a sinister cunning in his
full-moon countenance, "you are quide sure of being well
receifed."

"My affairs seem to be in a promising way," said Eugène to himself.—" 'Can you love me?' I asked her, and she did not resent it. The bit is in the horse's mouth, and I have only to mount and ride;" and with that he went to pay his respects to Mme. de Beauséant, who was leaving the theatre on d'Ajuda's arm.

The student did not know that the Baroness' thoughts had been wandering; that she was even then expecting a letter from de Marsay, one of those letters that bring about a rupture that rends the soul; so, happy in his delusion, Eugène went with the Vicomtesse to the peristyle, where people were waiting till their carriages were announced.

"That cousin of yours is hardly recognizable for the same man," said the Portuguese laughingly to the Vicomtesse, when Eugène had taken leave of them. "He will break the bank. He is as supple as an eel; he will go a long way, of that I am sure. Who else could have picked out a woman for him, as you did, just when she needed consolation?"

"But it is not certain that she does not still love the faithless lover," said Mme. de Beauséant.

The student meanwhile walked back from the Théâtre-Italien to the Rue Neuve-Sainte-Geneviève, making the most delightful plans as he went. He had noticed how closely Mme. de Restaud had scrutinized him when he appeared in the Vicomtesse's box, and again when he sat beside Mme. de Nucingen, and inferred that the Countess' doors would not be closed in future. Four important houses were now open to him —for he meant to stand well with the Maréchale; he had four supporters in the inmost circle of society in Paris. Even now it was clear to him that, once involved in this intricate social machinery, he must attach himself to a spoke of the wheel that was to turn and raise his fortunes; he would not examine himself too curiously as to the methods, but he was certain of the end, and conscious of the power to gain and keep his hold.

"If Mme. de Nucingen takes an interest in me, I will teach her how to manage her husband. That husband of hers is a great speculator; he might put me in the way of making a fortune by a single stroke."

He did not say this bluntly in so many words; as yet, indeed, he was not sufficient of a diplomatist to sum up a situation, to see its possibilities at a glance, and calculate the chances in his favor. These were nothing but hazy ideas that floated over his mental horizon; they were less cynical than Vautrin's notions; but if they had been tried in the crucible of conscience, no very pure result would have issued from the test. It is by a succession of such like transactions that men sink at last to the level of the relaxed morality of this epoch, when there have never been so few of those who square their courses with their theories, so few of those noble characters who do not yield to temptation, for whom the slightest deviation from the line of rectitude is a crime. To these magnificent types of uncompromising Right we owe two masterpieces —the Alceste of Molière, and, in our own day, the characters of Jeanie Deans and her father in Sir Walter Scott's novel. Perhaps a work which should chronicle the opposite course, which should trace out all the devious courses through which a man of the world, a man of ambitions, drags his conscience, just steering clear of crime that he may gain his end and yet save appearances, such a chronicle would be no less edifying and no less dramatic.

Rastignac went home. He was fascinated by Mme. de Nucingen; he seemed to see her before him, slender and graceful as a swallow. He recalled the intoxicating sweetness of her eyes, her fair hair, the delicate silken tissue of the skin, beneath which it almost seemed to him that he could see the blood coursing; the tones of her voice still exerted a spell over him; he had forgotten nothing; his walk perhaps heated his imagination by sending a glow of warmth through his veins. He knocked unceremoniously at Goriot's door.

"I have seen Mme. Delphine, neighbor," said he.

"Where?"

"At the Italiens."

"Did she enjoy it? . . . Just come inside," and the

old man left his bed, unlocked the door, and promptly returned again.

It was the first time that Eugène had been in Father Goriot's room, and he could not control his feeling of amazement at the contrast between the den in which the father lived and the costume of the daughter whom he had just beheld. The window was curtainless, the walls were damp, in places the varnished wall-paper had come away and gave glimpses of the grimy yellow plaster beneath. The wretched bed on which the old man lay boasted but one thin blanket, and a wadded quilt made out of large pieces of Mme. Vauquer's old dresses. The floor was damp and gritty. Opposite the window stood a chest of drawers made of rosewood, one of the old-fashioned kind with a curving front and brass handles, shaped like rings of twisted vine stems covered with flowers and leaves. On a venerable piece of furniture with a wooden shelf stood a ewer and basin and shaving apparatus. A pair of shoes stood in one corner; a night-table by the bed had neither a door nor marble slab. There was not a trace of a fire in the empty grate; the square walnut table with the cross-bar against which Father Goriot had crushed and twisted his posset-dish stood near the hearth. The old man's hat was lying on a broken-down bureau. An armchair stuffed with straw and a couple of chairs completed the list of ramshackle furniture. From the tester of the bed, tied to the ceiling by a piece of rag, hung a strip of some cheap material in large red and black checks. No poor drudge in a garret could be worse lodged than Father Goriot in Mme. Vauquer's lodging-house. The mere sight of the room sent a chill through you and a sense of oppression; it was like the worst cell in a prison. Luckily, Goriot could not see the effect that his surroundings produced on Eugène as the latter deposited his candle on the night-table. The old man turned round, keeping the bedclothes huddled up to his chin.

"Well," he said, "and which do you like the best, Mme. de Restaud or Mme. de Nucingen?"

"I like Mme. Delphine the best," said the law student, "because she loves you the best."

At the words so heartily spoken the old man's hand slipped out from under the bedclothes and grasped Eugène's.

"Thank you, thank you," he said, gratefully. "Then what did she say about me?"

The student repeated the Baroness' remarks with some embellishments of his own, the old man listening the while as though he heard a voice from Heaven.

"Dear child!" he said. "Yes, yes, she is very fond of me. But you must not believe all that she tells you about Anastasie. The two sisters are jealous of each other, you see, another proof of their affection. Mme. de Restaud is very fond of me too. I know she is. A father sees his children as God sees all of us; he looks into the very depths of their hearts; he knows their intentions; and both of them are so loving. Oh! if I only had good sons-in-law, I should be too happy, and I dare say there is no perfect happiness here below. If I might live with them—simply hear their voices, know that they are there, see them go and come as I used to do at home when they were still with me; why, my heart bounds at the thought. . . . Were they nicely dressed?"

"Yes," said Eugène. "But, M. Goriot, how is it that your daughters have such fine houses, while you live in such a den as this?"

"Dear me, why should I want anything better?" he replied, with seeming carelessness. "I can't quite explain to you how it is; I am not used to stringing words together properly, but it all lies there——" he said, tapping his heart. "My real life is in my two girls, you see; and so long as they are happy, and smartly dressed, and have soft carpets under their feet, what does it matter what clothes I wear or where I lie down of a night? I shall never feel cold so long as they are warm; I shall never feel dull if they are laughing. I have no troubles but theirs. When you, too, are a father, and you hear your children's little voices, you will say to yourself, 'That has all come from me.' You will feel that those little ones are akin to every drop in your veins, that they are the very flower of your life (and what else are they?); you will cleave so closely to them that you seem to feel every movement that they make. Everywhere I hear their voices sounding in my ears. If they are sad, the look in their eyes freezes my blood. Some day you will find out that there is far more happiness in another's happiness than in your own. It is something that I cannot explain, something within that sends a glow of warmth all through you. In short, I live my life three times over. Shall I tell you something funny? Well, then, since I have been a father, I have come to understand God. He is everywhere in the world, because the whole world comes from Him. And it is just the same with my children, monsieur. Only, I love my daughters better than God loves the world, for the world is not so beautiful as God Himself is, but my children are more beautiful than I am. Their lives are so bound up with mine that I felt somehow that you would see them this evening. Great Heaven! If any man would make my little Delphine as happy as a wife is when she is loved, I would black his boots and run on his errands. That miserable M. de Marsay is a cur; I know all about him from her maid. A longing to wring his neck comes over me now and then. He does not love her! does not love a pearl of a woman, with a voice like a nightingale and shaped like a model. Where can her eyes have been when she married that great lump of an Alsatian? They ought both of them to have married young men, good-looking and good-tempered—but, after all, they had their own way."

Father Goriot was sublime. Eugène had never yet seen his face light up as it did now with the passionate fervor of a father's love. It is worthy of remark that strong feeling has a very subtle and pervasive power; the roughest nature, in the endeavor to express a deep and sincere affection, communicates to others the influence that has put resonance into the voice, and eloquence into every gesture, wrought a change in the very features of the speaker; for under the inspiration of passion the stupidest human being attains to the highest eloquence of ideas, if not of language, and seems to move in some sphere of light. In the old man's tones and gesture there was something just then of the same spell that a great actor exerts over his audience. But does not the poet in us find expression in our affections?

"Well," said Eugène, "perhaps you will not be sorry to hear that she is pretty sure to break with de Marsay before long. That sprig of fashion has left her for the Princesse Gala-thionne. For my part, I fell in love with Mme. Delphine this evening."

"Stuff!" said Father Goriot.

"I did indeed, and she did not regard me with aversion. For a whole hour we talked of love, and I am to go to call on her on Saturday, the day after to-morrow."

"Oh! how I should love you, if she should like you. You are kind-hearted; you would never make her miserable. If you were to forsake her, I would cut your throat at once. A woman does not love twice, you see! Good heavens! what nonsense I am talking, M. Eugène! It is cold; you ought not to stay here. *Mon Dieu!* so you have heard her speak? What message did she give you for me?"

"None at all," said Eugène to himself; aloud he answered, "She told me to tell you that your daughter sends you a good kiss."

"Good-night, neighbor! Sleep well, and pleasant dreams to you! I have mine already made for me by that message from her. May God grant you all your desires! You have come in like a good angel on me to-night, and brought with you the air that my daughter breathes."

"Poor old fellow!" said Eugène as he lay down. "It is enough to melt a heart of stone. His daughter no more thought of him than of the Grand Turk."

Ever after this conference Goriot looked upon his neighbor as a friend, a confidant such as he had never hoped to find; and there was established between the two the only relation-ship that could attach this old man to another man. The passions never miscalculate. Father Goriot felt that this friendship brought him closer to his daughter Delphine; he thought that he should find a warmer welcome for himself if the Baroness should care for Eugène. Moreover, he had confided one of his troubles to the younger man. Mme. de Nucingen, for whose happiness he prayed a thousand times daily, had never known the joys of love. Eugène was certainly (to make use of his own expression) one of the nicest young men that he had ever seen, and some prophetic instinct seemed to tell him that Eugène was to give her the happiness which had not been hers. These were the beginnings of a friendship that grew up between the old man and his neighbor; but for this friendship the catastrophe of the drama must have remained a mystery.

The affection with which Father Goriot regarded Eugène, by whom he seated himself at breakfast, the change in Goriot's face, which, as a rule, looked as expressionless as a plaster cast, and a few words that passed between the two, surprised the other lodgers. Vautrin, who saw Eugène for the first time since their interview, seemed as if he would fain read the student's very soul. During the night Eugène had had some time in which to scan the vast field which lay before him; and now, as he remembered yesterday's proposal, the thought of Mlle. Taillefer's dowry came, of course, to his mind, and he could not help thinking of Victorine as the most exemplary youth may think of an heiress. It chanced that their eyes met. The poor girl did not fail to see that Eugène looked very handsome in his new clothes. So much was said in the glance, thus exchanged, that Eugène could not doubt but that he was associated in her mind with the vague hopes that lie dormant in a girl's heart and gather round the first attractive newcomer. "Eight hundred thousand francs!" a voice cried in his ears, but suddenly he took refuge in the memories of yesterday evening, thinking that his extemporized passion for Mme. de Nucingen was a talisman that would preserve him from this temptation.

"They gave Rossini's *Barber of Seville* at the Italiens yesterday evening," he remarked. "I never heard such delicious music. Good gracious! how lucky people are to have a box at the Italiens!"

Father Goriot drank in every word that Eugène let fall, and watched him as a dog watches his master's slightest movement.

"You men are like fighting cocks," said Mme. Vauquer; "you do what you like."

"How did you get back?" inquired Vautrin.

"I walked," answered Eugène.

"For my own part," remarked the tempter, "I do not care about doing things by halves. If I want to enjoy myself that way, I should prefer to go in my carriage, sit in my own box, and do the thing comfortably. Everything or nothing; that is my motto."

"And a good one, too," commented Mme. Vauquer.

"Perhaps you will see Mme. de Nucingen to-day," said Eugène, addressing Goriot in an undertone. "She will welcome you with open arms, I am sure; she would want to ask you for all sorts of little details about me. I have found out that she would do anything in the world to be known by my cousin Mme. de Beauséant; don't forget to tell her that I love her too well not to think of trying to arrange this."

Rastignac went at once to the École de Droit. He had no mind to stay a moment longer than was necessary in that odious house. He wasted his time that day; he had fallen a victim to that fever of the brain that accompanies the too vivid hopes of youth. Vautrin's arguments had set him meditating on social life, and he was deep in these reflections when he happened on his friend Bianchon in the Jardin du Luxembourg.

"What makes you look so solemn?" said the medical student, putting an arm through Eugène's as they went towards the Palais.

"I am tormented by temptations."

"What kind? There is a cure for temptation."

"What?"

"Yielding to it."

"You laugh, but you don't know what it is all about. Have you read Rousseau?"

"Yes."

"Do you remember that he asks the reader somewhere what he would do if he could make a fortune by killing an old mandarin somewhere in China by mere force of wishing it, and without stirring from Paris?"

"Yes."

"Well, then?"

"Pshaw! I am at my thirty-third mandarin."

"Seriously, though. Look here, suppose you were sure that you could do it, and had only to give a nod. Would you do it."

"Is he well stricken in years, this mandarin of yours? Pshaw! after all, young or old, paralytic, or well and sound, my word for it. . . . Well, then. Hang it, no!"

"You are a good fellow, Bianchon. But suppose you loved a woman well enough to lose your soul in hell for her, and that she wanted money, lots of money for dresses and a carriage, and all her whims, in fact?"

"Why, here you are taking away my reason, and want me to reason!"

"Well, then, Bianchon, I am mad; bring me to my senses. I have two sisters as beautiful and innocent as angels, and I want them to be happy. How am I to find two hundred thousand francs apiece for them in the next five years? Now and then in life, you see, you must play for heavy stakes, and it is no use wasting your luck on low play."

"But you are only stating the problem that lies before every one at the outset of his life, and you want to cut the Gordian knot with a sword. If that is the way of it, dear boy, you must be an Alexander, or to the hulks you go. For my own part, I am quite contented with the little lot I mean to make for myself somewhere in the country, when I mean to step into my father's shoes and plod along. A man's affections are just as fully satisfied by the smallest circle as they can be by a vast circumference. Napoleon himself could only dine once, and he could not have more mistresses than a house student at the Capuchins. Happiness, old man, depends on what lies between the sole of your foot and the crown of your head; and whether it costs a million or a hundred louis, the actual amount of pleasure that you receive rests entirely with you, and is just exactly the same in any case. I am for letting that Chinaman live."

"Thank you, Bianchon; you have done me good. We will always be friends."

"I say," remarked the medical student, as they came to the end of a broad walk in the Jardin des Plantes, "I saw the Michonneau and Poiret a few minutes ago on a bench chatting with a gentleman whom I used to see in last year's troubles hanging about the Chamber of Deputies; he seems to me, in fact, to be a detective dressed up like a decent retired tradesman. Let us keep an eye on that couple; I will tell you why some time. Good-bye; it is nearly four o'clock, and I must be in to answer to my name."

When Eugène reached the lodging-house, he found Father Goriot waiting for him.

"Here," cried the old man, "here is a letter from her. Pretty handwriting, eh?"

Eugène broke the seal and read:—

"SIR,—I have heard from my father that you are fond of Italian music. I shall be delighted if you will do me the pleasure of accepting a seat in my box. La Fodor and Pellegrini will sing on Saturday, so I am sure that you will not refuse me. M. de Nucingen and I shall be pleased if you will dine with us; we shall be quite by ourselves. If you will come and be my escort, my husband will be glad to be relieved from his conjugal duties. Do not answer, but simply come. —Yours sincerely, D. DE N."

"Let me see it," said Father Goriot, when Eugène had read the letter. "You are going, aren't you?" he added, when he had smelled the writing-paper. "How nice it smells! Her fingers have touched it, that is certain."

"A woman does not fling herself at a man's head in this

way," the student was thinking. "She wants to use me to bring back de Marsay; nothing but pique makes a woman do a thing like this."

"Well," said Father Goriot, "what are you thinking about?"

Eugène did not know the fever of vanity that possessed some women in those days; how should he imagine that to open a door in the Faubourg Saint-Germain a banker's wife would go to almost any length. For the coterie of the Faubourg Saint-Germain was a charmed circle, and the women who moved in it were at that time the queens of society; and among the greatest of these *Dames du Petit-Château,* as they were called, were Mme. de Beauséant and her friends the Duchesse de Langeais and the Duchesse de Maufrigneuse. Rastignac was alone in his ignorance of the frantic efforts made by women who lived in the Chaussée-d'Antin to enter this seventh heaven and shine among the brightest constellations of their sex. But his cautious disposition stood him in good stead, and kept his judgment cool, and the not altogether enviable power of imposing instead of accepting conditions.

"Yes, I am going," he replied.

So it was curiosity that drew him to Mme. de Nucingen; while, if she had treated him disdainfully, passion perhaps might have brought him to her feet. Still he waited almost impatiently for to-morrow, and the hour when he could go to her. There is almost as much charm for a young man in a first flirtation as there is in first love. The certainty of success is a source of happiness to which men do not confess, and all the charm of certain women lies in this. The desire of conquest springs no less from the easiness than from the difficulty of triumph, and every passion is excited or sustained by one or other of these two motives which divide the empire of love. Perhaps this division is one result of the great question of temperaments; which, after all, dominates social life. The melancholic temperament may stand in need of the tonic of coquetry, while those of nervous or sanguine complexion withdraw if they meet with a too stubborn resistance. In other words, the lymphatic temperament is essentially despondent, and the rhapsodic is bilious.

Eugène lingered over his toilette with an enjoyment of all its little details that is grateful to a young man's self-love, though he will not own to it for fear of being laughed at. He thought, as he arranged his hair, that a pretty woman's glances would wander through the dark curls. He indulged in childish tricks like any young girl dressing for a dance, and gazed complacently at his graceful figure while he smoothed out the creases of his coat.

"There are worse figures, that is certain," he said to himself.

Then he went downstairs, just as the rest of the household were sitting down to dinner, and took with good humor the boisterous applause excited by his elegant appearance. The amazement with which any attention to dress is regarded in a lodging-house is a very characteristic trait. No one can put on a new coat but every one else must say his say about it.

"Clk! clk! clk!" cried Bianchon, making the sound with his tongue against the roof of his mouth, like a driver urging on a horse.

"He holds himself like a duke and a peer of France," said Mme. Vauquer.

"Are you going a-courting?" inquired Mlle. Michonneau.

"Cock-a-doodle-doo!" cried the artist.

"My compliments to my lady your wife," from the employé at the Muséum.

"Your wife; have you a wife?" asked Poiret.

"Yes, in compartments, water-tight and floats, guaranteed fast color, all prices from twenty-five to forty sous, neat check patterns in the latest fashion and best taste, will wash, half-linen, half-cotton, half-wool; a certain cure for toothache and other complaints under the patronage of the Royal College of Physicians! children like it! a remedy for headache, indigestion, and all other diseases affecting the throat, eyes, and ears!" cried Vautrin, with a comical imitation of the volubility of a quack at a fair. "And how much shall we say for this marvel, gentlemen? Twopence? No. Nothing of the sort. All that is left in stock after supplying the Great Mogul. All the crowned heads of Europe, including the Gr-r-rand Duke of Baden, have been anxious to get a sight of it. Walk up! walk up! gentlemen! Pay at the desk as you go in! Strike up the music there! Brooum, la, la, trinn! la, la, boum! boum! Mister Clarinette, there you are out of tune!" he added gruffly; "I will rap your knuckles for you!"

"Goodness! what an amusing man!" said Mme. Vauquer to Mme. Couture; "I should never feel dull with him in the house."

This burlesque of Vautrin's was the signal for an outburst of merriment, and under cover of jokes and laughter Eugène caught a glance from Mlle. Taillefer; she had leaned over to say a few words in Mme. Couture's ear.

"The cab is at the door," announced Sylvie.

"But where is he going to dine?" asked Bianchon.

"With Madame la Baronne de Nucingen."

"M. Goriot's daughter," said the law student.

At this, all eyes turned to the old vermicelli maker; he was gazing at Eugène with something like envy in his eyes.

Rastignac reached the house in the Rue Saint-Lazare, one of those many-windowed houses with a mean-looking portico and slender columns, which are considered the thing in Paris, a typical banker's house, decorated in the most ostentatious fashion; the walls lined with stucco, the landings of marble mosaic. Mme. de Nucingen was sitting in a little drawing-room; the room was painted in the Italian fashion, and decorated like a restaurant. The Baroness seemed depressed. The effort that she made to hide her feelings aroused Eugène's interest; it was plain that she was not playing a part. He had expected a little flutter of excitement at his coming, and he found her dispirited and sad. The disappointment piqued his vanity.

"My claim to your confidence is very small, madame," he said, after rallying her on her abstracted mood; "but if I am in the way, please tell me so frankly; I count on your good faith."

"No, stay with me," she said; "I shall be all alone if you go. Nucingen is dining in town, and I do not want to be alone; I want to be taken out of myself."

"But what is the matter?"

"You are the very last person whom I should tell," she exclaimed.

"Then I am connected in some way in this secret. I wonder what it is?"

"Perhaps. Yet, no," she went on; "it is a domestic quarrel, which ought to be buried in the depths of the heart. I am very unhappy; did I not tell you so the day before yesterday? Golden chains are the heaviest of all fetters."

When a woman tells a young man that she is very unhappy, and when the young man is clever, and well dressed, and has fifteen hundred francs lying idle in his pocket, he is sure to think as Eugène said, and he becomes a coxcomb.

"What can you have left to wish for?" he answered. "You are young, beautiful, beloved, and rich."

"Do not let us talk of my affairs," she said, shaking her head mournfully. "We will dine together *tête-à-tête,* and afterwards we will go to hear the most exquisite music. Am I to your taste?" she went on, rising and displaying her gown of white cashmere, covered with Persian designs in the most superb taste.

"I wish that you were altogether mine," said Eugène; "you are charming."

"You would have a forlorn piece of property," she said, smiling bitterly. "There is nothing about me that betrays my wretchedness; and yet, in spite of appearances, I am in despair. I cannot sleep; my troubles have broken my night's rest; I shall grow ugly."

"Oh! that is impossible," cried the law student; "but I am curious to know what these troubles can be that a devoted love cannot efface."

"Ah! if I were to tell you about them, you would shun me,"

"Am I to your taste?"

she said. "Your love for me as yet is only the conventional gallantry that men use to masquerade in; and, if you really loved me, you would be driven to despair. I must keep silence, you see. Let us talk of something else, for pity's sake," she added. "Let me show you my rooms."

"No; let us stay here," answered Eugène; he sat down on the sofa before the fire, and boldly took Mme. de Nucingen's hand in his. She surrendered it to him; he even felt the pressure of her fingers in one of the spasmodic clutches that betray terrible agitation.

"Listen," said Rastignac; "if you are in trouble, you ought to tell me about it. I want to prove to you that I love you for yourself alone. You must speak to me frankly about your troubles, so that I can put an end to them, even if I have to kill half-a-dozen men; or I shall go, never to return."

"Very well," she cried, putting her hand to her forehead in an agony of despair, "I will put you to the proof, and this very moment. Yes," she said to herself, "I have no other resource left."

She rang the bell.

"Are the horses put in for the master?" she asked of the servant.

"Yes, madame."

"I shall take his carriage myself. He can have mine and my horses. Serve dinner at seven o'clock."

"Now, come with me," she said to Eugène, who thought as he sat in the banker's carriage beside Mme. de Nucingen that he must surely be dreaming.

"To the Palais-Royal," she said to the coachman; "stop near the Théâtre-Français."

She seemed to be too troubled and excited to answer the innumerable questions that Eugène put to her. He was at a loss what to think of her mute resistance, her obstinate silence.

"Another moment and she will escape me." he said to himself.

When the carriage stopped at last, the Baroness gave the

law student a glance that silenced his wild words, for he was almost beside himself.

"Is it true that you love me?" she asked.

"Yes," he answered, and in his manner and tone there was no trace of the uneasiness that he felt.

"You will not think ill of me, will you, whatever I may ask of you?"

"No."

"Are you ready to do my bidding?"

"Blindly."

"Have you ever been to a gaming-house?" she asked in a tremulous voice.

"Never."

"Ah! now I can breathe. You will have luck. Here is my purse," she said. "Take it! there are a hundred francs in it, all that such a fortunate woman as I can call her own. Go up into one of the gaming-houses—I do not know where they are, but there are some near the Palais-Royal. Try your luck with the hundred francs at a game they call roulette; lose it all, or bring me back six thousand francs. I will tell you about my troubles when you come back."

"Devil take me, I'm sure, if I have a glimmer of a notion of what I am about, but I will obey you," he added, with inward exultation, as he thought, "She has gone too far to draw back—she can refuse me nothing now!"

Eugène took the dainty little purse, inquired the way of a second-hand clothes-dealer, and hurried to number 9, which happened to be the nearest gaming-house. He mounted the staircase, surrendered his hat, and asked the way to the roulette-table, whither the attendant took him, not a little to the astonishment of the regular comers. All eyes were fixed on Eugène as he asked, without bashfulness, where he was to deposit his stakes.

"If you put a louis on one only of those thirty-six numbers, and it turns up, you will win thirty-six louis," said a respectable-looking, white-haired old man in answer to his inquiry.

Eugène staked the whole of his money on the number 21 (his own age). There was a cry of surprise; before he knew what he had done, he had won.

"Take your money off, sir," said the old gentleman; "you don't often win twice running by that system."

Eugène took the rake that the old man handed to him, and drew in his three thousand six hundred francs, and, still perfectly ignorant of what he was about, staked again on the red. The bystanders watched him enviously as they saw him continue to play. The disc turned, and again he won; the banker threw him three thousand six hundred francs once more.

"You have seven thousand two hundred francs of your own," the old gentleman said in his ear. "Take my advice and go away with your winnings; red has turned up eight times already. If you are charitable, you will show your gratitude for sound counsel by giving a trifle to an old prefect of Napoleon who is down on his luck."

Rastignac's head was swimming; he saw ten of his louis pass into the white-haired man's possession, and went downstairs with his seven thousand francs; he was still ignorant of the game, and stupefied by his luck.

"So that is over; and now where will you take me?" he asked, as soon as the door was closed, and he showed the seven thousand francs to Mme. de Nucingen.

Delphine flung her arms about him, but there was no passion in that wild embrace.

"You have saved me!" she cried, and tears of joy flowed fast.

"I will tell you everything, my friend. For you will be my friend, will you not? I am rich, you think, very rich; I have everything I want, or I seem as if I had everything. Very well, you must know that M. de Nucingen does not allow me the control of a single penny; he pays all the bills for the house expenses; he pays for my carriages and opera box; he does not give me enough to pay for my dress, and he reduces me to poverty in secret on purpose. I am too

proud to beg from him. I should be the vilest of women if
I could take his money at the price at which he offers it. Do
you ask how I, with seven hundred thousand francs of my
own, could let myself be robbed? It is because I was proud,
and scorned to speak. We are so young, so artless when our
married life begins! I never could bring myself to ask my
husband for money; the words would have made my lips
bleed, I did not dare to ask; I spent my savings first, and
then the money that my poor father gave me, then I ran into
debt. Marriage for me is a hideous farce; I cannot talk about
it; let it suffice to say that Nucingen and I have separate
rooms, and that I would fling myself out of the window
sooner than consent to any other manner of life. I suffered
agonies when I had to confess to my girlish extravagance, my
debts for jewelry and trifles (for our poor father had never
refused us anything, and spoiled us), but at last I found
courage to tell him about them. After all, I had a fortune
of my own. Nucingen flew into a rage; he said that I should
be the ruin of him, and used frightful language! I wished
myself a hundred feet down in the earth. He had my dowry,
so he paid my debts, but he stipulated at the same time that
my expenses in future must not exceed a certain fixed sum,
and I gave way for the sake of peace. And then," she went
on, "I wanted to gratify the self-love of some one whom you
know. He may have deceived me, but I should do him the
justice to say that there was nothing petty in his character.
But, after all, he threw me over disgracefully. If, at a
woman's utmost need, *somebody* heaps gold upon her, he
ought never to forsake her; that love should last for ever!
But you, at one-and-twenty, you, the soul of honor, with the
unsullied conscience of youth, will ask me how a woman can
bring herself to accept money in such a way? *Mon Dieu!*
is it not natural to share everything with the one to whom
we owe our happiness? When all has been given, why should
we pause and hesitate over a part? Money is as nothing between us until the moment when the sentiment that bound us
together ceases to exist. Were we not bound to each other for

life? Who that believes in love foresees such an end to love?
You swear to love us eternally; how, then, can our interests
be separate?

"You do not know how I suffered to-day when Nucingen
refused to give me six thousand francs; he spends as much as
that every month on his mistress, an opera dancer! I thought
of killing myself. The wildest thoughts came into my head.
There have been moments in my life when I have envied my
servants, and would have changed places with my maid. It
was madness to think of going to our father, Anastasie and
I have bled him dry; our poor father would have sold himself
if he could have raised six thousand francs that way. I
should have driven him frantic to no purpose. You have
saved me from shame and death; I was beside myself
with anguish. Ah! monsieur, I owed you this explanation
after my mad ravings. When you left me just now, as
soon as you were out of sight, I longed to escape, to run
away . . . where, I did not know. Half the women in
Paris lead such lives as mine; they live in apparent luxury,
and in their souls are tormented by anxiety. I know of poor
creatures even more miserable than I; there are women who
are driven to ask their tradespeople to make out false bills,
women who rob their husbands. Some men believe that an
Indian shawl worth a hundred louis only cost five hundred
francs, others that a shawl costing five hundred francs is
worth a hundred louis. There are women, too, with narrow
incomes, who scrape and save and starve their children to
pay for a dress. I am innocent of these base meannesses.
But this is the last extremity of my torture. Some women
will sell themselves to their husbands, and so obtain their
way, but I, at any rate, am free. If I chose, Nucingen would
cover me with gold, but I would rather weep on the breast
of a man whom I can respect. Ah! to-night, M. de Marsay
will no longer have a right to think of me as a woman whom
he has paid." She tried to conceal her tears from him, hiding her face in her hands; Eugène drew them away and
looked at her; she seemed to him sublime at that moment.

"It is hideous, is it not," she cried, "to speak in a breath of money and affection. You cannot love me after this," she added.

The incongruity between the ideas of honor which make women so great, and the errors in conduct which are forced upon them by the constitution of society, had thrown Eugène's thoughts into confusion; he uttered soothing and consoling words, and wondered at the beautiful woman before him, and at the artless imprudence of her cry of pain.

"You will not remember this against me?" she asked; "promise me that you will not."

"Ah! madame, I am incapable of doing so," he said, She took his hand and held it to her heart, a movement full of grace that expressed her deep gratitude.

"I am free and happy once more, thanks to you," she said. "Oh! I have felt lately as if I were in the grasp of an iron hand. But after this I mean to live simply and to spend nothing. You will think me just as pretty, will you not, my friend? Keep this," she went on, as she took only six of the banknotes. "In conscience I owe you a thousand crowns, for I really ought to go halves with you."

Eugène's maiden conscience resisted; but when the Baroness said, "I am bound to look on you as an accomplice or as an enemy," he took the money.

"It shall be a last stake in reserve," he said, "in case of misfortune."

"That was what I was dreading to hear," she cried, turning pale. "Oh, if you would that I should be anything to you, swear to me that you will never re-enter a gaming-house. Great heaven! that I should corrupt you! I should die of sorrow!"

They had reached the Rue Saint-Lazare by this time. The contrast between the ostentation of wealth in the house, and the wretched condition of its mistress, dazed the student; and Vautrin's cynical words began to ring in his ears.

"Seat yourself there," said the Baroness, pointing to a low chair beside the fire. "I have a difficult letter to write," she added. "Tell me what to say."

"Say nothing," Eugène answered her. "Put the bills in an envelope, direct it, and send it by your maid."

"Why, you are a love of a man," she said. "Ah! see what it is to have been well brought up. That is the Beauséant through and through," she went on, smiling at him.

"She is charming," thought Eugène, more and more in love. He looked round him at the room; there was an ostentatious character about the luxury, a meretricious taste in the splendor.

"Do you like it?" she asked, as she rang for the maid.

"Thérèse, take this to M. de Marsay, and give it into his hands yourself. If he is not at home, bring the letter back to me."

Thérèse went, but not before she had given Eugène a spiteful glance.

Dinner was announced. Rastignac gave his arm to Mme. de Nucingen, she led the way into a pretty dining-room, and again he saw the luxury of the table which he had admired in his cousin's house.

"Come and dine with me on opera evenings, and we will go to the Italiens afterwards," she said.

"I should soon grow used to the pleasant life if it could last, but I am a poor student, and I have my way to make."

"Oh! you will succeed," she said, laughing. "You will see. All that you wish will come to pass. *I* did not expect to be so happy."

It is the wont of women to prove the impossible by the possible, and to annihilate facts by presentiments. When Mme. de Nucingen and Rastignac took their places in her box at the Bouffons, her face wore a look of happiness that made her so lovely that every one indulged in those small slanders against which women are defenceless; for the scandal that is uttered lightly is often seriously believed. Those who know Paris, believe nothing that is said, and say nothing of what is done there.

Eugène took the Baroness' hand in his, and by some light pressure of the fingers, or a closer grasp of the hand, they found a language in which to express the sensations which the music gave them. It was an evening of intoxicating delight for both; and when it ended, and they went out together, Mme. de Nucingen insisted on taking Eugène with her as far as the Pont Neuf, he disputing with her the whole of the way for a single kiss after all those that she had showered upon him so passionately at the Palais-Royal; Eugène reproached her with inconsistency.

"That was gratitude," she said, "for devotion that I did not dare to hope for, but now it would be a promise."

"And will you give me no promise, ingrate?"

He grew vexed. Then, with one of those impatient gestures that fill a lover with ecstasy, she gave him her hand to kiss, and he took it with a discontented air that delighted her.

"I shall see you at the ball on Monday," she said.

As Eugène went home in the moonlight, he fell to serious reflections. He was satisfied, and yet dissatisfied. He was pleased with an adventure which would probably give him his desire, for in the end one of the prettiest and best-dressed women in Paris would be his; but, as a set-off, he saw his hopes of fortune brought to nothing; and as soon as he realized this fact, the vague thoughts of yesterday evening began to take a more decided shape in his mind. A check is sure to reveal to us the strength of our hopes. The more Eugène learned of the pleasures of life in Paris, the more impatient he felt of poverty and obscurity. He crumpled the banknote in his pocket, and found any quantity of plausible excuses for appropriating it.

He reached the Rue Neuve-Sainte-Geneviève at last, and from the stairhead he saw a light in Goriot's room; the old man had lighted a candle, and set the door ajar, lest the student should pass him by, and go to his room without "telling him all about his daughter," to use his own expression. Eugène, accordingly, told him everything without reserve.

"Then they think that I am ruined!" cried Father Goriot, in an agony of jealousy and desperation. "Why, I have still

thirteen hundred livres a year! *Mon Dieu!* Poor little
girl! why did she not come to me? I would have sold my
rentes; she should have had some of the principal, and I
would have bought a life-annuity with the rest. My good
neighbor, why did not *you* come to tell me of her difficulty?
How had you the heart to go and risk her poor little hundred
francs at play? This is heart-breaking work. You see what
it is to have sons-in-law. Oh! if I had hold of them, I would
wring their necks. *Mon Dieu! crying!* Did you say she was
crying?"

"With her head on my waistcoat," said Eugène.

"Oh! give it to me," said Father Goriot. "What! my daughter's tears have fallen there—my darling Delphine, who never
used to cry when she was a little girl! Oh! I will buy you
another; do not wear it again; let me have it. By the terms
of her marriage-contract, she ought to have the use of her
property. To-morrow morning I will go and see Derville;
he is an attorney. I will demand that her money should be
invested in her own name. I know the law. I am an old
wolf; I will show my teeth."

"Here, father; this is a banknote for a thousand francs
that she wanted me to keep out of our winnings. Keep them
for her, in the pocket of the waistcoat."

Goriot looked hard at Eugène, reached out and took the
law student's hand, and Eugène felt a tear fall on it.

"You will succeed," the old man said. "God is just, you
see. I know an honest man when I see him, and I can tell you,
there are not many men like you. I am to have another dear
child in you, am I? There, go to sleep; you can sleep; you are
not yet a father. She was crying! and I have to be told about
it!—and I was quietly eating my dinner, like an idiot, all
the time—I, who would sell the Father, Son, and Holy Ghost
to save one tear to either of them."

"An honest man!" said Eugène to himself as he lay down.
"Upon my word, I think I will be an honest man all my life;
it is so pleasant to obey the voice of conscience." Perhaps

none but believers in God do good in secret; and Eugène believed in a God.

The next day Rastignac went at the appointed time to Mme. de Beauséant, who took him with her to the Duchesse de Carigliano's ball. The Maréchale received Eugène most graciously. Mme. de Nucingen was there. Delphine's dress seemed to suggest that she wished for the admiration of others, so that she might shine the more in Eugène's eyes; she was eagerly expecting a glance from him, hiding, as she thought, this eagerness from all beholders. This moment is full of charm for the one who can guess all that passes in a woman's mind. Who has not refrained from giving his opinion, to prolong her suspense, concealing his pleasure from a desire to tantalize, seeking a confession of love in her uneasiness, enjoying the fears that he can dissipate by a smile? In the course of the evening the law student suddenly comprehended his position; he saw that, as the cousin of Mme. de Beauséant, he was a personage in this world. He was already credited with the conquest of Mme. de Nucingen, and for this reason was a conspicuous figure; he caught the envious glances of other young men, and experienced the earliest pleasures of coxcombry. People wondered at his luck, and scraps of these conversations came to his ears as he went from room to room; all the women prophesied his success; and Delphine, in her dread of losing him, promised that this evening she would not refuse the kiss that all his entreaties could scarcely win yesterday.

Rastignac received several invitations. His cousin presented him to other women who were present; women who could claim to be of the highest fashion; whose houses were looked upon as pleasant; and this was the loftiest and most fashionable society in Paris into which he was launched. So this evening had all the charm of a brilliant *début;* it was an evening that he was to remember even in old age, as a woman looks back upon her first ball and the memories of her girlish triumphs.

The next morning, at breakfast, he related the story of his

success for the benefit of Father Goriot and the lodgers. Vautrin began to smile in a diabolical fashion.

"And do you suppose," cried that cold-blooded logician, "that a young man of fashion can live here in the Rue Neuve-Sainte-Geneviève, in the Maison Vauquer—an exceedingly respectable boarding-house in every way, I grant you, but an establishment that, none the less, falls short of being fashionable? The house is comfortable, it is lordly in its abundance; it is proud to be the temporary abode of a Rastignac; but, after all, it is in the Rue Neuve-Sainte-Geneviève, and luxury would be out of place here, where we only aim at the purely *patriarchalorama*. If you mean to cut a figure in Paris, my young friend," Vautrin continued, with half-paternal jocularity, "you must have three horses, a tilbury for the mornings, and a closed carriage for the evening; you should spend altogether about nine thousand francs on your stables. You would show yourself unworthy of your destiny if you spent no more than three thousand francs with your tailor, six hundred in perfumery, a hundred crowns to your shoemaker, and a hundred more to your hatter. As for your laundress, there goes another thousand francs; a young man of fashion must of necessity make a great point of his linen; if your linen comes up to the required standard, people often do not look any further. Love and the Church demand a fair altar-cloth. That is fourteen thousand francs. I am saying nothing of losses at play, bets, and presents; it is impossible to allow less than two thousand francs for pocket money. I have led that sort of life, and I know all about these expenses. Add the cost of necessaries next; three hundred louis for provender, a thousand francs for a place to roost in. Well, my boy, for all these little wants of ours we had need to have twenty-five thousand francs every year in our purse, or we shall find ourselves in the kennel, and people laughing at us, and our career is cut short, good-bye to success, and good-bye to your mistress! I am forgetting your valet and your groom! Is Christophe going to carry your *billets-doux* for you? And do you mean to employ the stationery you use

at present? Suicidal policy! Hearken to the wisdom of
your elders!" he went on, his bass voice growing louder at
each syllable. "Either take up your quarters in a garret,
live virtuously, and wed your work, or set about the thing in
a different way."

Vautrin winked and leered in the direction of Mlle. Taillefer to enforce his remarks by a look which recalled the late
tempting proposals by which he had sought to corrupt the
student's mind.

Several days went by, and Rastignac lived in a whirl of
gaiety. He dined almost every day with Mme. de Nucingen,
and went wherever she went, only returning to the Rue
Neuve-Sainte-Geneviève in the small hours. He rose at mid-
day, and dressed to go into the Bois with Delphine if the day
was fine, squandering in this way time that was worth far
more than he knew. He turned as eagerly to learn the lessons of luxury, and was as quick to feel its fascination, as
the flowers of the date palm to receive the fertilizing pollen.
He played high, lost and won large sums of money, and at
last became accustomed to the extravagant life that young
men lead in Paris. He sent fifteen hundred francs out of
his first winnings to his mother and sisters, sending handsome presents as well as the money. He had given out that
he meant to leave the Maison Vauquer; but January came
and went, and he was still there, still unprepared to go.

One rule holds good of most young men—whether rich
or poor. They never have money for the necessaries of life,
but they have always money to spare for their caprices—an
anomaly which finds its explanation in their youth and in the
almost frantic eagerness with which youth grasps at pleasure. They are reckless with anything obtained on credit,
while everything for which they must pay in ready money
is made to last as long as possible; if they cannot have all
that they want, they make up for it, it would seem, by squandering what they have. To state the matter simply—a student is far more careful of his hat than of his coat, because
the latter being a comparatively costly article of dress, it is in

the nature of things that a tailor should be a creditor; but it is otherwise with the hatter; the sums of money spent with him are so modest, that he is the most independent and unmanageable of his tribe, and it is almost impossible to bring him to terms. The young man in the balcony of a theatre who displays a gorgeous waistcoat for the benefit of the fair owners of opera glasses, has very probably no socks in his wardrobe, for the hosier is another of the genus of weevils that nibble at the purse. This was Rastignac's condition. His purse was always empty for Mme. Vauquer, always full at the demand of vanity; there was a periodical ebb and flow in his fortunes, which was seldom favorable to the payment of just debts. If he was to leave that unsavory and mean abode, where from time to time his pretensions met with humiliation, the first step was to pay his hostess for a month's board and lodging, and the second to purchase furniture worthy of the new lodgings he must take in his quality of dandy, a course that remained impossible. Rastignac, out of his winnings at cards, would pay his jeweler exorbitant prices for gold watches and chains, and then, to meet the exigencies of play, would carry them to the pawnbroker, that discreet and forbidding-looking friend of youth; but when it was a question of paying for board or lodging, or for the necessary implements for the cultivation of his Elysian fields, his imagination and pluck alike deserted him. There was no inspiration to be found in vulgar necessity, in debts contracted for past requirements. Like most of those who trust to their luck, he put off till the last moment the payment of debts that among the bourgeoisie are regarded as sacred engagements, acting on the plan of Mirabeau, who never settled his baker's bill until it underwent a formidable transformation into a bill of exchange.

It was about this time when Rastignac was down on his luck and fell into debt, that it became clear to the law student's mind that he must have some more certain source of income if he meant to live as he had been doing. But while he groaned over the thorny problems of his precarious situation, he felt that he could not bring himself to renounce the pleasures of this extravagant life, and decided that he must continue it at all costs. His dreams of obtaining a fortune appeared more and more chimerical, and the real obstacles grew more formidable. His initiation into the secrets of the Nucingen household had revealed to him that if he were to attempt to use this love affair as a means of mending his fortunes, he must swallow down all sense of decency, and renounce all the generous ideas which redeem the sins of youth. He had chosen this life of apparent splendor, but secretly gnawed by the canker worm of remorse, a life of fleeting pleasure dearly paid for by persistent pain; like *Le Distrait* of La Bruyère, he had descended so far as to make his bed in a ditch; but (also like *Le Distrait*) he himself was uncontaminated as yet by the mire that stained his garments.

"So we have killed our mandarin, have we?" said Bianchon one day as they left the dinner table.

"Not yet," he answered, "but he is at the last gasp."

The medical student took this for a joke, but it was not a jest. Eugène had dined in the house that night for the first time for a long while, and had looked thoughtful during the meal. He had taken his place beside Mlle. Taillefer, and stayed through the dessert, giving his neighbor an expressive glance from time to time. A few of the boarders discussed the walnuts at the table, and others walked about the room, still taking part in a conversation which had begun among them. People usually went when they chose; the amount of time that they lingered being determined by the amount of interest that the conversation possessed for them, or by the difficulty of the process of digestion. In winter-time the room was seldom empty before eight o'clock, when the four women had it all to themselves, and made up for the silence previously imposed upon them by the preponderating masculine element. This evening Vautrin had noticed Eugène's abstractedness, and stayed in the room, though he had seemed to be in a hurry to finish his dinner and go. All through

the talk afterwards he had kept out of the sight of the law
student, who quite believed that Vautrin had left the room.
He now took up his position cunningly in the sitting-room
instead of going when the last boarders went. He had
fathomed the young man's thoughts, and felt that a crisis was
at hand. Rastignac was, in fact, in a dilemma, which many
another young man must have known.

Mme. de Nucingen might love him, or might merely be
playing with him, but in either case Rastignac had been made
to experience all the alternations of hope and despair of
genuine passion, and all the diplomatic arts of a Parisienne
had been employed on him. After compromising herself by
continually appearing in public with Mme. de Beauséant's
cousin she still hesitated, and would not give him the lover's
privileges which he appeared to enjoy. For a whole month
she had so wrought on his senses, that at last she had made an
impression on his heart. If in the earliest days the student
had fancied himself to be master, Mme. de Nucingen had
since become the stronger of the two, for she had skilfully
roused and played upon every instinct, good or bad, in the
two or three men comprised in a young student in Paris.
This was not the result of deep design on her part, nor was
she playing a part, for women are in a manner true to themselves even through their grossest deceit, because their actions
are prompted by a natural impulse. It may have been that
Delphine, who had allowed this young man to gain such an
ascendency over her, conscious that she had been too demonstrative, was obeying a sentiment of dignity, and either repented of her concessions, or it pleased her to suspend them.
It is so natural to a Parisienne, even when passion has almost
mastered her, to hesitate and pause before taking the plunge;
to probe the heart of him to whom she intrusts her future.
And once already Mme. de Nucingen's hopes had been betrayed, and her loyalty to a selfish young lover had been despised. She had good reason to be suspicious. Or it may
have been that something in Eugène's manner (for his rapid
success was making a coxcomb of him) had warned her that

the grotesque nature of their position had lowered her somewhat in his eyes. She doubtless wished to assert her dignity;
he was young, and she would be great in his eyes; for the
lover who had forsaken her had held her so cheap that she
was determined that Eugène should not think her an easy
conquest, and for this very reason—he knew that de Marsay
had been his predecessor. Finally, after the degradation
of submission to the pleasure of a heartless young rake, it
was so sweet to her to wander in the flower-strewn realms
of love, that it was not wonderful that she should wish to
dwell a while on the prospect, to tremble with the vibrations
of love, to feel the freshness of the breath of its dawn. The
true lover was suffering for the sins of the false. This inconsistency is unfortunately only to be expected so long as
men do not know how many flowers are mown down in a
young woman's soul by the first stroke of treachery.

Whatever her reasons may have been, Delphine was playing with Rastignac, and took pleasure in playing with him,
doubtless because she felt sure of his love, and confident that
she could put an end to the torture as soon as it was her
royal pleasure to do so. Eugène's self-love was engaged; he
could not suffer his first passage of love to end in a defeat,
and persisted in his suit like a sportsman determined to
bring down at least one partridge to celebrate his first Feast
of Saint-Hubert. The pressure of anxiety, his wounded self-
love, his despair, real or feigned, drew him nearer and
nearer to this woman. All Paris credited him with this conquest, and yet he was conscious that he had made no progress
since the day when he saw Mme. de Nucingen for the first
time. He did not know as yet that a woman's coquetry is
sometimes more delightful than the pleasure of secure possession of her love, and was possessed with helpless rage. If, at
this time, while she denied herself to love, Eugène gathered
the springtide spoils of his life, the fruit, somewhat sharp
and green, and dearly bought, was no less delicious to the
taste. There were moments when he had not a *sou* in his
pockets, and at such times he thought in spite of his con-

science of Vautrin's offer and the possibility of fortune by a marriage with Mlle. Taillefer. Poverty would clamor so loudly that more than once he was on the point of yielding to the cunning temptations of the terrible sphinx, whose glance had so often exerted a strange spell over him.

Poiret and Mlle. Michonneau went up to their rooms; and Rastignac, thinking that he was alone with the women in the dining-room, sat between Mme. Vauquer and Mme. Couture, who was nodding over the woolen cuffs that she was knitting by the stove, and looked at Mlle. Taillefer so tenderly that she lowered her eyes.

"Can you be in trouble, M. Eugène?" Victorine said after a pause.

"Who has not his troubles?" answered Rastignac. "If we men were sure of being loved, sure of a devotion which would be our reward for the sacrifices which we are always ready to make, then perhaps we should have no troubles."

For answer Mlle. Taillefer only gave him a glance, but it was impossible to mistake its meaning.

"You, for instance, mademoiselle; you feel sure of your heart to-day, but are you sure that it will never change?"

A smile flitted over the poor girl's lips; it seemed as if a ray of light from her soul had lighted up her face. Eugène was dismayed at the sudden explosion of feeling caused by his words.

"Ah! but suppose," he said, "that you should be rich and happy to-morrow, suppose that a vast fortune dropped down from the clouds for you, would you still love the man whom you loved in your days of poverty?"

A charming movement of the head was her only answer.

"Even if he were very poor?"

Again the same mute answer.

"What nonsense are you talking, you two?" exclaimed Mme. Vauquer.

"Never mind," answered Eugène; "we understand each other."

"So there is to be an engagement of marriage between

M. le Chevalier Eugène de Rastignac and Mlle. Victorine
Taillefer, is there?" The words were uttered in Vautrin's
deep voice, and Vautrin appeared at the door as he spoke.

"Oh! how you startled me!" Mme. Couture and Mme. Vauquer exclaimed together.

"I might make a worse choice," said Rastignac, laughing.
Vautrin's voice had thrown him into the most painful agitation that he had yet known.

"No bad jokes, gentlemen!" said Mme. Couture. "My
dear, let us go upstairs."

Mme. Vauquer followed the two ladies, meaning to pass
the evening in their room, an arrangement that economized
fire and candlelight. Eugène and Vautrin were left alone.

"I felt sure you would come round to it," said the elder
man with the coolness that nothing seemed to shake. "But
stay a moment! I have as much delicacy as anybody else.
Don't make up your mind on the spur of the moment; you
are a little thrown off your balance just now. You are in debt,
and I want you to come over to my way of thinking after
sober reflection, and not in a fit of passion or desperation.
Perhaps you want a thousand crowns. There, you can have
them if you like."

The tempter took out a pocketbook, and drew thence three
banknotes, which he fluttered before the student's eyes. Eugène was in a most painful dilemma. He had debts, debts of
honor. He owed a hundred louis to the Marquis d'Ajuda
and to the Count de Trailles; he had not the money, and for
this reason had not dared to go to Mme. de Restaud's house,
where he was expected that evening. It was one of those informal gatherings where tea and little cakes are handed
round, but where it is possible to lose six thousand francs at
whist in the course of a night.

"You must see," said Eugène, struggling to hide a convulsive tremor, "that after what has passed between us, I
cannot possibly lay myself under any obligation to you."

"Quite right; I should be sorry to hear you speak otherwise," answered the tempter. "You are a fine young fellow,

honorable, brave as a lion, and as gentle as a young girl. You would be a fine haul for the devil! I like youngsters of your sort. Get rid of one or two more prejudices, and you will see the world as it is. Make a little scene now and then, and act a virtuous part in it, and a man with a head on his shoulders can do exactly as he likes amid deafening applause from the fools in the gallery. Ah! a few days yet, and you will be with us; and if you would only be tutored by me, I would put you in the way of achieving all your ambitions. You should no sooner form a wish than it should be realized to the full; you should have all your desires—honors, wealth, or women. Civilization should flow with milk and honey for you. You should be our pet and favorite, our Benjamin. We would all work ourselves to death for you with pleasure; every obstacle should be removed from your path. You have a few prejudices left; so you think that I am a scoundrel, do you? Well, M. de Turenne, quite as honorable a man as you take yourself to be, had some little private transactions with bandits, and did not feel that his honor was tarnished. You would rather not lie under any obligation to me, eh? You need not draw back on that account," Vautrin went on, and a smile stole over his lips. "Take those bits of paper and write across this," he added, producing a piece of stamped paper, *"Accepted the sum of three thousand five hundred francs due this day twelvemonth,* and fill in the date. The rate of interest is stiff enough to silence any scruples on your part; it gives you the right to call me a Jew. You can call quits with me on the score of gratitude. I am quite willing that you should despise me to-day, because I am sure that you will have a kindlier feeling towards me later on. You will find out fathomless depths in my nature, enormous and concentrated forces that weaklings call vices, but you will never find me base or ungrateful. In short, I am neither a pawn nor a bishop, but a castle, a tower of strength, my boy."

"What manner of man are you?" cried Eugène. "Were you created to torment me?"

"Why, no; I am a good-natured fellow, who is willing to do a dirty piece of work to put you high and dry above the mire for the rest of your days. Do you ask the reason of this devotion? All right; I will tell you that some of these days. A word or two in your ear will explain it. I have begun by shocking you, by showing you the way to ring the changes, and giving you a sight of the mechanism of the social machine; but your first fright will go off like a conscript's terror on the battlefield. You will grow used to regarding men as common soldiers who have made up their minds to lose their lives for some self-constituted king. Times have altered strangely. Once you could say to a bravo, 'Here are a hundred crowns; go and kill Monsieur So-and-so for me,' and you could sup quietly after turning some one off into the dark for the least thing in the world. But nowadays I propose to put you in the way of a handsome fortune; you have only to nod your head, it won't compromise you in any way, and you hesitate. 'Tis an effeminate age."

Eugène accepted the draft, and received the banknotes in exchange for it.

"Well, well. Come, now, let us talk rationally," Vautrin continued. "I mean to leave this country in a few months' time for America, and set about planting tobacco. I will send you the cigars of friendship. If I make money at it, I will help you in your career. If I have no children—which will probably be the case, for I have no anxiety to raise slips of myself here—you shall inherit my fortune. That is what you may call standing by a man; but I myself have a liking for you. I have a mania, too, for devoting myself to some one else. I have done it before. You see, my boy, I live in a loftier sphere than other men do; I look on all actions as means to an end, and the end is all that I look at. What is a man's life to me? Not *that*," he said, and he snapped his thumb-nail against his teeth. "A man, in short, is everything to me, or just nothing at all. Less than nothing if his name happens to be Poiret: you can crush him like a bug, he is flat and he is offensive. But a man is a god when he is like you; he is not a machine covered with a skin, but a theatre in which the greatest sentiments are displayed —great thoughts and feelings—and for these, and these only, I live. A sentiment—what is that but the whole world in a thought? Look at Father Goriot. For him, his two girls are the whole universe; they are the clue by which he finds his way through creation. Well, for my own part, I have fathomed the depths of life, there is only one real sentiment —comradeship between man and man. Pierre and Jaffier, that is my passion. I know *Venice Preserved* by heart. Have you met many men plucky enough when a comrade says, 'Let us bury a dead body!' to go and do it without a word or plaguing him by taking a high moral tone? I have done it myself. I should not talk like this to just everybody, but you are not like an ordinary man; one can talk to you, you can understand things. You will not dabble about much longer among the tadpoles in these swamps. Well, then, it is all settled. You will marry. Both of us carry our point. Mine is made of iron, and will never soften, he! he!"

Vautrin went out. He would not wait to hear the student's repudiation, he wished to put Eugène at his ease. He seemed to understand the secret springs of the faint resistance still made by the younger man; the struggles in which men seek to preserve their self-respect by justifying their blameworthy actions to themselves.

"He may do as he likes; I shall not marry Mlle. Taillefer, that is certain," said Eugène to himself.

He regarded this man with abhorrence, and yet the very cynicism of Vautrin's ideas, and the audacious way in which he used other men for his own ends, raised him in the student's eyes; but the thought of a compact threw Eugène into a fever of apprehension, and not until he had recovered somewhat did he dress, call for a cab, and go to Mme. de Restaud's.

For some days the Countess had paid more and more attention to a young man whose every step seemed a triumphal progress in the great world; it seemed to her that he might be a formidable power before long. He paid Messieurs de Trailles and d'Ajuda, played at whist for part of the evening, and made good his losses. Most men who have their way to make are more or less of fatalists, and Eugène was superstitious; he chose to consider that his luck was heaven's reward for his perseverance in the right way. As soon as possible on the following morning he asked Vautrin whether the bill that he had given was still in the other's possession; and on receiving a reply in the affirmative, he repaid the three thousand francs with a not unnatural relief.

"Everything is going on well," said Vautrin.

"But I am not your accomplice," said Eugène.

"I know, I know," Vautrin broke in. "You are still acting like a child. You are making mountains out of molehills at the outset."

Two days later, Poiret and Mlle. Michonneau were sitting together on a bench in the sun. They had chosen a little frequented alley in the Jardin des Plantes, and a gentleman was chatting with them, the same person, as a matter of fact, about whom the medical student had, not without good reason, his own suspicions.

"Mademoiselle," this M. Gondureau was saying, "I do not see any cause for your scruples. His Excellency, Monseigneur the Minister of Police——"

"Ah!" echoed Poiret, "His Excellency Monseigneur the Minister of Police!"

"Yes, his Excellency is taking a personal interest in the matter," said Gondureau.

Who would think it probable that Poiret, a retired clerk, doubtless possessed of some notions of civic virtue, though there might be nothing else in his head—who would think it likely that such a man would continue to lend an ear to this supposed independent gentleman of the Rue de Buffon, when the latter dropped the mask of a decent citizen by that word "police," and gave a glimpse of the features of a detective from the Rue de Jérusalem? And yet nothing was more natural. Perhaps the following remarks from the hitherto unpublished records made by certain observers will throw a light on the particular species to which Poiret belonged in the great family of fools. There is a race of quill-drivers, confined in the columns of the budget between the first degree of latitude (a kind of administrative Greenland where the salaries begin at twelve hundred francs) to the third degree, a more temperate zone, where incomes grow from three to six thousand francs, a climate where the *bonus* flourishes like a half-hardy annual in spite of some difficulties of culture. A characteristic trait that best reveals the feeble narrow-mindedness of these inhabitants of petty officialdom is a kind of involuntary, mechanical, and instinctive reverence for the Grand Lama of every Ministry, known to the rank and file only by his signature (an illegible scrawl) and by his title—"His Excellency Monseigneur le Ministre," five words which produce as much effect as the *il Bondo Cani* of the *Calife de Bagdad,* five words which in the eyes of this low order of intelligence represent a sacred power from which there is no appeal. The Minister is administratively infallible for the clerks in the employ of the Government, as the Pope is infallible for good Catholics. Something of this peculiar radiance invests everything he does or says, or that is said or done in his name; the robe of office covers everything and legalizes everything done by his orders; does not his very title—His Excellency—vouch for the purity of his intentions and the righteousness of his will, and serve as a sort of passport and introduction to ideas that otherwise would not be entertained for a moment? Pronounce the words "His Excellency," and these poor folk will forthwith proceed to do what they would not do for their own interests. Passive obedience is as well known in a Government department as in the army itself; and the administrative system silences consciences, annihilates the individual, and ends (give it time enough) by fashioning a man into a vise or a thumbscrew, and he becomes part of the machinery of Government. Wherefore, M. Gondureau, who seemed to know something of human nature, recognized Poiret at once as one of these dupes of officialdom, and brought out for his benefit, at the proper moment, the *deus ex machinâ*, the magical words "His Excellency," so as to dazzle Poiret just as he himself unmasked his batteries, for he took Poiret and the Michonneau for the male and female of the same species.

"If his Excellency himself, his Excellency the Minister . . . Ah! that is quite another thing," said Poiret.

"You seem to be guided by this gentleman's opinion, and you hear what he says," said the man of independent means, addressing Mlle. Michonneau. "Very well, his Excellency is at this moment absolutely certain that the so-called Vautrin, who lodges at the Maison Vauquer, is a convict who escaped from penal servitude at Toulon, where he is known by the nickname *Trompe-la-Mort.*"

"Trompe-la-Mort?" said Pioret. "Dear me, he is very lucky if he deserves that nickname."

"Well, yes," said the detective. "They call him so because he has been so lucky as not to lose his life in the very risky businesses that he has carried through. He is a dangerous man, you see! He has qualities that are out of the common; the thing he is wanted for, in fact, was a matter which gained him no end of credit with his own set——"

"Then is he a man of honor?" asked Poiret.

"Yes, according to his notions. He agreed to take another man's crime upon himself—a forgery committed by a very handsome young fellow that he had taken a great fancy to, a young Italian, a bit of a gambler, who has since gone into the army, where his conduct has been unexceptionable."

"But if his Excellency the Minister of Police is certain that M. Vautrin is this *Trompe-la-Mort,* why should he want me?" asked Mlle. Michonneau.

"Oh yes," said Poiret, "if the Minister, as you have been so obliging as to tell us, really knows for a certainty——"

"Certainty is not the word; he only suspects. You will soon understand how things are. Jacques Collin, nicknamed *Trompe-la-Mort,* is in the confidence of every convict in the three prisons; he is their man of business and their banker.

He makes a very good thing out of managing their affairs, which want a *man of mark* to see about them."

"Ha! ha! do you see the pun, mademoiselle?" asked Poiret. "This gentleman calls him a *man of mark* because he is a *marked man*—branded, you know."

"This so-called Vautrin," said the detective, "receives the money belonging to my lords the convicts, invests it for them, and holds it at the disposal of those who escape, or hands it over to their families if they leave a will, or to their mistresses when they draw upon him for their benefit."

"Their mistresses! You mean their wives," remarked Poiret.

"No, sir. A convict's wife is usually an illegitimate connection. We call them concubines."

"Then they all live in a state of concubinage?"

"Naturally."

"Why, these are abominations that his Excellency ought not to allow. Since you have the honor of seeing his Excellency, you, who seem to have philanthropic ideas, ought really to enlighten him as to their immoral conduct—they are setting a shocking example to the rest of society."

"But the Government does not hold them up as models of all the virtues, my dear sir——"

"Of course not, sir; but still——"

"Just let the gentleman say what he has to say, dearie," said Mlle. Michonneau.

"You see how it is, mademoiselle," Gondureau continued. "The Government may have the strongest reasons for getting this illicit hoard into its hands; it mounts up to something considerable, by all that we can make out. Trompe-la-Mort not only holds large sums for his friends the convicts, but he has other amounts which are paid over to him by the Society of the Ten Thousand——"

"Ten Thousand Thieves!" cried Pioret in alarm.

"No. The Society of the Ten Thousand is not an association of petty offenders, but of people who set about their work on a large scale—they won't touch a matter unless there are ten thousand francs in it. It is composed of the most distinguished of the men who are sent straight to the Assize Courts when they come up for trial. They know the Code too well to risk their necks when they are nabbed. Collin is their confidential agent and legal adviser. By means of the large sums of money at his disposal he has established a sort of detective system of his own; it is widespread and mysterious in its workings. We have had spies all about him for a twelvemonth, and yet we could not manage to fathom his games. His capital and his cleverness are at the service of vice and crime; this money furnishes the necessary funds for a regular army of blackguards in his pay who wage incessant war against society. If we can catch Trompe-la-Mort, and take possession of his funds, we should strike at the root of this evil. So this job is a kind of Government affair—a State secret—and likely to redound to the honor of those who bring the thing to a successful conclusion. You, sir, for instance, might very well be taken into a Government department again; they might make you secretary to a Commissary of Police; you could accept that post without prejudice to your retiring pension."

Mlle. Michonneau interposed at this point with, "What is there to hinder Trompe-la-Mort from making off with the money?"

"Oh!" said the detective, "a man is told off to follow him everywhere he goes, with orders to kill him if he were to rob the convicts. Then it is not quite as easy to make off with a lot of money as it is to run away with a young lady of family. Besides, Collin is not the sort of fellow to play such a trick; he would be disgraced, according to his notions."

"You are quite right, sir," said Poiret, "utterly disgraced he would be."

"But none of all this explains why you do not come and take him without more ado," remarked Mlle. Michonneau.

"Very well, mademoiselle, I will explain—but," he added in her ear, "keep your companion quiet, or I shall never have done. The old boy ought to pay people handsomely for listening to him.—Trompe-la-Mort, when he came back here," he went on aloud "slipped into the skin of an honest man; he turned up disguised as a decent Parisian citizen, and took up his quarters in an unpretending lodging-house. He is cunning, that he is! You don't catch him napping. Then M. Vautrin is a man of consequence, who transacts a good deal of business."

"Naturally," said Poiret to himself.

"And suppose that the Minister were to make a mistake and get hold of the real Vautrin, he would put every one's back up among the business men in Paris, and public opinion would be against him. M. le Préfet de Police is on slippery ground; he has enemies. They would take advantage of any mistake. There would be a fine outcry and fuss made by the Opposition, and he would be sent packing. We must set about this just as we did about the Coignard affair, the sham Comte de Sainte-Hélène; if he had been the real Comte de Sainte-Hélène, we should have been in the wrong box. We want to be quite sure what we are about."

"Yes, but what you want is a pretty woman," said Mlle. Michonneau briskly.

"Trompe-la-Mort would not let a woman come near him," said the detective. "I will tell you a secret—he does not like them."

"Still, I do not see what I can do, supposing that I did agree to identify him for two thousand francs."

"Nothing simpler," said the stranger "I will send you a little bottle containing a dose that will send a rush of blood to the head; it will do him no harm whatever, but he will fall down as if he were in a fit. The drug can be put into wine or coffee; either will do equally well. You carry your man to bed at once, and undress him to see that he is not dying. As soon as you are alone, you give him a slap on the shoulder, and *presto!* the letters will appear."

"Why, that is just nothing at all," said Poiret.

"Well, do you agree?" said Gondureau, addressing the old maid.

"But, my dear sir, suppose there are no letters at all," said Mlle. Michonneau; "am I to have the two thousand francs all the same?"

"No."

"What will you give me then?"

"Five hundred francs."

"It is such a thing to do for so little! It lies on your conscience just the same, and I must quiet my conscience, sir."

"I assure you," said Poiret, "that mademoiselle has a great deal of conscience, and not only so, she is a very amiable person, and very intelligent."

"Well, now," Mlle. Michonneau went on, "make it three thousand francs if he is Trompe-la-Mort, and nothing at all if he is an ordinary man."

"Done!" said Gondureau, "but on condition that the thing is settled to-morrow."

"Not quite so soon, my dear sir; I must consult my confessor first."

"You are a sly one," said the detective as he rose to his feet. "Good-bye till to-morrow, then. And if you should want to see me in a hurry, go to the Petite Rue Saint-Anne at the bottom of the Cour de la Sainte-Chapelle. There is one door under the archway. Ask there for M. Gondureau."

Bianchon, on his way back from Cuvier's lecture, overheard the sufficiently striking nickname of *Trompe-la-Mort,* and caught the celebrated chief detective's *"Done!"*

"Why didn't you close with him? It would be three hundred francs a year," said Poiret to Mlle. Michonneau.

"Why didn't I?" she asked. "Why, it wants thinking over. Suppose that M. Vautrin is this Trompe-la-Mort, perhaps we might do better for ourselves with him. Still, on the other hand, if you ask him for money, it would put him on his guard, and he is just the man to clear out without paying, and that would be an abominable sell."

"And suppose you did warn him," Poiret went on, "didn't that gentleman say that he was closely watched? You would spoil everything."

"Anyhow," thought Mlle. Michonneau, "I can't abide him. He says nothing but disagreeable things to me."

"But you can do better than that," Poiret resumed. "As that gentleman said (and he seemed to me to be a very good sort of man, besides being very well got up), it is an act of obedience to the laws to rid society of a criminal, however virtuous he may be. Once a thief, always a thief. Suppose he were to take it into his head to murder us all? The deuce! We should be guilty of manslaughter, and be the first to fall victims into the bargain!"

Mlle. Michonneau's musings did not permit her to listen very closely to the remarks that fell one by one from Poiret's lips like water dripping from a leaky tap. When once this elderly babbler began to talk, he would go on like clockwork unless Mlle. Michonneau stopped him. He started on some subject or other, and wandered on through parenthesis after parenthesis, till he came to regions as remote as possible from his premises without coming to any conclusions by the way.

By the time they reached the Maison Vauquer he had tacked together a whole string of examples and quotations more or less irrelevant to the subject in hand, which led him to give a full account of his own deposition in the case of the Sieur Ragoulleau *versus* Dame Morin, when he had been sum- moned as a witness for the defence.

As they entered the dining-room, Eugène de Rastignac was talking apart with Mlle. Taillefer; the conversation appeared to be of such thrilling interest that the pair never noticed the two older lodgers as they passed through the room. None of this was thrown away on Mlle. Michonneau.

"I knew how it would end," remarked that lady, addressing Poiret. "They have been making eyes at each other in a heartrending way for a week past."

"Yes," he answered. "So she was found guilty."

"Who?"

"Mme. Morin."

"I am talking about Mlle. Victorine," said Mlle. Michonneau, as she entered Poiret's room with an absent air, "and you answer, 'Mme. Morin.' Who may Mme. Morin be?"

"What can Mlle. Victorine be guilty of?" demanded Poiret.

"Guilty of falling in love with M. Eugène de Rastignac, and going further and further without knowing exactly where she is going, poor innocent!"

That morning Mme. de Nucingen had driven Eugène to despair. In his own mind he had completely surrendered himself to Vautrin, and deliberately shut his eyes to the motive for the friendship which that extraordinary man professed for him, nor would he look to the consequences of such an alliance. Nothing short of a miracle could extricate him now out of the gulf into which he had walked an hour ago, when he exchanged vows in the softest whispers with Mlle. Taillefer. To Victorine it seemed as if she heard an angel's voice, that heaven was opening above her; the Maison Vauquer took strange and wonderful hues, like a stage fairy-palace. She loved and she was beloved; at any rate, she believed that she was loved; and what woman would not likewise have believed after seeing Rastignac's face and listening to the tones of his voice during that hour snatched under the Argus eyes of the Maison Vauquer? He had trampled on his conscience; he knew that he was doing wrong, and did it deliberately; he had said to himself that a woman's happiness should atone for this venial sin. The energy of desperation had lent new beauty to his face; the lurid fire that burned in his heart shone from his eyes. Luckily for him, the miracle took place. Vautrin came in in high spirits, and at once read the hearts of these two young creatures whom he had brought together by the combinations of his infernal genius, but his deep voice broke in upon their bliss.

> "A charming girl is my Fanchette
> In her simplicity,"

he sang mockingly.

Victorine fled. Her heart was more full than it had ever been, but it was full of joy, and not of sorrow. Poor child!

Vautrin came in in high spirits

A pressure of the hand, the light touch of Rastignac's hair against her cheek, a word whispered in her ear so closely that she felt the student's warm breath on her, the pressure of a trembling arm about her waist, a kiss upon her throat—such had been her betrothal. The near neighborhood of the stout Sylvie, who might invade that glorified room at any moment, only made these first tokens of love more ardent, more eloquent, more entrancing than the noblest deeds done for love's sake in the most famous romances. This *plain-song* of love, to use the pretty expression of our forefathers, seemed almost criminal to the devout young girl who went to confession every fortnight. In that one hour she had poured out more of the treasures of her soul than she could give in later days of wealth and happiness, when her whole self followed the gift.

"The thing is arranged," Vautrin said to Eugène, who remained. "Our two dandies have fallen out. Everything was done in proper form. It is a matter of opinion. Our pigeon has insulted my hawk. They will meet to-morrow in the redoubt at Clignancourt. By half-past eight in the morning Mlle. Taillefer, calmly dipping her bread and butter in her coffee cup, will be sole heiress of her father's fortune and affections. A funny way of putting it, isn't it? Taillefer's youngster is an expert swordsman, and quite cocksure about it, but he will be bled; I have just invented a thrust for his benefit, a way of raising your sword point and driving it at the forehead. I must show you that thrust; it is an uncommonly handy thing to know."

Rastignac heard him in dazed bewilderment; he could not find a word in reply. Just then Goriot came in, and Bianchon and a few of the boarders likewise appeared.

"That is just as I intended," Vautrin said. "You know quite well what you are about. Good, my little eaglet! You are born to command, you are strong, you stand firm on your feet, you are game! I respect you."

He made as though he would take Eugène's hand, but Rastignac hastily withdrew it, sank into a chair, and turned ghastly pale; it seemed to him that there was a sea of blood before his eyes.

"Oh! so we have still a few dubious tatters of the swaddling clothes of virtue about us!" murmured Vautrin. "But Papa Doliban has three millions; I know the amount of his fortune. Once have her dowry in your hands, and your character will be as white as the bride's white dress, even in your own eyes."

Rastignac hesitated no longer. He made up his mind that he would go that evening to warn the Taillefers, father and son. But just as Vautrin left him, Father Goriot came up and said in his ear, "You look melancholy, my boy; I will cheer you up. Come with me."

The old vermicelli dealer lighted his dip at one of the lamps as he spoke. Eugène went with him, his curiosity had been aroused.

"Let us go up to your room," the worthy soul remarked, when he had asked Sylvie for the law student's key. "This morning," he resumed, "you thought that *she* did not care about you, did you not? Eh? She would have nothing to say to you, and you went away out of humor and out of heart. Stuff and rubbish! She wanted you to go because she was expecting *me!* Now do you understand? We were to complete the arrangements for taking some chambers for you, a jewel of a place, you are to move into it in three days' time. Don't split upon me. She wants it to be a surprise; but I couldn't bear to keep the secret from you. You will be in the Rue d'Artois, only a step or two from the Rue Saint-Lazare, and you are to be housed like a prince! Any one might have thought we were furnishing the house for a bride. Oh! we have done a lot of things in the last month, and you knew nothing about it. My attorney has appeared on the scene, and my daughter is to have thirty-six thousand francs a year, the interest on her money, and I shall insist on having her eight hundred thousand invested in sound securities, landed property that won't run away."

Eugène was dumb. He folded his arms and paced up and down his cheerless, untidy room. Father Goriot waited till the student's back was turned, and seized the opportunity to go to the chimney-piece and set upon it a little red morocco case with Rastignac's arms stamped in gold on the leather.

"My dear boy," said the kind soul, "I have been up to the eyes in this business. You see, there was plenty of selfishness on my part; I have an interested motive in helping you to change lodgings. You will not refuse me if I ask you something; will you, eh?"

"What is it?"

"There is a room on the fifth floor, up above your rooms, that is to let along with them; that is where I am going to live, isn't that so? I am getting old; I am too far from my girls. I shall not be in the way, but I shall be there, that is all. You will come and talk to me about her every evening. It will not put you about, will it? I shall have gone to bed before you come in, but I shall hear you come up, and I shall say to myself, 'He has just seen my little Delphine. He has been to a dance with her, and she is happy, thanks to him.' If I were ill, it would do my heart good to hear you moving about below, to know when you leave the house and when you come in. It is only a step to the Champs-Élysées, where they go every day, so I shall be sure of seeing them, whereas now I am sometimes too late. And then—perhaps she may come to see you! I shall hear her, I shall see her in her soft quilted pelisse tripping about as daintily as a kitten. In this one month she has become my little girl again, so light-hearted and gay. Her soul is recovering, and her happiness is owing to you! Oh! I would do impossibilities for you. Only just now she said to me, 'I am very happy, papa!' When they say 'father' stiffly, it sends a chill through me; but when they call me 'papa,' it is as if they were little girls again, and it brings all the old memories back. I feel most their father then; I even believe that they belong to me, and to no one else."

The good man wiped his eyes, he was crying.

"It is a long while since I have heard them talk like that, a long, long time since she took my arm as she did to-day. Yes, indeed, it must be quite ten years since I walked side by side with one of my girls. How pleasant it was to keep step with

her, to feel the touch of her gown, the warmth of her arm!
Well, I took Delphine everywhere this morning; I went shopping with her, and I brought her home again. Oh! you must
let me live near you. You may want some one to do you a
service some of these days, and I shall be on the spot to do it.
Oh! if only that great dolt of an Alsatian would die, if his
gout would have the sense to attack his stomach, how happy
my poor child would be! You would be my son-in-law; you
would be her husband in the eyes of the world. Bah! she has
known no happiness, that excuses everything. Our Father
in heaven is surely on the side of fathers on earth who love
their children. How fond of you she is!" he said, raising
his head after a pause. "All the time we were going about
together she chatted away about you. 'He is nice-looking,
papa; isn't he? He is kind-hearted! Does he talk to you
about me?' Pshaw! she said enough about you to fill whole
volumes; between the Rue d'Artois and the Passage des Panoramas she poured her heart out into mine. I did not feel
old once during that delightful morning; I felt as light as a
feather. I told her how you had given that banknote to me;
it moved my darling to tears. But what can this be on your
chimney-piece?" said Father Goriot at last. Rastignac had
showed no sign, and he was dying of impatience.

Eugène stared at his neighbor in dumb and dazed bewilderment. He thought of Vautrin, of that duel to be fought
to-morrow morning, and of this realization of his dearest
hopes, and the violent contrast between the two sets of ideas
gave him all the sensations of nightmare. He went to the
chimney-piece, saw the little square case, opened it, and found
a watch of Bréguet's make wrapped in paper, on which these
words were written:

"I want you to think of me every hour, *because* . . .
"DELPHINE."

That last word doubtless contained an allusion to some
scene that had taken place between them. Eugène felt

touched. Inside the gold watch-case his arms had been wrought in enamel. The chain, the key, the workmanship and design of the trinket were all such as he had imagined, for he had long coveted such a possession. Father Goriot was radiant. Of course he had promised to tell his daughter every little detail of the scene and of the effect produced upon Eugène by her present; he shared in the pleasure and excitement of the young people, and seemed to be not the least happy of the three. He loved Rastignac already for his own as well as for his daughter's sake.

"You must go and see her; she is expecting you this evening. That great lout of an Alsatian is going to have supper with his opera-dancer. Aha! he looked very foolish when my attorney let him know where he was. He says he idolizes my daughter, does he? He had better let her alone, or I will kill him. To think that my Delphine is his"—he heaved a sigh —"it is enough to make me murder him, but it would not be manslaughter to kill that animal; he is a pig with a calf's brains.—You will take me with you, will you not?"

"Yes, dear Father Goriot; you know very well how fond I am of you——"

"Yes, I do know very well. You are not ashamed of me, are you? Not you! Let me embrace you," and he flung his arms round the student's neck.

"You will make her very happy; promise me that you will! You will go to her this evening, will you not?"

"Oh! yes. I must go out; I have some urgent business on hand."

"Can I be of any use?"

"My word, yes! Will you go to old Taillefer's while I go to Mme. de Nucingen? Ask him to make an appointment with me some time this evening; it is a matter of life and death."

"Really, young man!" cried Father Goriot, with a change of countenance; "are you really paying court to his daughter, as those simpletons were saying down below? . . . *Tonnerre de Dieu!* you have no notion what a tap *à la Goriot* is like, and if you are playing a double game, I shall put a stop to it by one blow of the fist. . . Oh! the thing is impossible!"

"I swear to you that I love but one woman in the world," said the student. "I only knew it a moment ago."

"Oh! what happiness!" cried Goriot.

"But young Taillefer has been called out; the duel comes off to-morrow morning, and I have heard it said that he may lose his life in it."

"But what business is it of yours?" said Goriot.

"Why, I ought to tell him so, that he may prevent his son from putting in an appearance——"

Just at that moment Vautrin's voice broke in upon them; he was standing at the threshold of his door and singing:

> "Oh! Richard, oh my king!
> All the world abandons thee!
> Broum! broum! broum! broum! broum!
>
> The same old story everywhere,
> A roving heart and a . . . tra la la."

"Gentlemen!" shouted Christophe, "the soup is ready, and every one is waiting for you."

"Here," Vautrin called down to him, "come and take a bottle of my Bordeaux."

"Do you think your watch is pretty?" asked Goriot. "She has good taste, hasn't she? Eh?"

Vautrin, Father Goriot, and Rastignac came downstairs in company, and, all three of them being late, were obliged to sit together.

Eugène was as distant as possible in his manner to Vautrin during dinner; but the other, so charming in Mme. Vauquer's opinion, had never been so witty. His lively sallies and sparkling talk put the whole table in good humor. His assurance and coolness filled Eugène with consternation.

"Why, what has come to you to-day?" inquired Mme. Vauquer. "You are as merry as a skylark."

"I am always in spirits after I have made a good bargain."

"Bargain?" said Eugène.

"Well, yes, bargain. I have just delivered a lot of goods, and I shall be paid a handsome commission on them—Mlle. Michonneau," he went on, seeing that the elderly spinster was scrutinizing him intently, "have you any objection to some feature in my face, that you are making those lynx eyes at me? Just let me know, and I will have it changed to oblige you . . . We shall not fall out about it, Poiret, I dare say?" he added, winking at the superannuated clerk.

"Bless my soul, you ought to stand as model for a burlesque Hercules," said the young painter.

"I will, upon my word! if Mlle. Michonneau will consent to sit as the Venus of Père-Lachaise," replied Vautrin.

"There's Poiret," suggested Bianchon.

"Oh! Poiret shall pose as Poiret. He can be a garden god!" cried Vautrin; "his name means a pear——"

"A sleepy pear!" Bianchon put in. "You will come in between the pear and the cheese."

"What stuff you are all talking!" said Mme. Vauquer; "you would do better to treat us to your Bordeaux; I see a glimpse of a bottle there. It would keep us all in a good humor, and it is good for the stomach besides."

"Gentlemen," said Vautrin, "the Lady President calls us to order. Mme. Couture and Mlle. Victorine will take your jokes in good part, but respect the innocence of the aged Goriot. I propose a glass or two of Bordeauxrama, rendered twice illustrious by the name of Laffite, no political allusions intended.—Come, you Turk!" he added, looking at Christophe, who did not offer to stir. "Christophe! Here! What, you don't answer to your own name? Bring us some liquor, Turk!"

"Here it is, sir," said Christophe, holding out the bottle.

Vautrin filled Eugène's glass and Goriot's likewise, then he deliberately poured out a few drops into his own glass, and sipped it while his two neighbors drank their wine. All at once he made a grimace.

"Corked!" he cried. "The devil! You can drink the rest of this, Christophe, and go and find another bottle; take from the right-hand side, you know. There are sixteen of us; take down eight bottles."

"If you are going to stand treat," said the painter, "I will pay for a hundred chestnuts."

"Oh! oh!"

"Booououh!"

"Prrr!"

These exclamations came from all parts of the table like squibs from a set firework.

"Come, now, Mamma Vauquer, a couple of bottles of champagne," called Vautrin.

"*Quien!* just like you! Why not ask for the whole house at once. A couple of bottles of champagne; that means twelve francs! I shall never see the money back again, I know! But if M. Eugène has a mind to pay for it, I have some currant cordial."

"That currant cordial of hers is as bad as a black draught," muttered the medical student.

"Shut up, Bianchon," exclaimed Rastignac; "the very mention of black draught makes me feel—— Yes, champagne, by all means; I will pay for it," he added.

"Sylvie," called Mme. Vauquer, "bring in some biscuits, and the little cakes."

"Those little cakes are mouldy graybeards," said Vautrin. "But trot out the biscuits."

The Bordeaux wine circulated; the dinner table became a livelier scene than ever, and the fun grew fast and furious. Imitations of the cries of various animals mingled with the loud laughter; the Museum official having taken it into his head to mimic a cat-call rather like the caterwauling of the animal in question, eight voices simultaneously struck up with the following variations:

"Scissors to grind!"

"Chick-weeds for singing bir-ds!"

"Brandy-snaps, ladies!"

"China to mend!"

"Boat ahoy!"

"Sticks to beat your wives or your clothes!"

"Old clo'!"

"Cherries all ripe!"

But the palm was awarded to Bianchon for the nasal accent with which he rendered the cry of "Umbrellas to me-end!"

A few seconds later, and there was a head-splitting racket in the room, a storm of tomfoolery, a sort of cats' concert, with Vautrin as conductor of the orchestra, the latter keeping an eye the while on Eugène and Father Goriot. The wine seemed to have gone to their heads already. They leaned back in their chairs, looking at the general confusion with an air of gravity, and drank but little; both of them were absorbed in the thought of what lay before them to do that evening, and yet neither of them felt able to rise and go. Vautrin gave a side glance at them from time to time, and watched the change that came over their faces, choosing the moment when their eyes drooped and seemed about to close, to bend over Rastignac and to say in his ear:—

"My little lad, you are not quite shrewd enough to outwit Papa Vautrin yet, and he is too fond of you to let you make a mess of your affairs. When I have made up my mind to do a thing, no one short of Providence can put me off. Aha! we were for going round to warn old Taillefer, telling tales out of school! The oven is hot, the dough is kneaded, the bread is ready for the oven; to-morrow we will eat it up and whisk away the crumbs; and we are not going to spoil the baking? . . . No, no, it is all as good as done! We may suffer from a few conscientious scruples, but they will be digested along with the bread. While we are having our forty winks, Colonel Count Franchessini will clear the way to Michel Taillefer's inheritance with the point of his sword. Victorine will come in for her brother's money, a snug fifteen thousand francs a year. I have made inquiries already, and I know that her late mother's property amounts to more than three hundred thousand——"

Eugène heard all this, and could not answer a word; his tongue seemed to be glued to the roof of his mouth, an irresistible drowsiness was creeping over him. He still saw the table and the faces round it, but it was through a bright mist. Soon the noise began to subside, one by one the boarders went. At last, when their numbers had so dwindled that the party consisted of Mme. Vauquer, Mme. Couture, Mlle. Victorine, Vautrin, and Father Goriot, Rastignac watched as though in a dream how Mme. Vauquer busied herself by collecting the bottles, and drained the remainder of the wine out of each to fill others.

"Oh! how uproarious they are! what a thing it is to be young!" said the widow.

These were the last words that Eugène heard and understood.

"There is no one like M. Vautrin for a bit of fun like this," said Sylvie. "There, just hark at Christophe, he is snoring like a top."

"Good-bye, mamma," said Vautrin; "I am going to a theatre on the boulevard to see M. Marty in *Le Mont Sauvage,* a fine play taken from *Le Solitaire.* . . . If you like, I will take you and these two ladies——"

"Thank you; I must decline," said Mme. Couture.

"What! my good lady!" cried Mme. Vauquer, "decline to see a play founded on the *Le Solitaire,* a work by Atala de Chateaubriand? We were so fond of that book that we cried over it like Magdalens under the *line-trees* last summer, and then it is an improving work that might edify your young lady."

"We are forbidden to go to the play," answered Victorine.

"Just look, those two yonder have dropped off where they sit," said Vautrin, shaking the heads of the two sleepers in a comical way.

He altered the sleeping student's position, settled his head more comfortably on the back of his chair, kissed him warmly on the forehead, and began to sing:

> "Sleep, little darlings;
> I watch while you slumber."

"I am afraid he may be ill," said Victorine.

"Then stop and take care of him," returned Vautrin. " 'Tis your duty as a meek and obedient wife," he whispered in her ear. "The young fellow worships you, and you will be his little wife—there's your fortune for you. In short," he added aloud, "they lived happily ever afterwards, were much looked up to in all the countryside, and had a numerous family. That is how all the romances end.—Now, mamma," he went on, as he turned to Madame Vauquer and put his arm round her waist, "put on your bonnet, your best flowered silk, and the countess' scarf, while I go out and call a cab—all my own self."

And he started out, singing as he went:

> "Oh! sun! divine sun!
> Ripening the pumpkins every one."

"My goodness! Well, I'm sure! Mme. Couture, I could live happily in a garret with a man like that.—There, now!" she added, looking round for the old vermicelli maker, "there is that Father Goriot half seas over. *He* never thought of taking me anywhere, the old skinflint. But he will measure his length somewhere. My word! it is disgraceful to lose his senses like that, at his age! You will be telling me that he couldn't lose what he hadn't got—Sylvie, just take him up to his room!"

Sylvie took him by the arm, supported him upstairs, and flung him just as he was, like a package, across the bed.

"Poor young fellow!" said Mme. Couture, putting back Eugène's hair that had fallen over his eyes; "he is like a young girl, he does not know what dissipation is."

"Well, I can tell you this, I know," said Mme. Vauquer,
"I have taken lodgers these thirty years, and a good many
have passed through my hands, as the saying is, but I have
never seen a nicer nor a more aristocratic looking young man
than M. Eugène. How handsome he looks sleeping! Just
let his head rest on your shoulder, Mme. Couture. Pshaw!
he falls over towards Mlle. Victorine. There's a special
providence for young things. A little more, and he would
have broken his head against the knob of the chair. They'd
make a pretty pair those two would!"

"Hush, my good neighbor," cried Mme. Couture, "you
are saying such things——"

"Pooh!" put in Mme. Vauquer, "he does not hear.—Here,
Sylvie! come and help me to dress. I shall put on my best
stays."

"What! your best stays just after dinner, madame?" said
Sylvie. "No, you can get some one else to lace you. I am
not going to be your murderer. It's a rash thing to do,
and might cost you your life."

"I don't care, I must do honor to M. Vautrin."

"Are you so fond of your heirs as all that?"

"Come, Sylvie, don't argue," said the widow, as she left
the room.

"At her age, too!" said the cook to Victorine, pointing
to her mistress as she spoke.

Mme. Couture and her ward were left in the dining-room,
and Eugène slept on on Victorine's shoulder. The sound
of Christophe's snoring echoed through the silent house;
Eugène's quiet breathing seemed all the quieter by force of
contrast, he was sleeping as peacefully as a child. Victorine was very happy; she was free to perform one of those
acts of charity which form an innocent outlet for all the
overflowing sentiments of a woman's nature; he was so close
to her that she could feel the throbbing of his heart; there
was a look of almost maternal protection and conscious pride
in Victorine's face. Among the countless thoughts that
crowded up in her young innocent heart, there was a wild
flutter of joy at this close contact.

"Poor, dear child!" said Mme. Couture, squeezing her hand.

The old lady looked at the girl. Victorine's innocent, pathetic face, so radiant with the new happiness that had befallen her, called to mind some naïve work of mediæval art, when the painter neglected the accessories, reserving all the magic of his brush for the quiet, austere outlines and ivory tints of the face, which seems to have caught something of the golden glory of heaven.

"After all, he only took two glasses, mamma," said Victorine, passing her fingers through Eugène's hair.

"Indeed, if he had been a dissipated young man, child, he would have carried his wine like the rest of them. His drowsiness does him credit."

There was a sound of wheels outside in the street.

"There is M. Vautrin, mamma," said the girl. "Just take M. Eugène. I would rather not have that man see me like this; there are some ways of looking at you that seem to sully your soul and make you feel as though you had nothing on."

"Oh, no, you are wrong!" said Mme. Couture. "M. Vautrin is a worthy man; he reminds me a little of my late husband, poor dear M. Couture, rough but kind-hearted; his bark is worse than his bite."

Vautrin came in while she was speaking; he did not make a sound, but looked for a while at the picture of the two young faces—the lamplight falling full upon them seemed to caress them.

"Well," he remarked, folding his arms, "here is a picture! It would have suggested some pleasing pages to Bernardin de Saint-Pierre (good soul), who wrote *Paul et Virginie.* Youth is very charming, Mme Couture!—Sleep on, poor boy," he added, looking at Eugène, "luck sometimes comes while we are sleeping.—There is something touching and attractive to me about this young man, madame," he continued; "I know that his nature is in harmony with his face. Just look, the head of a cherub on an angel's shoulder! He deserves to be loved. If I were a woman, I would die (no—not such a fool), I would live for him." He bent lower and spoke in the widow's ear. "When I see those two together, madame, I cannot help thinking that Providence meant them for each other; He works by secret ways, and tries the reins and the heart," he said in a loud voice. "And when I see you, my children, thus united by a like purity and by all human affections, I say to myself that it is quite impossible that the future should separate you. God is just."—He turned to Victorine. "It seems to me," he said, "that I have seen the line of success in your hand. Let me look at it, Mlle. Victorine; I am well up in palmistry, and I have told fortunes many a time. Come, now, don't be frightened. Ah! what do I see? Upon my word, you will be one of the richest heiresses in Paris before very long. You will heap riches on the man who loves you. Your father will want you to go and live with him. You will marry a young and handsome man with a title, and he will idolize you."

The heavy footsteps of the coquettish widow, who was coming down the stairs, interrupted Vautrin's fortune-telling. "Here is Mamma Vauquerre, fair as a starr-r-r, dressed within an inch of her life.—Aren't we a trifle pinched for room?" he inquired, with his arm round the lady; "we are screwed up very tightly about the bust, mamma! If we are much agitated, there may be an explosion; but I will pick up the fragments with all the care of an antiquary."

"There is a man who can talk the language of French gallantry!" said the widow, bending to speak in Mme. Couture's ear.

"Good-bye, little ones!" said Vautrin, turning to Eugène and Victorine. "Bless you both!" and he laid a hand on either head. "Take my word for it, young lady, an honest man's prayers are worth something; they should bring you happiness, for God hears them."

"Good-bye, dear," said Mme. Vauquer to her lodger. "Do you think that M. Vautrin means to run away with me?" she added, lowering her voice.

"Lack-a-day!" said the widow.

"Oh! mamma dear, suppose it should really happen as that kind M. Vautrin said!" said Victorine with a sigh as she looked at her hands. The two women were alone together.

"Why, it wouldn't take much to bring it to pass," said the elderly lady; "just a fall from his horse, and your monster of a brother——"

"Oh! mamma."

"Good Lord! Well, perhaps it is a sin to wish bad luck to an enemy," the widow remarked. "I will do penance for it. Still, I would strew flowers on his grave with the greatest pleasure, and that is the truth. Black-hearted, that he is! The coward couldn't speak up for his own mother, and cheats you out of your share by deceit and trickery. My cousin had a pretty fortune of her own, but unluckily for you, nothing was said in the marriage-contract about anything that she might come in for."

"It would be very hard if my fortune is to cost some one else his life," said Victorine. "If I cannot be happy unless my brother is to be taken out of the world, I would rather stay here all my life."

"*Mon Dieu!* it is just as that good M. Vautrin says, and he is full of piety, you see," Mme. Couture remarked. "I am very glad to find that he is not an unbeliever like the rest of them that talk of the Almighty with less respect than they do of the Devil. Well, as he was saying, who can know the ways by which it may please Providence to lead us?"

With Sylvie's help the two women at last succeeded in getting Eugène up to his room; they laid him on the bed, and the cook unfastened his clothes to make him more comfortable. Before they left the room, Victorine snatched an opportunity when her guardian's back was turned, and pressed a kiss on Eugène's forehead, feeling all the joy that this stolen pleasure could give her. Then she looked round the room, and gathering up, as it were, into one single thought all the untold bliss of that day, she made a picture of her memories, and dwelt upon it until she slept, the happiest creature in Paris.

That evening's merry-making, in the course of which Vautrin had given the drugged wine to Eugène and Father Goriot, was his own ruin. Bianchon, flustered with wine, forgot to open the subject of Trompe-la-Mort with Mlle. Michonneau. The mere mention of the name would have set Vautrin on his guard; for Vautrin, or, to give him his real name, Jacques Collin, was in fact the notorious escaped convict.

But it was the joke about the Venus of Père-Lachaise that finally decided his fate. Mlle. Michonneau had very nearly made up her mind to warn the convict and to throw herself on his generosity, with the idea of making a better bargain for herself by helping him to escape that night; but as it was, she went out escorted by Poiret in search of the famous chief of detectives in the Petite Rue Saint-Anne, still thinking that it was the district superintendent—one Gondureau— with whom she had to do. The head of the department received his visitors courteously. There was a little talk, and the details were definitely arranged. Mlle. Michonneau asked for the draught that she was to administer in order to set about her investigation. But the great man's evident satisfaction set Mlle. Michonneau thinking; and she began to see that this business involved something more than the mere capture of a runaway convict. She racked her brains while he looked in a drawer in his desk for the little phial, and it dawned upon her that in consequence of treacherous revelations made by the prisoners the police were hoping to lay their hands on a considerable sum of money. But on hinting her suspicions to the old fox of the Petite Rue Saint-Anne, that officer began to smile, and tried to put her off the scent.

"A delusion," he said. "Collin's *sorbonne* is the most dangerous that has yet been found among the dangerous classes. That is all, and the rascals are quite aware of it. They rally round him; he is the backbone of the federation, its Bonaparte, in short; he is very popular with them all. The rogue will never leave his *chump* in the Place de Grève."

As Mlle. Michonneau seemed mystified, Gondureau explained the two slang words for her benefit. *Sorbonne* and *chump* are two forcible expressions borrowed from thieves' Latin, thieves, of all people, being compelled to consider the human head in its two aspects. A *sorbonne* is the head of a living man, his faculty of thinking—his council; a *chump* is a contemptuous epithet that implies how little a human head is worth after the axe has done its work.

"Collin is playing us off," he continued. "When we come across a man like a bar of steel tempered in the English fashion, there is always one resource left—we can kill him if he takes it into his head to make the least resistance. We are reckoning on several methods of killing Collin to-morrow morning. It saves a trial, and society is rid of him without all the expense of guarding and feeding him. What with getting up the case, summoning witnesses, paying their expenses, and carrying out the sentence, it costs a lot to go through all the proper formalities before you can get quit of one of these good-for-nothings, over and above the three thousand francs that you are going to have. There is a saving in time as well. One good thrust of the bayonet into Trompe-la-Mort's paunch will prevent scores of crimes, and save fifty scoundrels from following his example; they will be very careful to keep themselves out of the police courts. That is doing the work of the police thoroughly, and true philanthropists will tell you that it is better to prevent crime than to punish it."

"And you do a service to our country," said Poiret.

"Really, you are talking in a very sensible manner to-night, that you are," said the head of the department. "Yes, of course, we are serving our country, and we are very hardly used too. We do society very great services that are not recognized. In fact, a superior man must rise above vulgar prejudices, and a Christian must resign himself to the mishaps that doing right entails, when right is done in an out-of-the-way style. Paris is Paris, you see! That is the explanation of my life.—I have the honor to wish you a good-evening, mademoiselle. I shall bring my men to the Jardin du Roi in the morning. Send Christophe to the Rue du Buffon, tell him to ask for M. Gondureau in the house where you saw me before.—Your servant, sir. If you should ever have anything stolen from you, come to me, and I will do my best to get it back for you."

"Well, now," Poiret remarked to Mlle. Michonneau, "there are idiots who are scared out of their wits by the word police. That was a very pleasant-spoken gentleman, and what he wants you to do is as easy as saying 'Good-day.'"

The next day was destined to be one of the most extra-ordinary in the annals of the Maison Vauquer. Hitherto the most startling occurrence in its tranquil existence had been the portentous, meteor-like apparition of the sham Comtesse de l'Ambermesnil. But the catastrophes of this great day were to cast all previous events into the shade, and supply an inexhaustible topic of conversation for Mme. Vauquer and her boarders so long as she lived.

In the first place, Goriot and Eugène de Rastignac both slept till close upon eleven o'clock. Mme. Vauquer, who came home about midnight from the Gaîté, lay a-bed till half-past ten. Christophe, after a prolonged slumber (he had finished Vautrin's first bottle of wine), was behindhand with his work, but Poiret and Mlle. Michonneau uttered no complaint, though breakfast was delayed. As for Victorine and Mme. Couture, they also lay late. Vautrin went out before eight o'clock, and only came back just as breakfast was ready. Nobody protested, therefore, when Sylvie and Christophe went up at a quarter past eleven, knocked at all the doors, and announced that breakfast was waiting. While Sylvie and the man were upstairs, Mlle. Michonneau, who came down first, poured the contents of the phial into the silver cup belonging to Vautrin—it was standing with the others in the bain-marie that kept the cream hot for the morning coffee. The spinster had reckoned on this custom of the house to do her stroke of business. The seven lodgers were at last collected together, not without some difficulty. Just as Eugène came downstairs, stretching himself and yawning, a commissionaire handed him a letter from Mme. de Nucingen. It ran thus:—

"I feel neither false vanity nor anger where you are concerned, my friend. Till two o'clock this morning I waited for you. Oh, that waiting for one whom you love! No one that had passed through that torture could inflict it on another. I know now that you have never loved before. What can have happened? Anxiety has taken hold of me. I would have come myself to find out what had happened, if I had not feared to betray the secrets of my heart. How can I walk out or drive out at this time of day? Would it not be ruin? I have felt to the full how wretched it is to be a woman. Send a word to reassure me, and explain how it is that you have not come after what my father told you. I shall be angry, but I will forgive you. One word, for pity's sake. You will come to me very soon, will you not? If you are busy, a line will be enough. Say, 'I will hasten to you,' or else, 'I am ill.' But if you were ill my father would have come to tell me so. What can have happened? . . ."

"Yes, indeed, what has happened?" exclaimed Eugène, and, hurrying down to the dining-room, he crumpled up the letter without reading any more. "What time is it?"

"Half-past eleven," said Vautrin, dropping a lump of sugar into his coffee.

The escaped convict cast a glance at Eugène, a cold and fascinating glance; men gifted with this magnetic power can quell furious lunatics in a madhouse by such a glance, it is said. Eugène shook in every limb. There was the sound of wheels in the street, and in another moment a man with a scared face rushed into the room. It was one of M. Taillefer's servants; Mme. Couture recognized the livery at once.

"Mademoiselle," he cried, "your father is asking for you —something terrible has happened! M. Frédéric has had a sword thrust in the forehead in a duel, and the doctors have given him up. You will scarcely be in time to say good-bye to him! he is unconscious."

"Poor young fellow!" exclaimed Vautrin. "How can people brawl when they have a certain income of thirty thousand livres? Young people have bad manners, and that is a fact."

"Sir!" cried Eugène.

"Well, what then, you big baby!" said Vautrin, swallowing down his coffee imperturbably, an operation which Mlle. Michonneau watched with such close attention that she had no emotion to spare for the amazing news that had struck the others dumb with amazement. "Are there not duels every morning in Paris?" added Vautrin.

"I will go with you, Victorine," said Mme. Couture, and the two women hurried away at once without either hats or shawls. But before she went, Victorine, with her eyes full of tears, gave Eugène a glance that said—"How little I thought that our happiness should cost me tears!"

"Dear me, you are a prophet, M. Vautrin," said Mme. Vauquer.

"I am all sorts of things," said Vautrin.

"Queer, isn't it?" said Mme. Vauquer, stringing together a succession of commonplaces suited to the occasion. "Death takes us off without asking us about it. The young often go before the old. It is a lucky thing for us women that we are not liable to fight duels, but we have other complaints that men don't suffer from. We bear children, and it takes a long time to get over it. What a windfall for Victorine! Her father will have to acknowledge her now!"

"There!" said Vautrin, looking at Eugène, "yesterday she had not a penny; this morning she has several millions to her fortune."

"I say, M. Eugène!" cried Mme. Vauquer, "you have landed on your feet!"

At this exclamation, Father Goriot looked at the student, and saw the crumpled letter still in his hand.

"You have not read it through! What does this mean? Are you going to be like the rest of them?" he asked.

"Madame, I shall never marry Mlle. Victorine," said Eu-

gène, turning to Mme. Vauquer with an expression of terror
and loathing that surprised the onlookers at this scene.

Father Goriot caught the student's hand and grasped it
warmly. He could have kissed it.

"Oh, ho!" said Vautrin, "the Italians have a good proverb
—*Col tempo.*"

"Is there any answer?" said Mme. de Nucingen's messenger, addressing Eugéne.

"Say that I will come directly."

The man went. Eugène was in a state of such violent excitement that he could not be prudent.

"What is to be done?" he exclaimed aloud. "There are no
proofs!"

Vautrin began to smile. Though the drug he had taken
was doing its work, the convict was so vigorous that he rose
to his feet, gave Rastignac a look, and said in hollow tones,
"Luck comes to us while we sleep, young man," and fell
stiff and stark, as if he were struck dead.

"So there is a Divine Justice!" said Eugène.

"Well, if ever! What has come to that poor dear M. Vautrin?"

"A stroke!" cried Mlle. Michonneau.

"Here, Sylvie! girl, run for the doctor," called the widow.
"Oh, M. Rastignac, just go for M. Bianchon, and be as
quick as you can; Sylvie might not be in time to catch our
doctor, M. Grimprel."

Rastignac was glad of an excuse to leave that den of horrors, his hurry for the doctor was nothing but a flight.

"Here, Christophe, go round to the chemist's and ask for
something that's good for the apoplexy."

Christophe likewise went.

"Father Goriot, just help us to get him upstairs."

Vautrin was taken up among them, carried carefully up
the narrow staircase, and laid upon his bed.

"I can do no good here, so I shall go to see my daughter,"
said M. Goriot.

"Selfish old thing!" cried Mme. Vauquer. "Yes, go; I wish you may die like a dog."

"Just go and see if you can find some ether," said Mlle. Michonneau to Mme. Vauquer; the former, with some help from Poiret, had unfastened the sick man's clothes.

Mme. Vauquer went down to her room, and left Mlle. Michonneau mistress of the situation.

"Now! just pull down his shirt and turn him over, quick! You might be of some use in sparing my modesty," she said to Poiret, "instead of standing there like a stock."

Vautrin was turned over; Mlle. Michonneau gave his shoulder a sharp slap, and the two portentous letters appeared, white against the red.

"There, you have earned your three thousand francs very easily," exclaimed Poiret, supporting Vautrin while Mlle. Michonneau slipped on the shirt again.—"Ouf! How heavy he is," he added, as he laid the convict down.

"Hush! Suppose there is a strong-box here!" said the old maid briskly; her glances seemed to pierce the walls, she scrutinized every article of the furniture with greedy eyes. "Could we find some excuse for opening that desk?"

"It mightn't be quite right," responded Poiret to this.

"Where is the harm? It is money stolen from all sorts of people, so it doesn't belong to any one now. But we haven't time, there is the Vauquer."

"Here is the ether," said that lady. "I must say that this is an eventful day. Lord! that man can't have had a stroke; he is as white as curds."

"White as curds?" echoed Poiret.

"And his pulse is steady," said the widow, laying her hand on his breast.

"Steady?" said the astonished Poiret.

"He is all right."

"Do you think so?" asked Poiret.

"Lord! Yes, he looks as if he were sleeping. Sylvie has gone for a doctor. I say, Mlle. Michonneau, he is sniffing the ether. Pooh! it is only a spasm. His pulse is good. He is as strong as a Turk. Just look, mademoiselle, what a fur tippet he has on his chest; that is the sort of man to live till he is a hundred. His wig holds on tightly, however. Dear me! it is glued on, and his own hair is red; that is why he wears a wig. They always say that red-haired people are either the worst or the best. Is he one of the good ones, I wonder?"

"Good to hang," said Poiret.

"Round a pretty woman's neck, you mean," said Mlle. Michonneau, hastily. "Just go away, M. Poiret. It is a woman's duty to nurse you men when you are ill. Besides, for all the good you are doing, you may as well take yourself off," she added. "Mme. Vauquer and I will take great care of dear M. Vautrin."

Poiret went out on tiptoe without a murmur, like a dog kicked out of the room by his master.

Rastignac had gone out for the sake of physical exertion; he wanted to breathe the air, he felt stifled. Yesterday evening he had meant to prevent the murder arranged for half-past eight that morning. What had happened? What ought he to do now? He trembled to think that he himself might be implicated. Vautrin's coolness still further dismayed him.

"Yet, how if Vautrin should die without saying a word?" Rastignac asked himself.

He hurried along the alleys of the Luxembourg Gardens as if the hounds of justice were after him, and he already heard the baying of the pack.

"Well?" shouted Bianchon, "you have seen the *Pilote?*"

The *Pilote* was a Radical sheet, edited by M. Tissot. It came out several hours later than the morning papers, and was meant for the benefit of country subscribers; for it brought the morning news into provincial districts twenty-four hours sooner than the ordinary local journals.

"There is a wonderful history in it," said the house student of the Hôpital Cochin. "Young Taillefer called out Count Franchessini, of the Old Guard, and the Count put a couple of inches of steel into his forehead. And here is little Victorine one of the richest heiresses in Paris! If we had known that, eh? What a game of chance death is! They said Victorine was sweet on you; was there any truth in it?"

"Shut up, Bianchon; I shall never marry her. I am in love with a charming woman, and she is in love with me, so——"

"You said that as if you were screwing yourself up to be faithful to her. I should like to see the woman worth the sacrifice of Master Taillefer's money!"

"Are all the devils of hell at my heels?" cried Rastignac.

"What is the matter with you? Are you mad? Give us your hand," said Bianchon, "and let me feel your pulse. You are feverish."

"Just go to Mother Vauquer's," said Rastignac; "that scoundrel Vautrin has dropped down like one dead."

"Aha!" said Bianchon, leaving Rastignac to his reflections, "you confirm my suspicions, and now I mean to make sure for myself."

The law student's long walk was a memorable one for him. He made in some sort a survey of his conscience. After a close scrutiny, after hesitation and self-examination, his honor at any rate came out scatheless from this sharp and terrible ordeal, like a bar of iron tested in the English fashion. He remembered Father Goriot's confidences of the evening before; he recollected the rooms taken for him in the Rue d'Artois, so that he might be near Delphine; and then he thought of his letter, and read it again and kissed it.

"Such a love is my anchor of safety," he said to himself. "How the old man's heart must have been wrung! He says nothing about all that he has been through; but who could not guess? Well, then, I will be like a son to him; his life shall be made happy. If she cares for me, she will often come to spend the day with him. That grand Comtesse de Restaud is a heartless thing; she would make her father into her hall porter. Dear Delphine! she is kinder to the old man; she is worthy to be loved. Ah! this evening I shall be very happy!"

He took out his watch and admired it.

"I have had nothing but success! If two people mean to love each other for ever, they may help each other, and I can take this. Besides, I shall succeed, and I will pay her a hundredfold. There is nothing criminal in this *liaison;* nothing that could cause the most austere moralist to frown. How many respectable people contract similar unions! We deceive nobody; it is deception that makes a position humiliating. If you lie, you lower yourself at once. She and her husband have lived apart for a long while. Besides, how if I called upon that Alsatian to resign a wife whom he cannot make happy?"

Rastignac's battle with himself went on for a long while; and though the scruples of youth inevitably gained the day, an irresistible curiosity led him, about half-past four, to return to the Maison Vauquer through the gathering dusk.

Bianchon had given Vautrin an emetic, reserving the contents of the stomach for chemical analysis at the hospital. Mlle. Michonneau's officious alacrity had still further strengthened his suspicions of her. Vautrin, moreover, had recovered so quickly that it was impossible not to suspect some plot against the leader of all frolics at the lodging-house. Vautrin was standing in front of the stove in the dining-room when Rastignac came in. All the lodgers were assembled sooner than usual by the news of young Taillefer's duel. They were anxious to hear any detail about the affair, and to talk over the probable change in Victorine's prospects. Father Goriot alone was absent, but the rest were chatting. No sooner did Eugène come into the room, than his eyes met the inscrutable gaze of Vautrin. It was the same look that had read his thoughts before—the look that had such power to waken evil thoughts in his heart. He shuddered.

"Well, dear boy," said the escaped convict, "I am likely to cheat death for a good while yet. According to these ladies, I have had a stroke that would have felled an ox, and come off with flying colors."

"A bull you might say," cried the widow.

"You really might be sorry to see me still alive," said Vautrin in Rastignac's ear, thinking that he guessed the student's thoughts. "You must be mighty sure of yourself."

"Mlle. Michonneau was talking the day before yesterday about a gentleman nicknamed *Trompe-la-Mort*," said Bianchon; "and, upon my word, that name would do very well for you."

Vautrin seemed thunderstruck. He turned pale, and staggered back. He turned his magnetic glance, like a ray of vivid light, on Mlle. Michonneau; the old maid shrank and trembled under the influence of that strong will, and collapsed into a chair. The mask of good-nature had dropped from the convict's face; from the unmistakable ferocity of that sinister look, Poiret felt that the old maid was in danger, and hastily stepped between them. None of the lodgers understood this scene in the least, they looked on in mute amazement. There was a pause. Just then there was a sound of tramping feet outside; there were soldiers there, it seemed, for there was a ring of several rifles on the pavement of the street. Collin was mechanically looking round the walls for a way of escape, when four men entered by way of the sitting-room.

"In the name of the King and the Law!" said an officer, but the words were almost lost in a murmur of astonishment.

Silence fell on the room. The lodgers made way for three of the men, who had each a hand on a cocked pistol in a side pocket. Two policemen, who followed the detectives, kept the entrance to the sitting-room, and two more men appeared in the doorway that gave access to the staircase. A sound of footsteps came from the garden, and again the rifles of several soldiers rang on the cobblestones under the window. All chance of salvation by flight was cut off for Trompe-la-Mort, to whom all eyes instinctively turned. The chief walked straight up to him, and commenced operations by giving him a sharp blow on the head, so that the wig fell off, and Collin's face was revealed in all its ugliness. There was a terrible suggestion of strength mingled with cunning in the short, brick-red crop of hair, the whole head was in harmony with his powerful frame, and at that moment the fires of hell seemed to gleam from his eyes. In that flash the real Vautrin shone forth, revealed at once before them all; they understood his past, his present, and future, his pitiless doctrines, his actions, the religion of his own good pleasure, the majesty with which his cynicism and contempt for mankind invested him, the physical strength of an organization proof against all trials. The blood flew to his face, and his eyes glared like the eyes of a wild cat. He started back with savage energy and a fierce growl that drew exclamations of alarm from the lodgers. At that leonine start the police caught at their pistols under cover of the general clamor. Collin saw the gleaming muzzles of the weapons, saw his danger, and instantly gave proof of a power of the highest order. There was something horrible and majestic in the spectacle of the sudden transformation in his face; he could only be compared to a cauldron full of the steam that can send mountains flying, a terrific force dispelled in a moment by a drop of cold water. The drop of water that cooled his wrathful fury was a reflection that flashed across his brain like lightning. He began to smile, and looked down at his wig.

"You are not in the politest of humors to-day," he remarked to the chief, and he held out his hands to the policemen with a jerk of his head.

"Gentlemen," he said, "put on the bracelets or the handcuffs. I call on those present to witness that I make no resistance."

A murmur of admiration ran through the room at the sudden outpouring like fire and lava flood from this human volcano, and its equally sudden cessation.

"There's a sell for you, master crusher," the convict added, looking at the famous director of police.

"Come, strip!" said he of the Petite Rue Saint-Anne, contemptuously.

"Why?" asked Collin. "There are ladies present; I deny nothing, and surrender."

He paused, and looked round the room like an orator who is about to overwhelm his audience.

"Take this down, Daddy Lachapelle," he went on, addressing a little, white-haired old man who had seated himself at the end of the table; and after drawing a printed form from a portfolio, was proceeding to draw up a document. "I acknowledge myself to be Jacques Collin, otherwise known as Trompe-la-Mort, condemned to twenty years' penal servitude, and I have just proved that I have come fairly by my nickname.—If I had as much as raised my hand," he went on, addressing the other lodgers, "those three sneaking wretches yonder would have drawn claret on Mamma Vauquer's domestic hearth. The rogues have laid their heads together to set a trap for me."

Mme. Vauquer felt sick and faint at these words.

"Good Lord!" she cried, "this does give one a turn; and me at the Gaîté with him only last night!" she said to Sylvie.

"Summon your philosophy, mamma," Collin resumed. "Is it a misfortune to have sat in my box at the Gaîté yesterday evening? After all, are you better than we are? The brand upon our shoulders is less shameful than the brand set on your hearts, you flabby members of a society rotten to the core. Not the best man among you could stand up to me." His eyes rested upon Rastignac, to whom he spoke with a pleasant smile that seemed strangely at variance with the savage expression in his eyes.—"Our little bargain still holds good, dear boy; you can accept any time you like! Do you understand?" And he sang:

> "A charming girl is my Fanchette
> In her simplicity."

"Don't you trouble yourself," he went on; "I can get in my money. They are too much afraid of me to swindle me."

The convicts' prison, its language and customs, its sudden sharp transitions from the humorous to the horrible, its appalling grandeur, its triviality and its dark depths, were all revealed in turn by the speaker's discourse; he seemed to be no longer a man, but the type and mouthpiece of a degenerate race, a brutal, supple, clear-headed race of savages. In one moment Collin became the poet of an inferno, wherein all thoughts and passions that move human nature (save repentance) find a place. He looked about him like a fallen archangel who is for war to the end. Rastignac lowered his eyes, and acknowledged this kinship claimed by crime as an expiation of his own evil thoughts.

"Who betrayed me?" said Collin, and his terrible eyes traveled round the room. Suddenly they rested on Mlle. Michonneau.

"It was you, old cat!" he said. "That sham stroke of apoplexy was your doing, lynx eyes! . . . Two words from me, and your throat would be cut in less than a week, but I forgive you, I am a Christian. You did not sell me either. But who did?—— Aha! you may rummage upstairs," he shouted, hearing the police officers opening his cupboards and taking possession of his effects. "The nest is empty, the birds flew away yesterday, and you will be none the wiser. My ledgers are here," he said, tapping his forehead. "Now I know who sold me! It could only be that blackguard Fil-de-Soie. That is who it was, old catchpoll, eh?" he said, turning to the chief. "It was timed so neatly to get the banknotes up above there. There is nothing left for you— spies! As for Fil-de-Soie, he will be under the daisies in less than a fortnight, even if you were to tell off the whole force to protect him. How much did you give the Michonnette?" he asked of the police officers. "A thousand crowns? Oh you Ninon in decay, Pompadour in tatters, Venus of the graveyard, I was worth more than that! If you had given me warning, you should have had six thousand francs. Ah! you had no suspicion of that, old trafficker in flesh and blood, or I should have had the preference. Yes, I would have given six thousand francs to save myself an inconvenient journey and some loss of money," he said, as they fastened the handcuffs on his wrists. "These folks will amuse themselves by dragging out this business till the end of time to keep me idle. If they were to send me straight to jail, I should soon be back at my old tricks in spite of the duffers at the Quai des Orfèvres. Down yonder they will all turn themselves inside out to help their general—their good Trompe-la-Mort —to get clear away. Is there a single one among you that can say, as I can, that he has ten thousand brothers ready to do anything for him?" he asked proudly. "There is some good there," he said, tapping his heart; "I have never betrayed any one!—Look you here, you slut," he said to the old maid, "they are all afraid of me, do you see? but the sight of you turns them sick. Rake in your gains."

He was silent for a moment, and looked round at the lodgers' faces.

"What dolts you are, all of you! Have you never seen a convict before? A convict of Collin's stamp, whom you see before you, is a man less weak-kneed than others; he lifts up his voice against the colossal fraud of the Social Contract, as Jean Jacques did, whose pupil he is proud to declare himself. In short, I stand here single-handed against a Government and a whole subsidized machinery of tribunals and police, and I am a match for them all."

"Ye gods!" cried the painter, "what a magnificent sketch one might make of him!"

"Look here, you gentleman-in-waiting to his highness the gibbet, master of ceremonies to the widow" (a nickname full of sombre poetry, given by prisoners to the guillotine), "be a good fellow, and tell me if it really was Fil-de-Soie who sold me. I don't want him to suffer for some one else, that would not be fair."

But before the chief had time to answer, the rest of the party returned from making their investigations upstairs. Everything had been opened and inventoried. A few words passed between them and the chief, and the official preliminaries were complete.

"Gentlemen," said Collin, addressing the lodgers, "they

will take me away directly. You have all made my stay
among you very agreeable, and I shall look back upon it with
gratitude. Receive my adieux, and permit me to send you
figs from Provence."

He advanced a step or two, and then turned to look once
more at Rastignac.

"Good-bye, Eugène," he said, in a sad and gentle tone, a
strange transition from his previous rough and stern manner. "If you should be hard up, I have left you a devoted
friend," and, in spite of his shackles, he managed to assume
a posture of defence, called, "One, two!" like a fencing-master, and lunged. "If anything goes wrong, apply in that
quarter. Man and money, all at your service."

The strange speaker's manner was sufficiently burlesque,
so that no one but Rastignac knew that there was a serious
meaning underlying the pantomime.

As soon as the police, soldiers, and detectives had left the
house, Sylvie, who was rubbing her mistress' temples with
vinegar, looked round at the bewildered lodgers.

"Well," said she, "he was a man, he was, for all that."

Her words broke the spell. Every one had been too much
excited, too much moved by very various feelings to speak.
But now the lodgers began to look at each other, and then
all eyes were turned at once on Mlle. Michonneau, a thin,
shriveled, dead-alive, mummy-like figure, crouching by the
stove; her eyes were downcast, as if she feared that the green
eye-shade could not shut out the expression of those faces
from her. This figure and the feeling of repulsion she had
so long excited were explained all at once. A smothered
murmur filled the room; it was so unanimous, that it seemed
as if the same feeling of loathing had pitched all the voices
in one key. Mlle. Michonneau heard it, and did not stir.
It was Bianchon who was the first to move; he bent over his
neighbor, and said in a low voice, "If that creature is going
to stop here, and have dinner with us, I shall clear out."

In the twinkling of an eye it was clear that every one in
the room, save Poiret, was of the medical student's opinion,

so that the latter, strong in the support of the majority, went up to that elderly person.

"You are more intimate with Mlle. Michonneau than the rest of us," he said; "speak to her, make her understand that she must go, and go at once."

"At once!" echoed Poiret in amazement.

Then he went across to the crouching figure, and spoke a few words in her ear.

"I have paid beforehand for the quarter; I have as much right to be here as any one else," she said, with a viperous look at the boarders.

"Never mind that! we will club together and pay you the money back," said Rastignac.

"Monsieur is taking Collin's part" she said, with a questioning, malignant glance at the law student; "it is not difficult to guess why."

Eugène started forward at the words, as if he meant to spring upon her and wring her neck. That glance, and the depths of treachery that it revealed, had been a hideous enlightenment.

"Let her alone!" cried the boarders.

Rastignac folded his arms and was silent.

"Let us have no more of Mlle. Judas," said the painter, turning to Mme. Vauquer. "If you don't show the Michonneau the door, madame, we shall all leave your shop, and wherever we go we shall say that there are only convicts and spies left there. If you do the other thing, we will hold our tongues about the business; for when all is said and done, it might happen in the best society until they brand them on the forehead, when they send them to the hulks. They ought not to let convicts go about Paris disguised like decent citizens, so as to carry on their antics like a set of rascally humbugs, which they are."

At this Mme. Vauquer recovered miraculously. She sat up and folded her arms; her eyes were wide open now, and there was no sign of tears in them.

"Why, do you really mean to be the ruin of my establishment, my dear sir? There is M. Vautrin—— Goodness," she cried, interrupting herself, "I can't help calling him by the name he passed himself off by for an honest man! There is one room to let already, and you want me to turn out two more lodgers in the middle of the season, when no one is moving——"

"Gentlemen, let us take our hats and go and dine at Flicoteaux's in the Place Sorbonne," cried Bianchon.

Mme. Vauquer glanced round, and saw in a moment on which side her interest lay. She waddled across to Mlle. Michonneau.

"Come, now," she said; "you would not be the ruin of my establishment, would you, eh? There's a dear, kind soul. You see what a pass these gentlemen have brought me to; just go up to your room for this evening."

"Never a bit of it!" cried the boarders. "She must go, and go this minute!"

"But the poor lady has had no dinner," said Poiret, with piteous entreaty.

"She can go and dine where she likes," shouted several voices.

"Turn her out, the spy!"

"Turn them both out! Spies!"

"Gentlemen," cried Poiret, his heart swelling with the courage that love gives to the ovine male, "respect the weaker sex."

"Spies are of no sex!" said the painter.

"A precious sexorama!"

"Turn her into the streetorama!"

"Gentlemen, this is not manners! If you turn people out of the house, it ought not to be done so unceremoniously and with no notice at all. We have paid our money, and we are not going," said Poiret, putting on his cap, and taking a chair beside Mlle. Michonneau, with whom Mme. Vauquer was remonstrating.

"Naughty boy!" said the painter, with a comical look; "run away, naughty little boy!"

"Look here," said Bianchon; "if you do not go, all the rest of us will," and the boarders, to a man, made for the sitting-room-door.

"Oh! mademoiselle, what is to be done?" cried Mme. Vauquer. "I am a ruined woman. You can't stay here; they will go further, do something violent."

Mlle. Michonneau rose to her feet.

"She is going!—She is not going!—She is going!—No, she isn't."

These alternate exclamations, and a suggestion of hostile intentions, borne out by the behavior of the insurgents, compelled Mlle. Michonneau to take her departure. She made some stipulations, speaking in a low voice in her hostess' ear, and then—"I shall go to Mme. Buneaud's," she said, with a threatening look.

"Go where you please, mademoiselle," said Mme. Vauquer, who regarded this choice of an opposition establishment as an atrocious insult. "Go and lodge with the Buneaud; the wine would give a cat the colic, and the food is cheap and nasty."

The boarders stood aside in two rows to let her pass; not a word was spoken. Poiret looked so wistfully after Mlle. Michonneau, and so artlessly revealed that he was in two minds whether to go or stay, that the boarders, in their joy at being quit of Mlle. Michonneau, burst out laughing at the sight of him.

"Hist!—st!—st! Poiret," shouted the painter. "Hallo! I say, Poiret, hallo!" The employé from the Muséum began to sing:

"Partant pour la Syrie,
  Le jeune et beau Dunois . . . "

"Get along with you; you must be dying to go, *trahit sua quemque voluptas!*" said Bianchon.

"Every one to his taste—free rendering from Virgil," said the tutor.

Mlle. Michonneau made a movement as if to take Poiret's arm, with an appealing glance that he could not resist. The two went out together, the old maid leaning upon him, and there was a burst of applause, followed by peals of laughter.

"Bravo, Poiret!"

"Who would have thought it of old Poiret!"

"Apollo Poiret!"

"Mars Poiret!"

"Intrepid Poiret!"

A messenger came in at that moment with a letter for Mme. Vauquer, who read it through, and collapsed in her chair.

"The house might as well be burned down at once," cried she, "if there are to be any more of these thunderbolts! Young Taillefer died at three o'clock this afternoon. It serves me right for wishing well to those ladies at that poor young man's expense. Mme. Couture and Victorine want me to send their things, because they are going to live with her father. M. Taillefer allows his daughter to keep old Mme. Couture with her as lady companion. Four rooms to let! and five lodgers gone! . . ."

She sat up, and seemed about to burst into tears.

"Bad luck has come to lodge here, I think," she cried.

Once more there came a sound of wheels from the street outside.

"What! another windfall for somebody!" was Sylvie's comment.

But it was Goriot who came in, looking so radiant, so flushed with happiness, that he seemed to have grown young again.

"Goriot in a cab!" cried the boarders; "the world is coming to an end."

The good soul made straight for Eugène, who was standing wrapped in thought in a corner, and laid a hand on the young man's arm.

"Come," he said, with gladness in his eyes.

"Then you haven't heard the news?" said Eugène. "Vautrin was an escaped convict; they have just arrested him; and young Taillefer is dead."

"Very well, but what business is it of ours?" replied Father Goriot. "I am going to dine with my daughter *in your house,* do you understand? She is expecting you. Come!"

He carried off Rastignac with him by main force, and they departed in as great a hurry as a pair of eloping lovers.

"Now, let us have dinner," cried the painter, and every one drew his chair to the table.

"Well, I never," said the portly Sylvie. "Nothing goes right to-day! The haricot mutton has caught! Bah! you will have to eat it, burned as it is, more's the pity!"

Mme. Vauquer was so dispirited that she could not say a word as she looked round the table and saw only ten people where eighteen should be; but every one tried to comfort and cheer her. At first the dinner contingent, as was natural, talked about Vautrin and the day's events; but the conversation wound round to such topics of interest as duels, jails, justice, prison life, and alterations that ought to be made in the laws. They soon wandered miles away from Jacques Collin and Victorine and her brother. There might be only ten of them, but they made noise enough for twenty; indeed, there seemed to be more of them than usual; that was the only difference between yesterday and to-day. Indifference to the fate of others is a matter of course in this selfish world, which, on the morrow of a tragedy, seeks among the events of Paris for a fresh sensation for its daily renewed appetite, and this indifference soon gained the upper hand. Mme. Vauquer herself grew calmer under the soothing influence of hope, and the mouthpiece of hope was the portly Sylvie.

That day had gone by like a dream for Eugène, and the sense of unreality lasted into the evening; so that, in spite of his energetic character and clear-headedness, his ideas were a chaos as he sat beside Goriot in the cab. The old man's voice was full of unwonted happiness, but Eugène had been shaken by so many emotions that the words sounded in his ears like words spoken in a dream.

"It was finished this morning! All three of us are going to dine there together, together! Do you understand? I have not dined with my Delphine, my little Delphine, these four years, and I shall have her for a whole evening! We have been at your lodging the whole time since morning. I have been working like a porter in my shirt sleeves, helping to carry in the furniture. Aha! you don't know what pretty ways she has; at table she will look after me, 'Here, papa, just try this, it is nice.' And I shall not be able to eat. Oh, it is a long while since I have been with her in quiet every-day life as we shall have her."

"It really seems as if the world had been turned upside down."

"Upside down?" repeated Father Goriot. "Why, the world has never been so right-side up. I see none but smiling faces in the streets, people who shake hands cordially and embrace each other, people who all look as happy as if they were going to dine with their daughter, and gobble down a nice little dinner that she went with me to order of the chef at the Café des Anglais. But, pshaw! with her beside you gall and worm-wood would be as sweet as honey."

"I feel as if I were coming back to life again," said Eugène.

"Why, hurry up there!" cried Father Goriot, letting down the window in front. "Get on faster; I will give you five francs if you get to the place I told you of in ten minutes time."

With this prospect before him the cabman crossed Paris with miraculous celerity.

"How that fellow crawls!" said Father Goriot.

"But where are you taking me?" Eugène asked him.

"To your own house," said Goriot.

The cab stopped in the Rue d'Artois. Father Goriot stepped out first and flung ten francs to the man with the recklessness of a widower returning to bachelor ways.

"Come along upstairs," he said to Rastignac. They crossed a courtyard, and climbed up to the third floor of a new and handsome house. Here they stopped before a door; but before Goriot could ring, it was opened by Thérèse, Mme. de Nucingen's maid. Eugène found himself in a charming set of chambers; an ante-room, a little drawing-room, a bedroom, and a study, looking out upon a garden. The furniture and the decoration of the little drawing-room were of the most daintily charming description, the room was full of soft light, and Delphine rose up from a low chair by the fire and stood before him. She set her fire-screen down on the chimney-piece, and spoke with tenderness in every tone of her voice.

"So we had to go in search of you, sir, you who are so slow to understand!"

Thérèse left the room. The student took Delphine in his arms and held her in a tight clasp, his eyes filled with tears of joy. This last contrast between his present surroundings and the scenes he had just witnessed was too much for Rastignac's over-wrought nerves, after the day's strain and excitement that had wearied heart and brain; he was almost overcome by it.

"I felt sure myself that he loved you," murmured Father Goriot, while Eugène lay back bewildered on the sofa, utterly unable to speak a word or to reason out how and why the magic wand had been waved to bring about this final transformation scene.

"But you must see your rooms," said Mme. de Nucingen. She took his hand and led him into a room carpeted and furnished like her own; indeed, down to the smallest details, it was a reproduction in miniature of Delphine's apartment.

"There is no bed," said Rastignac.

"No, monsieur," she answered, reddening, and pressing his hand. Eugène, looking at her, understood, young though he yet was, how deeply modesty is implanted in the heart of a woman who loves.

"You are one of those beings whom we cannot choose but to adore for ever," he said in her ear. "Yes, the deeper and truer love is, the more mysterious and closely veiled it should be; I can dare to say so, since we understand each other so well. No one shall learn our secret."

"Oh! so I am nobody, I suppose," growled the father.

"You know quite well that 'we' means you."

"Ah! that is what I wanted. You will not mind me, will you? I shall go and come like a good fairy who makes himself felt everywhere without being seen, shall I not? Eh, Delphinette, Ninette, Dedel—was it not a good idea of mine to say to you, 'There are some nice rooms to let in the Rue d'Artois; let us furnish them for him?' And she would not hear of it! Ah! your happiness has been all my doing. I am the author of your happiness and of your existence. Fathers must always be giving if they would be happy themselves; always giving—they would not be fathers else."

"Was that how it happened?" asked Eugène.

"Yes. She would not listen to me. She was afraid that people would talk, as if the rubbish that they say about you were to be compared with happiness! Why, all women dream of doing what she has done——"

Father Goriot found himself without an audience, for Mme. de Nucingen had led Rastignac into the study; he heard a kiss given and taken, low though the sound was.

The study was furnished as elegantly as the other rooms, and nothing was wanting there.

"Have we guessed your wishes rightly?" she asked, as they returned to the drawing-room for dinner.

"Yes," he said, "only too well, alas! For all this luxury so well carried out, this realization of pleasant dreams, the elegance that satisfies all the romantic fancies of youth, appeals to me so strongly that I cannot but feel that it is my rightful possession, but I cannot accept it from you, and I am too poor as yet to——"

"Ah! ah! you say me nay already," she said with arch imperiousness, and a charming little pout of the lips, a woman's way of laughing away scruples.

But Eugène had submitted so lately to that solemn self-questioning, and Vautrin's arrest had so plainly shown him the depths of the pit that lay ready to his feet, that the instincts of generosity and honor had been strengthened in him, and he could not allow himself to be coaxed into abandoning his high-minded determinations. Profound melancholy filled his mind.

"Do you really mean to refuse?" said Mme. de Nucingen. "And do you know what such a refusal means? That you are not sure of yourself, that you do not dare to bind yourself to me. Are you really afraid of betraying my affection? If you love me, if I—love you, why should you shrink back from such a slight obligation? If you but knew what a pleasure it has been to see after all the arrangements of this bachelor establishment, you would not hesitate any longer, you would ask me to forgive you for your hesitation. I had some money that belonged to you, and I have made good use of it, that is all. You mean this for magnanimity, but it is very little of you. You are asking me for far more than this. . . . Ah!" she cried, as Eugène's passionate glance was turned on her, "and you are making difficulties about the merest trifles. Oh, if you feel no love whatever for me, refuse, by all means. My fate hangs on a word from you. Speak!—Father," she said after a pause, "make him listen to reason. Can he imagine that I am less nice than he is on the point of honor?"

Father Goriot was looking on and listening to this pretty quarrel with a placid smile, as if he had found some balm for all the sorrows of life.

"Child that you are!" she cried again, catching Eugène's hand. "You are just beginning life; you find barriers at the outset that many a man finds insurmountable; a woman's hand opens the way, and you shrink back! Why, you are sure to succeed! You will have a brilliant future. Success is written on that broad forehead of yours, and will you not be able to repay me my loan of to-day? Did not a lady in olden times arm her knight with sword and helmet and coat of mail, and find him a charger, so that he might fight for her in the tournament? Well, then, Eugène, these things that I offer you are the weapons of this age; every one who means to be something must have such tools as these. A pretty place your

garret must be if it is like papa's room! See, dinner is waiting all this time. Do you want to make me unhappy?—
Why don't you answer?" she said, shaking his hand. *"Mon
Dieu!* papa, make up his mind for him, or I will go away
and never see him any more."

"I will make up your mind," said Goriot, coming down
from the clouds. "Now, my dear M. Eugène, the next thing
is to borrow money of the Jews, isn't it?"

"There is positively no help for it," said Eugène.

"All right, I will give you credit," said the other, drawing
out a cheap leather pocket-book, much the worse for wear.
"I have turned Jew myself; I paid for everything; here are
the invoices. You do not owe a penny for anything here. It
did not come to very much—five thousand francs at most, and
I am going to lend you the money myself. I am not a woman
—you cannot refuse me. You shall give me a receipt on a
scrap of paper, and you can return it some time or other."

Delphine and Eugène looked at each other in amazement,
tears sprang to their eyes. Rastignac held out his hand and
grasped Goriot's warmly.

"Well, what is all this about? Are you not my children?"

"Oh! my poor father," said Mme. de Nucingen, "how did
you do it?"

"Ah! now you ask me. When I made up my mind to move
him nearer to you, and saw you buying things as if they were
wedding presents, I said to myself, 'She will never be able to
pay for them.' The attorney says that those law proceedings
will last quite six months before your husband can be made
to disgorge your fortune. Well and good. I sold out my
property in the funds that brought in thirteen hundred and
fifty livres a year, and bought a safe annuity of twelve hundred francs a year for fifteen thousand francs. Then I paid
your tradesmen out of the rest of the capital. As for me,
children, I have a room upstairs for which I pay fifty
crowns a year; I can live like a prince on two francs a day,
and still have something left over. I shall not have to spend
anything much on clothes, for I never wear anything out.

This fortnight past I have been laughing in my sleeve, thinking to myself, 'How happy they are going to be!' and—well, now, are you not happy?"

"Oh papa! papa!" cried Mme. de Nucingen, springing to her father, who took her on his knee. She covered him with kisses, her fair hair brushed his cheek, her tears fell on the withered face that had grown so bright and radiant.

"Dear father, what a father you are! No, there is not another father like you under the sun. If Eugène loved you before, what must he feel for you now?"

"Why, children, why, Delphinette!" cried Goriot, who had not felt his daughter's heart beat against his breast for ten years, "do you want me to die of joy? My poor heart will break! Come, Monsieur Eugène, we are quits already." ·And the old man strained her to his breast with such fierce and passionate force that she cried out.

"Oh! you are hurting me!" she said.

"I am hurting you!" He grew pale at the words. The pain expressed in his face seemed greater than it is given to humanity to know. The agony of this Christ of paternity can only be compared with the masterpieces of those princes of the palette who have left for us the record of their visions of an agony suffered for a whole world by the Saviour of men. Father Goriot pressed his lips very gently against the waist that his fingers had grasped too roughly.

"Oh! no, no," he cried. "I have not hurt you, have I?" and his smile seemed to repeat the question. *"You* have hurt me with that cry just now.—The things cost rather more than that," he said in her ear, with another gentle kiss, "but I had to deceive him about it, or he would have been angry."

Eugène sat dumb with amazement in the presence of this inexhaustible love; he gazed at Goriot, and his face betrayed the artless admiration which shapes the beliefs of youth.

"I will be worthy of all this," he cried.

"Oh! my Eugène, that is nobly said," and Mme. de Nucingen kissed the law student on the forehead.

"He gave up Mlle. Taillefer and her millions for you," said

Father Goriot. "Yes, the little thing was in love with you, and now that her brother is dead she is as rich as Crœsus."

"Oh! why did you tell her?" cried Rastignac.

"Eugène," Delphine said in his ear, "I have one regret now this evening. Ah! how I will love you! and for ever!"

"This is the happiest day I have had since you two were married!" cried Goriot. "God may send me any suffering, so long as I do not suffer through you, and I can still say, 'In this short month of February I had more happiness than other men have in their whole lives.'—Look at me, Fifine!" he said to his daughter. "She is very beautiful, is she not? Tell me, now, have you seen many women with that pretty soft color—that little dimple of hers? No, I thought not. Ah, well, and but for me this lovely woman would never have been. And very soon happiness will make her a thousand times lovelier, happiness through you. I could give up my place in heaven to you, neighbor, if needs be, and go down to hell instead. Come, let us have dinner," he added, scarcely knowing what he said, "everything is ours."

"Poor dear father!"

He rose and went over to her, and took her face in his hands, and set a kiss on the plaits of hair. "If you only knew, little one, how happy you can make me—how little it takes to make me happy! Will you come and see me sometimes? I shall be just above, so it is only a step. Promise me, say that you will!"

"Yes, dear father."

"Say it again."

"Yes, I will, my kind father."

"Hush! hush! I should make you say it a hundred times over if I followed my own wishes. Let us have dinner."

The three behaved like children that evening, and Father Goriot's spirits were certainly not the least wild. He lay at his daughter's feet, kissed them, gazed into her eyes, rubbed his head against her dress; in short, no young lover could have been more extravagant or more tender.

"You see!" Delphine said with a look at Eugène, "so long

as my father is with us, he monopolizes me. He will be rather in the way sometimes."

Eugène had himself already felt certain twinges of jealousy, and could not blame this speech that contained the germ of all ingratitude.

"And when will the rooms be ready?" asked Eugène, looking round. "We must all leave them this evening, I suppose."

"Yes, but to-morrow you must come and dine with me," she answered, with an eloquent glance. "It is our night at the Italiens."

"I shall go to the pit," said her father.

It was midnight. Mme. de Nucingen's carriage was waiting for her, and Father Goriot and the student walked back to the Maison Vauquer, talking of Delphine, and warming over their talk till there grew up a curious rivalry between the two violent passions. Eugène could not help seeing that the father's self-less love was deeper and more steadfast than his own. For this worshiper Delphine was always pure and fair, and her father's adoration drew its fervor from a whole past as well as a future of love.

They found Mme. Vauquer by the stove, with Sylvie and Christophe to keep her company; the old landlady, sitting like Marius among the ruins of Carthage, was waiting for the two lodgers that yet remained to her, and bemoaning her lot with the sympathetic Sylvie. Tasso's lamentations as recorded in Byron's poem are undoubtedly eloquent, but for sheer force of truth they fall far short of the widow's cry from the depths.

"Only three cups of coffee in the morning, Sylvie! Oh dear! to have your house emptied in this way is enough to break your heart. What is life, now my lodgers are gone? Nothing at all. Just think of it! It is just as if all the furniture had been taken out of the house, and your furniture is your life. How have I offended heaven to draw down all this trouble upon me? And haricot beans and potatoes laid in for twenty people! The police in my house, too! We shall have to live on potatoes now, and Christophe will have to go!"

The Savoyard, who was fast asleep, suddenly woke up at this, and said, "Madame," questioningly.

"Poor fellow!" said Sylvie, "he is like a dog."

"In the dead season, too! Nobody is moving now. I would like to know where the lodgers are to drop down from. It drives me distracted. And that old witch of a Michonneau goes and takes Poiret with her! What can she have done to him to make him so fond of her? He runs about after her like a little dog."

"Lord!" said Sylvie, flinging up her head, "those old maids are up to all sorts of tricks."

"There's that poor M. Vautrin that they made out to be a convict," the widow went on. "Well, you know that is too much for me, Sylvie; I can't bring myself to believe it. Such a lively man as he was, and paid fifteen francs a month for his coffee of an evening, paid you every penny on the nail too."

"And open-handed he was!" said Christophe.

"There is some mistake," said Sylvie.

"Why, no there isn't! he said so himself!" said Mme. Vauquer. "And to think that all these things have happened in my house, and in a quarter where you never see a cat go by. On my word as an honest woman, it's like a dream. For, look here, we saw Louis XVI. meet with his mishap; we saw the fall of the Emperor; and we saw him come back and fall again; there was nothing out of the way in all that, but lodging-houses are not liable to revolutions. You can do without a king, but you must eat all the same; and so long as a decent woman, a de Conflans born and bred, will give you all sorts of good things for dinner, nothing short of the end of the world ought to—but there, it is the end of the world, that is just what it is!"

"And to think that Mlle. Michonneau who made all this mischief is to have a thousand crowns a year for it, so I hear," cried Sylvie.

"Don't speak of her, she is a wicked woman!" said Mme.
Vauquer. "She is going to the Buneaud, who charges less
than cost. But the Buneaud is capable of anything; she
must have done frightful things, robbed and murdered people in her time. *She* ought to be put in jail for life instead
of that poor dear——"

Eugène and Goriot rang the door-bell at that moment.

"Ah! here are my two faithful lodgers," said the widow,
sighing.

But the two faithful lodgers, who retained but shadowy
recollections of the misfortunes of their lodging-house, announced to their hostess without more ado that they were
about to remove to the Chaussée d'Antin.

"Sylvie!" cried the widow, "this is the last straw.—Gentlemen, this will be the death of me! It has quite upset me!
There's a weight on my chest! I am ten years older for this
day! Upon my word, I shall go out of my senses! And what
is to be done with the haricots?—Oh, well, if I am to be left
here all by myself, you shall go to-morrow, Christophe.—
Good-night, gentlemen," and she went.

"What is the matter now?" Eugène inquired of Sylvie.

"Lord! everybody is going about his business, and that has
addled her wits. There! she is crying upstairs. It will do
her good to snivel a bit. It's the first time she has cried since
I've been with her."

By the morning, Mme. Vauquer, to use her own expression, had "made up her mind to it." True, she still wore a
doleful countenance, as might be expected of a woman who
had lost all her lodgers, and whose manner of life had been
suddenly revolutionized, but she had all her wits about her.
Her grief was genuine and profound; it was real pain of
mind, for her purse had suffered, the routine of her existence
had been broken. A lover's farewell glance at his lady-love's
window is not more mournful than Mme. Vauquer's survey
of the empty places round her table. Eugène administered
comfort, telling the widow that Bianchon, whose term of residence at the hospital was about to expire, would doubtless

take his (Rastignac's) place; that the official from the
Muséum had often expressed a desire to have Mme. Couture's
rooms; and that in a very few days her household would be on
the old footing.

"God send it may, my dear sir! but bad luck has come to
lodge here. There'll be a death in the house before ten days
are out, you'll see," and she gave a lugubrious look round the
dining-room. "Whose turn will it be, I wonder?"

"It is just as well that we are moving out," said Eugène
to Father Goriot in a low voice.

"Madame," said Sylvie, running in with a scared face, "I
have not seen Mistigris these three days."

"Ah! well, if my cat is dead, if *he* has gone and left us,
I——"

The poor woman could not finish her sentence; she clasped
her hands and hid her face on the back of her armchair,
quite overcome by this dreadful portent.

By twelve o'clock, when the postman reaches that quarter,
Eugène received a letter. The dainty envelope bore the
Beauséant arms on the seal, and contained an invitation to
the Vicomtesse's great ball, which had been talked of in Paris
for a month. A little note for Eugène was slipped in with
the card.

"I think, monsieur, that you will undertake with pleasure
to interpret my sentiments to Mme. de Nucingen, so I am
sending the card for which you asked me to you. I shall be
delighted to make the acquaintance of Mme. de Restaud's
sister. Pray introduce that charming lady to me, and do not
let her monopolize all your affection, for you owe me not a
little in return for mine.

"VICOMTESSE DE BEAUSÉANT."

"Well," said Eugène to himself, as he read the note a second time, "Mme. de Beauséant says pretty plainly that she
does not want the Baron de Nucingen."

He went to Delphine at once in his joy. He had procured

this pleasure for her, and doubtless he would receive the price of it. Mme. de Nucingen was dressing. Rastignac waited in her boudoir, enduring as best he might the natural impatience of an eager temperament for the reward desired and withheld for a year. Such sensations are only known once in a life. The first woman to whom a man is drawn, if she is really a woman—that is to say, if she appears to him amid the splendid accessories that form a necessary background to life in the world of Paris—will never have a rival.

Love in Paris is a thing distinct and apart; for in Paris neither men nor women are the dupes of the commonplaces by which people seek to throw a veil over their motives, or to parade a fine affectation of disinterestedness in their sentiments. In this country within a country, it is not merely required of a woman that she should satisfy the senses and the soul; she knows perfectly well that she has still greater obligations to discharge, that she must fulfil the countless demands of a vanity that enters into every fibre of that living organism called society. Love, for her, is above all things, and by its very nature, a vainglorious, brazen-fronted, ostentatious, thriftless charlatan. If at the Court of Louis XIV. there was not a woman but envied Mlle. de la Vallière the reckless devotion of passion that led the grand monarch to tear the priceless ruffles at his wrists in order to assist the entry of a Duc de Vermandois into the world—what can you expect of the rest of society? You must have youth and wealth and rank; nay, you must, if possible, have more than these, for the more incense you bring with you to burn at the shrine of the god, the more favorably will he regard the worshiper. Love is a religion, and his cult must in the nature of things be more costly than those of all other deities; Love the Spoiler stays for a moment, and then passes on; like the urchin of the streets, his course may be traced by the ravages that he has made. The wealth of feeling and imagination is the poetry of the garret; how should love exist there without that wealth?

If there are exceptions who do not subscribe to these Draconian laws of the Parisian code, they are solitary examples. Such souls live so far out of the main current that they are not borne away by the doctrines of society; they dwell beside some clear spring of everflowing water, without seeking to leave the green shade; happy to listen to the echoes of the infinite in everything around them and in their own souls, waiting in patience to take their flight for heaven, while they look with pity upon those of earth.

Rastignac, like most young men who have been early impressed by the circumstance of power and grandeur, meant to enter the lists fully armed; the burning ambition of conquest possessed him already; perhaps he was conscious of his powers, but as yet he knew neither the end to which his ambition was to be directed, nor the means of attaining it. In default of the pure and sacred love that fills a life, ambition may become something very noble, subduing to itself every thought of personal interest, and setting as the end—the greatness, not of one man, but of a whole nation.

But the student had not yet reached the time of life when a man surveys the whole course of existence and judges it soberly. Hitherto he had scarcely so much as shaken off the spell of the fresh and gracious influences that envelop a childhood in the country, like green leaves and grass. He had hesitated on the brink of the Parisian Rubicon, and in spite of the prickings of ambition, he still clung to a lingering tradition of an old ideal—the peaceful life of the noble in his château. But yesterday evening, at the sight of his rooms, those scruples had vanished. He had learned what it was to enjoy the material advantages of fortune, as he had already enjoyed the social advantages of birth; he ceased to be a provincial from that moment, and slipped naturally and easily into a position which opened up a prospect of a brilliant future.

So, as he waited for Delphine, in the pretty boudoir, where he felt that he had a certain right to be, he felt himself so far away from the Rastignac who came back to Paris a year ago, that, turning some power of inner vision upon this latter, he asked himself whether that past self bore any resemblance to the Rastignac of that moment.

"Madame is in her room," Thérèse came to tell him. The woman's voice made him start.

He found Delphine lying back in her low chair by the fireside, looking fresh and bright. The sight of her among the flowing draperies of muslin suggested some beautiful tropical flower, where the fruit is set amid the blossom.

"Well," she said, with a tremor in her voice, "here you are."

"Guess what I bring for you," said Eugène, sitting down beside her. He took possession of her arm to kiss her hand.

Mme. de Nucingen gave a joyful start as she saw the card. She turned to Eugène; there were tears in her eyes as she flung her arms about his neck, and drew him towards her in a frenzy of gratified vanity.

"And I owe this happiness to you—to *thee*" (she whispered the more intimate word in his ear); "but Thérèse is in my dressing-room, let us be prudent.—This happiness—yes, for I may call it so, when it comes to me through *you*—is surely more than a triumph for self-love? No one has been willing to introduce me into that set. Perhaps just now I may seem to you to be frivolous, petty, shallow, like a Parisienne, but remember, my friend, that I am ready to give up all for you; and that if I long more than ever for an entrance into the Faubourg Saint-Germain, it is because I shall meet you there."

"Mme. de Beauséant's note seems to say very plainly that she does not expect to see the *Baron* de Nucingen at her ball; don't you think so?" said Eugène.

"Why, yes," said the Baroness as she returned the letter. "Those women have a talent for insolence. But it is of no consequence, I shall go. My sister is sure to be there, and sure to be very beautifully dressed.—Eugène," she went on, lowering her voice, "she will go to dispel ugly suspicions. You do not know the things that people are saying about her. Only this morning Nucingen came to tell me that they had been discussing her at the club. Great heavens! on what does a woman's character and the honor of a whole family depend! I feel that I am nearly touched and wounded in my poor sister. According to some people, M. de Trailles must have put his name to bills for a hundred thousand francs, nearly all of them are overdue, and proceedings are threatened. In this predicament, it seems that my sister sold her diamonds to a Jew—the beautiful diamonds that belonged to her husband's mother, Mme. de Restaud the elder,—you have seen her wearing them. In fact, nothing else has been talked about for the last two days. So I can see that Anastasie is sure to come to Mme. de Beauséant's ball in tissue of gold, and ablaze with diamonds, to draw all eyes upon her; and I will not be outshone. She has tried to eclipse me all her life; she has never been kind to me, and I have helped her so often, and always had money for her when she had none.— But never mind other people now, to-day I mean to be perfectly happy."

At one o'clock that morning Eugène was still with Mme. de Nucingen. In the midst of their lovers' farewell, a farewell full of hope of bliss to come, she said in a troubled voice, "I am very fearful, superstitious. Give what name you like to my presentiments, but I am afraid that my happiness will be paid for by some horrible catastrophe."

"Child!" said Eugène.

"Ah! have we changed places, and am I the child to-night?" she asked, laughingly.

Eugène went back to the Maison Vauquer, never doubting but that he should leave it for good on the morrow; and on the way he fell to dreaming the bright dreams of youth, when the cup of happiness has left its sweetness on the lips.

"Well?" cried Goriot, as Rastignac passed by his door.

"Yes," said Eugène; "I will tell you everything to-morrow."

"Everything, will you not?" cried the old man. "Go to bed. To-morrow our happy life will begin."

Next day, Goriot and Rastignac were ready to leave the

lodging-house, and only awaited the good pleasure of a porter to move out of it; but towards noon there was a sound of wheels in the Rue Neuve-Sainte-Geneviève, and a carriage stopped before the door of the Maison Vauquer. Mme. de Nucingen alighted, and asked if her father was still in the house, and, receiving an affirmative reply from Sylvie, ran lightly upstairs.

It so happened that Eugène was at home all unknown to his neighbor. At breakfast time he had asked Goriot to superintend the removal of his goods, saying that he would meet him in the Rue d'Artois at four o'clock; but Rastignac's name had been called early on the list at the École de Droit, and he had gone back at once to the Rue Neuve-Sainte-Geneviève. No one had seen him come in, for Goriot had gone to find a porter, and the mistress of the house was likewise out. Eugène had thought to pay her himself, for it struck him that if he left this, Goriot in his zeal would probably pay for him. As it was, Eugène went up to his room to see that nothing had been forgotten, and blessed his foresight when he saw the blank bill bearing Vautrin's signature lying in the drawer where he had carelessly thrown it on the day when he had repaid the amount. There was no fire in the grate, so he was about to tear it into little pieces, when he heard a voice speaking in Goriot's room, and the speaker was Delphine! He made no more noise, and stood still to listen, thinking that she should have no secrets from him; but after the first few words, the conversation between the father and daughter was so strange and interesting that it absorbed all his attention.

"Ah! thank heaven that you thought of asking him to give an account of the money settled on me before I was utterly ruined, father. Is it safe to talk?" she added.

"Yes, there is no one in the house," said her father faintly.

"What is the matter with you?" asked Mme. de Nucingen.

"God forgive you! you have just dealt me a staggering blow, child!" said the old man. "You cannot know how much I love you, or you would not have burst in upon me like this, with such news, especially if all is not lost. Has something so important happened that you must come here about it? In a few minutes we should have been in the Rue d'Artois."

"Eh! does one think what one is doing after a catastrophe? It has turned my head. Your attorney has found out the state of things now, but it was bound to come out sooner or later. We shall want your long business experience; and I come to you like a drowning man who catches at a branch. When M. Derville found that Nucingen was throwing all sorts of difficulties in his way, he threatened him with proceedings, and told him plainly that he would soon obtain an order from the President of the Tribunal. So Nucingen came to my room this morning, and asked if I meant to ruin us both. I told him that I knew nothing whatever about it, that I had a fortune, and ought to be put into possession of my fortune, and that my attorney was acting for me in the matter; I said again that I knew absolutely nothing about it, and could not possibly go into the subject with him. Wasn't that what you told me to tell him?"

"Yes, quite right," answered Goriot.

"Well, then," Delphine continued, "he told me all about his affairs. He had just invested all his capital and mine in business speculations; they have only just been started, and very large sums of money are locked up. If I were to compel him to refund my dowry now, he would be forced to file his petition; but if I will wait a year, he undertakes, on his honor, to double or treble my fortune, by investing it in building land, and I shall be mistress at last of the whole of my property. He was speaking the truth, father dear; he frightened me! He asked my pardon for his conduct; he has given me my liberty; I am free to act as I please on condition that I leave him to carry on my business in my name. To prove his sincerity, he promised that M. Derville might inspect the accounts as often as I pleased, so that I might be assured that everything was being conducted properly. In short, he put himself into my power, bound hand and foot. He wishes the present arrangements as to the expenses of housekeeping to continue for two more years, and entreated me not to exceed my allowance. He showed me plainly that it was all that he could do to keep up appearances; he has broken with his opera dancer; he will be compelled to practise the most strict economy (in secret) if he is to bide his time with unshaken credit. I scolded, I did all I could to drive him to desperation, so as to find out more. He showed me his ledgers—he broke down and cried at last. I never saw a man in such a state. He lost his head completely, talked of killing himself, and raved till I felt quite sorry for him."

"Do you really believe that silly rubbish?" . . . cried her father. "It was all got up for your benefit! I have had to do with Germans in the way of business; honest and straightforward they are pretty sure to be, but when with their simplicity and frankness they are sharpers and humbugs as well, they are the worst rogues of all. Your husband is taking advantage of you. As soon as pressure is brought to bear on him he shams dead; he means to be more the master under your name than in his own. He will take advantage of the position to secure himself against the risks of business. He is as sharp as he is treacherous; he is a bad lot! No, no; I am not going to leave my girls behind me without a penny when I go to Père-Lachaise. I know something about business still. He has sunk his money in speculation, he says; very well then, there is something to show for it—bills, receipts, papers of some sort.   Let him produce them, and come to an arrangement with you. We will choose the most promising of his speculations, take them over at our own risk, and have the securities transferred into your name; they shall represent the separate estate of Delphine Goriot, wife of the Baron de Nucingen.   Does that fellow really take us for idiots? Does he imagine that I could stand the idea of your being without fortune, without bread, for forty-eight hours? I would not stand it a day—no, not a night, not a couple of hours! If there had been any foundation for the idea, I should never get over it. What! I have worked hard for forty years, carried sacks on my back, and sweated and pinched and saved all my life for you, my darlings, for you who made the toil and every burden borne for you seem light; and now, my fortune, my whole life, is to vanish in smoke! I should die raving mad if I believed a word of it. By all that's holiest in heaven and earth, we will have this cleared up at once; go through the books, have the whole business looked thoroughly into! I will not sleep, nor rest, nor eat until I have satisfied myself that all your fortune is in existence. Your money is settled upon you, God be thanked! and, luckily, your attorney, Maître Derville, is an honest man. Good Lord! you shall have your snug little million, your fifty thousand francs a year, as long as you live, or I will raise a racket in Paris, I will so! If the Tribunals put upon us, I will appeal to the Chambers. If I knew that you were well and comfortably off as far as money is concerned, that thought would keep me easy in spite of bad health and troubles. Money? why, it is life! Money does everything. That great dolt of an Alsatian shall sing to another tune! Look here, Delphine, don't give way, don't make a concession of half a quarter of a farthing to that fathead, who has ground you down and made you miserable. If he can't do without you, we will give him a good cudgeling, and keep him in order. Great heavens! my brain is on fire; it is as if there were something redhot inside my head. My Delphine lying on straw! You! my Fifine! Good gracious! Where are my gloves? Come, let us go at once; I mean to see everything with my own eyes—books, cash, and correspondence, the whole business. I shall have no peace until I know for certain that your fortune is secure."

"Oh! father dear, be careful how you set about it! If there is the least hint of vengeance in the business, if you show yourself openly hostile, it will be all over with me. He knows whom he has to deal with; he thinks it quite natural that if you put the idea into my head, I should be uneasy about my money; but I swear to you that he has it in his own hands, and that he had meant to keep it. He is just the man to abscond with all the money and leave us in the lurch, the scoundrel! He knows quite well that I will not dishonor the name I bear by bringing him into a court of law. His position is strong and weak at the same time. If we drive him to despair, I am lost."

"Why, then, the man is a rogue?"

"Well, yes, father," she said, flinging herself into a chair. "I wanted to keep it from you to spare your feelings," and she burst into tears; "I did not want you to know that you had married me to such a man as he is. He is just the same in private life—body and soul and conscience—the same through and through—hideous! I hate him; I despise him! Yes, after all that that despicable Nucingen has told me, I cannot respect him any longer. A man capable of mixing himself up in such affairs, and of talking about them to me as he did, without the slightest scruple,—it is because I have read him through and through that I am afraid of him. He, my husband, frankly proposed to give me my liberty, and do you know what that means? It means that if things turn out badly for him, I am to play into his hands, and be his stalk-ing-horse."

"But there is law to be had! There is a Place de Grève for sons-in-law of that sort," cried her father; "why, I would guillotine him myself if there was no headsman to do it."

"No, father, the law cannot touch him. Listen, this is what he says, stripped of all his circumlocutions—'Take your choice, you and no one else can be my accomplice; either everything is lost, you are ruined and have not a farthing, or you will let me carry this business through myself.' Is that plain speaking? He *must* have my assistance. He is assured that his wife will deal fairly by him; he knows that I shall leave his money to him and be content with my own. It is an unholy and dishonest compact, and he holds out threats of ruin to compel me to consent to it. He is buying my con-science, and the price is liberty to be Eugène's wife in all but name. 'I connive at your errors, and you allow me to com-mit crimes and ruin poor families!' Is that sufficiently ex-plicit? Do you know what he means by speculations? He buys up land in his own name, then he finds men of straw to run up houses upon it.   These men make a bargain with a contractor to build the houses, paying them by bills at long dates; then in consideration of a small sum they leave my husband in possession of the houses, and finally slip through the fingers of the deluded contractors by going into bankruptcy.   The name of the firm of Nucingen has been used to dazzle the poor contractors.   I saw that.   I noticed, too, that Nucingen had sent bills for large amounts to Amsterdam, London, Naples, and Vienna, in order to prove if necessary that large sums had been paid away by the firm.   How could we get possession of those bills?"

Eugène heard a dull thud on the floor; Father Goriot must have fallen on his knees.

"Great heavens! what have I done to you?   Bound my daughter to this scoundrel who does as he likes with her!—Oh! my child, my child! forgive me!" cried the old man.

"Yes, if I am in the depths of despair, perhaps you are to blame," said Delphine.   "We have so little sense when we marry!   What do we know of the world, of business, or men, or life?   Our fathers should think for us!   Father dear, I am not blaming you in the least, forgive me for what I said.   This is all my own fault.   Nay, do not cry, papa," she said, kissing him.

"Do not you cry either, my little Delphine.   Look up and let me kiss away the tears.   There!   I shall find my wits and unravel this skein of your husband's winding."

"No, let me do that; I shall be able to manage him.   He is fond of me, well and good; I shall use my influence to make him invest my money as soon as possible in landed property in my own name.   Very likely I could get him to buy back Nucingen in Alsace in my name; that has always been a pet idea of his.   Still, come to-morrow and go through the books, and look into the business.   M. Derville knows little of mercantile matters.   No, not to-morrow though.   I do not want to be upset.   Mme. de Beauséant's ball will be the day after to-morrow, and I must keep quiet, so as to look my best and

freshest, and do honor to my dear Eugène! . . . Come,
let us see his room."

But as she spoke a carriage stopped in the Rue Neuve-
Sainte-Geneviève, and the sound of Mme. de Restaud's voice
came from the staircase. "Is my father in?" she asked of
Sylvie.

This accident was luckily timed for Eugène, whose one
idea had been to throw himself down on the bed and pretend
to be asleep.

"Oh, father, have you heard about Anastasie?" said Delphine, when she heard her sister speak. "It looks as though
some strange things had happened in that family."

"What sort of things?" asked Goriot. "This is like to be
the death of me. My poor head will not stand a double misfortune."

"Good-morning, father," said the Countess from the
threshold. "Oh! Delphine, are you here?"

Mme. de Restaud seemed taken aback by her sister's
presence.

"Good-morning, Nasie," said the Baroness. "What is there
so extraordinary in my being here? I see our father every
day."

"Since when?"

"If you came yourself you would know."

"Don't tease, Delphine," said the Countess fretfully. "I
am very miserable, I am lost. Oh! my poor father, it is hopeless this time!"

"What is it, Nasie?" cried Goriot. "Tell us all about it,
child! How white she is! Quick, do something, Delphine;
be kind to her, and I will love you even better, if that were
possible."

"Poor Nasie!" said Mme. de Nucingen, drawing her sister
to a chair. "We are the only two people in the world whose
love is always sufficient to forgive you everything. Family
affection is the surest, you see."

The Countess inhaled the salts and revived.

"This will kill me!" said their father. "There," he went

on, stirring the smouldering fire, "come nearer, both of you. It is cold. What is it, Nasie? Be quick and tell me, this is enough to——"

"Well, then, my husband knows everything," said the Countess. "Just imagine it; do you remember, father, that bill of Maxime's some time ago? Well, that was not the first. I had paid ever so many before that. About the beginning of January M. de Trailles seemed very much troubled. He said nothing to me; but it is so easy to read the hearts of those you love, a mere trifle is enough; and then you feel things instinctively. Indeed, he was more tender and affectionate than ever, and I was happier than I had ever been before. Poor Maxime! in himself he was really saying good-bye to me, so he has told me since; he meant to blow his brains out! At last I worried him so, and begged and implored so hard; for two hours I knelt at his knees and prayed and entreated, and at last he told me—that he owed a hundred thousand francs. Oh! papa! a hundred thousand francs! I was beside myself! You had not the money, I knew; I had eaten up all that you had——"

"No," said Goriot; "I could not have got it for you unless I had stolen it. But I would have done that for you, Nasie! I will do it yet."

The words came from him like a sob, a hoarse sound like the death rattle of a dying man; it seemed indeed like the agony of death when the father's love was powerless. There was a pause, and neither of the sisters spoke. It must have been selfishness indeed that could hear unmoved that cry of anguish that, like a pebble thrown over a precipice, revealed the depths of his despair.

"I found the money, father, by selling what was not mine to sell," and the Countess burst into tears.

Delphine was touched; she laid her head on her sister's shoulder, and cried too.

"Then it is all true," she said.

Anastasie bowed her head, Mme. de Nucingen flung her arms about her, kissed her tenderly, and held her sister to her heart.

"I shall always love you and never judge you, Nasie," she said.

"My angels," murmured Goriot faintly. "Oh, why should it be trouble that draws you together?"

This warm and palpitating affection seemed to give the Countess courage.

"To save Maxime's life," she said, "to save all my own happiness, I went to the money-lender you know of, a man of iron forged in hell-fire; nothing can melt him; I took all the family diamonds that M. de Restaud is so proud of—his and mine too—and sold them to that M. Gobseck. *Sold them!* Do you understand? I saved Maxime, but I am lost. Restaud found it all out."

"How? Who told him? I will kill him," cried Goriot.

"Yesterday he sent to tell me to come to his room. I went. . . . 'Anastasie,' he said in a voice—oh! such a voice; that was enough, it told me everything—'where are your diamonds?'—'In my room——'—'No,' he said, looking straight at me, 'there they are on that chest of drawers——' and he lifted his handkerchief and showed me the casket. 'Do you know where they come from?' he said. I fell at his feet. . . . I cried; I besought him to tell me the death he wished to see me die."

"You said that!" cried Goriot. "By God in heaven, who-ever lays a hand on either of you so long as I am alive may reckon on being roasted by slow fires! Yes, I will cut him in pieces like . . ."

Goriot stopped; the words died away in his throat.

"And then, dear, he asked something worse than death of me. Oh! heaven preserve all other women from hearing such words as I heard then!"

"I will murder that man," said Goriot quietly. "But he has only one life, and he deserves to die twice.—And then, what next?" he added, looking at Anastasie.

"Then," the Countess resumed, "there was a pause, and he looked at me. 'Anastasie,' he said, 'I will bury this in silence; there shall be no separation; there are the children.

I will not kill M. de Trailles. I might miss him if we fought, and as for other ways of getting rid of him, I should come into collision with the law. If I killed him in your arms, it would bring dishonor on *those* children. But if you do not want to see your children perish, nor their father nor me, you must first of all submit to two conditions. Answer me. Have I a child of my own?' I answered, 'Yes.'—'Which?' —'Ernest, our eldest boy.'—'Very well,' he said, 'and now swear to obey me in this particular from this time forward.' I swore. 'You will make over your property to me when I require you to do so.' "

"Do nothing of the kind!" cried Goriot. "Aha! M. de Restaud, you could not make your wife happy; she has looked for happiness and found it elsewhere, and you make her suffer for your own ineptitude? He will have to reckon with me. Make yourself easy, Nasie. Aha! he cares about his heir! Good, very good. I will get hold of the boy; isn't he my grandson? What the blazes! I can surely go to see the brat! I will stow him away somewhere; I will take care of him, you may be quite easy. I will bring Restaud to terms, the monster! I shall say to him, 'A word or two with you! If you want your son back again, give my daughter her property, and leave her to do as she pleases.' "

"Father!"

"Yes. I am your father, Nasie, a father indeed! That rogue of a great lord had better not ill-treat my daughter. *Tonnerre!* What is it in my veins? There is the blood of a tiger in me; I could tear those two men to pieces! Oh! children, children! so this is what your lives are! Why, it is death! . . . What will become of you when I shall be here no longer? Fathers ought to live as long as their children. Ah! Lord God in heaven! how ill Thy world is ordered! Thou hast a Son, if what they tell us is true, and yet Thou leavest us to suffer so through our children. My darlings, my darlings! to think that trouble only should bring you to me, that I should only see you with tears on your faces! Ah! yes, yes, you love me, I see that you love me.

Come to me and pour out your griefs to me; my heart is large enough to hold them all. Oh! you might rend my heart in pieces, and every fragment would make a father's heart. If only I could bear all your sorrows for you! . . . Ah! you were so happy when you were little and still with me. . . ."

"We have never been happy since," said Delphine. "Where are the old days when we slid down the sacks in the great granary?"

"That is not all, father," said Anastasie in Goriot's ear. The old man gave a startled shudder. "The diamonds only sold for a hundred thousand francs. Maxime is hard pressed. There are twelve thousand francs still to pay. He has given me his word that he will be steady and give up play in future. His love is all that I have left in the world. I have paid such a fearful price for it that I shall die if I lose him now. I have sacrificed my fortune, my honor, my peace of mind, and my children for him. Oh! do something, so that at the least Maxime may be at large and live undisgraced in the world, where he will assuredly make a career for himself. Something more than my happiness is at stake; the children have nothing, and if he is sent to Sainte-Pélagie all his prospects will be ruined."

"I haven't the money, Nasie. I have *nothing*—nothing left. This is the end of everything. Yes, the world is crumbling into ruin, I am sure. Fly! Save yourselves! Ah!—I have still my silver buckles left, and half-a-dozen silver spoons and forks, the first I ever had in my life. But I have nothing else except my life annuity, twelve hundred francs . . ."

"Then what has become of your money in the funds?"

"I sold out, and only kept a trifle for my wants. I wanted twelve thousand francs to furnish some rooms for Delphine."

"In your own house?" asked Mme. de Restaud, looking at her sister.

"What does it matter where they were?" asked Goriot. "The money is spent now."

"I see how it is," said the Countess. "Rooms for M. de Rastignac. Poor Delphine, take warning by me!"

"M. de Rastignac is incapable of ruining the woman he loves, dear."

"Thanks! Delphine. I thought you would have been kinder to me in my troubles, but you never did love me."

"Yes, yes, she loves you, Nasie," cried Goriot; "she was saying so only just now. We were talking about you, and she insisted that you were beautiful, and that she herself was only pretty!"

"Pretty!" said the Countess. "She is as hard as a marble statue."

"And if I am?" cried Delphine, flushing up, "how have you treated me? You would not recognize me; you closed the doors of every house against me; you have never let an opportunity of mortifying me slip by. And when did I come, as you were always doing, to drain our poor father, a thousand francs at a time, till he is left as you see him now? That is all your doing, sister! I myself have seen my father as often as I could. I have not turned him out of the house, and then come and fawned upon him when I wanted money. I did not so much as know that he had spent those twelve thousand francs on me. I am economical, as you know; and when papa has made me presents, it has never been because I came and begged for them."

"You were better off than I. M. de Marsay was rich, as you have reason to know. You always were as slippery as gold. Good-bye; I have neither sister nor——"

"Oh! hush, hush, Nasie!" cried her father.

"Nobody else would repeat what everybody has ceased to believe. You are an unnatural sister!" cried Delphine.

"Oh, children, children! hush! hush! or I will kill myself before your eyes."

"There, Nasie, I forgive you," said Mme. de Nucingen; "you are very unhappy. But I am kinder than you are. How could you say *that* just when I was ready to do anything in the world to help you, even to be reconciled with my hus-

band, which for my own sake I—— Oh! it is just like you;
you have behaved cruelly to me all through these nine years."

"Children, children, kiss each other!" cried the father.
"You are angels, both of you."

"No. Let me alone," cried the Countess shaking off the
hand that her father had laid on her arm. "She is more
merciless than my husband. Any one might think she was a
model of all the virtues herself!"

"I would rather have people think that I owed money to
M. de Marsay than own that M. de Trailles had cost me more
than two hundred thousand francs," retorted Mme. de
Nucingen.

"*Delphine!*" cried the Countess, stepping towards her
sister.

"I shall tell you the truth about yourself if you begin to
slander me," said the Baroness coldly.

"Delphine! you are a——"

Father Goriot sprang between them, grasped the Countess'
hand, and laid his own over her mouth.

"Good heavens, father! What have you been handling
this morning?" said Anastasie.

"Ah! well, yes, I ought not to have touched you," said the
poor father, wiping his hands on his trousers, "but I have
been packing up my things; I did not know that you were
coming to see me."

He was glad that he had drawn down her wrath upon himself.

"Ah!" he sighed, as he sat down, "you children have
broken my heart between you. This is killing me. My head
feels as if it were on fire. Be good to each other and love
each other! This will be the death of me! Delphine! Nasie!
come, be sensible; you are both in the wrong. Come, Dedel,"
he added, looking through his tears at the Baroness, "she
must have twelve thousand francs, you see; let us see if we
can find them for her. Oh, my girls, do not look at each other
like that!" and he sank on his knees beside Delphine. "Ask

her to forgive you—just to please me," he said in her ear "She is more miserable than you are. Come now, Dedel."

"Poor Nasie!" said Delphine, alarmed at the wild extravagant grief in her father's face, "I was in the wrong, kiss me——"

"Ah! that is like balm to my heart," cried Father Goriot. "But how are we to find twelve thousand francs? I might offer myself as a substitute in the army——"

"Oh! father dear!" they both cried, flinging their arms about him. "No, no!"

"God reward you for the thought. We are not worth it, are we, Nasie?" asked Delphine.

"And besides, father dear, it would only be a drop in the bucket," observed the Countess.

"But is flesh and blood worth nothing?" cried the old man in his despair. "I would give body and soul to save you, Nasie. I would do a murder for the man who would rescue you. I would do, as Vautrin did, go to the hulks, go——" he stopped as if struck by a thunderbolt, and put both hands to his head. "Nothing left!" he cried, tearing his hair. "If I only knew of a way to steal money, but it is so hard to do it, and then you can't set to work by yourself, and it takes time to rob a bank. Yes, it is time I was dead; there is nothing left me to do but to die. I am no good in the world; I am no longer a father! No. She has come to me in her extremity, and, wretch that I am, I have nothing to give her. Ah! you put your money into a life annuity, old scoundrel; and had you not daughters? You did not love them. Die, die in a ditch, like the dog that you are! Yes, I am worse than a dog; a beast would not have done as I have done! Oh! my head . . . it throbs as if it would burst."

"Papa!" cried both the young women at once, "do, pray, be reasonable!" and they clung to him to prevent him from dashing his head against the wall. There was a sound of sobbing.

Eugène, greatly alarmed, took the bill that bore Vautrin's signature, saw that the stamp would suffice for a larger sum, altered the figures, made it into a regular bill for twelve thousand francs, payable to Goriot's order, and went to his neighbor's room.

"Here is the money, madame," he said, handing the piece of paper to her. "I was asleep; your conversation awoke me, and by this means I learned all that I owed to M. Goriot. This bill can be discounted, and I shall meet it punctually at the due date."

The Countess stood motionless and speechless, but she held the bill in her fingers.

"Delphine," she said, with a white face, and her whole frame quivering with indignation, anger, and rage, "I forgave you everything; God is my witness that I forgave you, but I cannot forgive this! So this gentleman was there all the time, and you knew it! Your petty spite has led you to wreak your vengeance on me by betraying my secrets, my life, my children's lives, my shame, my honor! There, you are nothing to me any longer. I hate you. I will do all that I can to injure you. I will . . ."

Anger paralyzed her; the words died in her dry parched throat.

"Why, he is my son, my child; he is your brother, your preserver!" cried Goriot. "Kiss his hand, Nasie! Stay, I will embrace him myself," he said, straining Eugène to his breast in a frenzied clasp. "Oh my boy! I will be more than a father to you; I would be everything in the world to you; if I had God's power, I would fling worlds at your feet. Why don't you kiss him, Nasie? He is not a man, but an angel, an angel out of heaven."

"Never mind her, father; she is mad just now."

"Mad! am I? And what are you?" cried Mme. de Restaud.

"Children, children, I shall die if you go on like this," cried the old man, and he staggered and fell on the bed as if a bullet had struck him.—"They are killing me between them," he said to himself.

The Countess fixed her eyes on Eugène, who stood stock-still; all his faculties were numbed by this violent scene.

"Sir? . . ." she said, doubt and inquiry in her face, tone, and bearing; she took no notice now of her father nor of Delphine, who was hastily unfastening his waistcoat.

"Madame," said Eugène, answering the question before it was asked, "I will meet the bill, and keep silence about it."

"You have killed our father, Nasie!" said Delphine, pointing to Goriot, who lay unconscious on the bed. The Countess fled.

"I freely forgive her," said the old man, opening his eyes; "her position is horrible; it would turn an older head than hers. Comfort Nasie, and be nice to her, Delphine; promise it to your poor father before he dies," he asked, holding Delphine's hand in a convulsive clasp.

"Oh! what ails you, father?" she cried in real alarm.

"Nothing, nothing," said Goriot; "it will go off. There is something heavy pressing on my forehead, a little headache. . . . Ah! poor Nasie, what a life lies before her!"

Just as he spoke, the Countess came back again and flung herself on her knees before him. "Forgive me!" she cried.

"Come," said her father, "you are hurting me still more."

"Monsieur," the Countess said, turning to Rastignac, "misery made me unjust to you. You will be a brother to me, will you not?" and she held out her hand. Her eyes were full of tears as she spoke.

"Nasie," cried Delphine, flinging her arms round her sister, "my little Nasie, let us forget and forgive."

"No, no," cried Nasie; "I shall never forget!"

"Dear angels," cried Goriot, "it is as if a dark curtain over my eyes had been raised; your voices have called me back to life. Kiss each other once more. Well, now, Nasie, that bill will save you, won't it?"

"I hope so. I say, papa, will you write your name on it?"

"There! how stupid of me to forget that! But I am not feeling at all well, Nasie, so you must not remember it against me. Send and let me know as soon as you are out of your strait. No, I will go to you. No, after all, I will not go; I might meet your husband, and I should kill him on the spot. And as for signing away your property, I shall have a word to say about that. Quick, my child, and keep Maxime in order in future."

Eugène was too bewildered to speak.

"Poor Anastasie, she always had a violent temper," said Mme. de Nucingen, "but she has a good heart."

"She came back for the endorsement," said Eugène in Delphine's ear.

"Do you think so?"

"I only wish I could think otherwise. Do not trust her," he answered, raising his eyes as if he confided to heaven the thoughts that he did not venture to express.

"Yes. She is always acting a part to some extent."

"How do you feel now, dear Father Goriot?" asked Rastignac.

"I should like to go to sleep," he replied.

Eugène helped him to bed, and Delphine sat by the bedside, holding his hand until he fell asleep. Then she went.

"This evening at the Italiens," she said to Eugène, "and you can let me know how he is. To-morrow you will leave this place, monsieur. Let us go into your room.—Oh! how frightful!" she cried on the threshold. "Why, you are even worse lodged than our father. Eugène, you have behaved well. I would love you more if that were possible; but, dear boy, if you are to succeed in life, you must not begin by flinging twelve thousand francs out of the windows like that. The Comte de Trailles is a confirmed gambler. My sister shuts her eyes to it. He would have made the twelve thousand francs in the same way that he wins and loses heaps of gold."

A groan from the next room brought them back to Goriot's bedside; to all appearance he was asleep, but the two lovers caught the words, "They are not happy!" Whether he was awake or sleeping, the tone in which they were spoken went to his daughter's heart. She stole up to the pallet-bed on which her father lay, and kissed his forehead. He opened his eyes.

"Ah! Delphine!" he said.

"How are you now?" she asked.

"Quite comfortable. Do not worry about me; I shall get up presently. Don't stay with me, children; go, go and be happy."

Eugène went back with Delphine as far as her door; but he was not easy about Goriot, and would not stay to dinner, as she proposed. He wanted to be back at the Maison Vauquer. Father Goriot had left his room, and was just sitting down to dinner as he came in. Bianchon had placed himself where he could watch the old man carefully; and when the old vermicelli maker took up his square of bread and smelled it to find out the quality of the flour, the medical student, studying him closely, saw that the action was purely mechanical, and shook his head.

"Just come and sit over here, hospitaller of Cochin," said Eugène.

Bianchon went the more willingly because his change of place brought him next to the old lodger.

"What is wrong with him?" asked Rastignac.

"It is all up with him, or I am much mistaken! Something very extraordinary must have taken place; he looks to me as if he were in imminent danger of serous apoplexy. The lower part of his face is composed enough, but the upper part is drawn and distorted. Then there is that peculiar look about the eyes that indicates an effusion of serum in the brain; they look as though they were covered with a film of fine dust, do you notice? I shall know more about it by to-morrow morning."

"Is there any cure for it?"

"None. It might be possible to stave death off for a time if a way could be found of setting up a reaction in the lower extremities; but if the symptoms do not abate by to-morrow evening, it will be all over with him, poor old fellow! Do you know what has happened to bring this on? There must have been some violent shock, and his mind has given way."

"Yes, there was," said Rastignac, remembering how the

two daughters had struck blow on blow at their father's heart.

"But Delphine at any rate loves her father," he said to himself.

That evening at the opera Rastignac chose his words carefully, lest he should give Mme. de Nucingen needless alarm.

"Do not be anxious about him," she said, however, as soon as Eugène began, "our father has really a strong constitution, but this morning we gave him a shock. Our whole fortunes were in peril, so the thing was serious, you see. I could not live if your affection did not make me insensible to troubles that I should once have thought too hard to bear. At this moment I have but one fear left, but one misery to dread —to lose the love that has made me feel glad to live. Everything else is as nothing to me compared with your love; I care for nothing else, for you are all the world to me. If I feel glad to be rich, it is for your sake. To my shame be it said, I think of my lover before my father. Do you ask why? I cannot tell you, but all my life is in you. My father gave me a heart, but you have taught it to beat. The whole world may condemn me; what does it matter if I stand acquitted in your eyes, for you have no right to think ill of me for the faults which a tyrannous love has forced me to commit for you! Do you think me an unnatural daughter? Oh! no, no one could help loving such a dear kind father as ours. But how could I hide the inevitable consequences of our miserable marriages from him? Why did he allow us to marry when we did? Was it not his duty to think for us and foresee for us? To-day I know he suffers as much as we do, but how can it be helped? And as for comforting him, we could not comfort him in the least. Our resignation would give him more pain and hurt him far more than complaints and upbraidings. There are times in life when everything turns to bitterness."

Eugène was silent; the artless and sincere outpouring made an impression on him.

Parisian women are often false, intoxicated with vanity,

selfish and self-absorbed, frivolous and shallow; yet of all women, when they love, they sacrifice their personal feelings to
their passion; they rise but so much the higher for all the
pettiness overcome in their nature, and become sublime. Then
Eugène was struck by the profound discernment and insight
displayed by this woman in judging of natural affection,
when a privileged affection had separated and set her at a
distance apart. Mme. de Nucingen was piqued by the silence.

"What are you thinking about?" she asked.

"I am thinking about what you said just now. Hitherto
I have always felt sure that I cared far more for you than you
did for me."

She smiled, and would not give way to the happiness she
felt, lest their talk should exceed the conventional limits of
propriety. She had never heard the vibrating tones of a sincere and youthful love; a few more words, and she feared for
her self-control.

"Eugène," she said, changing the conversation, "I wonder whether you know what has been happening? All Paris
will go to Mme. de Beauséant's to-morrow. The Rochefides
and the Marquis d'Ajuda have agreed to keep the matter a
profound secret, but to-morrow the king will sign the marriage-contract, and your poor cousin the Vicomtesse knows
nothing of it as yet. She cannot put off her ball, and the
Marquis will not be there. People are wondering what will
happen?"

"The world laughs at baseness and connives at it. But this
will kill Mme. de Beauséant."

"Oh, no," said Delphine, smiling, "you do not know that
kind of woman. Why, all Paris will be there, and so shall
I; I ought to go there for your sake."

"Perhaps, after all, it is one of those absurd reports that
people set in circulation here."

"We shall know the truth to-morrow."

Eugène did not return to the Maison Vauquer. He could
not forego the pleasure of occupying his new rooms in the

Rue d'Artois. Yesterday evening he had been obliged to leave Delphine soon after midnight, but that night it was Delphine who stayed with him until two o'clock in the morning. He rose late, and waited for Mme. de Nucingen, who came about noon to breakfast with him. Youth snatches eagerly at these rosy moments of happiness, and Eugène had almost forgotten Goriot's existence. The pretty things that surrounded him were growing familiar; this domestication in itself was one long festival for him, and Mme. de Nucingen was there to glorify it all by her presence. It was four o'clock before they thought of Goriot, and of how he had looked forward to the new life in that house. Eugène said that the old man ought to be moved at once, lest he should grow too ill to move. He left Delphine, and hurried back to the lodging-house. Neither Father Goriot nor young Bianchon was in the dining-room with the others.

"Aha!" said the painter as Eugène came in, "Father Goriot has broken down at last. Bianchon is upstairs with him. One of his daughters—the Comtesse de Restaurama—came to see the old gentleman, and he would get up and go out, and made himself worse. Society is about to lose one of its brightest ornaments."

Rastignac sprang to the staircase.

"Hey! Monsieur Eugène!"

"Monsieur Eugène, the mistress is calling you," shouted Sylvie.

"It is this, sir," said the widow. "You and M. Goriot should by rights have moved out on the 15th of February. That was three days ago; to-day is the 18th, I ought really to be paid a month in advance; but if you will engage to pay for both, I shall be quite satisfied."

"Why can't you trust him?"

"Trust him, indeed! If the old gentleman went off his head and died, those daughters of his would not pay me a farthing, and his things won't fetch ten francs. This morning he went out with all the spoons and forks he has left, I don't know why. He had got himself up to look quite young, and—Lord, forgive me—but I thought he had rouge on his cheeks; he looked quite young again."

"I will be responsible," said Eugène, shuddering with horror, for he foresaw the end.

He climbed the stairs and reached Father Goriot's room. The old man was tossing on his bed. Bianchon was with him.

"Good-evening, father," said Eugène.

The old man turned his glassy eyes on him, smiled gently, and said:

"How is *she?*"

"She is quite well. But how are you?"

"There is nothing much the matter."

"Don't tire him," said Bianchon, drawing Eugène into a corner of the room.

"Well?" asked Rastignac.

"Nothing but a miracle can save him now. Serous congestion has set in; I have put on mustard plasters, and luckily he can feel them, they are acting."

"Is it possible to move him?"

"Quite out of the question. He must stay where he is, and be kept as quiet as possible——"

"Dear Bianchon," said Eugène, "we will nurse him between us."

"I have had the head physician round from my hospital to see him."

"And what did he say?"

"He will give no opinion till to-morrow evening. He promised to look in again at the end of the day. Unluckily, the preposterous creature must needs go and do something foolish this morning; he will not say what it was. He is as obstinate as a mule. As soon as I begin to talk to him he pretends not to hear, and lies as if he were asleep instead of answering, or if he opens his eyes he begins to groan. Some time this morning he went out on foot in the streets, nobody knows where he went, and he took everything that he had of any value with him. He has been driving some confounded bargain, and it has been too much for his strength. One of his daughters has been here."

"Was it the Countess?" asked Eugène. "A tall, dark-haired woman, with large bright eyes, slender figure, and little feet?"

"Yes."

"Leave him to me for a bit," said Rastignac. "I will make him confess; he will tell me all about it."

"And meanwhile I will get my dinner. But try not to excite him; there is still some hope left."

"All right."

"How they will enjoy themselves to-morrow," said Father Goriot when they were alone. "They are going to a grand ball."

"What were you doing this morning, papa, to make yourself so poorly this evening that you have to stop in bed?"

"Nothing."

"Did not Anastasie come to see you?" demanded Rastignac.

"Yes," said Father Goriot.

"Well, then, don't keep anything from me. What more did she want of you?"

"Oh, she was very miserable," he answered, gathering up all his strength to speak. "It was this way, my boy. Since that affair of the diamonds, Nasie has not had a penny of her own. For this ball she had ordered a golden gown like a setting for a jewel. Her mantuamaker, a woman without a conscience, would not give her credit, so Nasie's waiting-woman advanced a thousand francs on account. Poor Nasie! reduced to such shifts! It cut me to the heart to think of it! But when Nasie's maid saw how things were between her master and mistress, she was afraid of losing her money, and came to an understanding with the dressmaker, and the woman refuses to send the ball-dress until the money is paid. The gown is ready, and the ball is to-morrow night! Nasie was in despair. She wanted to borrow my forks and spoons to pawn them. Her husband is determined that she shall go and wear the diamonds, so as to contradict the stories that are told all over Paris. How can she go to that heartless scoundrel and say, 'I owe a thousand francs to my dress-maker; pay her for me!' She cannot. I saw that myself. Delphine will be there too in a superb toilette, and Anastasie ought not to be outshone by her younger sister. And then— she was drowned in tears, poor girl! I felt so humbled yesterday when I had not the twelve thousand francs, that I would have given the rest of my miserable life to wipe out that wrong. You see, I could have borne anything once, but latterly this want of money has broken my heart. Oh! I did not do it by halves; I titivated myself up a bit, and went out and sold my spoons and forks and buckles for six hundred francs; then I went to old Daddy Gobseck, and sold a year's interest in my annuity for four hundred francs down. Pshaw! I can live on dry bread, as I did when I was a young man; if I have done it before, I can do it again. My Nasie shall have one happy evening, at any rate. She shall be smart. The banknote for a thousand francs is here under my pillow; it warms me to have it lying there under my head, for it is going to make my poor Nasie happy. She can turn that bad girl Victoire out of the house. A servant that can-not trust her mistress, did any one ever hear the like! I shall be quite well to-morrow. Nasie is coming at ten o'clock. They must not think that I am ill, or they will not go to the ball; they will stop and take care of me. To-morrow Nasie will come and hold me in her arms as if I were one of her children; her kisses will make me well again. After all, I might have spent the thousand francs on physic; I would far rather give them to my little Nasie, who can charm all the pain away. At any rate, I am some comfort to her in her misery; and that makes up for my unkindness in buying an annuity. She is in the depths, and I cannot draw her out of them now. Oh! I will go into business again, I will buy wheat in Odessa; out there, wheat fetches a quarter of the price it sells for here. There is a law against the im-portation of grain, but the good folk who made the law forgot to prohibit the introduction of wheat products and food stuffs made from corn. Hey! hey! . . . That struck me this morning. There is a fine trade to be done in starch."

Eugène, watching the old man's face, thought that his friend was light-headed.

"Come," he said, "do not talk any more, you must rest——" Just then Bianchon came up, and Eugène went down to dinner.

The two students sat up with him that night, relieving each other in turn. Bianchon brought up his medical books and studied; Eugène wrote letters home to his mother and sisters. Next morning Bianchon thought the symptoms more hopeful, but the patient's condition demanded continual attention, which the two students alone were willing to give —a task impossible to describe in the squeamish phraseology of the epoch. Leeches must be applied to the wasted body, the poultices and hot foot-baths, and other details of the treatment required the physical strength and devotion of the two young men. Mme. de Restaud did not come; but she sent a messenger for the money.

"I expected she would come herself; but it would have been a pity for her to come, she would have been anxious about me," said the father, and to all appearance he was well content.

At seven o'clock that evening Thérèse came with a letter from Delphine.

"What are you doing, dear friend? I have been loved for a very little while, and am I neglected already? In the confidences of heart and heart, I have learned to know your soul —you are too noble not to be faithful for ever, for you know that love with all its infinite subtle changes of feeling is never the same. Once you said, as we were listening to the Prayer in *Mosè in Egitto,* 'For some it is the monotony of a single note; for others, it is the infinite of sound.' Remember that I am expecting you this evening to take me to Mme. de Beauséant's ball. Every one knows now that the

King signed M. d'Ajuda's marriage-contract this morning, and the poor Vicomtesse knew nothing of it until two o'clock this afternoon. All Paris will flock to her house, of course, just as a crowd fills the Place de Grève to see an execution. It is horrible, is it not, to go out of curiosity to see if she will hide her anguish, and whether she will die courageously? I certainly should not go, my friend, if I had been at her house before; but, of course, she will not receive society any more after this, and all my efforts would be in vain. My position is a very unusual one, and besides, I am going there partly on your account. I am waiting for you. If you are not beside me in less than two hours, I do not know whether I could forgive such treason."

Rastignac took up a pen and wrote:

"I am waiting till the doctor comes to know if there is any hope of your father's life. He is lying dangerously ill. I will come and bring you the news, but I am afraid it may be a sentence of death. When I come you can decide whether you can go to the ball.—Yours a thousand times."

At half-past eight the doctor arrived. He did not take a very hopeful view of the case, but thought that there was no immediate danger. Improvements and relapses might be expected, and the good man's life and reason hung in the balance.

"It would be better for him to die at once," the doctor said as he took leave.

Eugène left Goriot to Bianchon's care, and went to carry the sad news to Mme. de Nucingen. Family feeling lingered in her, and this must put an end for the present to her plans of amusement.

"Tell her to enjoy her evening as if nothing had happened," cried Goriot. He had been lying in a sort of stupor, but he suddenly sat upright as Eugène went out.

Eugène, half heartbroken, entered Delphine's. Her hair

had been dressed; she wore her dancing slippers; she had only to put on her ball-dress; but when the artist is giving the finishing stroke to his creation, the last touches require more time than the whole groundwork of the picture.

"Why, you are not dressed!" she cried.

"Madame, your father——"

"My father again!" she exclaimed, breaking in upon him. "You need not teach me what is due to my father, I have known my father this long while. Not a word, Eugène. I will hear what you have to say when you are dressed. My carriage is waiting, take it, go round to your rooms and dress, Thérèse has put out everything in readiness for you. Come back as soon as you can; we will talk about my father on the way to Mme. de Beauséant's. We must go early; if we have to wait our turn in a row of carriages, we shall be lucky if we get there by eleven o'clock."

"Madame——"

"Quick! not a word!" she cried, darting into her dressing-room for a necklace.

"Do go, Monsieur Eugène, or you will vex madame," said Thérèse, hurrying him away; and Eugène was too horror-stricken by this elegant parricide to resist.

He went to his rooms and dressed, sad, thoughtful, and dispirited. The world of Paris was like an ocean of mud for him just then; and it seemed that whoever set foot in that black mire must needs sink into it up to the chin.

"Their crimes are paltry," said Eugène to himself. "Vautrin was greater."

He had seen society in its three great phases—Obedience, Struggle, and Revolt; the Family, the World, and Vautrin; and he hesitated in his choice. Obedience was dull, Revolt impossible, Struggle hazardous. His thoughts wandered back to the home circle. He thought of the quiet uneventful life, the pure happiness of the days spent among those who loved him there. Those loving and beloved beings passed their lives in obedience to the natural laws of the hearth, and in that obedience found a deep and constant serenity, unvexed by torments such as these. Yet, for all his good impulses, he could not bring himself to make profession of the religion of pure souls to Delphine, nor to prescribe the duties of piety to her in the name of love. His education had begun to bear its fruits; he loved selfishly already. Besides, his tact had discovered to him the real nature of Delphine; he divined instinctively that she was capable of stepping over her father's corpse to go to the ball; and within himself he felt that he had neither the strength of mind to play the part of mentor, nor the strength of character to vex her, nor the courage to leave her to go alone.

"She would never forgive me for putting her in the wrong over it," he said to himself. Then he turned the doctor's dictum over in his mind; he tried to believe that Goriot was not so dangerously ill as he had imagined, and ended by collecting together a sufficient quantity of traitorous excuses for Delphine's conduct. She did not know how ill her father was; the kind old man himself would have made her go to the ball if she had gone to see him. So often it happens that this one or that stands condemned by the social laws that govern family relations; and yet there are peculiar circumstances in the case, differences of temperament, divergent interests, innumerable complications of family life that excuse the apparent offence.

Eugène did not wish to see too clearly; he was ready to sacrifice his conscience to his mistress. Within the last few days his whole life had undergone a change. Woman had entered into his world and thrown it into chaos, family claims dwindled away before her; she had appropriated all his being to her uses. Rastignac and Delphine found each other at a crisis in their lives when their union gave them the most poignant bliss. Their passion, so long proved, had only gained in strength by the gratified desire that often extinguishes passion. This woman was his, and Eugène recognized that not until then had he loved her; perhaps love is only gratitude for pleasure. This woman, vile or sublime, he adored for the pleasure she had brought as her

dower; and Delphine loved Rastignac as Tantalus would
have loved some angel who had satisfied his hunger and
quenched the burning thirst in his parched throat.

"Well," said Mme. de Nucingen when he came back in
evening dress, "how is my father?"

"Very dangerously ill," he answered; "if you will grant
me a proof of your affection, we will just go in to see him
on the way."

"Very well," she said. "Yes, but afterwards. Dear Eugène, do be nice, and don't preach to me. Come."

They set out. Eugène said nothing for a while.

"What is it now?" she asked.

"I can hear the death-rattle in your father's throat," he
said, almost angrily. And with the hot indignation of youth,
he told the story of Mme. de Restaud's vanity and cruelty,
of her father's final act of self-sacrifice, that had brought
about this struggle between life and death, of the price that
had been paid for Anastasie's golden embroideries. Delphine
cried.

"I shall look frightful," she thought. She dried her tears.

"I will nurse my father; I will not leave his bedside," she
said aloud.

"Ah! now you are as I would have you," exclaimed Rastignac.

The lamps of five hundred carriages lit up the darkness
about the Hôtel de Beauséant. A gendarme in all the glory
of his uniform stood on either side of the brightly lighted
gateway. The great world was flocking thither that night in
its eager curiosity to see the great lady at the moment of her
fall, and the rooms on the ground floor were already full to
overflowing, when Mme. de Nucingen and Rastignac appeared. Never since Louis XIV. tore her lover away from
La grande Mademoiselle, and the whole court hastened to
visit that unfortunate princess, had a disastrous love affair
made such a sensation in Paris. But the youngest daughter
of the almost royal house of Burgundy had risen proudly
above her pain, and moved till the last moment like a queen

in this world—its vanities had always been valueless for her,
save in so far as they contributed to the triumph of her passion. The salons were filled with the most beautiful women
in Paris, resplendent in their toilettes, and radiant with
smiles. Ministers and ambassadors, the most distinguished
men at court, men bedizened with decorations, stars, and rib-
bons, men who bore the most illustrious names in France,
had gathered about the Vicomtesse.

The music of the orchestra vibrated in wave after wave
of sound from the golden ceiling of the palace, now made
desolate for its queen.

Madame de Beauséant stood at the door of the first salon
to receive the guests who were styled her friends. She was
dressed in white, and wore no ornament in the plaits of hair
braided about her head; her face was calm; there was no
sign there of pride, nor of pain, nor of joy that she did not
feel. No one could read her soul; she stood there like some
Niobe carved in marble. For a few intimate friends there was
a tinge of satire in her smile; but no scrutiny saw any change
in her, nor had she looked otherwise in the days of the glory
of her happiness. The most callous of her guests admired her
as young Rome applauded some gladiator who could die smiling. It seemed as if society had adorned itself for a last audience of one of its sovereigns.

"I was afraid that you would not come," she said to Rastignac.

"Madame," he said, in an unsteady voice, taking her
speech as a reproach, "I shall be the last to go, that is why
I am here."

"Good," she said, and she took his hand. "You are perhaps the only one that I can trust here among all these. Oh,
my friend, when you love, love a woman whom you are sure
that you can love always. Never forsake a woman."

She took Rastignac's arm, and went towards a sofa in the
card-room.

"I want you to go to the Marquis," she said. "Jacques,
my footman, will go with you; he has a letter that you will

take. I am asking the Marquis to give my letters back to
me. He will give them all up, I like to think that. When
you have my letters, go up to my room with them. Some one
shall bring me word."

She rose to go to meet the Duchesse de Langeais, her
most intimate friend, who had.come like the rest of the
world.

Rastignac went. He asked for the Marquis d'Ajuda at
the Hôtel Rochefide, feeling certain that the latter would
be spending his evening there, and so it proved. The Marquis went to his own house with Rastignac, and gave a casket
to the student, saying as he did so, "They are all there."

He seemed as if he was about to say something to Eugène, to ask about the ball, or the Vicomtesse; perhaps he
was on the brink of the confession that, even then, he was in
despair, and knew that his marriage had been a fatal mistake;
but a proud gleam shone in his eyes, and with deplorable
courage he kept his noblest feelings a secret.

"Do not even mention my name to her, my dear Eugène."
He grasped Rastignac's hand sadly and affectionately, and
turned away from him. Eugène went back to the Hôtel
Beauséant, the servant took him to the Vicomtesse's room.
There were signs there of preparations for a journey. He
sat down by the fire, fixed his eyes on the cedar wood casket,
and fell into deep mournful musings. Mme. de Beauséant
loomed large in these imaginings, like a goddess in the
Iliad.

"Ah! my friend! . . ." said the Vicomtesse; she
crossed the room and laid her hand on Rastignac's shoulder.
He saw the tears in his cousin's uplifted eyes, saw that one
hand was raised to take the casket, and that the fingers of
the other trembled. Suddenly she took the casket, put it
in the fire, and watched it burn.

"They are dancing," she said. "They all came very early;
but death will be long in coming. Hush! my friend," and
she laid a finger on Rastignac's lips, seeing that he was about
to speak. "I shall never see Paris again. I am taking my

leave of this world. At five o'clock this morning I shall set
out on my journey; I mean to bury myself in the remotest
part of Normandy. I have had very little time to make my
arrangements; since three o'clock this afternoon I have been
busy signing documents, setting my affairs in order; there
was no one whom I could send to . . ."

She broke off.

"He was sure to be . . ."

Again she broke off; the weight of her sorrow was more
than she could bear. In such moments as these everything
is agony, and some words are impossible to utter.

"And so I counted upon you to do me this last piece of
service this evening," she said. "I should like to give you
some pledge of friendship. I shall often think of you. You
have seemed to me to be kind and noble, fresh-hearted and
true, in this world where such qualities are seldom found.
I should like you to think sometimes of me. Stay," she said,
glancing about her, "there is this box that has held my gloves.
Every time I opened it before going to a ball or to the theatre, I used to feel that I must be beautiful, because I was so
happy; and I never touched it except to lay some gracious
memory in it: there is so much of my old self in it, of a Madame de Beauséant who now lives no longer. Will you take
it? I will leave directions that it is to be sent to you in the
Rue d'Artois.—Mme. de Nucingen looked very charming this
evening. Eugène, you must love her. Perhaps we may never
see each other again, my friend; but be sure of this, that
I shall pray for you who have been kind to me.—Now, let
us go downstairs. People shall not think that I am weeping. I have all time and eternity before me, and where I
am going I shall be alone, and no one will ask me the reason of my tears. One last look round first."

She stood for a moment. Then she covered her eyes with
her hands for an instant, dashed away the tears, bathed her
face with cold water, and took the student's arm.

"Let us go!" she said.

This suffering, endured with such noble fortitude, shook

Eugène with a more violent emotion than he had felt before.
They went back to the ballroom, and Mme. de Beauséant
went through the rooms on Eugène's arm—the last delicately gracious act of a gracious woman. In another moment
he saw the sisters, Mme. de Restaud and Mme. de Nucingen.
The Countess shone in all the glory of her magnificent diamonds; every stone must have scorched like fire, she was
never to wear them again. Strong as love and pride might
be in her, she found it difficult to meet her husband's eyes.
The sight of her was scarcely calculated to lighten Rastignac's
sad thoughts; through the blaze of those diamonds he
seemed to see the wretched pallet-bed on which Father Goriot was lying. The Vicomtesse misread his melancholy;
she withdrew her hand from his arm.

"Come," she said, "I must not deprive you of a pleasure."
Eugène was soon claimed by Delphine. She was delighted
with the impression that she had made, and eager to lay at
her lover's feet the homage she had received in this new world
in which she hoped to live and move henceforth.

"What do you think of Nasie?" she asked him.

"She has discounted everything, even her own father's
death," said Rastignac.

Towards four o'clock in the morning the rooms began to
empty. A little later the music ceased, and the Duchesse
de Langeais and Rastignac were left in the great ballroom.
The Vicomtesse, who thought to find the student there alone,
came back there at the last. She had taken leave of M. de
Beauséant, who had gone off to bed, saying again as he went,
"It is a great pity, my dear, to shut yourself up at your age!
Pray stay among us."

Mme. de Beauséant saw the Duchess, and, in spite of herself, an exclamation broke from her.

"I saw how it was, Clara," said Mme. de Langeais. "You
are going from among us, and you will never come back. But
you must not go until you have heard me, until we have understood each other."

She took her friend's arm, and they went together into the

next room. There the Duchess looked at her with tears in her eyes; she held her friend in a close embrace and kissed her cheek.

"I could not let you go without a word, dearest; the remorse would have been too hard to bear. You can count upon me as surely as upon yourself. You have shown yourself great this evening; I feel that I am worthy of our friendship, and I mean to prove myself worthy of it. I have not always been kind; I was in the wrong; forgive me, dearest; I wish I could unsay anything that may have hurt you; I take back those words. One common sorrow has brought us together again, for I do not know which of us is the more miserable. M. de Montriveau was not here to-night; do you understand what that means?—None of those who saw you to-night, Clara, will ever forget you. I mean to make one last effort. If I fail, I shall go into a convent. Clara, where are you going?"

"Into Normandy, to Courcelles. I shall love and pray there until the day when God shall take me from this world. —M. de Rastignac!" called the Vicomtesse, in a tremulous voice, remembering that the young man was waiting there.

The student knelt to kiss his cousin's hand.

"Good-bye, Antoinette!" said Mme. de Beauséant. "May you be happy."—She turned to the student. "You are young," she said; "you have some beliefs still left. I have been privileged, like some dying people, to find sincere and reverent feeling in those about me as I take my leave of this world."

It was nearly five o'clock that morning when Rastignac came away. He had put Mme. de Beauséant into her traveling carriage, and received her last farewells, spoken amid fast-falling tears; for no greatness is so great that it can rise above the laws of human affection, or live beyond the jurisdiction of pain, as certain demagogues would have the people believe. Eugène returned on foot to the Maison Vauquer through the cold and darkness. His education was nearly complete.

"There is no hope for poor Father Goriot," said Bianchon, as Rastignac came into the room. Eugène looked for a while at the sleeping man, then he turned to his friend. "Dear fellow, you are content with the modest career you have marked out for yourself; keep to it. I am in hell, and I must stay there. Believe everything that you hear said of the world, nothing is too impossibly bad. No Juvenal could paint the horrors hidden away under the covering of gems and gold."

At two o'clock in the afternoon Bianchon came to wake Rastignac, and begged him to take charge of Goriot, who had grown worse as the day wore on. The medical student was obliged to go out.

"Poor old man, he has not two days to live, maybe not many hours," he said; "but we must do our utmost, all the same, to fight the disease. It will be a very troublesome case, and we shall want money. We can nurse him between us, of course, but, for my own part, I have not a penny. I have turned out his pockets, and rummaged through his drawers—result, *nix*. I asked him about it while his mind was clear, and he told me he had not a farthing of his own. What have you?"

"I have twenty francs left," said Rastignac; "but I will take them to the roulette table, I shall be sure to win."

"And if you lose?"

"Then I shall go to his sons-in-law and his daughters and ask them for money."

"And suppose they refuse?" Bianchon retorted. "The most pressing thing just now is not really money; we must put mustard poultices, as hot as they can be made, on his feet and legs. If he calls out, there is still some hope for him. You know how to set about doing it, and besides, Christophe will help you. I am going round to the dispensary to persuade them to let us have the things we want on credit. It is a pity that we could not move him to the hospital; poor fellow, he would be better there. Well, come along, I leave you in charge; you must stay with him till I come back."

The two young men went back to the room where the old man was lying. Eugène was startled at the change in Goriot's face, so livid, distorted, and feeble.

"How are you, papa?" he said, bending over the pallet-bed. Goriot turned his dull eyes upon Eugène, looked at him attentively, and did not recognize him. It was more than the student could bear; the tears came into his eyes.

"Bianchon, ought we to have curtains put up in the windows?"

"No, the temperature and the light do not affect him now. It would be a good thing for him if he felt heat or cold; but we must have a fire in any case to make tisanes and heat the other things. I will send round a few sticks; they will last till we can have in some firewood. I burned all the bark fuel you had left, as well as his, poor man, yesterday and during the night. The place was so damp that the water stood in drops on the walls; I could hardly get the room dry. Christophe came in and swept the floor, but the place is like a stable; I had to burn juniper, the smell was something horrible.

"*Mon Dieu!*" said Rastignac. "To think of those daughters of his."

"One moment, if he asks for something to drink, give him this," said the house student, pointing to a large white jar. "If he begins to groan, and the belly feels hot and hard to the touch, you know what to do; get Christophe to help you. If he should happen to grow much excited, and begin to talk a good deal and even to ramble in his talk, do not be alarmed. It would not be a bad symptom. But send Christophe to the Hospice Cochin. Our doctor, my chum, or I will come and apply moxas. We had a great consultation this morning while you were asleep. A surgeon, a pupil of Gall's came, and our house surgeon, and the head physician from the Hôtel-Dieu. Those gentlemen considered that the symptoms were very unusual and interesting; the case must be carefully watched, for it throws a light on several obscure and rather important scientific problems. One of the authorities says that if there

is more pressure of serum on one or other portion of the
brain, it should affect his mental capacities in such and such
directions. So if he should talk, notice very carefully what
kind of ideas his mind seems to run on; whether memory, or
penetration, or the reasoning faculties are exercised; whether
sentiments or practical questions fill his thoughts; whether
he makes forecasts or dwells on the past; in fact, you must
be prepared to give an accurate report of him. It is quite
likely that the extravasation fills the whole brain, in which
case he will die in the imbecile state in which he is lying now.
You cannot tell anything about these mysterious nervous
diseases. Suppose the crash came here," said Bianchon,
touching the back of the head, "very strange things have been
known to happen; the brain sometimes partially recovers,
and death is delayed. Or the congested matter may pass out
of the brain altogether through channels which can only be
determined by a post-mortem examination. There is an old
man at the Hospital for Incurables, an imbecile patient, in
his case the effusion has followed the direction of the spinal
cord; he suffers horrid agonies, but he lives."

"Did they enjoy themselves?" It was Father Goriot who
spoke. He had recognized Eugène.

"Oh! he thinks of nothing but his daughters," said Bianchon. "Scores of times last night he said to me, 'They are
dancing now! She has her dress.' He called them by their
names. He made me cry, the devil take it, calling with that
tone in his voice, for 'Delphine! my little Delphine! and
Nasie!' Upon my word," said the medical student, "it was
enough to make any one burst out crying."

"Delphine," said the old man, "she is there, isn't she? I
knew she was there," and his eyes sought the door.

"I am going down now to tell Sylvie to get the poultices
ready," said Bianchon. "They ought to go on at once."

Rastignac was left alone with the old man. He sat at the
foot of the bed, and gazed at the face before him, so horribly
changed that it was shocking to see.

"Noble natures cannot dwell in this world," he said;

"Mme. de Beauséant has fled from it, and there he lies dying. What place indeed is there in the shallow petty frivolous thing called society for noble thoughts and feelings?"

Pictures of yesterday's ball rose up in his memory, in strange contrast to the deathbed before him. Bianchon suddenly appeared.

"I say, Eugène, I have just seen our head surgeon at the hospital, and I ran all the way back here. If the old man shows any signs of reason, if he begins to talk, cover him with a mustard poultice from the neck to the base of the spine, and send round for us."

"Dear Bianchon," exclaimed Eugène.

"Oh! it is an interesting case from a scientific point of view," said the medical student, with all the enthusiasm of a neophyte.

"So!" said Eugène. "Am I really the only one who cares for the poor old man for his own sake?"

"You would not have said so if you had seen me this morning," returned Bianchon, who did not take offence at this speech. "Doctors who have seen a good deal of practice never see anything but the disease, but, my dear fellow, I can see the patient still."

He went. Eugène was left alone with the old man, and with an apprehension of a crisis that set in, in fact, before very long.

"Ah! dear boy, is that you?" said Father Goriot, recognizing Eugène.

"Do you feel better?" asked the law student, taking his hand.

"Yes. My head felt as if it were being screwed up in a vise, but now it is set free again. Did you see my girls? They will be here directly; as soon as they know that I am ill they will hurry here at once; they used to take such care of me in the Rue de la Jussienne! Great Heavens! if only my room was fit for them to come into! There has been a young man here, who has burned up all my bark fuel."

"I can hear Christophe coming upstairs," Eugène answered. "He is bringing up some firewood that that young man has sent you."

"Good, but how am I to pay for the wood. I have not a penny left, dear boy. I have given everything, everything. I am a pauper now. Well, at least the golden gown was grand, was it not? (Ah! what pain this is!) Thanks, Christophe! God will reward you, my boy; I have nothing left now."

Eugène went over to Christophe and whispered in the man's ear, "I will pay you well, and Sylvie too, for your trouble."

"My daughters told you that they were coming, didn't they, Christophe? Go again to them, and I will give you five francs. Tell them that I am not feeling well, that I should like to kiss them both and see them once again before I die. Tell them that, but don't alarm them more than you can help."

Rastignac signed to Christophe to go, and the man went.

"They will come before long," the old man went on. "I know them so well. My tender-hearted Delphine! If I am going to die, she will feel it so much! And so will Nasie. I do not want to die; they will cry if I die; and if I die, dear Eugène, I shall not see them any more. It will be very dreary there where I am going. For a father it is hell to be without your children; I have served my apprenticeship already since they married. My heaven was in the Rue de la Jussienne. Eugène, do you think that if I go to heaven I could come back to earth, and be near them in spirit? I have heard some such things said. Is it true? It is as if I could see them at this moment as they used to be when we all lived in the Rue de la Jussienne. They used to come downstairs of a morning. 'Good-morning, papa!' they used to say, and I would take them on my knees; we had all sorts of little games of play together, and they had such pretty coaxing ways. We always had breakfast together, too, every morning, and they had dinner with me—in fact, I was a father then. I enjoyed my children. They did not think for themselves so long as they lived in the Rue de la Jussienne; they knew nothing of the world; they loved me with all their hearts. *Mon Dieu!* why could they not always be little girls? (Oh! my head! this racking pain in my head!) Ah! ah! forgive me, children; this pain is fearful; it must be agony indeed, for you have used me to endure pain. *Mon Dieu!* if only I held their hands in mine, I should not feel it at all.—Do you think that they are on the way? Christophe is so stupid; I ought to have gone myself. *He* will see them. But you went to the ball yesterday; just tell me how they looked. They did not know that I was ill, did they, or they would not have been dancing, poor little things? Oh! I must not be ill any longer. They stand too much in need of me; their fortunes are in danger. And such husbands as they are bound to! I must get well! (Oh! what pain this is! what pain this is! . . . ah! ah!)—I must get well, you see; for they *must* have money, and I know how to set about making some. I will go to Odessa and manufacture starch there. I am an old hand, I will make millions. (Oh! this is agony!)"

Goriot was silent for a moment; it seemed to require his whole strength to endure the pain.

"If they were here, I should not complain," he said. "So why should I complain now?"

He seemed to grow drowsy with exhaustion, and lay quietly for a long time. Christophe came back; and Rastignac, thinking that Goriot was asleep, allowed the man to give his story aloud.

"First of all, sir, I went to Madame la Comtesse," he said; "but she and her husband were so busy that I couldn't get to speak to her. When I insisted that I must see her, M. de Restaud came out to me himself, and went on like this: 'M. Goriot is dying, is he? Very well, it is the best thing he can do. I want Mme. de Restaud to transact some important business, when it is all finished she can go.' The gentleman looked angry, I thought. I was just going away when Mme. de Restaud came out into an ante-chamber through a door that I did not notice, and said, 'Christophe, tell my father that my husband wants me to discuss some matters with him, and I cannot leave the house, the life or death of my children is at stake; but as soon as it is over, I will come.' As for Madame la Baronne, that is another story! I could not speak to her either, and I did not even see her. Her waiting-woman said, 'Ah yes, but madame only came back from a ball at a quarter to five this morning; she is asleep now, and if I wake her before mid-day she will be cross. As soon as she rings, I will go and tell her that her father is worse. It will be time enough then to tell her bad news!' I begged and I prayed, but, there! it was no good. Then I asked for M. le Baron, but he was out."

"To think that neither of his daughters should come!" exclaimed Rastignac. "I will write to them both."

"Neither of them!" cried the old man, sitting upright in bed. "They are busy, they are asleep, they will not come! I knew that they would not. Not until you are dying do you know your children. . . . Oh! my friend, do not marry; do not have children! You give them life; they give you your deathblow. You bring them into the world, and they send you out of it. No, they will not come. I have known that these ten years. Sometimes I have told myself so, but I did not dare to believe it."

The tears gathered and stood without overflowing the red sockets.

"Ah! if I were rich still, if I had kept my money, if I had not given all to them, they would be with me now; they would fawn on me and cover my cheeks with their kisses! I should be living in a great mansion; I should have grand apartments and servants and a fire in my room; and *they* would be about me all in tears, and their husbands and their children. I should have had all that; now—I have nothing. Money brings everything to you; even your daughters. My money. Oh! where is my money? If I had plenty of money to leave behind me, they would nurse me and tend me; I should hear their voices, I should see their faces. Ah, God! who knows? They both of them have hearts of stone. I loved them too much; it was not likely that they should love me. A father ought always to be rich; he ought to keep his children well in hand, like unruly horses. I have gone down on my knees to them. Wretches! this is the crowning act that brings the last ten years to a proper close. If you but knew how much they made of me just after they were married. (Oh! this is cruel torture!) I had just given them each eight hundred thousand francs; they were bound to be civil to me after that, and their husbands too were civil. I used to go to their houses: it was, 'My kind father' here, 'My dear father' there. There was always a place for me at their tables. I used to dine with their husbands now and then, and they were very respectful to me. I was still worth something, they thought. How should they know? I had not said anything about my affairs. It is worth while to be civil to a man who has given his daughters eight hundred thousand francs apiece; and they showed me every attention then—but it was all for my money. Grand people are not great. I found that out by experience! I went to the theatre with them in their carriage; I might stay as long as I cared to stay at their evening parties. In fact, they acknowledged me their father; publicly they owned that they were my daughters. But I always was a shrewd one, you see, and nothing was lost upon me. Everything went straight to the mark and pierced my heart. I saw quite well that it was all sham and pretence, but there is no help for such things as these. I felt less at my ease at their dinner-table than I did downstairs here. I had nothing to say for myself. So these grand folks would ask in my son-in-law's ear, 'Who may that gentleman be?'—'The father-in-law with the dollars; he is very rich.'—'The devil, he is!' they would say, and look again at me with the respect due to my money. Well, if I was in the way sometimes, I paid dearly for my mistakes. And besides, who is perfect? (My head is one sore!) Dear Monsieur Eugène, I am suffering so now, that a man might die of the pain; but it is nothing, nothing to be compared with the pain I endured when Anastasie made me feel, for the first time, that I had said something stupid. She looked at me, and that glance of hers opened all my veins. I used to want to know everything, to be learned; and one thing I did learn thoroughly—I knew that I was not wanted here on earth.

"The next day I went to Delphine for comfort, and what should I do there but make some stupid blunder that made her angry with me. I was like one driven out of his senses. For a week I did not know what to do; I did not dare to go to see them for fear they should reproach me. And that was how they both turned me out of the house.

"Oh God! Thou knowest all the misery and anguish that I have endured; Thou hast counted all the wounds that have been dealt to me in these years that have aged and changed me and whitened my hair and drained my life; why dost Thou make me to suffer so to-day? Have I not more than expiated the sin of loving them too much? They themselves have been the instruments of vengeance; they have tortured me for my sin of affection.

"Ah, well! fathers know no better; I loved them so; I went back to them as a gambler goes to the gaming table. This love was my vice, you see, my mistress—they were everything in the world to me. They were always wanting something or other, dresses and ornaments, and what not; their maids used to tell me what they wanted, and I used to give them the things for the sake of the welcome that they bought for me. But, at the same time, they used to give me little lectures on my behavior in society; they began about it at once. Then they began to feel ashamed of me. That is what comes of having your children well brought up. I could not go to school again at my time of life. (This pain is fearful! *Mon Dieu!* These doctors! these doctors! If they would open my head, it would give me some relief!) Oh, my daughters, my daughters! Anastasie! Delphine! If I could only see them! Send for the police, and make them come to me! Justice is on my side, the whole world is on my side, I have natural rights, and the law with me. I protest! The country will go to ruin if a father's rights are trampled under foot. That is easy to see. The whole world turns on fatherly love; fatherly love is the foundation of society; it will crumble into ruin when children do not love their fathers. Oh! if I could only see them, and hear them, no matter what they said; if I could simply hear their voices, it would soothe the pain. Delphine! Delphine most of all. But tell them when they come not to look so coldly at me as they do. Oh! my friend, my good Monsieur Eugène, you do not know what it is when all the golden light in a glance suddenly turns to a leaden gray. It has been one long winter here since the light in their eyes shone no more for me. I have had nothing but disappointments to devour. Disappointment has been my daily bread; I have lived on humiliation and insults. I have swallowed down all the affronts for which they sold me my poor stealthy little moments of joy; for I love them so! Think of it! a father hiding himself to get a glimpse of his children! I have given all my life to them, and to-day they will not give me one hour! I am hungering and thirsting for them, my heart is burning in me, but they will not come to bring relief in the agony, for I am dying now, I feel that this is death. Do they not know what it means to trample on a father's corpse? There is a God in heaven who avenges us fathers whether we will or no.

"Oh! they will come! Come to me, darlings, and give me one more kiss; one last kiss, the Viaticum for your father, who will pray God for you in heaven. I will tell Him that you have been good children to your father, and plead your cause with God! After all, it is not their fault. I tell you they are innocent, my friend. Tell every one that it is not their fault, and no one need be distressed on my account. It is all my own fault, I taught them to trample upon me. I loved to have it so. It is no one's affair but mine; man's justice and God's justice have nothing to do in it. God would be unjust if He condemned them for anything they may have done to me. I did not behave to them properly; I was stupid enough to resign my rights. I would have hum-

bled myself in the dust for them. What could you expect?
The most beautiful nature, the noblest soul, would have been
spoiled by such indulgence. I am a wretch, I am justly punished. I, and I only, am to blame for all their sins; I spoiled
them. To-day they are as eager for pleasure as they used to
be for sugar-plums. When they were little girls I indulged
them in every whim. They had a carriage of their own when
they were fifteen. They have never been crossed. I am
guilty, and not they—but I sinned through love.

"My heart would open at the sound of their voices. I can
hear them; they are coming. Yes! yes! they are coming.
The law demands that they should be present at their father's
deathbed; the law is on my side. It would only cost them
the hire of a cab. I would pay that. Write to them, tell
them that I have millions to leave to them! On my word
of honor, yes. I am going to manufacture Italian paste
foods at Odessa. I understand the trade. There are millions to be made in it. Nobody has thought of the scheme
as yet. You see, there will be no waste, no damage in tran-
sit, as there always is with wheat and flour. Hey! hey! and
starch too; there are millions to be made in the starch trade!
You will not be telling a lie. Millions, tell them; and even
if they really come because they covet the money, I would
rather let them deceive me; and I shall see them in any case.
I want my children! I gave them life; they are mine, mine!"
and he sat upright. The head thus raised, with its scanty
white hair, seemed to Eugène like a threat; every line that
could still speak spoke of menace.

"There, there, dear father," said Eugène, "lie down again;
I will write to them at once. As soon as Bianchon comes
back I will go for them myself, if they do not come before."

"If they do not come?" repeated the old man, sobbing.
"Why, I shall be dead before then; I shall die in a fit of rage,
of rage! Anger is getting the better of me. I can see my
whole life at this minute. I have been cheated! They do
not love me—they have never loved me all their lives! It is
all clear to me. They have not come, and they will not come.

The longer they put off their coming, the less they are likely to give me this joy. I know them. They have never cared to guess my disappointments, my sorrows, my wants; they never cared to know my life; they will have no presentiment of my death; they do not even know the secret of my tenderness for them. Yes, I see it all now. I have laid my heart open so often, that they take everything I do for them as a matter of course. They might have asked me for the very eyes out of my head and I would have bidden them to pluck them out. They think that all fathers are like theirs. You should always make your value felt. Their own children will avenge me. Why, for their own sakes they should come to me! Make them understand that they are laying up retribution for their own deathbeds. All crimes are summed up in this one. . . . Go to them; just tell them that if they stay away it will be parricide! There is enough laid to their charge already without adding that to the list. Cry aloud as I do now, 'Nasie! Delphine! here! Come to your father; the father who has been so kind to you is lying ill!' —Not a sound; no one comes! Then am I to die like a dog? This is to be my reward—I am forsaken at the last. They are wicked, heartless women; curses on them, I loathe them. I shall rise at night from my grave to curse them again; for, after all, my friends, have I done wrong? They are behaving very badly to me, eh? . . . What am I saying? Did you not tell me just now that Delphine was in the room? She is more tender-hearted than her sister. . . . Eugène, you are my son, you know. You will love her; be a father to her! Her sister is very unhappy. And there are their fortunes! Ah, God! I am dying, this anguish is almost more than I can bear! Cut off my head; leave me nothing but my heart."

"Christophe!" shouted Eugène, alarmed by the way in which the old man moaned, and by his cries, "go for M. Bianchon, and send a cab here for me.—I am going to fetch them, dear father; I will bring them back to you."

"Make them come! Compel them to come! Call out the

Guard, the military, anything and everything, but make them come!" He looked at Eugène, and a last gleam of intelligence shone in his eyes. "Go to the authorities, to the Public Prosecutor, let them bring them here; come they shall!"

"But you have cursed them."

"Who said that!" said the old man in dull amazement. "You know quite well that I love them, I adore them! I shall be quite well again if I can see them. . . . Go for them, my good neighbor, my dear boy, you are kind-hearted; I wish I could repay you for your kindness, but I have nothing to give you now, save the blessing of a dying man. Ah! if I could only see Delphine, to tell her to pay my debt to you. If the other cannot come, bring Delphine to me at any rate. Tell her that unless she comes, you will not love her any more. She is so fond of you that she will come to me then. Give me something to drink! There is a fire in my bowels. Press something against my forehead! If my daughters would lay their hands there, I think I should get better. . . . _Mon Dieu!_ who will recover their money for them when I am gone? . . . I will manufacture vermicelli out in Odessa; I will go to Odessa for their sakes."

"Here is something to drink," said Eugène, supporting the dying man on his left arm, while he held a cup of tisane to Goriot's lips.

"How you must love your own father and mother!" said the old man, and grasped the student's hand in both of his. It was a feeble, trembling grasp. "I am going to die; I shall die without seeing my daughters; do you understand? To be always thirsting, and never to drink; that has been my life for the last ten years. . . . I have no daughters, my sons-in-law killed them. No, since their marriages they have been dead to me. Fathers should petition the Chambers to pass a law against marriage. If you love your daughters, do not let them marry. A son-in-law is a rascal who poisons a girl's mind and contaminates her whole nature. Let us have no more marriages! It robs us of our daughters; we are left alone upon our deathbeds, and they are not with us then.

They ought to pass a law for dying fathers. This is awful!
It cries for vengeance! They cannot come, because my sons-
in-law forbid them! . . . Kill them! . . . Restaud
and the Alsatian, kill them both! They have murdered me
between them! . . . Death or my daughters! . . .
Ah! it is too late, I am dying, and they are not here! . . .
Dying without them! . . . Nasie! Fifine! Why do you
not come to me? Your papa is going——"

"Dear Father Goriot, calm yourself. There, there, lie
quietly and rest; don't worry yourself, don't think."

"I shall not see them. Oh! the agony of it!"

"You *shall* see them."

"Really?" cried the old man, still wandering. "Oh! shall
I see them; I shall see them and hear their voices. I shall
die happy. Ah! well, after all, I do not wish to live; I cannot stand this much longer; this pain that grows worse and
worse. But, oh! to see them, to touch their dresses—ah!
nothing but their dresses, that is very little; still, to feel something that belongs to them. Let me touch their hair with
my fingers . . . their hair . . ."

His head fell back on the pillow, as if a sudden heavy blow
had struck him down, but his hands groped feebly over the
quilt, as if to find his daughters' hair.

"My blessing on them . . ." he said, making an effort,
"my blessing . . ."

His voice died away. Just at that moment Bianchon came
into the room

"I met Christophe," he said; "he is gone for your cab."

Then he looked at the patient, and raised the closed eyelids with his fingers. The two students saw how dead and
lustreless the eyes beneath had grown.

"He will not get over this, I am sure," said Bianchon. He
felt the old man's pulse, and laid a hand over his heart.

"The machinery works still; more is the pity, in his state
it would be better for him to die."

"Ah! my word, it would!"

"What is the matter with you? You are as pale as death."

"Dear fellow, the moans and cries that I have just heard. . . . There is a God! Ah! yes, yes, there is a God, and He has made a better world for us, or this world of ours would be a nightmare. I could have cried like a child; but this is too tragical, and I am sick at heart."

"We want a lot of things, you know; and where is the money to come from?"

Rastignac took out his watch.

"There, be quick and pawn it. I do not want to stop on the way to the Rue du Helder; there is not a moment to lose, I am afraid, and I must wait here till Christophe comes back. I have not a farthing; I shall have to pay the cabman when I get home again."

Rastignac rushed down the stairs, and drove off to the Rue du Helder. The awful scene through which he had just passed quickened his imagination, and he grew fiercely indignant. He reached Mme. de Restaud's house only to be told by the servant that his mistress could see no one.

"But I have brought a message from her father, who is dying," Rastignac told the man.

"The Count has given us the strictest orders, sir——"

"If it is M. de Restaud who has given the orders, tell him that his father-in-law is dying, and that I am here, and must speak with him at once."

The man went.

Eugène waited for a long while. "Perhaps her father is dying at this moment," he thought.

Then the man came back, and Eugène followed him to the little drawing-room. M. de Restaud was standing before the fireless grate, and did not ask his visitor to seat himself.

"Monsieur le Comte," said Rastignac, "M. Goriot, your father-in-law, is lying at the point of death in a squalid den in the Latin Quarter. He has not a penny to pay for firewood; he is expected to die at any moment, and keeps calling for his daughter——"

"I feel very little affection for M. Goriot, sir, as you probably are aware," the Count answered coolly. "His character has been compromised in connection with Mme. de Restaud; he is the author of the misfortunes that have embittered my life and troubled my peace of mind. It is a matter of perfect indifference to me if he lives or dies. Now you know my feelings with regard to him. Public opinion may blame me, but I care nothing for public opinion. Just now I have other and much more important matters to think about than the things that fools and chatterers may say about me. As for Mme. de Restaud, she cannot leave the house; she is in no condition to do so. And, besides, I shall not allow her to leave it. Tell her father that as soon as she has done her duty by her husband and child she shall go to see him. If she has any love for her father, she can be free to go to him, if she chooses, in a few seconds; it lies entirely with her——"

"Monsieur le Comte, it is no business of mine to criticise your conduct; you can do as you please with your wife, but may I count upon your keeping your word with me? Well, then, promise me to tell her that her father has not twenty-four hours to live; that he looks in vain for her, and has cursed her already as he lies on his deathbed,—that is all I ask."

"You can tell her yourself," the Count answered, impressed by the thrill of indignation in Eugène's voice.

The Count led the way to the room where his wife usually sat. She was drowned in tears, and lay crouching in the depths of an armchair, as if she were tired of life and longed to die. It was piteous to see her. Before venturing to look at Rastignac, she glanced at her husband in evident and abject terror that spoke of complete prostration of body and mind; she seemed crushed by a tyranny both mental and physical. The Count jerked his head towards her; she construed this as a permission to speak.

"I heard all that you said, monsieur. Tell my father that if he knew all he would forgive me. . . . I did not think there was such torture in the world as this; it is more than I can endure, monsieur!—But I will not give way as long as I live," she said, turning to her husband. "I am a mother.

—Tell my father that I have never sinned against him in spite of appearances!" she cried aloud in her despair.

Eugène bowed to the husband and wife; he guessed the meaning of the scene, and that this was a terrible crisis in the Countess' life. M. de Restaud's manner had told him that his errand was a fruitless one; he saw that Anastasie had no longer any liberty of action. He came away mazed and bewildered, and hurried to Mme. de Nucingen. Delphine was in bed.

"Poor dear Eugène, I am ill," she said. "I caught cold after the ball, and I am afraid of pneumonia. I am waiting for the doctor to come."

"If you were at death's door," Eugène broke in, "you must be carried somehow to your father. He is calling for you. If you could hear the faintest of those cries, you would not feel ill any longer."

"Eugène, I dare say my father is not quite so ill as you say; but I cannot bear to do anything that you do not approve, so I will do just as you wish. As for *him,* he would die of grief I know if I went out to see him and brought on a dangerous illness. Well, I will go as soon as I have seen the doctor.— Ah!" she cried out, "you are not wearing your watch, how is that?"

Eugène reddened.

"Eugène, Eugène! if you have sold it already or lost it. . . . Oh! it would be very wrong of you!"

The student bent over Delphine and said in her ear, "Do you want to know? Very well, then, you shall know. Your father has nothing left to pay for the shroud that they will lay him in this evening. Your watch has been pawned, for I had nothing either."

Delphine sprang out of bed, ran to her desk, and took out her purse. She gave it to Eugène, and rang the bell, crying:

"I will go, I will go at once, Eugène. Leave me, I will dress. Why, I should be an unnatural daughter! Go back; I will be there before you.—Thérèse," she called to the waiting-woman, "ask M. de Nucingen to come upstairs at once and speak to me."

Eugène was almost happy when he reached the Rue Neuve-Sainte-Geneviève; he was so glad to bring the news to the dying man that one of his daughters was coming. He fumbled in Delphine's purse for money, so as to dismiss the cab at once; and discovered that the young, beautiful, and wealthy woman of fashion had only seventy francs in her private purse. He climbed the stairs and found Bianchon supporting Goriot, while the house surgeon from the hospital was applying moxas to the patient's back—under the direction of the physician, it was the last expedient of science, and it was tried in vain.

"Can you feel them?" asked the physician. But Goriot had caught sight of Rastignac, and answered, "They are coming, are they not?"

"There is hope yet," said the surgeon; "he can speak."

"Yes," said Eugène, "Delphine is coming."

"Oh! that is nothing!" said Bianchon; "he has been talking about his daughters all the time. He calls for them as a man impaled calls for water, they say——"

"We may as well give up," said the physician, addressing the surgeon. "Nothing more can be done now; the case is hopeless."

Bianchon and the house surgeon stretched the dying man out again on his loathsome bed.

"But the sheets ought to be changed," added the physician. "Even if there is no hope left, something is due to human nature. I shall come back again, Bianchon," he said, turning to the medical student. "If he complains again, rub some laudanum over the diaphragm."

He went, and the house surgeon went with him.

"Come, Eugène, pluck up heart, my boy," said Bianchon, as soon as they were alone; "we must set about changing his sheets, and put him into a clean shirt. Go and tell Sylvie to bring some sheets and come and help us to make the bed."

Eugène went downstairs, and found Mme. Vauquer engaged in setting the table; Sylvie was helping her. Eugène had scarcely opened his mouth before the widow walked up to him with the acidulous sweet smile of a cautious shopkeeper who is anxious neither to lose money nor to offend a customer.

"My dear Monsieur Eugène," she said, when he had spoken, "you know quite as well as I do that Father Goriot has not a brass farthing left. If you give out clean linen for a man who is just going to turn up his eyes, you are not likely to see your sheets again, for one is sure to be wanted to wrap him in. Now, you owe me a hundred and forty-four francs as it is, add forty francs to that for the pair of sheets, and then there are several little things, besides the candle that Sylvie will give you; altogether, it will all mount up to at least two hundred francs, which is more than a poor widow like me can afford to lose. Lord! now, Monsieur Eugène, look at it fairly. I have lost quite enough in these five days since this run of ill-luck set in for me. I would rather than ten crowns that the old gentleman had moved out as you said. It sets the other lodgers against the house. It would not take much to make me send him to the workhouse. In short, just put yourself in my place. I have to think of my establishment first, for I have my own living to make."

Eugène hurried up to Goriot's room.

"Bianchon," he cried, "the money or the watch?"

"There it is on the table, or the three hundred and sixty odd francs that are left of it. I paid up all the old scores out of it before they let me have the things. The pawn ticket lies there under the money."

Rastignac hurried downstairs.

"Here, madame" he said in disgust, "let us square accounts. M. Goriot will not stay much longer in your house, nor shall I——"

"Yes, he will go out feet foremost, poor old gentleman," she said, counting the francs with a half-facetious, half-lugubrious expression.

"Let us get this over," said Rastignac.

"Sylvie, look out some sheets, and go upstairs to help the gentlemen."

"You won't forget Sylvie," said Mme. Vauquer in Eugène's ear; "she has been sitting up these two nights."

As soon as Eugène's back was turned, the old woman hurried after her handmaid.

"Take the sheets that have had the sides turned into the middle, number 7. Lord! they are plenty good enough for a corpse," she said in Sylvie's ear.

Eugène, by this time, was part of the way upstairs, and did not overhear the elderly economist.

"Quick," said Bianchon, "let us change his shirt. Hold him upright."

Eugène went to the head of the bed and supported the dying man, while Bianchon drew off his shirt; and then Goriot made a movement as if he tried to clutch something to his breast, uttering a low inarticulate moaning the while, like some dumb animal in mortal pain.

"Ah! yes!" cried Bianchon. "It is the little locket and the chain made of hair that he wants; we took it off a while ago when we put the blisters on him. Poor fellow! he must have it again. There it lies on the chimney-piece."

Eugène went to the chimney-piece and found a little plait of faded golden hair—Mme. Goriot's hair, no doubt. He read the name on the little round locket, ANASTASIE on the one side, DELPHINE on the other. It was the symbol of his own heart that the father always wore on his breast. The curls of hair inside the locket were so fine and soft that it was plain they had been taken from two childish heads. When the old man felt the locket once more, his chest heaved with a long deep sigh of satisfaction, like a groan. It was something terrible to see, for it seemed as if the last quiver of the nerves were laid bare to their eyes, the last communication of sense to the mysterious point within whence our sympathies come and whither they go. A delirious joy lighted up the distorted face. The terrific and vivid force of the feeling that had survived the power of thought made such an impression on the students, that the dying man felt their hot tears falling on him, and gave a shrill cry of delight.

"Nasie!   Fifine!"

"There is life in him yet," said Bianchon

"What does he go on living for?" said Sylvie

"To suffer," answered Rastignac.

Bianchon made a sign to his friend to follow his example, knelt down and passed his arms under the sick man, and Rastignac on the other side did the same, so that Sylvie, standing in readiness, might draw the sheet from beneath and replace it with the one that she had brought. Those tears, no doubt, had misled Goriot; for he gathered up all his remaining strength in a last effort, stretched out his hands, groped for the students' heads, and as his fingers caught convulsively at their hair, they heard a faint whisper:

"Ah! my angels!"

Two words, two inarticulate murmurs, shaped into words by the soul which fled forth with them as they left his lips.

"Poor dear!" cried Sylvie, melted by that exclamation; the expression of the great love raised for the last time to a sublime height by that most ghastly and involuntary of lies.

The father's last breath must have been a sigh of joy, and in that sigh his whole life was summed up; he was cheated even at the last. They laid Father Goriot upon his wretched bed with reverent hands. Thenceforward there was no expression on his face, only the painful traces of the struggle between life and death that was going on in the machine; for that kind of cerebral consciousness that distinguishes between pleasure and pain in a human being was extinguished; it was only a question of time—and the mechanism itself would be destroyed.

"He will lie like this for several hours, and die so quietly at last, that we shall not know when he goes; there will be no rattle in the throat. The brain must be completely suffused."

As he spoke there was a footstep on the staircase, and a young woman hastened up, panting for breath.

"She has come too late," said Rastignac.

But it was not Delphine; it was Thérèse, her waiting woman, who stood in the doorway.

"Monsieur Eugène," she said, "monsieur and madame have had a terrible scene about some money that Madame (poor thing!) wanted for her father. She fainted, and the doctor came, and she had to be bled, calling out all the while, 'My father is dying; I want to see papa!' It was heartbreaking to hear her——"

"That will do, Thérèse. If she came now, it would be trouble thrown away. M. Goriot cannot recognize any one now."

"Poor, dear gentleman, is he as bad as that?" said Thérèse.

"You don't want me now, I must go and look after my dinner; it is half-past four," remarked Sylvie. The next instant she all but collided with Mme. de Restaud on the landing outside.

There was something awful and appalling in the sudden apparition of the Countess. She saw the bed of death by the dim light of the single candle, and her tears flowed at the sight of her father's passive features, from which the life had almost ebbed. Bianchon with thoughtful tact left the room.

"I could not escape soon enough," she said to Rastignac.

The student bowed sadly in reply. Mme. de Restaud took her father's hand and kissed it.

"Forgive me, father! You used to say that my voice would call you back from the grave; ah! come back for one moment to bless your penitent daughter. Do you hear me? Oh! this is fearful! No one on earth will ever bless me henceforth; every one hates me; no one loves me but you in all the world. My own children will hate me. Take me with you, father; I will love you, I will take care of you. He does not hear me . . . I am mad . . ."

She fell on her knees, and gazed wildly at the human wreck before her.

"My cup of misery is full," she said, turning her eyes upon Eugène. "M. de Trailles has fled, leaving enormous debts behind him, and I have found out that he was deceiving me. My husband will never forgive me, and I have left my fortune in his hands. I have lost all my illusions. Alas! I have forsaken the one heart that loved me (she pointed to her father as she spoke), and for whom? I have held his kindness cheap, and slighted his affection; many and many a time I have given him pain, ungrateful wretch that I am!"

"He knew it," said Rastignac.

Just then Goriot's eyelids unclosed; it was only a muscular contraction, but the Countess' sudden start of reviving hope was no less dreadful than the dying eyes.

"Is it possible that he can hear me?" cried the Countess. "No," she answered herself, and sat down beside the bed. As Mme. de Restaud seemed to wish to sit by her father, Eugène went down to take a little food. The boarders were already assembled.

"Well," remarked the painter, as he joined them, "it seems that there is to be a death-orama upstairs."

"Charles, I think you might find something less painful to joke about," said Eugène.

"So we may not laugh here?" returned the painter. "What harm does it do? Bianchon said that the old man was quite insensible."

"Well, then," said the employé from the Muséum, "he will die as he has lived."

"My father is dead!" shrieked the Countess.

The terrible cry brought Sylvie, Rastignac, and Bianchon; Mme. de Restaud had fainted away. When she recovered they carried her downstairs, and put her into the cab that stood waiting at the door. Eugène sent Thérèse with her, and bade the maid take the Countess to Mme. de Nucingen.

Bianchon came down to them.

"Yes, he is dead," he said.

"Come, sit down to dinner, gentlemen," said Mme. Vauquer, "or the soup will be cold."

The two students sat down together.

"What is the next thing to be done?" Eugène asked of Bianchon.

"I have closed his eyes and composed his limbs," said Bianchon. "When the certificate has been officially registered at the Mayor's office, we will sew him in his winding sheet and bury him somewhere. What do you think we ought to do?"

"He will not smell at his bread like this any more," said the painter, mimicking the old man's little trick.

"Oh, hang it all!" cried the tutor, "let Father Goriot drop, and let us have something else for a change. He is a standing dish, and we have had him with every sauce this hour or more. It is one of the privileges of the good city of Paris that anybody may be born, or live, or die there without attracting any attention whatsoever. Let us profit by the advantages of civilization. There are fifty or sixty deaths every day; if you have a mind to do it, you can sit down at any time and wail over whole hecatombs of dead in Paris. Father Goriot has gone off the hooks, has he? So much the better for him. If you venerate his memory, keep it to yourselves, and let the rest of us feed in peace."

"Oh, to be sure," said the widow, "it is all the better for him that he is dead. It looks as though he had had trouble enough, poor soul, while he was alive."

And this was all the funeral oration delivered over him who had been for Eugène the type and embodiment of Fatherhood.

The fifteen lodgers began to talk as usual. When Bianchon and Eugène had satisfied their hunger, the rattle of spoons and forks, the boisterous conversation, the expressions on the faces that bespoke various degrees of want of feeling, glutfony, or indifference, everything about them made them shiver with loathing. They went out to find a priest to watch that night with the dead. It was necessary to measure their last pious cares by the scanty sum of money that remained. Before nine o'clock that evening the body was laid out on the bare sacking of the bedstead in the desolate room; a lighted candle stood on either side, and the priest watched at the foot. Rastignac made inquiries of this latter as to the expenses of the funeral, and wrote to the Baron de Nucingen and the Comte de Restaud, entreating both gentlemen to authorize their man of business to defray the charges of lay-

ing their father-in-law in the grave. He sent Christophe with
the letters; then he went to bed, tired out, and slept.

Next day Bianchon and Rastignac were obliged to take the
certificate to the registrar themselves, and by twelve o'clock
the formalities were completed. Two hours went by; no
word came from the Count nor from the Baron; nobody appeared to act for them, and Rastignac had already been
obliged to pay the priest. Sylvie asked ten francs for sewing
the old man in his winding-sheet and making him ready for
the grave, and Eugène and Bianchon calculated that they
had scarcely sufficient to pay for the funeral, if nothing was
forthcoming from the dead man's family. So it was the
medical student who laid him in a pauper's coffin, despatched
from Bianchon's hospital, whence he obtained it at a cheaper
rate.

"Let us play those wretches a trick," said he "Go to the
cemetery, buy a grave for five years at Père-Lachaise, and
arrange with the Church and the undertaker to have a third-
class funeral. If the daughters and their husbands decline
to repay you, you can carve this on the headstone—'*Here lies
M. Goriot, father of the Comtesse de Restaud and the Baronne de Nucingen, interred at the expense of two students.*'"

Eugène took part of his friend's advice, but only after he
had gone in person first to M. and Mme. de Nucingen, and
then to M. and Mme. de Restaud—a fruitless errand. He
went no further than the doorstep in either house. The servants had received strict orders to admit no one.

"Monsieur and madame can see no visitors. They have
just lost their father, and are in deep grief over their loss."

Eugène's Parisian experience told him that it was idle to
press the point. Something clutched strangely at his heart
when he saw that it was impossible to reach Delphine.

"Sell some of your ornaments," he wrote hastily in the
porter's room, "so that your father may be decently laid in
his last resting-place."

He sealed the note, and begged the porter to give it to Thérèse for her mistress; but the man took it to the Baron de Nucingen, who flung the note into the fire. Eugène, having finished his errands, returned to the lodging-house about three o'clock. In spite of himself, the tears came into his eyes. The coffin, in its scanty covering of black cloth, was standing there on the pavement before the gate, on two chairs. A withered sprig of hyssop was soaking in the holy water bowl of silver-plated copper; there was not a soul in the street, not a passer-by had stopped to sprinkle the coffin; there was not even an attempt at a black drapery over the wicket. It was a pauper who lay there; no one made a pretence of mourning for him; he had neither friends nor kindred— there was no one to follow him to the grave.

Bianchon's duties compelled him to be at the hospital, but he had left a few lines for Eugène, telling his friend about the arrangements he had made for the burial service. The house student's note told Rastignac that a mass was beyond their means, that the ordinary office for the dead was cheaper, and must suffice, and that he had sent word to the undertaker by Christophe. Eugène had scarcely finished reading Bianchon's scrawl, when he looked up and saw the little circular gold locket that contained the hair of Goriot's two daughters in Mme. Vauquer's hands.

"How dared you take it?" he asked.

"Good Lord! is that to be buried along with him?" retorted Sylvie. "It is gold."

"Of course it shall!" Eugène answered indignantly; "he shall at any rate take one thing that may represent his daughters into the grave with him."

When the hearse came, Eugène had the coffin carried into the house again, unscrewed the lid, and reverently laid on the old man's breast the token that recalled the days when Delphine and Anastasie were innocent little maidens, before they began "to think for themselves," as he had moaned out in his agony.

Rastignac and Christophe and the two undertaker's men

were the only followers of the funeral. The Church of Saint-Étienne du Mont was only a little distance from the Rue Neuve-Sainte-Geneviève. When the coffin had been deposited in a low, dark, little chapel, the law student looked round in vain for Goriot's two daughters or their husbands. Christophe was his only fellow-mourner; Christophe, who appeared to think it was his duty to attend the funeral of the man who had put him in the way of such handsome tips. As they waited there in the chapel for the two priests, the chorister, and the beadle, Rastignac grasped Christophe's hand. He could not utter a word just then.

"Yes, Monsieur Eugène," said Christophe, "he was a good and worthy man, who never said one word louder than another; he never did any one any harm, and gave nobody any trouble."

The two priests, the chorister, and the beadle came, and said and did as much as could be expected for seventy francs in an age when religion cannot afford to say prayers for nothing.

The ecclesiastics chanted a psalm, the *Libera nos* and the *De profundis*. The whole service lasted about twenty minutes. There was but one mourning coach, which the priest and chorister agreed to share with Eugène and Christophe.

"There is no one else to follow us," remarked the priest, "so we may as well go quickly, and so save time; it is half-past five."

But just as the coffin was put in the hearse, two empty carriages, with the armorial bearings of the Comte de Restaud and the Baron de Nucingen, arrived and followed in the procession to Père-Lachaise. At six o'clock Goriot's coffin was lowered into the grave, his daughters' servants standing round the while. The ecclesiastic recited the short prayer that the students could afford to pay for, and then both priest and lackeys disappeared at once. The two grave diggers flung in several spadefuls of earth, and then stopped and asked Rastignac for their fee. Eugène felt in vain in his pocket, and was obliged to borrow five francs of Christophe. This thing, so trifling in itself, gave Rastignac a terrible pang of distress. It was growing dusk, the damp twilight fretted his nerves; he gazed down into the grave, and the tears he shed were drawn from him by the sacred emotion, a single-hearted sorrow. When such tears fall on earth, their radiance reaches heaven. And with that tear that fell on Father Goriot's grave, Eugène Rastignac's youth ended. He folded his arms and gazed at the clouded sky; and Christophe, after a glance at him, turned and went—Rastignac was left alone.

He went a few paces further, to the highest point of the cemetery, and looked out over Paris and the windings of the Seine; the lamps were beginning to shine on either side of the river. His eyes turned almost eagerly to the space between the column of the Place Vendôme and the cupola of the Invalides; there lay the shining world that he had wished to reach. He glanced over that humming hive, seeming to draw a foretaste of its honey, and said magniloquently:

"Henceforth there is war between us."

And by way of throwing down the glove to Society, Rastignac went to dine with Mme. de Nucingen.

THE UNCONSCIOUS HUMORISTS

To M. le Comte Jules de Castellane.

LEON DE LORA, the famous French landscape painter, belongs to one of the noblest families of Roussillon. The Loras came originally from Spain; and while they are distinguished for their ancient lineage, for the last century they have faithfully kept up the traditions of the hidalgo's proverbial poverty. Léon himself came up to Paris on foot from his department of the Pyrénées-Orientales with the sum of eleven francs in his pocket for all viaticum; and in some sort forgot the hardships of childhood and the poverty at home in the later hardships which a young dauber never lacks when his whole fortune consists in an intrepid vocation. Afterwards the absorbing cares brought by fame and success still further helped him to forget.

If you have followed the tortuous and capricious course of these Studies, you may perhaps recollect one of the heroes of *Un Début dans la Vie,* Schinner's pupil, Mistigris, who re-appears from time to time in various Scenes.

You would not recognize the frisky penniless dauber in the landscape painter of 1845, the rival of Hobbema, Ruysdael, and Claude Lorrain. Lora is a great man. He lives near his old master Hippolyte Schinner in a charming house (his own property) in the Rue de Berlin, not very far from the Hôtel de Brambourg, where his friend Bridau lives. He is a member of the Institut and an officer of the Legion of Honor, he has twenty thousand francs a year, his work fetches its weight in gold; and, fact even more extraordinary (as he thinks) than the invitations to court balls which he sometimes receives —the fame of a name published abroad over Europe by the press for the last sixteen years at length reached the valley in the Pyrénées-Orientales, where three Loras of the old stock were vegetating—to wit, his elder brother, his father, and a paternal aunt, Mlle. Urraca y Lora.

On the mother's side no relatives remained to the painter save a cousin, aged fifty, living in a little manufacturing town in the department, but that cousin was the first to remember Léon. So far back as 1840 Léon de Lora received a letter from M. Sylvestre Palafox-Castel-Gazonal (usually known as plain Gazonal), to which letter Lora replied that he really was himself—that is to say, that he really was the son of the late Léonie Gazonal, wife of Comte Fernand Didas y Lora.

Upon this, in the summer of 1841, Cousin Sylvestre Gazonal went to apprise the illustrious but obscure house of Lora of the fact that young Léon had not sailed for the River Plate, nor was he dead, as they supposed; but he was one of the finest geniuses of the modern French school—which they refused to believe. The elder brother, Don Juan de Lora, told his cousin Gazonal that he, Gazonal, had been hoaxed by some Parisian wag.

Time went on, and the said Gazonal found himself involved in a lawsuit, which the prefect of the Pyrénées-Orientales summarily stopped on a question of disputed jurisdiction and transferred to the Council of State. Gazonal proposed to himself to go to Paris to watch his case, and at the same time to clear up this matter, and to call the Parisian painter to account for his impertinence. To this end, M. Gazonal sallied forth from his furnished lodgings in the Rue Croix des Petits Champs, and was astonished at the sight of the palace in the Rue de Berlin; and, learning on inquiry that its owner was traveling in Italy, renounced for the time being the intention of asking him for satisfaction. His mind misgave him whether the great man would consent to own his mother's nephew.

Through 1843 and 1844 Gazonal followed the fortunes of his lawsuit. The local authorities, supported by the riparian owners, proposed to remove a weir on the river. The very existence of Gazonal's factory was threatened. In 1845 he looked on the case as lost beyond hope. The secretary of the Master of Requests, who drew up the report, told him in confidence that it was unfavorable to his claims, and his own barrister confirmed the news. Gazonal, at home a commandant of the National Guard, and as shrewd a manufacturer as you would find in his department, in Paris felt so utterly insignificant, and found the cost of living so high, that he kept close in his shabby lodging.

The child of the South, deprived of the sun, poured maledictions upon Paris, that "rheumatism factory," as he called it; and when he came to reckon up the expenses of his stay, vowed to himself to poison the prefect or to "minotaurize" him on his return. In gloomier moments he slew the prefect outright; then he cheered up a little, and contented himself with "minotaurizing" the culprit.

One morning after breakfast, inwardly storming, he snatched the newspaper up savagely, and the following lines caught his eye at the end of a paragraph: "Our great landscape painter, Léon de Lora, returned from Italy a month ago. He is sending a good deal of his work to the Salon this year, so we may look forward to a very brilliant exhibition——" The words rang in Gazonal's ears like the inner voice which tells the gambler that he will win. With Southern impetuosity, Gazonal dashed out of the house, hailed a cab, and went to his cousin's house in the Rue de Berlin.

Léon de Lora happened to be engaged at this moment, but he sent a message asking his relative to breakfast with him next day at the Café de Paris. Gazonal, like a man of the South, poured out his woes to the valet.

Next morning, overdressed for the occasion in a coat of corn-cockle blue, with gilt buttons, a frilled shirt, white waistcoat, and yellow kid gloves, Gazonal fidgeted up and down the boulevard for an hour and a half, after learning from the *cafetier* (so provincials call the proprietor of a café) that gentlemen usually breakfasted between eleven and twelve.

"About half-past eleven," so he used to tell the story afterwards to everybody at home, "two Parisians in plain surtouts, looking like nobodies, came along the boulevard, and cried out as soon as they saw me, 'Here comes your Gazonal!——' "

The second comer was Bixiou, brought on purpose to "draw out" Léon's cousin.

"And then," he would continue, "young Léon hugged me in his arms and cried, 'Do not be cross, dear cousin; I am very much yours.'—The breakfast was sumptuous. I rubbed my eyes when I saw so many gold pieces put down on the bill. These fellows must be making their weight in gold, for my cousin gave the waiter thirty *sols*—a whole day's wages!"

Over that monster breakfast, in the course of which they consumed six dozen Ostend oysters, half a dozen cutlets à la Soubise, a chicken à la Marengo, a lobster mayonnaise, mushrooms on toast, and green peas, to say nothing of *hors d'œuvres,* washed down with three bottles of bordeaux, three of champagne, several cups of coffee and liqueurs, Gazonal launched forth into magnificent invective on the subject of Paris. The noble manufacturer complained of the length of the four-pound loaves, of the height of the houses, of the callous indifference towards each other displayed by the passersby, of the cold, of the rain, of the fares charged by the "demifiacres"—and all so amusingly, that the pair of artists warmed towards him and asked for the story of his lawsuit.

"The histor-r-ry of my lawsuit," said he, rolling his r's and accentuating every word in Provençal fashion, "the histor-r-ry of my lawsuit is quite simple. They want my factory. I find a fool of a barrister, I give him twenty francs every time to keep his eyes open, and always find him fast asleep. He is a shell-less snail that rolls about in a carriage while I go on foot. They have swindled me shamefully; I do nothing but go from one to another and I see that I ought to have gone in a carriage. They will not look at you here unless you hide yourself out of sight in a carriage. On the other hand, in the Council of State they are a pack of do-nothings that leave a set of little rascals in our prefect's pay to do their work for them. . . . That is the history of my lawsuit. They want my factory! *E bé* they will get it. . . . And they can fight it out with my workpeople, a hundred strong, that will give them a cudgeling which will make them change their minds——"

"Come now, cousin, how long have you been here?" inquired the landscape painter.

"For two whole years. Oh that prefect and his 'disputed jurisdiction,' he shall pay dear for it; I will have his life, and give mine for it at the Assize Court——"

"Which Councillor is chairman of your committee?"

"An ex-journalist, not worth ten *sols,* though they call him Massol."

Lora and Bixiou exchanged glances.

"And the commissioner?"

"Funnier still! It is a Master of Requests, a professor of something or other at the Sorbonne; he used to write for some review. I pr-r-rofess the deepest disrespect for him——"

"Claude Vignon?" suggested Bixiou.

"That is the name—Massol and Vignon, that is the style of the unstable firm of bandits (*Trestaillons*) in league with my prefect."

"There is hope for it yet," said Léon de Lora. "You can do anything, you see, in Paris, cousin—anything, good or bad, just or unjust. Anything can be done or undone, or done over again here."

"I will be hanged if I will stop in it for another ten seconds; it is the dullest place in France."

As he spoke, the three were pacing up and down that stretch of asphalt on which you can scarcely walk of an afternoon without meeting somebody whose name has been proclaimed from Fame's trumpet, for good or ill. The ground shifts. Once it used to be the Place Royale, then the Pont Neuf possessed a privilege transferred in our day to the Boulevard des Italiens.

The landscape painter held forth for his cousin's benefit. "Paris," said he, "is an instrument which a man must learn to play. If we stop here for ten minutes, I will give you a lesson. There! look," he continued, raising his cane to point out a couple that issued from the Passage de l'Opéra.

"What is it?" inquired Gazonal.

"It" was an elderly woman dressed in a very showy gown, a faded tartan shawl, and a bonnet that had spent six months in a shop window. Her face told of a twenty years' residence in a damp porter's lodge, and her bulging market-basket showed no less clearly that the ex-portress had not improved her social position. By her side walked a slim and slender damsel. Her eyes, shaded with dark lashes, had lost their expression of innocence, her complexion was spoiled with overwork, but her features were prettily cut, her face was fresh, her hair looked thick, her brows pert and engaging, her figure lacked fulness—in two words, it was a green apple.

"It," answered Bixiou, "is a 'rat' equipped with her mother."

"A r-r-rat? *Quésaco?*"

Léon favored Mlle. Ninette with a little friendly nod.

"The 'rat' may win your lawsuit for you," he said. Gazonal started, but Bixiou had him by the arm. It had struck him as they left the café that the Southern countenance was a trifle flushed.

"The rat has just come from a rehearsal at the Opéra. It is on its way home to its scanty dinner. In three hours' time it will come back to dress, if it comes on this evening in the ballet, that is, for to-day is Monday The rat has reached the age of thirteen; it is an old rat already. In two years' time the creature's market-price will be sixty thousand francs; she will be everything or nothing, a great dancer or a super, she will have a name in the world or she will be a common prostitute. Her working life began at the age of eight. Such as you see her to-day she is exhausted; she overtired herself this morning at the dancing class; she has just come out of a rehearsal as full of head-splitting ins and outs as a Chinese puzzle; and she will come back again to-night. The rat is one of the foundation stones of the Opéra; the rat is to the leading lady of the ballet as the little clerk is to the notary. The rat is Hope."

"Who brings the rat into the world?" asked Gazonal.

"Porters, poor folk, actors, and dancers," said Bixiou. "Nothing but the direst poverty could induce an eight-year-old child to bear such torture of feet and joints, to lead a well-conducted life till she is sixteen or eighteen years old (simply as a business speculation), and to keep a hideous old woman always with her like stable-litter about some choice plant.— You will see genius of every kind go past—artists in the bud and artists run to seed—all of them engaged in rearing that ephemeral monument to the glory of France, called the Opéra; a daily renewed combination of physical and mental strength, will and genius, found nowhere but in Paris."

"I have already seen the Opéra," Gazonal remarked with a self-sufficient air.

"Yes, from your bench at three francs sixty centimes, as you have seen Paris from the Rue Croix des Petits Champs— without knowing anything about it. What did they give at the Opéra when you went?"

"*William Tell.*"

"Good," returned Léon, "you must have enjoyed Mathilde's great duet. Well, what do you suppose the prima donna did as soon as she went off the stage?"

"Did?—What?"

"Sat down to two mutton cutlets, underdone, which her servant had prepared for her——"

"Ah! *bouffre!*"

"Malibran kept herself up with brandy—it was that that killed her. Now for something else. You have seen the ballet; now you have just seen the ballet go past in plain morning dress, not knowing that your lawsuit depends upon those feet?"

"My lawsuit?"

"There, cousin, there goes a *marcheuse,* as she is called."

Léon pointed out one of the superb creatures that have lived sixty years of life at five-and-twenty; a beauty so unquestioned, so certain to be sought, that she keeps in the shade. She was tall, she walked well, with a dandy's assured air, and her toilette was striking by reason of its ruinous simplicity.

"That is Carabine," said Bixiou, as he and the painter nodded slightly, and Carabine answered with a smile.

"There goes another who can cashier your prefect."

"A *marcheuse* is often a very handsome 'rat' sold by her real or pretended mother so soon as it is certain that she can neither rank as a first, nor second, nor third-rate dancer; or else she prefers her calling of *coryphée* to any other, perhaps because she has spent her youth in learning to dance and knows how to do nothing else. She met no doubt with rebuffs at the minor theatres; she cannot hope to succeed in the three French cities which maintain a *corps de ballet,* she has no money, or no wish to go abroad, for you must know that the great Paris school trains dancers for the rest of the civilized world. If a rat becomes a *marcheuse,* that is to say, a *figurante,* she must have had some weighty reason for staying in Paris—some rich man whom she did not love, that is to say, or a poor young fellow whom she loved too well. The one that passed just now will dress or undress three times in an evening as a princess, a peasant-girl, a Tyrolese, and the like, and gets perhaps two hundred francs a month."

"She is better dressed than our pr-r-refect's wife."

"If you went to call on her, you would find a maid, a cook, and a man-servant in her splendid establishment in the Rue Saint-Georges," said Bixiou. "But, after all, as modern incomes are to the revenues of the eighteenth century noblesse, so is she to the eighteenth century Opera girl, a mere wreck of former greatness. Carabine is a power in the land. At this moment she rules du Tillet, a banker with a good deal of influence in the Chamber——"

"And the higher ranks of the ballet, how about them?"

"Look!" said Lora, pointing out an elegant carriage which crossed the Boulevard and disappeared down the Rue de la Grange-Batelière, "there goes one of our leading ladies of the ballet; put her name on the placards, and she will draw all Paris; she is making sixty thousand francs per annum, she lives like a princess. The price of your factory would not buy you the right of wishing her a good morning thirty times."

"*Eh bé!* I can easily say it to myself; it will cost less."

"Do you see that good-looking young man on the front seat? He is a vicomte bearing a great name, and he is her first gentleman of the chamber; he arranges with the newspapers for her; he carries peace or declares war of a morning on the manager of the Opéra; or he makes it his business to superintend the applause when she comes on or off the stage."

"My good sirs, this beats everything; I had not a suspicion of Paris as it is."

"Oh well, at any rate you may as well find out what may be seen in ten minutes in the Passage de l'Opéra.—There!" exclaimed Bixiou.

Two persons, a man and a woman, came out as he spoke. The woman was neither pretty nor plain; there was a certain distinction that revealed the artist in the fashion and color of her gown. The man looked rather like a minor canon.

"That is a double-bass and a *second premier sujet*," continued Bixiou. "The double-bass is a tremendous genius; but the double-bass, being a mere accessory in the score, scarcely makes as much as the dancer. The *second sujet* made a great name before Taglioni and Elssler appeared; she preserved the traditions of the character dance among us; she would have been in the first rank to-day if the other two had not come to reveal undreamed-of poetry in the dance; as it is, she is only in the second rank, and yet she draws her thirty thousand francs, and has a faithful friend in a peer of France with great influence in the Chamber. Look! here comes the third-rate dancer, a dancer that owes her (professional) existence to the omnipotent press. If her engagement had not been renewed, the men in office would have had one more enemy on their backs. The *corps de ballet* is the great power at the Opéra; for which reason, in the upper ranks of dandyism and politics, it is much better form to make a connection among the dancers than among the singers.

'Monsieur goes in for music,' is a kind of joke among the frequenters of the Opéra in the orchestra."

A short, ordinary-looking, plainly-dressed man went past.

"At last here comes the other half of the receipts—the tenor. There is no poetry, no music, no acting possible without a famous tenor that can take a certain high note. The tenor means the element of love, a voice that reaches the heart, that thrills the soul; and when this voice resolves itself into figures, it means a larger income than a cabinet minister's. A hundred thousand francs for a throat, a hundred thousand for a pair of ankles—behold the two financial scourges of the Opéra."

"It fills me with amazement to see so many hundred thousand francs walking about," said Gazonal.

"You will soon see a great deal more, dear cousin of mine. Come with us.—We will take Paris as an artist takes up the violoncello, and show you how to play the great instrument, show you how we amuse ourselves in Paris in fact."

"It is a kaleidoscope seven leagues round," cried Gazonal.

"Before we begin to pilot this gentleman, I must see Gaillard," began Bixiou

"And Gaillard may help us in the cousin's affairs."

"What is the new scene?"

"It is not a scene, but a scene-shifter. Gaillard is a friend of ours; he has come at last to be the managing director of a newspaper; his character, like his cash-box, is chiefly remarkable for its tidal ebb and flow. Gaillard possibly may help to win your lawsuit."

"It is lost——"

"Just the time to win it then!" returned Bixiou.

Arrived at Théodore Gaillard's house in the Rue de Ménars, the friends were informed by the footman that his master was engaged. It was a private interview.

"With whom?" inquired Bixiou.

"With a man that is driving a bargain to imprison a debtor that cannot be caught," said a voice, and a very handsome woman appeared in a dainty morning gown.

"In that case, dear Suzanne, the rest of us may walk in——"

"Oh! what a lovely creature!" cried Gazonal.

"That is Mme. Gaillard," said Léon de Lora; and, lowering his voice for his cousin's ear, he added, "You see before you, dear fellow, as modest a woman as you will find in Paris; she has retired from public life, and is contented with one husband."

"What can I do for you, my lords?" said the facetious managing director, imitating Frederick Lemaître.

Théodore Gaillard had been a clever man; but, as so often happens in Paris, he had grown stupid with staying too long in the same groove. The principal charm of his conversation consisted in tags of quotation with which it was garnished, bits from popular plays mouthed after the manner of some well-known actor.

"We have come for a chat," said Léon

"*Encôre, jeûne hôme!*" (Odry in *Les Salimbanques.*)

"This time we shall have him for certain," said Gaillard's interlocutor by way of conclusion.

"Are you quite sure of that, Daddy Fromenteau? This is the eleventh time that we have had him fast at night, and in the morning he was gone."

"What can you do? I never saw such a debtor. He is like a locomotive, he goes to sleep in Paris and wakes up in Seine-et-Oise. He is a puzzle for a locksmith."

Seeing Gaillard smile, he added, "That is how we talk in our line. You 'nab' a man, or you lock him up; that means you arrest him. They talk differently in the criminal police. Vidocq used to say to his man, 'They have got it ready for you!' which was all the funnier because 'it' meant the guillotine."

Bixiou jogged Gazonal's elbow, and at once the visitor became all eyes and ears. "Does monsieur give palm oil?" continued Fromenteau, quite quietly, though there was a perceptible shade of menace in the tone.

"It is a matter of fifty centimes," said Gaillard (a reminiscence of Odry in *Les Saltimbanques*), as he handed over five francs to Fromenteau.

"And for the blackguards?" the man went on.

"Who are they?"

"Those in my employ," Fromenteau replied imperturbably.

"Is there any one lower yet," asked Bixiou.

"Oh yes, sir," the detective replied. "There are some that give us information unconsciously and get no pay for it. I put flats and noodles lower than blackguards."

"The blackguards are often very good-looking and clever," exclaimed Léon.

"Then do you belong to the police?" asked Gazonal, uneasily and curiously eyeing this little wizened, impassive person, dressed like a solicitor's under clerk.

"Which kind do you mean?" returned Fromenteau.

"Are there several kinds?"

"As many as five," said Fromenteau. "There is the Criminal Department (Vidocq used to be at the head of it) ; the Secret Superintendence (no one knows the chief) ; the Political Department (Fouché's own) ; and the Château, the system directly in the employ of the Emperor and Louis XVIII., and so on. The Château was always squabbling with the other department at the Quai Malaquais. That came to an end with M. Decazes. I used to belong to Louis XVIII.; I have been in the force ever since 1793 along with poor Contenson."

The listeners looked at one another, each with one thought in their minds—"How many men's heads has he cut off?"

"And now they want to do without us—tomfoolery!" added the little man that had grown so terrific all on a sudden. "Since 1830 they will only employ respectable people at the prefecture; I sent in my resignation, and learned my little knack of nabbing prisoners for debt."

"He is the right hand of the commercial police," said Gaillard, lowering his voice for Bixiou; "but you can never tell whether debtor or creditor pays him most."

"The dirtier the business, the more need for strict honesty," said Fromenteau sententiously; "I am for those that pay best. You want to recover fifty thousand francs, and you higgle over farthings. Give me five hundred francs, and to-morrow morning we will have him in quod."

"Five hundred francs for you yourself!" cried Théodore Gaillard.

"Lisette wants a shawl," answered the detective without moving a muscle of his countenance. "I call her 'Lisette' because of Béranger."

"You have a Lisette, and still you stay in your line!" cried the virtuous Gazonal.

"It is so amusing. Talk of field sports; it is far more interesting to run a man to earth in Paris!"

"They must be uncommonly clever to do it, and that is a fact," said Gazonal, thinking aloud.

"Oh, if I were to reckon up all the qualities that a man needs if he is to make his mark in our line, you would think I was describing a man of genius," replied Fromenteau, taking Gazonal's measure at a glance. "You must be lynx-eyed, must you not? Bold—for you must drop into a house like a bombshell, walk up to people as if you had known them all your life, and propose the never-refused dirty business, and so on.—You must have Memory, Sagacity, Invention—for you must be quick to think of expedients, and never repeat yourself; espionage must always be moulded on the individual character of those with whom you have to do—but invention is a gift of Heaven. Then you need agility, strength, and so on. All these faculties, gentlemen, are painted up over the door of Amoros' Gymnasium as virtues. All these things we must possess under penalty of forfeiting the salary of a hundred francs per month paid us by the Government, in the Rue de Jérusalem, or the commercial police."

"And you appear to me to be a remarkable man," said Gazonal. Fromenteau looked at him, but he neither answered nor showed any sign of feeling, and went away without taking leave, an unmistakable sign of genius.

"Well, cousin, you have just seen the police incarnate," said Léon.

"I have had quite as much as I want," returned the honest manufacturer. Gaillard and Bixiou chatted together meanwhile in an undertone.

"I will send round an answer to-night to Carabine's," Gaillard said aloud; and sitting down to his desk, he took no further notice of Gazonal.

"Insolence!" fumed the child of the South on the threshold.

"His paper has twenty-two thousand subscribers," said Léon de Lora. "He is one of the great powers of the age; he has not time to be polite of a morning."

"If go we must to the Chamber to arrange this lawsuit, let us take the longest way round," said Léon.

"Great men's sayings are like silver gilt," retorted Bixiou; "use wears the gilt off the silver, and all the sparkle goes out of the sayings if they are repeated. But where are we going?"

"To see our hatter near by," returned Léon.

"Bravo! If we go on like this, we may perhaps have some fun."

"Gazonal," began Léon, "I will draw him out for your benefit. Only—you must look as solemn as a king on a five-franc piece, for you are going to see *gratis* an uncommonly queer quiz; the man's self-importance has turned his head. In these days, my dear fellow, everybody wants to cover himself with glory, and a good many cover themselves with ridicule, and hence we have entirely new living caricatures——"

"When everybody is glorious together, how is a man to distinguish himself?" asked Gazonal.

"Distinguish yourself?" repeated Bixiou—"be a noodle. Your cousin wears a ribbon; I am well dressed, and people look at me, not at him."

After this remark, which may perhaps explain why so many orators and other great politicians never appear in the streets with a ribbon in their button-holes, Léon de Lora pointed out a name painted in gilt letters over a shop front. It was the illustrious name of an author of a pamphlet on hats, a person who pays newspaper proprietors as much for advertisements as any three vendors of sugar-plums or patent pills—VITAL, it ran (LATE FINOT), HAT MANUFACTURER, not plain HATTER, as heretofore.

Bixiou called Gazonal's attention to the glories of the shop window. "Vital, my dear boy, is making forty thousand francs per annum."

"And he is still in business as a hatter!" exclaimed Gazonal, nearly breaking Bixiou's arm with a violent wrench.

"You shall see the man directly," added Léon; "you want a hat, you shall have one gratis."

"Is M. Vital not in?" asked Bixiou, seeing no one at the desk.

"Monsieur is correcting proofs in his private office," said the assistant.

"What do you think of that, hey?" said Léon, turning to his cousin Then to the assistant, "Can we speak to him without disturbing his inspirations?"

"Let the gentlemen come in," called a voice—a bourgeois voice, a voice to inspire confidence in voters, a powerful voice, suggestive of a good steady income, and Vital vouchsafed to show himself. He was dressed in black from head to foot, and carried a diamond pin in his resplendent shirt-frill. Beyond him the three friends caught a glimpse of a young and pretty woman sitting at a desk with a piece of embroidery in her hands.

Vital was between thirty and forty years of age; native joviality had been repressed in him by ambitions. It is the privilege of a fine organization to be neither tall nor short, and Vital enjoyed that advantage. He was tolerably stout, and careful of his appearance; and if the hair had grown rather thin on his forehead, he turned the partial baldness to account, to give himself the airs of a man consumed by thought. You could see by the way that his wife looked at him that she admired her husband for a great man and a genius. Vital loved artists. Not that he had himself any taste for the arts, but he felt that he was one of the confraternity; he believed that he was an artist, and brought the fact home to you by sedulously disclaiming all right to that noble title, and constantly relegating himself to an enormous distance from the arts to draw out the remark, "Why, you have raised the manufacture of hats to the dignity of a science."

"Have you found the hat for me at last?" inquired Léon de Lora.

"What, sir, in one fortnight! A hat for *you!*" remonstrated Vital. "Why, two months will scarcely be long enough to strike out a shape to suit you! Look, here is your lithograph, there it lies. I have studied you very carefully already. I would not take so much trouble for a prince, but you are something more, you are an artist. And you understand me, my dear sir."

"Here is one of our great inventors; he would be as great a man as Jacquart if he would but consent to die for a bit," said Bixiou, introducing Gazonal. "Our friend here is a cloth weaver, the inventor of a way of restoring the indigo color in old clothes; he wanted to see you as a great phenomenon, for it was you who said, 'The hat is the man.' It sent this gentleman into ecstasies. Ah! Vital, you have faith! You believe in something; you have a passion for your work!"

Vital scarcely heard the words, his face had grown pale with joy.

"Rise, wife. This gentleman is one of the princes of science!"

Mme. Vital rose at a sign from her husband; Gazonal bowed.

"Shall I have the honor of finding a hat for you?" continued Vital, radiant and officious.

"At my price," said Bixiou.

"Quite so. I ask nothing but the pleasure of an occasional mention from you, gentlemen. Monsieur must have a picturesque hat, something in M. Lousteau's style," he continued, looking at Bixiou with the air of one laying down the law. "I will think of a shape."

"You take a great deal of trouble," said Gazonal.

"Oh! only for a few persons; only for those who can appreciate the value of the pains that I take. Why, among the aristocracy there is but one man who really understands a hat —the Prince de Béthune. How is it that men do not see, as women do, that the hat is the first thing to strike the eye? Why do they not think of changing the present state of things, which is disgraceful, it must be said? But a Frenchman, of all people, is the most persistent in his folly. I quite know the difficulties, gentlemen! I am not speaking now of my writings on a subject which I believe I have approached in a philosophical spirit; but simply as a practical hatter I have discovered the means of individualizing the hideous head-gear which Frenchmen are privileged to wear until I can succeed in abolishing it altogether."

He held up an example of the hideous modern hat.

"Behold the enemy, gentlemen. To think that the most intelligent nation under the sun should consent to put this 'stove-pipe' (as one of our own writers has said), this 'stove-pipe' upon their heads! . . . Here you see the various curves which I have introduced into those dreadful lines," he added, pointing out one of his own "creations." "Yet, although I understand how to suit the hat to the wearer—as you see, for here is a doctor's hat, this is for a trades-man, and that for a dandy or an artist, a stout man, a thin man—still, the hat in itself is always hideous. There! do you fully grasp my whole idea?"

He took up a broad-brimmed hat with a low crown.

"This is an old hat belonging to Claude Vignon, the great critic, independent writer, and free liver. . . . He has gone to the support of the ministry, he is a professor and librarian, he only writes for the *Débats* now, he has gained the post of Master of Requests. He has an income of sixteen thousand francs, he makes four thousand francs by his journalistic work, he wears a ribbon at his buttonhole.—Well, here is his new hat."

Vital exhibited a head covering, the *juste milieu* visible in every line.

"You ought to have made him a harlequin's hat," exclaimed Gazonal.

"Your genius rises over other people's heads, M. Vital," said Léon.

Vital bowed, unsuspicious of the joke.

"Can you tell me why your shops are the last of all to close here in Paris? They are open even later than the cafés and drinking bars. It really tickles my curiosity," said Gazonal.

"In the first place, our windows look their best when lighted up at night; and for one hat that we sell in the daytime, we sell five at night."

"Everything is queer in Paris," put in Léon.

"Well, in spite of my efforts and my success" (Vital pursued his panegyric), "we must come to the round crown. I am working in that direction."

"What hinders you?" asked Gazonal.

"Cheapness, sir. You start with a stock of fine silk hats at fifteen francs—the price would kill the trade; Parisians never have fifteen francs of ready money to invest in a new hat. A beaver costs thirty francs, but the problem is the same as ever. Beaver, I say, though there are not ten pounds' weight of real beaver skins bought in France in a year. The article is worth three hundred and fifty francs per pound, and an ounce is needed for a hat. And besides, the beaver hat is not good for much, the skin dyes badly; it turns rusty in the sunshine in ten minutes, it subsides at once in the heat. What we call 'beaver' is really nothing but hare-skin; the best hats are made from the backs, the second quality from the sides, and the third from the bellies. I am telling you trade secrets, you are men of honor. But whether you carry beaver or hare-skin on your head, the problem is equally insoluble—how to find fifteen or thirty francs of ready money. A man must pay cash for his hat—you behold the consequences! The honor of the garb of Gaul will be saved when a round gray hat shall cost a hundred francs. When that day comes we shall give credit, like the tailors. To that end people must be persuaded to wear the buckle, the gold galoon, the plumes, and satin-lined brims of the times of Louis XIII. and Louis XIV. Our business would expand ten times over if we went into the fancy line. France would be the hat-mart of the world, just as Paris always sets the fashion in women's dress. The present hat may be made anywhere. Ten million francs of export trade to be secured for Paris is involved in the question——"

"A revolution!" cried Bixiou, working up enthusiasm.

"Yes, a radical revolution. The form must be remodeled."

"You are happy after Luther's fashion," said Léon, always on the lookout for a pun. "You are dreaming of a reformation."

"Yes, sir. Ah! if the twelve or fifteen artists, capitalists, or dandies that set the fashion would but have courage for twenty-four hours, there would be a great commercial victory won for France. See here! as I tell my wife, I would give my fortune to succeed. Yes, it is my one ambition to regenerate the hat—and to disappear."

"The man is stupendous," remarked Gazonal, when they had left the shop, "but all your eccentrics have a touch of the South about them, I do assure you——"

"Let us go along the Rue Saint-Marc," said Bixiou.

"Are we to see something else?"

"Yes, you are going to see a money-lender—a money-lender among the 'rats' and *marcheuses*. A woman that has more hideous secrets in her keeping than gowns in her shop window," said Bixou.

He pointed as he spoke to a dirty-looking shop like a blot on the dazzling expanse of modern street. It had last been painted somewhere about the year 1820, a subsequent bankruptcy must have left it in a dubious condition on the owner's hands, and now the color was obscured by a thick coating of grime and dust. The windows were filthy, the door handle had that significant trick of turning of its own accord, characteristic of every place which people enter in a hurry, only to leave more promptly still.

"What do you say to this? Death's cousin-german, is she not?" Léon muttered in Gazonal's ear, pointing out a terrific figure behind the counter. "She is Mme. Nourrisson."

"How much for the guipure, madame?" asked Gazonal, not to be behindhand.

"To you, monsieur, only a hundred crowns, as you come from so far." Then remarking a certain Southern start of surprise, she added, with a touch of pathos in her voice, "It belonged to the Princesse de Lamballe, poor thing."

"What! here! right under the Tuileries?" cried Bixiou.

"Monsieur, 'they' don't believe it," said she.

"We did not come here as buyers, madame," Bixiou began valiantly.

"So I see, monsieur," retorted Mme. Nourrisson.

"We have several things to sell," continued the illustrious caricaturist. "I live at number 112 Rue de Richelieu, sixth floor. If you like to look in, in a moment, you may pick up a famous bargain——"

"Perhaps monsieur would like a bit of muslin; it is very much worn just now?" smiled she.

"No. It is a matter of a wedding dress," Léon de Lora said with much gravity.

Fifteen minutes later, Mme. Nourrisson actually appeared at Bixiou's rooms. Léon and Gazonal had come home with him to see the end of the jest, and Mme. Nourrisson found the trio looking as sober as three authors whose work (written in collaboration) has not met with that success which it deserved.

Bixiou unblushingly produced a pair of lady's slippers. "These, madame, belonged to the Empress Josephine," said he, giving Mme. Nourrisson, as in duty bound, the small change for her Princesse de Lamballe.

"*That?* . . ." cried she. "Why, it was new this year; look at the mark on the sole."

"Can you not guess that the pair of slippers is a prelude

Fifteen minutes later, Mme. Nourrisson actually appeared at Bixiou's
rooms

to the romance," said Léon; "and not, as usual, the se-
quel?"

"My friend here from the South," put in Bixiou, "wishes to
marry a certain young lady, very well-to-do and well connected; but he would like to know beforehand (huge family
interests being at stake) whether there has been any slip in
the past."

"How much is monsieur willing to pay?" she asked, eyeing
the prospective bridegroom.

"A hundred francs," said Gazonal, no longer astonished at
anything.

"Many thanks," said she, with a grimace which a monkey
might despairingly envy.

"Come, now, how much do you want, Mme. Nourrisson?"
asked Bixiou, putting his arm round her waist.

"First of all, my dear gentlemen, never since I have been
in business have I seen any one, man or woman, beating down
the price of happiness. And, in the second place, you are
all three of you chaffing me," she added, and a smile that
stole over her hard lips was reinforced by a gleam of cat-like
suspicion in her eyes. "Now, if your happiness is not involved, your fortune is at stake, and a man that lives up so
many pair of stairs is still less the person to haggle over a
rich match.—Come, now, what is it all about, my lambs?"
with sudden affability.

"We want to know about the firm of Beunier and Company," said Bixiou, very well pleased to pick up some information concerning a person in whom he was interested.

"Oh! a louis will be enough for that——"

"And why?"

"I have all the mother's jewels. She is hard up from one
quarter to another; why, it is all she can do to pay interest on
the money she owes me. Are you looking for a wife in that
quarter? You noodle! Hand me over forty francs, and I
will give you a good hundred crowns' worth of gossip."

Gazonal brought a forty-franc piece to light, and Mme.
Nourrisson gave them some startling stories of the straits to

which some so-called ladies are reduced. The old wardrobe-dealer grew lively as she talked, sketching her own portrait in the course of the conversation. Without betraying a single confidence, without letting fall a single name, she made her audience shudder by allowing them to see how much prosperity in Paris is based on the quaking foundation of borrowed money. In her drawers she had keepsakes set in gold and brilliants, memorials of grandmothers long dead and gone, of children still in life, of husbands or grandchildren laid in the grave. She had heard ghastly stories wrung from anger, passion, or pique, told, it may be, by one customer of another, or drawn from borrowers in the necessary course of sedative treatment which ends in a loan.

"Why did you enter this line of business?" asked Gazonal.

"For my son's sake," she replied simply.

Women that go up and down back stairs to ply their trade are always brimful of excuses based on the best of motives. Mme. Nourrisson, by her own account, had lost three matches, three daughters that turned out very badly, and all her illusions to boot. She produced pawn-tickets for some of her best goods, she said, just to show the risks of the trade. How she should meet the end of the month, she did not know; people "robbed" her to such a degree.

The word was a little too strong. The artists exchanged glances.

"Look here, boys, I will just show you how we get taken in. This did not happen to me, but to my neighbor over the way, Mme. Mahuchet, a ladies' shoemaker. I had been lending money to a Countess, a woman with more crazes than she can afford. She swaggers it with a fine house and grand furniture; she has At Homes, she makes a deuce of a dash.

"Well, she owed her shoemaker three hundred francs, and was giving a dinner and a party no further back than the day before yesterday. Mme. Mahuchet, hearing of this from the cook, came to me about it, and we got excited over the news. She was for making a fuss, but for my own part—'My dear Mother Mahuchet,' I said, 'where is the use of it? Just to get a bad name; it is better to get good security. It is diamond cut diamond, and you save your bile.'—But go she would; she asked me to back her up, and we went together. —'Madame is not at home.'—'Go on!' said Mother Mahuchet. 'We will wait for her if I stop here till midnight!'—So we camped down in the ante-chamber and chatted together. Well, doors opened and shut; by and by there was a sound of little footsteps and low voices; and, for my own part, I felt sorry. The company was coming to dinner. You can judge of the turn things took.

"The Countess sent in her own woman to wheedle la Mahuchet—'You shall be paid to-morrow'—and all the rest of the ways of trying it on.—No go.—Then the Countess, in her Sunday best, as you may say, comes into the dining-room. La Mahuchet hears her, flings open the door, and walks in. Lord! at the sight of the dinner-table, all sparkling like a jewel-case, the dish-covers and the plate and the candle-sconces, she went off like a soda-water bottle. She flings out her bomb—'Those that spend other people's money have no business to give dinner-parties; they ought to live quietly. You a Countess! and you owe a hundred francs to a poor shoemaker's wife with seven children!'—You can imagine how she ran on, an uneducated woman as she is. At the first word of excuse—'No money'—from the Countess, la Mahuchet cries out, 'Eh! my lady, but there is silver-plate here! Pawn your spoons and forks and pay me!'—'Take them yourself,' says the Countess, catching up half-a-dozen and slipping them into her hand, and we hurried away downstairs pell-mell.—What a success! Bah! no. Out in the street tears came into la Mahuchet's eyes, she is a good soul; she took the things back, and apologized. She found out the depths of the Countess' poverty—they were German silver!"

"Dishcovered that she had no cover," commented Léon de Lora, in whom the Mistigris of old was apt to reappear.

The pun flashed a sudden light across Mme. Nourrisson's brain. "Aha! my dear sir, you are an artist, a dramatic writer, you live in the Rue du Helder, you have kept com-

pany with Madame Antonia, I know a few of your little
ways! . . . Come, now, do you want something out of
the common in the grand style, Carabine or Mousqueton, for
instance, or Malaga or Jenny Cadine?"

"Malaga and Carabine, forsooth! when we have made
them what they are!" cried Léon.

"My dear Mme. Nourrisson, I solemnly swear to you that
we wanted nothing but the pleasure of making your acquaintance; and as we wish to hear about your antecedents, we
should like to know how you came to drop into your way of
business," said Bixiou.

"I was a confidential servant in the household of a Marshal of France," she said, posing like a Dorine; "he was the
Prince d'Ysembourg. One morning one of the finest ladies
at the Emperor's court came to speak privately with the Marshal. I took care at once to be within hearing. Well, my
Countess bursts into tears, and tells that simpleton of a Marshal (the Prince d'Ysembourg, the Condé of the Republic,
and a simpleton to boot), she tells him that her husband was
away at the wars in Spain, and had left her without a single
note for a thousand francs, and that unless she can have one
or two at once, her children must starve, she had literally
nothing for to-morrow. Well, my Marshal, being tolerably
free-handed in those days, takes a couple of thousand-franc
notes out of his desk.—I watched the fair Countess down the
stairs. She did not see me; she was laughing to herself with
not altogether motherly glee, so I slipped out and heard her
tell the *chasseur* in a low voice to drive to Leroy's. I rushed
round. My mother of a family goes to the famous shop in
the Rue de Richelieu—you know the place—and orders and
pays for a dress that cost fifteen hundred francs. You used
to pay for one dress by ordering another then. Two nights
afterwards she could appear at an ambassador's ball, decked
out as a woman must be when she wishes to shine for all the
world and for one besides. That very day said I to myself,
'Here is an opening for me! When I am no longer young,
I will lend money to fine ladies on their things; passion can-

not reckon, and pays blindly.' If it is a subject for a comedy that you want I will let you have some for a consideration——"

And making an end of a harangue, colored by all the phases of her past life, she departed, leaving Gazonal in dismay, caused partly by the matter of her discourse, but at least as much by an exhibition of five yellow teeth which she meant for a smile.

"What are we to do next?" he inquired.

"Find some banknotes," said Bixiou, whistling for his porter; "I want money, and I am going to teach you the uses of a porter. You imagine that they are meant to open doors; whereas their real use is to help vagrants like me out of difficulties, and to assist the artists whom they take under their protection, for which reason mine will take the Montyon prize some of these days."

The common expression, "eyes like saucers," found sufficient illustration in Gazonal's countenance at that moment.

The man that suddenly appeared in the doorway was of no particular age, a something between a private detective and a merchant's clerk, but more unctuous and sleeker than either; his hair was greasy, his person paunchy, his complexion of the moist and unwholesome kind that you observe in the superiors of convents. He wore a black cloth jacket, drab trousers, and list slippers.

"What do you want, sir?" inquired this personage, with a half-patronizing, half-servile manner.

"Oh, Ravenouillet—(his name is Ravenouillet," said Bixiou, turning to Gazonal)—"have you your 'bills receivable' about you?"

Ravenouillet felt in a side-pocket, and produced the stickiest book that Gazonal had even seen in his life.

"Just enter a note of these two bills for five hundred francs at three months, and put your name to them for me."

Bixiou brought out a couple of notes made payable to his order as he spoke. Ravenouillet accepted them forthwith, and noted them down on the greasy page among his wife's entries of various sums due from other lodgers.

"Thanks, Ravenouillet. Stay, here is an order for the Vaudeville."

"Ah, my child will enjoy herself very much to-night," said Ravenouillet, as he went away.

"There are seventy-one of us in the house," said Bixiou, "among us, on an average, we owe Ravenouillet six thousand francs per month, eighteen thousand francs per quarter for advances and postage, to say nothing of rent. He is our Providence—at thirty per cent. We pay him that without being so much as asked."

"Oh, Paris! Paris!" exclaimed Gazonal.

"On the way," said Bixiou, filling in his signature "(for I am going to show you another actor, Cousin Gazonal, and a charming scene he shall play, *gratis,* for you)——"

"Where?" Gazonal broke in.

"In a money-lender's office. On the way, I repeat, I will tell you how friend Ravenouillet started in Paris."

As they passed the door of the lodge, Gazonal heard Mlle. Lucienne Ravenouillet, a student at the Conservatoire, practising her scales, her father was reading the newspaper, and Mme. Ravenouillet came out with letters in her hand for the lodgers above.

"Thank you, M. Bixiou," called the little one.

"That is not a 'rat,'" said Léon! "it is a grasshopper in the larva state."

"It seems that here, as all the world over, you win the favor of those in office by good offices," began Gazonal. Léon was charmed with the pun.

"He is coming on in our society!" he cried.

"Now for Ravenouillet's history," said Bixiou, when the three stood outside on the boulevard. "In 1831, Massol (your chairman of committee, Gazonal) was a journalist barrister. At that time he merely intended to be Keeper of the Seals some day; he scorned to oust Louis-Philippe from the throne: pardon his ambition, he comes from Carcassonne. One fine morning a fellow-countryman turned up.—'*Monsu* Massol,' he said, 'you know me very well, my father is your neighbor the grocer; I have just come from down yonder, for they tell us that every one who comes here gets a place.' At those words a cold shiver ran through Massol. He thought within himself that if he were so ill advised as to oblige a compatriot, who for that matter was a perfect stranger, he should have the whole department tumbling in upon him. He thought of the wear and tear to bell-pulls, door hinges, and carpets, he saw his only servant giving notice, he had visions of trouble with his landlord, of complaints from the other tenants of the combined odors of garlic and *diligence* introduced into the house. So he fixed upon his petitioner such an eye as a butcher turns upon a sheep brought into the shambles. In vain. His fellow-countryman survived that gaze, or rather that stab, and continued his discourse, much on this wise, according to Massol's report of it:—

" 'I have my ambitions, like every one else,' said he; 'I shall not go back again until I am rich, if indeed I go back at all, for Paris is the ante-chamber of Paradise. They tell me that you write for the newspapers, and do anything you like with people here, and that for you it is ask and have with the Government. I have abilities, like all of us down yonder, but I know myself: I have no education; I cannot write (which is a pity, for I have ideas) ; so I do not think of coming into competition with you; I know myself; I should not make anything out. But since you can do anything, and we are brothers, as you may say, having played together as children, I count upon you to give me a start in life, and to use your influence for me.—Oh, you must. I want a place, the kind of place to suit my talents, a place that I, being I, am fitted to fill with a chance of making my fortune——'

"Massol was just on the point of brutally thrusting his fellow-countryman out at the door with a rough word in his ear, when the said countryman concluded thus:—

" 'So I do not ask for a place in the civil service, where a man gets on as slowly as a tortoise, for there is your cousin that has been a tax collector these twenty years, and is a tax collector still—no; I simply thought of going——?'—'On the stage?' put in Massol, greatly relieved by the turn things were taking.—'No. It is true, I have the figure for it, and the memory, and the gesticulation; but it takes too much out of you. I should prefer the career of a—porter.' Massol kept his countenance—'It will take far more out of you,' he said, 'but you are not so likely, at any rate, to perform to an empty house.'—So he found Ravenouillet's first-door-string for him, as he says."

"I was the first to take an interest in porters as a class," said Léon. "Your moral humbugs, your charlatans from vanity, your latter-day sycophants, your Septembrists disguised in trappings of decorous solemnity, your discoverers of problems palpitating with present importance, are all preaching the emancipation of the negro, the improvement of the juvenile offender, and philanthropic efforts on behalf of the ticket-of-leave man; while they leave their porters in a worse plight than the Irish, living in dens more loathsome than dark cells, upon a scantier pittance than the Government grants per head for convicts. I have done but one good deed in my life, and that is my porter's lodge."

"Yes," said Bixiou. "Suppose that a man has built a set of huge cages, divided up like a beehive or a menagerie, into hundreds of cells or dens, in which living creatures of every species are intended to ply their various industries; suppose that this animal, with the face of an owner of house-property, should come to a man of science and say: 'Sir, I want a specimen of the order *Bimana*, which shall live in a sink ten feet square, filled with old boots and plague-stricken rags. I want him to live in it all his life, and rear a family of children as pretty as cherubs; he must use it as a workshop, kitchen, and promenade; he must sing and grow flowers in it, and never go out; he must shut his eyes, and yet see everything that goes on in the house.'—Assuredly the man of science could not invent the Porter; Paris alone, or the Devil if you like to have it so, was equal to the feat."

"Parisian industrialism has gone even further into the

regions of the Impossible," added Gazonal. "You in Paris exhibit all kinds of manufactures; but there are by-products of which you know nothing. . . . There are your working classes.—They bear the brunt of competition with foreign industries, hardship against hardship, just as the regiments bore the brunt of Napoleon's duel with Europe."

"Here we are. This is where our friend Vauvinet lives," said Bixiou. "People who paint contemporary manners are too apt to copy old portraits; it is one of their greatest mistakes. In our own times every calling has been transformed. Tradesmen are peers of France, artists are capitalists, writers of vaudevilles have money in the funds. Some few figures remain as before; but, generally speaking, most professions have dropped their manners and customs along with their distinctive dress. Gobseck, Gigonnet, Chaboisseau, and Samanon were the last of the Romans; to-day we rejoice in the possession of our Vauvinet, the good fellow, the dandy-denizen of the greenroom, the frequenter of the society of *lorettes,* the owner of a neat little one-horse brougham. Watch my man carefully, friend Gazonal, and you shall see a comedy of money. First, the cool, indifferent man that will not give a penny; and second, the hot and eager man smelling a profit. Of all things, listen to him."

With that, the three mounted to a second-floor lodging in a very fine house on the Boulevard des Italiens, and at once found themselves amid elegant surroundings in the height of the fashion. A young man of eight-and-twenty, or thereabouts, came forward almost laughingly at sight of Léon de Lora, held out a hand to all appearance in the friendliest possible way to Bixiou, gave Gazonal a distant bow, and brought the three into his private office. All the man's bourgeois tastes lurked beneath the artistic decorations of the room in spite of the unimpeachable statuettes and numberless trifles appropriated to the uses of *petits appartements* by modern art, grown petty to supply the demand. Like most young men of business, Vauvinet was extremely carefully dressed, a man's clothes being as it were a kind of prospectus among them.

"I have come to you for money," said Bixiou, laughing as he held out his bills.

Vauvinet's countenance immediately grew so grave that Gazonal was amused at the difference between the smiles of a minute ago and the professional bill-discounting visage he turned on Bixiou.

"I would oblige you with the greatest pleasure, my dear fellow," said he, "but I have no cash at the moment."

"Oh, pshaw!"

"No. I have paid it all away, you know where. Poor old Lousteau is going to run a theatre. He has gone into partnership with an ancient playwright that stands very well with the ministry—Ridal, his name is—they wanted thirty thousand francs of me yesterday. I am drained dry, so dry indeed that I am just about to borrow a hundred louis of Cérizet to pay for my losses this morning at lansquenet, at Jenny Cadine's."

"You must be drained dry indeed if you cannot oblige poor Bixiou," put in Léon de Lora, "for he can say very nasty things when he is driven to it——"

"I can only speak well of a man so well off," said Bixiou.

"My dear fellow, even if I had the money, it would be quite impossible to discount bills accepted by your porter, even at fifty per cent. There is no demand for Ravenouillet's paper. He is not exactly Rothschild. I warn you that this sort of thing is played out. You ought to try another firm. Look up an uncle, for the friend that will back your bills is extinct, materialism is so frightfully on the increase——"

Bixiou turned to Gazonal.

"I have a friend here," he said, "one of the best known cloth manufacturers in the South. His name is Gazonal. His hair wants cutting," continued Bixiou, surveying the provincial's luxuriant and somewhat disheveled crop, "but I am just about to take him to Marius, and his resemblance to a poodle, so deleterious to his credit and ours, will presently disappear."

"A Southern name is not good enough for me, without

offence to this gentleman be it said," returned Vauvinet, and Gazonal was so much relieved that he passed over the insolence of the remark. Being extremely acute, he thought that Bixiou and the painter meant to make him pay a thousand francs for the breakfast at the Café de Paris by way of teaching him to know the town. He had not yet got rid of the suspicion in which the provincial always intrenches himself.

"How should I do business in the Pyrenees, six hundred miles away?" added Vauvinet.

"So there is no more to be said?" returned Bixiou.

"I have twenty francs at home."

"I am sorry for you," said the author of the hoax. "I thought I was worth a thousand francs," he added, drily.

"You are worth a hundred thousand francs," Vauvinet rejoined; "sometimes you are even beyond all price—but I am drained dry."

"Oh, well, we will say no more about it. I had contrived as good a bit of business as you could wish at Carabine's to-night—do you know?"

Vauvinet's answer was a wink. So does one dealer in horseflesh convey to another the information that he is not to be deceived.

"You have forgotten how you took me by the waist, exactly as if I were a pretty woman, and said with coaxing words and looks, 'I will do anything for you, if only you will get me shares at par in this railway that du Tillet and Nucingen are bringing out,' said you. Very well, my dear fellow, Maxime and Nucingen are coming to-night to meet several political folk at Carabine's. You are losing a fine chance, old man. Come. Good-day, dabbler."

And Bixiou rose to go, leaving Vauvinet to all appearance indifferent, but in reality as vexed as a man can be with himself after a blunder of his own making.

"One moment, my dear fellow, I have credit if I have no cash. If I can get nothing for your bills, I can keep them till they fall due, and give you other bills in exchange from my portfolio. After all, we might possibly come to an understanding about those railway shares; we could divide the profits in a certain proportion, and I would give you a draft on myself on account of the prof——"

"No, no," returned Bixiou, "I must have money; I must cash my Ravenouillet elsewhere——"

"And Ravenouillet is a good man," resumed Vauvinet; "he has an account at the savings bank; a very good man——"

"Better than you are," said Léon; "he has no rent to pay, he does not squander his money on *lorettes,* nor does he rush into speculation and shake in his shoes with every rise and fall."

"You are pleased to laugh, great man. You have given us the quintessence of La Fontaine's fable of the *Oak and the Reed,*" said Vauvinet, grown jovial and insinuating all at once.—"Come, Gubetta, my good fellow-conspirator," he continued, taking Bixiou by the waist, "you want money, do you? Very well, I may just as well borrow three as two thousand francs of my friend Cérizet. And 'Cinna, let us be friends!' . . . Hand us over those two leaves that grow from the root of all evil. If I refused at first, it was because it is very hard on a man that can only do his bit of business by passing on bills to the Bank to make him keep your Ravenouillets locked up in the drawer of his desk. It is hard, very hard——"

"What discount?"

"Next to nothing," said Vauvinet. "At three months it will cost you a miserable fifty francs."

"You shall be my benefactor, as Émile Blondet used to say."

"It is borrowing money at twenty per cent per annum, interest included——" Gazonal began in a whisper, but for all answer he received a blow from Bixiou's elbow directed at his windpipe.

"I say," said Vauvinet, opening a drawer, "I perceive an odd note for five hundred francs sticking to the cloth. I did not know I was so rich. I was looking for a bill to offer you.

I have one almost due for four hundred and fifty. Cérizet
will take it off you for a trifle; and that makes up the amount.
But no tricks, Bixiou. I am going to Carabine's to-night,
eh? Will you swear——?"

"Are we not friends again?" asked Bixiou, taking the
banknote and the bill. "I give you my word of honor that
you shall meet du Tillet to-night and plenty of others that
have a mind to make their (rail) way."

Vauvinet came out upon the landing with the three friends,
cajoling Bixiou to the last.

Bixiou listened with much seriousness while Gazonal on
the way downstairs tried to open his eyes to the nature of the
transaction just completed. Gazonal proved to him that if
Cérizet, this crony of Vauvinet's, charged no more than
twenty francs for discounting a bill for four hundred and
fifty francs, then he (Bixiou) was borrowing money at the
rate of forty per cent per annum.

Out upon the pavement Bixiou burst into a laugh, the
laugh of a Parisian over a successful hoax, a soundless, joy-
less chuckle, a labial northeaster which froze Gazonal into
silence.

"The grant of the concession to the railway will be postponed at the Chamber," he said; "we knew that yesterday
from the *marcheuse* whom we met just now. And if I win five
or six thousand francs at lansquenet, what is a loss of sixty
or seventy francs so long as you have something to stake?"

"Lansquenet is another of the thousand facets of Paris life
to-day," said Léon. "Wherefore, cousin, count upon our introducing you to one of the duchesses of the Rue Saint-
Georges. In her house you see the aristocracy of lorettes,
and may perhaps gain your lawsuit. But you cannot possibly
show yourself with that Pyrenean crop, you look like a hedgehog; we will take you to Marius, close by in the Place de la
Bourse. He is another of our humorists."

"What is the new humorist?"

"Here comes the anecdote," said Bixiou. "In 1800 a young
wigmaker named Cabot came from Toulouse, and set up shop

(to use your jargon) in Paris. This genius—he retired afterwards with an income of twenty thousand francs to Libourne
—this genius, consumed with ambition, saw that the name
of Cabot could never be famous. M. Parny, whom he attended professionally, called him Marius, a name infinitely
superior to the 'Armands' and 'Hippolytes' beneath which
other victims of that hereditary complaint endeavor to conceal the patronymic. All Cabot's successors have been named
Marius. The present Marius is Marius V.; his family name
is Mougin. This is the way with many trades, with *Eau de
Botot* for example, and La Petite-Vertu's ink. In Paris a
man's name becomes a part of his business, and at length
confers a certain status; the signboard ennobles. Marius left
pupils behind him, too, and created (it is said) the first
school of hair-dressing in the world."

"I noticed before this as I traveled across France a great
many names upon signboards—So-and-so, *from Marius.*"

"All his pupils are bound to wash their hands after each
customer," continued Bixiou; "and Marius will not take
every one, a pupil must have a shapely hand and tolerable
good looks. The most remarkable of these, for figure or eloquence, are sent out to people's houses; Marius only puts
himself about for titled ladies. He has a cab and a
'groom.' "

"But, after all, he is only a barber (*merlan*)," Gazonal
cried indignantly.

"A barber!" repeated Bixiou. "You must know that he is
a captain in the National Guard, and wears the Cross because
he was the first to leap a barricade in 1832."

"Be careful. He is neither a hair-dresser nor a wigmaker; he is the manager of *salons de coiffure,*" said Léon
on the sumptuously carpeted staircase between the mahogany
hand-rails and cut-glass balusters.

"And, look here, do not disgrace us," added Bixiou. "The
lackeys in the ante-chamber will take off your coat and hat
to brush them, open the door of the salon and close it after
you. Which is worth knowing, my friend Gazonal," Bixiou
continued slily, "or you might cry 'Thieves!' "

"The three salons are three boudoirs," said Léon; "the manager has filled them with all that modern luxury can devise. There are fringed lambrequins over the windows, flower-stands everywhere, and silken couches, on which you await your turn and read the newspapers if all the dressing-rooms are occupied. As you come in, you begin to finger your waistcoat pockets, and imagine that they will charge you five francs at least; but no pocket is mulcted of more than half a franc if the hair is curled, or a franc if the hair-dresser cuts it. Elegant toilet-tables stand among the flowers, there are jets of water playing, you see yourself reflected everywhere in huge mirrors. So try to look as if you were used to it. When the client comes in (Marius uses the elegant term 'client' instead of the common word 'customer'), when the client appears on the threshold, Marius appraises him at a glance; for him you are a 'head' more or less worthy of his interest. From Marius' point of view, there are no men—only heads."

"We will tune Marius to concert-pitch for you," said Bixiou, "if you will follow our lead."

When Gazonal appeared upon the scenes, Marius at once gave him an approving glance. "Regulus!" cried he, "take this head. Clip with the small shears first of all."

At a sign from Bixiou, Gazonal turned to the pupil. "Pardon me," he said, "I wish to have M. Marius himself."

Greatly flattered by this speech, Marius came forward, leaving the head on which he was engaged.

"I am at your service, I am just at an end. Be quite easy, my pupil will prepare you, I myself will decide on the style."

Marius, a little man, his face seamed with the smallpox, his hair frizzed after Rubini's fashion, was dressed in black from head to foot. He wore white cuffs and a diamond in his shirt-frill. He recognized Bixiou, and saluted him as an equal power.

"A commonplace head," he remarked to Léon, indicating the subject under his fingers, "a philistine. But what can one do? If one lived by art alone, one would end raving mad at Bicêtre." And he returned to his client with an inimitable gesture and a parting injunction to Regulus, "Be careful with that gentleman, he is evidently an artist."

"A journalist," said Bixiou.

At that word Marius passed the comb two or three times over the "commonplace head," swooped down upon Gazonal just as the small shears were brought into play, and caught Regulus by the arm with:

"I will take this gentleman.—Look, see yourself in the large mirror, sir (if the glass can stand it)," he said, addressing the relinquished philistine.—"Ossian!"

A lackey came in and carried off the "client."

"Pay at the desk, sir," said Marius as the bewildered customer drew out his purse.

"Is it any use, my dear fellow, to proceed to this operation with the small shears?" asked Bixiou.

"A head never comes under my hands until it has been brushed," said the great man; "but on your account I will take this gentleman from beginning to end. The blocking out I leave to my pupils, I do not care to take it. Everybody, like you, is for 'M. Marius himself'; I can only give the finishing touches. For what paper does monsieur write?"

"In your place I would have three or four editions of Marius."

"Ah! monsieur is a feuilletoniste, I see," said Marius. "Unluckily, a hairdresser must do his work himself, it cannot be done by a deputy. . . . Pardon me."

He left Gazonal to give an eye to Regulus, now engaged with a newly-arrived head, and made a disapproving comment thereon, an inarticulate sound produced by tongue and palate, which may be rendered thus—"titt, titt, titt."

"Goodness gracious! come now, that is not broad enough, your scissors are leaving furrows behind them. . . . Stay a bit; look here, Regulus, you are not clipping poodles, but *men*—men with characters of their own; and if you continue to gaze at the ceiling instead of dividing your attention between the glass and the face, you will be a disgrace to 'my house.'"

"You are severe, M. Marius."

"I must do my duty by them, and teach them the mysteries of the art——"

"Then it is an art, is it?"

Marius stopped in indignation, the scissors in one hand, the comb in the other, and contemplated Gazonal in the glass."

"Monsieur, you talk like a ——— child. And yet, from your accent, you seem to come from the South, the land of men of genius."

"Yes. It requires taste of a kind, I know," returned Gazonal.

"Pray say no more, monsieur! I looked for better things from you. I mean to say that a hairdresser (I do not say a *good* hairdresser, for one is either a hairdresser or one is not), a hairdresser is not so easily found as—what shall I say?—as—I really hardly know—as a Minister—(sit still) no, that will not do, for you cannot judge of the value of a Minister, the streets are full of them.—A Paganini?—no, that will not quite do.—A hairdresser, monsieur, a man that can read your character and your habits, must have that in him which makes a philosopher. And for the women! But there, women appreciate us, they know our value; they know that their triumphs are due to us when they come to us to prepare them for conquest . . . which is to say that a hairdresser is—but no one knows what he is. I myself, for instance, you will scarcely find a—well, without boasting, people know what I am. Ah! well, no, I think there should be a better yet. . . . Execution, that is the thing! Ah, if women would but give me a free hand; if I could but carry out all the ideas that occur to me!—for I have a tremendous imagination, you see—but women will not co-operate with you, they have notions of their own, they *will* run their fingers or their combs through the exquisite creations that ought to be engraved and recorded, for our works only live for a few hours, you see, sir! Ah! a great hairdresser should be something like what Carême and Vestris are in their lines.—

(Your head this way, if you please, I am catching the expression. That will do.)—Bunglers, incapable of understanding their epoch or their art, are the ruin of our profession.—They deal in wigs, for instance, or hair-restorers, and think of nothing but selling you a bottle of stuff, making a trade of the profession; it makes one sorry to see it. The wretches cut your hair and brush it anyhow. Now, when I came here from Toulouse, it was my ambition to succeed to the great Marius, to be a true Marius, and in my person to add such lustre to the name as it had not known with the other four. 'Victory or death!' said I to myself. (Sit up, I have nearly finished.) I was the first to aim at elegance. My salons excited curiosity. I scorn advertisements; I spend the cost of advertisements on comfort, monsieur, on improvements. Next year I shall have a quartette in a little salon; I shall have music, and the best music. Yes, one must beguile the tedium of the time spent in the dressing-room. I do not shut my eyes to the unpleasant aspects of the operation. (Look at yourself.) A visit to the hairdresser is perhaps quite as tiring as sitting for a portrait. Monsieur knows the famous M. de Humboldt? (I managed to make the most of the little hair that America spared to him, for science has this much in common with the savage—she is sure to scalp her man.) Well, the great man said, as monsieur perhaps knows, that if it was painful to go to be hanged, it was only less painful to sit for your portrait. I myself am of the opinion of a good many women, that a visit to the hairdresser is more trying than a visit to the studio. Well, monsieur, I want people to come here for pleasure. (You have a rebellious tuft of hair.) A Jew suggested Italian opera-singers to pluck out the gray hairs of young fellows of forty in the intervals; but his signoras turned out to be young persons from the Conservatoire, or pianoforte teachers from the Rue Montmartre.—Now, monsieur, your hair is worthy of a man of talent.—Ossian!" (to the lackey in livery) "brush this gentleman's coat, and go to the door with him.—Who comes next?" he added, majestically, glancing round a group of customers waiting for their turn.

"Do not laught, Gazonal," said Léon as they reached the foot of the stairs. "I can see one of our great men down yonder," he continued, exploring the Place de la Bourse with his eyes. "You shall have an opportunity of making a comparison; when you have heard him talk, you shall tell me which is the queerer of the two—he or the hairdresser."

" 'Do not laugh, Gazonal,' " added Bixiou, imitating Léon's manner. "What is Marius' business, do you think?"

"He is a hairdresser."

"He has gradually made a monopoly of the wholesale trade in human hair, just as the provision dealer of whom we shall shortly buy a Strasbourg pie for three francs has the truffle trade entirely in his hands. He discounts bills in his line of business, he lends money to customers at a pinch, he deals in annuities, he speculates on 'Change, he is a shareholder in all the fashion papers; and finally, under the name of a chemist, he sells an abominable drug which brings him in thirty thousand francs per annum as his share of the profits, and costs a hundred thousand francs in advertisements."

"Is it possible?"

"Bear this in mind," Bixiou, replied with gravity, "in Paris there is no such thing as a small trade; everything here is done on a large scale, be it frippery or matches. The barkeeper standing with a napkin under his arm to watch you enter his shop very likely has an income of fifty thousand francs from investments in the funds. The waiter has a vote, and may offer himself for election; a man whom you might take for a beggar in the street carries a hundred thousand francs' worth of unmounted diamonds in his waistcoat pocket, and does not steal them."

The three, inseparable for that day at least, were piloted by Léon de Lora in such sort that at the corner of the Rue Vivienne they ran against a man of forty or thereabouts with a ribbon in his buttonhole.

"My dear Dubourdieu, what are you dreaming about? Some beautiful allegorical composition?" asked Léon.—"My dear cousin, I have the pleasure of introducing you to the well-known painter Dubourdieu, celebrated no less for his genius than for his humanitarian convictions.—Dubourdieu, my cousin Palafox!"

Dubourdieu, a pallid little man with melancholy blue eyes, nodded slightly while Gazonal bowed low to the man of genius.

"So you have nominated Stidmann instead of——"

"How could I help it! I was away," returned Léon de Lora.

"You are lowering the standard of the Académie," resumed the painter. "To think of choosing such a man as that! I do not wish to say any harm of him, but he really is a crafts-man. . . . What is to become of the first and most per-manent of all the arts, of sculpture that reveals the life of a nation when everything else, even the memory of its exist-ence, has passed away—of sculpture that sets the seal of eternity upon the great man? The sculptor's office is sacred. He sums up the thought of his age, and you, forsooth, fill the ranks of the priesthood by taking in a bungling mantel-piece maker, a designer of drawing-room ornaments, one of those that buy and sell in the Temple! Ah! as Chamfort said, 'If you are to endure life in Paris, you must begin by swal-lowing a viper every morning. . . .' After all, Art re-mains to us; no one can prevent us from cultivating Art."

"And besides, my dear fellow, you have a consolation which few among artists possess—the future is yours," put in Bixiou. "When every one is converted to our doctrine, you will be the foremost man in your art, for the ideas which you put into your work will be comprehensible to all—when they are common property. In fifty years' time you will be for the world at large what you are now for us—a great man. It is only a question of holding out till then."

The artist's face smoothed itself out, after the wont of mortal man when flattered on his weak side. "I have just finished an allegorical figure of Harmony," he said. "If you care to come to see it, you will understand at once how I managed to put two years' work into it. It is all there. At

a glance you see the Destiny of the Globe. She is a queen
holding a bishop's crozier, the symbol of the aggrandizement
of races useful to man; on her head she wears the cap of
Liberty, and after the Egyptian fashion (the ancient Egyp-
tians seem to have had foreshadowings of Fourier) she has
six breasts. Her feet rest upon two clasped hands, which
enclose the globe between them, to signify the brotherhood of
man; beneath her lie broken fragments of cannon, because all
war is abolished, and I have tried to give her the serenity of
Agriculture triumphant. At her feet, besides, I have put an
enormous Savoy cabbage, the Master's symbol of Concord.
Oh, it is not Fourier's least claim to our veneration that he
revived the association of plants and ideas; every detail in
creation is linked to the rest by its significance as a part of a
whole, and no less by its special language. In a hundred
years' time the globe will be much larger than it is now——"

"And how will that come to pass?" inquired Gazonal,
amazed to hear a man outside a lunatic asylum talking in
this way.

"By the increase of production. If people make up their
minds to apply the System, it should react upon the stars; it
is not impossible——"

"And in that case what will become of painting?" asked
Gazonal.

"Painting will be greater than ever."

"And will our eyes be larger?" continued Gazonal, looking
significantly at his friends.

"Man will be once more as in the days before his degradation; our six-foot men will be dwarfs when that time
comes——"

"How about your picture," interrupted Léon; "is it finished?"

"Quite finished," said Dubourdieu. "I tried to see Hiclar
about a symphony. I should like those who see the picture to
hear music in Beethoven's manner at the same time; the
music would develop the ideas, which would thus reach the
intelligence through the avenues of sight and sound. Ah!

if the Government would only lend me one of the halls in the
Louvre——"

"But I will mention it if you like. Nothing that can strike
people's minds should be left undone."

"Oh! my friends are preparing articles, but I am afraid
that they may go too far."

"Pshaw!" said Bixiou, "they will go nothing like as far as
the Future——"

Dubourdieu eyed Bixiou askance and went on his way.

"Why, the man is a lunatic," said Gazonal, "moonstruck
and mad."

"He has technical skill and knowledge," said Léon, "but
Fourier has been the ruin of him. You have just seen one
way in which ambition affects an artist. Too often here in
Paris, in his desire to reach fame (which for an artist means
fortune) by some short cut, he will borrow wings of circumstance; he will think to increase his stature by identifying
himself with some Cause, or advocating some system, hoping in time to widen his coterie into a public. Such an one
sets up to be a Republican, such another a Saint-Simonian, an
aristocrat or a Catholic, or he is for the *juste milieu,* or the
Middle Ages, or for Germany. But while opinions cannot
give talent, they inevitably spoil it; witness this unfortunate
being whom you have just seen. An artist's opinion ought to
be a faith in works; and his one way to success is to work
while Nature gives him the sacred fire."

"Let us fly, Léon is moralizing," said Bixiou.

"And did the man seriously mean what he said?" cried
Gazonal; he had not yet recovered from his amazement.

"Very seriously," replied Bixiou; "he was quite as much
in earnest as the king of hairdressers just now."

"He is crazy," said Gazonal.

"He is not the only man driven crazy by Fourier's notions," returned Bixiou. "You know nothing of Paris. Ask
for a hundred thousand francs to carry out some idea most
likely to be useful to the species (to try a steam-engine, for
instance), you will die like Salomon de Caus at Bicêtre; but

when it comes to a paradox, any one will be cut in pieces for it—he and his fortune. Well, here it is with systems as with practical matters. Impossible newspapers have consumed millions of francs in the last fifteen years. The very fact that you are in the right of it makes your lawsuit so difficult to win; taken together with the other fact that your prefect has his own private ends to gain, as you say."

"Can you understand how a clever man can live anywhere but in Paris when once he knows the psychology of the city?" asked Léon.

"Suppose that we take Gazonal to Mother Fontaine," suggested Bixiou, beckoning a hackney cab, "it would be a transition from the severe to the fantastic.—Drive to the Rue Vieille-du-Temple," he called to the man, and the three drove away in the direction of the Marais.

"What are you taking me to see?"

"Ocular demonstration of Bixiou's remarks," said Léon; "you are to be shown a woman who makes twenty thousand francs per annum by exploiting an idea."

"A fortune-teller," explained Bixiou, construing Gazonal's expression as a question. "Among folk that wish to know the future Mme. Fontaine is held to be even wiser than the late Mlle. Lenormand."

"She must be very rich!"

"She has fallen a victim to her idea since lotteries came into existence. In Paris, you see, great receipts always mean a large expenditure. Every hard head has a crack in it somewhere, like a safety-valve, as it were, for the steam. Every one that makes a great deal of money has his weaknesses or his fancies, a provision of nature probably to keep the balance."

"And now that lotteries are abolished?"

"Oh, well, she has a nephew, and is saving for him."

Arrived in the Rue Vieille-du-Temple, the three friends entered one of the oldest houses in the street, and discovered a tremulous staircase, with wooden steps laid on a foundation of concrete. Up they went in the perpetual twilight, through the fetid atmosphere peculiar to houses with a passage entry, till they reached the third story, and a door which can only be described by a drawing; any attempt to give an adequate idea of it in words would consume too much midnight oil.

An old crone, so much in keeping with the door that she might have been its living counterpart, admitted the three into a room which did duty as an ante-chamber, icy cold as a crypt, while the streets outside were sweltering in the heat. Puffs of damp air came up from an inner court, a sort of huge breathing-hole in the building; a box full of sickly-looking plants stood on the window-ledge. A gray daylight filled the room. Everything was glazed over with a greasy fuliginous deposit; the chairs and table, the whole room, in fact, was squalid; the damp oozed up through the brick floor like water through the sides of a Moorish jar. There was not a single detail which did not harmonize with the hook-nosed, pallid, repulsive old hag in the much-mended rags, who asked them to be seated, and informed them that MADAME never saw more than one person at a time.

Gazonal screwed up his courage and went boldly forwards.

The woman whom he confronted looked like one of those whom Death has forgotten, or more probably left as a copy of himself in the land of the living. Two gray eyes, so immovable that it tired you to look at them, glittered in a fleshless countenance on either side of a sunken, snuff-bedabbled nose. A set of knuckle-bones, firmly mounted with sinews almost like bone, made as though they were human hands, thrumming like a piece of machinery thrown out of gear upon a pack of cards. The body, a broomstick decently draped with a gown, enjoyed the advantages of still life to the full; it did not move a hair's-breadth. A black velvet cap rose above the automaton's forehead. Mme. Fontaine, for she was really a woman, sat with a black fowl on her right hand, and a fat toad named Ashtaroth on her left. Gazonal did not notice the creature at first.

The toad, an animal of portentous size, was less alarming in himself than by reason of a couple of topazes, each as large as a fifty centime piece, that glowed like lamps in his head. Their gaze was intolerable. "The toad is a mysterious creature," as the late M. Lassailly used to say, after lying out in the fields to have the last word with a toad that fascinated him. Perhaps, all creation, man included, is summed up in the toad; for Lassailly tells us that it lives on almost indefinitely, and it is well known that, of all animals, its mating lasts the longest.

The black fowl's cage stood two feet away from a table covered with a green cloth; a plank like a drawbridge lay between.

When the woman, the least real of the strange company about a table worthy of Hoffmann, bade Gazonal "Cut!"— the honest manufacturer shuddered in spite of himself. The secret of the formidable power of such creatures lies in the importance of the thing we seek to learn of them. Men and women come to buy hope of them; and they know it.

The sibyl's cave was a good deal darker than the antechamber, so much so, in fact, that you could not distinguish the color of the wall paper. The smoke-begrimed ceiling, so far from reflecting, seemed rather to absorb such feeble light as struggled in through a window blocked up with bleached sickly-looking plant-life; but all the dim daylight in the place fell full upon the table at which the sorceress sat. Her armchair and a chair for Gazonal completed the furniture of a little room cut in two by a garret, where Mme. Fontaine evidently slept. A little door stood ajar, and the murmur of a pot boiling on the fire reached Gazonal's ears. The sounds from the kitchen, the compound of odors in which effluvia from the sink predominated, called up an incongruous association of ideas—the necessities of everyday life and the sense of the supernatural. Disgust was mingled with curiosity. Gazonal caught sight of the lowest step of the deal staircase which led to the garret; he saw all these particulars at a glance, and his gorge rose. The kind of terror inspired by similar scenes in romances and German plays was somehow so different; the absence of illusion, the prosaic sensation caught him by the throat. He felt heavy and dizzy in that atmosphere; the gloom set his nerves on edge. With the very coxcombry of courage, he turned his eyes on the toad, and with sickening sensation of heat in the pit of the stomach, felt a sort of panic such as a criminal might feel at sight of a policeman. Then he sought comfort in a scrutiny of Mme. Fontaine, and found a pair of colorless, almost white eyes, with intolerable unwavering black pupils. The silence grew positively appalling.

"What does monsieur wish?" asked Mme. Fontaine. "His fortune for five francs, or ten francs, or the *grand jeu?*"

"Five francs is quite dear enough," said the Provençal, making unspeakable efforts to fight against the influences of the place. But just as he strove for self-possession, a diabolical cackle made him start on his chair. The black hen emitted a sound.

"Go away, my girl. Monsieur only wishes to spend five francs."

The hen seemed to understand, for when she stood within a step of the cards, she turned and walked solemnly back to her place.

"Which is your favorite flower?" asked the old crone, in a voice hoarse with the accumulation of phlegm in her throat.

"The rose."

"Your favorite color?"

"Blue."

"What animal do you like best?"

"The horse. Why do you ask?" queried Gazonal in turn.

"Man is linked to other forms of life by his own previous existences," she said sententiously, "hence his instincts, and his instincts control his destiny.—Which kind of food do you like best; fish, game, grain, butcher meat, sweet things, fruit, or vegetables?"

"Game."

"In what month were you born?"

"September."

"Hold out your hand."

Mme. Fontaine scanned the palm put forth for her inspection with close attention. All this was done in a business-like way, with no attempt to give a supernatural color to the proceedings; a notary asking a client's wishes with regard to the drafting of a lease could not have been more straightforward. The cards being sufficiently shuffled, she asked Gazonal to cut and make them up into three packs. This done, she took up the packs, spread them out one above another, and eyed them as a gambler eyes the thirty-six numbers at roulette before he stakes his money.

Gazonal felt a cold chill freeze the marrow of his bones; he scarcely knew where he was; but his surprise grew more and more when this repulsive hag in the greasy, flabby green skull-cap, and false front that exhibited more black silk than hair curled into points of interrogation, began to tell him, in her rheumy voice, of all the events, even the most intimate history of his past life. She told him his tastes, his habits, his character, his ideas even as a child; she knew all that might have influenced his life. There was his projected marriage, for instance; she told him why and by whom it was broken off, giving him an exact description of the woman he had loved; and finally she named his district, and told him about his lawsuit, and so on, and so on.

Gazonal thought at first that the whole thing was a hoax got up for his benefit by his cousin; but the absurdity of this theory struck him almost at once, and he sat in gaping astonishment. Opposite sat the infernal power incarnate, a power that, from among all human shapes, had borrowed that one which has struck the imagination of poets and painters throughout all time as the most appalling—a cold-blooded, shrunken, asthmatic, toothless hag, with hard lips, flat nose, and pale eyes. Nothing was alive about Mme. Fontaine's face save the eyes; some gleam from the depths of the future or the fires of hell sparkled in them.

Gazonal, scarcely knowing what he said, interrupted her to ask the uses of the fowl and the toad.

"To foretell the future. The 'consultant' himself scatters

some seeds over the cards; Cleopatra comes to pick them up; and Ashtaroth creeps over them to seek the food that the client gives him. Their wonderful intelligence is never deceived. Would you like to see them at work and hear your future read? It costs a hundred francs."

But Gazonal, dismayed by Ashtaroth's expression, bade the terrible Mme. Fontaine good-day, and fled into the next room. He was damp with perspiration; he seemed to feel an unclean spirit brooding over him.

"Let us go out of this," he said. "Has either of you ever consulted this witch?"

"I never think of taking a step in life until Ashtaroth has given his opinion," said Léon, "and I am always the better for it."

"I am still expecting the honest competence promised me by Cleopatra," added Bixiou.

"I am in a fever!" cried the child of the South. "If I believed all that you tell me, I should believe in witchcraft, in a supernatural power."

"It can only be natural," put in Bixiou. "Half the artists alive, one-third of the lorettes, and one-fourth of the statesmen consult Mme. Fontaine. It is well known that she acts as Egeria to a certain statesman."

"Did she tell you your fortune?" inquired Léon.

"No. I had quite enough of it with the past." A sudden idea struck Gazonal. "But if she and her disgusting collaborators can foretell the future," he said, "how is it that she is unlucky in the lottery?"

"Ah! there you have set your finger on one of the great mysteries of occult science," answered Léon. "So soon as the personal element dims the surface of that inward mirror, as it were, which reflects past and future, so soon as you introduce any motive foreign to the exercise of this power that they possess, the sorcerer or sorceress at once loses the power of vision. It is the same with the artist who systematically prostitutes art to gain advancement or alien ends; he loses his gift. Mme. Fontaine once had a rival, a man who told

fortunes on the cards; he fell into criminal courses, yet he
never foresaw his own arrest, conviction, and sentence. Mme.
Fontaine is right eight times out of ten, yet she never could
tell that she should lose her stake in the lottery."

"It is the same with magnetism," Bixiou remarked. "A
man cannot magnetize himself."

"Good! Now comes magnetism. What next! Do you
really know everything?"

"My friend Gazonal, before you can laugh at everything,
you must know everything," said Bixiou with gravity. "For
my own part, I have known Paris since I was a boy, and my
pencil helps me to laugh for a livelihood at the rate of five
caricatures per month. So I very often laugh at an idea in
which I have faith."

"Now, let us go in for something else," said Léon. "Let us
drive to the Chamber and arrange the cousin's business."

"This," continued Bixiou, burlesquing Odry and Gaillard,
"is High Comedy; we will draw out the first great speaker
that we meet in the Salle des Pas-Perdus; and there, as
everywhere else, you shall hear the Parisian harping upon two
eternal strings—Self-interest and Vanity."

As they stepped into the cab again, Léon noticed a man
driving rapidly past, and signaled his wish to speak a word
with the newcomer.

"It is Publicola Masson," he told Bixiou; "I will just ask
him for an interview this evening at five o'clock when the
House rises. The cousin shall see the queerest of all characters."

"Who is it?" asked Gazonal, while Léon went across to
speak to his man.

"A chiropodist, that will cut your corns by contract, an
author of a treatise on chiropody. If the Republicans triumph for six months, he will without doubt have a place in
history."

"And does he keep a carriage?"

"No one but a millionaire can afford to go about on foot
here, my friend."

"The Chamber!" Léon called to the driver.

"Which, sir?"

"The Chamber of Deputies," said Léon, exchanging a smile with Bixiou.

"Paris is beginning to confuse me," sighed Gazonal.

"To show you its immensity—moral, political, and literary —we are copying the Roman cicerone that shows you a thumb of the statue of St. Peter, which you take for a life-size figure until you find out that a finger is more than a foot long. You have not so much as measured one of the toes of Paris yet——"

"And observe, cousin Gazonal, that we are taking things as they come, we are not selecting."

"You shall have a Belshazzar's feast to-night; you shall see Paris, *our* Paris, playing at lansquenet, staking a hundred thousand francs without winking an eye."

Fifteen minutes later their hackney cab set them down by the flight of steps before the Chamber of Deputies on that side of the Pont de la Concorde which leads to discord.

"I thought the Chambers were unapproachable," said Gazonal, surprised to find himself in the great Salle des Pas-Perdus.

"That depends," said Bixiou. "Physically speaking, it costs you thirty sous in cab hire; politically speaking, rather more. A poet says that the swallows think that the Arc de Triomphe de l'Étoile was built for them; and we artists believe that this public monument was built to console the failures on the stage of the Théâtre-Français and to amuse us; but these state-paid play-actors are more expensive than the others, and it is not every day that we get our money's worth."

"So this is the Chamber! . . ." repeated Gazonal. He strode through the great hall, almost empty now, looking about him with an expression which Bixiou noted down in his memory for one of the famous caricatures in which he rivals Gavarni. Léon on his side walked up to one of the ushers who come and go constantly between the Salle des Séances it-

self and the lobby, where the reporters of the *Moniteur* are at
work while the House is sitting, with some persons attached
to the Chamber.

"The Minister is here," the usher was telling Léon as Gazonal came up, "but I do not know whether M. Giraud has
gone or not; I will see——" He opened one of the folding
doors through which no one is allowed to pass save deputies,
ministers, or royal commissioners, when a man came out,
young as yet, as it seemed to Gazonal, in spite of his forty-
eight years. To this newcomer the usher pointed out Léon
de Lora.

"Aha! you here!" he said, shaking hands with Léon and
Bixiou. "You rascals! what do you want in the innermost
sanctuary of law?"

"Gad! we have come for a lesson in the art of humbug,"
said Bixiou. "One gets rusty if one does not."

"Then let us go out into the garden," said the newcomer,
not knowing that Gazonal was one of the company.

Gazonal was at a loss how to classify the well-dressed
stranger in plain black from head to foot, with a ribbon and
an order; but he followed to the terrace by the river once
known as the Quai Napoléon. Out in the garden the *ci-devant* young man gave vent to a laugh, suppressed since his
appearance in the Salle des Pas-Perdus.

"Why, what is the matter with you?" asked Léon.

"My dear friend, we are driven to tell terrific lies with incredible coolness to prove the sincerity of the constitutional
government. Now I myself have my moods. There are days
when I can lie like a political programme, and others when
I cannot keep my countenance. This is one of my hilarious
days. Now the Opposition has called upon the chief secretary to disclose secrets of diplomacy which he would not impart if they were in office, and at this moment he is on his
legs preparing to go through a gymnastic performance. And
as he is an honest man that will not lie on his own account,
he said confidentially to me before he mounted to the breach,
'I have not a notion what to tell them.' So, when I saw him

there, an uncontrollable desire to laugh seized me, and I went out, for you cannot very well have your laugh out on the Ministerial benches, where my youth occasionally revisits me unseasonably."

"At last!" cried Gazonal. "At last! I have found an honest man in Paris. You must be indeed great!" he continued, looking at the stranger.

"I say, who is this gentleman?" inquired the other, scrutinizing Gazonal as he spoke.

"A cousin of mine," Léon put in hastily. "I can answer for his silence and loyalty as for my own. We have come here on his account; he has a lawsuit on hand, it depends on your department; his prefect simply wishes to ruin him, and we have come to see you about it and to prevent the Council of State from confirming injustice."

"Who is the chairman?"

"Massol."

"Good."

"And our friends Claude Vignon and Giraud are on the committee," added Bixiou.

"Just say a word to them, and let them come to Carabine's to-night," said Léon. "Du Tillet is giving a party, ostensibly a meeting of railway shareholders, for they rob you more than ever on the highways now."

"But, I say, is this in the Pyrénées?" inquired the young-looking stranger, grown serious by this time.

"Yes," said Gazonal.

"And you do not vote for us at the general election," he continued, fixing his eyes on Gazonal.

"No; but the remarks you made just now have corrupted me. On the honor of a Commandant of the National Guard, I will see that your candidate is returned——"

"Very well. Can you further guarantee your cousin?" asked the young-looking man, addressing Léon.

"We are forming him," said Bixiou, in a very comical tone.

"Well, I shall see," said the other, and he hurried back to the Salle des Séances.

"I say, who is that?"

"The Comte de Rastignac; he is the head of the department in which your affair is going on."

"A Minister! Is that all?"

"He is an old friend of ours as well, and he has three hundred thousand livres a year, and he is a peer of France, and the King has given him the title of Count. He is Nucingen's son-in-law, and one of the two or three statesmen produced by the Revolution of July. Now and then, however, he finds office dull, and comes out to have a laugh with us."

"But, look here, cousin, you did not tell us that you were on the other side down yonder," said Léon, taking Gazonal by the arm. "How stupid you are! One deputy more or less to the Right or Left, will you sleep any the softer for that?"

"We are on the side of the others——"

"Let them be," said Bixiou—Monrose himself could not have spoken the words more comically—"let them be, they have Providence on their side, and Providence will look after them without your assistance and in spite of themselves.—A manufacturer is bound to be a necessarian."

"Good! here comes Maxime with Canalis and Giraud," cried Léon.

"Come, friend Gazonal; the promised actors are arriving on the scene."

The three went towards the newcomers, who to all appearance were lounging on the terrace.

"Have they sent you about your business that you are doing like this?" inquired Bixiou, addressing Giraud.

"No. We have come out for a breath of air till the ballot is over."

"And how did the chief secretary get out of it?"

"He was magnificent!" said Canalis.

"Magnificent!" from Giraud.

"Magnificent!" from Maxime.

"I say! Right, Left, and Centre all of one mind!"

"Each of us has a different idea in his head though," Maxime de Trailles remarked. (Maxime was a **Ministerialist.**)

"Yes," laughed Canalis. Canalis had once been in office, but he was now edging away towards the Right.

"You have just enjoyed a great triumph," Maxime said, addressing Canalis, "for you drove the Minister to reply."

"Yes, and to lie like a charlatan," returned Canalis.

"A glorious victory!" commented honest Giraud. "What would you have done in his place?"

"I should have lied likewise."

"Nobody calls it 'lying,'" said Maxime; "it is called 'covering the Crown,'" and he drew Canalis a few paces aside.

Léon turned to Giraud.

"Canalis is a very good speaker," he said.

"Yes and no," returned the State Councillor. "He is an empty drum, an artist in words rather than a speaker. In short, 'tis a fine instrument, but it is not music, and therefore he has not had and never will have 'the ear of the House.' He thinks that France cannot do without him; but whatever happens, he cannot possibly be 'the man of the situation.'"

Canalis and Maxime rejoined the group just as Giraud, deputy of the Centre-Left, delivered himself of this verdict. Maxime took Giraud by the arm and drew him away, probably to give the same confidences that Canalis had received.

"What an honest, worthy fellow he is!" said Léon, indicating Giraud.

"That kind of honesty is the ruin of a government," replied Canalis.

"Is he a good speaker in your opinion?"

"Yes and no," said Canalis. "He is wordy and prosy. He is a plodding reasoner, a good logician; but he does not comprehend the wider logic—the logic of events and of affairs—for which reason he has not and never will have 'the ear of the House'——"

Canalis was in the midst of his summing-up when the subject of his remarks came towards them with Maxime; and, forgetting that there was a stranger present whose discretion was not so certain as Léon's or Bixiou's, he took Canalis' hand significantly.

"Very good," said he, "I agree to M. le Comte de Trailles' proposals. I will ask the question, but it will be pressed hard."

"Then we shall have the House with us on the question, for a man of your capacity and eloquence 'always has the ear of the House,'" returned Canalis. "I will undertake to crush you and no mistake."

"You very likely will bring about a change of ministry, for on such ground you can do anything you like with the House, and you will be 'the man of the situation'——"

"Maxime has hocussed them both," said Léon, turning to his cousin. "That fine fellow is as much at home in parliamentary intrigue as a fish in water."

"Who is he?" asked Gazonal.

"He *was* a scamp; he *is* in a fair way to be an ambassador," answered Bixiou.

"Giraud," said Léon, "do not go until you have asked Rastignac to say something, as he promised me he would, about a lawsuit that will come up for decision before you the day after to-morrow; it affects my cousin here. I will come round to-morrow morning to see you about it." And the three friends followed the three politicians, at a certain distance, to the Salle des Pas-Perdus.

"Now, cousin, look at the two yonder," said Léon, pointing out a retired and very famous Minister and the leader of the Left Centre, "those are two speakers that always 'have the ear of the House'; they have been called in joke the leaders of His Majesty's Opposition; they have the ear of the House, so much so indeed that they very often pull it."

"It is four o'clock. Let us go back to the Rue de Berlin," said Bixiou.

"Yes. You have just seen the heart of the Government; now you ought to see the parasites and ascarides, the tapeworm, or, since one must call him by his name—the Republican."

The friends were no sooner packed into their cab than Gazonal looked maliciously at his cousin and Bixiou; there was a pent-up flood of southern and splenetic oratory within him.

"I had my suspicions before of this great jade of a city," he burst out in his thick southern accent, "but after this morning I despise it. The poor country district, for so shabby as she is, is an honest girl; but Paris is a prostitute, rapacious, deceitful, artificial, and I am very glad to escape with my skin——"

"The day is not over yet," Bixiou said sententiously, with a wink at Léon.

"And why complain like a fool of a so-called prostitution by which you will gain your case?" added Léon. "Do you think yourself a better man, less hypocritical than we are, less rapacious, less ready to make a descent of any sort, less taken up with vanity than all those whom we have set dancing like marionettes?"

"Try to tempt me."

"Poor fellow!" shrugged Léon. "Have you not promised your vote and influence, as it is, to Rastignac?"

"Yes; because he is the only one among them that laughed at himself."

"Poor fellow!" echoed Bixiou. "And you distrust *me* when I have done nothing but laugh! You remind me of a cur snapping at a tiger.—Ah, if you had but seen us making game of somebody or other. Do you realize that we are capable of driving a sane man out of his wits?"

At this point they reached Léon's house. The splendor of its furniture cut Gazonal short and put an end to the dispute. Rather later in the day it began to dawn upon him that Bixiou had been drawing *him* out.

At half-past five, Léon de Lora was dressing for the evening, to Gazonal's great bewilderment. He counted up his cousin's thousand-and-one superfluities, and admired the valet's seriousness, when "monsieur's chiropodist" was announced, and Publicola Masson entered the room, bowed to Gazonal and Bixiou, set down a little case of instruments, and took a low chair opposite Léon. The newcomer, a little man of fifty, bore a certain resemblance to Marat.

"How are things going?" inquired Léon, holding out a foot, previously washed by the servant.

"Well, I am compelled to take a couple of pupils, two young fellows that have given up surgery in despair and taken to chiropody. They were starving, and yet they are not without brains——"

"Oh, I was not speaking of matters pedestrian; I was asking after your political programme——"

Masson's glance at Gazonal was more expressive than any spoken inquiry.

"Oh! speak out; that is my cousin, and he is all but one of you; he fancies that he is a Legitimist."

"Oh, well, we are getting on; we are getting on. All Europe will be with us in five years' time. Switzerland and Italy are in full ferment, and we are ready for the opportunity if it comes. Here, for instance, we have fifty thousand armed men, to say nothing of two hundred thousand penniless citizens——"

"Pooh!" said Léon, "how about the fortifications?"

"Pie crusts made to be broken," Masson retorted. "In the first place, we shall never allow artillery to come within range; and in the second, we have a little contrivance more effectual than all the fortifications in the world, an invention which we owe to the doctor who cured folk faster than all the rest of the faculty could kill them while his machine was in operation."

"What a rate you are going!" said Gazonal. The sight of Publicola made his flesh creep.

"Oh, there is no help for it. We come after Robespierre and Saint-Just, to improve upon them. They were timid, and you see what came of it—an emperor, the elder branch and then the younger. The Mountain did not prune the social tree sufficiently."

"Look here, you that will be consul, or tribune, or something like it, don't forget that I have asked for your protection any time these ten years," said Bixiou.

"Nothing will happen to you. We shall need jesters, and you could take up Barère's job."

"And I?" queried Léon.

"Oh, you are my client; that will save you; for genius is an odious privileged class that receives far too much here in France. We shall be forced to demolish a few of our great men to teach the rest the lesson that they must be simple citizens."

This was said with a mixture of jest and earnest that sent a shudder through Gazonal.

"Then will there be an end of religion?" he asked.

"An end of a *State religion*," said Masson, laying a stress on the last two words; "every one will have his own belief. It is a very lucky thing that the Government just now is protecting the convents; they are accumulating the wealth for our Government. Everybody is conspiring to help us. For instance, all those who pity the people, and bawl so much over the proletariat and the wage-earning classes, or write against the Jesuits, or interest themselves in the amelioration of anybody whatsoever—communists, humanitarians, philanthropists, you understand,—all these folk are our advanced guard. While we lay in powder they are braiding the fuse, and the spark of circumstance will set fire to it."

"Now, pray, what do you want for the welfare of the country?"

"Equality among the citizens, cheap commodities of every kind. There shall be no starving folk on one hand, no millionaires on the other; no blood-suckers, no victims—that is what we want."

"Which is to say the *maximum* and the *minimum*?" queried Gazonal.

"You have said," the other returned laconically.

"An end of manufacturers?"

"Manufactures will be carried on for the benefit of the State; we shall all have a life interest in France. Every man will have his rations served out as if he were on board ship, and everybody will do the work for which he is fitted."

"Good. And meanwhile, until you can cut your aristocrats' heads off——"

"I pare their nails," said the Republican-Radical, shutting up his case of instruments and finishing the joke himself. Then with a very polite bow he withdrew.

"Is it possible? In 1845?" cried Gazonal.

"If we had time we could show you all the characters of 1793; and you should talk with them. You have just seen Marat. Well, we know Fouquier-Tinville, Collot-d'Herbois, Robespierre, Chabot, Fouché, Barras, and even a magnificent Mme. Roland."

"Ah, well, tragedy has not been left unrepresented on this stage," said Gazonal.

"It is six o'clock. We will take you to see Odry in *Les Saltimbanques* this evening, but first we must call upon Mme. Cadine, an actress, very intimate with Massol your chairman; you must pay your court assiduously to her to-night."

"As it is absolutely necessary that you should conciliate this power, I will just give you a few hints," added Bixiou. "Do you employ women in your factory?"

"Assuredly."

"That was all that I wanted to know," said Bixiou. "You are not a married man, you are a great——"

"Yes," interrupted Gazonal. "You have guessed; women are my weak point."

"Very good. If you decide to execute a little manœuvre which I will teach you, you shall know something of the charm of intimacy with an actress without spending one farthing."

Bixiou, intent on playing a mischievous trick upon the cautious Gazonal, had scarcely finished tracing out his part for him, when they reached Mme. Cadine's house in the Rue de la Victoire. But a hint was enough for the southern brain, as will shortly be seen.

They climbed the stair of a tolerably fine house, and discovered Jenny Cadine finishing her dinner. She was to play in the second piece at the Gymnase. Gazonal introduced to the power, Léon and Bixiou went aside ostensibly to see a new piece of furniture, really to leave the two alone together; but not before Bixiou had whispered to her that "this was Léon's cousin, a manufacturer worth millions of francs. —He wants to gain his lawsuit against the prefect in the Council of State," he added, "so he wishes to win you first, to have Massol on his side."

All Paris knows Jenny Cadine's great beauty; no one can wonder, therefore, that Gazonal stood dumfounded at sight of her. She had received him almost coldly at first, but during those few minutes that he spent alone with her she was very gracious to him. Gazonal looked contemptuously round at the drawing-room furniture through the door left ajar by his fellow-conspirators, and made a mental estimate of the contents of the dining-room.

"How any man can leave such a woman as you in such a dog-hole as this!——" he began.

"Ah! there it is. It cannot be helped. Massol is not rich. I am waiting until he is a Minister——"

"Happy man!" exclaimed Gazonal, heaving a sigh from the depths of a provincial heart.

"Good," thought the actress, "I shall have new furniture; I can rival Carabine now."

Léon came in. "Well, dear child," he said, "you are coming to Carabine's this evening, are you not? Supper and lansquenet."

"Will monsieur be there?" Jenny asked artlessly and sweetly.

"Yes, madame," said Gazonal, dazzled by his rapid success.

"But Massol will be there too," rejoined Bixiou.

"Well, and what has that to do with it?" retorted Jenny. "Now let us go, my treasures, I must be off to my theatre."

Gazonal handed her down to the cab that was waiting for her at the door, and squeezed her hands so tenderly, that Jenny wrung her fingers.

"Eh!" she cried, "I have not a second set."

Once in the carriage, Gazonal tried to hug Bixiou. "She is hooked!" he cried; "you are a most unmitigated scoundrel!"

"So the women say," returned Bixiou.

At half-past eleven, after the play, a hackney cab brought the trio to Mlle. Séraphine Sinet's abode. Every well-known lorette either takes a pseudonym, or somebody bestows one upon her, and Séraphine is better known as Carabine, possibly because she never fails to bring down her "pigeon." She had come to be almost indispensable to du Tillet the famous banker, and member of the Left Centre, and at that time she was living in charming rooms in the Rue Saint-Georges. There are certain houses in Paris that seem fated to carry on a tradition; this particular house had already seen seven reigns of courtesans. A stockbroker had installed Suzanne du Val-Noble in it somewhere about the year 1827. The notorious Esther had here driven the Baron de Nucingen to commit the only follies of his life. Here Florine, and she whom some facetiously call the *"late* Madame Schontz," had shone in turn, and finally when du Tillet tired of his wife he had taken the little modern house and established Carabine in it; her lively wit, her off-hand manners, her brilliant shamelessness provided him with a counterpoise for the cares of life, domestic, public, and financial.

Ten covers were always laid; dinner was served (and splendidly) whether du Tillet and Carabine were at home or no. Artists, men of letters, journalists, and frequenters of the house dined there, and there was play of an evening. More than one member of the Chamber came hither to seek the pleasure that is paid for in Paris by its weight in gold. A few feminine eccentrics, certain falling stars of doubtful significance that sparkle in the Parisian firmament, appeared here in all the splendor of their toilettes. The conversation was good, for talk was unrestrained, and anything might be said and was said. Carabine, a rival of the no less celebrated Malaga, had fallen heir as it were to several salons; the coteries belonging to Florine (now Mme. Nathan), Tullia (afterwards Comtesse du Bruel), and Madame Schontz (who became the wife of President du Ronceret) had all rallied to Carabine.

Gazonal made but one remark as he came in, but his observation was both legitimate and Legitimist—"It is finer than the Tuileries," said he; and, indeed, his provincial eyes found so much employment with satins, velvets, brocades, and gilding, that he did not see Jenny Cadine in a dress that commanded respect, hidden behind Carabine. She was taking mental notes of her litigant's entry while she chatted with her hostess.

"This is my cousin, my dear," said Léon, addressing Carabine; "he is a manufacturer; he dropped in upon me this morning from the Pyrénées. He knows nothing as yet of Paris; he wants Massol's help in a case that has gone up to the Council of State; so we have taken the liberty of bringing him here to supper, beseeching you at the same time to leave him in full possession of his faculties——"

"As he pleases; wine is dear," said Carabine, scanning the provincial, who struck her as in no wise remarkable.

As for Gazonal, dazzled by the women's dresses, the lights, the gilding, and the chatter of various groups, all concerned, as he supposed, with him and his affairs, he could only stammer out incoherent words.

"Madame—madame—you are—you are very kind."

"What do you manufacture?" asked the mistress of the house, smiling at him.

"Say lace," prompted Bixiou in a whisper, "and offer her pillow-lace or guipures."

"P-p-pill——"

"Pills!" said Carabine. "I say, Cadine, child, you have been taken in."

"Lace," Gazonal got out, comprehending that he must pay for his supper. "It will give me the greatest pleasure to offer you—er—a dress—a scarf—a mantilla of my own manufacture."

"What, three things! Well, well, you are nicer than you look," returned Carabine.

"Paris has caught me," said Gazonal to himself, as he caught sight of Jenny Cadine, and went to pay his respects to her.

"And what should *I* have?" asked the actress.

"Why, my whole fortune!" cried Gazonal, shrewdly of the opinion that to offer all was to offer nothing.

Massol, Claude Vignon, du Tillet, Maxime de Trailles, Nucingen, Du Bruel, Malaga, M. and Mme. Gaillard, Vauvinet, and a host of others crowded in.

In the course of conversation, Massol and Gazonal went to the bottom of the dispute; the former, without committing himself, remarked that the report was not yet drawn up, and that citizens might put confidence in the lights and the independent opinion of the Council of State. After this cut-and-dried response, Gazonal, losing hope, judged it necessary to win over the charming Jenny Cadine, with whom he fell head over ears in love. Léon de Lora and Bixiou left their victim in the clutches of the most mischief-loving woman in their singular set, for Jenny Cadine was the famous Déjazet's sole rival.

At the supper-table Gazonal was fascinated by the work of Froment Meurice, the modern Benvenuto Cellini—by costly plate, with contents worth the interest on the wrought silver that held them. The two perpetrators of the hoax had taken care to sit as far away from him as possible; but furtively they watched the wily actress' progress. Ensnared by that insidious hint of new furniture, she had set herself to carry Gazonal home with her; and never did lamb in the Fête-Dieu procession submit to be led by his St. John the Baptist with a better grace than Gazonal showed in his obedience to this siren.

Three days afterwards, Léon and Bixiou having meanwhile seen and heard nothing of their friend, repaired to his lodging about two o'clock in the afternoon

"Well, cousin, the decision has been given in your favor."

"Alas! it makes no difference now, cousin," Gazonal answered, turning his melancholy eyes upon them; "I have turned Republican again."

"*Quésaco?*" asked Léon.

"I have nothing left, not even enough to pay my counsel.

Mme. Jenny Cadine holds bills of mine for more than I am worth——"

"It is a fact that Cadine is rather expensive, but——"

"Oh! I have had my money's worth. Ah! what a woman! After all, Paris is too much for a provincial. I am about to retire to La Trappe."

"Good," said Bixiou. "Now you talk sensibly. Here, acknowledge the sovereign power of the capital——"

"And of capital!" cried Léon, holding out Gazonal's bills. Gazonal stared at the papers in bewilderment.

"You cannot say that we have no notion of hospitality; we have educated you, rescued you from want, treated you, and —amused you," said Bixiou.

"And nothing to pay!" added Léon, with the gesture by which a street-boy conveys the idea that somebody has been successfully "done."

PARISIANS IN THE COUNTRY

GAUDISSART THE GREAT

To Madame la Duchesse de Castries.

Is not the commercial traveler—a being unknown in earlier times—one of the most curious types produced by the manners and customs of this age? And is it not his peculiar function to carry out in a certain class of things the immense transition which connects the age of material development with that of intellectual development? Our epoch will be the link between the age of isolated forces rich in original creativeness, and that of the uniform but leveling force which gives monotony to its products, casting them in masses, and following out an unifying idea—the ultimate expression of social communities. After the Saturnalia of intellectual communism, after the last struggles of many civilizations concentrating all the treasures of the world on a single spot, must not the darkness of barbarism invariably supervene?

The commercial traveler is to ideas what coaches are to men and things. He carts them about, he sets them moving, brings them into impact. He loads himself at the centre of enlightenment with a supply of beams which he scatters among torpid communities. This human *pyrophoros* is an ignorant instructor, mystified and mystifying, a disbelieving priest who talks all the more glibly of arcana and dogmas. A strange figure! The man has seen everything, he knows everything, he is acquainted with everybody. Saturated in Parisian vice, he can assume the rusticity of the countryman. Is he not the link that joins the village to the capital, though himself not essentially either Parisian or provincial?

For he is a wanderer. He never sees to the bottom of things; he learns only the names of men and places, only the surface of things; he has his own foot-rule, and measures everything by that standard; his glance glides over all he sees, and never penetrates the depths. He is inquisitive about everything, and really cares for nothing. A scoffer, always ready with a political song, and apparently equally attached to all parties, he is generally patriotic at heart. A good actor, he can assume by turns the smile of liking, satisfaction, and obligingness, or cast it off and appear in his true character, in the normal frame which is his state of rest.

He is bound to be an observer or to renounce his calling. Is he not constantly compelled to sound a man at a glance, and guess his mode of action, his character, and, above all, his solvency; and, in order to save time, to calculate swiftly the chances of profit? This habit of deciding promptly in matters of business makes him essentially dogmatic; he settles questions out of hand, and talks as a master, of the Paris theatres and actors, and of those in the provinces. Besides, he knows all the good and all the bad places in the kingdom, *de actu et visu.* He would steer you with equal confidence to the abode of virtue or of vice. Gifted as he is with the eloquence of a hot-water tap turned on at will, he can with equal readiness stop short or begin again, without a mistake, his stream of ready-made phrases, flowing without pause, and producing on the victim the effect of a moral douche. He is full of pertinent anecdotes, he smokes, he drinks. He wears a chain with seals and trinkets, he impresses the "small fry," is looked at as a *milord* in the villages, never allows himself to be "got over"—a word of his slang—and knows exactly when to slap his pocket and make the money jingle so as not to be taken for a "sneak" by the women servants— a suspicious race—of the houses he calls at.

As to his energy, is it not the least of the characteristics of this human machine? Not the kite pouncing on its prey, not the stag inventing fresh doublings to escape the hounds and put the hunter off the trail, not the dogs coursing the game, can compare with the swiftness of his rush when he scents a commission, the neatness with which he trips up a rival to gain upon him, the keenness with which he feels, sniffs, and spies out an opportunity for "doing business." How many special talents must such a man possess! And how many will you find in any country of these diplomates of the lower class, profound negotiators, representatives of the calico, jewelry, cloth, or wine trades, and often with more acumen than ambassadors, who are indeed for the most part but superficial?

Nobody in France suspects the immense power constantly wielded by the commercial traveler, the bold pioneer of the transactions which embody to the humblest hamlet the genius of civilization and Parisian inventiveness in its struggle against the common sense, the ignorance, or the habits of rustic life. We must not overlook these ingenious laborers, by whom the intelligence of the masses is kneaded, moulding the most refractory material by sheer talk, and resembling in this the persevering polishers whose file licks the hardest porphyry smooth. Do you want to know the power of the tongue, and the coercive force of mere phrases on the most tenacious coin known—that of the country freeholder in his rustic lair?— Then listen to what some high dignitary of Paris industry can tell you, for whose benefit these clever pistons of the steam engine called Speculation work, and strike, and squeeze.

"Monsieur," said the director-cashier-manager-secretary-and-chairman of a famous Fire Insurance Company to an experienced economist, "in the country, out of five hundred thousand francs to be collected in renewing insurances, not more than fifty thousand are paid willingly. The other four hundred and fifty thousand are only extracted by the persistency of our agents, who go to dun the customers who are in arrears till they have renewed their policies, and frighten and excite them by fearful tales of fires.—Eloquence, the gift of the gab, is, in fact, nine-tenths of the matter in the ways and means of working our business."

To talk—to make oneself heard—is not this seduction? A nation with two Chambers, a woman with two ears, alike are lost! Eve and the Serpent are the perennial myth of a daily recurring fact which began, and will probably only end with the world.

"After two hours' talk you ought to have won a man over to your side," said an attorney who had retired from business.

Walk round the commercial traveler! Study the man. Note his olive-green overcoat, his cloak, his morocco stock, his pipe, his blue-striped cotton shirt. In that figure, so genuinely original that it can stand friction, how many different natures you may discover. See! What an athlete, what a circus, and what a weapon! He—the world—and his tongue.

A daring seaman, he embarks with a stock of mere words to go and fish for money, five or six hundred thousand francs, say, in the frozen ocean, the land of savages, of Iroquois—in France! The task before him is to extract by a purely mental process and painless operation the gold that lies buried in rural hiding-places. The provincial fish will not stand the harpoon or the torch; it is only to be caught in the seine or the landing-net—the gentlest snare.

Can you ever think again without a shudder of the deluge of phrases which begins anew every day at dawn in France? —You know the genus; now for the individual.

There dwells in Paris a matchless bagman, the paragon of his kind, a man possessing in the highest degree every condition indispensable to success in his profession. In his words vitriol mingles with bird-lime; bird-lime to catch the victim, besmear it and stick it to the trapper, vitriol to dissolve the hardest limestone.

His "line" was hats—he *traveled in hats;* but his gifts, and the skill with which he ensnared folks, had earned him such commercial celebrity that dealers in *l'Article Paris,* the dainty novelties invented in Paris workshops, positively courted him to undertake their business. Thus, when he was in Paris on his return from some triumphant progress, he was perpetually being feasted; in the provinces the agents made much of him; in Paris the largest houses were respectful to him. Welcomed, entertained, and fed wherever he went, to him a breakfast or a dinner in solitude was a pleasure and a debauch. He led the life of a sovereign—nay, better, of a journalist. And was he not the living organ of Paris trade?

His name was Gaudissart; and his fame, his influence, and the praises poured on him had gained him the epithet of Gaudissart the Great. Wherever he made his appearance, whether in a counting house or an inn, in a drawing-room or a diligence, in a garret or a bank, each one would exclaim on seeing him, "Ah, ha! here is Gaudissart the Great!"

Never was a nickname better suited to the appearance, the manners, the countenance, the voice, or the language of a man. Everything smiled on the Traveler, and he smiled on all. *Similia Similibus;* he was for homœopathy: Puns, a horse-laugh, the complexion of a jolly friar, a Rabelaisian aspect; dress, mien, character, and face combined to give his whole person a stamp of jollification and ribaldry.

Blunt in business, good-natured and capital fun, you would have known him at once for a favorite of the *grisette*—a man who can climb with a grace to the top of a coach, offer a hand to a lady in difficulties over getting out, jest with the postilion about his bandana, and sell him a hat; smile at the inn-maid, taking her by the waist—or by the fancy; who at table will imitate the gurgle of a bottle by tapping his cheek while putting his tongue in it, knows to make beer go off by drawing the air between his lips, or can hit a champagne glass a sharp blow with a knife without breaking it, saying to the others, "Can you do that?"—who chaffs shy travelers, contradicts well-informed men, is supreme at table, and secures all the best bits.

A clever man too, he could on occasion put aside all such pleasantries, and look very serious when, throwing away the end of his cigar, he would look out on a town and say, "I mean to see what the folks here are made of." Then Gaudissart was the most cunning and shrewd of ambassadors. He knew how to be the official with the préfet, the capitalist with the banker, orthodox and monarchical with the royalist, the blunt citizen with the citizen—in short, all things to all men, just what he ought to be wherever he went, leaving Gaudissart outside the door, and finding him again as he went out.

Until 1830 Gaudissart the Great remained faithful to the *Article Paris.* This line of business, in all its branches, appealing to the greater number of human fancies, had enabled him to study the secrets of the heart, had taught him the uses of his persuasive eloquence, the way to open the most closely tied money bags, to incite the fancy of wives and husbands, of children and servants, and to persuade them to gratify it. None so well as he knew how to lure a dealer by the temptations of a job, and to turn away at the moment when his desire for the bait was at a climax. He acknowledged his indebtedness to the hatter's trade, saying that it was by studying the outside of the head that he had learned to understand its inside, that he was accustomed to find caps to fit folks, to throw himself at their head, and so forth. His jests on hats were inexhaustible.

Nevertheless, after the August and October of 1830, he gave up traveling in hats and the *Article Paris,* and left off trading in all things mechanical and visible to soar in the loftier spheres of Parisian enterprise. He had given up matter for mind, as he himself said, and manufactured products for the infinitely more subtle outcome of the intellect.

This needs explanation.

The stir and upset of 1830 gave rise, as everybody knows, to the new birth of various antiquated ideas which skilful speculators strove to rejuvenate. After 1830 ideas were more than ever a marketable commodity; and, as was once said by a writer who is clever enough to publish nothing, more ideas than pocket-handkerchiefs are filched nowadays. Some day, perhaps, there may be an Exchange for ideas; but even now, good or bad, ideas have their price, are regarded as a crop imported, transferred, and sold, can be realized, and are viewed as an investment. When there are no ideas in the market speculators try to bring words into fashion, to give them the consistency of an idea, and live on those words as birds live on millet.

Nay, do not laugh! A word is as good as an idea in a country where the ticket on the bale is thought more of than the contents. Have we not seen the book trade thriving on the word *picturesque* when literature had sealed the doom of the word *fantastic*.

Consequently, the excise has levied a tax on the intellect; it has exactly measured the acreage of advertisements, has assessed the prospectus, and weighed thought—Rue de la Paix *Hôtel du Timbre* (the Stamp Office). On being constituted taxable goods, the intellect and its products were bound to obey the method used in manufacturing undertakings. Thus the ideas conceived after drinking in the brain of some of those apparently idle Parisians who do battle on intellectual ground while emptying a bottle or carving a pheasant's thigh, were handed over the day after their mental birth to commercial travelers, whose business it was to set forth, with due skill, *urbi et orbi,* the fried bacon of advertisement and prospectus by which the departmental mouse is tempted into the editor's trap, and becomes known in the vulgar tongue as a subscriber, or a shareholder, a corresponding member, or, perhaps, a backer or a part owner—and being always a flat.

"What a flat I am!" has more than one poor investor exclaimed after being tempted by the prospect of *founding* something, which has finally proved to be the founding that melts down some thousand or twelve hundred francs.

"Subscribers are the fools who cannot understand that it costs more to forge ahead in the realm of intellect than to travel all over Europe," is the speculator's view.

So there is a constant struggle going on between the dilatory public which declines to pay the Paris taxes and the collectors who, living on their percentages, baste that public with new ideas, lard it with undertakings, roast it with prospectuses, spit it on flattery, and at last eat it up with some new sauce in which it gets caught and intoxicated like a fly in treacle. What has not been done in France since 1830 to stimulate the zeal, the conceit of the *intelligent* and *progres-*

sive masses? Titles, medals, diplomas, a sort of Legion of Honor invented for the vulgar martyrs, have crowded on each other's heels. And then every manufacturer of intellectual commodities has discovered a spice, a special condiment, his particular makeweight. Hence the promises of premiums and of anticipated dividends; hence the advertisements of celebrated names without the knowledge of the hapless artists who own them, and thus find themselves implicated unawares in more undertakings than there are days in the year; for the Law could not foresee this theft of names. Hence, too, this rape of ideas which the contractors for public intelligence—like the slave merchants of the East—snatch from the paternal brain at a tender age, and strip and parade before the Greenhorn, their bewildered Sultan the terrible public, who, if not amused, beheads them by stopping their rations of gold.

This mania of the day reacted on Gaudissart the Great, and this was how. A company got up to effect insurances on life and property heard of his irresistible eloquence, and offered him extraordinarily handsome terms, which he accepted. The bargain concluded, the compact signed, the bagman was weaned of the past under the eye of the Secretary to the Society, who freed Gaudissart's mind of its swaddling-clothes, explained the dark corners of the business, taught him its lingo, showed him all the mechanism bit by bit, anatomized the particular class of the public on whom he was to work, stuffed him with cant phrases, crammed him with repartees, stocked him with peremptory arguments, and, so to speak, put an edge on the tongue that was to operate on life in France. The puppet responded admirably to the care lavished on him by Monsieur the Secretary.

The directors of the Insurance Company were so loud in their praises of Gaudissart the Great, showed him so much attention, put the talents of this living prospectus in so favorable a light in the higher circles of banking and of intellectual diplomacy, that the financial managers of two newspapers, then living but since dead, thought of employing him to tout for subscriptions. The *Globe,* the organ of the doctrines of Saint-Simon, and the *Mouvement,* a Republican paper, invited Gaudissart the Great to their private offices and promised him, each, ten francs a head on every subscriber if he secured a thousand, but only five francs a head if he could catch no more than five hundred. As the *line* of the political paper did not interfere with that of the Insurance Company, the bargain was concluded. At the same time, Gaudissart demanded an indemnity of five hundred francs for the week he must spend in "getting up" the doctrine of Saint-Simon, pointing out what efforts of memory and brain would be necessary to enable him to become thoroughly conversant with this *article,* and to talk of it so coherently as to avoid, said he, "putting his foot in it."

He made no claim on the Republicans. In the first place, he himself had a leaning to Republican notions—the only views according to the Gaudissart philosophy that could bring about rational equality; and then Gaudissart had ere now dabbled in the plots of the French *carbonari.* He had even been arrested, but released for lack of evidence; and finally, he pointed out to the bankers of the paper that since July he had allowed his moustache to grow, and that he now only needed a particular shape of cap and long spurs to be representative of the Republic.

So for a week he went every morning to be Saint-Simonized at the *Globe* office, and every evening he haunted the bureau of the Insurance Company to learn the elegancies of financial slang. His aptitude and memory were so good, that he was ready to start by the 15th of April, the date at which he usually set out on his first annual circuit.

Two large commercial houses, alarmed at the downward tendency of trade, tempted the ambitious Gaudissart still to undertake their agency, and the King of Commercial Travelers showed his clemency in consideration of old friendship and of the enormous percentage he was to take.

"Listen to me, my little Jenny," said he, riding in a hackney cab with a pretty little flower-maker.

Every truly great man loves to be tyrannized over by some feeble creature, and Jenny was Gaudissart's tyrant; he was seeing her home at eleven o'clock from the *Gymnase* theatre, where he had taken her in full dress to a private box on the first tier.

"When I come back, Jenny, I will furnish your room quite elegantly. That gawky Mathilde, who makes you sick with her innuendoes, her real Indian shawls brought by the Russian Ambassador's messengers, her silver-gilt, and her Russian Prince—who is, it strikes me, a rank humbug—even she shall not find a fault in it. I will devote all the 'Children' I can get in the provinces to the decoration of your room."

"Well, that is a nice story, I must say," cried the florist. "What, you monster of a man, you talk to me so coolly of your children! Do you suppose I will put up with anything of that kind?"

"Pshaw! Jenny, are you out of your wits? It is a way of talking in my line of business."

"A pretty line of business indeed!"

"Well, but listen; if you go on talking so much, you will find yourself in the right."

"I choose always to be in the right! I may say you are a cool hand to-night."

"You will not let me say what I have to say? I have to push a most capital idea, a magazine that is to be brought out for children. In our walk of life a traveler, when he has worked up a town and got, let us say, ten subscriptions to the *Children's Magazine,* says I have got ten *Children;* just as, if I had ten subscriptions to the *Mouvement,* I should simply say I have got ten *Mouvements.*—Now do you understand?"

"A pretty thing too!—So you are meddling in politics? I can see you already in Sainte-Pélagie, and shall have to trot there to see you every day. Oh, when we love a man, my word! If we knew what we are in for, we should leave you to manage for yourselves, you men!—Well, well, you are going to-morrow, don't let us get the black dog on our shoulders; it is too silly."

The cab drew up before a pretty house, newly built in the Rue d'Artois, where Gaudissart and Jenny went up to the fourth floor. Here resided Mademoiselle Jenny Courand, who was commonly supposed to have been privately married to Gaudissart, a report which the traveler did not deny. To maintain her power over him, Jenny Courand compelled him to pay her a thousand little attentions, always threatening to abandon him to his fate if he failed in the least of them. Gaudissart was to write to her from each town he stopped at and give an account of every action.

"And how many *Children* will you want to furnish my room?" said she, throwing off her shawl and sitting down by a good fire.

"I get five sous on each subscription."

"A pretty joke! Do you expect to make me a rich woman —five sous at a time. Unless you are a Wandering Jew and have your pocket sewn up tight."

"But, Jenny, I shall get thousands of *Children*. Just think, the little ones have never had a paper of their own. However, I am a great simpleton to try to explain the economy of business to you—you understand nothing about such matters."

"And pray, then, Gaudissart, if I am such a gaby, why do you love me?"

"Because you are such a sublime gaby! Listen, Jenny. You see, if I can get people to take the *Globe* and the *Mouvement,* and to pay their insurances, instead of earning a miserable eight or ten thousand francs a year by trundling around like a man in a show, I may make twenty to thirty thousand francs out of one round."

"Unlace my stays, Gaudissart, and pull straight—don't drag me askew."

"And then," said the commercial traveler, as he admired the girl's satin shoulders, "I shall be a shareholder in the papers, like Finot, a friend of mine, the son of a hatter, who has thirty thousand francs a year, and will get himself made a peer! And when you think of little Popinot!—By the way, I forgot to tell you that Monsieur Popinot was yesterday made Minister of Commerce. Why should not I too be ambitious? Ah, ha! I could easily catch the cant of the Tribune, and I might be made a Minister—something like a Minister too! Just listen:

" 'Gentlemen,' " and he took his stand behind an armchair, " 'the Press is not a mere tool, not a mere trade. From the point of view of the politician, the Press is an Institution. Now we are absolutely required here to take the political view of things, hence' "—he paused for breath—" 'hence we are bound to inquire whether it is useful or mischievous, whether it should be encouraged or repressed, whether it should be taxed or free—serious questions all. I believe I shall not be wasting the precious moments of this Chamber by investigating this article and showing you the conditions of the case. We are walking on to a precipice. The Laws indeed are not so guarded as they should be——'

"How is that?" said he, looking at Jenny. "Every orator says that France is marching towards a precipice; they either say that or they talk of the Chariot of the State and political tempests and clouds on the horizon. Don't I know every shade of color! I know the dodges of every trade.—And do you know why? I was born with a caul on. My grandmother kept the caul, and I will give it to you. So, you see, I shall soon be in power!"

"You!"

"Why shouldn't I be Baron Gaudissart and Peer of France? Has not Monsieur Popinot been twice returned deputy for the fourth *Arrondissement?*—And he dines with Louis-Philippe. Finot is to be a Councillor of State, they say. Oh! if only they would send me to London as Ambassador, I am the man to nonplus the English, I can tell you. Nobody has ever caught Gaudissart napping—Gaudissart the Great. No, no one has ever got the better of me, and no one ever shall in any line, politics or impolitics, here or anywhere. But for the present I must give my mind to insuring property, to the *Globe,* to the *Mouvement,* to the *Children's* paper, and to the *Article de Paris.*"

"You will be caught over your newspapers. I will lay a wager that you will not get as far as Poitiers without being done."

"I am ready to bet, my jewel."

"A shawl!"

"Done. If I lose the shawl, I will go back to trade and hats. But, get the better of Gaudissart? Never! never!"

And the illustrious commercial traveler struck on attitude in front of Jenny, looking at her haughtily, one hand in his waistcoat, and his head half turned in a Napoleonic pose.

"How absurd you are! What have you been eating this evening?"

Gaudissart was a man of eight-and-thirty, of middle height, burly and fat, as a man is who is accustomed to go about in mail-coaches; his face was as round as a pumpkin, florid, and with regular features resembling the traditional type adopted by sculptors in every country for their statues of Abundance, of Law, Force, Commerce, and the like. His prominent stomach was pear-shaped, and his legs were thin, but he was wiry and active. He picked up Jenny, who was half undressed, and carried her to her bed.

"Hold your tongue, *free woman,*" said he. "Ah, you don't know anything about the free woman and Saint-Simonism, and antagonism, and Fourierism, and criticism, and determined push—well it is—in short, it is ten francs on every subscription, Madame Gaudissart."

"On my honor, you are going crazy, Gaudissart."

"Always more and more crazy about you," said he, tossing his hat on to the sofa.

Next day, after breakfasting in style with Jenny Courand, Gaudissart set out on horseback to call in all the market towns which he had been particularly instructed to work up by the various companies to whose success he was devoting his genius. After spending forty-five days in beating the country lying between Paris and Blois, he stayed for a fortnight in this little city, devoting the time to writing letters and visiting the neighboring towns. The day before leaving for Tours he wrote to Mademoiselle Jenny Courand the following letter, of which the fulness and charm cannot be matched by any narrative, and which also serves to prove the peculiar legitimacy of the ties that bound these two persons together.

Letter from Gaudissart to Jenny Courand.

"MY DEAR JENNY,—I am afraid you will lose your bet. Like Napoleon, Gaudissart has his star, and will know no Waterloo. I have triumphed everywhere under the conditions set forth. The Insurance business is doing very well. Between Paris and Blois I secured near on two millions; but towards the middle of France heads are remarkably hard, and millions infinitely scarcer. The *Article Paris* toddles on nicely, as usual; it is a ring on your finger. With my usual rattle, I can always come round the shopkeepers. I got rid of sixty-two Ternaux shawls at Orleans; but, on my honor, I don't know what they will do with them unless they put them back on the sheep.

"As to the newspaper line, the Deuce is in it! that is quite another pair of shoes. God above us! what a deal of piping those good people take before they have learned a new tune. I have got no more than sixty-two *Mouvements* so far; and that in my whole journey is less than the Ternaux shawls in one town. These rascally Republicans won't subscribe at all; you talk to them, and they talk; they are quite of your way of thinking, and you soon are all agreed to upset everything that exists. Do you think the man will fork out? Not a bit of it. And if he has three square inches of ground, enough to grow a dozen cabbages, or wood enough to cut a toothpick, your man will talk of the settlement of landed estate, of taxation, and crops, and compensation—a pack of nonsense, while I waste my time and spittle in patriotism. Business is bad, and the *Mouvement* generally is dull. I am writing to the owners to say so. And I am very sorry as a matter of opinion.

"As to the *Globe,* that is another story. If I talk of the

new doctrines to men who seem likely to have a leaning to
such quirks, you might think it was a proposal to burn their
house down. I tell them it is the coming thing, the most
advantageous to their interests, the principle of work by which
nothing is lost;—that men have oppressed men long enough,
that woman is a slave, that we must strive to secure the triumph of the great Idea of thrift, and achieve a more rational
co-ordination of Society—in short, all the rhodomontade at
my command. All in vain! As soon as I start on this subject, these country louts shut up their cupboards as if I had
come to steal something, and beg me to be off.

"What fools these owls are! The *Globe* is nowhere.—I
told them so. I said, 'You are too advanced. You are getting forward, and that is all very well; but you must have
something to show. In the provinces they want to see results.'
However, I have got a hundred *Globes;* and, seeing the den-
sity of these country noodles, it is really a miracle. But I
promise them such a heap of fine things, that be hanged if I
know how the Globules, or Globists, or Globites, or Globians
are ever going to give them. However, as they assured me
that they would arrange the world far better than it is arranged at present, I lead the way and prophesy good things
at ten francs per head.

"There is a farmer who thought it must have to do with
soils, by reason of the name, and I rammed the *Globe* down
his throat; he will take to it, I feel sure; he has a prominent
forehead, and men with prominent foreheads are always ideologists.

"But as to the *Children!* give me the *Children.* I got two
thousand Children between Paris and Blois—a nice little
turn! And there is less waste of words. You show the picture to the mother on the sly, so that the child wants to see;
then, of course, the child sees; and he tugs at mamma's skirts
till he gets his paper, because 'Daddy has hisn paper.' Mamma's gown cost twenty francs, and she does not want it torn
by the brat; the paper costs but six francs, that is cheaper;
so the subscription is dragged out. It is a capital, and meets

a real want—something between the sugar-plum and the pict-
ure-book, the two eternal cravings of childhood. And they
can read, too, these frenzied brats.

"Here, at the table-d'hôte, I had a dispute about newspapers and my opinions. I was sitting, peacefully eating,
by the side of a man in a white hat who was reading the *Débats*. Said I to myself, 'I must give him a taste of my eloquence. Here is a man who is all for the dynasty; I must
try to catch him. Such a triumph would be a splendid fore-
cast of success as a Minister.' So I set to work, beginning by
praising his paper. It was a precious long job, I can tell you.
From one thing to another I began to overrule my man, giving him four-horse speeches, arguments in F sharp, and all
the precious rhodomontade. Everybody was listening, and I
saw a man with *July* in his moustaches, ready to bite for the
Mouvement. But, by ill-luck, I don't know how I let slip the
word *ganache* (old woman). Away went my dynastic white
hat—and a bad hat too, a Lyons hat, half silk and half cotton
—with the bit between his teeth in a fury. So I put on my
grand air—you know it—and I say to him, 'Heyday, monsieur, you are a hot pot! If you are vexed, I am ready to
answer for my words. I fought in July——'—'Though I am
the father of a family,' says he, 'I am ready——' —'You are
the father of a family, my dear sir,' say I. 'You have children?'—'Yes, monsieur.'—'Of eleven?'—'Thereabouts.'—
'Well, then, monsieur, *The Children's Magazine* is just about
to be published—six francs *per annum,* one number a month,
two columns, contributors of the highest literary rank, got up
in the best style, good paper, illustrations from drawings by
our first artists, genuine India paper proofs, and colors that
will not fade.' And then I give him a broadside. The father
is overpowered! The squabble ends in a subscription.

"'No one but Gaudissart can play that game,' cried little
tomtit Lamard to that long noodle Bulot when he told him
the story at the café.

"To-morrow I am off to Amboise. I shall do Amboise in
two days, and write next from Tours, where I am going to

try my hand on the deadliest country from the point of view of intelligence and speculation. But on the honor of Gaudissart, they will be done, they *shall* be done! Done brown! By-bye, little one; love me long, and be true to me. Fidelity through thick and thin is one of the characteristics of the free woman. Who kisses your eyes?

"Yours, FELIX for ever."

Five days later Gaudissart set out one morning from the *Faisan* hotel, where he put up at Tours, and went to Vouvray, a rich and populous district where the public mind seemed to him to be open to conviction. He was trotting along the river quay on his nag, thinking no more of the speeches he was about to make than an actor thinks of the part he has played a hundred times. Gaudissart the Great cantered on, admiring the landscape, and thinking of nothing, never dreaming that the happy valleys of Vouvray were to witness the overthrow of his commercial infallibility.

It will here be necessary to give the reader some insight into the public spirit of Touraine. The peculiar wit of a sly romancer, full of banter and epigram, which stamps every page of Rabelais' work, is the faithful expression of the Tourangeau nature, of an intellect as keen and polished as it must inevitably be in a province where the Kings of France long held their court; an ardent, artistic, poetical, and luxurious nature, but prompt to forget its first impulse. The softness of the atmosphere, the beauty of the climate, a certain ease of living and simplicity of manners, soon stifle the feeling for art, narrow the most expansive heart, and corrode the most tenacious will.

Transplant the native of Touraine, and his qualities develop and lead to great things, as has been proved in the most dissimilar ways, by Rabelais and by Semblançay; by Plantin the printer and by Descartes; by Boucicault, the Napoleon of his day; by Pinaigrier, who painted the greater part of our Cathedral glass; by Verville and Courier. But, left at home, the countryman of Touraine, so remarkable elsewhere, re-

mains like the Indian on his rug, like the Turk on his divan.
He uses his wit to make fun of his neighbor, to amuse himself, and to live happy to the end of his days. Touraine is
the true Abbey of Thelema, so much praised in Gargantua's
book. Consenting nuns may be found there, as in the poet's
dream, and the good cheer sung so loudly by Rabelais is supreme.

As to his indolence, it is sublime, and well characterized
in the popular witticism: "Tourangeau, will you have some
broth?"—"Yes."—"Then bring your bowl."—"I am no longer
hungry."

Is it to the glee of the vinedresser, to the harmonious beauty
of the loveliest scenery in France, or to the perennial peace
of a province which has always escaped the invading armies
of the foreigner, that the soft indifference of those mild and
easy habits is due? To this question there is no answer. Go
yourself to that Turkey in France, and there you will stay,
indolent, idle, and happy. Though you were as ambitious as
Napoleon, or a poet like Byron, an irresistible, indescribable
influence would compel you to keep your poetry to yourself,
and reduce your most ambitious schemes to day-dreams.

Gaudissart the Great was fated to meet in Vouvray one
of those indigenous wags whose mockery is offensive only by
its absolute perfection of fun, and with whom he had a deadly
battle. Rightly or wrongly, your Tourangeau likes to come
into his father's property. Hence the doctrines of Saint-
Simon were held particularly odious, and heartily abused in
those parts; still, only as things are hated and abused in Touraine, with the disdain and lofty pleasantry worthy of the land
of good stories and jokes played between neighbors—a spirit
which is vanishing day by day before what Lord Byron called
English Cant.

After putting up his horse at the *Soleil d'Or,* kept by one
Mitouflet, a discharged Grenadier of the Imperial Guard, who
had married a wealthy mistress of vinelands, and to whose
care he solemnly confided his steed, Gaudissart, for his sins,
went first to the prime wit of Vouvray, the life and soul of

the district, the jester whose reputation and nature alike made it incumbent on him to keep his neighbor's spirits up. This rustic Figaro, a retired dyer, was the happy possessor of seven or eight thousand francs a year, of a pretty house on the slope of a hill, of a plump little wife, and of robust health. For ten years past he had had nothing to do but to take care of his garden and his wife, to get his daughter married, to play his game of an evening, to keep himself informed of all the scandal that came within his jurisdiction, to give trouble at elections, to squabble with the great landowners, and arrange big dinners; to air himself on the quay, inquire what was going on in the town, and bother the priest; and, for dramatic interest, to look out for the sale of a plot of ground that cut into the ring fence of his vineyard. In short, he lived the life of Touraine, the life of a small country town.

At the same time, he was the most important of the minor notabilities of the place, and the leader of the small proprietors—a jealous and envious class, chewing the cud of slander and calumny against the aristocracy, and repeating them with relish, grinding everything down to one level, hostile to every form of superiority, scorning it indeed, with the admirable coolness of ignorance.

Monsieur Vernier—so this little great man of the place was named—was finishing his breakfast, between his wife and his daughter, when Gaudissart made his appearance in the dining-room—one of the most cheerful dining-rooms for miles round, with a view from the windows over the Loire and the Cher.

"Is it to Monsieur Vernier himself that I have the honor —— ?" said the traveler, bending his vertebral column with so much grace that it seemed to be elastic.

"Yes, monsieur," said the wily dyer, interrupting him with a scrutinizing glance, by which he at once took the measure of the man he had to do with.

"I have come, monsieur," Gaudissart went on, "to request the assistance of your enlightenment to direct me in this district where, as I learn from Mitouflet, you exert the greatest influence. I am an emissary, monsieur, to this Department in behalf of an undertaking of the highest importance, backed by bankers who are anxious——"

"Anxious to swindle us!" said Vernier, laughing, long since used to deal with the commercial traveler and to follow his game.

"Just so," replied Gaudissart the Great with perfect impudence. "But, as you very well know, sir, since you are so clear-sighted, people are not to be swindled unless they think it to their interest to allow themselves to be swindled. I beg you will not take me for one of the common ruck of commercial gentlemen who trust to cunning or importunity to win success. I am no longer a *traveler;* I was one, monsieur, and I glory in it. But I have now a mission of supreme importance, which ought to make every man of superior mind regard me as devoted to the enlightenment of his fellow-countrymen. Be kind enough to hear me, monsieur, and you will find that you will have profited greatly by the half hour's conversation I beg you to grant me. The great Paris bankers have not merely lent their names to this concern, as to certain discreditable speculations such as I call mere rat-traps. No, no, nothing of the kind. I can assure you, I would never allow myself to engage in promoting such booby-traps. No, monsieur, the soundest and most respectable houses in Paris are concerned in the undertaking, both as shareholders and as guarantors——"

And Gaudissart unrolled the frippery of his phrases, while Monsieur Vernier listened with an affectation of interest that quite deceived the orator. But at the word guarantor, Vernier had, in fact, ceased to heed this bagman's rhetoric; he was bent on playing him some sly trick, so as to clear off this kind of Parisian caterpillar, once for all, from a district justly regarded as barbarian by speculators, who can get no footing there.

At the head of a delightful valley, known as the *Vallée coquette,* from its curves and bends, new at every step, and each more charming than the last, whether you go up or down the winding slope, there dwelt, in a little house surrounded by a vineyard, a more than half-crazy creature named Margaritis. This man, an Italian by birth, was married, but had no children, and his wife took care of him with a degree of courage that was universally admired; for Madame Margaritis certainly ran some risk in living with a man who, among other manias, insisted on always having two long knives about him, not unfrequently threatening her with them. But who does not know the admirable devotion with which country people care for afflicted creatures, perhaps in consequence of the discredit that attaches to a middle-class wife if she abandons her child or her husband to the tender mercies of a public asylum? Again, the aversion is well known which country folks feel for paying a hundred louis, or perhaps a thousand crowns, the price charged at Charenton or in a private asylum. If any one spoke to Madame Margaritis of Dubuisson, Esquirol, Blanche, or other mad-doctors, she preferred, with lofty indignation, to keep her three thousand francs and her goodman.

The inexplicable caprices of this worthy's insanity being closely connected with the course of my story, it is needful to mention some of his more conspicuous vagaries. Margaritis would always go out as soon as it began to rain, to walk bareheaded among his vines. Indoors he was perpetually asking for the newspaper; just to satisfy him, his wife or the maid-servant would give him an old *Journal d'Indre-et-Loire* and for seven years he had never discovered that it was always the same copy. A doctor might perhaps have found it interesting to note the connection between his attacks of asking for the paper and the variations in the weather. The poor madman's constant occupation was to study the state of the sky and its effect on the vines.

When his wife had company, which was almost every evening—for the neighbors, in pity for her position, came in to play boston with her—Margaritis sat in silence in a corner, never moving; but when ten o'clock struck by a clock in a tall wooden case, he rose at the last stroke with the mechanical precision of the figures moved by a spring in a German toy, went slowly up to the card-players, looked at them with eyes strangely like the automatic gaze of the Greeks and Turks to be seen in the Boulevard du Temple in Paris, and said, "Go away!"

At times, however, this man recovered his natural wits, and could then advise his wife very shrewdly as to the sale of her wine; but at those times he was exceedingly troublesome, stealing dainties out of the cupboards and eating them in secret.

Occasionally when the customary visitors came in, he answered their inquiries civilly, but he more often replied quite at random. To a lady who asked him, "How are you to-day, Monsieur Margaritis?"—"I have shaved," he would reply, "and you?"

"Are you better, monsieur?" another would say. "Jerusalem! Jerusalem!" was the answer. But he usually looked at them with a blank face, not speaking a word, and then his wife would say, "The goodman cannot hear anything to-day." Twice or thrice in the course of five years, always about the time of the equinox, he had flown into a rage at this remark, had drawn a knife, and shrieked, "That hussy disgraces me!"

Still, he drank, ate, and walked out like any man in perfect health; and by degrees every one was accustomed to pay him no more respect or attention than if he had been a clumsy piece of furniture.

Of all his eccentricities, there was one to which no one had ever been able to discover a clue; for the wise heads of the district had in the course of time accounted for, or explained, most of the poor lunatic's maddest acts. He insisted on always having a sack of flour in the house, and on keeping two casks of wine from the vintage, never allowing any one to touch either the flour or the wine. But when the month of June came round, he began to be anxious to sell the sack and the wine-barrels with all the fretfulness of a madman. Madame Margaritis generally told him that she had sold the two puncheons at an exorbitant price, and gave him the money, which he then hid without his wife or his servant ever having succeeded, even by watching, in discovering the hiding-place.

The day before Gaudissart's visit to Vouvray, Madame Margaritis had had more difficulty than ever in managing her husband, who had had an attack of lucid reason.

"I declare I do not know how I shall get through to-morrow," said she to Madame Vernier. "Only fancy, my old man insisted on seeing his two casks of wine. And he gave me no peace all day till I showed him two full puncheons. Our neighbor, Pierre Champlain, luckily had two casks he had not been able to sell, and at my request he rolled them into our cellar. And then what must he want, after seeing the casks, but nothing will content him but selling them himself."

Madame Vernier had just been telling her husband of this difficult state of things when Gaudissart walked in. At the commercial traveler's very first words Vernier determined to let him loose on old Margaritis.

"Monsieur," replied the dyer, when Gaudissart the Great had exhausted his first broadside, "I will not conceal from you that your undertaking will meet with great obstacles in this district. In our part of the world the good folks go on, bodily, in a way of their own; it is a country where no new idea can ever take root. We live as our fathers did, amusing ourselves by eating four meals a day, occupying ourselves by looking after our vineyards, and selling our wine at a good price. Our notion of business is, very honestly, to sell things for more than they cost. We shall go on in that rut, and neither God nor the devil can get us out of it. But I will give you some good advice, and good advice is worth an eye. We have in this neighborhood a retired banker, in whose judgment I myself have the utmost confidence, and if you win his support you shall have mine. If your proposals offer any substantial prospects, and we are convinced of it, Monsieur Margaritis' vote carries mine with it, and there are twenty well-to-do houses in Vouvray where purses will be opened and your panacea will be tried."

As she heard him mention the madman, Madame Vernier looked up at her husband.

"By the way, I believe my wife was just going to call on Madame Margaritis with a neighbor of ours. Wait a minute, and the ladies will show you the way.—You can go round and pick up Madame Fontanier," said the old dyer with a wink at his wife.

This suggestion that she should take with her the merriest, the most voluble, the most facetious of all the merry wives of Vouvray, was as much as to tell Madame Vernier to secure a witness to report the scene which would certainly take place between the bagman and the lunatic, so as to amuse the country with it for a month to come. Monsieur and Madame Vernier played their parts so well that Gaudissart had no suspicions, and rushed headlong into the snare. He politely offered his arm to Madame Vernier, and fancied he had quite made a conquest of both ladies on the way, being dazzlingly witty, and pelting them with waggery and puns which they did not understand.

The so-called banker lived in the first house at the opening into the Vallée coquette. It was called La Fuye, and was not particularly remarkable. On the ground floor was a large paneled sitting-room, with a bedroom on each side for the master and mistress. The entrance was through a hall, where they dined, opening into the kitchen. This ground floor, quite lacking the external elegance for which even the humblest dwellings in Touraine are noted, was crowned by attics, to which an outside stair led up, built against one of the gable ends, and covered by a lean-to roof. A small garden, full of marigolds, seringa, and elder, divided the house from the vineyard. Round the courtyard were the buildings for the wine-presses and storage.

Margaritis, seated in a yellow Utrecht velvet chair by the window in the drawing-room, did not rise as the ladies came in with Gaudissart; he was thinking of the sale of his butts of wine. He was a lean man, with a pear-shaped head, bald above the forehead, and furnished with a few hairs at the

back. His deep-set eyes, shaded by thick black brows, and
with dark rings round them, his nose as thin as the blade of
a knife, his high cheek-bones and hollow cheeks, his generally
oblong outline—everything, down to his absurdly long flat
chin, contributed to give a strange look to his countenance,
suggesting that of a professor of rhetoric—or of a rag-picker.

"Monsieur Margaritis," said Madame Vernier, "come,
wake up! Here is a gentleman sent to you by my husband,
and you are to hear him with attention. Put aside your
mathematical calculations and talk to him."

At this speech the madman rose, looked at Gaudissart,
waved to him to be seated, and said:

"Let us talk, monsieur."

The three women went into Madame Margaritis' room,
leaving the door open so as to hear all that went on, and in-
tervene in case of need. Hardly were they seated when Monsieur Vernier came in quietly from the vineyard, and made
them let him in through the window without a sound.

"You were in business, monsieur?" Gaudissart began.

"Public business," replied Margaritis, interrupting him.
"I pacified Calabria when Murat was King."

"Heyday, he has been in Calabria now!" said Vernier in
a whisper.

"Oh, indeed!" said Gaudissart. "Then, monsieur, we cannot fail to come to an understanding."

"I am listening," replied Margaritis, settling himself in
the attitude of a man sitting for his portrait.

"Monsieur," said Gaudissart, fidgeting with his watch
key, which he twisted round and round without thinking of
what he was doing, with a regular rotary twirl which engaged
the madman's attention, and perhaps helped to keep him
quiet; "monsieur, if you were not a man of superior intelligence"—Margaritis bowed—"I should restrict myself to setting forth the material advantages of this concern; but its
psychological value is worthy of your attention. Mark me!
Of all forms of social wealth, time is the most precious; to
save time is to grow rich, is it not? Now is there anything

which takes up more time in our lives than anxiety as to what I may call boiling the pot—a homely metaphor, but clearly stating the question? Or is there anything which consumes more time than the lack of a guarantee to offer as security to those of whom you ask money when, though impecunious for a time, you yet are rich in prospects?"

"Money—you have come to the point."

"Well, then, monsieur, I am the emissary to the departments of a company of bankers and capitalists, who have perceived what enormous loss of time, and consequently of productive intelligence and activity, is thus entailed on men with the future before them. Now, the idea has occurred to us that, to such men, we may capitalize the future, we may discount their talents, by discounting what?—why, their time, and securing its value to their heirs. This is not merely to economize time; it is to price it, to value it, to represent in a pecuniary form the products you may expect to obtain in a certain unknown time by representing the moral qualities with which you are gifted, and which are, monsieur, a living force, like a waterfall, or a steam engine of three, ten, twenty, fifty horse-power. This is progress, a great movement towards a better order of things, a movement due to the energy of our age—an essentially progressive age, as I can prove to you when we come to the conception of a more logical co-ordination of social interests.

"I will explain myself by tangible instances. I quit the purely abstract argument which we, in our line, call the mathematics of ideas. Supposing that instead of being a man of property, living on your dividends, you are a painter, a musician, a poet——"

"I am a painter," the other put in by way of parenthesis.

"Very good, so be it, since you take my metaphor; you are a painter, you have a great future before you. But I am going further——"

At those words the lunatic studied Gaudissart uneasily to see if he meant to go away, but was reassured on seeing him remain seated.

"You are nothing at all," Gaudissart went on, "but you feel yourself——"

"I feel myself," said Margaritis.

"You say to yourself, 'I shall be a Minister'; very good. You, the painter, you, the artist, the man of letters, the future Minister, you calculate your prospects, you value them at so much—you estimate them, let us say—at a hundred thousand crowns——"

"And you have brought me a hundred thousand crowns?" said the lunatic.

"Yes, monsieur, you will see. Either your heirs will get them without fail, in the event of your death, since the company pledges itself to pay, or, if you live, you get them by your works of art or your fortunate speculations. Nay, if you have made a mistake, you can begin all over again. But, when once you have fixed the value, as I have had the honor of explaining to you, of your intellectual capital—for it is intellectual capital, bear that clearly in mind, monsieur——"

"I understand," said the madman.

"You sign a policy of insurance with this company, which credits you with the value of a hundred thousand francs— you, the painter——"

"I am a painter," said Margaritis.

"You, the musician, the Minister—and promises to pay that sum to your family, your heirs, if, in consequence of your demise, the hopes of the income to be derived from your intellectual capital should be lost. The payment of the premium is thus all that is needed to consolidate your——"

"*Your* cash-box," said the madman, interrupting him.

"Well, of course, monsieur; I see that you understand business."

"Yes," said Margaritis, "I was the founder of the Banque Territoriale, Rue des Fossés-Montmartre in Paris, in 1798."

"For," Gaudissart went on, "in order to repay the intellectual capital with which each of us credits himself, must not all who insure pay a certain premium—three per cent, annually three per cent? And thus, by paying a very small sum, a mere nothing, you are protecting your family against the disastrous effects of your death."

"But I am alive," objected the lunatic.

"Ah, yes, and if you live to be old—that is the objection commonly raised, the objection of the vulgar, and you must see that if we had not anticipated and annihilated it, we should be unworthy to become—what? What are we, in fact?—The book-keepers of the Great Bank of Intellect.

"Monsieur, I do not say this to you; but wherever I go, I meet with men who pretend to teach something new, to bring forward some fresh argument against those who have grown pale with studying the business—on my word of honor, it is contemptible! However, the world is made so, and I have no hope of reforming it.—Your objection, monsieur, is ab-surd——"

"*Quésaco?* (What!)" said Margaritis.

"For this reason. If you should live, and if you have the money credited to you in your policy of insurance against the chances of death—you follow me——"

"I follow."

"Well, then, it is because you have succeeded in your un-dertakings! And you will have succeeded solely in conse-quence of that policy of insurance; for, by ridding yourself of all the anxieties which are involved in having a wife at your heels, and children whom your death may reduce to beggary, you simply double your chances of success. If you are at the top of the tree, you have grasped the intellectual capital compared with which the insurance money is a trifle, a mere trifle."

"An admirable idea!"

"Is it not, monsieur?—I call this beneficent institution the Mutual Insurance against beggary!—or, if you prefer it, the Office for discounting Talent. For talent, sir, talent is a bill of exchange, bestowed by Nature on a man of genius, and which is often at long date—ha, hah!"

"Very handsome usury," cried Margaritis.

"The deuce! He is sharp enough, this old boy! I have

made a mistake; I must attack this man on higher ground with palaver A 1," thought Gaudissart.—"Not at all, monsieur," said he aloud. "To you who——"

"Will you take a glass of wine?" asked Margaritis.

"With pleasure," said Gaudissart."

"Wife! give us a bottle of the wine of which two casks are left.—You are here in the headquarters of Vouvray," said the master, pointing to his vines. "The clos Margaritis."

The maid brought in glasses and a bottle of the wine of 1819. The worthy lunatic filled a glass with scrupulous care, and solemnly presented it to Gaudissart, who drank it.

"But you are playing me some trick, monsieur," said the commercial traveler. "This is Madeira, genuine Madeira!"

"I should think it is!" replied the lunatic. "The only fault of the Vouvray wine, monsieur, is that it cannot be used as an *ordinaire,* as a table wine. It is too generous, too strong; and it is sold in Paris as Madeira after being doctored with brandy. Our wine is so rich that many of the Paris merchants, when the French crop is insufficient for Holland and Belgium, buy our wine to mix with the wine grown about Paris, and so manufacture a Bordeaux wine.— But what you are drinking at this moment, my dear and very amiable sir, is fit for a king; it is the head of Vouvray. I have two casks, only two casks of it. Persons who appreciate the finest wines, high-class wines, and like to put a wine on their table which has a character not to be met with in the regular trade, apply direct to us. Now, do you happen to know any one——"

"Let us go back to our business," said Gaudissart.

"We are there, monsieur," replied the madman. "My wine is heady, and you are talking of capital; the etymology of capital is *caput*—head.—Heh?—The Head of Vouvray—the connection is obvious."

"As I was saying," persisted Gaudissart, "either you have realized your intellectual capital——"

"I have realized, monsieur.—Will you take my two puncheons? I will give you favorable terms."

"No," said Gaudissart the Great, "I allude to the insurance of intellectual capital and policies on life. I will resume the thread of my argument."

The madman grew calmer, sat down, and looked at Gaudissart.

"I was saying, monsieur, that if you should die, the capital is paid over to your family without difficulty."

"Without difficulty."

"Yes, excepting in the case of suicide——"

"A question for the law."

"No, sir. As you know, suicide is an act that is always easily proved."

"In France," said Margaritis. "But——"

"But abroad," said Gaudissart. "Well, monsieur, to conclude that part of the question, I may say at once that death abroad, or on the field of battle, are not included——"

"What do you insure, then? Nothing whatever," cried the other. "Now, my bank was based on——"

"Nothing whatever, sir?" cried Gaudissart, interrupting him. "Nothing whatever? How about illness, grief, poverty, and the passions? But we need not discuss exceptional cases."

"No, we will not discuss them," said the madman.

"What, then, is the upshot of this transaction?" exclaimed Gaudissart. "To you, as a banker, I will simply state the figures.—You have a man, a man with a future, well dressed, living on his art—he wants money, he asks for it—a blank. Civilization at large will refuse to advance money to this man, who, in thought, dominates over civilization, who will some day dominate over it by his brush, his chisel, by words, or ideas, or a system. Civilization is merciless. She has no bread for the great men who provide her with luxuries; she feeds them on abuse and mockery, the gilded slut! The expression is a strong one; but I will not retract it.—Well, your misprized great man comes to us; we recognize his greatness, we bow to him respectfully, we listen to him, and he says to us:

" 'Gentlemen of the Insurance Company, my life is worth so much; I will pay you so much per cent on my works.'— Well, what do we do? At once, without grudging, we admit him to the splendid banquet of civilization as an important guest——"

"Then you must have wine," said the madman.

"As an important guest. He signs his policy, he takes our contemptible paper rags—mere miserable rags, which, rags as they are, have more "power than his genius had. For, in fact, if he wants money, everybody on seeing that sheet of paper is ready to lend to him. On the Bourse, at the bankers', anywhere, even at the money-lenders', he can get money— because he can offer security.—Well, sir, was not this a gulf that needed filling in the social system?

"But, sir, this is but a part of the business undertaken by the Life Insurance Company. We also insure debtors on a different scale of premiums. We offer annuities on terms graduated by age, on an infinitely more favorable calculation than has as yet been allowed in tontines based on tables of mortality now known to be inaccurate. Our Society operating on the mass, our annuitants need have no fear of the reflections that sadden their latter years, in themselves sad enough; such thoughts as must necessarily invade them when their money is in private hands. So, you see, monsieur, we have taken the measure of life under every aspect——"

"Sucked it at every pore," said Margaritis.—"But take a glass of wine; you have certainly earned it. You must lay some velvet on your stomach if you want to keep your jaw in working order. And the wine of Vouvray, monsieur, is, when old enough, pure velvet."

"And what do you think of it all?" said Gaudissart, emptying his glass.

"It is all very fine, very new, very advantageous; but I think better of the system of loans on land that was in use in my bank in the Rue des Fossés-Montmartre."

"There you are right, monsieur," said Gaudissart, "that has been worked and worked out, done and done again. We now have the Mortgage Society which lends on real estate, and works that system on a large scale. But is not that a mere trifle in comparison with our idea of consolidating possibilities. Consolidating hopes, coagulating—financially— each man's desires for wealth, and securing their realization. It remained for our age, sir, an age of transition—of transition and progress combined!"

"Ay, of progress," said the lunatic. "I like progress, especially such as brings good times for the wine trade——"

"The *Times—le Temps*——!" exclaimed Gaudissart, not heeding the madman's meaning. "A poor paper, sir; if you take it in, I pity you."

"The newspaper?" cried Margaritis. "To be sure, I am devoted to the newspaper.—Wife, wife! where is the newspaper?" he went on, turning towards the door.

"Very good, monsieur; if you take an interest in the papers, we shall certainly agree."

"Yes, yes; but before you hear the paper, confess that this wine is——"

"Delicious," said Gaudissart.

"Come on, then, we will finish the bottle between us." The madman a quarter filled his own glass, and poured out a bumper for Gaudissart.

"As I say, sir, I have two casks of that very wine. If you think it is good, and are disposed to deal——"

"The fathers of the Saint-Simonian doctrine have, in fact, commissioned me to forward them such products as—— But let me tell you of their splendid newspaper. You, who understand the insurance business, and are ready to help me to extend it in this district——"

"Certainly," said Margaritis, "if——"

"Of course, if I take your wine. And your wine is very good, monsieur; it goes to the spot."

"Champagne is made of it. There is a gentleman here, from Paris, who has come to make champagne at Tours."

"I quite believe it.—The *Globe,* which you must have heard mentioned——"

"I know it well," said Margaritis.

"I was sure of it," said Gaudissart. "Monsieur, you have a powerful head—a bump which is known as the equine head. There is something of the horse in the head of every great man. Now a man can be a genius and live unknown. It is a trick that has happened often enough to men who, in spite of their talents, live in obscurity, and which nearly befell the great Saint-Simon and Monsieur Vico, a man of mark who is making his way. He is coming on well is Vico, and I am glad. Here we enter on the new theory and formula of the human race. Attention, monsieur——"

"Attention!" echoed Margaritis.

"The oppression of man by man ought to have ended, monsieur, on the day when Christ—I do not say Jesus Christ, I say Christ—came to proclaim the equality of men before God. But has not this equality been hitherto the most illusory chimera?—Now, Saint-Simon supplements Christ. Christ has served His time——"

"Then, is He released?" asked Margaritis.

"He has served His time from the point of view of Liberalism. There is something stronger to guide us now—the new creed, free and individual creativeness, social co-ordination by which each one shall receive his social reward equitably, in accordance with his work, and no longer be the hireling of individuals who, incapable themselves, make *all* labor for the benefit of one alone. Hence the doctrine——"

"And what becomes of the servants?" asked Margaritis.

"They remain servants, monsieur, if they are only capable of being servants."

"Then of what use is the doctrine?"

"Oh, to judge of that, monsieur, you must take your stand on the highest point of view whence you can clearly command a general prospect of humanity. This brings us to Ballanche! Do you know Monsieur Ballanche?"

"It is my principal business," said the madman, who misunderstood the name for *la planche* (boards or staves).

"Very good," said Gaudissart. "Then, sir, if the palingenesis and successive developments of the spiritualized Globe touch you, delight you, appeal to you,—then, my dear sir, the newspaper called the *Globe,* a fine name, accurately expressing its mission—the *Globe* is the *cicerone* who will explain to you every morning the fresh conditions under which, in quite a short time, the world will undergo a political and moral change."

"*Quésaco?*" said Margaritis.

"I will explain the argument by a simile," said Gaudissart. "If, as children, our nurses took us to Séraphin, do not we older men need a presentment of the future?—These gentlemen——"

"Do they drink wine?"

"Yes, monsieur. Their house is established, I may say, on an admirable footing—a prophetic footing; handsome receptions, all the bigwigs, splendid parties."

"To be sure," said the madman, "the laborers who pull down must be fed as well as those who build."

"All the more so, monsieur, when they pull down with one hand and build up with the other, as the apostles of the *Globe* do."

"Then they must have wine, the wine of Vouvray; the two casks I have left—three hundred bottles for a hundred francs —a mere song!"

"How much a bottle does that come to?" said Gaudissart. "Let us see; there is the carriage, and the town dues—not seven sous—a very good bargain." ("I have caught my man," thought Gaudissart. "You want to sell me the wine which I want, and I can get the whip hand of you.") "They pay more for other wine," he went on. "Well, monsieur, men who haggle are sure to agree.—Speak honestly; you have considerable influence in the district?"

"I believe so," said the madman. "The head of Vouvray, you see."

"Well, and you perfectly understand the working of the Intellectual Capital Insurance?"

"Perfectly."

"You have realized the vast proportions of the *Globe?*"

"Twice—on foot."

Gaudissart did not heed him; he was entangled in the maze of his own thoughts, and listening to his own words, assured of success.

"Well, seeing the position you hold, I can understand that at your age you have nothing to insure. But, monsieur, you can persuade those persons in this district to insure who, either by their personal merits or by the precarious position of their families, may be anxious to provide for the future. And so, if you will subscribe to the *Globe,* and if you will give me the support of your authority in this district to invite the investment of capital in annuities—for annuities are popular in the provinces—well, we may come to an agreement as to the purchase of the two casks of wine.—Will you take in the *Globe?*"

"I live on the globe."

"Will you support me with the influential residents in the district?"

"I support——"

"And——"

"And?——"

"And I—— But you will pay your subscription to the *Globe?*"

"The *Globe*—a good paper—an annuity?"

"An annuity, monsieur?—Well, yes, you are right; for it is full of life, of vitality, and learning; choke full of learning; a handsome paper, well printed, a good color, thick paper. Oh, it is none of your flimsy shoddy, mere wastepaper that tears if you look at it. And it goes deep, gives you reasoning that you may think over at leisure, and pleasant occupation here in the depths of the country."

"That is the thing for me," said the madman.

"It costs a mere trifle—eighty francs a year."

"That is not the thing for me," said Margaritis.

"Monsieur," said Gaudissart, "of course you have little children?"

"Some," said Margaritis, who misunderstood *have* for *love*.

"Well, then, the *Journal des Enfants,* seven francs a year——"

"Buy my two casks of wine," said Margaritis, "and I will subscribe to your children's paper; that is the thing for me; a fine idea. Intellectual tyranny—a child—heh? Does not man tyrannize over man?"

"Right you are," said Gaudissart.

"Right I am."

"And you consent to steer me round the district?"

"Round the district."

"I have your approbation?"

"You have."

"Well, then, sir, I will take your two casks of wine at a hundred francs——"

"No, no, a hundred and ten."

"Monsieur, a hundred and ten, I will say a hundred and ten, but it is a hundred and ten to the gentlemen of the paper and one hundred to me. If I find you a buyer, you owe me a commission."

"A hundred and twenty to them. No commission to the commissioners."

"Very neat. And not only witty, but spirited."

"No, spirituous."

"Better and better—like Nicolet."

"That is my way," said the lunatic. "Come and look at my vineyards?"

"With pleasure," said Gaudissart. "That wine goes strangely to the head."

And Gaudissart the Great went out with Monsieur Margaritis, who led him from terrace to terrace, from vine to vine.

The three ladies and Monsieur Vernier could laugh now at their ease, as they saw the two men from the window gesticulating, haranguing, standing still, and going on again, talking vehemently.

"Why did your good man take him out of hearing?" said Vernier. At last Margaritis came in again with the commercial traveler; they were both walking at a great pace as if in a hurry to conclude the business.

"And the countryman, I bet, has been too many for the Parisian," said Vernier.

In point of fact, Gaudissart the Great, sitting at one end of the card-table, to the great delight of Margaritis, wrote an order for the delivery of two casks of wine. Then, after reading through the contract, Margaritis paid him down seven francs as a subscription to the children's paper.

"Till to-morrow, then, monsieur," said Gaudissart the Great, twisting his watch-key; "I shall have the honor of calling for you to-morrow. You can send the wine to Paris direct to the address I have given you, and forward it as soon as you receive the money."

Gaudissart was from Normandy; there were two sides to every bargain he made, and he required an agreement from Monsieur Margaritis, who with a madman's glee in gratifying his favorite whim, signed, after reading, a contract to deliver two casks of wine of *Clos Margaritis.*

So Gaudissart went off in high spirits, humming *Le roi des mers, prends plus bas,* to the *Golden Sun* Inn, where he naturally had a chat with the host while waiting for dinner. Mitouflet was an old soldier, simple but cunning, as peasants are, but never laughing at a joke, as being a man who is accustomed to the roar of cannon, and to passing a jest in the ranks.

"You have some very tough customers hereabouts," said Gaudissart, leaning against the door-post and lighting his cigar at Mitouflet's pipe.

"How is that?" asked Mitouflet.

"Well, men who ride roughshod over political and financial theories."

"Whom have you been talking to, if I may make so bold?" asked the innkeeper guilelessly, while he skilfully expectorated after the manner of smokers.

"To a wideawake chap named Margaritis."

Mitouflet glanced at his customer, twice, with calm irony.

"Oh yes, he is wideawake, no doubt! He knows too much for most people; they don't follow him——"

"I can quite believe it. He has a thorough knowledge of the higher branches of finance."

"Yes, indeed," said Mitouflet; "and for my part, I have always thought it a pity that he should be mad."

"Mad? How?"

"How? Why, mad, as a madman is mad," repeated the innkeeper. "But he is not dangerous, and his wife looks after him.—So you understand each other? That's funny," said the relentless Mitouflet, with the utmost calm.

"Funny?" cried Gaudissart. "Funny? But your precious Monsieur Vernier was making a fool of me!"

"Did he send you there?" said Mitouflet.

"Yes."

"I say, wife," cried the innkeeper, "listen to that! Monsieur Vernier actually sent monsieur to talk to old Margaritis——"

"And what did you find to say to each other, my good gentleman," said the woman, "since he is quite mad?"

"He sold me two casks of wine."

"And you bought them?"

"Yes."

"But it is his mania to want to sell wine; he has none."

"Very good!" cried the bagman. "In the first place, I will go and thank Monsieur Vernier."

Gaudissart, boiling with rage, went off to the house of the ex-dyer, whom he found in his parlor laughing with the neighbors, to whom he was already telling the story.

"Monsieur," said the Prince of Bagmen, his eyes glaring with wrath, "you are a sneak and a blackguard; and if you are not the lowest of turnkeys—a class I rank below the convicts—you will give me satisfaction for the insult you have done me by placing me in the power of a man whom you knew to be mad. Do you hear me, Monsieur Vernier, the dyer?"

This was the speech Gaudissart had prepared, as a tragedian prepares his entrance on the stage.

"What next?" retorted Vernier, encouraged by the presence of his neighbors. "Do you think we have not good right to make game of a gentleman who arrives at Vouvray with an air and a flourish, to get our money out of us under pretence of being great men—painters, or verse-mongers—and who thus gratuitously places us on a level with a penniless horde, out at elbows, homeless and roofless? What have we done to deserve it, we who are fathers of families? A rogue, who asks us to subscribe to the *Globe,* a paper which preaches as the first law of God, if you please, that a man shall not inherit what his father and mother can leave him? On my sacred word of honor, old Margaritis can talk more sense than that.

"And, after all, what have you to complain of? You were quite of a mind, you and he. These gentlemen can bear witness that if you had speechified to all the people in the country-side you would not have been so well understood."

"That is all very well to say, but I consider myself insulted, monsieur, and I expect satisfaction."

"Very good, sir; I consider you insulted if that will be any comfort to you, and I will not give you satisfaction, for there is not satisfaction enough in the whole silly business for me to give you any. Is he absurd, I ask you?"

At these words Gaudissart rushed on the dyer to give him a blow; but the Vouvrillons were on the alert, and threw themselves between them, so that Gaudissart the Great only hit the dyer's wig, which flew off and alighted on the head of Mademoiselle Claire Vernier.

"If you are not satisfied now, monsieur, I shall be at the inn till to-morrow morning; you will find me there, and ready to show you what is meant by satisfaction for an insult. I fought in July, monsieur!"

"Very well," said the dyer, "you shall fight at Vouvray;

and you will stay here rather longer than you bargained for."

Gaudissart departed, pondering on this reply, which seemed to him ominous of mischief. For the first time in his life he dined cheerlessly.

The whole borough of Vouvray was in a stir over the meeting between Gaudissart and Monsieur Vernier. A duel was a thing unheard of in this benign region.

"Monsieur Mitouflet, I am going to fight Monsieur Vernier to-morrow morning," said Gaudissart to his host. "I know nobody here; will you be my second?"

"With pleasure," said Mitouflet.

Gaudissart had hardly finished his dinner when Madame Fontanieu and the Mayor's deputy came to the *Golden Sun,* took Mitouflet aside, and represented to him what a sad thing it would be for the whole district if a violent death should occur; they described the frightful state of affairs for good Madame Vernier, and implored him to patch the matter up so as to save the honor of the community.

"I will see to it," said the innkeeper with a wink.

In the evening Mitouflet went up to Gaudissart's room carrying pens, ink, and paper.

"What is all that?" asked Gaudissart.

"Well, as you are to fight to-morrow, I thought you might be glad to leave some little instructions, and that you might wish to write some letters, for we all have some one who is dear to us. Oh! that will not kill you. Are you a good fencer? Would you like to practise a little? I have some foils."

"I should be glad to do so."

Mitouflet fetched the foils, and two masks.

"Now, let us see."

The innkeeper and the bagman stood on guard. Mitouflet, who had been an instructor of grenadiers, hit Gaudissart sixty-eight times, driving him back to the wall.

"The devil! you are good at the game!" said Gaudissart, out of breath.

"I am no match for Monsieur Vernier."

"The deuce! Then I will fight with pistols."

"I advise you to.—You see, if you use large horse pistols and load them to the muzzle, they are sure to kick and miss, and each man withdraws with unblemished honor. Leave me to arrange it. By the Mass, two good men would be great fools to kill each other for a jest."

"Are you sure the pistols will fire wide enough? I should be sorry to kill the man," said Gaudissart.

"Sleep easy."

Next morning the adversaries, both rather pale, met at the foot of the Pont de la Cise.

The worthy Vernier narrowly missed killing a cow that was grazing by the roadside ten yards off.

"Ah! you fired in the air!" exclaimed Gaudissart, and with these words the enemies fell into each other's arms.

"Monsieur," said the traveler, "your joke was a little rough, but it was funny. I am sorry I spoke so strongly, but I was beside myself.—I hold you a man of honor."

"Monsieur, we will get you twenty subscribers to the children's paper," replied the dyer, still rather pale.

"That being the case," said Gaudissart, "why should we not breakfast together? Men who have fought are always ready to understand each other."

"Monsieur Mitouflet," said Gaudissart, as they went in, "there is a bailiff here, I suppose?"

"What for?"·

"I mean to serve a notice on my dear little Monsieur Margaritis, requiring him to supply me with two casks of his wine."

"But he has none," said Vernier.

"Well, monsieur, I will say no more about it for an indemnity of twenty francs. But I will not have it said in your town that you stole a march on Gaudissart the Great."

Madame Margaritis, afraid of an action, which the plaintiff would certainly gain, brought the twenty francs to the clement bagman, who was also spared the pains of any further propaganda in one of the most jovial districts of France, and at the same time the least open to new ideas.

On his return from his tour in the southern provinces, Gaudissart the Great was traveling in the coupé of the Laffite-Caillard diligence, and had for a fellow-passenger a young man to whom, having passed Angoulême, he condescended to expatiate on the mysteries of life, fancying him, no doubt, but a baby.

On reaching Vouvray, the youth exclaimed:

"What a lovely situation !"

"Yes, monsieur," said Gaudissart, "but the land is uninhabitable by reason of the inhabitants. You would have a duel on your hands every day. Why only three months ago I fought on that very spot"—and he pointed to the bridge—"with a confounded dyer—pistols; but—I fleeced him !"

PARIS, *November* 1832.